Selar

KATHRYN LYNN DAVIS

POCKET BOOKS

New York   London   Toronto   Sydney   Tokyo

An *Original* Publication of POCKET BOOKS

POCKET BOOKS, a division of Simon & Schuster Inc.
1230 Avenue of the Americas, New York, NY 10020

Copyright © 1989 by Kathryn Lynn Davis
Cover illustration copyright © 1989 Osyczka Limited
Inside cover art copyright © 1990 Charles Gehm

ISBN: 0-671-67269-X

First Pocket Books paperback printing January 1990

10 9 8 7 6 5 4 3 2 1

Printed in the U.S.A.

With inexpressible gratitude—

To my friend Page Ashley
Without whom this book would never have been conceived,

And to my husband Michael
Without whom it would never have been completed.

Acknowledgments

Too Deep for Tears is the culmination of a five-year project that has been sustained and encouraged through many turbulent changes by the support and forbearance of my friends and family. The exaltation its publication makes me feel is due in part to these people, without whom I might have long since lost hope.

My close friend and fellow author Brenda Trent has read, reread, and commented on each revision of the manuscript; her astute, honest criticism and her friendship have been invaluable. Jill Gardner, at a difficult and uncomfortable time in her own life, nevertheless listened, calmed, and advised me through each crisis and was never unwilling or too busy to help. Maiu Espinosa, the Estonian lioness, has been part of the pain and growth of the last year, constantly ready to listen and inspire with her intuitive gifts. My parents, Ann and Mickey Davis, believed from the beginning that I could attain the unattainable; I have always been able to depend on their faith in me, along with their thoughtful advice.

There are several others I wish to thank: Murray, who respected me enough to say, "Do it so *you* feel it's right. Trust your instincts—they will not mislead you"; Dorris, who, almost two years ago, took me on a treasure hunt and unknowingly helped me articulate the major themes of this book; Susan Grode, who—with tact and sensitivity—helped me make some difficult decisions that changed the direction of my career; Jim Parsons, a history professor at the University of California, Riverside, who first instilled in me a love

ACKNOWLEDGMENTS

of China—both its wonder and its brutality; John Phillips, another of my major history professors who has, over the years, shared his enthusiasm and scholarly expertise, making my research much easier.

Many friends have been involved in the continuing saga of choosing a title for this book. The Bear Flag Café was often the scene of heated discussions among Jonathan Kinsman, Bill Odien, Jeff Odien, Chris Krummenacher, Jane Laning, Steve Goodyear, Steve and Chuck, and especially Virginia Magnuson Odien, who were willing to offer endless suggestions and inspiration. I am also grateful to my friend and teacher Esther F. Gobrecht, with whom I sat for hours, read poetry, and wept while we sought the perfect title.

Finally, my sincere appreciation to my editor, Linda Marrow, a kindred spirit who, through her sensitivity and wisdom, has made working on this book a joy; and to my agent, Andrea Cirillo, who understood from the beginning that I don't do things the easy way, but nevertheless chose to take the risk.

Thanks to the human heart by which we live,
Thanks to its tenderness, its joys, and fears,
To me the meanest flower that blows can give
Thoughts that do often lie too deep for tears.

—*from* William Wordsworth's
"Ode: Intimations of Immortality
from Recollections of Early
Childhood"

BOOK

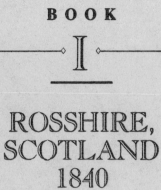

I

ROSSHIRE,
SCOTLAND
1840

Prologue

Mairi hurried, barefoot, over the soft earth while the wind sighed through the pine and hawthorn trees, echoing the rush of her chilled breath as she ran. The mist obscured the faint path ahead, but that did not matter; she had known these woods since childhood and found her way by instinct through the low branches and thick green ferns. The cool darkness enfolded her as she listened to the sounds of birds and small chattering animals. Then the murmur of the stream drifted through the settling silence and she paused where the trees parted to reveal the water. One foot on a flat boulder, she stood at the edge of the stream and closed her eyes; she wanted to absorb the music of wind and water that rose toward the dark, brackened mountains in the distance.

She drew her wool plaid half across her face, so it pressed damp hair against her cheek, while the familiar voices of the glen spoke to her. Head thrown back, she listened, feeling the breeze caress her skin, until the flutter of her pulse faded into the sound of these beloved voices, became one of them.

The rhythm of the music changed slightly and she opened her eyes to see a wildcat on the far bank. She froze when his yellow eyes met hers, appraisingly. She did not blink or look away but only smiled a little. The wildcat raised its head, less wary now, as if she had spoken words of reassurance, though she had not moved. Then, at the same moment, each turned away—she to her simple stone croft, he to the safety of the shadowed woods.

Her long skirts swung about her ankles as Mairi hurried across the clearing to the thatched croft built into a sloped

3

bank. Fingers curled tightly around the rusted latch, she turned back for one more breath of summer-scented air. The mist had woven itself among the firs and pines until it concealed the mountain peaks; the cries of wind and water were slowly silenced by the shimmering white moisture. Mairi gazed around her at the glen she had always known—constant and unchanging despite the turmoil inside her. It would never change, no matter how much happiness or pain she knew. That was the wonder of it; the secrets of the hills could not be altered by human feelings.

She smiled with bitter sweetness and pulled the oak door open. For a moment she paused to gaze wonderingly at her husband, who lay asleep on the rough-hewn bed. With the golden firelight on his face, glinting off his light brown hair, he looked so young, so vulnerable. It was true that Charles was twenty-four, five years older than she, but there was so much he did not know. So much he did not wish to know.

Her violet eyes darkened to slate as an image rose in her mind of that same bed, empty and cold after Charles had gone. He was wrong for her; she had known it from the beginning. She wondered why she had married him at all, then. What foolish instinct had bidden her love him?

As if in answer to her unspoken question, Charles opened his eyes and reached for her. "Mairi, I've been waiting."

Then she knew why—because he was Charles. She needed no more reason than that.

"Where have you been?" he asked as he took her hands, drawing her into the warmth of the room.

"About the glen." It was all she could say. She did not mention the tiny dell ringed by forbidding hills where she had huddled among the rocks. She did not tell him how the eerie silence, broken only by the cry of the wind, had surrounded her like the spirits of the dead that hovered in the crevices of those rocks. These things Charles would never understand.

"I went to look for you, but the wind was so cold and I could feel the animals watching me from the edge of the woods." He shivered. "Then the fog began to rise and I was afraid I would lose my way. I felt that you were already lost in those unfriendly hills, that I couldn't follow you there.''

"The hills are no' unfriendly," she cried. "Ye just don't understand them."

Charles shook his head and touched her cheek where he could feel the chill of approaching evening. "You'll miss your hills, won't you, when we get to England?"

She hesitated, then murmured, "Ye don't realize what this place means to me. 'Tis all I've ever known or cared to know."

Charles did not hear the desperation in her voice. "You'll soon forget all that once we begin to travel. I promise. There's so much I want to show you—Europe, Asia, America. You've seen nothing outside the Highlands," he continued, filling the silence that had fallen between them. "Not the pyramids in the middle of the bleak Egyptian desert, or the magnificence of the mountains in Switzerland. Mairi, there are wonders beyond these hills that you can't begin to imagine."

As he spoke, he moved away from her and paced the floor, unable to stay still. "And the beauty of the Orient . . ." He gestured widely as if to encompass that beauty and make her understand. Blue eyes sparkling with excitement, he added, "I want to share these things with you. There are many worlds to conquer and I intend to find them all." His hands described mountains, cathedrals, and vast foreign plains while he moved restlessly toward the door, as if he could not wait to be gone.

Closing her eyes against the denial that rose inside her, Mairi looked away. She tried, for an instant, to imagine leaving the glen, but even the thought made her shiver with apprehension.

"Mairi?" Charles raised her chin so he could see her face. Her cheeks had lost their chill and were flushed now from the heat of the fire. Her violet eyes were cloudy gray. "What is it?"

She glanced away, unable, for the moment, to find her voice.

"I love you," he said firmly, as if the simple words had the power to heal her pain and ease her panic.

5

"And I ye," she whispered.

Charles smiled. "Then nothing can be wrong between us."

"What we feel cannot change what has been," she said in agitation. "Ye are English. Your people have been the enemies of my people for centuries."

"But what has that to do with you and me?"

"Do ye not know how many horrors the English have committed against us? How much sufferin' and death and sorrow they have left behind over the years?"

Charles took her shoulders and forced her to meet his gaze. "Surely you don't blame me for what my ancestors did?"

"Ye don't understand!" she cried, pulling free of his grasp. "Your friends, your family, everyone ye know will blame *me*."

He stared at her in disbelief. "For what?"

"For the past, for the battles and slaughters and rebellions, for their fear of our fierce pride, but most of all, for bein' what I am—a Scot." Before he could interrupt, she added, "And worst of all, *mo-charaid*, they'll blame ye for marryin' me."

Her husband shook his head, unconvinced. "I don't care what they say or think. You're my wife and I'll protect you."

Mairi knew, though Charles did not, that there could be no protection from a hatred so old, so deep and strong. She knew how brutal that hatred could be; she had seen it with her own eyes. She shuddered. She would not think about that, or the fear would come back, as real now as on the day when it had begun. No love was great enough to free her from that remembered horror. Only here, among the hills and moors her family had always known, could she find peace. She sensed that Charles would stagnate in the isolated Highlands, yet she could not survive anywhere else.

For a moment, when her gaze met his, he caught a glimpse of her distress. "Let nothing trouble you, Mairi. I've told you, I'll make you happy. You'll forget the glen in time."

She looked into his eyes, vibrant with the glow of

confidence, and knew if she told him she could not leave this place, he would not believe her. He would try to force her to go with him, thinking she would change, that in time his friends would come to accept her, but she knew differently. Charles was too young and eager to recognize the wisdom in her eyes; he would simply refuse to see the truth.

So she said nothing, but only shook her head so her plaid fell back, revealing her tangled, damp red hair. She started away, but he reached out to draw her back to him. He cupped her face in his palms, mesmerized by the secrets she concealed in her eyes. His only fear was that he would somehow lose her. The wedding ring of several intertwined gold bands was not strong enough to hold a spirit like hers.

Mairi knew he was about to speak and she stopped his lips with hers. Just now, she wanted him to hold her, to make her forget tomorrow would ever come. Tonight, with the blazing fire to obliterate the starless night beyond the windows, she wanted to lose herself in the warmth of his arms, which would be closed against her in the morning, cold and unforgiving.

Charles sighed when her lips moved against his. With an effort, he suppressed the fierce need to feel her body at once, naked beneath his seeking fingers. Instead he began to unwind the plaid that wrapped her from her head to the hem of her plain linen gown. With great care, he uncovered the rest of her hair, her shoulders, and the curve of her breasts. While his hands circled her, she began to spin, away from him and back again, until she was free of the plaid, and he dropped it on the fur rug.

His fingers trembled as he undid the strings of her gown, then drew it down her body until she stepped away from it. Mairi discarded her chemise and drawers, eyes dark and lips parted. She was not shy of his hungry gaze. From the beginning she had sensed that it was right to love him this way. She had known, too, that her desire was too great to deny. Now she stood waiting while he removed his own clothes and drew her down beside him onto the thick fur rug.

He ran his hands over her body, roughly; he could no longer hold in check the need to touch her everywhere. He

7

cupped her breasts, circling the dark nipples until they rose into his open palms. With his tongue, he caressed the pulse at the base of her throat as his hands moved down to her waist, then her hips.

"Charlie, my Charlie," Mairi whispered. She dug her fingers into his shoulders, followed the curves and hollows of the body she had only just begun to know. Her cheeks were flushed as she pushed him onto his back, then ran her hands over his chest; she wanted to feel the heat of his skin beneath her palms, to enjoy the touch of curling blond hairs that caught her fingers and held them in a silken web.

Charles and Mairi's heated breath rose to mingle with the scent of burning peat while the blood began to pound furiously in her head. With a desperation born of sorrow, she clung to her husband, holding him so tightly that he gasped in surprise. Skin to skin and mouth to mouth, they turned and turned again until they were wrapped in the long red plaid that held them gently bound together. In their youthful passion they rolled across the fur rug, desperate to know every inch of each other's bodies, to swallow each other's breath as their tongues met and circled, circled and clung.

'Tis the last time, Mairi thought. She pulled her husband closer until there was no part of him that did not touch her. From his shoulders to his waist to his long muscled legs, she caressed him, memorizing every inch for the long cold nights to come. When he entered her and began to rock, Mairi moved with him, answered his thrusts with her own, pressed her fingernails into his back as her body trembled more and more violently. The colors blurred and altered until a brilliant light splintered within her. She cried out once just as Charles shuddered and buried his face in the wild, tangled hair at her neck.

In that instant, she forgot her disturbing knowledge, the years of emptiness she had seen before her. Almost, she could believe that with the magic of his touch he had carried her back in time to a day when the mountains would have welcomed him, when the heather and wild grasses would have protected them from the cold and quelling mist. Furiously, she clung to that impalpable vision and prayed to the

Tuatha De Danann, the ancient Celtic gods, that it would never leave her.

"Mairi," Charles said softly when he could find the breath to speak, "tell me again that you love me."

She shifted beneath the plaid that still lay across their glistening bodies. She could see his love for her in every line of his face. The sight of him now was a joy beyond words, the thought of his loss an inconceivable darkness. "I love ye," she answered through the constriction in her throat, though she knew he was really asking for more.

She could not lie to him, but she also could not tell him the truth. She was afraid to do so; she knew too well the power of his enthusiasm, the lure of his clear blue eyes. He might, for a moment, make her believe in his foolish dreams, convince her to go away with him, though she knew in her heart she would wither and die, stifled by the hatred that awaited her outside the Highlands. She wondered, fleetingly, if he would leave her anything out of the few lost months that they had shared? Or would she have no more than aching memories?

Finally Charles glanced out the window at the gloaming, then drew away from her. "I didn't realize how late it was. I want to go into town for a few things."

"Tonight?" she cried. Not so soon, she added silently. I thought I would at least have these few hours. Don't take those from me, too.

"It's better that way. Then we can leave first thing in the morning. There'll be nothing further to keep us here."

Mairi bowed her head.

"Come kiss me good-bye." Charles drew her up and wrapped the plaid more tightly around her. Numbly, she watched as he put on his linen shirt, wool trousers, and fine, worsted coat. Without a word, she followed him to the door.

"Don't look so grim," he said. "I'll only be gone for a couple of hours."

"Aye," she whispered, "I know." But when he returned, she would be gone, hidden away in the mountains where he would never find her. She looked up and, for an instant, could not hide the grief that swept through her.

Charles saw the pain but did not understand it. He only

knew that Mairi needed comfort. He held her close before he brushed his lips across her forehead. "I'll hurry," he murmured.

Mairi nodded but did not speak. She stood on the threshold with the warmth of the fire behind her and watched her husband go. In that moment, the urge to call him back, to bind him to her forever in spite of what she knew, overpowered her. But when she opened her mouth to cry out, the fear rose within her, so sudden and uncontrollable that it stopped the words in her throat. She could not ignore it, and beyond this glen, without the comfort of the ancient gods who dwelt here, she would never escape it. That knowledge kept her silent now as, step by step, Charles Kittridge moved away from her. Slowly, the mist curled around his shoulders, then enveloped him completely until it blocked him from her sight.

Knowing he had disappeared for the last time into the hills she loved, Mairi shuddered at a pain of loss so deep, so much a part of the pulse of her blood, that even the passage of months could not dislodge it. Instead it grew and lingered, curving through her body until it touched, and colored, the forming memory of the child that had begun to grow inside her that night.

ROSSHIRE, SCOTLAND 1858

Come away, O human child!
To the waters and the wild
With a fairy, hand in hand,
For the world's more full of weeping
Than you can understand.

—WILLIAM BUTLER YEATS

1

Ailsa Rose did not remember exactly when it had happened—the slow awakening of her body, her mind, which before had been slumbering. Perhaps soon after she had turned sixteen, nearly a year ago, though she was not certain of that. She only knew that one day she had ceased to follow her mother through the glen and begun to seek out her own hills and hollows—private places where she let the cool darkness enfold her, where she sat among the curled fronds of bracken and played her flute in celebration of streams and mountains and in wonder at the strange new feelings that had begun to grow inside her. Only one person knew of these secret places and shared them with her. Ian Fraser, her childhood friend.

Today she had finished her chores long since, then left the croft, basket in hand, to gather the lichens, bog myrtle, birch bark, and whinberry her mother used in her dyes. She had set the full creel nearby. Ailsa was free now to do as she wished.

With her knees pressed into the damp bank of the one wide stretch of calm in the boisterous river Affric, she leaned forward to stare at her face in the water. Her freshly washed chestnut hair, touched with glimmers of red, hung limp and tangled across her cheeks and forehead. She pushed the tangles aside, pleased by the image of her face, though she knew her mother Mairi, with her red Highland hair and violet eyes, was much prettier. Ailsa did not mind. Her own softly rounded cheeks and straight nose were pleasant enough. She stared at the reflection of her eyes, surprised, as always, by the striated combination of blue and violet that turned to gray with the movement of the sunlight.

13

She was proud of her eyes and her aristocratic nose, because she knew they had come from her father, the Englishman Charles Kittridge. She had never met him, but Mairi had shown her a miniature he had painted of himself when he was young. The first time Ailsa had seen her face reflected in a pail of clear water, she had recognized the marks of her father, who had left the Highlands before she was born. She was glad of these reminders that he had once been here, for they were all she had to cling to of the man she knew only as a shadow, remembered through her mother's eyes. The familiar ache of loss began within her, but she refused to let it disturb her peace today.

Warmed by an unexpected rush of sunlight, Ailsa thought how pleasant it would be to join her image in the water. Glancing around to make certain she was alone, she tossed her plaid on the ground and untied the strings of her gown. She discarded her chemise and drawers as well; she wanted to feel the water everywhere. The wind dipped through the treetops, rattled the leaves as she stood naked on the bank. Ailsa nodded as if the breeze had spoken a word of approval.

She stepped in, shivering. It was late in April, and the pond had not yet lost its winter chill, but she did not mind. The cold invigorated her as she moved toward the far end, where a waterfall cascaded over tumbled rocks from the stream bed above. Ailsa stretched out her arms and floated on the surface, closed her eyes as the water lapped around her, caressing her bare skin.

She ducked beneath the waterfall so the liquid brightness rushed over her face and down her shoulders. She paused, head tilted, as a lark began to sing, then another and another. Their song seemed to spring from the rushing water, to meld with it in a harmony so beautiful that she stood still to listen. Then the wind returned, undulating through the dimness, making the leaves shiver in a rhythm of wavering shadow and sunlight. Birds, wind, and water seemed to have been created for the wonder of this moment, this burst of harmony so perfect it could never be equaled by man.

But Ailsa had to try. She moved with agility toward the

bank, shuddered at the cold as she stepped onto the bracken and picked up her plaid to wrap around herself. She had no time for more. In an instant the song would be gone. She searched the wide pockets of her gown, found her flute, and began to play, to echo the ripple of water on stones, the rustle of leaves, and the lovely song of the larks overhead. It came naturally to her, this making of everyday sounds into music.

She could not remember a time when she had not loved the music of nature and wanted to re-create it. Ian had recognized her desire and carved her this flute of rosewood long ago. She took it with her everywhere. Not a day went by when she didn't stop, the flute to her lips, to make up a little song.

She closed her eyes, but the image of the copse did not leave her; instead it grew brighter. She was not aware that her body trembled in the insufficient plaid, nor that her skin was thoroughly chilled from the cold. These things did not matter. Then she heard a rich, deep voice.

> "A lark sang, aye so clear and true
> That the wind picked up its lovely song,
> And touched the water, woven through
> With streams of sunlight, frail yet strong."

Ailsa looked up in delight as Ian parted the leaves of the hawthorn tree where he'd been sitting. Without a word, she began the tune again so she would not forget it. Then she and Ian repeated the words together, their voices caught on the back of the wind.

Ian tumbled to the ground, rolled once, then jumped to his feet. Ailsa smiled at the dark hair that framed his face and curled down his neck to his shoulders. Her eyes met his, startlingly green in his tanned, dusky face.

Ian winked and gazed at her body, ill-concealed by her long, red plaid. It clung to her damply, flung carelessly over one shoulder so the other was bare and one breast only just covered by the wet wool. Crouched as she was on the marshy bank, her legs were bare from the knee down, as were her graceful arms. Her wet hair fell down her back to her waist. Even disordered as it was, he thought it beautiful when, as now, the scattered sunlight touched the clinging drops that glittered among the tangles.

Shivering, Ailsa noticed he was staring at her body as he had not done before, much as she had been looking at his of late—with more than just childish curiosity.

"Come," he murmured, scrutinizing the leaves overhead with pretended interest, "put your flute aside for a bit. There's somethin' I want to show ye." His hands shook when he shifted the black, yellow, and red Fraser plaid on his shoulder; suddenly he could not contain his impatience.

Ailsa's heart began to beat in expectation. Daily, Ian wandered the hills and valleys of Glen Affric, chasing his father's sheep and cattle, sometimes just exploring the deeply carved caves and mountains all around. As he went, he kept his eyes open for anything new or mysterious; his discoveries were varied and wonderful.

When she started to rise eagerly, Ian stopped her with a wave of his hand.

"Don't ye think ye'll get a bit cold, dressed that way?"

Ailsa blushed, clutching her damp plaid to her chest. She picked up her gown and underthings and motioned him away, uneasy, all at once, with her exposed limbs and clinging wool garment. "Be gone with ye, Ian Fraser, while I make myself decent."

Swiftly, he faded into the trees. When she was dressed once more in her linsey-woolsey gown, she moved downstream, past the broad pond, to leap barefoot over the burn, trailing her wet plaid behind her.

"Ye didn't have to dress up for me, lass," Ian said, grinning when he caught sight of her. His collie, Torran, named in the Gaelic for the sound of his growl, which was like the low rumble of distant thunder, pranced at his side, eager to be gone.

" 'Twasn't for ye," she responded playfully. "I did it for the spirits of the hills so they would welcome us." She picked up a twig, and as they walked she ran it through her hair until the last of the tangles were gone.

The wind whistled above them, urging them on. They hurried their steps until they were running through the bracken. The dog raced in front of them, barked at groups of sheep and cattle they passed now and then, and stopped to look back reproachfully when his master fell too far behind.

They paused when the magnificent hills and crags rose before them. Ian motioned to the dog. "Home, Torran," he said firmly. With a last regretful wag of his tail, the animal turned away. Taking Ailsa's hand, Ian guided her up the granite incline, much scarred from ancient water and ice. When the incline became steeper, he began to climb, hand over hand, while Ailsa followed, placing her feet carefully in the spots where he'd stepped in his loose leather sandals.

"We've no' yet been to this side," she said.

"But 'twas waitin' for us all the time," Ian said mysteriously. "Just waitin' for today."

"Tell me what ye found!" she demanded.

"Ye'll see soon enough." He hoisted himself over a fallen boulder, then reached back to help her after him.

Ailsa stopped to stare in wonder at a narrow dell she had never seen before. It was circled on all sides by jagged rocks as well as carefully placed standing stones that made the wind echo in eerie imitation of a lost human voice. This must have been a Druid temple once, though now it contained only three cairns—graves covered with tiny stones piled one upon the other—nearly hidden in the shadow of the rocks. The cairns were huge, as if they had been built upon year after year in careful reverence for the dead. The wind was caught here, circling madly among the ring of stones, screaming at its own impotence.

She knew instinctively that some tragedy had occurred in this place, felt an inexplicable need to drop her own stones onto the cairns, to show her respect for those who had been long dead. Then the wind howled, circled once above the dell, and disappeared into the wide, cloud-woven sky. With a sigh of relief, Ailsa turned to find Ian beside her.

" 'Tis just the beginnin'," he said. "Come."

He grasped her hand more tightly as they traversed the ledge, then, abruptly, he ducked beneath an overhang of rock and drew her down into a cavern. At first it was dark— too dark to see the rough walls, but slowly Ian and Ailsa moved toward a distant light and she saw that the top of the cave had crashed in.

Ian glanced up, eyes narrowed against the sunlight. "It can't have been over long this way," he whispered, "or what I found would have been destroyed by the light and air."

He pointed to a carved chest against the farthest wall of the cavern, nearly concealed by an overhang of rock. "What is't?" she gasped, startled by the overloud sound of her voice.

"I don't know yet," Ian admitted. "I wanted to open it with ye."

Touched that he had waited, Ailsa knelt beside the chest to lay her hands on the seasoned wood.

"We'll need light. I brought a torch." Ian ducked around a bend in the wall, then reappeared with a pine torch in his hand. He held it high so they could see, carved on the lid, "Chisholm, 1746."

"I'll wager the people who left this here were part of the '45," he murmured. He referred to the rebellion over a hundred years earlier when the Scottish clans had followed bonny Prince Charlie into battle. The Jacobite rebels had tried to take the throne of England from the Hanoverians and restore it to King James, Prince Charlie's father, the last of the royal Stewarts.

Ian held the torch steady and lifted one side of the lid while Ailsa lifted the other. They bent together to touch the bolt of Chisholm tartan that covered the contents. The plaid with stripes of white, blue, and green on a greenish-yellow background was easily recognizable. As small children they had memorized the Highland tartans along with their morning and evening prayers.

Ailsa lifted the plaid to admire the fine wool. It was whole and unharmed by either moths or dampness. The Chisholms had chosen their hiding place well. Beneath the plaid lay a miniature of the prince himself, the paint rubbed thin by the imprint of many reverent fingers. Beside it was a claymore, the heavy Highland sword banned by the English after the rebellion had failed. Ian touched the weapon respectfully, noticing the chips along the sides, the traces of dried blood. This blade had seen much service before it was hidden away.

Ailsa touched the cold metal and her anger at the English rose anew. It was not the last time they had come here to drive the Scottish inhabitants from their homes. Her mother had lost her family in the final Highland Clearances when greedy landlords had enlisted the aid of the English in removing the tenants from the hills to make way for more profitable sheep. Mairi had hidden herself and managed to stay, with a few others, in the area.

The image of her father came to Ailsa unbidden. He, too, was English—a stranger, a foreigner. But she had never thought of him that way. Somehow she had kept him separate in her mind from the history of his countrymen. It was necessary to her that he remain unstained by the sins of others.

When Ian removed the sword, Ailsa saw a fragile lace and satin wedding gown. Gently, she moved it aside to reveal an ancient hand harp. "A clarsach!" she cried in wonder. She had heard of the beautiful sounds such an instrument could make, but never had she seen one. She drew in her breath as Ian held it out to her. The wood was damaged on one side; it had cracked from age and usage no doubt. Still she was enchanted with the carved instrument that had been the only possession of the ancient Gaelic bards who had written and recorded the history of the Highlands in their songs.

As she ran her hand over the nine strings, they broke with a discordant twang. They had been too long hidden away, too long unused, too old to stand the pressure. Ailsa's eyes filled with tears. She believed, as had her Celtic ancestors, that the sin of all sins was to destroy beauty.

"Never mind," Ian said comfortingly, laying his hand on hers. The warmth of his touch diminished her sadness and she looked away from the harp. Next to the place where it had lain in the chest was an old diary. She had just opened the cover when Ian cried out, "Look!"

He held in his palm a circular brooch, carved silver with the Chisholm crest—the fern—worked into the intricate design. Around the graceful leaves were several emeralds.

Even in the poor light, they glittered. Ailsa sighed and reached out to touch it. " 'Tis the most beautiful thing I've ever seen," she whispered. "How could they leave it behind?"

"Some things are too precious to take to a strange land. Maybe they felt they left part of themselves here with these treasures."

At last, while Ian leaned over her shoulder, she began to flip through the diary. The name on the flyleaf was Janet Chisholm and the pages told a common story in those years of turmoil, 1745 and 1746. This woman's husband had been at the prince's side at the Battle of Culloden Moor and had been injured by an English bayonet that had cost him the use of his arm. When he returned at last, it was to tell Janet that the British army, under the command of William, Duke of Cumberland, was not far behind. Already, by his brutal actions against the vanquished Highlanders, Cumberland had earned himself the nickname the Butcher. The Chisholms had hidden in the cave and listened as the English marched through the town and over the countryside, burning, killing, raping, destroying. The footsteps had grown louder until they crossed the very rock above and echoed down the rough stone walls. But the English had not found the family.

Then, when the use of the Gaelic, the wearing of the tartan and kilt had been proscribed, and their weapons taken from them, the family had realized they had to leave the Highlands where they were no longer free. So they had hidden this chest and fled. Ailsa read the final entry aloud.

"Our last day among the hills we love, and, we pray, our last grief, though 'twill haunt us for the rest of our lives. We'll no' be forgettin' the Highlands, nor the voices of the past that speak to us here. We'll no' forget the burns, the tumblin' water over stones, the heather and the swirlin' mist. To forget these things would be to lose all hope, all beauty, all that we hold dear. We want to come back someday, but cannot know what will happen in the darkness ahead. If we don't return, and someone finds this place and shelters here, I wish them joy of my possessions. I take what joy I have with me across the wide sea. Let Niethe, God of

Waters, keep us safe. Mayhap in a new land, the horror will no' follow anymore.''

"I wonder if they made it to Canada or America," Ailsa said. ''But 'tis clear that after so long they'll no' be back for this. What shall we do?''

"Mayhap we were meant to find these things, to bring them into the light,'' Ian suggested.

Ailsa could not be certain of that, but one thing she did know: Ian had not found this cave by accident. He had been drawn here by some instinct beyond his knowledge, the same instinct that had bidden him return with her beside him. "Aye, these have been too long hidden away. We should take them from here and treasure them for the sake of those who left them behind.'' Her voice echoed upward, faded into the dark crevices of the cave. There was no other sound, no sigh of wind to deny her.

"So it shall be,'' Ian murmured solemnly.

"I think ye should have the tartan and the claymore.''

He nodded. "I'll hang them above the door.'' He said it fiercely as if, by displaying these things, he would defy the law that had been repealed long since. For the absent Chisholms he would do it; he would remember their plight each time he stepped beneath the doorframe. He would leave the claymore for another time. It was heavy and he could not easily get it down the steep hill. "Ye must have the harp,'' he said.

Ailsa shook her head. It hurt her to look at the instrument that had once made lovely music, but would do so no more.

"Then I'll take it,'' he said, "but ye have the brooch. And look, these ribbons might have been made for your hair.'' He held up several purple satin ribbons that fell like rippled midnight through his fingers.

"The ribbons, aye,'' she said, smiling with pleasure as she put them into her pocket. "But no' the brooch.'' She touched the circle of carved silver set with stones. '' 'Tis too valuable. I couldn't do it.''

"Well then, if no' for yourself, take it for your mother. She doesn't have many pretty things.''

Ailsa reread Janet Chisholm's words and reluctantly

nodded her head. Then she closed the book. "I'll leave this here," she said, "where it belongs." But as she turned to lay the diary in the chest, she hesitated. "I think I'll keep it after all," she whispered in a voice so low that Ian could barely hear her. "Because," she said slowly, enunciating each word as if she were uncertain of what the next might be, "I feel a strange kinship with this woman who lived and died a hundred years ago. As if we share a loss somehow."

Ian was disturbed as Ailsa seemed to retreat from him. "I don't know what ye mean."

"Neither do I. I just know I was meant to take it."

At last she became aware of the burst of colored light that filtered through the hole in the roof of the cave. The sun was setting outside. She turned to look at her friend, shook her head as if awakened from a dream, then slid the brooch and diary into her pocket. Ian draped the Chisholm plaid over his shoulder and, carrying the harp in his other hand, helped Ailsa to her feet. In silence, they moved toward the wash of reddish light that was softened and, oddly, warmed, by the mist that crept through the hole in the stone. "I don't like it when I can't reach ye," Ian said softly.

"Ye can always reach me, Ian. Ye know that." Ailsa glanced up at the red-streaked sky. The mauve and violet light swirled around them, shimmering over their upturned faces. "We must go," she added.

"Aye," he agreed half-heartedly. "But ye'll no' be goin' home in that wet plaid." He removed the garment and draped it over his arm. Then he wrapped her gently in the piece of Chisholm tartan.

She smiled in gratitude, clasped his hand, and drew him out of the cave. Carefully, one foot at a time, she climbed down the rocky hillside they had ascended an hour earlier.

When her feet met the springy earth, she paused to let the mist surround her; it was an old friend that touched the familiar landscape with mystery, making it new, unknown, exciting.

She heard Ian drop to the ground beside her.

"Home," Ailsa said with a smile as Ian shifted the harp in the crook of his arm.

"Ye go first," he told her. "And ye choose the poem."

She thought for a moment. "LOVE was a pilgrim dressed in gray."

Ian responded with the second line. "LOVE was a Minstrel blithe and gay."

As soon as he'd finished, Ailsa was off. She moved lithely, staring at the ground to make out familiar rocks and hillocks so she did not stumble. The fog parted to reveal the copse ahead, then shifted to cover the group of trees with a thin veil of white. Aware of the growing chill, she clutched her plaid tightly as she made her way at last to the group of tall birches. Here she stopped, her back against a smooth trunk, to whistle a single, lingering note.

Ian stood at the foot of the hillside, listening intently for Ailsa's whistle. With the shifting of the wind, it was not easy to judge the direction from which it had come. That made it more difficult to find her. But that was part of the fun.

They had played this game of tag in the mist since they were children, making an adventure and a challenge of what might otherwise have been a threat. When he heard Ailsa's signal, Ian grinned. Clever, the way she could put so many nuances of tone into a single note. At once he started after her, head bent to search for braes and clumps of bracken, until he caught up with her in the copse. She was looking the other way so he crept up to grasp her around the waist. She gasped with surprise, then laughter.

"LOVE was a maid that wouldna stay," she chanted, picking up the words of the song where they had left off.

"LOVE was a bairn that ran away," he answered.

"O LOVE COME BACK TO ME," they said together.

"Ye made no' a sound," Ailsa scolded when the verse was done. " 'Tisn't fair that ye should have such quiet footsteps. My own seem to echo up and down the glen."

Ian grinned. "LOVE was the gentle seneschal."

"Did carefully provide for all," she replied without hesitation.

"Hush," he whispered suddenly. "I think I hear a mountain blackbird."

Ailsa looked up, listening for the song of the rare bird. Before she realized it, Ian was gone. He had disappeared as silently as he had come.

She waited breathlessly until she heard his whistle carried on the wind. Some instinct led her sideways and back, rather than forward. It was one of Ian's favorite tricks to confuse her and make the game last longer. This time she was not fooled. She caught up to him at the edge of the moor that stretched across the hollow toward the distant mountains.

"Who came with flowers and water sweet," Ian murmured.

"LOVE wore the wreaths and bathed the feet."

"O LOVE COME BACK TO ME," they sang in unison.

"Ian Fraser," Ailsa cried, grasping his arm in chilled fingers, "we'll never get home if ye keep runnin' backward."

He smiled. "Mayhap I don't wish ye to get home."

She leaned toward him. As he reached out to touch her, she slipped away. "LOVE was fire and LOVE was ice."

Before the last word had faded, Ian added, "LOVE bidden once came ever twice."

Then Ailsa was gone.

When he caught up to her, she leaned close to whisper in his ear. "LOVE came to scorn as well as sighs."

"LOVE was the pearl without a price."

Together they chanted, "O LOVE COME BACK TO ME."

Thus they covered the landscape they could walk in their dreams, laughing as they repeated the ancient song. Sometimes they stopped to catch their breath and stared at each other through wisps of white silence that dimmed their imperfections and drew them closer somehow. In those moments, they did not speak, but only listened to the rise and fall of each other's breath, their faces so close that their lips nearly touched—but only nearly. One or the other always turned away at the last moment.

Once, Ailsa was certain she had lost Ian; she had heard no sound from him for so long. She was nearing home and wondered if he had decided to veer off to his own croft on the way. She peered about her curiously and whistled once more. At the same instant, she heard a whistle behind her and realized she and Ian stood back to back. They laughed, for neither had known how close the other was, then turned slowly as the thick mist changed to rain.

Ian watched the tiny drops collect on Ailsa's chestnut hair, her forehead, and the bridge of her nose, like a fine soft veil. She smiled at him shyly, disconcerted by his perusal. "LOVE was the happy weddin' tide."

"LOVE was the granted, the denied," she answered.

"LOVE was the bridegroom, LOVE the bride."

"LOVE was all in the world beside."

They stood with the rain falling between them. Slowly Ian raised his left hand and Ailsa her right. They touched palms while the moisture gathered on their skin. "O LOVE COME BACK TO ME," they whispered together.

He had touched her thus many times before. As children they had clasped hands, run, and tumbled on the moors. But somehow this moment was different. Ailsa stood perfectly still, her palm pressed to Ian's. The rain swirled around, isolating them, so there was nothing but their two bodies, their hands, their eyes, feverish with a dissatisfaction neither could explain.

"I must go," she said at last.

Ian nodded, but still they stood, their fingers locked together until the mist dried on their palms and the warmth of their sweat replaced it.

"Go," Ian said finally, though he released her with reluctance. " 'Tis long past time."

"Long past time," she repeated dreamily. "Aye, so 'tis." She smiled, then turned toward the shelter of her mother's croft built into the nearby hillside. With her plaid over her head, she went, looking back only once to see Ian absorbed by the rain, consumed by it, until she could see him no more.

2

Ailsa pushed the door inward and ducked beneath the low, warped doorframe. She stood for a moment, blinking, confused by the rush of warmth that greeted her. The mist seemed to follow her inside; she felt that only the twilight was real and not the packed dirt floor or blackened stone walls of the croft. For a moment more, she was caught in the web of her waking dreams. Then, slowly, the fire in the center of the room and the smell of roasting mutton brought her back to earth.

She focused on the everyday things that made up her home—the loom in the corner, the spinning wheel, the huge black pot over the fire, the simple oak table where her mother sat with a newly finished bolt of cloth.

Ailsa frowned when she saw a momentary reflection of the gloaming in Mairi Rose's eyes. Once, her mother had known this feeling, too. "I've brought ye somethin'," the girl said. She picked up the brooch and displayed it with pride.

Mairi stared at the jewelry in her daughter's hand. The silver gleamed dully and the firelight touched the emerald facets, making them glow.

"I couldn't take such a thing. Where did it come from, anyway?"

" 'Twas a gift from Anu," Ailsa said with a playful smile.

Anu was the Celtic goddess of abundance and prosperity whom the Highlanders still worshiped while the minister of the local kirk looked the other way. Mairi shook her head. "Fools make feasts and wisemen eat 'em, and I'll no' be cookin' tonight. Tell me the truth."

26

"Ian and I found it in a chest hidden in a cave. Please listen," Ailsa added quickly when she saw her mother was going to object again. She reached into her voluminous pocket, found the diary, and read the last page. "Janet Chisholm would have wanted ye to have it. I know she would."

Mairi considered, brow furrowed. "Aye," she said at last, "she might at that." She rose and went to the dresser against the far wall to put the brooch in her special place—a carved rosewood box that had once been her mother's, in which she kept all her treasures.

Ailsa held her breath, as she always did when the box was opened. Beside it stood the miniature of Charles Kittridge he had left behind. Inside the box were the letters he had sent since, one or two a year, along with the gifts he had included from many countries. As a member of the British Diplomatic Service, he traveled all over the Empire in Queen Victoria's service. Everywhere he went, he found something for Mairi.

Ailsa had examined each gift, held it in her hands, tried to imagine what her father must have felt bundling it up to send to the woman who had turned him away. She soon realized that the objects carried no feeling within them; they were poor attempts to lure her mother to him with tokens of the splendor of a world she would never see.

But the letters were different; they were a part of her father. Ailsa had read each one of them many times, beginning with the note Charles had written on the day he discovered his wife had left him. That single piece of parchment revealed anguish, accusation, and a regret so real that Ailsa felt it each time she touched the well-worn page. All the others were the same, full of sadness, though the words were cheerful and Charles spoke with excitement and wonder of the places he was discovering. The words enchanted his daughter, made her want to join him, to see those worlds, to know their mysteries, to share their strange, exotic magic with the man who was her father.

Each time her mother opened the box, Ailsa expected a wisp of smoke to rise in the air, a residue of all the hopes and secrets hidden inside.

27

Mairi looked at the Chisholm brooch once more, long-ingly. "I'll keep it here in trust for the day when 'tis wanted again." Then she laid it among her other treasures.

Ailsa noticed that her mother's fingers brushed the image of Charles Kittridge and lingered there a moment. Then, with an effort, she shrugged her thoughts away and turned back to her daughter, eyes twinkling. "There's to be mutton for supper, as ye can tell."

The girl sniffed appreciatively at the fragrance of mutton seasoned with rosemary, thyme, and garlic that filled the room. "I thought we'd eaten the last of the meat weeks ago."

"And so we did," Mairi agreed. "But Angus Fraser brought us a leg o' lamb today. Said he had to slaughter another sheep and we might as well share in the feast. Bless him."

Ailsa nodded. She sometimes wondered if she and her mother would have survived without the help of Ian, his father, and brother Duncan, before that young man had gone away to Glasgow to make his fortune. The two women had no man to see to their needs, so the Frasers and others in the glen had taken on that responsibility, though Mairi never asked for their help. They said it was in payment for the cloth she wove and made into clothing. They said they could never repay her for her knowledge of the secrets of herbs which had saved many a life in the isolated hills of Glen Affric.

They said these things, but it was not quite the truth, at least not all of it. Angus Fraser had once voiced the real reason. "We have struggled long and hard just to stay among the hills we love. There's been sufferin' enough without lettin' our neighbors go hungry. The world outside the glen doesn't care for us, so we must see to ourselves."

Ailsa closed her eyes, enjoyed the smell of cooking meat. The small house welcomed her, put her at ease. She touched the thick stone walls with affection.

"Ye'd best get your things off and dry yourself out," Mairi cautioned when Ailsa drew off the plaid to reveal her wet hair. "Sit by the fire and tell me your stories."

Ailsa did as her mother asked, drawing a stool next to

the peat fire, holding her chilled hands above the flames. She
began to recount her day. Only then did she remember the
plants she had gathered, then left in the basket near the
river.

"Don't fret," Mairi said calmly. "They'll be where ye
left them tomorrow, no doubt, unless the deer are at them."
As she spoke, she began to prepare the cabbage for dinner.

Ailsa helped by clearing the fabric and rowans of wool
from the table. She folded the tartan cloth carefully, placing
it on the chest in the corner, and laid the rowans beside the
spinning wheel to be worked into thread later. Finally, she
set out wooden bowls and horn spoons worn smooth by
years of use.

"Jenny Mackensie came to see ye today," Mairi said.

Ailsa looked up, barely conscious of the nimble movement of her fingers as she pared carrots to add to the huge
cooking pot over the fire. She had seen less and less of her
friend of late. Now her time was spent alone or with Ian;
once the three of them had often been together. She missed
Jenny sometimes. Missed the way they used to giggle at
nothing and the secrets they had shared, hiding them gleefully from the adults. Now her secrets belonged to Ian.

"She and her family will be by after supper, and the
Frasers as well no doubt. Mayhap even the Macdonnells."

Ailsa grinned in expectation. The evenings when friends
gathered in the croft were always great fun. She would have
time enough alone with her thoughts after she'd crawled
between the sheets and drawn the quilt over her head.

After supper was eaten and the meat stored away for
tomorrow's brose, Ailsa laid out butter, cheese, milk, and
oatcakes for the guests. She brewed two large pots of precious tea and checked to see that they had lager enough.
She was excited as she laid the griddle over the fire and
prepared *bannoch claiche*—stone cakes to be cooked on a
flat, round pan.

She had brushed out her hair and washed her feet, then
removed the first bannoch from the fire when Angus Fraser
entered the croft with his family behind him. They did not
knock, for the door was never closed, except in the un-

friendly winter. It was so all over the Highlands; the Scots were proud of their hospitality and would no more think to turn a guest away than they would to waste a piece of meat or take the life of a friend.

Ailsa greeted Angus and Flora Fraser, Flora's mother, Anne Macdonnell and Ian's sisters Megan and Kirstie before she met Ian's gaze. He grinned, depositing his bagpipe in a corner out of the way.

"Hoots!" Angus called in his booming voice. "Come away from your spinnin' for the while, Mairi Rose, and enjoy the company of your friends."

"I'll enjoy your company from here. Just because my hands are busy doesn't mean my ears can't hear nor my mouth speak."

Flora punched her husband in the arm. "Give up, ye fool. Ye've been tryin' for years to make her leave her wheel and ye've never won yet."

Angus turned as his daughters tumbled, laughing, over the wooden settle by the fire, spilling their dolls onto the floor. "Be soft, ye noisy bairns," Anne Macdonnell shouted so loudly that her voice echoed off the walls, "else how am I to hear myself think?"

While Angus poured ale into the cup he'd brought with him, Anne settled into the rocking chair. The children sat at her feet while the others drew up polished birch chairs.

Flora helped Ailsa arrange the bannochs on a wooden platter as others began to arrive. First came Jenny Mackensie, her mother Christian and her father Callum as well as his father Geordie, who hovered at the door. Finally, Colin Munro tramped in, shaking the earth from his leather sandals and the droplets of moisture from his hair. He was followed by the Grants, Andrew and Catriona, who'd apparently left the children at home.

As always, every man had brought his favorite *quach;* each cup was different, formed of pieces of colored wood and hooped in brass or silver. Ailsa scurried about pouring ale while Flora served the ladies tea in the carved wooden cups she had taken from the press in the kitchen. When everyone was seated, except Andrew Grant, who stood in the doorway, and Geordie Mackensie, who stood outside beneath the stars, smoking his horn pipe and listening, Angus Fraser began to talk about the expected rise in temperature and the heavy rains that were sure to fall. He asked Andrew how his cattle were faring and there followed a heated discussion of the best feed for cows in spring.

The women listened and watched the children as they tumbled about on the floor, rattling the strings of red rowan berries they wore around their necks. The girls had spent most of the afternoon stringing the berries they'd picked from the mountain ash, and wanted everyone to notice their new treasures. Ailsa took a string in her hand and admired it, which brought a dimpled smile to Megan Fraser's face.

Finally, Flora turned to Ailsa. "Ian tells me ye found a chest of treasures in a cave today. Seems as though the Chisholms left it behind when they fled."

"Aye," Ailsa said. She met Ian's gaze and he smiled slowly, knowingly. "There were treasures indeed."

Before she could continue, Geordie Mackensie stooped beneath the doorframe and moved closer to the fire. "The Chisholms fought on both sides in the '45, ye ken. Brother against brother 'twas, and a sadder sight ye'll never see. My mother told me how 'twas." He puffed on his long, graceful pipe and stared at the soot-blackened ceiling, as if trying to recall the details.

The others leaned forward eagerly. Geordie could be counted on to tell a good tale. Stories of the disastrous '45 were always favorites, even though the Highlanders had lost, because, against appalling odds, they had risked everything to try.

" 'Twas the Laird Chisholm's great grief that his older sons, John and James, chose to fight with the Sassenach, the English enemy," Geordie continued. He stared out the tiny window, looking into the past, winding together the threads of a life he had never lived. Yet he was as familiar with that life as he was with his own. " 'Twas a greater grief by far when so many of his men were killed at the Battle of Culloden Moor. The wailin' that rose from that field, from all Scotland for years after 'twas long over, was more than man nor beast could bear. Those who survived were like to die of sorrow at the sound."

Silence had fallen. The only light was the glow from the fire, but it was enough to show the concentration on every face. Even the children had abandoned their wooden dolls to listen.

Geordie rubbed his chin, ran his fingers through his gray beard. "After Culloden, 'twas three Chisholms who hid in the cave with our prince in Glen Moriston to wait out the fury of the Butcher. 'Tis said that the Laird Hugh shook the prince's hand when they parted and never offered it to another thereafter."

"I wonder why the Chisholms never came back," young Jenny Mackensie mused aloud.

Geordie shrugged. "Ye know what they say, lass: A burnt bairn fire dreads."

Angus Fraser raised his cup. "To the '45! May we never forget!"

Every cup was raised as all cried in unison, "To the '45!"

Even Mairi stopped spinning long enough to take a drink.

" 'Tis time for a song, Angus, don't ye think?" she suggested, turning back to her rowans of wool.

" 'Tis indeed," her friend replied with enthusiasm. He picked up the fiddle he'd left under his chair. He ran the bow across the strings once or twice, then began to play and sing.

"Come ye by Athol, lad with the philabeg,
Down by the Tummel, or banks o' the Garry,
Saw ye our lads, with their bonnets and white cockades,
Leavin' their mountains to follow Prince Charlie?"

Ailsa, Ian, and the others joined in the refrain, repeating the words they had known from childhood.

"Follow thee! follow thee! who wouldna follow thee?
Long hast thou loved and trusted us fairly!
Charlie, Charlie, who wouldna follow thee,
King o' the Highland hearts, bonny Prince Charlie?"

Ailsa's voice rose as she thought of the men who had rushed to answer the prince's cry for help. The same men who, a few months later, had hidden in caves like hunted animals. Men who, had the prince called them again, would have answered again, even knowing before they went what the cost would be.

"I have but one son, my gallant young Donald;
But if I had ten, they should follow Glengarry!
Health to McDonnell and gallant Clan-Ranald,
For these are the men that will die for their Charlie!"

Ailsa took her flute from her pocket and began to play as Flora, Jenny, and Christian stamped their feet on the floor.

"Down through the Lowlands, down with the Whigamore!
Loyal true Highlanders, down with them rarely!
Ronald an' Donald, drive on, with broad claymore,
Over the necks of the foes o' Prince Charlie!

"Follow thee! follow thee! who wouldna follow thee? . . ."

By the time the song was finished, the guests were clapping and stamping their feet so loudly that the clatter drowned the sound of their own voices. Through the din, Andrew Grant called, "To your pipes, Ian Fraser! I've a mind to hear the cry of the Son o' the Wind."

Ian retrieved the instrument from the corner. With the bag under his right arm, he caught one pipe in his mouth and poised his fingers over the chanter. He tuned the reeds and nodded to Ailsa, who took up her flute and began to play, a slow tune that grew more lively note by note until it raced and tumbled over itself. Slowly, Ian backed into the doorway and picked up the song. The sound of the pipes reverberated through the night air. It rushed and trembled, flowed like rumbling water, sang like the birds with a hundred different voices.

Angus watched his son with pride, then propped his fiddle under his chin and joined in the song. The two little girls clasped hands and began to dance around the fire. Flora

Fraser could not resist joining her daughters. Together, they stamped out a Highland reel just beyond the reach of the flames.

Ian's face was flushed with exertion, his eyes bright. Ailsa sensed his exhilaration and played more fiercely, until her notes rose and mingled with his like the wild sweetness of wind in the trees. It was as if, without speaking, they touched each other across the flames, so instinctively did they respond to the slightest change in tone or rhythm.

Jenny Mackensie shook her straight brown hair over her shoulders and moved away from the glow of the fire. She did not want anyone to read the thoughts in her hazel eyes. She saw how Ian and Ailsa looked at each other across the room, communicating without words. The sight left her feeling hollow. She had dreamed of Ian Fraser for many long nights, and the end of the dream was always the same. Jenny stood alone, surrounded by shadows, watching Ian and Ailsa dance together in the sunlight.

"Come out of the darkness and dance, Jenny," Ian cried. "Your feet are itchin' to be movin' and well ye know it. Dance!"

She rose at the sound of his voice, could not resist doing so. She forced a smile when her father joined her. Callum grasped his daughter's hand on one side and Flora's on the other, while Christian and Geordie joined the dancers. Linked together now, they circled the fire to the skirling music of the pipes, laughing and stamping, dipping and turning.

Mairi glanced up to see a long look pass between her daughter and Ian. She felt a flutter of unease and wondered why. She had known this was coming, known it long before the two children ever suspected the strength of the tie that bound them together. But now that the moment had come, she remembered Charles and her heart felt heavy. She dropped the rowan of wool she'd been spinning into yarn and the motion of the wheel ceased.

There were more songs, many peats added to the fire, much laughter when Anne Macdonnell pulled a carved jumping jack from her pocket and began to dance it on her knee for her fascinated but sleepy-eyed granddaughters. The dancers collapsed, exhausted and laughing, in the warm light of the flames.

When the moon began to sink behind the mountains, the first guests drifted away. Ian moved from the doorway so the others could go. He stood watching Ailsa as she took the cups and stacked them on the table, bade her guests good-bye, and glanced once or twice at her mother, who seemed oddly silent tonight.

Finally, only the Frasers were left.

"I thank ye kindly for the cakes and ale," Angus said formally. "I'll no' even mention that ye stopped your spinnin' half the night. 'Tisn't in my nature to gloat."

"Be off with ye," his wife said, grinning. " 'Tisn't in your nature to keep your mouth shut when 'tis wise."

They all laughed, and the Frasers, carrying their two tired daughters between them, stepped out into the darkness. Ian was the last to go. He paused in the doorway, smiled at Mairi, and nodded to Ailsa, who smiled in return. No word passed between them, indeed none had all night, but they had spoken many promises in that moment, and Mairi knew it as well as they.

When Ian's footsteps had faded away, and silence fell once again over the croft, Mairi lit a tallow candle and went to sit at the table with her wooden comb in her hand. Slowly, while Ailsa watched, perplexed, she began to braid her long red hair.

Mairi usually wore her hair down or pulled back with a leather thong or piece of colorful ribbon. Never had she braided it as she did now, carefully, intently, each turn of her fingers slow and deliberate.

"Why are ye doin' that?" Ailsa asked.

Mairi did not look up from her task. "Because ye're a woman now. 'Tis time I learned to act my age."

The girl gasped. "Ye're no' old," she cried. "Ye couldn't ever be old."

Now Mairi glanced up. "Ye may be a woman, but ye've a deal yet to learn." She turned back to her task, winding and weaving, twisting and turning. Thus she also wove her cloth, as if the pattern of her hair mattered as much. She used the rhythm of her movements to help her think, just as

35

she did when she worked at the loom. "Sit down, Ailsa," she said at last, when she had fastened the end of the long braid with a leather thong.

Ailsa did as her mother bade her. "What is't, Mother, that troubles ye?"

Mairi took her daughter's hand. "There are things ye should know, lass, before ye become a woman indeed. 'Tis well in some ways to leave childhood behind; there are many wonders bairns can't know. But ye must take care."

"I don't understand."

Mairi frowned. "How can ye, Ailsa-*mo-ghray*, when ye've known so little pain in your life? I don't think ye realize that 'tis possible to love someone too much, then find that after all, he's no more than a stranger." She was thinking back to the few short months she had shared with Charles—a man called by a voice she could not hear, to explore a world she could not understand. Yet she had always known that, from the first moment she laid eyes on him. She had simply refused to face it.

Ailsa shook her head. "I know Ian as I know myself."

"Aye," Mairi replied. "But still ye can make a mistake and find great sorrow."

Her daughter did not believe it. "The only sorrow in my life is because I've never known my father," she said.

Mairi smiled her sad, knowing smile. Only now did she realize how much she wanted to protect Ailsa from the grief she guessed awaited her. In that way, Mairi was unlike the other Highlanders, who raised their children by strict rules, showing them little affection or softness. Mairi could not be harsh with her daughter; she gave to Ailsa all the gentle care and tenderness she would have given Charles, had he stayed with her.

The girl considered her mother doubtfully. "I don't think—"

Mairi sighed. "Ye'll no' believe till ye see for yourself. 'Tis enough for the moment that ye think about what I've said. Off to bed with ye, birdeen. Ye'll be needin' your rest."

Ailsa was reluctant to leave her mother while she had that dark, shadowed look in her eyes. "Shall I stay with ye awhile?"

Mairi looked up in surprise. "No. I would be alone tonight, to think and remember."

Ailsa nodded and rose from the table. On the way to her bed against the far wall, she stopped to look at the miniature of her father. She did not need the light of day, nor a candle or lamp to see by; she knew the lines and hollows of that face by heart.

She touched the tiny painting reverently, unaware that her mother watched her in distress, disturbed by the look on her daughter's face. Mairi wondered, not for the first time, about the letter she had sent Charles soon after Ailsa's birth. Why had he not responded? Had he even received it? She thought that she would never know.

Mayhap tomorrow he'll return, Ailsa thought. Make it tomorrow, she prayed silently, as she did each night. She turned, saw the look of hurt on her mother's face, and felt an unexpected flash of anger at the shadowed image of Charles Kittridge. She had never hated him simply for being English, as many Highlanders would have. But for her own sake, and for Mairi's, she hated him sometimes. "Why hasn't he come back?" she demanded. "Doesn't he know how much we need him?"

"Mayhap he doesn't," Mairi replied without rancor. No matter how much anger she felt when she thought of Charles, she had never let Ailsa see it. Perhaps she had been wrong.

"But he's traveled all over the world. He knows so much; I've seen it in his letters. Why doesn't he know that?" Ailsa turned, the dying firelight on her face, to wait for an answer.

"He's just a man, Ailsa. He makes mistakes like ye and me."

Ailsa shook her head in denial. Mairi loved him, didn't she? Enough that she had never taken another man, though some had offered. Enough to choose solitude over the warmth and comfort of a husband beside her at night. Enough that, even after seventeen years, her grief at his loss still showed in her eyes.

"Why didn't ye go with him, Mother?" Ailsa asked unexpectedly.

"Because I was afraid." Her mother was surprised into telling the truth.

"Of what?" It was the one answer the girl had not anticipated, the only one she could not believe. She had never known her mother to feel fear.

Mairi took a deep breath. "Of myself, of my feelin's, and of somethin'—" She broke off, unable to continue. " 'Twill be a day when ye need to know about that other fear, but 'tis no' yet come. Now go."

Ailsa saw the stubborn glint in her mother's eyes and knew she would learn no more tonight. She went to open the sliding doors of her box bed, revealing the heather mattress and the quilt her mother had made for her. Silently, still aware of Mairi sitting at the table, chin in hand, her daughter took off her gown and put on a warm nightrail. Then she removed Janet Chisholm's diary from her pocket and put it beside her pillow. The forgotten purple ribbons scattered across the pillowcase and she picked them up, rubbed the soft satin against her cheek, let the strands spill through her fingers. She would put them in her kist, she decided.

Ailsa went to the carved chest where she kept the linens and undergarments she had made over the years, the needlework and ribbons and lace she had collected, which made up her "providing" for the day when she became a wife. Everything was stored in this chest until she should need it. As she opened the lid, the fragrance of herbs rose to meet her: they kept the garments free of moths and smelling sweet. She reached for the shottle in the corner—the tiny box where she kept the most precious of her possessions. She touched the piece of heather Ian had picked on the hillside one day, the dried wild rose he had given her last Beltaine, a few colored ribbons, but none as bright and soft as these. She let the satin slide from her hand into the box, ran her fingers over the neatly folded linens, sniffed the fragrant herbs once more, then closed the lid.

Finally she returned to bed. Though the image of Charles's face was still with her, she knew she would not dream of him tonight, but of Ian and that moment in the mist-shrouded gloaming.

She was wrong.

Much later, when the moon had cast its light over the hills outside her window, Ailsa dreamed of a woman standing on a high crag above the sea. She saw chestnut hair whipped by the wind, the slight, long-legged figure of the woman, and thought it was herself. Then she realized that the woman was old and the landscape unfamiliar—bleak, barren, completely unknown.

As the woman stood looking out across the water, Ailsa had the sense that she was reaching back in time and place to another moment, another life. There was an infinite sadness about her; her face was lined and worn from work and grief. She cried out once, a single mournful note, and extended her arms as if to ease the aching need to touch a familiar hand. But there was no one to answer.

Ailsa cried out, wanting to soothe the woman's sorrow, but as their hands met over the turbulent, blue-gray water, she awakened.

She sat up in bed, the image of the dream still strong within her, and realized that the woman had worn the Chisholm plaid. There'd been something in the stranger's eyes meant for Ailsa alone—a warning without words of pain and suffering to come. The girl shivered, even with the warmth of the quilt around her. She leaned her head against the tiny square of the window, pushing the leather aside to let the cold air touch her, remind her of the beauty of the hills and glen she loved.

But tonight those things did not console her. She felt instead a sense of impermanence, of impending loss. Strangely, in that moment, she did not think of Ian, but of Charles, the stranger in a foreign land. She missed him tonight, wanted so desperately to know him, even for a moment, if that were all she could have. How, she wondered, could she grieve so much for a man she had never even met?

3

Ailsa woke just before dawn to the sound of her mother working at the loom. Mairi had placed an oil lamp nearby, which cast a pool of yellow light around her, though her fingers were so deft that she could weave her fabrics in the dark.

Mairi smiled as she tamped down the meshwork of newly woven wool. There was a pleasant feel to the morning, whose pale gray light had begun, slowly, to filter through the leather squares that covered the windows to keep out cold and rain.

Ailsa sensed her mother's tranquillity; despite her mood last night, there would be no shadows in Mairi's eyes today. The girl rose, quickly smoothed the handmade linen sheets and slid the doors to her box bed closed. Shivering at the early morning chill, she dressed in chemise and drawers covered by a plain green linsey-woolsey gown. While Mairi continued to work, Ailsa prepared the porridge for breakfast, laying out leftover scones, along with nutmeg and butter. She poured two wooden cups full of milk from the bucket in the coolest corner of the kitchen.

"Why don't ye stop a minute and have somethin' to eat?" she asked her mother at last.

Mairi nodded. "Soon, *mo-graidh*, soon."

Ailsa stood beside the loom as her mother moved the shuttle through warp and weft, creating a vivid pattern of red and green. " 'Tis to be the royal Stewart tartan, then?" she asked.

"Aye, again. 'Twill be a blanket for those at the Hill o' the Hounds. The English never seem to tire of the Scottish royal pattern." Mairi looked up for the first time. "Ye'd

40

think they'd seen enough of the Stewarts long since. I can only suppose," she added dryly, "that to a Sassenach mind, bedcovers have nothin' to do with politics."

She rose, stretched her cramped muscles, and sat across from Ailsa while they ate warm porridge with butter melted through it and nutmeg sprinkled on top.

"Today I'm for the Hill to learn what I can learn," Ailsa said, placing her empty cup on the table. The English Lord and Lady Williston lived at the Hill o' the Hounds and Mairi wove much of the fabric for the Lady and her daughter. On one of Lady Williston's visits to choose a new bolt of cloth, she had heard Ailsa playing her flute outside. She had listened for a full half hour, then insisted that the girl be given lessons right along with the Lord's children. It was partial payment, she said, for the fine and unusual fabrics Mairi created.

"I'd best be at my chores early or the bairns will have worn Master James down before I even arrive."

"Be off with ye, then," Mairi said. "But 'tis back to the royal Stewart I'm goin'."

Her daughter hummed with the rhythm of the loom as she rinsed the dishes in a pail of clear water and set them away in the cupboard. When she had swept the floor of the croft, she took a bowl of dried corn to feed the chickens and a pail for milking the cow. These tasks completed, she turned to weeding the low-walled garden, where cabbage, potatoes, carrots, leeks, beans, and peas grew in abundance. Finally she cared for the secluded corner where Mairi grew her precious herbs. Ailsa watered them lightly and picked some of the thyme and rosemary. Not until she had placed the herbs on the windowsill to dry and gone to find the creel for gathering peats did she remember that she had left the basket full of plants and roots by the river the day before.

She hurried away without her plaid; she liked to feel the fine mist drift through her hair. While the sun burned away the pearly light of early morning, she ran across the clearing toward the woods, leaving the imprint of her bare feet on the grass.

Ailsa found the basket at the base of a rowan tree where she had left it. She noticed with relief that the deer had not discovered it during the night. Picking up the laden creel, she started toward home, taking the long way past the rocky outcroppings beyond the woods.

She stopped when she saw Ian crouched beneath a ledge, his face hidden by the shadow of the overhang. Torran bounded through the heather nearby, growling at a rabbit.

"What ails ye?" she asked breathlessly as she sat by Ian's side. She knew from his expression that all was not well.

He looked up, frowning. "I was out lookin' to find my father's missin' sheep, and when I stopped to rest beneath this ledge, a strange feelin' came over me—" He broke off abruptly and reached for her hand. "Don't go to the Hill today, Ailsa. Come with me instead." His eyes were glittering, wild.

He had said the same many times, but never with so much vehemence. "I want to go, *mo-charaid*. Please try to understand. I know so little about music and there is so much to learn."

"Ye know enough," he said obstinately. "Your heart tells ye what to do and your ear. Ye need only listen to the voices of the glen to know how to make music."

"I can't learn to play the harp and piano by listenin' to the wind on the water. There are things beyond the glen, Ian. Things I wish to know."

"Why can't ye be happy with what ye have? Pianos and harps don't belong among these mountains and well ye know it. They don't belong any more than those Sassenach strangers do. 'Tis our glen, no' theirs."

"They let us be, Ian Fraser. Why can't ye let them be?"

"Why must ye always defend them?"

"My father is one of them," she reminded him.

"Aye, and that's why ye go to the Hill to learn their London ways. 'Tis for him, isn't it?"

" 'Tis for me alone," Ailsa replied fiercely.

"I know ye too well to believe that. 'Tis for your father."

"I have to go." She rose quickly so he would not see the truth in her eyes. "I'll be late and they'll no' be waitin' for me. I'll come to ye later, when I'm free."

" 'Tis one thing ye'll never be free of," Ian called after her, "those dreams of your father that fill your head both day and night."

He was angry, and more; she could feel his distress in her own racing pulse. But she did not stop or turn around. When she could no longer hear his voice, she prayed for silence, but instead heard the soft-spoken question Mairi had asked her long ago. "Ye go to the Hill as if 'twere a kirk and ye a worshiper there. Why is't so important to ye?"

"Because of my father," the girl had said before she stopped to think. "I want to learn all I can so I'll be ready when he comes for me."

Mairi had looked away. "He'll no' be comin' back, birdeen. 'Tis time ye realize that."

"He'll be back," her daughter had insisted. "I know it."

The despair in her mother's eyes had filled her with fear. "What is't?" Ailsa had asked.

"Only that sometimes I see a trace of your father in ye."

" 'Tis nothin' to weep for," the girl had said, relieved.

"No," Mairi had whispered. "No' yet."

Ailsa had not understood, and her mother had refused to explain. The girl had not let Mairi change her mind then; she did not let Ian do so now. She must continue her lessons at the Hill, no matter what anyone said. She did not question the need that drove her; she only knew she must follow where it led.

Ailsa stopped at the croft only long enough to leave the creel beside the settle, then she set out again, hurrying through the woods. In a short time, she reached the edge of the trees, where the moor stretched to the base of the Hill. The Willistons' huge, formal house sat at the top, overlooking the loch on one side and the glen on the other. Where the moor ended, Scotland seemed to end. The English had attempted to tame and control the landscape, to shape it into a memory of home. The gardeners spent hours every day fighting a hopeless battle against nature, which wanted to take back this land and make it as wild as it had once been.

Slowly, Ailsa went up the hill and lifted the heavy brass knocker. A maid appeared at once, dressed in a plain black gown with a single white ruffle around the neckline. Not a hair was out of place, nor was there a single crease in her gown. "Good morning, Miss Ailsa. The master is waiting in the music room. You know the way."

"Aye, Katie. And good mornin' to ye."

When Ailsa entered the hall, the door closed behind her with a thud, shutting out the glen as completely as if it had never been. She walked through the drawing room, dim and elegant with its Chippendale furniture, brocade settees, and heavy velvet drapes. The ceiling was high and vaulted, painted with cupids, angels, and gold-foil greenery. The muted light gave a touch of softness to the ornate furniture and huge, gold-framed portraits on the walls. Ailsa paused to listen to the ponderous silence that gave no hint of the wind that could shriek and moan through the hills beyond these walls.

Each time she entered this house, she felt that she was entering her father's world. When she moved down the long hall, she imagined Charles by the window, looking out at the view of the loch below. As elegant and refined as his surroundings, he would lean nonchalantly, one hand on the windowsill. His brow would be furrowed, his light brown hair falling over his forehead as he stared pensively through the glass and considered the landscape below. He was trying to understand the view, to absorb its beauty and comprehend it all at once.

In her mind he stood, staring, until he felt her presence. Then he would turn, see her, and smile. "Good morning, Ailsa," he would say.

" 'Tis a lovely day," she would answer as she stood beside him at the window.

"Even lovelier now that you're here," he'd tell her with a grin. She would blush and smile, pleased at the compliment.

The image was so real that she reached out to touch her father's arm, as if she would find cloth and flesh and bone instead of empty air.

"I won't!"

The illusion faded when the shout reverberated down the hall. A little boy barreled toward her, his cheeks vivid red. "I won't, I won't, I won't!" he repeated to the harassed woman who followed in his turbulent wake.

"Richard, darling, don't be difficult," his mother called, struggling to catch her breath. "You know it's time for your music lesson."

"I don't care," Richard puffed vehemently. "I don't want to stay in that stuffy old room. I want to go outside."

"But, darling, I've told you, it's dangerous in those woods. Why, you might be attacked by a wildcat or anything."

Richard paused and turned to face his mother. "I'm not afraid of a little old wildcat. I'd shoot it down before it had a chance to move."

Lady Williston shuddered. "Please don't talk like that. Can't you, just this once, be a good little boy? You're behaving quite badly in front of Ailsa. She's terribly shocked, I'm sure. Good morning, Ailsa," she added as an afterthought.

Richard crossed his chubby arms over his chest. "I don't care."

With a glimmer of a smile, Ailsa leaned down. "Mayhap if ye come with me to the music room, and if ye pay attention to the master, I'll tell ye a story after."

The boy frowned, considering. "A ghost story?"

"Aye, if ye like, so long as ye don't scare your sister."

Richard's eyes lit with expectation, but when he spoke, his tone was nonchalant. "All right then, but only for a little."

Lady Williston gave Ailsa a grateful smile and disappeared down the hall.

With Richard beside her, Ailsa reached the end of the hall, turned the crystal doorknob, and pushed the boy ahead of her into the music room. This was the brightest room in the house, situated at a corner with windows on two sides. Here the curtains were flowered chintz rather than velvet or brocade and the chairs were spidery and graceful. The tutor was already seated behind a music stand with Cecilia beside him. A thin man with perpetually untidy straw-colored hair,

45

he pointed hopefully to a series of notes while the girl repeated them again and again on her violin. Ailsa winced.

Master James looked up, smiling in relief. "Ah, there you are. I'd begun to think you weren't coming." He glanced down, as he always did, at her bare feet. He could not help himself. The idea of a young lady running about without shoes and stockings was abhorrent to him. But he would forgive Ailsa anything, because she had fingers that drew magic from piano and harp. She alone, of his students, had a natural ear for music; it was a delight to teach someone so eager to learn. If only she would wash her feet and wear button-top boots like a normal girl.

"Ye know I wouldn't miss a lesson, Master James."

He nodded. "Would you like to begin at the piano with Master Richard while I attempt to teach Cecilia this new song?"

Ailsa seated herself on the bench and folded back the piano lid. For a moment, she was unaware of the boy sliding onto the bench beside her as she ran her fingers gently over the keys, pleased by the trill of notes she created.

Richard reminded her forcefully of his presence when he pressed down as many keys as he could reach with all the strength in his small, round arms.

Ailsa shook her head. "No' like that, Master Richard. Like this." She positioned his hands over the keys and showed him how to touch them lightly, to follow her lead as she ran through the scales. To her, even that simple exercise had beauty. But Richard was being particularly difficult today and his discordant notes ruined her concentration more than once.

She tried again, reaching around him to demonstrate which keys to strike, while he wriggled on the bench and stared longingly out the window.

"I'll tell ye what," Ailsa said in desperation. "Pretend this hand is a fox in the woods and this one a rabbit, and one is chasin' t'other. Ye see, the fox takes a few steps—" she played a few light, sharp notes—"then the rabbit—" a few more. "The fox, then the rabbit, then the fox again. Sometimes they even run together." She used both hands at once, creating a lively tune that caught the boy's attention at last.

He bit his lip and made a small effort. But while her fingers moved lightly on the keys, his repeatedly got tangled like twine in the wind. He simply could not hit the right notes.

"I've spoiled it," he cried in frustration. "I can't make it sound like you, so why should I try?" With a bellow, he pounded all the keys at once with his elbows and forearms.

Ailsa drew a deep breath. "Ye mustn't do that. Ye might bruise the soul of the piano."

He looked up skeptically. "A piano doesn't have a soul."

"O' course it does. Ye just don't give it a chance to come out."

"That's silly," Richard declared.

Ailsa noticed that Cecilia and Master James had stopped their exercises to listen. "If ye'll wait, Master Richard," she said firmly, "I'll show ye that every musical instrument has a soul."

"How?" he demanded in disbelief.

She rose and went to the harp in the corner. She seated herself on the tiny petit-point stool before drawing the harp down onto her shoulder. Ailsa loved this instrument best of all; the sounds it made lingered and echoed, long after the bright, brittle notes of the flute had faded away. As she ran her fingers over the strings, she remembered the hand harp she and Ian had found in the chest. A momentary sadness came over her. She would never know how the clarsach sounded, so this harp would have to do.

Closing her eyes, she shut out the three expectant faces, the room in which she sat, and the dimness of the house beyond. By the strength of her will, she transported herself to the edge of the river where the waterfall made a jubilant noise and water splintered into rainbows with every flash of light through the leaves. Slowly, she began to play.

The music rose like a whisper from beneath her nimble fingers, curled like smoke through the bright stillness, lingered in a fine, soft haze. She played, smiling, her cheek on the heavy gilded harp frame.

Her fingers began to move more quickly, to echo the rush and sparkle of leaping water. Ailsa sensed that the others were listening; even Richard had stopped squirming for the moment.

Slowly, she began to sing.

> "Be, if thou wilt, unfair, contemptuous,
> Listenin' to none, self-praised, contentious;
> But sit beside me, let me touch thy hand,
> And I will stay content forever thus."

She paused to listen as the last note quivered in the still air. Then she looked up at Richard. "Do ye see now that this harp has a soul? Didn't ye hear it sing?"

He shook his head. "I only heard *you* sing. 'Tisn't the same, you know."

Ailsa sighed. This boy would never understand; he had no trace of Celtic spirit in his heart.

"Well now, I think we should all begin in earnest," Master James announced at this opportune moment. He gathered the children and Ailsa around him and began to explain the sheet music he held in his hand. Ailsa settled back to listen and watch as he demonstrated first on the violin and then the piano, then had each of them try a different piece. Ailsa had been working on Haydn for some weeks, and though Master James was ecstatic over her efforts, she was never quite satisfied. She repeated phrases again and again while he looked over her shoulder and made suggestions, then moved on to the children.

Finally Richard had had enough. "You promised to tell a story," he reminded Ailsa. He stood with arms crossed, daring her to deny it.

"And so I shall, if Master James doesn't mind."

"Please," he said fervently. When Ailsa was here the children were quiet, and at no other time. Whatever method she used to keep them so, he would not object.

Ailsa sat on the wide window seat, curling her bare feet beneath her. Cecilia sat beside her and Richard at her feet, while Master James kept his place by the forgotten music stand.

"Now," Ailsa said, in a deep, quavering voice, "look outside and imagine a tall kirk standin'—old, battered, and long-abandoned. Imagine its broken cross tiltin' madly in the wind. Imagine its windows, once bright with colored glass, now dark and coated with dust, the shingles fallin' from its sides. 'Tis called the Kirk o' Kilchriosd and 'twas set afire once and said to be haunted by the ghosts of the worshipers who died there.''

''Did the ghosts come out at night and kill their enemies?'' Richard demanded.

''No, for a ghost can't kill a man. But he can lead him into peril so the man dies by his own foolishness. That's why many a moon passed before anyone dared approach the kirk at night.''

''I would have taken my rifle and gone right in,'' the boy declared rashly.

Ailsa smiled. ''That's as may be, but no' part of my story. It seems one day some men were talkin' outside the coopersmith's shop about the horrible cries that came from the kirk. They bet a poor young tailor a large sum of money that he couldn't stay the night there—or as much of the night as it took him to make a pair of hose. He wanted to get married, ye see, and had no money, so he took the wager.''

''Wasn't he terrified?'' Cecilia asked.

''I'm guessin' he was sore afraid, but he took his tallow candle just the same, sat in one of the back pews, and began to sew. 'Twas no' a sound in the empty kirk, and he worked quickly, as frightened by the silence as he was by the thought of ghosts.

''For a long time, nothin' happened and he began to think 'twas a pack of lies the other men had told him. Then, when the clock rang the last stroke of midnight, the specter appeared.''

''What was it?'' Richard cried eagerly.

'' 'Twas a skull with the flesh rotted all away. It smiled with its bare, gapin' jaws and stared from hollow holes where its eyes had once been. Then it spoke to the tailor in a gravelly voice like stones rattlin' down a great granite mountain.

'' 'See'st thou this big gray head without food, O Tailor?'

'' 'That I see, but this I sew,' the little man said with a quiver in his voice. Then he bent his head to his work.

" 'See'st thou this long rotted trunk without food, O Tailor?' As it spoke, the spirit came closer till much of its skeletal body was visible.

" 'That I see, but this I sew,' the tailor whispered. His hands trembled with terror as he sewed more furiously.

" 'See'st thou this frail, fleshless arm without food, O Tailor?' The specter extended its hand with a horrible rattle of bone on bone.

"Teeth clenched and cheeks pale, the tailor made the last few passes with his needle through the fabric, tied a knot, and broke the thread. Just then the creature reached out to seize him.

" 'See'st thou this great bony paw without food, O Tailor?'

"The little man jumped up and ran to the door. As he pulled it open, the spirit caught at his leg, but he wrenched himself free and fled, closin' the door behind him. With a sigh of relief, he stopped to catch his breath. Then he heard the ghost reach for the latch. Blind, unable to locate the rusted metal, the spirit banged and clawed at the wood. The tailor carried the bruises for many a day from the grasp of those spectral hands, and the next day the people from the nearby village found the dents and scratches those same bony hands had made in the wood. Some say they can be seen even today."

"So the tailor won his wager?" Cecilia asked.

Ailsa patted the girl's blond head in reassurance. "Aye, that he did. He was married within the week to his bride."

Richard was silent, but there was a pinched look about his nostrils.

"So," Ailsa added, "if a Scotsman ever says to ye, 'That I see, but this I sew,' it means ye'll no' be talkin' him out of whatever purpose he has in mind. Like the poor tailor, he'll no' give in till the last stitch is taken."

Richard eyed her doubtfully. "Do all Scots know the story?"

"All Scots know all stories. 'Tis part of our schoolin' to learn each legend by heart."

The boy was unimpressed. "We learn facts, Ailsa Rose, about history and books and such. Everyone knows that's better."

"But stories are more fun, ye must admit."

Richard nodded reluctantly while his sister responded with more enthusiasm. The girl hugged Ailsa as she prepared to leave.

"You aren't going already? It's terribly dull without you."

Ailsa looked at the tutor apologetically, but he seemed to agree with the child. He nodded and smiled at her.

"I've a great many things to do before gloamin'," Ailsa said, hugging the girl, then gently disentangling herself. "But I'll come back soon. Ye know that."

Cecilia sighed while Richard pranced toward the door. "Are we free then?" he called to Master James. "Can I go hunting?"

The man raised his hands in a gesture of defeat. "Go."

Ailsa curtsied toward the master as Lady Williston had taught her. "Thank ye for the lesson," she said.

"I think it was you who taught us today," he replied. "But you're welcome just the same."

Suddenly Ailsa herself was eager to be gone. Through the window she saw that the morning mist had burned away and the loch glimmered blue, gemlike, and inviting far below. The woods would be beautiful today. She'd take Mairi's herbs and sort them for drying on her favorite rock. With a wave of her hand, she was gone, following in Richard's noisy wake. He pounded his fist on the wall as he ran, as if trying to break it down and make his escape more rapid. At last they reached the front door. While the boy hurried off to the gun room, Ailsa headed toward the cool, dark woods.

She found Ian waiting for her in the shade of a Caledonian pine. "I don't wish to fight with ye," he said. "Will ye forgive me?"

"Always," she told him. With a smile, she raised her hand and he pressed his palm to hers.

◇ 4 ◇

A few nights later, Ailsa lay in her bed and dreamed. At first there was only the stillness of nighttime, the soft flutter of insect wings around her. In her dream, she stirred uncomfortably, staring through the gap in the bed curtains. The room was cold, filled with shadows that danced along the walls, whispers that crept, unwanted, about her head. The partition between her room and the salon was open; in the light of a hanging lantern, she saw her mother's averted face—the curve of her cheek, the deep black of her restless, watching eyes.

The girl sensed her mother's unease; it filled her own lungs until every breath brought effort and pain. Then came a tap on the gauze-covered latticework—the brush of a bird's wing on a swaying branch. Her mother rose swiftly to open the door.

When she closed it again, Charles Kittridge stood beside her, gasping, his hair disordered, his face flushed. He glanced over his shoulder furtively. The girl followed his gaze, expecting to see the shadows of his enemies rise along the paper walls, but there was nothing. He crouched with her mother in a corner, whispered to her urgently. The girl strained to hear, but could make out nothing. All she knew was the alarming rhythm of the words, the dips and panicked rises that fueled her fear.

The figures of her parents stretched and wavered in the lantern light like shadow puppets on a distant screen. They kissed, clung together, then the child's father leaned over her to whisper, "Take care, little one. Don't forget me."

She reached up, desperate to catch his face in her hands. "Do not go, my Father," she cried. "Do not leave

52

us alone. When you've gone, they will come and take us away."

"No," he whispered. "It's me they want, not you. You'll be safe now, little one. Go back to sleep."

Then he was gone. He pushed the cane mat aside and slipped into the garden just as shadows loomed outside the house, twice the size of normal men. They beat on the wooden frame until the walls shook; the child trembled as if the fists were striking her own body. The noise became louder, more insistent; the sound beat its way into the girl's brain and an ache began in her temples. The pounding, the throbbing, the pain became one, became her whole world as the men burst in, swords in hand.

There was a flurry of movement, the clatter of chairs pushed over, the breaking of glass, the crash of tables against the marble floor. The sounds came closer until the girl's voice left her, and her breath, and the beat of her heart. Only the terror remained. The soldiers whose shadows stretched so high ripped the bed curtains open with their swords.

"Where is he?" they demanded.

"I do not know."

"Tell us where he is!" They dragged the girl from her bed and she stood staring at the floor. She dared not look up and meet their eyes. "Where?" they bellowed, waving their bright swords in the air. "Where? Where? Where?"

She fell to her knees, beaten down by the threat of their voices. Her head throbbed with a pain so piercing she knew she could not bear it. "I do not know." She felt their hatred and disbelief. The pain grew more intense.

She heard one of the soldiers raise his sword. She knew in an instant he would strike her dead because she would not tell him what she did not know. "My Father!" she screamed. "Help me, my Father!" There was no answer as the pain splintered into shards of brilliant glass that left her blind.

Ailsa sat up abruptly. She rose, held her head in her hands, prayed for the pain to cease, the pressure behind her lids to ease so she might see again. She stumbled through the room, calling for her father, though she knew the shadows had swallowed him long since. She searched for him in every corner of the room, but found only a still, cold silence.

Mairi heard her daughter trip and nearly fall. Ailsa stumbled around the room as if it were unfamiliar and she had to find her way by touch. Mairi started toward the girl then stopped, astonished at the sounds coming from her mouth. They were not words, but rather guttural noises that rose from deep in Ailsa's throat. She seemed to be pleading, from the way she reached out and called a single word over and over.

Mairi looked at her daughter's eyes, full of a terror so deep it changed her face into that of a stranger.

"What is't?" Mairi cried. She stopped Ailsa in the middle of the room, grasping her arms in a painful grip. "What ails ye?"

Her daughter looked at her blankly, and babbled more of the unfamiliar sounds. She was speaking, or thought she was, but the words had no meaning. Mairi realized with a quiver of fear that Ailsa was lost in another world.

She drew the girl close, smoothing her tangled hair. " 'Tis all right, lass. Ye're safe with me. Wake up, Ailsa!"

It was a long time before the strange sounds faded into silence. A longer time yet until the girl eased the pressure of her fingers on her temples and her shadowed eyes grew clear.

"Ye're all right," Mairi repeated. " 'Twas only a dream."

Ailsa blinked at the woman who held her. Who was she? The girl began to move about the tiny room, confused and bewildered. Where was she? Where was the matting, the painted paper walls, the lacquered furniture and hanging lanterns?

What was this rough stone wall, the roof of woven reeds above? She touched the worn and polished table. She had seen it before. She ran her hands over the wood, trying to reacquaint herself with a distant memory. She stopped to stare into the coals that burned inside a circle of stones. She had known the smell of that fire, the musty odor of peat that filled the room. She moved on until she touched the top of the dresser and her fingers came to rest on the carved rosewood box.

Then she knew. This was her home. She was in Glen Affric and the woman watching in concern was her mother.

Ailsa closed her eyes. What had happened to her? She felt shaken, drained, as if she had been wrenched from one world to another, then sent spinning backward again, as though she had traveled many miles and cried many tears during this night. She tried to steady her breathing while the nightmare came back to her a little at a time.

Mairi sighed with relief that her daughter had returned and gently drew the girl into a chair. "Ye had a bad dream," she said quietly. She kept her hand on Ailsa's protectively, reassuringly. "Tell me what 'twas that changed ye so."

Ailsa tried to reconnect the jumbled images in her mind. "I was lyin' awake in a strange bed. I couldn't sleep because of the shadows. Then my father came, but no' to this house. 'Twas altogether different. I've never seen one like it. He spoke to ye in whispers—" She broke off. "No, 'twasn't ye. 'Twas a woman with looped black hair and golden skin and slanted dark eyes. She was my mother, and she was afraid. They were both afraid; I could feel it like a cold wind all around me. Then he came to bid me good-bye." She frowned. " 'Twas no' really me, yet 'twas. I was only a bairn and I had long black hair and the same slanted eyes, but the color was blue, like my father's eyes." She shook her head in confusion. "I don't understand."

A suspicion began to form in Mairi's mind. "Go on."

"He told me no' to forget him. Then he was gone and the soldiers came. They wore strange, jeweled helmets and their armor—I can't even describe it. Their swords were long and graceful, with carved silver handles. They tried to make me tell them where my father was, but I didn't know. I told them so, but they didn't believe me. They raised their swords and—" She stopped, shuddering. Her head throbbed dully. "Oh, Mother, 'twas horrible. 'Twas so real that I believed I was there, even after I woke. How can that be?"

Mairi squeezed her daughter's hand. "It doesn't matter now. 'Tis over. Try to forget it."

For a long time they sat, gripping each other's hands, until the chill left Ailsa's skin. Then Mairi retrieved a precious bottle of sherry from the press She poured a little into

55

a glass and gave it to the girl. " 'Twill warm ye," she said, but her voice was cold—cold and brittle.

Ailsa could not stop trembling, could not quite convince herself the dream had not been real, that a sword was not now raised above her head, ready to descend. While Mairi dressed, she sipped the sherry gratefully.

"Let go of the dream," Mairi said firmly. "The fear is no' yours to feel. It belongs to another. Let it go, Ailsa-*aghray*."

"How do ye know these things?" Ailsa asked, looking up at her mother's pinched face in the somber half-light before dawn.

"Because I know, 'tis all. I can't tell ye why. Are ye all right now? Can I leave ye for a time?"

"Aye, but—"

Mairi raised a hand and Ailsa knew she dared ask no more questions. She watched in astonishment as Mairi took the miniature of her husband from the dresser and slipped it into her pocket. Then she was gone, but before she went, Ailsa caught a glimpse of the raw pain in her mother's eyes.

Mairi hurried away from the croft, fighting back waves of nausea. Ailsa might not understand the dream, but her mother did. Charles had written to her last when he was sent to China, that strange and distant land in which she could never quite believe. She had not received a letter for several years and had not understood his silence. Until now.

The dream had been so vivid, had transformed her daughter so completely, that it must be more than a fleeting vision. Ailsa had, for one night, slipped inside another girl's mind to see and feel her fear. That girl might be her sister, Charles Kittridge's daughter by a Chinese woman. Otherwise, why had Ailsa been so certain that the two people were her parents? Why had it been so hard for her to shake away the influence of the dream? Because it was real. Somewhere in the world, this woman had waited, this child had suffered, and Charles had fled from a group of angry soldiers.

Mairi guessed that he had not written in so long because he had found another woman. She bowed her head, oblivious to the swirled darkness in the sky above. She had known this would happen someday, known from the beginning that Charles was not a man who could bear to be alone. But the reality was more painful than she'd realized, the knowledge that there was probably a child, another daughter—a child he knew and to whom he had taken the time to say goodbye.

Mairi moved by instinct to the sheltered place circled by rocks that she called the Valley of the Dead. She stood staring at the three cairns covered with years of stones, of offerings and prayers for forgiveness, but all she saw was Charles smiling gently as he disappeared into the woods. She took out the miniature and touched the painted image of her husband's face.

The gods forgive her, she still loved him as she had when she was nineteen. She sank to her knees and gazed into the darkness that circled with clouds and mist and the weeping wind.

Mairi turned with her back to the graves, the cold stones against the bare soles of her feet, to watch the first streaks of morning appear at the top of the granite circle. Slowly, the light moved upward in swathes of mauve, purple, and pink that slashed the darkness with vibrant color. The sky grew lighter, the colors deepened, undulating with the force of the wind.

At last the sun burst into the sky, so bright she had to close her eyes against it. For an instant, she forgot herself in the face of the breathtaking sunrise. She ached with the beauty of it, ached to remember it with this sense of wonder laced with pain, ached to capture it in the palm of her hand as she had once wanted to capture Charles. Yet she knew the moment would pass and leave her behind, just as her husband had done.

The new light of dawn enfolded her and the wind whispered softly, "The sun sets in one land and rises in another." Mairi could not deny that simple truth of nature; in her heart she had always known it.

" 'Twas your choice," she reminded herself. But this time it was not enough. She covered her face with her hands. Through her fingers she could see the dew-wet grass, the light that touched the drops of moisture and was caught there, glittering. The prisms of color within those tiny drops mesmerized her. Visions glistened on her lids like brief blazing stars. She saw moments of the future in those fragments of tinted light, saw the meeting, the parting, the pain that was deeper than sorrow. She saw all she would learn and all she would lose, and the weight of the seeing was more than she could bear. While the sun rose, majestic and golden in a cloud-drifted sky, she crouched there, silent, with the dream upon her eyes, and wept.

Ailsa watched her mother disappear into the woods. Often when Mairi had that distant look in her eyes, she would slip away just before dawn. Once Ailsa had tried to follow. The woman had drawn her daughter close and explained, "There are times, wee one, when a person needs to be alone to think. We each have a secret place where we do not wish to be found. My place is sacred, if only to me. I must know that when I go there, I'll no' be disturbed."

"But why?"

"Ye'll learn for yourself someday," Mairi had assured her.

Ailsa had understood when, a year later, she discovered her own secret place—a promontory high on the side of a mountain that overlooked the whole of the glen. She had known from the moment she set foot on that ledge that this one discovery she would not share. This was her sacred and private place.

As she stood alone in the doorway, Ailsa began to tremble. The memory of the nightmare paled, but not the feeling of unease it had left behind. She knew that, even deep in sleep, she had been as much a part of the girl in the dream as she was of Ian. Mairi was wrong when she said the fear belonged to another. Somehow, in a way she could not explain, Ailsa felt that fear and shared it. It had touched Mairi as well; she knew from the strained look on her mother's face. Suddenly Ailsa needed light and air. She was stifling in the tiny room, heavy with the scent of peat smoke.

She threw on a gown, took her plaid from the hook by the door, and started toward her mountain ledge—the one place where she knew she would find peace. As she climbed the scarred gray and purple mountainside, scattered with heather and clumps of gorse, her unease lingered. When at last she stood on the precipice, she looked southward, toward the imagined glitter of London, her father's city. Would she ever see it? Would she ever know the man who had made it real to her with a few vivid words on polished paper?

Thoughts of Charles Kittridge were strong within her. His face seemed to hover above her, always just beyond her reach. Eyes closed in prayer, she called to him and waited for an answer that never came. How often had she waited like this, alone, listening, in the desperate hope that this time he would answer her plea? Yet the only sound in the pre-dawn stillness was the wind that swooped and moaned around her.

At last the dawn song began—the awakening of the birds from their night's sleep. The lapwings cried their mournful greeting, so frail and poignant beside the melodic song of the mavis, the warbling of linnets, and the strong, clear notes of the mountain blackbirds. The sound filled the morning as the sun rose slowly, revealing bit by bit the world spread at her feet.

Ailsa gasped at the beauty of the landscape she had known since birth. The moor spread below her like a sea turned to gems by the glimmer of light on dew. Beyond the moor was the river, rushing through the woods like liquid silver. The tall birches swayed, twined their branches with the supple pines that bent at the wind's urging to meet and part and meet again.

How magnificent the rest of the world—her father's world—must be, Ailsa thought, if this small corner held so much beauty.

Then she saw a movement at the edge of the woods—men who brought wood and peats to build bonfires while barefoot women carried stones to set about the stacked wood in a circle. Only then did she remember that today was Beltaine, the first day of May, the Celtic sun festival. The celebrations would begin after dark when bonfires blazed and the people gathered to welcome the return of spring.

Ailsa felt a sense of expectation that eclipsed the dream, the fear, the memory of Mairi's troubled face. When she saw a kite wheel upward with its narrow wings and graceful forked tail, she smiled and spread her hands wide. Perhaps today her father would come. With her head thrown back, she felt the stinging touch of the wind, the light of the sun so bright it hurt her eyes. She did not close them, but let the light burn its way into her mind until it warmed her, filled her, consumed her.

Ian opened his eyes, wide-awake, though he had been sleeping deeply a moment before. He was up and out of bed in an instant. Today was Beltaine and he meant to finish his chores early so he'd be free to enjoy the festivities. He dressed quickly in his shirt, trousers, and wool socks of the red, black, and yellow Fraser plaid. Then he slipped on his sandals, wound the leather thongs up his legs, and tied them at the top. His father was already up and away, he noticed, but his mother and sister still slept. He wondered if Ailsa lay as they did, her hair tumbled on the pillow, her cheeks flushed with the pleasure of a dream.

As he stepped out into the chilly air, he realized the glen was still draped in the half darkness that came before dawn. Despite the many tasks before him, he could not resist the lure of the sunrise.

His collie appeared at his side, barking a joyful greeting. "Hush, Torran," he said. " 'Tis the whole of the glen ye'll be wakin' and me who'll be payin' the price." The dog grew quiet, though he continued to wag his tail energetically.

When Ian started away, the collie followed. The two moved quickly through the trees to the knoll where Ian often stood to watch the dawn. From here he could see the mountains rising steeply in the shadowed light; he shivered, awed by the power they embodied, even half shrouded by darkness. He felt a thrill of exhilaration as the sky grew lighter, more vibrant with splashes of color that softened the harsh edges of stone, tinted the thin curls of mist, and dyed the water pale shimmering pink.

At last the sun rose, blindingly bright. The light touched the mountains, giving them life and breath and warmth. In that instant, Ian saw the spirit within those towering peaks, saw it glitter in the streams of water that descended, roaring, down their granite sides.

He glimpsed movement on a stone ledge high on the hill. Perhaps the fairies were out today to celebrate Beltaine. But when the light struck the figure poised against the mountain, he saw that it was Ailsa, arms outstretched, palms raised.

She was far away, and though her features were obscured, he could see as clearly as if she stood beside him the look of rapture on her face. The sun set her aflame, engulfed her; in a moment, Belenus the Sun God would lift her into the center of the raging light above. She was consumed by her own longing, a longing so intense that he could not understand it. Torran whimpered when he sensed his master's distress, but at a movement of Ian's hand, fell silent.

The sun rose a fraction higher; the light spread and dissipated until Ailsa became no more than a dark silhouette on a distant mountain. She dropped her hands and turned; the moment had passed. He had imagined it, Ian told himself, that inner fire that burned beyond his comprehension or control. It had been a trick of the dawn light, which everyone knew created illusions, even lured men into madness or miracles.

Though he knew Ailsa could not see him, he raised his palm to his lips and sent a kiss floating toward her. Only then did he hear the song of the birds, the harmony that rose from among the hidden greenery to fill the morning. He stopped for a moment more to listen, then, smiling to himself, he turned away.

"Dear me! I can't imagine what possessed me to come on this ghastly journey to the middle of nowhere!" Sarah Worthy exclaimed, patting at her damp forehead with a small lace handkerchief. The mist seemed to creep in no matter how tightly she closed the windows against it. This trip had been a mistake; she knew it already. Why *had* she decided to come along? As the coach she and her friends were traveling in barreled over the rough Highland countryside, she glanced wistfully at the man on her right and knew the answer to her own question.

"You were hoping to find a husband," her friend Agatha replied snippily. "There are always so many unattached men at these dreadful hunting parties. I suppose that's why so many young ladies find it prudent to attend." When she saw the horrified look on Sarah's face, Agatha gasped and put a gloved hand to her mouth. "Oh dear, forgive me, William, I didn't—"

But William Sinclair, the only unmarried man in the coach, had not heard her. He was too engrossed in staring at the landscape, trying to determine shapes and colors. A fine veil of mist coated the hills and moors; he could feel the moisture in the air. He realized with a shock that he wanted nothing more than to breathe in that mist along with the gust of clean wind that touched his face.

"I don't know why you *will* bring me on your hunting holidays," Agatha said to her husband, relieved that the other man had not noticed her outburst. "There's nothing to do but watch while you go dashing off into the brush waving your gun."

Her husband, Gerald Harcourt, was wondering himself why he had come. "Don't remember these carriages being so blasted uncomfortable," he remarked, running his fingers inside the tight rim of his high starched collar, wishing he had the nerve to loosen his perfectly tied cravat. "Shan't sit comfortably for a week, I'm sure, after perching on these springs for so long."

"I don't see why they don't bring the railroad up here and make the trip a little more civilized," Sarah interjected. She had recovered from her mortification when she realized William was paying no attention to the conversation. Now she felt neglected. "All that horrible dust, and the damp seems to creep right under the windowsills. I'm sure we'll all have ague before the day is out."

William frowned. He could not imagine preferring thick, gritty London fog to air that smelled fresh, free of soot and grime. He had never heard Sarah complain about the fog at home. He did not turn toward the other passengers, who sat on the edges of their seats as if they could not wait for the trip to be over. William was enjoying himself, though he would never have said so. They would have been shocked by such an admission.

He lowered the window and leaned out, hoping to catch a glimpse of the scenery now that the sky had begun to lighten. He could see the outline of a distant range of mountains and the sound of water grew louder. He gasped as layer upon layer of vivid colors swirled across the sky. He had never seen the dawn in London; the buildings where he lived and worked were crowded too close together and built too high, while the smoke from the factories stained the sky a perpetual dingy gray.

He strained to see more clearly the shades of lilac that painted the low clouds, fading to rose, then pink, until the entire sky was suffused with color. The mountains dominated the scene, casting their purple shadows over the sloping moors. William clutched the windowsill with chilled fingers. It was too beautiful; he wanted to close his eyes against the image. Then the sun touched the topmost peak and exploded into the sky, sending the colored light spinning away. He did not understand the pain in his chest, the sense of unreality that assailed him. He had never before felt anything like it, and it frightened him.

"Heaven preserve us, look at those heathens!" Agatha cried.

This time William turned, relieved at the excuse to shut out the painful beauty of the sunrise. Through the far window, he could see women running barefoot, skirts gathered around their knees, carrying heavy stones, and men in open shirts and knee-length breeches gathering wood to stack in huge piles. He heard a strange sound and, intrigued, leaned so far forward that he pressed against Sarah. She gasped in surprise.

"Terribly sorry," he murmured. He turned back to his own window and saw that there were other Scots on the bank of the river that now ran beside the coach. He strained to hear better. Then he realized what it was that had drawn his attention. These people were singing as they worked, strange lilting songs whose words he could not understand. But more than that, they were laughing. It came to him then with a flash of regret that he had seldom heard laughter, real laughter, since he was a child. Once or twice, after his fifth birthday, he had laughed aloud, but his parents had usually shushed him to silence. After they died, his aunt had done the same.

"I heard they were savages," Sarah gasped. "But I had no idea. How dreadfully dirty they are." In self-defense, she checked the buttons on her high-necked wool traveling suit and patted her braided and coiled hair, just visible beneath the edge of her bonnet. Shuddering, she brushed at the sleeves of her jacket as if to protect herself from contamination by the laughter that spilled through the open window.

William shook his head. It wasn't like Sarah to judge others so harshly. His frown disappeared when he heard the distant song of a bagpipe. The people on the riverbank paused to listen. William felt a flutter of excitement for the first time in years. The tiny, nagging part of his mind that rebelled against Victorian rules and restraints reveled in the apparent freedom of the Highlanders as they sang and laughed and laid their fires. "I think"—he paused uncertainly, then plunged ahead—"I think they look rather charming. Perhaps things are different here."

"Different indeed," Gerald said, "and damned dangerous if you ask me. Running about half-naked, men and women together. Appalling behavior. I'll tell you the truth, old man, those savages frighten me."

William brushed the windblown hair out of his face. In a way, he shared Gerald's disquiet. In London he had always felt safe. He knew the rules, the boundaries, what to expect. Yet sometimes he experienced a faint stirring of restlessness, a desire for something more.

"What do you suppose they're doing out there?" he asked, unable to contain his curiosity.

"Some barbaric tradition of lighting bonfires on May Day. They say the church has changed Scotland, but I don't believe it for a minute. All a bunch of pagans worshiping fairies and dragons, if you ask me. You think they look like savages now, you should catch a glimpse of them around the fires tonight. Scare the wits out of any sane man." He turned back to the women. "You would probably faint dead away, m'dear."

"I'm sure I shouldn't like it," Agatha agreed with a shiver.

When the mountains loomed nearer, Gerald coughed with relief. "Begun to recognize the lay of the land, don't you know. We should be at the Hill o' the Hounds soon."

William did not hear him. He thought he saw a movement in the forest, a flicker of light among the shadows, but the mist had settled along the ground, obscuring his vision. Then the veil of moisture parted and he saw a flash of red. He peered more intently, determined to catch sight of whatever had made those flashes of light and color. Suddenly a girl emerged from among the trees, moving swiftly. She ran, her head thrown back, and crossed the river in one long, graceful leap. Her chestnut hair hung about her shoulders, caught up by the wind to mingle with her red, flowing plaid.

William blinked, shook his head, and looked again, but she had already disappeared, faded without a sound into the mist.

5

On the way back through the woods, Ailsa noticed red berries hidden among the leaves of the rowan trees. She decided to pick some for the ceremonies that night. Tucking her gown around her hips, she climbed the nearest mountain ash. She hung with one hand from the swaying branch while she picked berries with the other. She dropped several fistfuls into her pockets, then jumped to the ground. A few of the berries in her hand, she rubbed the sacred food of the Celtic gods over her face, leaving her cheek wet with dew. Her sense of anticipation grew.

When Ailsa came to the river, she chose to cross where the turbulent water widened into a pond. She drew a deep breath, backed several feet away, then ran and leaped, legs extended. With a cry of triumph, she landed safely on the far bank. She had not known she could jump so far, but today she felt like taking chances. The sunrise had imbued her with new courage, an urge to experience all that she had ever missed.

At the edge of the clearing, she knelt to cup her hands around the long blades of grass, collecting drops of dew in her palms. Then she raised her hands toward the sky and cried, "I cleanse myself for thee, Belenus, God of the Sun, and to welcome the return of spring." She washed her face with her dew-wet hands and tilted her head toward the warmth above. Already the mist had begun to burn away; it would be a bright and clear Beltaine. Ailsa shivered with the pleasure of expectation, rose from her knees, and returned to the croft.

Mairi was waiting there. She had left the door wide open, thrown back the leather from the windows, and lit two oil lamps. Now she sat, head bent in concentration, threading the loom. Ailsa saw that her mother had put aside the Stewart tartan, unfinished, and replaced it with a combination wool thread that she'd soaked for weeks in a vat of precious indigo, bought from Dundreggan months earlier. There was also silk that she had dyed deep purple with crowberry and dandelion before fixing the colors with fir-club moss. Most of Mairi's fabrics were simple and inexpensive, prepared with natural dyes from the wool of local sheep. This piece would be the most costly she had ever made: she had purchased the finest indigo, as well as rowans from sheep in the south whose soft, pliant wool took the dye more easily. Finally, the cloth would be shot with silk, the pattern an intricate alternation of blue and purple that would take much time and effort to create. Perhaps Lady Williston had come to order the fabric for a gown. Ailsa could not imagine who else could afford such luxury.

" 'Tis lovely," she said reverently as she ran her finger over the soft threads and sighed with appreciation. "Who is't for?"

"For a special occasion," Mairi said shortly. She did not look up or pause in her task. Her fingers moved deftly as she wound the threads around the frame of the loom, setting up the subtle pattern of alternating blue and purple.

"It must be the midsummer ball at the Hill."

Her mother did not reply.

The girl was disturbed by the tint of gray in Mairi's violet eyes, as if she were weary with grieving. "Has somethin' happened to upset ye?" her daughter asked anxiously.

"Only that I've seen the sunrise, and the light on the dew."

Ailsa understood from those few words that Mairi had had a vision. They often came with the dawn that was neither day nor night, the dew that was not sea nor river nor rain. At such times, in such things, the spirits hovered and magic occurred. Ailsa also guessed that her mother did not want to discuss it further. Her concentration on her task was absolute, as if, through hard work, she could push the vision to the back of her mind where it would bother her no more.

Although Ailsa was curious, she left her mother in

peace. She had learned over the years that there were some questions Mairi could not answer. All day as she went about her tasks, she was aware of her mother's uneasy silence, the movement of her feet on the pedals, the sweep of the shuttle through warp and weft. Most disturbing of all were the shadows clustered about the loom, even in the midday light.

As the sun began to slide toward the mountains, Ailsa prepared a huge oatcake for the ceremony that night. Each year it was provided by a different family, and like the seasons, the cycle never changed. This year it was the Roses' turn. When it was ready, she wrapped the oatcake in cheesecloth and put it at the bottom of the creel. Then she mixed a caudle of milk, eggs, oatmeal, and butter, poured it into a deep wooden bowl, and covered that too with cheesecloth, bound around the outside by a leather thong to keep it from spilling.

While the sound of the loom echoed in her ears, Ailsa readied herself for the evening. Tonight she would wear her one good muslin gown, a simple design with a square neck, puffed sleeves, and a wide, full skirt. It had taken her mother many days of soaking the fabric in a tormentil dye, then rinsing and soaking it again until she attained the color she desired. She had grinned when she gave it to her daughter. "The color is Rose red, ye see, and no one can wear it with as much right as ye."

Ailsa had laughed in delight, pleased with a fabric so much softer than the wool she was accustomed to. The color was beautiful, like a swath of dawn light that swirled about her ankles just as it moved through the morning sky. Now, while she slipped the dress over her head, she watched her mother curiously out of the corner of her eye.

Mairi had not spoken since their conversation early that morning, nor had she left the loom. Ailsa had never seen her work so intently for so long. " 'Tis nearly time to meet Ian," the girl said at last. "Will ye no' come out for the while?"

Mairi shook her head. "Beltaine is no' for the likes of me. 'Tis for the young."

"Flora and Angus Fraser will be there, and the Grants and Geordie Mackensie. Besides, I don't like to leave ye alone."

For the first time in hours, her mother looked up. "I've been alone before, *mo-run*, and shall be again. I have learned to find peace in silence."

The Gaelic endearment reassured Ailsa, though she did not like the cast on her mother's eyes that turned them as dark as the silk on her loom.

When the girl continued to hesitate, Mairi said softly, "Get ye gone. The others will be waitin'."

"If ye're certain—"

"Go," her mother repeated. "Mayhap I'll weave my gloom away while ye're out."

"I hope ye do." Ailsa leaned down to kiss Mairi's cheek, then hurried to take the creel from the kitchen table. She placed the oatcake on top of the bowl and started to leave, but could not resist turning when she reached the door. "Spring is back," she said. "Ye should rejoice."

"Rejoice *ye*, Ailsa-my-heart, for there is more joy in ye who have no' yet seen the *Amadan Dhu*—the Dark Fool."

"And have ye seen him? Is that why ye grieve?"

Mairi turned to meet her daughter's perplexed gaze. "Many times have I seen him, but tonight isn't the time to talk of that. Go out to the fires and find ye the wonder there."

Still puzzled, Ailsa nevertheless did as her mother asked. With the creel under her arm, she stepped out into the chilly evening. The moment the croft was behind her, her sense of anticipation returned. She knew the night was full of promise; she felt it in the fading twilight. As she crossed the clearing, Ailsa stopped to pick some of the wild roses and tiny white starflowers scattered through the grass. She placed them carefully in the basket, then hurried to meet Ian.

He waited at the edge of the woods, his hands full of daffodils, which he put in the creel. "Good Beltaine, *mo-charaid*," he murmured. "Have ye the oatcake?"

Ailsa nodded, and twined her fingers with his as they found their way through the trees toward the far side where the bonfires had been built earlier in the day.

"The fairies will be out tonight, I'll wager," Ailsa said.

"Aye, so they will. Ye'd best take care or they'll carry

ye away with them to the land beyond the dew and the moonshine."

"More like they'll be stealin' the milk from the kine, or tryin' to," she replied, grinning. "But Belenus will watch over us. I'm no' afraid of the *Aes Sidhe*."

As they walked slowly through the woods, the moon rose, casting a pale light over the water.

"Listen!" Ian whispered.

Ailsa tilted her head and heard the last mournful cry of a lapwing ripple through the leaves like a strand of ribbon through long, curling hair.

"Come welcome the spring! Come bury the winter!" The call rang through the trees, breaking the spell of the moonlight. Ian and Ailsa turned toward the huge clearing where the twin bonfires already burned a few yards apart.

The flames rose into the night, turned the sky an incandescent gold, transforming the young people who approached into ever-changing shadows of themselves.

When the others saw Ailsa, they called out, "The offerin'!"

Ian removed the oatcake from the basket and handed it to Alistair Munro, who set it on a round griddle that he pushed close to the fire with a long stick. He made certain that only part of the cake was near the flames, then, satisfied, joined the other men who arranged the stones and placed the bowls of caudle around the bonfires.

Jenny Mackensie and Megan and Anne Macdonnell, along with several other girls with baskets of flowers under their arms, joined Ailsa on the grass at the edge of the trees. They sat close together, full of excitement as they wove crowns of wild roses and starflowers and daffodils. Then, while the men began to form two circles, the girls set the flowers on their heads and joined the growing numbers who linked hands in the feverish light of the fires. Ailsa recognized Flora, Angus, and Geordie Mackensie, though their faces were altered by the shimmering flames. She could not find the Grants, but the crowd was so large by now that she gave up the attempt.

The talk among the men and women grew louder until the rumble of excited voices echoed upward to the sky. Then everyone fell silent at the same moment. The ceremonies were about to begin.

Ian appeared at Ailsa's side to take her hand. She took Jenny's on the other side and Jenny took Malcolm Drummond's and he Anne Macdonnell's until each person was linked to the one beside him and the two circles were complete. Everyone raised their hands in the air as they began to revolve around the bonfires. They murmured incantations in the Gaelic, each choosing his own favorite. The voices rose and faded, rose and faded as the people moved close to the flames, hands raised, and away again, dropping their clasped hands as they went.

"Hear us, Brigit, Goddess of Fire and Hearth and Poetry," Archibald Maclennan cried. "Hear our song to thee!" He began, softly, to sing. The other men joined in until their voices rose above the hiss and crackle of the flames.

> "Passion hath votaries, but thou hast none,
> Thou silent icon, cloistered in a cell. . . ."

The women answered in their sweet, high voices:

> "Love and Affection flaunt them in the sun,
> Unto the few thy secrets dost thou tell."

The men took up the next line, chanting:

> "And such of mortals who by listenin' well . . ."

Before the last word had faded away, the women replied,

> "Learn and perceive the marvels thou hast done."

Finally, everyone chanted together:

> "Securely sheltered, gently nurtured one,
> Involve us in thy wonder-woven spell."

The Highlanders stopped still and released each other's hands. While the men stood silent, expectant, the women moved forward. As she drew close to the blaze, Ailsa took the rowan berries from her pocket and tossed them into the fire. Others who had brought handfuls of the bright red fruit did the same. Each woman bent to pick up a bowl of caudle, then raised it high above her head, crying, "*Tuatha De-Danann*, gods of our Celtic past, this to ye we offer in gratitude for the comin' once again of spring, for the promise of life and sun and growth. By the three most ancient cries, we praise ye—the call of the curlew, the moanin' of the wind, and the sighin' of the sea."

They spilled some caudle on the ground for the gods to consume. Finally each woman leaned forward so the heat touched her cheeks with a flush of red, and set the bowl on the warm stones that surrounded the fire. Slowly, the women grasped hands and revolved; beyond them, the men circled in the other direction until the caudle was done. Then the women held out the bowls to the men, who dipped their fingers in the thickening mixture while the women took their share. As one, they raised their fingers to their lips and ate, sharing, for this one night, the food and power of the gods. When the caudle was gone, the women rejoined the circle and clasped hands as their voices rose in triumph:

"Now hath heaven to earth descended,
And cloud and clay and stone and star are blended."

Ailsa, Ian, and the others swayed inward, then out again, forward and backward, hands locked in the air. The circles began to move more quickly until the people were running, turning, leaping. Inspired by the mood of celebration, the revelers broke free and began to spin, dancing private tributes to the fire that symbolized the rising of the sun, in bursts of glory, from its long winter sleep.

Ailsa danced, mesmerized by the blaze that melded past and present, light and shadow, until there was nothing but this moment, this radiance, this flame of reckless abandon within her and without. The fire rose, terrifying and magnificent, beautiful beyond words, but not beyond feeling. She raised her skirts and twirled barefoot over the tamped-down grass. She sang to herself, exulting. Ian caught her hand and they whirled together while the sweat covered their faces and the glow of the flames lit their eyes with madness.

For that one hour, as she responded to the demands of the fire that ruled them all, she felt she was part of the Celtic glory that had disappeared long since into the darkness beyond these hills. Tonight, when she looked up at the stars, caught each in its own white silence across the night sky, she knew that miracles were possible.

The dancers paused and held their breath, so suddenly still that they might have been a ring of stones at an ancient Druid temple. Shadows they were, flickering yet unmoving, frozen with waiting, burning with heat from the bonfires they circled. The adults took the moment of quiet to slip away and leave the young ones to their celebration. Slowly, those who remained began to sway once more, releasing their breath like a rush of warm wind against the cold mist. Now they danced wildly, fiercely; the last of their inhibitions had been consumed by the flames.

Ailsa whirled, breathless, moved closer and closer to the fire, tempting it to reach out and draw her into its white-hot center. When the hem of her dress caught the edge of a flame, she fell out of the circle. She laughed and rolled in the dew-wet grass until the fire was out.

She lay for a moment, too exhausted to rise. Then she felt a presence nearby. She looked up to find Jenny Mackensie staring at her in terror. "Are ye all right?"

Ailsa took her friend's trembling hand. "Don't fret over me. 'Tis happy I am this night, and happy I shall be forever."

Jenny was taken aback by the laughter. "Ye're no' afraid of anythin', are ye?"

Ailsa frowned. "What is there to fear?" She noticed as she spoke that Ian had come to join them. He knelt beside Jenny, who could not stop shaking.

"Loneliness," Jenny replied, "and darkness and storms and the wind on the mountains." She turned to look at the dancers spinning frantically in the weird light. "And these people. Look at the fire in their eyes." Her own hazel eyes were wide with dread. " 'Tis as if the fire comes from within them, no' from without. 'Tis no longer a reflection of the flames, but the flames themselves." She shuddered and looked away.

Ian put a gentle hand on her shoulder. "There's nothin' here to be afraid of, Jenny. These are the people ye've always known. The ones ye played with as a bairn, who laughed with ye and tumbled with ye on the moors. They're havin' a bit of fun is all. 'Twill no' hurt anyone."

When she still looked doubtful, he pointed toward the dancers. "Look, isn't that Malcolm with Alistair beside him, and Anne and Archibald and Megan and Janet? Look at them, Jenny. Remember who they are, who they will always be."

Jenny listened, hypnotized by the sound of Ian's voice, the touch of his hand on her shoulder. When she looked into his eyes, she believed what he said.

"Come, Ian!" Alistair called. " 'Tis time for the oatcake." Now that the fires had begun to burn low, the last ritual of the night was to be performed. Ian and Ailsa rose together.

"Don't leave me!" Jenny cried.

Ian smiled. "Then come with us, birdeen, and welcome."

Jenny nodded but did not move when Ian and Ailsa ran back to the fire. They watched while Alistair drew the oatcake away from the stones and left it to cool for a moment. He took off his bonnet and, with great ceremony, crumbled the cake into it, offering it to each of the boys in turn. Ian reached in with the others, then moved closer to the light to examine his fragment.

" 'Tis burnt blacker than the devil's own teeth!" Alistair exclaimed, displaying his own lightly browned piece. "Ye're to be the one."

Everyone present had passed between the two fires in the traditional rite of purification, but Ian had been chosen to perform the sacred act that would cleanse them of all sins for the year to come. He would leap across the fire three times. Ailsa's heart began to beat more rapidly with the sense of anticipation that had grown in her since dawn.

Before the ceremony began, the men turned their backs

to the flames and tossed the remnants of the cake into the bonfire, calling, "This to you, O mists and storms, spare ye our pastures and our corn; this to you, O eagle, spare ye our lambs and our kids; this to you, O fox and falcon, spare ye our poultry."

This done, they turned while Ian backed away, trying to judge the distance he would need to clear the low-burning fire.

Ailsa watched him with pride and fear mingled. It was an honor to be chosen, but not all managed to escape unharmed. Ian ran from the shadows into the light, reached the edge of the ring, and leaped across the fire to land with both feet on the far side.

A cheer went up and several people patted his back and applauded his prowess. If he succeeded in the next two tries, all would have good luck for the rest of the year. Ailsa's eyes glowed and her heart pounded. How magnificent Ian had looked when he rose above the flames, a moving star that blazed for an instant, then fell into the darkness. She felt his exhilaration and wanted, suddenly, to share in it.

As Ian backed away on the other side of the ring, Ailsa found the place where he had begun the last jump. He took a deep breath; so did she. He raised his head; she raised hers, too. He began to run, gathering speed as he went; Ailsa also ran. At the same instant, his feet and hers left the ground on opposite sides of the fire. Encouraged by the shouts of the other revelers, the two young people leaped high. Ian's eyes widened in surprise as he passed Ailsa, legs extended, arms spread to the open sky. Then the two landed together, safely, the low flames still between them. The cheers rose around them like thunder.

"Again!" Ian called above the other voices.

"Again!" Ailsa replied.

Slowly, inch by inch, they moved backward until they stood equal distances from the bonfire. They stared at each other, eyes locked, then began to move forward. This time they ran faster—so fast that Ailsa gasped for breath, but she did not falter. Then they leaped, meeting in the center above the last of the flames. To those who watched, the two seemed to hover for an instant, suspended in time, plaids streaming behind them. Simultaneously, they raised their hands and brushed palms, then plunged downward and collapsed, laughing in triumph on the two sides of the circle.

All the revelers joined hands again while Ian made his way to Ailsa's side. He did not speak, did not need to; she read the approval and pride in his eyes. They began to revolve, more slowly this time.

Jenny stood outside the circle, her mouth open, quivering with horror over what her friends had done. At the same moment, Ian and Ailsa broke their grasp and pulled the other girl into the ring. "Don't be a stranger, Jenny. Don't let the magic go without even tryin' to catch it in your hand."

Jenny moved with them, reluctantly, but as the rhythm of the flames and the movement of bodies in flickering light caught her up, her fear receded.

Ailsa and Ian sensed the change in their friend and their gazes met over her head. It was, just then, as it had been in that instant when they stared at each other, palm to palm, poised above the flames. They stood alone in the center of the fire and around them all was darkness without meaning or light.

William Sinclair was restless after an endless dinner of mock turtle soup, salmon, roast leg of mutton, grouse, venison, wild duck, carrots, potatoes, and bread pudding. He turned when Sarah spoke to him, nodded as John Williston discussed the good hunting this year, smiled at Gerald Harcourt's harmless jokes, and wished himself as far away as possible from the table cluttered with lace and silver and fine bone china. He wanted to be outside, where the air was clear with the fresh night unclouded by London fog. Finally, in desperation, he suggested that they watch the Beltaine festivities. To his surprise, the others agreed, though Agatha Harcourt and Lady Williston were less than enthusiastic.

"Really, William, what can you be thinking of? Standing about in the ghastly fog while the Scots dance around a fire like children gone wild?" Agatha sniffed.

"I always stay inside on May Day," Eleanor Williston added. She leaned forward to whisper confidentially, "These Scots aren't like us, you know. Not a bit of it. They actually *enjoy* losing all control and cavorting about in a frenzy. It makes my skin crawl even to think of it.''

When they realized that not only William, but also John and Gerald were determined, the ladies reluctantly joined the party.

"Brisk walk after dinner will do you good, m'dear," John Williston told his wife.

Sarah Worthy said nothing, glancing at William to see if he had noticed her calm acquiescence. He smiled absently in her direction and headed for the front door. There was no need to ask directions; once the party was assembled outside, they could see the glare of the bonfires and hear the singing. The women drew their pelisses protectively around them while the men led the way toward the edge of the forest where they could watch the celebration without being seen.

William's heart began to beat in anticipation as he watched the dancers circle the flames. He leaned forward to try to catch some of the words they were chanting.

"Do you hear?" Sarah demanded in consternation, her good intentions forgotten. "They're calling to their heathen gods to protect them as if . . ." She sputtered and could not go on.

"As if what?" William asked.

Sarah opened her mouth, closed it, then opened it again. "As if the devil himself were looking over their shoulders."

"Perhaps he is," William suggested mildly. "Perhaps that's why they need protection."

Though his expression was perfectly serious, Sarah had the strangest feeling he was laughing at her.

"Well, I, for one, do not intend to stand by and watch such depravity any longer." She pulled her bonnet forward to block the sight from her eyes, then turned and walked away. Her wide skirt swayed from side to side, catching on branches and twigs as she went. She cursed under her breath in annoyance, then glanced back to see if anyone had noticed. The others were apparently transfixed by the spectacle in the clearing. "Damn!" she said, more loudly, but no one turned or inclined a head. With a heartfelt sigh, she returned to the Hill alone.

William moved closer to the edge of the trees, frowning

in concentration. Once or twice he thought he saw the girl he had caught a glimpse of earlier that morning, but now that her face was ablaze with firelight, he could not be sure. His gaze was drawn again and again to the girl, who wore a red gown that revealed her bare feet and ankles when she leaped. He saw how she threw back her head in pure joy. Free and unencumbered, she danced and sang, unaware and uncaring of what anyone thought.

He should have been appalled; the girl was everything he'd been taught to despise. But he could not despise her. As she moved, her chestnut hair swung out behind her, scattering dew in the firelight. Her eyes, turned toward him once or twice, seemed to be all colors, yet none at all. She was not human; she was a spirit woven of flame and mist.

He edged forward, as close as he dared. Then the girl— he was certain now that it was she whom he'd seen at dawn—danced too near the flames and broke away from the others, her skirt ablaze.

"Dear God, she's on fire!" Gerald exclaimed. All three men instinctively stepped forward, then saw that she had already extinguished the flames by rolling in the damp grass.

Agatha Harcourt gasped. "Would you look at that?" she cried. "The girl is laughing. Actually *laughing*, when she might have been burnt or even killed."

"Yes," William whispered. "Isn't she marvelous?"

The others did not hear him. "I think," Eleanor Williston said weakly, "that I shall join Sarah at the hall."

"And I shall come with you," Agatha declared. "I'd rather not watch while these savages throw themselves into the flames. I'm sure it's only a matter of time."

William hardly heard; he was staring at the girl. He saw others go to her, saw her pick up her crown of flowers and set it back on her hair, then rejoin the dancers.

"Terribly sorry, old man," Gerald huffed, "but it's been a long day, you know, what with that blasted coach ride and all. Craving my bed, don't you know."

"Very long day," John concurred. "Better see to my guests."

With a wave of his hand, William dismissed his friends. He knew he should go back, but something held him there, immobile.

"The fire's cast a spell over him, poor chap," John whispered to Gerald. "Seen it happen often. Terrible business. Don't bother to argue. The man won't hear a word you say."

He was right. All William could hear was the roar of the fires and the calls of the dancers. He held his breath when he saw the young man leap across the flames, released it in a rush when the Highlander landed safely on the other side. Then he saw the girl back toward the trees, her eyes on the low-burning fire. Somehow he sensed her intention. William clutched a thin birch so tightly his hands ached. She was near enough that he could hear her breathing. He could have put out a hand and tried to stop her. Before he could move, it was too late and she was gone. She flew through the air, hovered above the bonfire, then hit the ground without a sound. At once she turned and leaped again, meeting the young man in midair.

William gasped; he could not help himself. He could have sworn those two were suspended in the air, touching palms for an endless moment. Then they parted and hit the ground while the clearing resounded with thunderous cheers. He released his breath in a weary sigh, though why he should feel so tired and drained he did not know. His only clear thought was that he had never known a woman braver than that girl, perhaps not even a man. Certainly he himself did not possess such courage.

The dancers gathered again, clasped hands, and began to circle, but soon they dropped out one by one and sat on the ground. Several moved away from the fires and stretched out to stare at the sky, their heads resting on their cupped hands.

William heard a shout and a young man raised his head, then started toward the woods. Suddenly William realized he might be seen. It struck him then, forcibly, that he was nothing more than an intruder, an interloper; the young man would be shocked to find him watching this celebration with the unimaginative eyes of an Englishman. William Sinclair could never understand their Highland rituals, nor would they want him to. He was a stranger here, would probably never even know that girl's name.

Depressed all at once, he turned back toward the Hill o' the Hounds, thinking without pleasure of the comfortable feather bed that awaited him.

The dancers began to fall back one at a time, drained and exhausted. Even Ailsa and Ian eventually sat on the grass, then lay back, gazing at the midnight sky.

"Ian Fraser, to the pipes!" someone called. "Bring ye these dead men back to life."

Ian rose at once. He had been waiting for this moment. Earlier, he had left his pipes in a hollow tree trunk; now he went to retrieve them. With the bag under his right arm, he grasped a pipe with his lips and held the chanter between his fingers. Quietly at first, he began to play, a thin, curling tune that wove itself among the weary dancers, weighting their eyelids with a whisper of sleep. Then he blew louder, worked an intricate tune on the chanter, full of wind and motion and the rush of clear water.

One by one, the listeners raised their heads as the primitive notes swept through the darkness. The song caressed the men with drooping shoulders, the girls with heads on bent knees; it laughed and pleaded and skirled its way inside them until they rose, unable to resist the call of the Son o' the Wind.

Ian was not the best among the pipers in the glen—he was too young and inexperienced—but they called for Ian Fraser on Beltaine because of the passion he played into his songs, the magic he wove like ribbons of mist through the clear night air.

Jenny Mackensie came up beside Ailsa. "He's playin' for ye, isn't he?" she said.

"Och, no! 'Tis for Beltaine, for the comin' of spring."

Jenny shook her head. " 'Tis for ye," she repeated wistfully.

Ailsa stared at her friend in surprise. For the first time, she saw the longing in Jenny's eyes when she looked at Ian—longing mingled with resignation. In the rise and fall of a single breath, the other girl understood how much Jenny wanted Ian, understood, too, that she knew she would never have him.

Ailsa did not know what to say. If it were anyone but Ian, she would have shaken Jenny, told her she was a fool to give up without trying, that she must fight with all her strength to make him hers. But Jenny Mackensie was not a fighter. She trembled at the beauty of Ian's song, yet dared not even meet his eyes. Ailsa took the other girl's hand in silence. She, of all people, could not give Jenny comfort, only compassion and a sad smile of her own that echoed the wailing cry of the pipes.

By the time the few remaining dancers left the clearing, it was nearly dawn and the fires were no more than smoldering ashes enclosed within circles of stone. By unspoken agreement, the revelers started homeward, exhausted, sweat-soaked, aching, and deeply happy.

When they reached the river Affric at the place where the waterfall tumbled into the pond, Ian called out, "To the water!" and fell in, fully clothed. Ailsa followed him promptly, relieved to feel the cool, refreshing water close around her. It washed away the sweat and the smell of the fire, along with her heavy-lidded weariness.

The others hesitated briefly, then jumped in all at once, sending the water rushing over the bracken in a wave. Only Jenny Mackensie stayed safely on the bank.

Alistair and Anne, Malcolm, and Archibald ducked beneath the water, then began to flail about. They splashed and called to one another like children. Ian and Ailsa swam toward the tumbled stones; they wanted to feel the water on their upturned faces. Together, they stood beneath the rushing waterfall until it knocked their feet from under them.

They caught at each other and rose to the surface, laughing and choking, then stopped still when their eyes met with the sheen of the crystal spray between them. At the same instant, they leaned forward to touch their lips together. Then Ian drew Ailsa closer and his kiss deepened, became a command and a plea all at once.

Ailsa shivered at the pressure of his lips on hers, his tongue in her mouth, circling, seeking, twining with her own. She put her arms around him, held him so tightly that he gasped. Then his grip tightened and he took her breath away.

Her heart raced, filled her body with its rhythmic pulse. She was dazed, she was enchanted, she could not breathe. Gasping, she looked up to meet Ian's gaze, and saw reflected there the same turmoil that raged within her. He kissed her again, fiercely, ran his hands up her back, pressed her breasts against his chest until the meeting of their bodies was fire and ice, agony and pleasure, yearning and pain.

Her heart was pounding, her head spinning, her legs trembling until she could no longer stand. It was too much, this glorious blaze—too bright, too fierce, too sweet to bear.

She broke away just as Ian did and they stood, unable to move or speak, frightened by the rise of their passion as they had not been, would never be, by the incandescent flames of the bonfire they had left behind.

◦ 6 ◦

The next morning, Ailsa awoke to the cry of a lapwing outside her window. She moaned, huddling deeper into the heather mattress. She had stumbled in at dawn, too weary to do more than remove her wet clothes and drape them over a chair by the fire. She had smiled as she curled under the quilt, remembering the exhilaration of those dangerous leaps across the bonfire. She had taken the risk and won. The knowledge of her victory filled her with a new and wonderful sense of power.

The lapwing gave its plaintive cry again. Ailsa closed her eyes tight. Perhaps if she refused to recognize the aches in every part of her body, they might go away. But she could not make herself comfortable and sleep eluded her.

When the bird sang out for the third time, she sighed and pushed the covers aside. As she sat up, she paused, one hand caught in her tangled hair. It could not have been a lapwing that awakened her; the notes had been too high and clear. She smiled and bent to find a gown and undergarments in one of the drawers beneath the bed. It must have been Ian.

He often whistled like a bird as a sign that he was waiting for her. He had become so adept at imitating the various songs that sometimes she could not tell the difference. Quickly she tied the strings of her gown, glanced about, and saw that Mairi had already left the cottage. And no wonder. When she looked outside, Ailsa realized the sun was high in the sky. She had slept until noon.

Stopping only long enough to rinse her face in the pail of water by the table, Ailsa ran her fingers through her hair and stepped outside. Ian was not in sight, which puzzled her. Usually he waited at the edge of the clearing. She frowned, trying to recall from which direction the bird whistle had come. She could not remember; her mind was still fogged with sleep. She had just begun to give up hope when she heard the cry again. It was coming from the woods.

She hurried forward, but when she stepped under the second sky of fluttering leaves, she saw only a red squirrel, who watched her intently. She shook her head, glad that the day was clear and sparkling. There was mist enough in her thoughts without the deceptive swirls of white moisture to lead her astray. She waited, eyes narrowed, until the lapwing called again.

When the cry came, it caught her by surprise, it was so near. She ducked under the low branch of a pine, startling the squirrel, who scurried away. This time she was sure Ian would be waiting, but once again she was disappointed. Three times he called to her; three times she followed. She started to enjoy the game as her mind cleared and the movement of her muscles began to ease the ache.

Finally she realized Ian was leading her to the pond. He was always a little ahead of her, but near enough, she was certain, to smile at her confusion. When she reached the spot where the river widened, she stepped into the clearing expectantly. Once again, he was nowhere in sight.

There was no sign that Ian had been here, not even the print of his sandals on the damp bracken. Then she saw it— the hand harp from the Chisholm chest propped against the base of a tree. She froze, unable to believe her eyes. The wood had been repaired, sanded down and polished where the splinters had broken free. And the strings were obviously new.

Reluctant to touch the ancient instrument, Ailsa knelt to gaze at it in stunned silence. Then she reached out to run her hand over the fine wood. It felt smooth against her skin. Finally, holding her breath, she touched the strings, afraid they would break under the pressure of her fingers. But they held. The sound of the notes that trembled briefly at her touch was clear, sweet, and full of promise.

Ailsa felt a constriction in her throat. She had thought

the clarsach lost, but Ian had taken the time and care to save it. Lifting the harp, she leaned against the tree and held the instrument in her lap. It was small and fragile compared to the harp at the Hill, but the sounds it made were even more lovely.

She played tentatively at first, testing the nine strings, the combinations of sound she could coax from them. Then she began an ancient song.

William Sinclair made his way through the forest, cursing his uncomfortable high-topped boots as they sank into the marshy earth. He knew the bracken that curled about his feet would ruin his fine wool trousers, but did not care. He was listening to the warbling birds, enthralled by a harmony he had not heard since the early summers he had spent at his parents' country home. After they died, the house had been sold to pay his father's debts.

He smiled to himself, astonished that he should feel such peace, surrounded by windblown trees and dark, rugged mountains. Now that the mist had burned away, his uneasiness at the compelling landscape dissipated. He was enjoying himself, enjoying the freedom to walk so far without seeing a starved and hollow-eyed child or a single gray, imposing building. Actually, he was on an errand for Eleanor Williston, and now that he was free of that house, he did not intend to hurry.

He paused when he heard a new song rise above the voices of the birds.

> "When he woke from his long swoon,
> Full upon him fell the Moon. . . ."

To William's surprise, he changed course, drawn by the lilting notes. He could not have turned away from that music any more than he could from the celebration last night.

> "Makin' visions strange and white
> In the middle of the night."

The song swirled around him, shivered over his skin like the brush of gentle fingertips. He stopped to peer through the protective greenery to see who it was that had lured him here.

He drew in his breath when he saw a girl seated with her back to a tree, strumming a tiny harp. Her hair was loose and wild around her face, as if she had not combed it yet this morning. The glorious disorder pleased him, not only because he knew it would have shocked the ladies at the Hill.

He recognized her at once—the girl who had danced with abandon, then leaped over the bonfire. It came to him then that he had dreamed of her last night. She had twirled and swayed in the firelight, her hair free and flowing, her hem touched with flame, a carved flute in her hand. As she danced she had played a spell upon him and it clung to him now like a shadow.

He could hardly believe that the girl who had danced so recklessly, who had been so full of passion, even a little madness, was the same one who coaxed this fragile, plaintive song from the little harp. He had thought her wild, untamed, yet the music she made was more lovely, more touched with sensitivity than any he had heard in the drawing rooms in London.

Her head was bent, her face suffused with joy as she sang:

"O Lady Moon, how many dreams . . ."

William turned, perplexed, when another voice responded.

"Lit by thy elusive beams,
Have I mingled with pale thought—
Dreams and musin's come to naught."

Startled from his waking dream, William realized that for the second time in twenty-four hours, he was eavesdropping on a private moment, intruding where he had not been invited, and would not, he knew, be welcome.

Appalled at his behavior, he turned away. Long after he

had left the copse behind, the notes of the harp followed, singing to him, beguiling him, calling him back.

As the sound of Ian's voice faded, Ailsa raised her head, waiting. Just as he had before, he dropped from the branches of the tree on the opposite bank. " 'Tis a gift in honor of the day of your birth," he told her.

She looked at him in surprise. She had forgotten that today was her birthday. The excitement of Beltaine had sent everything else from her head.

"Do ye like it?" he asked unnecessarily.

Ailsa nodded, too moved to speak. Instead she began to play again, to him and for him, letting her music express what she could not. Finally she found her voice. "Ian-*mocharaid*, 'tis the most wonderful gift I've ever received. Thank ye."

She moved closer to the water until she knelt on the marshy bank, unaware of the moisture that soaked through her gown to her bare legs. As she looked at Ian's familiar face, at his eyes, full of joy at her delight, at his dark hair with twigs and leaves caught in the strands, she felt a longing she had never known. Gently she laid the harp aside, placing it on a high boulder, out of the reach of the water.

"Now," he said, "ye are a true *Seanachaidh*."

"I don't think the ancient bards would be happy to hear ye call me one of them." But she was pleased by the compliment, just the same. For a long moment, she was poised beside the river, transfixed by the fragments of sunlight on water. The sight of crowns of flowers floating on the surface—the last scattered remnants of the Beltaine celebration—brought back to her the moment when Ian had kissed her beneath the waterfall.

"Shall we go in?" he asked.

"Aye," Ailsa replied without hesitation. "But let's no' ruin all our clothes this time."

While Ian removed his shirt, breeches, socks, and sandals, leaving only his underdrawers, she slid her gown over her head and tossed it aside. She turned to find him waiting on the bank.

"Now!" they cried, and fell forward. The icy water

closed around them, and in a shower of bubbles they reached out to grasp each other's hands. Their toes slid over smooth stones, curled in the soft silty bottom of the pond. They drew closer, clung together as water ran down their bodies in rivulets.

Ailsa trembled, shaken by the touch of his skin on hers, and backed away. She wanted to look at him. She stared, fascinated by the black hair on his chest, then reached out shyly to run her fingers over the wet curls. He stood motionless, holding his breath as she explored his glistening shoulders, his arms, the curve of his throat. "Ye're beautiful," she whispered.

"And ye," he replied. He trailed a fingertip from the curve of her ear to the rapid pulse at the base of her throat. When she did not speak, he continued slowly downward, caressing her shoulders through her clinging chemise. Then he cupped her breasts in his hands until she sighed in pleasure and her nipples hardened into his palms. He shivered when she leaned closer, eyes closed, lips slightly parted.

Ian kissed her again, lingeringly. "I want to see all of ye," she murmured against his lips. "I want nothin' between us but clear flowin' water."

He held her at arm's length. "Are ye certain?"

"Come, don't tell me ye're a coward after all," Ailsa teased. "Ye've always told me ye feared nothin'." She gave him no chance to answer, but began to unfasten her chemise. When she slipped it down her arms and tossed it aside, Ian sucked in his breath at the sight of her bare shoulders, the pale curve of her breasts beneath the water.

She moved away and bent to remove her drawers while he did the same. They turned, the lap and swell of the water carried them forward, and their bodies met, skin to skin. Ailsa slid her arms around him and began to learn with her fingertips the breadth of his shoulders, the firm, rounded muscles of his back curving down to his buttocks, which she cupped in her hands. Ian gasped and pulled her closer.

She kissed him briefly, then drew away. The hair on Ian's chest brushed her bare nipples and she sighed in pleasure, aware, all at once, of the pressure of his need against her thigh. The spinning began in her head, but she forced it into silence and opened her mouth to his probing tongue. She moaned when he ran his hands up her side until he cupped her breasts in widespread fingers. Leaning back, she let her legs slide between his as he circled her nipples first with his hands, then with his tongue.

Ailsa floated, eyes closed, glorying in the slow-burning heat that moved through her body. She trembled at the gentle pressure of his fingertips on her skin. Slowly, arrestingly, he traced the droplets of water that glistened between her breasts, down to the white curve of her stomach. Then he slid his hand between her thighs.

She clutched at him, digging her fingernails into his back until he, too, began to tremble. Ailsa gasped, unable to breathe. She wanted him so much that her need was a sharp pain through her heart. Her face was flushed, her eyes dark with longing.

"Dear God!" Ian cried, as shaken as she. "Ye will drive me mad with wantin' ye."

She swallowed, her throat dry and parched. Ian's pulse went wild at the feather-light touch of her fingers on his chest, his hip, his thigh. Ailsa reached lower, toward the curling hair between his legs. Suddenly she was overcome by the rage in her blood that was too fierce and bright to bear, too achingly beautiful to end.

But she had to end it or be drawn into the whirlpool of her passion, where she would turn endlessly, crying out at the flames that threatened to consume her from within. "I can't," she gasped as she broke away from him, her hands pressed to her chest to stop the frantic beating of her heart. The fear was with him, too. She could see it in his luminous eyes, the way his hands shook when he released her.

"No, *mo-charaid*," he managed to whisper. " 'Tisn't yet the time for us." He took her hand and held it toward the sun, kissing the palm until even that pleasure was too intense. With an effort, he added shakily, "We must wait, lass."

The two stood rigid, afraid to move, craving comfort, peace. He wanted to brush the hair from her face but dared not. She wanted to twine her fingers with his, but could not.

They wanted to hold each other, to soothe away the frenzy and fear, but they knew a single touch would bring it rushing back. For a long moment, the cool water flowed between and around them while the passion, with no fire to feed it, receded.

Abruptly, Ian turned away. He swam to the opposite side of the pond, ducked beneath the water. He came toward her, hands extended, and gripped her ankles. Then he tugged until he pulled her legs from under her. She tumbled with him through the water, and finally rose to the surface, choking with laughter. As always, he had known how to distract her. She caught her breath, ducked low, so her hair spread around her like wild, rippled wings. "Come to me," she said in invitation. "Come."

He grinned. "Ye'll no' be foolin' me with your wanton ways, Ailsa Rose. I see the wickedness in your eyes."

She lunged for him, grasped his shoulders, and pushed him back under the water. He rolled, tried to pull her down with him, but she swam away just as he surfaced, blowing bubbles and waving his arms threateningly. When he started toward her, Ailsa raised her hands in a gesture of surrender. "No more, Ian Fraser, or I'll be too weary to find my way home."

He collapsed next to her and they sat laughing near the bank, where the water murmured at their waists.

"Hush!" Ailsa said suddenly. "Someone is comin'."

Ian peered through the trees. They heard low, sonorous voices and saw flashes of the hunting green Mackensie plaid.

"I forgot 'tis the Sabbath," Ailsa whispered. "They must be on their way to the kirk." Her mother, like Ian's parents, had not insisted that Ailsa receive her religious education in the strict Scottish kirk. The two children had learned to read from the Bible during many evenings by the peat fire at home.

At the same moment, Ian and Ailsa heard Jenny's soft-spoken voice. She was walking through the trees, head bowed. She had always observed the Sabbath as the other Highlanders did, refusing to work or play on Sunday. Jenny spent the day praying and reading the Bible, meditating on her sins. Ailsa grimaced at the thought. To her, the fairies and Celtic gods were far more real than the grim, forbidding God the others worshiped.

"They would be gey shocked if they saw us here on the Sabbath," Ian whispered. "They might even find the need to pray for our souls."

"They would be as shocked if 'twere any other day of the week. And I fear they've been prayin' for our souls long since."

"Well then," he said with a wicked grin, "I suppose we are damned, thee and me, Ailsa Rose."

"Hush," Ailsa said, pinching his arm. "Do ye want them to hear ye?"

Ian raised an eyebrow. "No, my heart. For I fear they would want to join us, and the pond isn't wide enough to hold us and the whole Clan Mackensie as well."

" 'Twas wide enough last night," she reminded him.

"Aye," he said, "but last night there was magic in the air, birdeen. Remember?"

She shivered, smiled, and wanted to weep. "So I do."

Mairi sat at the loom, weaving the magnificent blue and purple fabric. She looked up occasionally at a sound from outside and wondered where her daughter might be. If Ailsa had forgotten that this was her birthday, her mother had not. She had saved a special piece of mutton for dinner and intended to bake black buns, Ailsa's favorite. She had already prepared the currants and apples, nuts, cloves, and ginger for the filling. The pastry would not take long.

Mairi frowned in concentration as she worked. She had not yet freed herself of the premonition that had troubled her since yesterday. Perhaps that was why, when she heard a gentle knock at the half-open door, she jumped in alarm. Highlanders never knocked; they always came right in.

She drew a steadying breath and rose. Pulling the door further open, she stared in surprise at the man in morning coat, silk waistcoat, and fine wool trousers who stood outside. She knew he was an Englishman. If his clothes had not told her as much, his top hat would have. No man wore a formal top hat among these hills unless he were mad or English or both.

The man opened his mouth and closed it again. He felt immensely uncomfortable, not only because his clothes were too warm for this spring day and the long walk he had already taken. There was something about Mairi's penetrating gaze that disconcerted him. After an awkward pause, he removed his hat and bowed. "Good morning, madam. I hope I'm not disturbing you?"

Mairi stifled a smile at his formality. "Ye're welcome here, whoever ye be."

"Oh dear," he muttered. "I'd completely forgotten that we haven't been introduced. Difficult to remember to follow the rules in a place like this, don't you agree?"

"Impossible," she said, no longer able to hide her smile. "I wouldn't even bother to try if I were ye."

He looked at her suspiciously. Was she laughing at him? But her smile was warm and there had been a genuine note of welcome in her voice when she greeted him. Running his hands nervously around the brim of his hat, he said at last, "William Sinclair, barrister. I'm staying with the Willistons on the Hill. And you would be Mairi Rose?"

She inclined her head. He seemed uncertain how to proceed. Out of pity, Mairi prompted, "Can I help ye in some way?"

When he nodded, his light brown hair fell into his gray eyes. He brushed it back impatiently. "Lady Williston sent me, in point of fact. Her son has been sleeping badly and she said you might know a way to help."

"Come in," Mairi said. "I can give ye what she needs. 'Tis only the tops of nettles, chopped very small. I've some here in the press." When he seemed reluctant to follow, she touched his arm to draw him inside.

He stared about him in wonder as she went to get her leather bag of medicinal cures out of the kitchen cupboard. The house was tiny and dark and smelled strongly of peat. He wondered how the Highlanders could spend their lives in such a place. But perhaps they were outside more often than not.

"Here ye be." Mairi offered a small leather bag. "Tell Lady Williston to mix this with the whites of eggs and apply it to the boy's temples when 'tis bedtime. It should ease him."

"Thank you." William put the bag in his pocket, took out a coin, and offered it to her.

Mairi stared at him, shocked. "I couldn't take that. 'Tis helpin' a friend I am, no' makin' a profit from their misery."

He took a step back, as if her anger were a wind so strong he could not stand before it. Strange, he thought, that a woman like this should call Lady Williston a friend. Or perhaps she was only being courteous. He wondered if Eleanor would return that particular courtesy, but thought it unlikely. "Forgive me," he stammered. "I didn't know—"

He was actually blushing, Mairi realized, ashamed of her outburst. How could he have known? He was from a world where everything was bought and paid for. " 'Tis nothin'," she told him gently. " 'Tis forgotten."

Before he could respond, Ailsa brushed past the open door. "Look what Ian gave me!"

William and Mairi turned in astonishment. Even her mother had not heard her approach. Ailsa's face was flushed and she danced across the floor, unable to stay still. Oblivious to everything but her own exuberance, she did not notice William standing, mouth agape.

Ailsa offered the harp to her mother, but paused when Mairi frowned. The girl turned, startled, to see a stranger with a top hat in his hand, running his fingers around and around the brim. She gasped and the color faded from her cheeks.

Mairi opened her mouth to make the introductions, then saw the expression on William's face. He was clearly dumbfounded by the sight of her daughter, but more than that, he was enchanted. He looked as though he had been given a gift straight from the hands of the gods. Mairi's heartbeat slowed. So it had come already. Too soon, she wanted to cry. 'Tis too soon! With an effort of will, she forced herself to speak. "My daughter, Ailsa," she said tonelessly. "And this is Mr. William Sinclair, a guest of the Willistons come to get some nettles for the lady."

Ailsa nodded, attempted a polite smile. "Forgive me," she said softly. "I didn't know ye were here."

William shook his head emphatically; he was having difficulty finding his voice. He had never thought to meet this girl, yet here she stood, apologizing for her behavior. He could not allow it. "There's no need for all that. It was entirely my fault for intruding," he managed at last. Then he bowed to atone for his blunder.

Ailsa grinned at his obvious sincerity. Apparently it was important to him that *she* forgive *him*, though she was not certain why. She could not know that he had intruded on her privacy more than once before. "Don't be daft," she said. "How were ye to know that I'd come in so full of the wonder of my clarsach that I wouldn't see if Dagda himself were waitin' here?"

William did not understand what she said, but the sound of her voice was so musical, compared to the clipped and precise sentences of his friends, that he thought he could listen to it all day. He straightened his shoulders to shake away such thoughts. The two women stood idle, waiting, no doubt, for him to leave. "I shall be on my way, ladies. I've taken more than enough of your time. I thank you, madam, for the packets," he told Mairi. Then he turned to Ailsa. "And you for—" He broke off, flushing in confusion.

"For what?" she asked with a curious smile.

Her smile left him momentarily speechless; it was so natural, with no hint of pinched nostrils or rigid lips. "I shall be going," he repeated. Then, before he could make more of a fool of himself, he hurried out the door.

Ailsa watched him go, perplexed. She turned to Mairi with a question on her lips but was stopped by the look on her mother's face. Mairi was glowering after William Sinclair as if he had indeed offended her, as if she would like to slam the door to make certain he never returned. Perhaps he reminded her, painfully, of her husband. To Ailsa, the sight of another Englishman was exciting. So few had come to the glen since her father left it.

"Mother," Ailsa said, drawing Mairi's attention back to herself, "just look! We found this clarsach in the Chisholm chest, but 'twas old and broken. Ian took it home and fixed it for me. Isn't it wonderful?" She held out the harp and her mother took it gingerly. She ran her hands along the wood as Ailsa had done earlier.

" 'Tis very beautiful," she said. "Ian is most wise."

Ailsa went to place the harp in her kist, out of reach of the damp. As she passed the door, she saw that the Englishman stood several yards away, scratching his muttonchop sideburns and looking about him in confusion.

"I think Mr. Sinclair is lost," she said.

Mairi glanced out the door and sighed. "I don't know why they come at all, when they can't even find their way home." She turned away in anger.

Ailsa was puzzled by her mother's response. Was it so odd that a stranger could not find his way through woods and hills he had never known?

Despite Mairi's strange behavior, Ailsa called out, "Can I show ye the way to the Hill o' the Hounds, Mr. Sinclair?"

He turned, trying to hide his embarrassment. "I'm afraid I don't quite remember—"

"Never mind. I'll take ye there. 'Tis a lovely day for a walk anyway."

As Ailsa took down her plaid, Mairi shook her head wildly, even reached out to grasp her daughter's arm and hold her back.

"What is't, Mother?"

"I don't want ye to go."

"But why?" Ailsa asked.

Mairi clasped her hands together and stared down at them. "Never mind, birdeen. Ye go and do what ye must."

"So I shall." Still puzzled, Ailsa nevertheless threw the plaid around her shoulders and went to join William. "This way," she said. " 'Tis through the woods, ye ken, and up the hill."

The Englishman looked around at the intimidating landscape—the hills, growing darker by the moment; the wind, wailing through the trees; the sky, which, though it had been clear a few minutes before, was filled now with gray threatening clouds. Ailsa had run ahead and he followed with care, watching for hillocks or roots or clumps of gorse that might trip him up. He had to move slowly, even in his heavy boots, though the girl moved carelessly over the same ground in bare feet. "What is that noise?" he asked, uneasy at the low, deep groan that seemed to rise from the distant mountains.

Ailsa stopped to listen. "Mayhap 'tis the *me'h'ing*."

"I beg your pardon?" he said to her back.

She waited until he caught up to her and explained, "The melancholy bleatin' of the sheep on the hills. Or," she said, leaning forward to whisper dramatically, "mayhap 'tis the Spirit o' the Mountain."

He blinked at her in confusion.

" 'Tis the deep, sad sound that 'tis neither wind nor water nor thunder nor rain, but the sighin' of the hills when a storm is on the way." She closed her eyes to listen more carefully. "Aye," she said. " 'Tis the Spirit indeed. 'Tis magnificent, don't ye think?"

William shivered at the mournful drone and glanced at the clouds overhead. They had swept quickly across the sky, engulfed it, making a long, gray shadow on the land. Now they rumbled, dark and heavy with moisture. "I do believe it's going to rain," he said.

"Aye," Ailsa agreed. "I can't wait." Then she saw his frown. "Och, but ye wouldn't care for it, would ye? I've been thinkin' too much of myself and no' of ye. We'll hurry."

She was off before he could stop her, running through the bracken, ducking under swaying leaves. By the time William caught up to her, he was breathing heavily. "Don't hurry," he said, "I think I might enjoy this after all." His voice shook a little, for in truth he did not like the looks of the jagged mountains circled by clouds, but he knew too that he did not want this walk to end. "I saw the harp you brought home," he said when she began to walk more slowly beside him. "Are you interested in music?"

"I love it as much as a storm in the glen," she told him. "To me 'tis magic, just like the wind and the rain."

There was no pretense in her answer. She did not stop to wonder what he wanted to hear, or what she ought to say, or what was most polite; whatever thought flew into her head flew out of her mouth the same way.

"I go to the opera often in London. Verdi is my favorite."

Ailsa stopped in the middle of the path. "I've never heard an opera. Tell me what 'tis like," she asked eagerly.

"I've never tried to describe it, actually." He felt inadequate, certain he could never do it properly. Yet for her he had to try. "The music is wonderful, powerful, when the orchestra is right and the singers are good. The songs rise from the stage and echo through the hall until they seem to fill every niche with the sound. I've seen women weep, so moved were they by a performance."

Ailsa leaned closer, eyes wide. "And what about the hall itself? Tell me what 'tis like inside."

"There are many opera houses, but my favorite is the Royal Italian. It's a beautiful building with a huge circular ceiling and crystal chandeliers that tinkle with the vibration of voices sometimes. The stage is carved all round with figures that seem frozen in fascination as they listen to the music. There are rows and rows of private boxes with velvet curtains and comfortable seats, and the women who use them come dressed in satin and silk with their wide skirts and fur-trimmed pelisses—" William broke off, astonished that he had gone on for so long. It was not like him to chatter.

"Och, don't stop!" Ailsa cried, eyes sparkling. "Tell me more about the city." Without realizing it, she touched his arm. "I heard once of a palace made of glass. Is't true?"

All at once, William found it difficult to catch his breath. "You must mean the Crystal Palace. Yes, it's true. It was built for the Great Exhibition of 1851. It's beautiful, like a huge fairy tale in glass. But I can't really describe it. You have to see it for yourself." He recognized her disappointment and added quickly, "There's more than just the building, you know. You can also wander through groves of tropical trees in the pleasure gardens, where they have musical concerts and exhibitions of painting and sculpture."

"It sounds like a miracle," Ailsa breathed. "I've always wanted to go to London. My father was born there, ye ken."

"Is he English, then?"

"Aye. Ye might even know him," she said hopefully. "His name is Charles Kittridge. He's a diplomat in Queen Victoria's service."

William frowned and tried to remember. "I've heard of the family, certainly. They've an estate in Kent. I believe I recall hearing that the younger son had joined the Diplomatic Service. Never met him, though. From what I understand, he doesn't return to London often. Off seeing the world, you know."

"I know," she said wistfully.

"Tell me—" William stopped abruptly when they reached the edge of the woods. The moor stretched ahead, a strange, glowing green in the light of the approaching storm. Now that the sky was not hidden by trees, he could see how the clouds hovered low above the hills, more threatening than ever. As he paused, reluctant to leave the forest, the rain began to fall.

Ailsa stepped from beneath the protection of the leaves and raised her face to the sky. The wind came up, moaning, and she looked about at the swaying trees, the shadowed mountains, the lake, whose deep blue had changed to leaden silver in the past few moments. " 'Tis beautiful, isn't it? Sometimes I ache inside with the beauty."

William forgot the storm when he looked at Ailsa's face, altered by the translucent light into an image too radiant to be real. Her blue and violet eyes glistened with tears at the scene that moved her so deeply. He felt a film of moisture on his own eyes, an urge to weep and laugh together that he did not understand.

When the wind howled more fiercely, Ailsa turned. " 'Tis time to go inside. Soon ye'll no' be able to find your way." She pointed to the loch, a churning mass of gray and silver waves that leaped and beat against the shore. " 'Tis *Marcach Sine*," she whispered, "the Rider o' the Storm. He comes on the back of the wind and blows the waters from below till they spit and snarl like wildcats. He slips into the heart of a burn or loch and casts a *sian* upon it—a spell that fills it with the force of his own drivin' fury."

William listened, breathless, not daring to move, afraid she would stop and the sound of her voice fade into a chilled silence. She had cast a *sian* on him in his dream last night, weaving it tighter as they walked together. If she told him now to join the Rider o' the Storm in the heart of that raging loch, he would do it, and gladly.

Ailsa saw how he stared, eyes glazed. She did not know

what it meant: she only knew no one had ever looked at her that way before. She felt strangely drawn to him in that instant, but the rain was falling faster, like sheets of beaten silver that blurred and transformed the landscape. "Ye'd best hurry," she said firmly. " 'Tis dangerous to linger now. I shouldn't have tarried. Will ye forgive me?"

He stood with the rain streaming around him, so heavy he could barely see her face. "Anything," he said. "I would forgive you anything."

She smiled—he could tell, even through the downpour. "Ye may not say so tomorrow when ye can't rise from your bed for the gatherin' of fog in your head and the coughin' in your throat."

"I will always think so," he said. He reached up to tip his hat but the rain had knocked it off, or perhaps he had lost it in the woods. He neither remembered nor cared.

"Go," Ailsa repeated, "or ye'll be ill."

She turned away, but he reached for her, uncertain, for a moment, if he held only rain and wind in his hand. Then he felt the rough texture of her sleeve. "Will I see you again?"

The urgency of his question, the touch of his hand on her arm made her feel somehow unreal, a part of someone else's dream. "I come to the Hill on Tuesday for music lessons. But now, be off with ye!" she cried. "For the Kelpies will be out soon and they'll carry ye away." Then with a smile, she was gone.

She did not turn and walk away; she simply faded into the downpour like a spirit. But he knew now she was real. Despite her admonition, he stood for a long time, staring at the place where she had been while the rain poured down around him. The sound of her laughter came to him, a fragment of light in the darkening storm, a whisper, an echo—or was it only in his mind?

It did not matter which, he realized as he peered through the shimmering light at the dance of trees in the furious wind. Echo or whisper, dream or reality, spirit or woman—Ailsa Rose was the answer to a prayer he had carried inside him for years but had never once voiced, even to himself.

William Sinclair had fallen deeply in love for the first and last time in his life.

7

William stood at the sideboard, staring blankly at milk, eggs, muffins, bread, butter, cold fowl, ham, and tongue. He felt vaguely ill. He had lost his appetite a few days past in the midst of a storm. Taking only a cup of coffee, he sat at the far end of the table. Agatha, Sarah, and Eleanor were chattering about the gowns they would have made for the summer ball, while Gerald Harcourt and John, Lord Williston discussed the number of grouse and partridge they were likely to bag on today's shoot. William had already declined to attend. It was Tuesday and he meant to stay close to the house.

He stared into his swirling coffee and saw the lake roil and spit in fury. The rain had ceased yesterday, but the storm went on inside him. He did not speak a word, but left the table and wandered into the morning room, his half-filled cup in his hand.

The curtains had been carefully drawn to keep out the morning light. William felt ill at ease in the unnatural dimness. He sank into a chair and stared at the buffet covered with china figurines placed carefully among gold-framed photographs of Williston relatives. To him, the faces were all the same, as were the Oriental vases on the Chippendale tables that flanked the two sets of wing-backed chairs. He was hemmed in, suddenly, by the clutter.

"William, whatever is the matter with you?"

He half turned to find Sarah Worthy approaching, a silver tray in her hand.

"You didn't eat a thing at breakfast. I was worried about you. I noticed you'd forgotten to put milk and sugar in your coffee. You always drink it with milk and sugar, you know."

Had he imagined it, or was there a hint of accusation in her voice?

"So I've brought it along to you. I thought you might like a bit of company." She noticed he had forgotten to button his jacket again and his cravat was tied in an uneven bow; he had not taken the time to do it properly. But she did not mention these things. He might think she was criticizing.

"Thank you," William replied without enthusiasm. "Most kind, I'm sure." He hadn't actually noticed that the coffee tasted more bitter than usual. His thoughts were on a pair of blue-violet eyes and the sound of laughter in the wind.

Sarah sat primly beside him, took his cup to add milk and sugar, stirred the mixture with an ornate silver spoon. "There, that should be better."

He frowned. It sounded as if she were giving him medicine, assuring him it wouldn't taste as dreadful as he supposed.

"I was just thinking, now that that wretched rain has stopped, it might be a nice day for a walk," the lady continued, somewhat abashed because William's eyes had not met hers since she entered the room. She had worn her best morning gown, pale spring green with tiny pink roses, a lace scalloped bodice, and bell-shaped skirt. She also wore her widest crinoline. The dress made her waist look particularly small, and the color was good for her skin, she knew. She had even allowed a few curls to escape from her crown of braids to make her face look softer. She patted her forehead with her handkerchief. William had not even noticed her careful preparations. In fact, he spoke fewer words to her every day.

He did not answer now, but stared at the crack in the heavy drapes that allowed a single ray of light into the murky room.

"I said, I thought it would be nice to take a walk," she repeated.

Again he did not answer.

"William!" Sarah snapped, then covered her mouth

with her lace-gloved hand. She was relieved when the others arrived, each with their coffee or tea in hand. She had left her own chocolate on the dining table in her agitation at William's abrupt departure. She noticed that he still had not looked up, even when she raised her voice so rudely. Sarah sighed, rose, and went to stand at the window.

"William, my dear," Agatha proclaimed, taking in the scene at a single glance, "whatever possessed you to leave the table like that? We've all been wondering what the matter is."

He looked up, unable to ignore the piercing quality of Agatha Harcourt's voice. "Bit bilious this morning, you know. Couldn't eat a thing," he lied.

She raised her eyebrows skeptically. "Well, it's really such a shame, after all the trouble the Willistons have gone to—"

"No trouble at all," John Williston declared. "Leave the man in peace." He and his wife seated themselves on the opposite side of the room on an apple-green brocade sofa.

Gerald Harcourt rested his elbow on the marble mantel. "Dashed peculiar the way you've been acting these past few days," he said to William. "Climate must not agree with you."

"It was that ghastly storm," Agatha said. "Ever since you got yourself drenched, you've been behaving as if we don't exist. Must have caught a chill or something." She leaned down to whisper, "Someone must give you a talking to, William. You need to settle down and straighten out your priorities." She paused, took a deep breath, and added, "If you ask me—"

"Which he most assuredly did not," Gerald interjected.

Agatha ignored her husband. "If you ask me, you need a woman to take you in hand. It's time you married, indeed it is." She glanced at Sarah, caught in a ray of sunlight at the window. "Long past time, actually."

"You're right," William agreed. "You are absolutely right." He rose abruptly, set his cup and saucer on the table, and left the room, closing the door behind him with fervor.

Agatha stared after him, shocked, for once, beyond words.

◊ ◊ ◊

Her chores completed, Ailsa made her way through the cool woods. She had taken some time to play her hand harp, as she did each day, becoming more adept with every try, and more delighted with the sounds that spilled from those nine strings. When she touched the clarsach, the past enveloped her and there was nothing in the world but the music she created. Still, she had been restless and unable to concentrate this morning, so she'd started for the Hill earlier than usual.

Ian was waiting beside the river, half concealed by the morning mist. "I'll walk ye to the moor," he said softly.

"Aye," she whispered, "aye."

They walked in silence. Ailsa wondered why today Ian did not try to keep her away from the Hill o' the Hounds. He only held her hand tightly and did not turn to kiss or draw her near. There was danger in those things; he knew it as well as she. When they reached the edge of the woods, he turned to face her.

"I'll be waitin' when you're through."

She nodded and swayed toward him. They paused with their lips a breath apart and stood, staring into each other's eyes at the naked, hungry souls beyond. They shivered, their fingers locked in a painful grip. This time Ian was the first to draw away. "I'll be waitin'," he repeated.

"I'll be here." She turned away, her heart beating rapidly, but the memory of his touch did not go. The raw emptiness she felt each time they parted rose inside and with it the words of a long-forgotten song.

> "I have a tumult in my brain
> A monster in my thoughts."

Then she realized Ian was speaking the words, voicing her turmoil aloud and calling it his own.

> "A drivin', hectorin' pain
> That goes, but comes again."

All at once, Ailsa began to hurry. She craved the dim silence of the house on the Hill—her father's world of order, precision, and elegance. She wanted peace, a momentary freedom from the joyful savagery of her feelings for Ian.

When she entered the house, the stillness welcomed her, cool, dark, and comforting. The drawing-room doors were shut, so she continued down the hall, touching the wainscotting, the flowered wallpaper, catching a glimpse now and then of the loch that shimmered far below.

She paused when she realized a man stood in the embrasure near the end of the hall, staring out the window. William Sinclair. In his silk waistcoat, dark brown morning coat, and trousers cut close to his legs, he blended with the elegant setting, yet still seemed ill at ease. He gazed through the glass pensively, a trace of sadness in the curve of his mouth, his brown hair falling untidily into his eyes. His expression was intent, as if by contemplating the loch carefully enough, he would come at last to understand it.

With one hand he leaned on the windowsill, with the other he grasped the velvet curtains. Suddenly he raised his head. He had sensed Ailsa's presence. He turned, saw the girl who stood barefoot in her plain brown linsey-woolsey gown with her red plaid draped around her shoulders. The sadness left him in an instant and he smiled, awkwardly, uncertain of her response. "Good morning, Ailsa."

She moved forward, troubled, caught in the web of memory. She missed her father suddenly, acutely, yearned to see his unknown but familiar face. Ailsa reached William's side and looked out at the loch. The water was calm now that the storm had passed. Sunlight sparkled on the surface like pale yellow gems on an undulating cloth of blue. " 'Tis so beautiful," Ailsa murmured.

William took a deep breath and managed to stammer, "It's not as—" He broke off and gripped the drapes more tightly.

Ailsa looked up curiously. "No' as what?"

He swallowed, then plunged ahead, "Not as beautiful as you."

She closed her eyes and the ache of her loss became greater. When William drummed his fingers on the windowsill, she looked down to see him shift from one foot to the other. He was clearly uncomfortable. "Why did ye come here?" she asked, in order to divert her thoughts.

He turned back to the window. "My aunt talked me into it, actually. She said I'd been working too hard and needed some rest. I didn't want to come, you know. I'm not really certain why I agreed. At least I didn't know then. Now I do." He did not look at her, dared not.

"Why?"

She asked only because she was curious. She did not wish to tease or tempt him. He caught his breath, unable to speak. What should he tell her? It came to him then that this girl, of all the women he knew, deserved the truth. "I was meant to come because—" The words stuck in his throat after all, but he made himself go on. "So that I could meet you."

Unable to bear the disbelief or pity he might see in her expressive eyes, he turned away before she could respond. He slipped into the study, closing the doors behind him. Ailsa stood with the sunlight on her face to stare mutely at the place where he had been a moment since.

As she finished her lesson, Ailsa noticed that the door, which had been ajar, was closed softly from without. She rose in a trance, picked up her plaid, bade farewell to the children and Master James, and went into the hall. William was standing at the window where she had first seen him. She knew he had been listening as she played. When he saw her, he flushed.

"I've come to apologize," he said. "I shouldn't have spoken to you like that. It was quite appallingly—"

" 'Twas kind," she interrupted, "to say such lovely things about a person ye hardly know."

He turned to look at her. "Since the moment I left you, I've been planning what to say, how to apologize, but then I heard you playing. I knew it had to be you. Who else could make a harp sound like an angel singing without words? You made me forget everything while I listened." He paused to take a breath, unaccustomed to saying so much all at once. "I've always enjoyed music, but I never understood—how very beautiful it could be." He swallowed and gathered his courage. "Not until now." He looked away, more embarrassed than ever. The sight of Ailsa with her hair over her shoulder, her eyes wide, her lips parted in a half smile was too much for him just then.

All her life, Ailsa had waited to hear the words he had just spoken. Ian, Mairi and her friends had always taken her music for granted, had never thought it necessary to praise the talent she'd been born with. She felt a soaring sense of satisfaction she could not express.

She was silent for so long that William's heart began to beat erratically. "Perhaps I shouldn't have said anything."

Ailsa touched his arm. "Och, but ye should have. And I thank ye. From my heart I thank ye."

He found he could not speak, not with the pressure of her fingers on his arm. He could feel it even through the layers of wool and fine linen. When he shivered, she withdrew her hand. In a moment she would be gone and he could not bear to let that happen. "Do you like coming here?" he asked. It was the only question that came to mind.

Ailsa smiled broadly. "Oh, aye. There's so much to learn. 'Tisn't only the music I come for, though 'tis most of it. But the house itself teaches me things. I want to know all I can about the world I haven't seen." She paused. "I can't really explain what the Hill o' the Hounds means to me."

Somehow William had to keep her here, keep her talking in that lilting Scottish brogue that turned words into magic. "It's a strange name, that, don't you think? How'd the Willistons come by it, anyway?"

Ailsa grinned. "Och, 'twasn't the Willistons who chose it. A Scottish bard named it after a gey sad legend."

"Tell me," he said softly.

Ailsa did not blush or make him plead or ask him if he really did not wish to know. She simply leaned close to the glass to better absorb the sunlight. "Well," she began, "it happened long ago, when the Clan Grant had their keep on this very hill. 'Twas durin' the time of troubles when King Jamie IV chose to fight the English over an insult from their king that he couldn't forgive. He called the best men in Scotland to fight his battle with him, and the laird of the Grants and his sons answered out of honor and love."

She frowned and when she continued, her voice was full of bitterness. "There were some Macdonnells who were no' so loyal and stayed behind. Knowin' this keep to be poorly defended, they attacked, killin' every Grant who had the misfortune to cross their path that day. Then they set the keep afire and left the bodies to smolder in the flames.

"But they were overproud, those Macdonnells. They hadn't noticed the huntin' hounds locked in the kennel, bayin' mournfully as the Grants fell one by one under enemy swords. After the intruders had gone, the dogs jumped at the wooden door of the kennel, batterin' it till it weakened and collapsed. Snarlin' and snappin', they leaped through the flames as if they were no more than air, to follow the Macdonnells."

Ailsa stopped to take a breath. "The hounds tracked the men through burn and mountain, moor and wood. One by one the Macdonnells fell as the animals hurled their bodies at the enemy, rippin' out their throats and leavin' them to bleed their lives into the flowerin' purple heather. The dogs didn't stop till every Macdonnell who'd been at the keep that day was dead. Then, wearily, the animals made their way back to the hill and lay down to wait for their master's return."

Tears shimmered in her eyes. "The laird of the Clan Grant never came back. He'd fallen beside his king at the massacre of Flodden Field. So the brave hounds lay here, thirsty, hungry, forgotten, guardin' the castle that had become a tomb, till they, too, died, one by one. When a few of the survivin' Grants returned and saw what had happened, they buried the animals with great ceremony beside the members of the clan on top of the hill. They lie among the bones of the Grants, in peace at last, beneath the place where the house now stands."

William felt like weeping at the sad tale. Or was it the way Ailsa spoke, the way she trembled with grief for men and dogs who had died centuries before her own birth?

"There's been a lot of suffering in the Highlands because of us," he said. He felt responsible somehow for her pain.

"The glen is full of sufferin'," Ailsa murmured. " 'Tis part of its beauty. How could ye know the miracle of sunlight on the water if ye hadn't also known the darkness?" She stared out at the loch and saw there a reflection of the past—the pain, the joy, the celebration and sorrow that had rung through these hills for hundreds of years. The soul of the glen seemed to speak to her through voices of fragmented light and wind on the water.

"Will you marry me?" William asked.

Slowly, Ailsa turned from the window to look into his gray eyes, full of hope and fear and an adoration he could no longer hide. "Marry ye?" she repeated blankly.

"Yes. Become my wife and return to London with me. I don't want to lose you."

He was speaking the simple truth; she could see it in his eyes. "London?" she repeated in a reverent whisper.

"Of course." He had asked without thinking; now he began to shake at the audacity of what he'd done.

"I can't answer a question like that," she said. "I don't even know ye."

"But I know you." He struggled to find the words that would make her believe his life would end the moment she ceased to be part of it. But there was nothing he could say. "Please," he murmured at last, "just think about it."

Ailsa looked away in confusion. She did not understand the things she felt, could not explain her inclination to touch his face, his lips, to make him smile as he had this morning when he first caught sight of her. He was daft; that must be it. But his gaze was steady, his expression sincere. She opened her mouth to reply and found she had no answer. "I have to go," she said.

"Promise me you'll think about it." He was desperate now and reached out to grasp her arm, then stopped himself, his fingers curled tightly inward. He had no right to touch her, no right to try to make her stay. "Please."

No one had ever said please in quite that way, as if the world would be naught but a shadow if she refused. She took a step backward. "I'll think," she said. "But—"

He raised his hand to stop her. "It's enough," he said. "Enough for me."

She had given him so little, yet his face glowed with joy. She felt a pain in her chest that made her want to weep. Without another word, she left him.

The collie Torran met Ailsa halfway across the moor, barking a boisterous greeting while he pranced impatiently beside her in an attempt to make her hurry. His master was waiting in the shade of a Caledonian pine, his thumbs hooked in his wide leather belt. Ailsa ran to cup his face in her hands, running her fingertips over his features. She stared into his eyes, caught her fingers in his hair until the feeling of unreality slowly receded. "I missed ye," she said.

Ian covered her hands with his. "Ye've a look in your eyes, birdeen, like a lass who's been workin' overmuch and needs to take a day to simply wander through the woods." He kissed her palms one at a time, then twined his fingers with hers and led her into the forest. Torran ran ahead, his attention caught by a quick red squirrel, but when the tiny animal ran up an oak, the dog came racing back. He stood, tongue lolling, tail wagging, ready and waiting for an adventure.

"Come, Torran, and we'll find ye a rabbit to chase."

"Where are we goin'?" Ailsa asked. Ian walked with a purposeful stride that did not seem like "wandering" to her.

"To the heart of the hills, to the place of the wind and the rain," he told her mysteriously.

"Will ye no' let me go home for dinner? Or do ye think to starve me to death?"

"I've cheese and milk and bread hidden near a burn, and even a black bun or two. And I've already told Mairi ye'll no' be comin' home till gloamin'," Ian replied.

"Did ye no' think to ask me before ye planned my day?"

He paused to grin at her. "I thought to do it, aye, but ye've been an obstinate lass of late, so I judged it safer to see to things myself."

Ailsa wondered why she thought just then of William Sinclair's uncertainty, his whispered "please" that had touched her so deeply. She pushed the image to the back of her mind and broke away from Ian to run through the trees. She ducked beneath leaves and low-hanging branches, the damp earth clinging to the soles of her feet.

Ian caught up to her at the edge of a brae and grasped her around the waist. She spun toward him, laughing, but her foot slipped and she nearly sent them both tumbling down the hill into patches of heather and gorse below. Ian shifted his weight so they fell backward instead, landing in a bed of bracken that softened their fall.

Torran scrambled after them to see if they were hurt. He licked his master's face experimentally and Ian pushed him back with a groan. "Away with ye. I'm no' dead yet, though I soon will be if ye don't leave off your barkin' and kissin'."

While he struggled with the dog, Ailsa rose and was off again. She ran the other way now, toward the purple mountains and the strange, tilted shadows of rocks on the moor. She darted in and out among the boulders, climbing higher and slowly higher until she reached a huge standing stone that curved almost to a point at the top. Holding her breath, she drew herself to the narrow crown and stood, balanced precariously. The wind came up beside her with a cry of welcome. She spread her arms wide so her plaid streamed behind her like soaring crimson wings.

Ailsa smiled as she swayed in the force of the wind, then she saw Ian at the base of the stone. He reached up to her, called, "Come down, Ailsa Rose, before the wind takes ye." The tension in his voice, the fear in his eyes brought her back to her senses. The moor, streaked with shadows, lay stretched at her feet. For all the soft murmur of the breeze through the rippling grass, it would make a hard and painful place to land. Carefully, inching her body downward, she grasped Ian's hand, then leaped to the ground and collapsed among the stark outcroppings of stone.

"What madness has made ye so reckless today?" Ian asked as he crouched beside her.

"I don't know," she whispered. "All at once I couldn't seem to stay still." She turned to meet his gaze, glanced once more at the high, narrow boulder, and shivered. Which was more dangerous—the look of longing in Ian's eyes or the fall from the wind to the shadows below?

"Why can't I bear to look at ye sometimes?" She touched his arm briefly, tentatively.

"Because no matter how much we shout that we fear nothin', we're afraid now, ye and me, of the things inside us that we can't understand."

"Aye," she whispered.

For a while they sat in silence and watched Torran bark furiously as he ran from stone to stone, calling challenge after challenge. When he received no response but gray, rigid silence, he ran back to his master and lay down, panting.

"We must go," Ailsa said at last. "There are better places, warmer, where we'll be more welcome."

They rose to wander back across the moor until they reached the hollow tree where Ian had hidden his basket of food. Ailsa realized she was hungry when he drew out cheese and crisp black buns, bread, and a bowl. He removed the leather thong that bound the cheesecloth and they drank from opposite sides of the bowl, enjoying the thick, creamy milk. Once, he leaned forward to lick the ring of white from her lips, but did not kiss her. The madness was too near to take such a risk.

Breaking off pieces of cheese to bury in the bread, they ate while the collie growled at the tiny burn nearby. Ailsa frowned, feeling restless. There was something unfinished, something she had to do, but she did not know what it was. When the food was gone, she stared at the weave of the empty basket and thought of a bolt of plaid with stripes of white, blue, and green on a yellow background. "I want to go—"

"—to the cave where we found the Chisholm chest," Ian finished for her.

She could not help but smile. He knew her so well. "Aye," she agreed. "I want to be movin'."

Together they repacked the basket and stowed it in the hollow tree. When he saw them rise, Torran began to race about their heels, barking in rapture. "Home, Torran," his master told the dog. The barking ceased abruptly. With a last mournful wag of his tail, the animal turned toward home.

They made their way through the forest, tangled now with afternoon shadows, to the rugged stone hill that led to the cave. Hand over hand they climbed, as they had that first day, and stopped, as they had then, at the top of the ridge. Ailsa looked at the three graves ringed in stone, and grief lay like a weight around her heart.

At last she and Ian ducked inside, surrounded at once by cool, echoing stone. Ailsa moved toward the chest and knelt beside it, placing her hands on the lid. She closed her eyes and thought of Janet Chisholm, of the dream that had come to her the night they found the chest. She felt that, somehow, she had absorbed this woman's restless unhappiness. She remembered too vividly the thin, mournful stranger, the exile of her dream who had sent a warning across the turbulent sea.

Ian felt Ailsa shiver and noticed the pallid color of her cheeks. "What troubles ye?" When she did not answer, he drew her toward him so she sat with her back pressed to his chest.

She leaned her head on his shoulder and felt the soothing rhythm of his heartbeat. "William Sinclair, the Englishman I told ye about, asked me to marry him today." She did not know she was going to say it until the words were out of her mouth. What had William's proposal to do with Janet Chisholm and her sorrow?

"Is he mad?"

"So I thought for a time, but no," she murmured. " 'Tisn't that. I don't know why."

"Why does it fret ye, *mo-run?* All Sassenachs are touched by the English air—it makes them like bairns who don't know why they do what they do. He's a stranger who will soon be gone. Why should ye care?"

Ailsa frowned. She did care; that was the odd thing. She could not forget William's kindness, the way he had looked at her through the rain, his fumbling praise of her music. He made her heart ache, whether she wished for it or not.

"Ailsa-my-heart, don't concern yourself with such as him. Ye can't marry him anyway," Ian said teasingly.

She turned so she could see his face, his green eyes that she knew in every shade of mood and thought. "Why can't I?"

"Because ye're goin' to marry me."

He said it with such certainty, such a smile of contentment. "Why would I want to marry ye?" she teased back, a little angry that he should take her consent for granted.

"Because 'twas meant to be."

"Why?" She wanted something from him, though she was not certain what.

"Ye know why. We couldn't live without each other any more than the sheep could live without the grass on the hillsides."

Ailsa frowned. "Is't enough?"

"Of course 'tis enough. I love ye."

She turned to face him fully. "Why didn't ye ever say that before?"

Ian blinked at her as though she were a poor wandering lunatic who could not find her way. "Because ye've always known it. Just as I've always known that ye love me. Ye don't rise in the mornin', look in your glass, and say, 'Ailsa, I love ye.' Ye just know it here." He pointed to his heart, leaned forward to take her face in his hands. "Without me there is no ye, without ye there is no me. Together we are all and everything. Apart we are half finished, nothin' but shadows."

She was not breathing. She could feel the heat of his fingers on her skin, the tumult of despair and joy, hope and sorrow that came whenever he touched her. But just in that moment, it was not enough. Not now that she had seen the look on William Sinclair's face when he asked her to be his wife.

"Ye know in your heart 'tis true," Ian said.

When she did not answer, he felt that she had struck him in the chest. "Ye're thinkin' of tellin' that Sassenach 'aye.' "

She pulled away, unable to think clearly while he held her. But now that he had said the words, she realized it was true. "I know nothin' about the world but that I want to see it someday. Out there, beyond these hills, there's beauty and grace and elegance ye haven't even dreamed of. I know it."

Ian shook his head. "I heard my brother's stories of Glasgow. There's nothin' outside these hills but poverty, filth, and darkness that stains and swallows everyone it touches."

"How can ye be so certain?"

"Because ye are blind, is there no sight for those who can see?"

She bit her lip. His stubborn belief in his own rightness frightened her; it was a side of Ian she had never seen before. "Proverbs can't change the truth," she insisted. " 'Twas an old Highlander who said that, one who never set foot outside the glen. There's another world, Ian. A world full of wonder."

"Your father's world," he said bitterly. A pain that began deep inside him moved through his body one limb at a time. "And ye'll no' be content till ye've seen it for yourself."

"No," she agreed, while his pain flowed into her and became her own. "I must see it. I must find him and all the things he's made me dream about."

"Never mind how much I love ye, or how much Mairi needs ye to lift the sorrow from her life. 'Tis wrong for *ye*, Ailsa, that world of glitter that ye seek. 'Tis wrong and ye know it."

She felt tears building behind her eyes, and a bleak, hollow emptiness. But there was another voice that she could not ignore. "That I see," she said deliberately, "but this I sew." Before he could speak again, before he could twist her words and make her believe what she did not wish to believe, she turned for the first time in her life and fled from him.

— ◇ 8 ◇ —

Ian followed her to the mouth of the cave. Long after he was out of sight, Ailsa felt his gaze upon her. He was calling her back, but she only ran faster until her breath came in short gasps and her side began to ache. Yet she could not escape the turmoil of fear and hope, sorrow and longing inside her.

When she reached home, she stumbled over the threshold and slammed the door shut. She stood against it, breathing heavily.

Mairi looked up, startled, at her daughter's windblown hair, her glittering eyes, her hands that trembled with each harsh breath. "If 'tis the devil or the fairies ye're tryin' to keep out, an oaken door will no' help ye much."

"'Tisn't that," Ailsa whispered.

"No? Then what is't ye fear?"

Ailsa bit her lip. She could not tell her mother that she sought to avoid Ian's watching eyes. "'Tisn't fear, exactly," she murmured. "'Tis somethin'—" She broke off, flustered. She could not explain the thoughts that whirled in her head. "Mayhap the fairies have got me already."

Mairi arched her eyebrows knowingly as she returned to her work at the loom. "'Tis long before gloamin'," she observed without looking up again. "I didn't think to see ye so soon."

Reluctantly, Ailsa opened the door, leaned her cheek on the weathered oak. "I didn't want—I thought ye might need me."

Mairi ignored what she knew to be untrue. "Are ye certain ye know what ye want?"

Ailsa turned to her mother with feverish eyes. "No, I'm

115

not certain. I only know that I wanted to be away, to be free."

"Yet ye closed the door behind ye as if to shut yourself in."

Ailsa did not reply; she had no answer to give. Brow furrowed, she crossed the room and added unnecessary peats to those already smoldering within the circle of stones. Then she looked about frantically for something else to do. Her heart was beating in erratic bursts as she paced the packed dirt floor. With each step she felt the heat of Ian's eyes upon her. Yesterday she would have welcomed that familiar gaze. Why did she wish to run from it now? What, in the name of the *Tuatha De Danann*, was she running *to*?

"Mayhap ye should sit down for the while and play your harp," Mairi suggested.

"I can't sit. There are things to do." Ailsa touched the dried herbs laid out on the table but saw only Ian's face, and William's, one upon the other like a shadow on the water. Her hands shook as she put nettles, rosemary and thyme, hedge hyssop and spinewort in packets and stored them in the press. Without a word, she went outside to stir the fabrics that lay in vats of dye her mother had set out days ago. The wooden paddle beat a steady rhythm against the sides of the tub, but Ailsa heard only Ian's declaration, "Ye *are* me!" and William's whispered plea, "Will you think about it? Please?" Woven into the sound of those remembered voices was Janet Chisholm's tormented cry as she stood on a cliff across the ocean. Ailsa dropped the paddle into the dye. With a groan, she rose, too overwrought to think of removing the stirrer from the liquid.

She burst back into the croft and began to prepare supper. She tried to concentrate on the thick peppery soup made from leftover mutton. Carefully, she hung the huge black pot above the fire, stirred in pearl barley, then peeled and pared the onions, leeks, and carrots to add later. She was aware with each movement, each stroke of the knife that Ian was watching her, calling her back to him. Then she heard him singing, in rhythm with the motion of the loom:

"Tears in the heart and tears upon the eyes,
Believe me, Precious, are not composit.

So if I weep not, nor rain dewy sighs,
Nor wear a countenance all bleached and white . . ."

Ailsa glanced up, smiling in spite of herself, certain she would see Ian poised on the threshold. But the door hung open to the empty clearing and nothing moved but the wind in the grass. She turned to find Mairi watching her. "I thought I heard somethin'," she said uncomfortably.

Her mother had seen the tender smile that touched the girl's lips, the sigh of disappointment when she found the doorway empty. "Mayhap ye should listen more carefully."

Ailsa could not have done anything else.

"It isna, love, that I love thee less,
But that the deep well of passion deeper lies,
And at its depth hath more of tenderness.
For that which sudden blooms, most sudden dies."

She paused and waited, strained to hear each word.

"Thee would I worship in another wise,
Not tell it every minute nor each hour.
I would choose wait a consummation slower
And see love ripen like an openin' flower."

She closed her eyes, bereft, when he sang no more. Now there was only the sound of the loom to keep her company. For a long time, she sat with her head in her hands and tried to understand the pain in her chest that could not quell the sense of anticipation in her blood. She laid out wooden bowls and horn spoons, brewed a pot of tea, and filled cups for her mother and herself. "Supper is ready," she said in an overloud voice that could not begin to fill the stillness.

Mairi came to sit across from her daughter. "Tell me about your day, birdeen. Ye need to be talkin', no' sinkin' further into the gloom of your own makin'."

"What do ye mean?"

"I mean, tell me about your day. No more than that."

Ailsa tried to remember, but the past few hours came back to her in disconnected fragments. "Ian and I had a picnic in the woods while Torran tried to conquer the burn." She rubbed her forehead as another fragment fell into place. "Earlier, I went to the foot of the mountains and climbed a high, narrow rock. When the wind came up, I thought mayhap I could fly. But Ian called me down again."

"Bless him," Mairi murmured. "And what else?"

"The bairns at the Hill were very quiet, but I couldn't concentrate just the same. And William Sinclair was waitin' in the hall. I told him the story of the Hill o' the Hounds."

Mairi made no comment, but Ailsa did not notice. She was concentrating on shifting bits of memory that scattered like a flock of swallows when she tried to catch them in her hands. "And two men asked me to marry them today."

"Aye? Is't so?" her mother said, although she had known it would come. It was happening so quickly—too quickly.

"Well, no' exactly. One asked and one told me."

Reaching across the scarred tabletop, Mairi covered her daughter's hand with her own. "Don't let your pride and anger guide ye, *mo-run*. Don't be the fool your mother was."

Ailsa hardly heard her. " 'Tisn't anger that I feel."

"Well, what then?"

Abruptly, the girl rose from the table. " 'Tis only that William Sinclair has given me a choice. Before there was none—my life was, would always be, what it had to be. A life without my father, with no chance to know his world, or even see it. A life ringed by the boundaries of this glen."

Charlie, my Charlie, will ye never leave us in peace? Mairi thought. When will your long, dark shadow lift from your daughter's eyes? She focused on Ailsa. "It hasn't made ye happy, this choice. I've seen the madness in ye, the uncertainty, since ye returned home."

Ailsa could not deny it. Even now she moved incautiously close to the fire, whirling after each few steps, unable to stay still. She felt flushed with fever but knew she was not ill. The heat came from the questions, the doubts that spun in her head with the turbulence of the storm a few days past. "I didn't say the choice was easy," she cried. "But it exists. Don't ye see how much that matters?"

"I see that it matters to ye," Mairi said quietly. She kept her eyes lowered so Ailsa would not see the pain reflected there.

"I wish someone would tell me what to do."

Mairi shook her head. "Ye wouldn't listen anyway."

Ailsa started to object, but could not lie to herself with her mother's steady gaze upon her. "I'd no' be able to hear the sound above my own voices, I'm afraid."

"Ye should play your harp," Mairi suggested for the second time. "The music may help clear your mind."

The girl nodded and took her hand harp from the chest by the wall. She sat in the doorway for a long time with the clarsach cradled in her lap before she began to play. Then she ran her fingers over the strings until they cried with the depth of her sorrow, sang with the soaring sound of her hope.

Mairi sat at the loom as Ailsa played hour after hour, mournful songs, wild songs, songs of exaltation, full of a savagery of emotion that frightened her mother. Each time the strings cried out her daughter's distress, Mairi wanted to weep, but her eyes stayed painfully raw and dry.

Finally Ailsa returned the clarsach to its chest. "I'm for bed," she said softly. "Is there nothin' ye can say to help me?"

Mairi raised her head. "I can tell ye only this—to listen to your heart. 'Twill never lie to ye."

Ailsa considered her mother's advice as she took off her clothes, put on a warm wool gown, then slipped beneath the covers. There were many voices in her head tonight, but which came from her heart? She could not tell anymore. She lay with her eyes open, staring out the window Angus Fraser had carved in the solid wall of her box bed so she could look up at the moon and stars. But tonight in the glow of white silence across the heavens, she saw only Ian's eyes, his green, all-seeing eyes, his eyes that called her back to where he sat outside the cave.

Finally she closed her own eyes, but sleep eluded her. Why hadn't she told Ian she would stay with him, that she had always loved him and always would? Why couldn't she forget William Sinclair's face, half lit by blue reflected light as he turned, saw her, and smiled until there was no memory of the frown he had worn a moment since?

On that thought she fell asleep at last. She turned restlessly, waking, drifting back to sleep, waking again until she could no longer tell if the dreams or the waking were reality. Sometime before dawn she fell into exhausted slumber and dreamed.

She wandered down narrow, twisted streets. She had lost her way and the fog was closing around her, unfriendly, chilled, and dirty. As she walked, the streets grew narrower, the fog more dense, so she could not see her hand or hear the sound of her own footfalls. Despair stalked her; she began to run in order to escape it. The darkness moved faster, crept closer every minute. She ran, stumbling, terrified by the shadow of gloom that touched her heels as she fled. She cried out into the cold, gray night, but no sound escaped her raw throat.

Then she heard, faint and far away, the soft, trilling notes of a flute. Ian. He played to her, tried to lead her home. She turned toward the sound, slowed and weighted down by the fog that reached out with wispy ghostlike hands to hold her back. A brick wall—solid and impenetrable—rose up to block her way and the song of the flute grew fainter.

She went back the way she had come until the music grew louder, calling her back to light and warmth. As she ran the fog grew denser, grimier; it stopped the breath in her throat and the sound of the flute faded into the soot.

She whirled again, praying for the music to find her, praying, when it did, that she would reach it before the darkness at her heels enveloped her. The song came to her then, soft and alluring, but she could not find the way. She was sobbing now, gasping from lack of air. At the moment when she was weakest, the shadow caught up with her at last. She struggled but could not free herself. Her feet were like lead, too awkward and heavy to take another step. She would never find her way out of the fog to Ian. He was lost in the darkness beyond her reach. She would never see his face again.

Ailsa awakened, sobbing, rose in a daze, and ran to the

door in her nightrail. She had to feel the air on her face. She did not bother to dress, but took her plaid and slipped outside.

She ran frantically from the croft and the shadow of the dream. She was hardly aware of where she went. She felt moisture in the air and knew that clouds were gathering above. She could hear the approaching storm in the howl of wind that cried out her hopelessness over the hills and moors. The night absorbed her pain and confusion and called it back to her. The brooding clouds sank lower, touched her with their melancholy weight, unable to fill the gnawing emptiness inside. She fled to the river, to the sound of the water, to the soft mist that swirled in the moonlight. But she found no comfort in these things.

She was obsessed, pursued by the sound of her harsh breath that echoed in her ears. She continued to run in desperation, gasping, a bright hot pain in her chest, until she could run no more and she collapsed at the foot of a hawthorn tree. She shivered uncontrollably at the wind that would not leave her in peace. It circled, laughed at her desolation, whirled off into the black stormy clouds. It spoke to her, whispered that tonight she was a stranger here, lost, forgotten as surely as she had been lost in her dark dream.

Ailsa buried her head in her hands. She could not catch her breath and the pain in her chest grew worse by the minute. Her heart pounded wildly as she struggled, futilely, against the weakness of her body.

Then the cry of the wind stilled, the dark clouds retreated, and the beating of her heart began to ease. She found that she could breathe again; as she drew the air into her lungs, the pain in her chest faded until it disappeared. She did not raise her head at once, but sat with her forehead on her knees and slowly became aware of the touch of soothing hands upon her back.

Ian had found her. He caressed her with his fingertips, kneaded away the tension in her muscles with his circling thumbs. From her neck to her shoulders to the curve of her spine, he massaged her. And with each touch he pushed back the darkness a little further, threw a protective cape around her so the desolation could not reach her anymore.

He caught his fingers in her hair, holding the tangled strands to his cheek.

At last Ailsa raised her head and turned to look at him.

"Don't ever despair, Ailsa-*aghray*. I'm here for ye. I'll always be here." He leaned closer, slipped his arms under hers, and pulled her against him.

She nodded, spellbound by the rhythm of his heartbeat. They sat in silence for a long time—time enough for the darkness to fade and dawn to transform the landscape. Time enough for the songs of birds to rise from the treetops to meet the cloud-laden, violet sky. But Ian and Ailsa were unaware of these things. They merely sat, eyes closed, and enjoyed each other's warmth until the dream disappeared into memory.

"I should go back," Ailsa said reluctantly. "My mother will be worried."

"Aye, just as ye say." Ian did not move at once, but held her more tightly and buried his face in her hair with a sigh. Then, slowly, he drew away.

They rose and their eyes met, full of the secrets they had not spoken, the passion and madness they had made themselves forget. Ian opened his mouth, but Ailsa pressed her fingers to his lips. "No' just now, *mo-charaid*. Give me a little time to enjoy the peace ye've given me tonight."

He wanted to argue, but saw the look of determination on her face and knew it would not be wise. Instead they started toward the croft, hands linked. They stopped outside the door and stood smiling, unwilling to part.

"I've chores to do," Ian said at last.

"Aye."

He raised his left hand, she her right and they touched palms, briefly. Then he was gone, lost in the gloom the storm clouds had cast over the glen. The instant he was out of sight, Ailsa began to shiver at the chill, the emptiness he left behind. The despair was with her again, and a new kind of fear that bleached the color from her cheeks then sent it rushing back again. She drew a deep breath.

Mairi had seen her daughter come home with a smile on her lips, holding Ian's hand. She had seen the look of peace in Ailsa's eyes as she touched her palm to his and bade him

122

good-bye. Mairi saw, too, the change that came over the girl in an instant. Dropping the creel, she hurried to take her daughter's hand. "What is't?" her mother cried.

Ailsa turned, eyes tinted wintry gray. "Did ye see how easily he took my joy and gave me grief instead? 'Twas only by withdrawin' the touch of his hand. Dear God, what if he ever turned on me in anger?" Her voice shook with the effort to speak aloud a terror so deep. "Is't right that anyone should have such power over another?" Ailsa took Mairi's hands in a painful grip. "Tell me, should it be so?"

Her mother swallowed dryly. " 'Tisn't right, *mo-ghray,* but 'tis too often true, just the same."

"Was it true for ye?"

Mairi's eyes were so dry they ached. She wanted to lie, knowing where the truth would lead, but could not bring herself to do it. "Almost, but in the end, no, 'twasn't true."

Eyes narrowed, her daughter tried to understand, but then she saw a movement from the corner of her eye. She whirled. "Did ye see somethin'? Is someone there?"

Mairi hesitated. "Aye. Someone's there." She, too, had seen the rim of a top hat bobbing through the wisps of white that draped the landscape.

"I'm certain 'tis William. I have to go." Ailsa took one more steadying breath and hurried inside. Quickly, she threw on yesterday's gown and joined Mairi at the door.

Her mother put her hand on the girl's arm. "Ye can't run away from your fear. 'Twill follow wherever ye go."

"I'm no' runnin' away," Ailsa declared.

"Mayhap if ye opened your eyes, ye'd see things differently."

Ailsa did not wait to hear more. "William!" she called as she left her mother behind.

He had been moving carelessly, stumbling on the uneven ground, but now he stopped. She caught up with him at the edge of the woods. Slowly, he turned to face her.

"You should have told me about him," he said without preamble. "I would have understood."

"Ye saw us." It was not a question. Ailsa saw the anguish in William's face and felt like weeping. She did not want to cause him pain. She wanted to hold him, as Ian had held her, until the pain was gone.

William looked at her chestnut hair drifted with moisture. It was disheveled—she had not had time to comb it—and her eyes were turbulent seas of gray-streaked blue. Her cheeks were flushed with color. Was it from that boy's touch? His heart turned cold and he started away.

"Don't go," she cried.

He could not have ignored that plea even if he wanted to. He turned and stretched out a hand, not to touch her, but only to express his regret. "Forgive me for speaking so rashly yesterday. It was wrong."

"Wrong to tell me what ye felt? How can such a thing be wrong?"

"Because you were—you have another man. In England one simply does not speak to a woman already committed."

" 'Tisn't England ye're standin' in now. In the glen ye say whatever ye wish and ye regret it only if ye seek to deceive. Ye were tellin' me the truth, so it can't be wrong."

She spoke with a certainty that astonished him. "How can you be so sure? You hardly know me."

"I saw it in your eyes. I think the only way ye know how to lie is to keep silent and say nothin'. For if ye speak, ye speak the truth."

William looked away. No applause of his associates, no praise from his aunt or his friends, no success he had ever attained could equal the simple trust of this young girl. "I can never have you," he said, unable to hold in his grief. His voice shook with infinite pain and regret.

Ailsa placed her hand in the one he had extended a moment before. "I didn't say that, William Sinclair." She gasped and looked down at the ground. She had not intended to reassure him, but the words came of their own accord.

William smiled and his face was transformed. His eyes, which had been dull gray, glimmered with hope; the color rose in his pallid cheeks. "You mean, even though he wants you, you might choose me?"

He sounded incredulous, as if God could not possibly treat him so kindly. "If it's possible, even remotely, if there's some chance, I will be content to wait." He spoke breathlessly, his words tumbling one over the other. Then he frowned. "But if you mean to marry him, please tell me now. This I must know." The flush disappeared from his cheeks, leaving them sallow once again. "Please," he said softly. "Tell me which."

Ailsa was touched at his gentle question. Ian had not asked. He knew she would deny him nothing. She buried her hands in her pockets and tried to keep her voice steady. "I don't know what I want just now. I know only that I must think. I need to be alone to decide on my own. Can ye understand that?"

"I understand. I'll leave you to your thoughts. And when you know your answer, whatever it is, whenever that may be, please come to me and tell me." He wanted to take her in his arms, to hold her so tightly she could never get free, but he did not move. Ailsa was a spirit who would turn to mist and slip away if he tried to keep her against her will. Nor would he want her that way.

She recognized the struggle it cost him to say those words and she was grateful. "Thank ye," she said. Then she swept him a brief curtsy and was gone.

She did not stop to think but headed instinctively toward her precipice. She had to have a moment of peace in the midst of the turmoil; that ledge was the only place where she had ever found true silence. Her heart was racing as she ran. The landscape blurred and shimmered.

> "I have a tumult in my brain,
> A monster in my thoughts,
> A drivin', hectorin' pain
> That goes but comes again."

Ailsa raised her head. Was it she who had spoken those words, or had they come to her on the wind? She hurried faster, running from the demons that whirled in her head. At the bottom of the mountain, she began to climb, though several times her hands slipped or she lost her footing and slid backward.

She was breathing hard when she reached the top. She stopped to look down at the view. The chaotic landscape, scattered with sheep and cattle, leaping rabbits and deer, lapwings that rose from the trees to weave patterns in the sky, seemed to echo her confusion. There was no help for her there, only a beauty that broke her heart and healed it, all in a single glance. She grasped her upper arms so tightly that her nails dug into the skin. She cried out at the pain, but even that could not distract her from the image of William's face, Ian's eyes, his magic hands, Mairi's warning, her own doubts. They were jumbled together like the fragments of a nightmare and she did not know which way to turn.

Ailsa closed her eyes and thought of her father, of the incredible places he had seen, the worlds he had described in his letters, for these things had always brought her hope and comfort. She spread her arms toward the sky in a gesture of entreaty. She did not want to lose Ian, or William, or the memory of her father that burned inside her like a beacon.

"I don't know what to do," she cried silently. "Help me!"

Then, from far away, she heard a voice, softly at first, like a breath of air not seen but felt against her skin. She listened more intently, opened herself to that insubstantial sound, tried to hear it with her body and her mind. At last the words grew clearer and she understood.

"Come to me, Ailsa," a strange voice said. "Forgive me and come to me. I need you."

She had never heard Charles Kittridge speak, but she knew it was he who called. She had waited all her life to hear that voice, that plea. And she knew, as she had always known, that she could not refuse it. Finally, finally, her father had reached out to her and she would go.

Only then did the turbulence cease, the confusion and the fear. The stillness settled around her and she knew what she must do.

Mairi stood in the doorway of the croft to watch Ailsa approach. She could see that her daughter's eyes were still, her cheeks no longer flushed, her breathing normal. She had healed herself, but at what cost? With a weight like lead in her chest, Mairi held out her hands.

Ailsa took them, smiling. "I've made my choice."

"I know." Her mother drew Ailsa inside, to the two

birch chairs by the fire. "Ye'd better tell me," she said as she took one chair and her daughter the other.

Ailsa stared into the dying flames and gathered her courage in her hands. "It must be William. I have to take the chance." Her mother looked away. To fill the uncomfortable silence that fell between them, Ailsa added, "If I marry Ian, I'll never be leavin' the glen. And I couldn't bear that, Mother, truly I couldn't. Never to know what lies beyond the mountains, never to see the ocean or the beauty of the cities out there waitin' to be enjoyed. I want to wander like the Celts of long ago, to experience everything and tell my bairns of my journeys. I have the spirit of the old ones within me. I know it."

As she spoke she rose and moved around the room; she could not contain her excitement. "In London alone there are such wonders. William told me about the theaters and opera houses." She stopped to face her mother. "Do ye know what 'twould mean to me to see the Crystal Palace and walk in the pleasure gardens among strange and lovely plants whose names I don't even know?" She swayed and bent like a tropical tree in a sudden wind. "Or to hear an opera, a real orchestra whose music soars so high it fills every part of a huge, domed room?" She tilted her head as if listening and with her hands swept wide, graceful circles in the air to describe the power of the music. Her eyes were luminous as, drawn by the spell of her own creation, Ailsa headed toward the door. She wanted to see it now, did not want to waste a single moment.

Mairi felt as if some part of her were being torn away by an angry hand. She had seen and heard this all before, a long time ago, on the night when Charles had disappeared forever into the mist—the same night her daughter had been conceived. "Come," she said softly, "sit with me."

For an instant, Ailsa hesitated, stared longingly outside, then returned to her chair.

"Ye speak a great deal of the world out there. But what of the man ye are to marry?"

Her daughter blinked, tried to bring herself back to the small, dark croft in the middle of the glen. "William loves me very much, I think," she said with difficulty.

"And ye? How do ye feel about him?"

Ailsa considered the question, brow furrowed. "I care for him a great deal. He's good to me, and kind."

Mairi nodded. " 'Tis as I thought." She stared down at her fingers locked together, the knuckles white and bloodless. "Only remember this, *mo-run*. Ye go far about, seekin' the nearest."

"I don't understand."

For a long time her mother did not raise her head. When she did, her eyes were clouded gray, her face set in rigid lines. "Will ye come with me? There's somethin' I want to show ye."

In spite of her own exhilaration, Ailsa sensed Mairi's distress. "O' course I'll come. Ye don't need to ask."

Mairi rose and moved toward the door, slowly; she might have aged in the past hour, so that now she ached with every step. Ailsa followed and they went without speaking through the woods and around the base of a mountain, taking a path the girl had never traveled before. At last they came to a cleft in the rock and Mairi stepped through with her daughter close behind.

Ailsa found herself in a dell ringed by stone. The sides were scarred with jagged rocks and crevices full of moving shadows. It was eerily silent, except for the wind that moaned with the sound of human voices. There were ghosts here, sunk in the crevices and hidden in the shadows. She felt them like a cold hand on her shoulder.

While Mairi stood silent, Ailsa looked around until she saw the three cairns piled with stones. She gasped as she glanced up at the highest ridge. Surely this was the valley she and Ian had seen as they stood outside the cave? She turned to her mother and saw Mairi's pallid cheeks, the look of sorrow in her eyes. She knew then why the sight of this valley had disturbed her so deeply—because the desolation did not belong to a stranger whose secrets she would never know: the tragedy was her mother's.

Still in silence, Mairi went to the graves and knelt, head bent. Shaken by her realization, Ailsa moved forward slowly to kneel at her mother's side.

" 'Tis the Valley of the Dead," Mairi said, "where I come when the shadow is upon me."

" 'Tis your secret, sacred place," Ailsa whispered, "isn't it?"

"Sacred 'tis, though secret no more."

"Tell me," the girl said.

Mairi rose and began to pace. " 'Twas durin' the last great sorrow, when the Sassenach soldiers came to clear us from our homes. My mother is buried in the kirk yard in the glen and her mother before her and hers before her. We who still lived didn't wish to go from the place we loved, from our past, from the hills and burns and moors that were all in the world to us."

"But what could ye do against the English with their guns and sabers?"

Closing her eyes, Mairi said in a ragged voice, "We hid in this valley, my brother and father and me, hopin' they would pass us by. But then we heard a soldier comin'. We knew 'twas an Englishman by the arrogant stamp of his boots on stone. My father bid me hide among the rocks and told me no' to come out, no matter what. The look on his face frightened me so deeply that I did as he'd bid me.

"Then the Sassenach came. He climbed over the boulders and found his way to the place where they hid as if the devil himself had led him by the hand. He couldn't see them, but he raised his gun with the long, wicked bayonet on the end and shouted for whoever was there to come out or he'd fire among the rocks. My father and brother rose and stood to face him, for they were no' cowards. He told them to be gone, to find another place."

"But they didn't go," Ailsa whispered.

"No, they didn't. My father tried to tell him that there was no other place for a heart born to these hills, but the soldier didn't listen. He started to push them forward." She shivered at the memory. " 'Twas then that they drew from behind them the huge, gnarled sticks they'd hidden among the boulders. They raised them against the Sassenach and said they wouldn't go, would stand and fight, even kill to stay in the home of their hearts."

She stopped, her face pale and bloodless, her hands extended as if somehow, even now, she could help those cornered men. "I guessed then that they knew before they came they wouldn't leave this valley alive. But they chose to die rather than go at the command of an English soldier. They struck him only once before he fired his gun, killin' my father with one shot. My brother knelt beside him, tried to stop the bleedin', tho' 'twas clear he was already dead. And while he knelt, his hands covered with blood, grievin' for the father he had lost, the Sassenach reloaded his gun, raised it again, and shot my brother down."

Her voice faded out, and with it the wind. Now there was silence, which was worse by far than the moaning of the spirits. "He fell dead, his eyes open and starin', his face pale as dawn with the gray of night around the edges. Then the soldier, the Englishman who had no right to stand on this soil or breathe this air, dropped his gun in the grass, smiled, and stood lookin' down at the men he had killed. And he spit on them."

Her voice shook with the force of remembered fury. "A great anger rose inside me then. For I knew he had come, hopin' they would stand and fight. He didn't want them to leave the glen and find a new home in another land. He wanted them dead. He didn't even know them, Ailsa. 'Twas only because they were Scots that he wanted so much to spill their blood."

She fell silent and Ailsa grasped her hand, though she knew her touch would bring no comfort.

"I crept up behind him," Mairi said at last, "silent as the ghosts of my father and brother, picked up the gun, raised it high, and stabbed him through the heart with the bayonet. For he had destroyed the heart of me and 'twas right that his, too, should bleed in that place where he had committed such an act."

Mairi sank to the ground beside her daughter. "I never even knew his name. But the minute he was dead, I knew 'twas wrong, what I had done. I had made myself too much like him, killin' out of hate for a man I didn't know. Alone, I buried my father and brother and the stranger who'd taken them from me. It took me two days, but I did it, for I wanted no one else to know of my sin. And I didn't wish to leave the dell, for I feared I would meet another soldier."

She lowered her head. "The grief passed in time, but

no' the guilt it left behind. I've come here often in the years since, layin' stone upon stone on the three cairns, but each stone was another weight on my heart. I couldn't leave the glen from that day, for I'd seen what lay beyond it. I'd seen the hatred in the Sassenach's eyes."

Mairi rose, found three stones in the tumbled ruins, and placed one on each of the graves. Slowly, Ailsa did the same. There were tears on her cheeks when she murmured, "Are ye sayin' ye didn't go with my father because ye feared the English?"

Mairi looked away. "I couldn't leave my family behind, nor my sin. To abandon the dead, to deprive them of the reverence they deserved, would have been worse than the deed itself. Besides," she added fiercely, "I saw how deep that hatred was, how easily it could destroy our lives, our homes, our very past. I felt it, Ailsa. I only hope ye don't feel it, too."

"But 'twas only one man—"

"There are many others. The English have hated us since they first faced us across the border hundreds of years agone. Surely ye know that, who knows our history so well."

Ailsa did know it, but to her, it was not enough. When she gave in to her fear, Mairi had lost the only man she would ever love. But she had given up more than just Charles Kittridge; she had given up hope, the lure of mystery, all the beauty of the unknown world beyond the mountains. Ailsa would not do the same. She was not afraid.

"Ye'll no' be likin' the world ye find out there," her mother said, reading her thoughts in her eyes. " 'Twill make a different person of ye, a stranger to this place, to your home, to the people ye love."

"I couldn't ever be a stranger to ye or Ian." The girl's voice shook a little as she spoke the name.

Mairi cupped her daughter's face in her hands. "There are things ye believe, lass, and things that are true. Someday, mayhap, ye'll learn to know the difference."

◦ 9 ◦

William Sinclair walked with a sprightly step through tall grass strewn with daffodils and wood anemone, through blue splashes of violets and trails of wild roses. He hummed to himself as he went, something he had not done in many years.

He had been stunned when Ailsa came to him yesterday and stood at the window where he'd asked her to marry him. The setting sun had cast a golden glow over her face as she looked up with her compelling eyes to tell him she would be his wife.

The despair that had gripped him since he'd seen her with the boy—seen the way they looked at each other, the way their hands met in silent but binding communion—had left him in an instant. He had lain awake all night, dreaming, remembering the brush of her lips over his cheek, the heat in his chest when she'd looked at him with promise in her eyes. Ailsa did not break her promises; he knew that as surely as he knew how to tie his cravat or choose his waistcoat in the morning.

He was on his way now to speak to her mother and ask for the girl's hand. He meant to do this properly, no matter what his friends on the Hill said. Agatha had laughed at him, actually laughed aloud in a very unladylike manner, while Sarah had merely stared, stricken, pale. Gerald had exploded with a single vibrant curse, "Well, I'll be damned, see if I won't!" The Willistons had remained politely silent. But he had seen in their eyes that they did not understand, not even they, who had known Ailsa for so long, had heard her play and sing.

Their reaction had not dimmed his joy one bit. Rather,

132

it pleased him, for he had finally shocked every one of them out of their complacency. He was glad he had done it. He would do it again. He would do anything for Ailsa.

He reached the croft and stopped outside, suddenly ill at ease. He did not mind the disapproval of his friends, but he dreaded the chill he expected to see in Mairi Rose's eyes. Straightening his pale yellow waistcoat, he checked to see that his cravat was properly tied, his coat securely buttoned, then he knocked on the heavy door, even though it stood ajar.

Mairi started at the sound of the gentle rapping and misguided the shuttle, ruining one line of weave. She gripped the edge of the loom with stiff fingers. That must be William Sinclair. Ailsa had said he was coming today. Reluctantly, Mairi rose and went to the door.

"Good mornin', Mr. Sinclair." She smiled with as much warmth as she could manage. It was not this man's fault that her daughter was lost in the dreams her father had woven since he left the glen behind. "Come in and sit ye down."

He sat on a polished birch chair beside the peat fire that burned low because the day was warm.

"Would ye have some bannochs and milk? Or maybe some ale?"

He took one of the small round cakes she offered, but shook his head at the pitcher of milk. "You are too kind," he said. "I know you must wish I had never come to Glen Affric."

He did not shrink from her gaze; Mairi could see the sincerity in his gray eyes. She was surprised that he understood her feelings so well. "What I wish to be isn't often what is meant to be. I have learned to accept what I can't change."

"Can you accept me as your son-in-law? Ailsa has agreed to marry me, but I won't make her my wife without your consent."

He meant that, as well. Mairi realized how much power he had put into her hands, realized, too, that she could never use it. " 'Tis what Ailsa wishes. I wouldn't stop her from makin' her own choice, just as I made mine."

William dropped the bannoch into the flames, unaware that he had done so. "But you don't approve of her choice?"

She softened and gave him a sad half smile. "If ye love her enough, ye won't care if I approve or no'."

He did not understand the mournful knowledge in her eyes, but it did not really matter. "I love her enough," he said firmly.

Sinking onto the settle by the fire, Mairi leaned toward him, her work-roughened hands clasped together. "Will your friends no' think my daughter strange?"

William stiffened. Had she somehow guessed about the objections of those at the Hill? "I don't care what they think."

"Won't they laugh at her?" she persisted.

"Who could laugh at Ailsa? She is what every woman should be but few dare to be."

"What if they laugh just the same, if they cause her pain because they fear the woman she is? Ailsa has grown up free and wild, roamin' the glen at her will, choosin' her own path. 'Twill no' be easy for her to change."

William rose, suddenly impatient. "I don't want her to change! I've told you, I love her."

He said it with such conviction that Mairi began to believe him. He stared at her challengingly, as if daring her to deny it. Mayhap, she thought, beneath that tremblin' voice and those shakin' hands is a heart strong enough to protect Ailsa after all. "Ye will cherish her always?" she whispered, her eyes dry with unshed tears. "Ye'll no' forsake her because she can't be all that ye wish?"

"She will always be all that I wish, but even if she were not, I would never forsake her. Never!"

A week later, Ailsa lay awake in her bed. Tomorrow she would marry William Sinclair and go from these hills to the world of her dreams—Charles Kittridge's world. The ceremony would take place quietly in the kirk down the way. William had asked the minister, Reverend Ross, if he would forego the three-week waiting period, the calling of the banns, and marry them at once. The reverend had been shocked and had refused point-blank. But then Mairi had gone to talk to him—Mairi, who had nursed his wife and child day and night for nearly a week when the fever struck. She had saved them in the end, though her hands had shaken with fatigue and there'd been dark circles under her eyes by the time she left them sleeping peacefully. She had fallen ill herself afterward and only recovered with dedicated care from her daughter.

At Mairi's urging, the minister had changed his mind, though he could not understand why she should be so eager to give up her daughter to a Sassenach stranger. He could not know that once she realized it was inevitable, Mairi wanted it done as soon as possible. Waiting, watching day by day as Ailsa drifted away from her, was more painful than a sudden break would be.

Ailsa smiled sadly into the darkness. "Don't you want a real celebration," William had asked, "the kind of wedding your friends will have?"

She had shaken her head, recognizing the relief in his eyes, though he tried to hide it. She understood that he wanted a quiet ceremony so his English friends need not be invited. Ailsa did not tell him she could not bear the thought of the dances, the processions, the sharing of cakes and ale, the gifts exchanged at a true Highland wedding. She did not want to see her friends celebrate a marriage they could not approve, toast a love in which they could not believe. Most important, she could not do such a thing to Ian, whom she had not seen since she'd told him her decision and he'd turned without a word to leave her standing alone on the riverbank.

She leaned her head against the window. Her sadness grew as she watched the moonlight wash the earth, soften the harsh outlines of the mountains, turn the fluttering leaves to gossamer. She knew the light would pour like liquid silver upon the river, touch the water with a pearly glow that would linger until the moon sank behind the hills and darkness fell again.

At this moment Ian might be looking at the sky, thinking the same thoughts. She closed her eyes as a pain pierced her heart, so severe that she gasped and fell back onto the pillow. The sense of expectation and excitement that had kept her walking in a dream began to dim; she was leaving this place, the boy she had loved since childhood, for a world beyond her comprehension. She was leaving the spirits in the trees and wind and water—the ancient gods that had watched over her, unseen, since birth. She sensed they would not follow her from these hills any more than Mairi would, or Ian.

The pain grew more intense until she rocked, her mouth open in a silent plea for the agony to stop. But it would not stop. For the first time, she began to understand what it would mean to leave her home. For the first time she felt the tearing in her heart and soul, which had been born and shaped among mountains, moors, and woods; her body, which had felt the caress of mist like the hand of a welcome friend; her face, which had known the touch of rain pouring down her cheeks. And Ian.

She moaned silently so she would not disturb Mairi. Ailsa knew her mother had been agitated and unable to rest for the past week. Several times, the girl had awakened to find Mairi bent over a tallow candle, working intently, her back to her daughter's bed. Ailsa had asked once what she was doing. Mairi had told her to see to her dreams and not her mother's labor.

The girl turned away from the sight of Mairi sleeping. Ailsa realized she had been looking only forward—to William, to London, to meeting her father at last. Now, all at once, she had begun to look back. The pain was tearing her apart, the knowledge of a loss so great it was beyond words. She picked up her harp, which lay by her pillow, and touched the strings, but the pain grew worse. This anguish was beyond music, too. There was no way to express it. She must simply endure until it ceased, if it ever did.

Quietly, she slipped from her bed, took down her red plaid, and stepped into the moon-washed night. It was so beautiful that she closed her eyes against it. She soon opened them again; she had to keep moving, to try to lose herself in the woods where the pain could not find her. She stumbled often, but some instinct guided her across the moor, through woods and water to the stone ledge and, eventually, the stillness of the cave.

She dropped down next to the Chisholm chest, thinking to find silence, but someone was already there. When Ian moved toward her, the moonlight through the crumbled stones enwrapped him in a cape of woven light.

She reached for him and he for her. They knelt, trembling, sharing the pain beyond words until it burst within them like hot, searing stars, then faded as the stars fell to earth, chilled and dulled by their journey through the night.

Slowly, Ian raised his head and their eyes met. They stared, frozen in a moment of waiting, of time within time, time without motion, time in a world that had nothing to do with the glen or the hills or the stone cave around them.

At last the pain began to ease as they looked into each other's eyes and saw the truth there. Ian released her, ran his hand up her arm, leaving a path of fire and ice behind. He wove his fingers in her hair and with both hands, raised it like a bolt of velvet to bury his face in the rippling strands. Ailsa could not draw away; she did not have that kind of courage. Such a splitting apart of her own soul was impossible in that moment.

Ian breathed in the scent of her—of peat and flame and mist and birch buds—until it filled his lungs. Then, still without a word, he brushed her cheek with parted lips. She cupped his face in her hands to pull him closer, so their mouths met in a rush of heat that shocked them both with its intensity.

Tenderly, he unwound her plaid to reveal her body, clad only in a thin nightrail. He untied the strings of her gown, drew it down around her shoulders, uncovering her breasts, round and white and touched with moonlight. She rose to let the garment slide to her feet, then lifted it aside, so that it settled with a whisper into the darkness.

Ailsa freed the buttons of Ian's shirt, drew the rough linen away from his body so she could see his bare shoulders and the dark hairs on his chest. She helped him as he fumbled with the wide leather belt, then flung it after her gown. He removed his breeches, sandals, and finally, his high woolen socks, until there was nothing left to hide his body from her gaze.

As she stretched out on the damp earth, Ian kissed her

forehead, her cheeks, her chin, even the tip of her nose, but not her lips. He needed to know every inch of her, every dip and curve and soft, giving part of her body. With his tongue, he flicked the edge of her ear, the line of her throat where he could see the throbbing pulse.

Ailsa felt the heat of his touch on her skin and in her blood—everywhere within and without. Though she lay still, letting him explore, she wanted to draw him toward her, into her, to force him to put out the flame that raced now through her veins. Her hands shook as he traced the curve of her arm, then followed the path with his tongue, from her shoulder to the soft inside of her elbow. She shuddered with pleasure and cried out, wanting more, wanting everything.

Ian continued his slow arousal as he trailed his tongue down her throat to her chest. With the flicking tip he circled one breast, then the other. The hunger was hot and fierce within him; he pressed into her so she felt his hardness, his eagerness to have her completely. She moaned and caught her fingers in his hair, but he would not be hurried—not even by the urgency in his own blood.

With his hand, with the moonlight, with the fine sheen of mist, he created magic on her body, breathing with the rhythm of her rasping breath as she cried out for him again and again. He explored her abdomen with his fingertips, his tongue, then moved lower and lower still, circling, always circling. His moist tongue kindled trails of fever wherever he caressed her flesh.

Ailsa gasped when his mouth reached the warmth between her thighs. She shook from the heat, the brilliant colors, the agony of pleasure that became one with her beating heart. She screamed from within and her fear was burned away in one brief flash.

Ian raised his head in an attempt to steady his own ragged breath. He could feel his power over her, the way she shivered at each touch. The knowledge only fueled the fire that raged through his body. She clutched him with fingers bent, digging her nails into his skin. He smiled at the pain and held her closer. His heart pounded so madly that he shook with the force of it and beads of sweat covered his forehead. He could not take her now; it was too soon. Eyes closed, he concentrated on the colored light behind his lids until the madness eased a little, just enough.

With a smile, he moved his hands down the outside of Ailsa's legs while he caressed the inside with his lips and tongue. He circled the back of her knee, her ankle, even the bottoms of her feet until she cried out harshly, "No more!" Then, when she lay still, he cupped her buttocks in his hands and began once more to flick his tongue between her legs.

She shuddered, reached out for him, afraid of the spasms that shook her from head to toe, taking her breath away. She moaned and stiffened as lights and colors whirled furiously inside her, sent her spinning into the center of a whirlpool. "Ian!" she sobbed. "Ian!"

He stretched out beside her and held her close until the trembling ceased and she laid her cheek against the frenzied pulse in his throat. Her body was bathed in sweat and her breath came in harsh bursts. "Now?" she whispered.

"Now."

She lay back as he braced himself above her. For the first time, she saw his luminous eyes, the passion that glowed there, clear, savage, and unmistakable. She shivered and gripped him with widespread fingers, pulling him closer. When his body rested on hers, Ian kissed her deeply.

Ailsa threw her arms around him, caressed his back, his buttocks, slid her hands between his legs. She demanded with her touch that he feed the hunger that possessed them both. She stiffened at the searing pain when he finally entered her. She gasped, tried to roll away, but he rolled with her, held her closer, soothing her with the motion of his body. He pressed into her slowly, until the pain became a memory.

He began to move more forcefully and Ailsa moved with him, raising her hips to meet each thrust. She wrapped her legs around him, gripped him so tightly that he cried out in delight. The soft moonlight turned bright and piercing, swirled and shimmered, painfully vivid. She felt Ian's breath against her ear, his heart beating into hers, his hands, rough from the hillsides, moving over her back.

He could not catch his breath and did not care. He thrust and rocked, thrust and rocked, moaning when she ran her nails down his back, reveling in the glorious pain. Then the flames leaped within him, so wild, so fierce, that they became him. In an instant the blaze consumed his heart and soul and spirit.

"Ailsa!" he cried in terror and wonder just as she gasped, "Ian!"

She feared he would have disappeared in a wisp of smoke, but he was there, he was with her, trembling in disbelief at what had passed between them. She knew, even then, that she would never feel like this in William's arms, that never, for a single moment, would he touch her fevered soul, where Ian's spirit lay now, smoldering.

As they held each other, unmoving, their breath began to come more easily, their hearts to beat less violently. When the silence curled around them like a blessing in the moonlight, Ian pressed his cheek to Ailsa's and murmured softly:

"O Light that shinest in the untemper'd East,
Sitting in chambers gaudy, gladsomest,
Gild my Love's heart, Bright Lord, that she may be
To others pale, but golden fire to me."

When she recognized the words of the Celtic bridal pledge, Ailsa felt the pain begin again, deep inside. Then, because she could not stop herself, she answered:

"O light that reignest in an argent sphere,
Having a court of beauteous planets near,
Make pure my love that I may ever be
Married, the loving bond slave still of thee."

Palm to palm, they spoke in a single voice, a single thought.

"O rosy love and crimson heated fire,
And desperate heart, full of unsatisfied desire,
Come Hymen in his saffron silk attire,
And carrying torches, set thy conflagration higher."

They took a long, deep breath, then eyes and hands locked, they whispered,

"And, lo! thy house aflame, thy walls are razed,
But in the midst of the destruction where it blazed,
A hearth, a palace, home I see upraised,
And the Destroyer Love, the Builder—God be praised!"

Long after their voices had faded into the dark recesses of the cave, they sat, arms about each other's waists. As the perfect stillness of their communion dissipated, Ian said at last, "Ye can't go from me. We are one."

Ailsa looked into his eyes, full of secrets and magic and knowledge of things hidden, and tried to see a future with him. She saw flames and splendor, gold and scarlet, magic and silver rippled with blazing gold—the roaring, all-consuming passion of the night. But afterward came a dawn burnt to ashes by the force of the flames. She felt then a terror deeper than any she had ever known.

"Don't ye see," she cried, seeking any excuse but the true one. " 'Tis exactly why I must go. I know ye as I know myself. All my life, ye've been there, waitin', known, familiar. I want to know more, Ian, *mo-charaid,* so much more than the reflection of my own soul, my own thoughts, my own dreams."

"When ye say 'more,' ye mean ye wish to know *him*," he said bitterly.

"Aye," she began, "William—"

" 'Tisn't William!" he snarled as he moved away from her. "Ye can't lie to me, Ailsa. Ye know that. 'Tis Charles Kittridge ye seek and always will. If 'twere no' for that man, ye'd be happy here where ye belong."

"I can't say what I would be without the knowledge of my father," Ailsa told him honestly. "It has always been with me."

"Ye belong here," he repeated furiously, as if his anger could convince her when his passion had not.

"Mayhap," she said. "But I have to go."

"Ye love him that much?"

She wondered if he meant William or her father. "I don't know. I only know I have to go, to see what I have missed, to learn of the mysteries I haven't touched."

Ian rose and began to dress. "Ye haven't known the mysteries of that other world, Ailsa-*mo-ghraidh,* but neither have ye known the sorrow. Ye haven't ever felt real hurt. Ye don't even know what it means. Ye've lived all your life in the paradise of the glen. Ye can't begin to know the ugliness and pain that await ye out there. Ye've never known true loss, but if ye marry that man tomorrow, ye will know it, and soon."

"Are ye layin' a destiny upon me?" she asked. Thus had the ancient Celts cursed one another as Ian seemed to curse her now. When he did not answer, she found her gown and plaid and threw them about her. "Whatever I find, Ian Fraser, that I shall find. For I'm goin' and nothin' ye say can stop me."

He caught her as she tried to pass and wound his fingers in her hair. "Nothin'?" he asked as his lips met hers, teaching her lessons she would never learn from any other man.

She trembled, weakened, then remembered William's soft smile, the low, hoarse cry of Charles Kittridge's voice on the back of the wind. *Come to me. I need you.*

She drew away from Ian with her palms flat against his chest. "Nothin'," she said. The tears spilled down her cheeks and she did not try to stop them. "But I will miss ye, Ian, more than ye know or wish to know." She started away, then whirled and extended a hand. "Do ye hate me?" she asked.

"Aye," he answered fiercely, in a hollow, stranger's voice. "Almost as much as I love ye." He slipped past her and was gone before the first fingers of dawn had reached the sky.

◆ 10 ◆

Mairi lay still and watched Ailsa slip away. She knew she should stop the girl but did not have the heart. This was Ailsa's last night of freedom and her mother could not take it from her. Mairi waited until her daughter was gone, then rose to light the oil lamp on the table. She placed it by the huge wicker basket Ailsa had left beside the door after painstakingly packing and repacking the clothes she would take with her to London. In the flickering yellow light, Mairi went to pull a trunk and a soft leather bag from under her bed.

When she knelt, her nightrail settled in a pool around her on the floor. The moonlight caressed one side of her face, the lamplight the other. Her eyes were smoke gray, drained of their normal hue by the strange light and the sheen of her sorrow that eclipsed all color. Opening the basket, she found Ailsa's hand harp lying on top. Mairi lifted it in her arms, cradled it for a moment as if it were a helpless child. Her head ached and her chest, with a pain that was of her heart and not her body. How could she say good-bye to her daughter when even the sight of the clarsach was so painful that it took her breath away?

Closing her eyes, Mairi listened. She found in the moonlight and the silence of stars the strength she needed. With a murmured prayer of gratitude, she turned back to her task. She put the harp in the center of an uncut piece of the Rose plaid, wrapping the instrument gently in the soft folds. She opened the leather bag, slipped the harp inside, and pulled the drawstring tight. One by one, lovingly, she took each piece of clothing and placed it in the trunk. She closed it

143

with the leather straps, then returned the basket to its place next to the press.

Finally, she took out her handwork. Drawing the lamp close, she sat on a chair by the fire and began to work and wait. She sewed, brow furrowed in an effort to keep her attention on the small fine stitches she was making. The moon rose high above the shimmering leaves, hovered there, then sank behind the hills until the darkness grew deep and black. When the first hint of gray light appeared over the mountains, Mairi looked up in concern. What if the girl did not return? Her heart leaped with a last burst of hope, but then she heard Ailsa approach. Mairi put the fabric she'd been working on under her quilt just as her daughter appeared in the doorway.

The girl was wild-eyed, her skin pallid in the yellow glow of the lamp. Her cheeks were red and streaked; clearly she had been weeping. Ailsa stood for a moment staring blankly at her mother while she struggled to regain her composure. "I needed some air," she said in explanation.

"Aye," Mairi murmured.

"Is everything ready?" Ailsa asked breathlessly. She had thought the pain of parting would ease as she left Ian farther behind, but she had been wrong. She gripped the doorjamb as the realization hit her fully for the first time; this was her wedding day. Gasping at a new rush of fear, she took a step forward. She nearly tripped on the trunk near the door where she had left the basket earlier. "What . . .?" she began.

"Andrew and Catriona Grant found it in their cellar. They said they hadn't ever used it, nor would they likely do so now. They wanted ye to have it."

Ailsa swallowed dryly as she knelt to touch the small trunk as if it were made of fine silver. "That was kind," she managed to whisper. "And what of this?" She pointed to the leather bag.

"Alistair Munro brought it by yesterday for your bride gift. He made it for ye to take your clarsach in, for such a treasure didn't belong with common things like clothes, he said."

Biting her lip to hold back tears, Ailsa lifted the soft

144

leather, caressed the figures tooled around the top edge. There were wreaths of roses intertwined with the mistletoe and oak leaves sacred to the Druids, the mystic Celtic symbols of the sacred three—the center, the cross, and the circle as well as the circle broken into three swirling parts that met in three dark eyes at the center. Finally, there were two intricate birds, their wings, spread in flight, spiraled upward to entwine as did their beaks and necks until the two birds fused into one incredible snakelike animal. It was beautiful work, perhaps the best Alistair had done.

Ailsa fought to breathe evenly, but her hands trembled just the same. She set the precious hand harp down, then closed her eyes and said a little prayer to Neithe, God of Waters, who had always been her special deity. Give me courage, she said silently. Help me remember my joy and my hope in the midst of the partin's I will endure this day. She felt a momentary sense of calm as she rose. "Well," she said, turning away from the sight of the luggage, "I'd best begin to get ready. I'll be goin' down to the burn to bathe first, for I must come fresh to my groom and—" She hesitated and found she could not speak the word "pure." "And clean," she finished shakily. "I'll be as quick as I can."

"Ye don't need to hurry yet. Ye've plenty of time." Mairi handed the girl a linen towel and some handmade soap.

Ailsa dropped the rough bar of soap and knelt to pick it up. When she stood again, her eyes glittered feverishly. She started for the door, but whirled at the last moment. "Mother!" The single hoarse word was a plea for reassurance.

" 'Tis no' so strange that ye should be afraid, *moghray*. 'Twould be daft indeed if ye weren't. Just ye go about your business and don't let the fear become your master."

"I'll try," Ailsa said, but she did not sound very certain.

Mairi followed her daughter to the door and saw her disappear into the trees. She was headed for the secluded trickle of a burn that broke away from the river Affric.

Ailsa returned as the sun rose higher and dawn lightened the sky. She draped the towel over a birch chair by the fire

145

and met her mother's searching gaze. She trembled with nervousness and her stomach felt hollow.

"Don't fret, birdeen. Things will go well. 'Tis the Thursday of the growth of the moon, remember. Perfect for a weddin' day. Sit ye down and eat some porridge."

Ailsa pressed her hand to her stomach. "Och, I couldn't eat anythin' today. I feel like there's a bird trapped inside flappin' his wings, demandin' that I set him free."

Mairi smiled. "He'll fly away on his own in time. But if ye're no' goin' to eat, ye'd best be gettin' ready. When your hands are still, your mind roams and I don't think ye want that."

"No." For a moment, the girl seemed uncertain which way to turn. She whirled, took a few steps, and stopped still, remembering the sound of Ian's voice, the touch of his hands, the gnawing grief and emptiness inside her. In desperation, she went to kneel beside her kist. Pushing back the leather on the window, she allowed the pearly light to wash over the lid. Ailsa pressed her hands against the renderings of griffins, fairies, and winged horses carved there. She leaned so far forward that the raised figures became imprinted on her palms.

She loved this chest that held her "providing"—the clothing and linen she had collected since childhood for the day when she would marry. She had already taken from it the few things she would need. Although she tried to keep the image away, she remembered all too clearly the dismay she'd felt when Lady Williston had come to speak to her a few days earlier.

The Lady had explained what she feared William would fail to mention. Ailsa would have new clothes in London, and her new house was fully furnished, so she did not need the undergarments she had made so carefully, the linen sheets she had woven herself, the tablecloth she and Mairi had worked on together for nearly a year.

Resentment rose in Ailsa's throat. Why should these things, so precious to her, mean so little to her groom? But that was not fair and she knew it. Lady Williston had told her William did not even know of the visit. He assumed his friends would accept Ailsa as she was, but Eleanor Williston knew better. She had come out of kindness to prepare the girl for what she would find in London. Ailsa sighed. This would have been her torcher, her bridal portion. But more than once during the long walks she had taken with William in the past week, when they'd come to know each other better and had spoken about the future, he had insisted she need bring him nothing but herself. She would use the gown inside this chest, but that was all.

When she raised the lid, the fragrance of herbs rose to meet her in a rush. The sprigged muslin dress, made from one of the few bolts of cloth Mairi had purchased, lay on top. Ailsa took it out and spread it in her lap. She touched with sadness the linens and wool garments, the woven and patterned cloth. She had never thought to leave them behind, but Lady Williston had implied that in London these Highland products would be looked down upon, perhaps even laughed at. Ailsa treasured them too much to take that chance.

"What if I'm no' good enough for William?" she whispered. "What if I can't learn—"

"Ye're good enough for any man," her mother said fiercely. "And don't ye ever doubt it."

"But what if—"

"No more of that. Any Highlander with half a wit will tell ye, raise no more devils than ye can lay. Be at peace, for your choice is made."

Ailsa nodded, soothed by the sound of her mother's familiar voice, if not by her wisdom. She started to close the lid, but her eye was caught by the gleam of purple satin in the tiny box in the corner. She fingered the ribbons Ian had found in the Chisholm chest. When she held them up, she saw that beneath them lay the dried heather and roses he had picked for her years ago.

Her head ached horribly as the ribbons slipped from her numb fingers. Then her shoulders began to shake and the tears to slide down her cheeks. They fell onto the dress until it was damp with the weight of her sorrow. She was trembling so badly that she could not even grasp the gown to move it out of the way.

"Come, *mo-run*," Mairi said behind her. "Come to me."

Ailsa rose unsteadily to throw her arms around her mother. Mairi pulled her close and they stood, holding each other, while Ailsa sobbed.

"Ye've said farewell to Ian, haven't ye?" Mairi said at last.

"Aye," her daughter choked. "I must leave him, but I can't bear to. 'Tis too hard, too cruel."

"Ye'll find ye can bear a great many things that ye think too cruel, birdeen. Ye are strong, Ailsa. Never forget that. Never let anyone convince ye 'tisn't so," she said with passion.

Ailsa hugged Mairi more tightly, afraid to let go. She wept into her mother's hair, shaking with the force of her grief, while Mairi wept in her own way, silently, with dry shadowed eyes. It was then, as the two women clung together, that they said their true good-byes to one another.

William paced back and forth in the drawing room at the Hill. He had been up and dressed for hours, unable to stay in bed, unable to sit down or remain in one place for very long.

Eleanor entered the room to find him staring blankly at the Persian rug. She wanted to turn and flee, but forced herself to greet him. "Good morning, William," she said in a quavering voice. "You look very handsome today." She smiled weakly as she went to join him by the window.

She was a little surprised to realize she had spoken the truth. He did look handsome in his black cutaway coat, white linen shirt, and silver cravat, which had been retied at least ten times. It set off his dark gray waistcoat to perfection. His black boots gleamed with fresh polish. Even his light brown hair was combed neatly into place this morning. Not a single strand fell over his temple.

"Thank you," he murmured absently. He stood for a moment in the wash of dawn light that spilled through the open window. He had needed air so desperately that, against all convention, he had drawn back the drapes and thrown the windows open.

Eleanor put her hands on the sill and looked out. William's agitation was only making her more flustered.

"It's a lovely day," she managed at last. "Isn't it?" She spoke hesitantly, as if he might disagree.

William gulped. "Yes," he stammered, "yes indeed."

"Good morning," Agatha Harcourt snapped as she swept into the room with her husband Gerald tagging behind. "I thought you should know, Eleanor, that Sarah is in bed with a beastly headache and will not be down today. Something has made her quite ill."

"Oh dear," Eleanor muttered, glancing nervously at William. He did not seem to have noticed Agatha's biting tone. "How dreadful for her. Perhaps some chamomile tea—"

"Oh, nothing will be of the slightest help, I'm sure." Agatha turned pointedly away from William. Despite his wife's warning glare, Gerald went to slap the groom's back a bit too heartily.

"So today's to be the day. Big step, old man. Bit nervous are you? Not surprised, you know. Happens to everyone, indeed it does."

William smiled stiffly. Gerald was trying, but he shifted his weight from one foot to the other, making his discomfort obvious. And he would not meet his friend's gaze.

"If he's nervous," Agatha muttered under her breath, "it's probably because he knows what a mistake he's making."

This time William raised his head. He narrowed his eyes and his lips became a rigid line. He could cheerfully have throttled the woman just then, especially because, for once, she had hit a little too close to the truth. Today, for the first time, he *had* begun to wonder if this whole thing weren't a mistake. It was all happening so quickly. If he truly loved Ailsa, why did he feel this sick terror in the pit of his stomach?

"I'm going to breakfast," Agatha announced, flouncing from the room in a rustle of silk and crinoline. Gerald smiled a thin smile. "Not a bad idea. Best of luck, old man. Don't know if I'll see you before you go." He shook William's hand briefly, then hurried after his wife with a sigh of relief.

John Williston passed the Harcourts in the doorway. "You're a bit pale around the edges, don't you know," he observed, joining William. "Feeling a little doubtful, are you? There's no need to worry, actually. I felt the same way on my wedding day. Scared stiff, if you want to know the truth." He took his wife's hand to tuck it under his elbow. "But I've never regretted it since."

William stared at the man in surprise. He spoke with genuine sympathy; his brown eyes were steady and his reassuring smile sincere. William smiled back, grateful for one friendly face in a house full of strangers. Then he realized Eleanor, too, was smiling, though her lips trembled slightly with the strain.

"I'll tell you what," John continued. "Eleanor and I have talked it over and we want to give you a wedding gift. But not just another silver bowl that'll get thrust onto some back shelf. Is there anything you'd particularly like?"

"It's very kind of you, but—" William broke off, searching for the right words. "But it's really not necessary."

"It has nothing to do with necessity," Eleanor said with uncharacteristic firmness. "We want to do it. Truly. Ailsa has brought us a great deal of pleasure over the years." She flushed in embarrassment and added, "Besides, more than once she's rescued me from Richard's noisy clutches, and Cecilia worships her. You're our friend, William. Please take something."

William was touched. "I don't know," he began.

"Don't ruin our pleasure," John interrupted. "Isn't there something you want? Anything at all?"

For a moment more William hesitated. "Well, actually, there is something—"

"Madam! M'lady!" The maid's piercing voice drowned out William's murmur. Katie stood in the doorway, her cap awry and her cheeks flushed.

"What is it, Katie? What's wrong?"

"There's some men at the door and they won't go away," the girl announced shakily. "I've tried to tell them they're not wanted, but they won't listen."

Eleanor sighed. "I suppose I must see to it." She glanced at her husband pleadingly, but he was more concerned with William than the intruders at the door. With great reluctance, she followed the maid from the room. When she reached the front door and pulled it open, she found three Highlanders in full kilts who stood, hands on hips, feet spread challengingly.

"I told you," Katie whispered, and hurried away.

"Is there something I can do for you?" Lady Williston asked a little breathlessly, intimidated by the men's broad shoulders and the gleam of determination in their eyes.

"As a matter of fact," Alistair Munro declared, "we're waitin' for William Sinclair. We're to take him to the kirk to be married this day. And we'll no' be goin' till he comes with us." He glanced back over his shoulder. "Will we?"

"Not even the devil could drive us away," the other two answered in unison.

"Oh dear." Eleanor's hands fluttered like pale, awkward wings. When she saw how they flapped about, she twisted her fingers in the skirt of her gown. "I really don't know—"

"It doesn't matter if ye know or ye don't. We've come for the groom and we'll wait till he appears. 'Tis as simple as that."

Lady Williston saw that the man held a flask of whiskey in his hand. She wondered how many times he had drunk from it already. When he took a step closer, she backed away. "I'll go tell him you're here, but I can't say what he'll do." If he were wise, she thought as she made her way to the drawing room, he would slip out the back way. "Oh dear," she muttered under her breath. "Oh dear, oh dear, oh dear!"

"What is it, Eleanor?" John asked when he saw his wife's pale cheeks.

"Some Highlanders are looking for William. They say they're to escort him to the church. I've told them to go away, but they tell me they won't unless he comes."

"Is it time already?" William swallowed nervously. "I'd better go with them, then. I'd probably get lost anyway."

"Are you sure?" John demanded. "There's more than one way out of this house, you know."

"I'm sure." No doubt this was what Ailsa wanted and

he did not intend to disappoint her even in so small a way. He picked up his top hat from the table. "Thank you for everything," he said. "If you hadn't invited me, I never would have met her." The look of blank astonishment on their faces followed him all the way down the hall.

He found the three men standing where Eleanor had left them, arms crossed over their draped plaids. "You wanted me?" he said.

"That we do," Alistair replied. "I'm Alistair Munro, this is Malcolm Drummond and Archibald Maclennan. We're to see ye safely to the kirk." Without waiting for his permission, the two others flanked William and grasped his arms. "This way."

Archibald removed a flask from his pocket and handed it to the bridegroom. "Have ye a bittie dram, why don't ye? It'll calm your nerves."

William hesitated briefly, then raised the flask to take a deep drink of the whiskey that burned like fire down his throat. Alistair took a swig from his own flask and passed it to Malcolm while Archibald retrieved his and tilted it so the amber liquid spilled into his open mouth. William found the flask in his hand once more and took a second drink, though he refused a third.

As he followed the men over the moor and down to the loch, his nervousness retreated and he felt the first surge of anticipation at the thought of the coming ceremony. Today he would make Ailsa his. How could he have doubted for an instant that he was doing the right thing? The three Highlanders began to sing at the top of their lungs, some strange Gaelic song he could not understand. William smiled as Alistair pounded him on the back and bellowed out another verse. Suddenly the Englishman's pulse was racing. He walked more quickly, unable to contain his exhilaration.

The other men trudged ahead, plaids swinging, voices growing louder with each breath. William wanted to join them but did not know the words, and could not have pronounced them if he did. It was a long time before he realized they were moving unsteadily over long, curving paths that lost themselves in gorse and bracken and trees that crowded close on every side. It seemed to him that they had reached the far side of the loch. He stopped and leaned down, hands on knees as he tried to catch his breath. When he could speak again, he asked, "Are you certain this is the right way?"

The Scots finished another verse of their exuberant song before they replied. "I know this glen like the back of my own head," Alistair claimed. "Or is it my hand?" He scratched his head thoughtfully while he pondered the question. When he saw the pasty color of William's face, he grinned. "Have another dram and ye'll no' be worryin' about such things. 'Tis your weddin' day, man, and ye with the prettiest girl in the glen. Ye should be celebratin', no' fritterin'."

William took his advice and swallowed a third drink of whiskey as the three men took up their song once more and started off in the opposite direction.

"'Tis time to stop your weepin' and prepare for the ceremony," Mairi said. She drew away from her daughter and smoothed the hair from her wet cheeks. "Unless—" she added with a thread of hope in her voice.

"Aye," Ailsa said firmly, " 'tis time." She searched for her dress and realized it lay crumpled at her feet. "Look what I've done to my gown!" she cried. She had forgotten it was in her lap; it had fallen to the floor when she rose.

"It doesn't matter, birdeen, for ye'll no' be wearin' it anyway. Why should ye be married in an old gown when ye have a new?" She went to her bed and threw back the quilt to reveal a beautiful dress made of the deep blue wool shot with purple silk. "I told ye 'twas for a special occasion and I can't think of a better one than your weddin'."

Ailsa gaped. She knew how much the cloth was worth, how hard her mother had worked to weave the pattern perfectly. When Mairi handed her the gown, Ailsa took it gingerly. It fell in soft folds over her arm and she held the cool fabric up to her cheek. A constriction in her throat stopped her breath.

Mairi touched her daughter's hair. "I wanted to give ye a gift ye wouldn't forget."

"But 'tis your finest fabric. I know ye were savin' it to sell to the Willistons for a side of beef."

"What would I be needin' with a side of beef when there's only myself to be feedin'? I was savin' it, aye, but I didn't know for what till the dawn of Beltaine when I saw your comin' marriage. 'Tis for ye, Ailsa. I wish it so."

Ailsa knew how her mother felt about this marriage, yet she had spent hour after hour, day after day weaving the fabric, night after night making the gown. The girl's eyes filled with tears. "Thank ye," was all she could manage to say.

"There'll be no more tears on your weddin' day, Ailsa Rose. Now get ye dressed, and hurry."

"I'll be helpin' ye with that, as we always planned." Jenny Mackensie spoke unexpectedly from the doorway. At Ailsa's look of surprise, she added, " 'Tis tradition, ye ken. I didn't think ye would argue with that, knowin' how ye feel about the past."

Ailsa opened her mouth but no words came. She had not thought to see her friend today. Only then did it strike her how much she wanted Jenny here. The day would have been empty indeed with no friends to turn to now that Ian was gone.

"Where's to begin?" Jenny asked, glancing from the muslin gown to the wool one. "Ye're to wear the blue and purple, are ye no'? Bonnier by far, and just right for your eyes. Besides, these go better with that one." She held out a pair of beige leather slippers she had hidden in her pockets. "My father made them for ye. 'Tisn't right to go barefoot to the kirk on your weddin' day. He wanted ye to have somethin' finer than your sandals."

She handed the shoes to Ailsa, who put them on, sighing at the feel of pliable leather against her toes. "They're lovely, Jenny, and so soft I hardly know I have them on. Thank ye. And thank Callum for me, too. I don't think ye know what your kindness means to me."

Jenny brushed her gratitude aside. "Ye didn't think we'd forget ye today of all days, did ye?" She took the muslin gown and laid it back in the kist, closed the lid, then noticed the ribbons on the floor. "Och, Ailsa Rose, wherever did ye get these? They'll be perfect with your gown." She picked them up and raised her hand so the satin streamed between her fingers.

Ailsa blinked at her. The ribbons might have been made for the gown, so close was the match. But she saw beyond the purple strands to the look in Ian's eyes when he had given them to her. Abruptly, she turned and began to dress. She put on her best drawers and chemise, then raised her arms while Jenny and Mairi slipped the dress over her head.

Jenny fastened the hooks in back while Mairi piled Ailsa's chestnut hair on her head. As her mother worked, she twined the ribbons cleverly into the soft, gleaming strands. Then Jenny put sprigs of heather and violets and a few wild roses among the curls and the bride was ready.

Ailsa looked down in wonder at the gown with its low neckline that curved gracefully between her breasts. The sleeves, puffed at the top, began to narrow at the elbow and ended in points on the backs of her hands. The skirt was so wide that it swirled as she walked and the silk made it rustle like the whisper of fall leaves.

" 'Tis beautiful ye are," Jenny said in awe. Ailsa's hair was swept up and away from her face, emphasizing her wide cheekbones and high forehead. The color of the dress darkened her blue-violet eyes to the soft velvet purple of midnight. And the bodice, cut tight and narrowing to a point at her waist, made Ailsa look slender and elegant. Yet, as Jenny gazed at her friend, she could not hide a tiny, perplexed frown.

Ailsa saw the question in Jenny's expression and looked away.

"Ye'll cast a *sian* on your groom with those eyes of yours," Mairi whispered. "I'll be gey proud if he can even remember to say his vows."

There was a clatter of feet and clapping hands outside. "Where's the bride?" several voices cried in chorus. "Bring her out before the day turns into gloamin' and the Kelpies come lookin' for pretty young girls. Bring us the bride!"

Smoothing her skirt one last time, Ailsa drew a deep breath and crossed the threshold to find Megan and Anne Macdonnell, both of Jenny's parents, Geordie Mackensie, Andrew and Catriona Grant, and Colin Munro waiting for her. They cheered and smiled when she appeared, though their eyes mirrored Jenny's doubt.

"We wondered if ye'd ever be poppin' your head out the door," Angus Fraser cried from the back of the group. "We're here to escort ye to the kirk. Alistair and the others will be along with the groom before ye blink thrice."

The sight of Ian's father, come to celebrate Ailsa's marriage to another man, the sound of his voice, hearty with an enthusiasm that sounded sincere, broke the girl's heart. It was too much to ask of any man what Angus Fraser clearly intended to do for her today. Her throat was suddenly raw and dry. "I didn't think to see ye all this mornin'," she said.

"Come now, don't grieve," Geordie Mackensie called. "After all, a Sassenach groom is better than none. Besides," he added, grinning, "do ye think we'd miss a chance to drink a dram and wish ye well?"

"Let's be off, friends, or the devil will be at our heels," Angus said. Resting his fiddle beneath his chin, he tilted the bow dramatically, let it hover above the strings for an instant, then struck up a lively tune. The notes spilled over his shoulders like the singing of cheerful birds. Then the song became low and soft, curling through the air with the slow, hypnotic rhythm of a mountain stream.

Just when the music caught in Ailsa's chest and pressed against her heart, Angus changed the tune again. This one laughed and tumbled around her, singing of joy and celebration, of youth and the beauty of a clear spring day. The pressure in Ailsa's chest eased as the others began to clap their hands and walk more briskly. Thus, at the head of the procession, Angus played one mood after another onto those who followed. Many brides had gone this way in the past, but none, Ailsa suspected, with so deep a love for the friends who stood beside her now, even though they could never approve her marriage to an Englishman and, what was more, a stranger. Her eyes shimmered with moisture while drams of whiskey were passed among the group and Ailsa's health and happiness drunk time and again.

As they drew near the kirk, she heard a commotion behind her and saw Alistair, Malcolm, and Archibald escorting William, who looked a little taken aback by all the noise. He wobbled as he walked and she wondered how many drams of whiskey they had forced on him. His hair had long since fallen into his eyes and he carried his top hat in his hands. He was grinning as he approached, but when he caught sight of his bride, he stopped in the middle of the path.

William had thought Ailsa could never be more beautiful

than she had been in the midst of the raging storm, but he had been wrong. Before, she had looked young, fresh, and lovely, but today—with her hair piled on her head and the color of the gown reflected in her eyes—she was a girl no longer, but a woman. The other voices faded into silence; all he could hear was Ailsa's soft greeting.

"Good mornin', William. I hope my friends didn't lead ye too far astray."

The bleary-eyed drunkenness of his tramp through the woods disappeared abruptly. He took Ailsa's hand; his fingers closed around hers tightly, as if he were afraid she would slip away at any moment. "Not too far," he said. "They brought me to you in the end, and that's all that really matters."

Ailsa looked into his glowing eyes and suddenly her nervousness and doubts seemed unimportant. She covered his hand with hers. "Are ye ready?"

He nodded. He wanted to say more, to tell her that the sight of her, the touch of her hand made him ache with pleasure and gratitude, but he could not find the words.

The crowd fell silent as, hands clasped, bride and groom entered the church and moved down the aisle toward the simple altar where the minister waited. Jenny went next and the others followed until everyone was inside. Mairi was last. She paused with her fingers spread on the weathered oak doors, then pushed them closed. As she found her place in the first pew, an expectant stillness settled over the little group. The tiny building with a few narrow windows on each side of the plain, hard benches was shadowed and cool—a separate world within the circled mountains.

But the other world was there; Ailsa felt it in the chilly breeze that crept beneath the door, heard it in the low rumble of thunder, the rattling of leaves and the melancholy cry of the Spirit o' the Mountain. The glen could not be shut out by a few thin walls and the intimidating sound of a sonorous voice.

No one moved as Ailsa smiled and turned to her groom.

Ian wandered the hills restlessly with his bow under one arm, his pipes under the other, and Torran at his side. His father had several guns at home, but Ian did not like to use them. He preferred the ancient thrill of stalking an animal and meeting him on equal terms. But today, as Ian followed a red deer from a distance, moving on silent feet, the excitement was gone.

He made a sign to Torran and the collie barked, sending the deer running. That was better. Ian took off after the fleeing animal, ducked in and out among the trees, brushed past low-hanging branches, let the shadows rush over him like falling rain. He needed to be moving, gasping, using every last ounce of his energy so he would not think.

He lost the animal for a while and crouched, listening, while the dog rested its snout on his master's knee. Ian heard a distant crackle of branches, but still he did not move. He waited, the bow clutched in his hand. All his attention was concentrated on a light-speckled copse where the deer stood, head raised and nostrils quivering. The shadows concealed the graceful animal as the clouds moved over the sky, rumbling like the drums of the god of thunder and war.

Ian waited until the deer forgot him, began to move through the cool, dark forest toward the moor beyond. Then the young man followed, walking through bracken and wild grasses when he could, so he broke no twigs and made no sound. He crept slowly closer, his eyes and ears and body focused on the animal he stalked.

His heart began to pound when he drew nearer and saw that the animal was moving toward a stone ledge it could not possibly climb. Ian moved stealthily, like a wildcat full of fury unleashed, waiting for a chance to set that fury free. He crouched, his bow to his shoulder, then realized that the animal was turning restlessly away. Quickly Ian picked up his pipes, filled them with air, and placed the chanter in his mouth. He held the drone in his fingers and began, softly, to play.

The deer paused, raised its head to listen to the high plaintive notes. Mesmerized by the sweet wild song, the animal turned its huge eyes toward the place where Ian sat hidden among the branches of a pine. The pipes held the deer captive: he could not have fled even if he wished to. With a last, wailing note that lingered in the treetops, Ian traded the pipes for his bow, fitted an arrow, and drew the string taut. He raised the bow, sighted along the shaft, and prepared to let the arrow fly.

Freed from the spell of Ian's song, the deer turned its head and sniffed, startled by a deep roll of thunder that ran before the rising storm. Frightened by the reverberations that filled the sky, the animal leaped headlong up the rugged mountainside.

Ian stood staring in disbelief as the deer dislodged shower after shower of loose stones and gravel. He raced after the animal, but when he reached the top of the incline, he found himself looking down into the Valley of the Dead. On the far side, the deer ran, touched by the first raindrops as he escaped over the wild grass to a place behind the three cairns where the standing stones parted.

He was gone, free, lost forever. The rain began to splatter the rock at Ian's feet. With each second, it fell more fiercely. He tried to close his ears against the voice of the Spirit o' the Mountain, but the lament went on and on. Ian thought the mad mournful sound would never cease. He would stand here, battered by the force of the storm within him and without, until the moaning Spirit entered him, became him. From somewhere far away he thought he heard church bells. Ian closed his eyes.

Ailsa was leaving him. Not until this moment had he really believed it. His cheeks were wet, but whether with tears or rain he did not know. He only knew he could not bear the pain that sliced through him with every drop that struck his skin, his face, his naked throat. "Ailsa!" he cried into the savage confusion of wind and rain and thunder. "Ailsa!" The name rose in the torrent, carried from the heart of the storm inside him, a last desperate plea to one who was already lost. "Ailsa!"

"Ailsa, wilt ye have this man to be your husband?"

Ailsa stood frozen by the sound of her name, which echoed through the church as if every voice were crying it in anguish, as if the storm itself called out to her. She turned and saw that the others sat calmly, waiting for her response. Only Mairi seemed to notice her daughter's agitation, but even her mother's all-seeing eyes were blank. No one else could hear it then. The resounding echo was inside Ailsa's head. "Ailsa!" The single word was more than just a name, it was a *caiodh*, a wailing lamentation. "Ailsa!" She could not shut out the sound.

"Ailsa?"

The voice of Reverend Ross penetrated her trance at last. She looked up to find William watching in concern, his gray eyes full of fear that she would choose, in the end, not to answer.

"Aye," she said, laying her free hand over their clasped fingers. "Aye, that I will." Her voice trembled, but there was no other sign of the dying tumult of that echo in her head.

"Then 'tis done," the minister announced ponderously. "Ye are, by the grace of God and the angels, husband and wife."

The couple turned, hands still clasped, while Ailsa's friends parted to let them pass. Slowly, to the strange, sighing music of the storm, bride and groom walked down the aisle and out of the kirk. Ailsa paused for a moment, raised her face to the rain, and let it wash over her, uncaring of the flowers, ribbons, and curls that fell from their confinement on her head. "Och, William," she cried, "isn't it lovely? Have ye ever known such joy in your life?"

She was looking at the storm-ravaged heavens but he was looking at her. "No," he said softly. "Never."

Then they ran, heads bent, toward the distant shelter of Mairi Rose's croft. Once there, with the door closed against the rain and a peat fire burning in the center of the room, the guests took off their wet plaids and laid them out to dry. While the rain beat furiously on the roof, the women and men took turns standing close to the warmth of the fire. Ailsa smiled at them and with Jenny's help passed out bannochs and black buns and cups of ale.

The chill of the storm wore off at last. One at a time, the guests moved to where Ailsa stood beside her new husband. Jenny Mackensie was the first to present her offer of the bridal bread and cheese. Ailsa took it, bit off a portion of each, then offered both bread and cheese to William. One by one the others rose and repeated the ritual. Angus Fraser was the last. He found it difficult to meet Ailsa's eyes as he wished her joy.

While Mairi spoke to William, Angus drew the girl aside to murmur, "Forgive Flora. She couldn't come, but must stay at home and grieve today."

Ailsa looked away. "I understand."

"Do ye?" he said, pushing his iron-gray hair out of his eyes. "I wonder. Just remember, a willful lass should be very wise." He turned away and she heard him say to Geordie a moment later, "As does the mother, so does the bairn."

Ailsa frowned. Was Angus talking that way because she had married an Englishman? But surely Ailsa's choice was different. William would not leave her to grieve alone as Charles Kittridge had left Mairi. She looked up then and caught her husband's eye. He was smiling at her with affection and awe. She felt a flow of warmth in her chilled hands. This man would keep her safe from grief. She knew it.

The group dispersed as the time approached for the coach to depart for Glasgow. Before they started home, each of the guests left behind small gifts of cheese, home-made sweets, and baskets of food for the long trip to London. Soon the bride's arms were full, as were the groom's. Alistair had to carry the trunk down to the place where the coach would pass, but Ailsa insisted on keeping the leather bag that held her harp.

When they reached the edge of woods, Ailsa dropped the gifts into Mairi's arms. "I want to go back in alone, to say good-bye."

Her mother nodded in understanding and those who remained watched the girl run across the clearing, holding her skirt above the wet ground; the leather bag swung from her arm. They waited in silence, as reverent now as they had been in the kirk, while Ailsa made her private farewell to the house in which she had been born.

◊ ◊ ◊

Jenny slipped away as the group headed toward the stagecoach stop. She had bidden good-bye to the bride long since. Now there was something else she must do. Ailsa was among friends and did not need her. There was another who was alone today.

She went first to the Fraser croft, but Ian was not there. Flora sat staring into the flames, blinded by sorrow, and did not answer Jenny's questions. The girl left the woman to her grief and continued on her way, seeking out the places where Ian went when he was troubled. She found him at last, seated, head bent, at the foot of a mountain, his bagpipe under his arm, the rain falling on his dark head.

She paused uncertainly, recognizing his torment in the droop of his shoulders, the way he gripped the chanter in white, rigid fingers. She had come to cheer him, but now that she was here, she did not know what to say. She stood out of sight behind a tall birch, uncaring that her own gown was sodden and her bare feet chilled from the cold wet ground. In silence she watched him, hoping for an inspiration. It frightened her that he sat unmoving, staring at the ground that she knew he did not see any more than his mother had seen the leaping flames.

Jenny wanted to sit beside him, to touch his hand, to let him know he was not alone. But the longer she hesitated, the greater was her fear. Eventually, she dared not move from behind the shelter of her tree. Then the storm cleared for a moment and a drift of sun broke through the clouds. Ian looked up, so that Jenny saw his face for the first time.

She gasped at the sight of his pale, bloodless lips, his eyes, raw and red, his cheeks the color of lifeless ash. Then he began to sing. She strained to hear the words.

> "Here, by the banks and groves so green
> Where Yarrow's waters warblin' roll,
> The lovesick swain, unheard, unseen,
> Pours to the stream his secret soul;
> Sings to his bright charmer, and by turns,
> Despairs, and hopes, and fears, and burns."

Jenny knew then that there was nothing she could do for him. His face was ravaged by a sorrow so great that she could neither understand nor begin to ease it. Aching for him, her own face covered with tears, she turned away.

Just before Ailsa boarded the coach, Mairi tossed the bright red plaid about her daughter's head and hugged her close. Neither could speak. There was too much to say—too much to fear, to hope for, to promise. Then, while the horses stamped in impatience, William touched his wife's arm. She drew away from her mother, eyes burning, and allowed her new husband to help her aboard. Ailsa hung out the window as the coach rolled away with the mud heavy on its wheels and the harnesses jingling through the clearing air. The storm was over at last.

For a long time Mairi stood in the middle of the road and watched the carriage disappear from view. Longer she stood, staring at the rutted road, unwilling to face the emptiness that awaited her at the croft. But at last she turned away, her heart heavy with weariness and grief, with the weight of the smiles and reassurances she had given her daughter today, though she knew them to be lies.

Mairi paused in the doorway, gazing at the rough stone walls, the peat fire, the plain oak table and polished birch chairs that had been filled so recently with friends and noise and laughter. Now silence had settled upon the croft. She went to Ailsa's box bed and leaned against it for support. Then, one last time, she slid the doors open to look at the quilt her daughter had slept beneath for seventeen years. Her heart paused when she saw what lay on the heather mattress. Mairi moved closer, squinting through the yellow light, though she knew she had not been mistaken. The hand harp had been placed by careful hands in the center of the bed—the clarsach that Ailsa loved above all other possessions, the source of her music and her magic. How could her daughter have left it behind?

Mairi closed her eyes as the tears of many days and years began to fall at last. She touched the harp, so cold and lifeless without Ailsa's fingers to caress the strings, and knew with a chilling certainty that her daughter was never coming home.

◇ ◇ ◇

The stagecoach bounced and rattled over the uneven ground, but Ailsa did not notice. She listened to the jingle of the harnesses and tried to ignore the ache in her heart at the memory of her mother standing silent and forsaken in the road. She touched William's hand more than once and smiled when he laced his fingers with hers. She wanted him to know how grateful she was that he had given her not only his name and his heart, but also a chance to see the world.

Now and then she had to look away to hide her grief at leaving the glen behind. Ailsa put her head out the window and listened as the storm clouds retreated in the wind. Then she heard something strange within the whoosh and moan of the Spirit o' the Mountain. It was the wind, yet it was not—perhaps then, the Son o' the Wind, the song of the Highland pipes.

Her heart beat furiously as she looked back along the rolling hills, above the forest to the dark mountains in the distance, drawn by the plaintive rise and swirl of music through the cloud-laden sky. At last she saw a figure, small and dark against the mountainside, standing on the ledge that had been her special place. Ian. She did not need to see his face to know that it was he.

Ailsa found she could not catch her breath and her pulse grew sluggish in her veins. He was playing to her; she knew that, too. He was calling out one last time with the sound of the mountain waterfall, the cry of the birds in the trees, and the sweet, curling wonder of a song that rose above the woods, above the hills, above the last of the roiling storm. And the tune he played was "*Uighean bhoidheach, sian leibh*"—"Ye Pretty Maids, Farewell!"

There was a weight in her chest that pressed her back against the seat. Her eyes burned with dry tears that she dared not shed. Once they started, she feared that they would never cease. She could not do that to William—not today when he had given her so much.

Unable to stop herself, she leaned out the window once more, weeping without sound or tears until Ian and his mountain and his song had disappeared beyond her reach.

12

After a long while, when the threat of tears had passed for the moment, Ailsa drew a deep breath. "I didn't think a coach could go so fast," she said to William.

"This one's called the Zephyr, because it moves like a very fast wind."

"Och, how lovely!" she cried. "To be movin' inside the wind. Haven't ye always yearned to do that?"

He smiled. "I don't think so—" He paused, rubbing his chin between thumb and forefinger. "But then, perhaps I have, only I didn't know it until now. You've already taught me things about myself that I never would have known otherwise."

"Have I? Tell me what they are."

He was taken aback by her request. Brow furrowed, he stared at the muddy toes of his boots that had gleamed so brightly that morning. "First," he said, fumbling for the right words. "I suppose you've taught me how much I love music. And you've shown me that a storm can be as beautiful as it is violent. I know now, too, that there is one person in the world who is honest and without guile."

Ailsa touched his arm and he covered her fingers with his. "All of that?"

He nodded. "And one thing more."

"What is't?"

William looked away, unable to meet her curious gaze. "You've shown me how much I hate—" He broke off when he realized what he was saying. He could not tell her that she'd made his life before seem sterile and absurd, that it was her courage, not his, that had freed him from that prison. When he knew his voice would not quaver, he said instead, "I can hardly believe you're here beside me."

" 'Tis a little like magic, isn't it?" his wife replied, though for some reason the affection in his eyes made her hurt inside. She glanced out the window again. "Almost like the feelin' of movin' so fast that the trees and hills fly by ye just as shadows run through the woods in a breeze."

"Something like that," William said in a choked voice. The pressure of her fingers on his arm, the curve of her lips, the pensive look in her eyes made him want to draw her close and kiss her. He clenched his hands into fists. He could do no such thing, not here in a public coach, even if they were the only passengers. He had learned the lessons of his childhood too well.

Ailsa felt a sudden chill and leaned closer to her husband. She knew they had passed the boundaries of the glen by now. She had begun to miss it already. "Please hold me for a while, William," she whispered. "I feel so cold."

He hesitated until he saw her shiver. Then he wrapped his arms around her and she rested her head on his shoulder. William took a deep, ragged breath. His heart was beating wildly and his hands were damp with sweat. He held them rigid, afraid to feel the texture of her gown beneath his fingers, to imagine the length of her spine and the softness of her pale white skin. Dear God, he had not known it would feel like this merely to hold her. As he had on the first morning in the glen when he saw that magnificent sunrise, he wanted to close his mind to her beauty, to the scent of her hair, the curve of her cheek, the stirring and frightening feelings that moved through his body. She touched him so deeply that he could not bear the pleasure. He could not.

Ailsa felt him stiffen. "What is't, my husband? Ye're lookin' very gray, so ye are."

Her eyes were bright with concern and she touched his forehead with her palm to see if he felt overly warm or cool.

"It's nothing," he said a little too quickly. "I just— need a little air." Abruptly, he put his head out the window to draw in huge gulps of the moist Highland air. After a while his heartbeat slowed and he forced himself to breathe evenly.

"Has the motion made ye ill?" Ailsa asked when he leaned back against the cushioned seat. "I wish I'd thought to bring some of my mother's herbs. They'd make ye right again."

"I'll be fine," William muttered in the general direction of the buttons on his waistcoat. "Just need to rest a little. All the excitement, don't you know."

Ailsa patted his hand, which was still damp and cool. "I understand. I'll leave ye be for a time and watch the world go by." It was not really a hardship to turn her attention to the coach and the scenery. Ailsa was fascinated by everything around her—the lanterns affixed to the outside of the coach, the polished brass fittings that glittered like splintered stars when sunlight touched them, the driver perched precariously on his high seat above the coach. The man leaned forward, the reins in his hands, and though she could barely see his back, Ailsa imagined him smiling into the wind, his eyes alight with exhilaration as the coach barreled over the uneven roads.

She wanted to be up that high, in the seats on top where no padded walls blocked her view, where the wind and the rain could run through her hair. She had meant to ask William earlier, but knew he would not be comfortable there and so did not suggest it now.

Ailsa inhaled the cool air and gazed with delight at a loch that lay in the shadow of a mountain. The water was the color of blue midnight, except in the shallows where the shadow did not reach. There the clear water danced in small, rippled circles that touched the bank covered with fragile shoots of bracken. The song of the wind in the leaves seemed to echo the excited beat of Ailsa's heart.

A sense of breathless anticipation overcame her. The adventure she had waited for all her life had finally begun. She blinked, certain she felt her father's presence in the coach; Charles Kittridge was smiling and willing her on. The forest gave way at last to the wild beauty of a moor with the cloud-circled mountains behind it. Ailsa closed her eyes to see more clearly the images of dusky braes and purple heather made pale by the presence of black and silver mountains. This landscape was as beautiful, almost, as the glen she had left behind. But she did not want to think about Glen Affric, did not want to admit, even to herself, that she wished to be far away from her home as quickly as possible—not because she was glad to go, but because she loved it too much. Her exhilaration began to fade and she shook her head. She would not grieve—not today. Maybe, as she saw new wonders, the old affection would fade and the pain in her chest become a memory.

Ailsa leaned back, hoping to be lulled by the pleasant motion of the coach, the rhythmic clack of spoked wheels over the road. As the vehicle picked up speed, she was startled by the blurred landscape beyond the little window. It was like the forest in a storm—trees, leaves, clouds, branches, and sky whipped together in a frenzy of bright, vivid color. "Isn't it wonderful?" she asked, turning to William.

He was watching her, calmer now that the danger had passed, his eyes still luminous whenever they rested on her flushed face. "Aye," he said. His pleasure in her enthusiasm was so great that he did not even realize he had used a Highland word. Nor, in that moment, would he have cared.

Ailsa smiled to herself and said nothing. Instead she moved over to kiss William's cheek.

He flushed and looked around in distress.

"There's no one here but ye and me," she said, laughing. "And besides, ye're my husband now." She tilted her head to gaze at him intently. " 'Tis strange, isn't it, that this mornin' I was just plain Ailsa, but now I can call myself your wife."

William, who had intended to explain to her about propriety, decorum, and modesty, closed his mouth. He had told Mairi he did not want Ailsa to change and it was true. He twined his fingers with hers and she settled herself against his side with her head on his shoulder.

They traveled for five hours that first day. By the time gloaming fell, Ailsa had lost some of her sparkle. She was weary, worn down by the tumult of emotions she had struggled with since dawn. A soft rain began to fall when they were a mile outside the town of Aberfeldy. She let the drops cover her face and fall into her eyes. It was soothing, the touch of the rain on her cheeks, but it ceased too soon. She was grateful when they entered the town and the coach pulled up beside an inn.

William helped his bride down the metal steps and onto the muddy road. She leaned against him for a moment, too tired to take another step. When he stiffened, she looked up curiously. "What is't that troubles ye?"

He could not tell her, with the driver listening unabashed as he unloaded their luggage, that her nearness made his pulse race, that he wanted to pull her into his arms and kiss her right there, but did not wish for all the world to see his passion. Gently, he set her away from him. "We should go in, don't you think, and have some supper?"

Ailsa did not understand. "But William—"

"We'll talk when we're alone," he whispered, touching her cheek briefly.

She had to be satisfied with that. Moving awkwardly after her long confinement, she preceded him into the cozy inn. A fire crackled at one end of the room and the guests were gathered around long wooden tables as close to the flames as possible. The storm had left a chill behind that managed to creep inside wool cloaks no matter how tightly the travelers pulled them closed.

William directed the driver upstairs with the luggage, then guided Ailsa to a table with only two men at the far end. Husband and wife sat sipping brandy, which Ailsa had never tasted before and thought wonderful, while they waited for roast beef and potatoes to arrive. Afterward they had warm gingerbread with heavy cream.

Now that her stomach was full and the fire had warmed her chilled skin, Ailsa gazed around her with feigned interest. The fluttering nervousness of early morning had returned as she glanced up the stairs and saw how William avoided meeting her eyes. He dropped his spoon with a clatter on the marred tabletop. Ailsa realized he was as nervous as she.

Long after the food had been removed and the last sip of brandy swallowed, they sat in silence, staring into the flames. Finally William cleared his throat. "Shall we go up?"

Ailsa noticed the quaver in his voice; it echoed the beat of her pulse. "Aye," she said, "lest ye wish to sleep down here with our heads cradled on the tabletop."

Her husband could not help but smile, though the smile turned to a frown as he followed her up the stairs. He indicated a chamber, rested his hand on her waist for an instant, then pushed the door open. Ailsa was surprised to see that there were two rooms, a bedroom and sitting room connected by a single door. The accommodations were not luxurious, but comfortable enough, with heavy wool blankets on the bed and a blazing fire that filled the rooms with warmth and light.

"I'll leave you now," William said as soon as the outer door was closed behind them.

The color rose in Ailsa's cheeks when she realized she had to remove her gown. She was grateful for her husband's thoughtfulness in leaving her alone to make herself ready for him. The thought of disrobing in front of him dismayed her. A fleeting memory of Ian's body in the silver moonlight flickered through her mind, but that had been different. She had been safe in the glen last night with a young man she had known all her life. Ailsa stood still, her hands spread protectively over her skirt. William was not a stranger, she reminded herself. He was her husband. The word sounded so foreign that she repeated it aloud. "My husband."

Quickly, she slipped out of the wool and silk gown. She laid it gingerly over a chair, running her hands once more across the fine fabric. Then she discarded her chemise and drawers, found the small leather bag the Grants had given her, and lifted out the nightrail Mairi had made for her daughter's wedding night. It was far lovelier than any Ailsa had ever worn. The neckline, usually buttoned tightly at her throat, was curved and scalloped, made of simple lace; the wide sleeves were gathered gracefully at her wrists.

Shivering at the wind that wailed outside her window, she slipped the gown over her head, then sat in the chair before the fire. One by one, she took the ribbons and flowers from her hair. Finally she removed the few wooden pins and found the comb Jenny had given her as a wedding gift. She combed out her waist-length hair until it crackled and shimmered, touched with red by the light of the fire. She wanted to look soft and welcoming when William came to her. She wanted him to take her in his arms, to make her forget the touch of Ian's hands upon her body.

At last she slipped between the linen sheets and pulled the blanket up to her chin. She lay back against the thick pillows to wait, enjoying the comfort of a feather mattress, though she missed the subtle scent of heather. For nearly an hour she watched the door between the two rooms, but it remained firmly shut. She heard no sound from the other side. The flutter of wings in her stomach became a flock of birds fleeing before a storm.

The stillness was empty, chilled, and absolute. Ailsa realized with dismay that her husband was not going to return. She rose and went to tap softly on the door. There was no answer. She turned the knob and entered the sitting room, glancing around in apprehension. There was no light but the glow from the fire, which cast shadows like demons that leaped along the walls. Her husband was standing with his back to her, staring out into the night.

"William?" she said. He did not seem to hear. She moved closer, touched his arm lightly. He turned but his eyes were blank; he looked through her as if she were not there. At that moment, he was more like carved stone than living, breathing flesh and blood. "What ails ye?" she cried. "Are ye ill?"

He shook his head and turned back to the window. Ailsa felt a weight of lead settle in her stomach. "Mayhap ye're weary and should come to bed."

"No," he said in a hoarse voice. He was agonizingly aware of her presence, of the fresh scent of her hair, which fell shimmering around her in the firelight. He clenched his teeth and closed his eyes. He wanted her so much that the need to touch her was a violent, wrenching pain, but he could not touch her here.

He was so stiff, so strange and distant, like Mairi when she saw a disturbing vision. "Please," Ailsa murmured. "Come."

"No, I said." He had not meant to speak so harshly, but his frustration had grown until he thought he would explode with it.

When his wife reached out again, he flinched away. Ailsa took a step backward, wincing as if he had struck her. "Ye don't want me," she whispered. She drew her breath in sharply. Perhaps he knew what she had done with Ian and that was why he could not bear to touch her. Her throat grew dry with terror and remorse while her heart beat out the uneven rhythm of her guilt.

For the first time a flicker of emotion showed in William's eyes. "How can you believe such a thing? I want you so much—" He broke off. He should not be discussing this with her. She should not have asked such a question. But the hurt and fear in her blue-violet eyes was so bright and sharp that he wanted to make her understand.

Ailsa breathed a sigh of relief. Surely William would not look at her that way, with such tender longing, if he knew. "Then why?"

Her husband took a deep, labored breath. "Because it's not right to—be together in a place such as this. An unknown inn with strangers all around."

"There are walls aplenty to hide us from the strangers," Ailsa said, perplexed. "How can they know what passes between ye and me? I don't think they even care."

William sighed. "I have learned to live by certain rules."

"I don't care about your rules. I only know I want ye with me."

Her gaze was earnest and direct; she did not falter in embarrassment at speaking so openly. It was her husband who looked away. He realized then that he had been wrong to think Ailsa had freed him by becoming his wife. Her courage was not enough to break the bonds that imprisoned him. He needed some courage of his own. But he had used all he had in daring to marry her. Just now, he had no strength left to make her truly his. "It has to be right for us, Ailsa. The time, the place—they must be perfect," he said. But he knew it was a lie. Fear made him move away from her touch. Fear made him grasp the windowsill in a painful grip. He could not face the chaos of need and desire, pleasure and agony that had raged within him from the moment he caught sight of his wife in her clinging gown. He

173

had very nearly lost control and that had frightened him more than anything.

Ailsa frowned, trying to understand, "But I thought—"

From somewhere he found the strength to shake his head. "You should get some rest. The remainder of the journey will be long and tiring."

His wife realized then how much she wanted him to hold her, to fill her, to ease the emptiness inside her. But she could not tell him that. "Well then," she said, barely above a whisper, "I'll see ye in the mornin'."

William could not hide his relief as she moved away from him; the shape and texture of her body grew less defined, the fragrance of her hair and skin faded. "Good night," he said. He did not turn his head; he could not bear to see her go.

"Good night." Ailsa returned to her room, leaned against the door that shut her away from William, and wondered how many times today she had fought back the tears that burned now, dry and painful behind her closed lids.

The next day they reached the outskirts of Glasgow when the sun had burned its way to the top of the sky. Exhausted because she had slept so little, Ailsa did not stare out the window as she had yesterday. She was not even aware that she was entering the first real city she had ever been near. Thus it was that she did not see Glasgow unfolding around them. The coach rolled to a stop at another comfortable inn, where she stumbled blindly up the stairs, ate her dinner, and tossed and turned alone in her bed for the second time.

It was not until morning, when William took her to the train station, that she saw the factories, the smoke from chimneys that rose into the sky, covering the clouds and the last trace of blue. Ailsa stopped, unable to make her feet take another step, as she watched the grimy, stinking water rush down the cobbled streets and overflow the gutters. The stench was so great that she thought she would be ill. She had never breathed anything but clean Highland air and the filth here threatened to choke her.

As she moved in a trance, someone jostled her, knocking her off balance. She gasped and looked up at a tall, thin boy, shoulders bent, face dark with soot, trudging toward one of the factories.

"I'm sorry," she said, though she wanted to retreat in horror at the sight of his tattered clothes, blackened and worn thin from years of work. He neither saw nor heard her, but moved ahead, his face devoid of expression. In a single glimpse of his colorless eyes, she saw that his spirit was dead, and his joy, and his hope.

Though William tugged on her arm, she paused to look around, aware, suddenly, that there were many like the boy, some so young that it wrenched her heart to see them— bony, undernourished, their thin bodies visible beneath grease-smudged rags. She had heard of poverty, read about it, but never had she imagined a poverty so great that it took the heart from a city full of people, leaving them empty and broken. Her eyes filled with tears as she saw one after another pass beside her. They walked, not in a waking dream, but in a waking nightmare.

There's nothin' outside these hills but poverty and filth and darkness that stains and swallows everyone it touches. Ian's warning came back to her on a gust of foul air that whipped her plaid about her neck. Ailsa began to shiver and could not stop, not even when William pulled her close.

"I'm sorry you had to see this," he said. "But I chose the closest station. I wanted us to be on our way as quickly as possible." He saw from the look of horror in her eyes that she did not hear. Oblivious to the passersby or the rules he might be breaking, William slipped his arms around his wife and held her tightly, protectively. When her trembling stopped, he put his arm around her and led her to their modest first-class compartment on the train. He was glad he had insisted on a private coach. He had only just begun to recognize how difficult this trip would be for a girl who had lived all her life in the wild paradise of the glen.

William settled his wife in one of the two brocade armchairs, removed her plaid, and looked in concern at her pallid cheeks. For the first time since he'd known her, Ailsa's eyes had lost their glow. He had the porter bring her brandy and watched her drink it, cupping his hands around hers to steady the crystal glass as the train began to move jerkily out of the station. Soon they would be free of this place, out in the open countryside, and she would forget. In the meantime, he stayed beside her, until, a little at a time, she began to awaken from her stupor.

Ailsa blinked and touched her husband's face; she had to know that he was real. She had been aware of little in the past few minutes but the rhythm of his breath and the warmth of his hands on hers. Even had she been able to speak, she could not have told him how grateful she was for those things.

"Are you feeling better?" he asked hopefully.

She gazed at his familiar face with relief. "Aye," she said. She thought regretfully of her home, where people shared in poverty or abundance, where no one she knew had ever starved, where the air was clear and fresh and hope came with each new morning, no matter how dark the night. She had never seen such hopelessness and would not soon forget it, but as the train swayed along the tracks, the image became less painfully vivid.

For the first time, Ailsa looked around in curiosity at the room in which she sat. It was small but comfortably furnished with two beds, two armchairs, and a graceful Pembroke table. The floor was covered with a brightly patterned Brussels carpet and lamps with opaque white globes hung from the carved ceiling. She could feel the train vibrating and hear the clack of the wheels, but the sound was muffled by padded walls. When the factories had disappeared behind them, her husband drew her to the window.

"You see, it's not all like Glasgow, my dear. The countryside is really quite lovely, though in a peaceful kind of way—not at all like your glen."

Ailsa looked at the endless green fields and felt an urge to lean out and breathe the air, free of the soot that still clung to her face. She raised the thin glass an inch but the fumes billowed under the sill, along with sparks and smoke that rose from beneath the wheels. Ailsa closed the window quickly, coughing so hard that she collapsed in the chair.

"Have another brandy, or perhaps a glass of water. It will make you feel better," William suggested.

"Come sit beside me," she said shakily. "*That* will make me feel better."

William drew up a stool and gently covered the hand Ailsa rested on the arm of her chair. They sat in silence, watching the blurred images that passed beyond their window. The countryside was indeed lovely, dotted by cottages with tumbled stone fences and grazing sheep or cattle. But these things had no power to make Ailsa forget her distress as the jagged hills sliced with rushing silver water might have done. The world flew past so quickly that she looked away. "Is't safe to go so fast?"

"It's perfectly safe, I assure you," William said. He tried to coax a smile from her. "Yesterday you said you wanted to travel inside the wind. This wind is at least three times as fast as the Zephyr."

"Aye," she whispered, "the wind gone mad." But this was a madness she could not understand.

The rest of the journey went by in a blur. For three days they traveled, while Ailsa stared out the window and the hours crawled by. She gaped in disbelief at the trains that passed going the other way. The third-class passengers clung for dear life in low open wagons, some of which had wooden awnings that did little to protect the people from the rain. One man had fallen out and been crushed beneath the wheels. Ailsa had been ill for several hours afterward.

She never felt quite well now. Perhaps it was the constant motion of the train, or the slums of Newcastle, Leeds, and Manchester that they passed through. The cities all began to look the same—filthy, full of smoke and stench and dirty people with hopeless eyes. Was this the glittering world of wonder her father had described? Her own words came back to her like a taunting refrain within the endless clatter of the wheels: *Out there, beyond these hills, there's beauty and grace and elegance ye haven't even dreamed of.* What would Ian think if he saw her now, bent over a chamber pot, unable to hold down a meal or even a sip of water?

Ailsa huddled in her plaid and turned her head away when she felt William watching her. No doubt he was disgusted, as she was, by her weakness when the nausea rose again and again in her body. She had not been ill since she was very young, and even those bouts with childhood infection had not lasted long. She had had Mairi and her herbs and the clear air to restore her. Ailsa coughed, fighting back bile, ashamed that her husband should see her like this.

William watched her in concern. He wanted to hold her but sensed she would only pull away. "Isn't there something I can do for you?" he asked for what seemed to him the hundredth time.

" 'Tis nothin'," she told him as she always did. " 'Twill pass."

He swallowed dryly. She had become so pale in the past few days. His wife had eaten almost nothing since they boarded the train. He looked away to stare unseeing out the window. He had thought Ailsa so strong that she was above human frailty and illness. He realized now that she was very human, very frail. It hurt him to see her crouched in the corner, shivering, her face turned toward the wall. He would have given anything to make her better, to see her radiant smile and the light of daring in her eyes. She doubled up again and he clenched his hands into fists. For the first time he wondered if he had made a mistake in marrying her.

They reached the outskirts of London at dusk—that time which in the glen was soft and misted with possibilities, the breath of fairies, and the promise of falling night. But here, as Ailsa looked eagerly out the window, she saw that the light was gray and dim, concealing the wonders she knew to be beyond her grimy window. Now that they had arrived, she was certain things would be better. This was London, after all, the place where her father had been born, the center of all that was splendid, exotic, and entrancing. She felt a thrill of excitement that made her forget, for the moment, her tired and aching body.

William saw the flicker of life in his wife's eyes. With a sigh of profound relief, he stood beside her at the window with his arm around her waist. "We're nearly home now."

He could not hide his excitement. Ailsa turned to smile at him. "Aye," she said softly, "home."

The sound of that word on her lips made William ache.

He drew her closer as the train pulled into King's Cross Station.

When William helped Ailsa down, she stood on the platform for an instant, unused to the sudden lack of motion. Her legs wobbled briefly, but she took a deep breath and forced herself to remain standing. Then, while her husband called for a porter, she glanced at the high vaulted ceiling, the glass-roofed platforms farther down, and the confusion of tracks that wound through the station. It was huge and impressive, especially with the press of people hurrying on their way—women in bright, wide-skirted dresses with their pelisses flying, men holding their top hats with one hand while they motioned for a porter with the other. Everywhere there was talk and laughter and shouting and running feet. Ailsa smiled into the crowd, sensing their exhilaration and making it her own.

"I'm sorry to have left you for so long," William rasped as he came up beside her. "I was trying to get a hansom cab, but it seems we've come back at a difficult time of the evening. There's not an empty cab to be found at the moment. I've arranged for the porter to send our luggage round later, but I fear we'll have to take an omnibus," he finished apologetically.

Ailsa, who was feeling much better now that she was off the train and able to see the color and motion all around her, squeezed her husband's hand. "I don't mind, so long as ye're with me."

Pleased and flustered, William offered her his elbow. "There'll be a bus along in a minute that will take us down Fleet Street, then the Strand and straight to Westminster. You'll enjoy the ride, I think. There's a great deal to see."

"Och, as if I didn't know it. Tell me," she said, clinging to his arm, "will we pass the Crystal Palace?"

William hated to disappoint her. "Not today, I'm sorry to say. It's in Hyde Park, you see, and that's not precisely on our way."

"Well, then," she said philosophically, "we'll see it another day. It'll give me somethin' to look farward to."

Her husband smiled, grateful that her spirits had risen. "Here's the bus," he called.

All at once they were running with the others. William gripped his top hat while Ailsa's plaid whipped behind her like a vivid flag. She had time to notice the brightly colored advertisements on the outside of the vehicle before her husband pulled her on board and she found herself pressed between William and a woman who smelled strongly of fish. Ailsa realized with horror that there were several young men clinging precariously to the sides as the horse-drawn omnibus wound its way through the crowded streets. She was sure one of the men would lose his grip and go tumbling into the gutter at any moment, yet she envied them in a way.

The low-roofed, poorly ventilated bus was so crowded that she could not move. Whenever the vehicle jolted to a stop, the woman smelling of fish poked Ailsa in the ribs and the man across the way trampled her toes. She tried to crane her neck and look out the window, but the view was a chaos of cabs, trains, buses, horses, and even a few stray sheep that bleated plaintively as the shepherd tried to guide them across a bridge.

The bus rattled over the poorly paved streets, lost itself in the roar and movement of traffic. Above the odor of fish, Ailsa noticed the strong smell of horse dung that mingled with the mud that splattered from under hundreds of wheels.

She felt the bile rise in her throat again as the whoosh and clatter, babble and roar engulfed her—not like the wind, which even in its madness had been clean and clear and free, but like a rush of stifling heat that took her breath away. She covered her ears, but the sound penetrated just the same.

"Look to the right!" William called, hoping to distract his wife from the overpowering first impression of the City. "There's Covent Garden Market."

She did so, but could see little more than brightly colored canopies beneath which moved a mass of shouting, grasping men and women. Then there were tattered merchants who called out for passersby to stop and buy fruit or fabric or buttons from their rickety carts.

"There's the Palace of Whitehall," William shouted above the cacophony.

Ailsa looked to the left, had a brief impression of an elegant building with sweeping grounds, then a huge omnibus blocked her view and she leaned back against the hard seat—and the fish woman's sharp elbow—with a sigh. This was not the London she had imagined.

At last the bus turned down Victoria Street. Ailsa leaned forward as she caught a glimpse of narrow alleys strung with lines of clothes that were dusty gray, though they might have been clean once. There were children, seen dimly, playing in the closes, calling out across the damp cobbles. Hands and feet bare, they dipped water from the huge troughs in the center of the courts. She could smell the piles of garbage and the stench from stagnant gutters that rotted in the lane. She saw dark passages crowded with filth and houses so dilapidated she was certain they would crumble at a touch. The streets of neat brick houses in between with their tiny gardens and wrought-iron railings could not erase the memory of those narrow alleys.

Ailsa closed her eyes. She felt her husband watching her, brow furrowed, and reached blindly for his hand, but caught the callused fingers of the woman beside her instead. She could not suppress a shiver of revulsion. Then William touched her arm and whispered, "We're home."

She opened her eyes. "Truly?" she asked.

William winced at the disbelief, the despair, the hope that flickered in her eyes. "Truly." He took her hand and helped her through the crowd of people, not one of whom moved out of their way. Then she stepped down from the bus and was free of the smell, the dank air, the pressure of bodies. Ailsa took in huge gulps of air, which seemed fresher here somehow. She turned down Larkspur Crescent with her husband beside her, noticing with gratitude the trees that lined the walk and the small patches of grass behind lovely carved railings.

"Well," he asked when he paused in front of a large brick house, "what do you think?"

She looked up through the yellow glow of street lamps at three neat rows of windows, capped with stone cornices of leaves and flowers, at the wide front steps, clean, white, and welcoming. Here there was quiet and even, it seemed, a breath of clean air; the clatter and grime of the city had faded as they moved into this maze of squares and crescents.

Ailsa whispered a prayer of thanks. " 'Tis lovely," she said, and meant it.

"Saint James's Park is just behind us. You'll like that, too," William told her. "But now I think it's time to go inside where there'll be a fire and supper set out, I'm sure."

Ailsa thought it sounded heavenly. As her husband guided her up the steps, the front door opened, letting the light from inside pour out.

"Is that you, Mr. Sinclair?" a friendly voice asked. "We've been waitin' ever so impatiently for your return."

"Well, I'm back now, Lizzie," he replied. "You might watch for the luggage and tell Emma to make certain fires are laid in our rooms. You see, my wife is tired and eager to be home."

Lizzie curtsied prettily. "Yes sir, ma'am."

Ailsa nodded but was hardly aware of the young girl as she entered a narrow hall where light and blessed silence closed around her at last.

13

When William cleared his throat, Ailsa looked up to find a row of girls waiting at the end of the hall. Although they kept their eyes discreetly lowered, they somehow managed to stare curiously at the same time.

"The servants," William murmured at her look of surprise. He drew her forward. "This is my wife, Ailsa. You've already met Lizzie. She'll be your ladies' maid."

Ailsa managed a smile as the pretty girl with blond curly hair and blue eyes curtsied again.

"Here we have Martha, the kitchen girl, and Emma the parlormaid. Where, by the way," he said, "is Cook?"

Lizzie blushed. "She was sulkin' in the kitchen last time I looked," the girl replied. "She's had supper laid out for near an hour and you know how she gets."

"Shall I tell her you're wantin' her?" Martha, the dark-haired, dark-eyed kitchen girl asked shyly.

"Please," William said. "Let her know that we'll be eating at once. Just a light supper for tonight. We've had a long journey and my wife is rather badly in need of rest."

"Yes, sir." Martha curtsied and hurried off.

Ailsa listened in a daze, moving as if through a thin veil of smoke. She was so exhausted that she feared her legs would crumple beneath her, but somehow she continued to stand. She smiled half-heartedly when Lizzie removed her plaid. The other girls had already scattered.

"Come," William said, "the dining room is this way."

She followed him numbly into a room with lilac-and-pink-papered walls and a faded Turkish carpet on the floor. The narrow space was dominated by a mahogany table and chairs as well as an ornate buffet carved and crowded with figures that danced before Ailsa's tired eyes. She sat in the chair her husband pulled out for her and leaned her elbows on the heavy damask tablecloth, resting her chin in her hands. She stared blankly at the huge silver centerpiece filled with flowers and flanked by two intricate candelabras whose arms reached toward her with bony fingers that made wavering shadows on the cloth.

"I'm sorry, sir," Martha said nervously, appearing from a door at the far end of the room, "but Cook says there's nothin' edible but cold beef and bread puddin'."

William smiled at the girl. "That's all we require to-night, Martha. Thank you."

Sighing in relief, the servant slipped away. Before long, she returned with a platter in one hand and a large bowl in the other. Her hands shook as she placed the beef in front of her new mistress, but Ailsa did not notice.

"You may go now," William told the girl. "I'll have Cook clear up."

"Thank you, sir." Martha paused in the doorway for one last surreptitious glance at Mr. Sinclair's wife. She looked pale and lifeless with her chin cradled in her hands, not the kind of mistress to make enemies of the servants. Satisfied, Martha went on her way.

Hardly aware of what she was doing, Ailsa ate the beef and some of the pudding her husband served. She was surprised to find that the food made her feel better, but could not dispel the mist that clouded her thoughts. She did not realize she was eating off Wedgwood china, drinking from cut-crystal glasses with thick curved stems. She would not have cared if she had known.

"Have you had enough?" William asked at last.

"Aye. 'Tis only the comfort of my bed I'm wantin' now."

Just then the cook appeared, huffing and puffing as if she had had to climb five sets of stairs to answer her master's ring.

"Well, and it's about time you were comin' home. I'd lost all hope, so I had, with the soup cold, the turbot turned to jelly, the chickens burnt blacker than coal, and the spin-ach as thick as yesterday's butter."

Startled from her malaise, Ailsa raised her head to stare at the large, gray-haired woman who stood, arms akimbo, white cap quivering with the force of her indignation.

William ignored the woman's tirade and said softly, "The beef was quite good, actually, and the pudding excellent. So you see, no harm was done." Still, he was clearly uncomfortable under her piercing brown gaze. "Cook," he said at last, "this is my new wife and your new mistress, Ailsa Sinclair."

"Don't ye have another name?" Ailsa asked.

The woman turned to glare at her through narrowed eyes. " 'Cook' will do well enough for you, I'm sure."

Ailsa frowned at the hostility in her tone. "I only meant—"

"Never mind, my dear." William patted his wife's hand reassuringly. "It's late and we're all tired." He turned back to the servant. "We'll be retiring now. I've already told Martha she was free for the night. So if you could clear up—"

"Hummph," the woman interrupted grumpily.

She began to scoop up dishes with a tremendous clatter. William pulled back Ailsa's chair and she rose, grateful that he slipped her arm through his. She felt dizzy from the clink of silverware, the tinkle of glasses, and the too bright candlelight. Leaning against her husband, she started from the room. They were halfway to the door when a startled gasp made them turn.

Cook had dropped the dishes back onto the table. One hand was extended as far from her body as it would go; in it she held a pair of leather slippers. They were Callum Mackensie's wedding gift to Ailsa. She had not even realized she'd slipped them off her aching feet.

"Seems you've lost somethin'," Cook said, staring in open disapproval at Ailsa's bare toes. "I suppose in Scotland it's common to undress at table, but here in England—"

"That's quite enough," William began, but Ailsa stopped him.

"In Scotland," she said softly, " 'tis common to be polite to everyone and no' to draw attention to their mistakes. Besides," she added, "if the slippers were lost, ye wouldn't have found them so soon. But I thank ye for savin' me the trouble of comin' back down." She went to retrieve her shoes, then joined William, who was trying to suppress a smile of approval.

Without another word, they left the room. The silence that followed them was ominous. Ailsa did not care. Her husband squeezed her hand warmly as they stepped into the hall.

"Your first battle won," he murmured. He grinned at her and did not notice that Emma and Martha stood whispering in a nearby corner. They parted abruptly, blushing, when Ailsa saw them.

Wearily, she preceded William up the carpeted stairs. He paused at the first oak door on the left. "This is my room," he said, then pointed to the next two doors. "That one will be yours, and the dressing room beyond, of course."

Ailsa put her hand on his chest. "We'll no' be together?"

He stared at the floor, mumbled something incomprehensible, then said, "When we choose to be, we may be. But this is the way it's done in England. You have your rooms and I have mine."

"Oh." Her hands slipped from his waistcoat. She could not hide her disappointment.

"Get some rest," her husband said as he bent to kiss her cheek. "You'll find you'll get used to all this in time." Or would she? He turned quickly and disappeared into his room, hoping to escape the look of pain and confusion in his wife's eyes. With relief, he heard her door open and close, then the sound of voices in the room next door. Ailsa would feel better tomorrow, he told himself firmly.

His wife closed her bedroom door and leaned against it, so disoriented that for a moment she could not think what to do.

Lizzie, who had just finished folding back the covers on the bed, took pity on the pale girl whose face was covered with dust, her eyes clouded with distress and fatigue.

"Come in and get warm, ma'am. There's a nice roarin' fire that Emma laid for you and your bed's all ready."

Ailsa stared at the girl. "I don't remember—"

"I'm Lizzie, your ladies' maid." The girl put her arm around her mistress's shoulders and drew her toward the fire. "Don't you worry about a thing, ma'am. I'll see to it all."

Ailsa nodded, though she wasn't sure why.

"I thought you might like to wash up before bed. Here's your nightdress and your cap."

Ailsa stared at the linen gown with long sleeves, a high neck, and so many ruffles that they fluttered and flapped with each breath she took. The cambric cap, the purpose of which she could not even guess, was embroidered with flowers, birds, and clinging green leaves. The edge was ruffled with fine French lace. She held it by the satin ribbons and shook her head.

"I think you should wear it," Lizzie suggested, noting Ailsa's distaste. "Mr. Sinclair's aunt had them made for you especially. She'd be hurt if you tossed them away."

Ailsa could not imagine how the woman would know, but she no longer cared. She had to get into bed before she collapsed where she stood. "Aye," was all she could manage.

"There's a washstand in the dressing room with fresh water, soap, and towels," Lizzie told her cheerfully. "You'll feel much better once you've gotten rid of a little of that London grime."

No doubt the maid was right. Ailsa put the nightdress over her arm and went through the half-open door to find the washstand with its pitcher and bowl.

Lizzie watched her go, shaking her head. The woman— she was more of a girl, really—had obviously been poor until her marriage. Her rose-colored gown was very plain with no ruffles or lace or embroidery, no crinoline to make the skirt stand out, and if the maid wasn't mistaken, no corset underneath. Lizzie hadn't seen a grown woman with her hair in a single long braid like Ailsa's since she was a girl. But they could fix all that. There was a new wardrobe waiting in the armoire and the drawers were full to bursting with accessories and underthings. William's Aunt Abigail had seen to it all.

When Ailsa returned, her face clean, wearing the frilled white gown, she looked much better. "Here, sit you down by the fire while I brush out your hair," Lizzie suggested.

"But I can do that!" Ailsa protested.

"Not anymore. That's part of my job now."

In spite of her objections, Ailsa found she enjoyed sitting with the warmth of the fire on her still-tingling face and the soothing strokes of the brush through her hair. Her eyes began to droop, though she fought to keep them open. She did not want to be asleep if her husband came to her tonight.

"You've lovely hair, ma'am, really. So thick and splendid, and such a color!" Lizzie sighed and pushed her own thin blond curls away from her face. Then she set the cap on her mistress's head and tied the satin ribbons under her chin. "You're lucky, you know. And now it's to bed for you." The maid waved the silver-backed brush toward the huge feather bed with its heavy carved posts and curtains hung with bright green tassels at the corners.

Gratefully, Ailsa crawled between the sheets and drew the thick blue satin coverlet up to her neck.

"I'll see you in the morning then, shall I?" Lizzie said. "If you need me durin' the night, just use the bell pull." She pointed to an intricately embroidered strip of brocade with a heavy tassel on the end. "I'll come runnin' if you ring."

Ailsa smiled and nodded. "Thank you," she said as the maid curtsied and started for the door.

Lizzie paused in surprise. "Why you're welcome, ma'am."

When she was gone, Ailsa leaned back against the pillows, counting the days since she had stood among the heather-strewn hills of Glen Affric. It seemed like a lifetime ago. She welcomed the stillness of her room, where she could be alone with the ache of loss that had become, in the past five days, a part of the rush and flow of her blood. She had thought that it would ease as the world and all its wonders unfolded before her, but instead it had grown with each passing minute.

The ribbons of her nightcap were tied too tightly beneath her chin. She untied them, held them loose in her fingers for a moment, then tossed the cap onto the table beside the bed. She had never liked anything more binding than the curve of her plaid around her head and preferred nothing at all. She felt better now that the frilly cap was hidden behind the paraffin lamp.

She turned down the lamp until there was only a circle of light that did not touch the cluttered room beyond. She closed her eyes, feeling the warmth of the tiny pool of yellow radiance, and tried to pretend that she need only glance out the window to see hills and moors and to hear the murmur of water. Then she raised her head. She sensed that someone stood on the other side of the door, hesitating.

She waited, breath held in anticipation, but the stillness remained unbroken for so long that she began to despair. Yet she knew William was there as surely as if she could feel the pressure of his hand on the doorknob. She willed him to turn that knob, to come and hold her, to give her a little of his warmth and dissipate the chill inside her. Finally, in desperation, she called out, "William?"

He paused for a moment more, then pushed the door open and entered his wife's room. William found that he could not move. The pool of light illuminated her face with a soft glow that touched her hair, loose and flowing around her shoulders, with glints of red. She did not look away when he finally came closer, but smiled in welcome. Her eyes were so luminous that he feared he could never escape their power.

Ailsa was surprised to see that her husband wore a nightcap of his own with a bright red tassel that fell behind his ear. He also wore a dressing gown of burgundy velvet with a linen nightshirt beneath and slippers on his feet. He approached her without a word, then reached out to turn down the lamp. William sighed as the light faded, with relief rather than sadness. Ailsa wondered why. She heard him making his way to the far side of the bed, discarding his slippers and robe, moving about uncertainly in the darkness. He fumbled with the bedclothes, then paused and stood perfectly still.

"Come to bed, William," Ailsa said softly. " 'Tis warmer here. And besides, I've missed ye." She hoped he did not notice the quiver in her voice or realize what it meant.

Finally he slipped between the sheets, sat for a moment, then reached for his wife without warning. He kissed her quickly, barely brushing his lips over hers.

She craved his reassuring warmth, the weight of his hands and his body on hers, so she drew him closer, pressed her lips more urgently to his.

William froze and retreated. She could feel his embarrassment but did not understand it. For a long time, he was poised above her, undecided. Instinctively, Ailsa lay back among the pillows to wait. Her husband reached out slowly, touched her hair, her cheek, then ran his hand over her shoulder through the French lace gown. He trailed his fingers down her arm and finally, awkwardly, brushed her breast through the fabric.

Ailsa felt a comforting warmth move slowly through her veins. She wanted more, but realized that William must make his own pace. He stretched out beside her, drew his breath in sharply when he felt her nipple rise into his palm.

He kissed his wife again, more fiercely as the heat rose within him like wildfire. He could wait no longer to hold her, to feel every part of her, to assuage the yearning that had begun the first moment she touched him. He tried to raise her long, ruffled dressing gown, but when he moved, his legs became confused in the folds of his nightshirt and he caught his fingers in a bit of lace on hers. Husband and wife lay immobile, tangled together, breathing heavily.

"Wouldn't it be more comfortable," Ailsa suggested, "without these gowns?"

William stopped, one hand in midair, the other caught in the lace of her gown. He cleared his throat. "I suppose it would, but don't you see, it's not right. One doesn't—"

She stopped him with a finger on his lips. "William," she whispered. She moved her hand to cup his cheek and felt the heat there. She had embarrassed him again. She drew back in dismay. She could not seem to please him and did not understand why.

William looked down at his wife. He wanted desperately to draw her to him, to breathe her into his blood so she would be with him always. He wanted to feel her beneath him, naked and trembling with passion. But he didn't dare move too fast. She had led a sheltered life; he could not bear to push himself upon her only to see her shudder with revulsion as he had heard many women did on their wedding night. His aunt had talked little of sex, but enough to convince him that for men, making love was a pleasure. For women it was at best a responsibility and at worst a horror. He did not want to hurt Ailsa, ever, or make her fear him. Nor did he want her to know how much he feared her—the nearness of her woman's body, her parted lips, the rise and fall of her breasts with each breath she took.

"Never mind," he said. Slowly, with infinite tenderness, he raised her gown above her thighs, kissing her lips, her cheek. At last he held his breath and entered her.

He had not prepared her body for his entry and she stiffened at the pain, but he did not seem to notice. Not while the blood pounded in his ears and his heart beat wildly with his need. Jaws clenched to hold back the full force of his passion, he moved against her, cradling her like a fragile porcelain doll.

He felt the release build within him, making him tremble. He grasped her hair in both hands as if to anchor himself to the earth and shuddered at the waves of pleasure that moved through him. He cried out once, "Ailsa!" then, ashamed that he had lost control, he rolled away from her, gasping.

Ailsa felt chilled in spite of William's heat. He had not listened to her body, had not lit fires within her, but only held her like a child. She wanted to draw him back to her, to kiss him wildly, run her hand along his thigh until he responded, caressed her, made her one with him. But just as she reached out to pull him back to her, he slipped from the bed. Frozen with shock, she heard him put on his robe and slippers. Then he left her, simply faded into the darkness. As he reached the door he whispered, "Forgive me."

Ailsa stared after him, uncomprehending. When the door closed with a click, she felt cold, abandoned, bereft, and more alone than ever in her life before.

14

When Ailsa awoke, pale, watery sunlight filtered through the window. The satin drapes had been parted to reveal frilled muslin curtains beneath, which allowed the light to penetrate weakly. Ailsa gazed around her in astonishment. She must have been very tired last night. She had not even noticed the pastels that filled the room from floor to ceiling—the patterned wallpaper of large yellow and pink flowers twined with heavy vines and brilliant green leaves, the green and pale blue sofa by the window, covered with huge stuffed and embroidered pillows, the chairs and ottomans scattered over a carpet so bright and flowery it made her dizzy.

Ailsa shook her head, but nothing changed—not the ornate mantel crowded with vases and figurines or the painted fire screen or the dresser with intricate brass handles. The drawers curved outward strangely, as if the dresser had been so long overloaded that the wood had altered its shape. A huge armoire dominated one wall; nearby was a dressing table with a frilled lace and satin duster that fell from the marble top to the floor. The top was barely visible beneath a collection of bottles, jewelry cases, hairbrushes, combs and other things she could not identify. The walls were covered with gilt mirrors and paintings in large, dark frames. She shook her head again.

"It's real, all right, ma'am," Lizzie said, appearing soundlessly from the dressing room.

Ailsa stared, surprised that the girl had read her thoughts so easily.

"I don't suppose it's like this where you come from," the maid continued.

"No, 'tis nothin' like this." Ailsa glanced around again,

192

still unable to take it in. She felt trapped in a prison of chair legs and arms and gleaming, cluttered surfaces.

"I've left fresh water on the washstand," Lizzie said. "Your luggage arrived late last night and I packed it away this mornin'. I'll have your things for today laid out when you're done washin' up."

Reluctantly, Ailsa crawled out of bed and started for the dressing room. When she returned from using the flowered porcelain pitcher and the water closet hidden in the far corner of the hall, Ailsa watched the maid scurry about the room, the purple ribbon on her white cap flapping as she bent and rose, turned from dresser to armoire to bureau and back again. The girl looked quite pretty in her print lilac dress, white cotton stockings and black shoes. Somehow she was not at all what Ailsa had imagined a servant to be, but then nothing in London was as she had expected.

Lizzie blushed when she saw her mistress watching her and explained breathlessly, "Mr. Sinclair sent the news down that he had a wife and his aunt Abigail was to see to a wardrobe. You've some gowns and hats and underthings and shoes—"

"Wait!" Ailsa cried. "I really don't need ye to take out my clothes. I've always done it for myself."

Lizzie looked up, startled. "But this is London, ma'am. Things are different here. Heaven knows what they'd say if they thought you did your own toilet in the mornin'."

Ailsa frowned. She had just noticed the quantity of articles the maid had produced from within the numerous drawers and cupboards. She picked up what looked like a chemise with the waist squeezed in and bones slid through the seams. "What is't?" she cried, dropping it as if it might snap at her.

"A corset, ma'am. Every lady wears one to give her a slender waist."

Ailsa looked down at her own narrow waist and shook her head. "I don't think—"

"Oh, but ma'am, you must!" Lizzie exclaimed. "They'll know if you don't and we'll never hear the end of it."

Ailsa sighed, then glanced at the ankle-length linen

drawers, the cambric shift, and finally, the stiff circle of boned red flannel that lay at her feet. "And that?" she said.

"Your crinoline, ma'am. Every lady—"

"Wears one," Ailsa interrupted. "They'd rise groanin' from their graves to haunt me if I didn't." She sank onto the bed, wondering in despair who "they" were. She had already begun to dislike them intensely.

Lizzie giggled and considered her mistress with interest. "I didn't think you'd be so young."

Ailsa raised her head. "I'm seventeen. I might have been married long since in the glen."

The maid frowned. "Just seventeen!" She gasped and covered her mouth with her hand, but could not hide the flush that stained her cheeks. "Forgive me, ma'am. I shouldn't be talkin' that way, indeed I shouldn't."

Ailsa rose, hands on hips. "Why shouldn't ye if 'tis what ye think? Why are all ye Sassenachs worried day and night about what ye shouldn't do and say?"

"Things must be done properly, accordin' to the rules."

"Whose rules?" Ailsa persisted. "If ye act accordin' to what your heart tells ye, 'twould be just as proper as someone else's rule."

Biting her lip, Lizzie considered this for a moment. "But what if my heart doesn't agree with the Queen's?"

Ailsa sighed in defeat. "Don't ye *ever* listen to your own conscience instead of what 'they' tell ye to do?"

Lizzie glanced around, afraid someone would overhear. "Well, honestly, sometimes I do, but only when no one's lookin'."

"Well, birdeen, no one's lookin' now."

Smiling to herself, the maid went to remove a gown from the dark recesses of the armoire. "Your morning gown," she said, displaying the striped green and yellow dress with its high neck, lace undersleeves, and huge belled skirt.

Ailsa saw a hint of dark blue protruding from the cabinet and pulled the door open further.

"Don't worry, I'll see that that one's given to the secondhand man," Lizzie said as she drew out button boots and wool stockings. "I suppose the styles in Scotland are different."

With a sigh, Ailsa drew out the gown of blue wool and purple silk that she'd worn on her wedding day. Rubbing the fabric over her cheek, she felt the ache inside turn to a throb. This gown, which she had treasured more than any she'd ever owned, was not good enough for London. Tears stung her eyes, but she fought them back. *'Tis wrong for ye, that world of glitter that ye seek,* Ian had told her. *'Tis wrong and ye know it.*

Ailsa straightened abruptly. She was not ready to admit defeat so soon. She had barely arrived. Burying her face in the gown one last time, she inhaled, hoping to catch a lingering scent of Highland air, but the grime of the journey had tainted this fabric, too.

Lizzie stopped, a hairbrush in her hand, to stare at her mistress, who clutched the dress as if it were a talisman. She felt a rush of sympathy for the young girl who looked so lost just now. "Forgive me," the maid said softly. "I didn't know what that gown meant to you. I'll store it carefully in camphor so the moths don't get at it."

Ailsa closed her eyes and let the fabric fall from her fingers. The maid's simple kindness made tears rise to her eyes again. "Thank ye," she said. "Ye're very kind." Then she straightened her shoulders and added, "I'd best hurry if I'm to get all these clothes on before noon."

William, dressed in a dark morning coat and pants, gray waistcoat, and top hat, was waiting for his wife at the foot of the stairs. His mouth fell open when he saw her gown with its high neckline trimmed in satin. Her hair was parted neatly in the middle, looped at the back of her neck, and confined in a silver net. When she walked in the unfamiliar crinoline, her wide skirt swayed forward, revealing the button-top boots underneath. He smiled a little stiffly. This woman was lovely, but she was not Ailsa.

"Well?" She paused with her hand on the carved balustrade. "Do ye think I'll ever make a lady?"

"I sincerely hope not," he said without thinking.

Ailsa grinned and skipped down the last few steps to meet him. She took his arm and whispered in his ear, "If it means sufferin' day and night with cloth full of wires and bones and a skirt so big that it might be carried off by the wind at any moment, I'm no' certain I want to be a lady. But don't tell Lizzie. No doubt she'd fear that the gods would turn me to stone and then she'd never be able to dress me properly.''

William sighed with relief. This was Ailsa after all. He kissed her chastely on the cheek and murmured, ''I hope you feel more rested today.''

''Aye. I slept like a bairn after—'' She broke off when he swallowed nervously. ''Aye,'' she repeated. ''I'm better.''

''Good. Then before I go off to my chambers, I'd like to show you the rest of the house. And you should have a talk with Cook today. Get to know her, discuss the menus. Lizzie will know.'' He took his wife's hand and led her to the end of the hall.

''This is the sitting room,'' he told her, pushing a door open to reveal green papered walls, forest-green drapes with pale green tassels, back-to-back yellow-green settees, and a jumble of tables, shelves, cabinets, china, and glass. The heavy darkness from within seemed to billow into the hall. Ailsa stepped back.

William closed the door sharply and continued down the hall. ''The study.''

His wife glanced inside and felt the same instinctive withdrawal from the heavy mahogany furniture, tan walls, dark wainscoting, and brown drapes. Husband and wife moved from the sewing room to the dining room to the drawing room. With each step, Ailsa felt more uneasy while William's expression grew strained and distant. It was as if, under the influence of the shadows in this house, he had forgotten what it was to run with her through a storm, enjoying the rumble of thunder and the silver-blue fury of the loch.

Ailsa gaped, dazed by the proliferation of objects of all kinds—spindle-legged tables, vases, porcelains, mirrors, lamps, sculptures, woodwork carved, molded, and painted, wallpaper so covered with flowers and stripes that it hurt her eyes.

When they stopped in the front hall, William noticed her glazed expression. ''You don't like it,'' he said.

Ailsa looked up at him and tried to find an answer that was not a lie. " 'Tis only that there is so much of everythin'. Mayhap a little *too* much for me just now."

"My aunt had it decorated for me. At the time I didn't care much and I suppose I've grown used to it since. But if you don't like it, change it."

His wife tried to read the emotion in his eyes but failed. "Ye can't simply walk into another person's home and make it to your likin'," she objected.

William grasped her by the shoulders. "I took you from *your* home. Now I want you to make this one yours. Do with it what you like." He spoke with a passion that confused her.

"Mayhap in time," she murmured.

"Good," he said. "We'll talk about it later. But just now I must be going. Lizzie will make sure you're settled in. I'll see you at dinner." He looked down at her face, at the invitation of her slightly parted lips, the curious light in her eyes which made him want more than anything to draw her close. But he knew the servants were watching. Besides, the crinoline beneath her huge belled skirt made a barrier between them for which, at the moment, he was grateful. He ran his fingertip over a curl that had escaped Lizzie's careful ministrations, then turned and left his wife to stare after him, her lips unkissed and her heart heavy.

The day passed with agonizing slowness. Ailsa moved awkwardly in the rigid corset that pressed painfully into her tender skin. The boots had been an agony from the moment Lizzie slid them on; Ailsa's feet were used to the feel of damp grass and curling bracken, not the pinched confinement of new stiff leather. And she could not accustom herself to the swaying of her skirt, which rose up more than once like a wave intent on knocking her backward into the swirling sea.

"Don't worry yourself about it. You'll learn in time," Lizzie clucked.

Ailsa found herself envying the girl. As a servant she wore no crinoline or corset and her shoes were simple black pattens.

In the morning, Ailsa had gone to speak to Cook, whose name, she had discovered from Lizzie, was Mrs. O'Neil. The visit had not gone well. When Ailsa saw the menus the woman had planned, the endless list of meats and fowl, fish and soups, vegetables and desserts and breads, she had suggested that perhaps they did not need so much food for only William and herself. Cook had puffed up her chest until her face turned vivid red. "If you want to be embarrassin' Mr. Sinclair with your thriftiness and have everyone on the street snickerin' at us behind their hands, I'm tellin' you right now, I'll be havin' no part of it. This is how it's done in London—the right way, mind you—and until the master tells me different, this is how it *will* be done."

Ailsa had retreated in defeat. It was her first day here and she hadn't yet begun to keep straight all the articles of clothing she was supposed to wear. How could she know what to serve at meals? She had no right to criticize what she did not understand. From that moment on, as she moved through the house that was now her home, she'd begun to feel like an unwanted stranger in a land beyond her comprehension. Each room was more oppressive than the last.

Ailsa sat briefly at the piano in the drawing room but did not play. Her body ached too much from the train journey and the horribly restraining clothes. She felt that she could not breathe, and did not want to, from the glimpse she'd had of the air outside. Her feet throbbed at the unaccustomed pinching of her boots, and though her soles were impervious to the rough mountainsides and forests, in half a day these boots had given her blisters everywhere. She wanted William—to touch him, talk to him, see the smile in his eyes when he looked at her. But he was gone, lost somewhere in the noisy streets.

She rested her head on her folded arms, but the sound of Lizzie's admonishing voice brought her up sharply.

"Mrs. Fieldin' will be here soon, ma'am. You'll have to get ready right away."

"But I'm ready now," Ailsa said.

"Indeed you're not. You can't wear your mornin' gown for tea, nor your tea gown for dinner."

At Ailsa's look of bewildered dismay, the maid added,

"Don't worry. There's no need to remember which is which. I'll lay out your clothes for you. But come. You must change at once."

Soon, dressed in a pink satin gown with lace spilling from the sleeves and around the low bodice, Ailsa stood before the cheval glass in her room. She had never seen her reflection so clearly; a face in a pail of water was always distorted by the motion of the surface. The gown looked comely enough, but there were circles under her eyes and her cheeks were pale. She was not at all certain she liked the unfamiliar sight of her hair fastened at the back of her neck. It was not Ailsa she saw, but a pale, unhappy stranger.

Ye'll no' be likin' the world ye find out there. 'Twill make a different person of ye. The sound of Mairi's voice was so clear that Ailsa turned, expecting to find her mother standing behind her. But there was only the movement of the curtains in a desultory breeze. *'Twill make ye a stranger to this place, to your home, to the people ye love.* "No!" Ailsa said aloud, but she knew she was lying to herself.

"Ma'am?" Lizzie asked curiously. "Are you all right?"

Ailsa thought of her throbbing feet, hot, tired, and bruised beyond endurance. "No," she said abruptly. While the maid stood open-mouthed, she sat on the bed, dragged her unwieldy crinoline out of the way, and removed the offensive boots and stockings.

"But ma'am, you can't do that. They wouldn't approve."

Ailsa crossed her arms in determination. "If 'they' go about lookin' under ladies' skirts, then 'they' deserve a shock, don't ye think? Besides, who will ever know?"

Lizzie looked at her mistress with frank admiration. "I know a great many women who've always wanted to do that but never had the courage. God bless you, that's what I say." She leaned closer to whisper, "And if 'they' rise from their graves in horror, we'll just lock them in the kitchen with Cook."

Her mistress laughed. "Aye, so we will."

"But for now, it's time to greet your guests."

With a deep, steadying breath, Ailsa started down the stairs.

199

Three women waited in the drawing room, standing stiffly, their lace-gloved hands clasped before them. They wore flowered and frilled bonnets over parted hair pulled close to their heads and caught neatly at the backs of their necks.

"Good afternoon, ladies," Ailsa said, entering the room in a rustle of satin. All three turned to eye her up and down, their mouths pressed primly closed, their expressions cloaked as thoroughly as if they wore veils over their faces.

Ailsa's courage wavered. "I'm Ailsa Rose—that is, Sinclair." She turned to the eldest of the three, a gaunt woman in a black gown with gray hair and cold blue eyes. "And ye must be William's aunt Abigail. He's told me—"

"I am Mrs. Fielding," the woman interrupted in a clipped, precise voice. "And these are my dear friends, Mrs. Grantley and Mrs. Wells. They were kind enough to do you the honor of paying a call on your first day here." She gestured vaguely at the two women in pale blue and yellow gowns. "We were all quite shocked to receive the news of my nephew's marriage. When I sent him off to Scotland to rest, it never occurred to me that he might come back with a wife."

She sniffed. "Unless of course, it were Sarah Worthy. They've been acquainted for simply ages, and he always seemed to like her company. Naturally, we all assumed . . ." Mrs. Fielding trailed off and busied herself straightening her gloves on her bony wrists. "William was always such a sensible young man. He's never been one to act without thinking. Imagine his marrying someone so—well, so rural." She sighed heavily. "But then, I suppose what is done cannot be undone. I hope you enjoyed the nightdress I had made for you. French lace, you know. You haven't mentioned it."

Ailsa stared in astonishment at the woman's thinly disguised barbs. She fought back an angry response. She would not let Abigail Fielding make her behave rashly at their first meeting. Instead she said softly, "Of course I meant to thank ye for the gown, but I didn't want to speak without thinkin' and mayhap say the wrong thing. 'Tis why it took me so long to get to it." She caught the gleam of amusement in Lizzie's eyes and suppressed a smile of her own. " 'Tis a lovely gift—a perfect gown for an English lady."

Lizzie began to cough in order to hide her laughter. She knew quite well what her mistress thought of the clothes English ladies wore. "I'll go get Emma to bring the tea," the maid said when she could speak again. "Excuse me, ma'am." She hurried from the room, her hand over her mouth.

Mrs. Fielding, who had started in dismay at the sound of Ailsa's accent, paused, brow furrowed as the young woman continued. Her nephew's wife had been perfectly polite, yet Abigail had the distinct feeling that she had been made to look bad, though she was not certain how.

"They said she was Scottish, but my dear, that voice," Mrs. Grantley whispered to Mrs. Wells.

Ailsa ignored them. "Would ye like to sit down for a bit? Surely ye're gey tired of standin' about?"

"Certainly we wish to sit. It's what one does at teatime." Mrs. Fielding offered coolly. She had taken control once again.

The guests chose their seats on the red velvet settee, the overstuffed brocade chair, and an uncomfortable-looking spindle-legged chair flanked by a Pembroke table and a false marble plant stand. All three women removed their gloves and laid them neatly folded in their laps.

As the visitors finished arranging their skirts about them, Emma entered with a silver tea service in her hands. She laid the tray on the low rosewood table. Ailsa gazed in dismay at the thin china cups, ornate sugar bowl and creamer, spoons and forks and tiny lace napkins, as well as the diverse array of cakes and pastries. "Surely we don't need so much?" she said. "I saw some bairns on the way here last night who looked very hungry. Mayhap they would like some of these. Even if there were eight of us, we couldn't possibly eat all this ourselves."

Plain little Emma with the pale brown hair and eyes, stood, mouth agape, while the three ladies gasped in unison. "It's what we always serve, ma'am." The girl wrung her hands, uncertain what to do.

Color suffused Mrs. Fielding's face, then faded, leaving her skin sallow. "Well!" she huffed. Then she turned to Emma. "Never mind, dear. Obviously Mrs. Sinclair is not familiar with our way of doing things yet. She's from the hills of Scotland, you know. I hear they're really quite uncivilized."

"Ma'am?" The girl turned pleadingly toward her mistress who nodded stiffly. Emma curtsied and fled while Mrs. Grantley and Mrs. Wells grinned. Ailsa realized with a shock that they were enjoying her discomfort. Flustered by their rudeness, and even more by their unkindness, she reached for the teapot.

"I shall do that," Mrs. Fielding informed her piously. "I've had so much more practice, you know."

She poured the tea and passed the cakes while Ailsa watched helplessly. She was used to outbursts of anger and disappointment, to shouting and weeping and open accusations, but she had no defense against this kind of polite hostility.

When William's aunt held her delicate Wedgwood cup in her hand, she took a small sip and turned back to Ailsa. "My nephew tells me you enjoy music. Perhaps you'd play for us?"

Her tone was pleasant enough, but her eyes were cold and hard. Nevertheless, Ailsa agreed. Behind the piano was the one place where she would feel at home just now. She moved to the instrument, pushed the heavy curtains back from the window to give herself a little light, then sat on the bench. Lifting the lid, she placed her fingers on the familiar keys, tenderly, greeting an old friend.

Neither she nor the other women heard the front door close or saw William pause in the doorway, the *Times* under his arm. He had been restless all day, thinking of Ailsa—her chestnut hair, her clear honest gaze, her laughter, and the touch of her hand on his arm. He had left his chambers early and hurried home to assure himself she was still here. He was glad to see she was going to play. He had missed her music more than he realized.

Before his wife could strike a note, Abigail Fielding interrupted. "What about your sheet music? Surely you must have some?"

"Och, no!" Ailsa said. "What I play comes from inside my head, from my heart, no' from pages someone else has written."

The other woman was nonplussed. "Well, you *do* have a favorite composer, don't you? Handel, for instance, is very well thought of in London circles. Or Haydn?"

"Sometimes I play the works of others, sometimes my own. And sometimes I mix the two. I hear a piece, remember it, and when I feel that song again, I play it. But I don't bother to learn the name. To me 'tis the magic of the notes that matters."

William smiled to himself.

"I don't understand a bit of it, I'm sure," Mrs. Wells said.

"Ye don't have to understand. Just listen and let the music speak to ye." Ailsa ran her fingers over the keys, eyes closed as she leaned forward, a distant smile on her face. The notes rose from beneath her hands like flocks of graceful birds that dipped and hovered in the air. She played by instinct as images came to her of the wild hills and mountains she loved, of fierce slashing waterfalls, the wind and thunderous storms that shook the earth. She saw those things and played them into music, even though the playing hurt. The memories, the pain of loss, grew more vivid as the resounding notes echoed through the room. She forgot the women sitting primly in their chairs as she played out her loneliness, her love of the glen, and the savage pain of loss that moved through her in endless waves.

William listened, entranced, as his wife wove her spell ever more tightly around him. Yet beneath the pleasure was a vague unease at the violence with which she played and the anguish in her eyes.

When she finished, Ailsa spread her fingers on the silent keys and tried to free herself from the achingly beautiful spell of the song. Her head was lowered, so she did not see Abigail's flushed face and uneven breathing or the way she pressed her hands to her breast to stop her heart from pounding.

Mrs. Fielding opened her mouth several times but seemed to have trouble finding her voice. Finally she rasped,

"Quite, quite shocking. Have you never learned restraint? But no, in Scotland I don't suppose one does. Why the music was so wild it was positively immoral! Sounds like that have no place in a London drawing room, I'm sure!" Her heart would not stop beating, nor could she close out the memory of the haunting music, which made her all the more furious.

Ailsa felt as if she had been struck across the face. People had responded in many ways to her playing: some had swayed with the rhythm or listened, mesmerized, others had sung along or wept or danced or closed their eyes and slipped into another world, and a very few had seemed not to notice. But never had anyone stared at her, eyes brimming with horror, and called her music immoral. She struggled to catch her breath, but could not.

William stood on the threshold, too appalled to move, with Mairi's warning ringing in his head. *What if your friends cause Ailsa pain because they fear the woman she is?* He gripped the doorframe in stiff fingers. He knew he should say something, defend his wife, but he could not seem to make himself move.

Mrs. Fielding felt uneasy under the penetrating scrutiny of Ailsa's blue-violet eyes. Abigail looked down to hide her discomfort, then gasped, pointing at the floor while the stain of color faded from her cheeks, leaving them sickly gray. "Just look at that!"

Her friends leaned forward to get a better view. Ailsa's crinoline had risen as she turned, revealing her feet, bare of shoes or stockings. "Well, I never!" Mrs. Grantley exclaimed.

"And I hope to the Good Lord above," Mrs. Fielding said grimly, "that you never do again."

William could just see the pale blur of Ailsa's bare feet against the purple and scarlet Brussels carpet. Then he heard the women snickering. *Will your friends no' think my daughter strange? Won't they laugh at her?* Mairi had asked. *Who could laugh at Ailsa?* he had replied with confidence. Unwillingly, he raised his gaze to Ailsa's face. There were dark circles under her eyes, her cheeks were pale, and her hands trembled. She looked as ill as she had on the train and as out of place.

"I've heard you Scots were little more than savages, but this is simply too much." Mrs. Wells began to gather her gloves; she could not bear to remain in the room a moment longer.

William looked away from his wife. She was a little wax doll, turned out by the maid to appear just like her neighbors, but the corsets and petticoats, lace and satin could not hide her blazing soul or the hurt that shone now in her eyes. A pain sliced through his heart that made him gasp. He had thought Ailsa a spirit with the power to draw him into her world of mist and wind and shadowed mountains. He had thought that her voice, her smile, the sound of her music in the air around him would destroy all that was grim and unpleasant in his life. Selfishly, because he needed her so much, he had taken her from paradise and brought her here. And by that simple act, he had made her a prisoner, too.

Ailsa sat frozen at the sound of the women's laughter. She was surprised by how much it hurt—more even, than it had hurt to leave the glen. She thought, suddenly, of Charles Kittridge, of the image of his young and handsome face that she had come to know so well from the miniature he had left behind. Her father, who had cried out to her in need and brought her here. For this?

Then she glanced up to see her husband watching from the doorway. The look on his face, the regret, the horror, made her pain more intense. She had let him down again. She had embarrassed him so often since their arrival that she had lost count of her transgressions. Her throat was suddenly dry, her breathing labored. She could not let these women know what she felt. That much at least, she could do for her husband.

She rose slowly to her feet, took a deep breath. "Ye haven't touched your tea, Mrs. Fieldin'. Is't cold? Shall I send for some more?"

William saw the effort it took for his wife to speak calmly. When she held out the tray of cakes and pastries to her guests as if nothing had happened, he thought his heart would break. There was a smile on her lips, but the grief that cast a shadow on her strange Highland eyes was so deep that he knew he could never heal it.

— ◇ 15 ◇ —

As Ailsa descended the stairs one evening a week later, the gloom of the hallway closed around her. William had been gone since early morning. He had explained that he would plead before the High Court of Parliament today and so must leave the house at dawn, but she had sensed that he was glad to get away. She sighed and closed her fingers around the newel post, carved in the shape of a lion's head. Neither she nor her husband had spoken of the incident in the drawing room that first afternoon, but the knowledge was always between them like a wisp of smoke that tainted the air with an unpleasant smell.

Ailsa had waited hopefully but William had not come to her that night. Though she had wanted to weep into her feather pillows, her eyes had remained painfully dry. The following night he had crept into her room, furtively, as if he did not wish to be discovered there. He had slipped away as soon as his desire was satisfied, leaving her shivering and alone.

The ache of loss was with her always, every minute of every endless day. She spent much of her time reading in William's extensive library, but it was not enough. "How does a lady keep from goin' mad?" she asked Lizzie in desperation.

"Why, she keeps busy writin' letters or doin' fancy-work or makin' calls—" The maid had broken off in confusion. She knew what had happened with Mr. Sinclair's aunt, knew too that her new mistress could not make calls to houses where the women would have been warned against her.

Ailsa went slowly through the hall to the drawing room,

then stopped on the threshold in astonishment. A large beautiful harp had been placed next to the piano. She blinked at the fine instrument as if it were an apparition.

Finally she made herself move forward, stretched out a hand, and touched the pillar. A faint memory stirred within her. She had seen this harp before. She ran her fingers down the pillar and felt the nick Richard Williston had made when, frustrated by his failure to play a tune on the piano properly, he had thrown a vase at the harp in fury.

Ailsa swallowed dryly. How had it come to be in William's drawing room? Then she saw the envelope attached to the curved neck. With sudden resolution, she took it and withdrew the note.

To Mr. and Mrs. Sinclair,

We wish you joy in your marriage. May you, Ailsa, give your husband as much pleasure with your music in the future as you have given us in the past. He chose this gift above the others we offered because he knew, as we know, that it truly belongs in your care, and has since the first moment you made it sing.

Yours most sincerely,
John and Eleanor Williston

Ailsa felt the dry burning of tears that would not fall. This act of kindness, the first she had known in many days, only made her pain more difficult to bear. Yet for a moment, her instinct was stronger than her sorrow. She pulled up a chair and rested the harp on her shoulder. She ran her fingers over the strings, but the sound was strange and distant, like the people she had met in London. The notes sounded harsh and discordant; they were unfamiliar even after she had played them many times.

"Why that's lovely, ma'am," Lizzie said, popping in to gaze in admiration at the gold and white harp. "Like the sound of angels singin'."

Ailsa did not look up. William had said that once, long

207

ago in another world, before she had disappointed him time and again. She dropped her hands into her lap.

"Oh, won't you play some more? This house is so full of silence sometimes it makes me want to scream."

"I know what ye mean." Ailsa half smiled at the girl who was the only light in her long, dreary days. The pretty blonde with her bright blue eyes had become a friend and ally, though "they" would have been appalled by such a thought—"they," who had chosen her dinner gown of layers of filmy lace over Ottoman silk, caught at the throat with an ornate silver and ruby brooch. "They," who had proclaimed her an outcast because her music was too wild and because she had taken her shoes off at teatime.

Lizzie tilted her head, listening. "You'd best put on a smile and get rid of that dreadful frown," she suggested. "I'm thinkin' Mr. Sinclair won't like it at all."

Ailsa froze when the front door opened and closed. So William was home. She waited, holding her breath, to see if he would seek her out. She heard him pause in the foyer, heard his steps in the hall. At last he came in, unbuttoning his sober black coat as he crossed the threshold.

He smiled broadly for the first time in days when he saw her seated at the harp. "So it's finally arrived. I hope you like it, my dear."

"I love it, William. But ye knew I would."

Her husband leaned down to kiss the top of her head. "I hoped. It was all I could do."

Ailsa was glad he could not see her face at that moment. "Thank ye," she whispered, though she knew this gift had come from another time, from those few days in the glen when he had loved her.

William's hand brushed his wife's hair, encased in a silver net, and he grimaced. He wanted to rip the net away, discard the pins and combs, and let her glorious hair fall to her waist as it used to do. But he was afraid to touch her so intimately, afraid she would turn away or stare at him with empty eyes. Only at night, in the darkness, did he let his desire overpower him, because then he could not see her face, could pretend to himself that she welcomed his caresses.

As her husband seated himself in his chair by the fire, Ailsa asked softly, "Did ye have any news of my father today?"

William leaned forward, clasped his hands between his knees, shook his head with regret. "I'm sorry, but the Kittridge family is not willing to discuss their son. I did hear from another chap in the Diplomatic Corps that your father has left China. Says he won't be stopping back in England. This chap seems to think Kittridge doesn't particularly like his home and keeps away from it as much as possible."

Ailsa's melancholy deepened. She looked out the window at the smoke-stained sky. She would not find her father in London: she knew that now. Then why, *why* had he brought her here?

William saw the shadow that crossed her face and lingered in her eyes. He ached for her, wanted more than anything to comfort her, but did not know how. "Would you play for me, Ailsa? I haven't heard your music in so long."

She saw his longing and could not deny him; in this small way, at least, she could still please him. She rested her cheek on the cool wood and touched the familiar strings, creating the sounds that reminded her so wrenchingly of the hills she had left behind. The harp brought back to her the glen and its musical waters, its sighing winds and dark, cool forests. Ian, playing a plaintive tune that shook her like the sound of thunder—low, distant, and beyond her reach. Or the song of birds, so sweet that her body went cold at the sound. Some lines of a Wordsworth poem came to her unexpectedly, an echo of many lonely hours spent in William's library.

And O, ye Fountains, Meadows, Hills and Groves,
Forebode not any severing of our loves!

Her pulse slowed and grew labored.

Yet in my heart of hearts I feel your might;
I only have relinquished one delight
To live beneath your more habitual sway.

Ailsa's hands felt rigid on the strings. This was not music, not the kind she had come to love. Richard Williston had been right when he said this instrument had no soul; the songs had come from *her* soul, and now that voice was silent. The singing had ceased. Everywhere in her world, the music had ceased.

As she dropped her hands into her lap, her face revealed the depth of her unhappiness.

William buried his head in his hands. He could not bear to watch her.

Ailsa looked up, her eyes raw and dry. Her husband's face was not visible, but she knew what she would see there if he raised his head. She had seen too often that terrible look of regret and sadness that transformed him into a man broken, defeated. Because of her.

Ailsa and William exchanged few words as they sat at the elaborate dining table and were served soup, boiled salmon, sweetbreads, leg of mutton, carrots, soufflé or rice, and for dessert, a rhubarb tart. Neither ate much; Cook muttered and grumbled under her breath as she removed dish after dish that had barely been touched. Ailsa knew the food would be discarded and shook with anger when she thought of the waste.

After dinner, husband and wife sat in the drawing room for a while, but presently the silence began to weigh on them, so they rose and went each to the privacy of their own room. When Lizzie had slipped away for the night, Ailsa sat numbly at her dressing table in the frilled nightgown she hated and stared at her hollow-cheeked face in the mirror. The color had left her skin and her eyes were blank. She was suspended in time, living a nightmare that never changed.

This could not go on; eventually she would turn to stone like the standing monuments at the ancient Druid temples, like the tumbled rocks in the Valley of the Dead, where the voices of ghosts moaned in the wind.

I love the Brooks which down their channels fret,
Even more than when I tripped lightly as they;

The innocent brightness of a new-born day
Is lovely yet . . .

Wordsworth again. Why could she not put the poem out of her head tonight, when she could not believe in it? As she sat unmoving, the awful, empty silence descended. She thought she could bear anything but that silence—a stillness without sound or feeling.

She went to the door that stood between herself and William. She wanted to pound on it and shout how much she needed him, to tear it down so he could never close it against her again. She raised her fists, clenched so tightly that her nails pierced the skin of her palms, then let her hands fall to her sides.

She could not do such a thing. It was not right, it was not ladylike, William would not understand. He would be even more disappointed in her than he already was.

She turned when she heard a rap on the window. Narrowing her eyes, she looked more closely and saw that there were raindrops trailing down the glass. Then she heard the distant rumble of thunder and her heart began to beat more rapidly. A storm was on the way; she could smell it in the musty air. It had rained on and off since her arrival in London, but only in little showers without power or fury.

The glass shook with the force of the wind outside and Ailsa ran to open the casements wide. It had been so long since she'd felt the rain on her face, the roar of thunder in her ears, the wind in her hair. As she drew the window inward, she shivered at the cold, sharp drops that struck her mercilessly, like an enemy who had waited for a chance to release its rage upon her. She opened her mouth to cry out, but the rain fell on her tongue, bitter with the taste of city grime. The heavy, tainted drops pounded brutally against the glass. There was no hint in this storm of the caress of soft green earth by the rain in the hills of Scotland. The wind rose, howling, angry, like a trapped animal. Ailsa shuddered at the vicious assault and tried to shut the window.

The wind fought her, forcing the casements inward as she struggled to close out the storm. The deluge fell more furiously until the panes of glass quivered. Finally one shattered, sending slivered fragments spinning. Ailsa gathered all her strength and with one last effort pushed the casements shut, latching them and drawing the heavy curtains closed. But even that barrier could not keep out the cry of the wind and the drops that splattered through the broken glass to make a wide stain on the rug.

Ailsa gasped at a pain in her hand and looked down to see her palm covered with blood. She stood mesmerized by the sight of the sluggish flow of red over her pale skin. She gripped her wrist until her knuckles were white and the pain brought tears to her eyes. It came to her then, sharp and clear—the knowledge that there were no miracles for her in London. She was a stranger in this house, this city, and could never be anything else. Her mother had known that. *There are things ye believe, lass, and things that are true. Someday, mayhap, ye'll learn to know the difference.* The echo of the English poem rose out of the memory of Mairi's voice.

The clouds that gather round the setting sun
Do take a sober coloring from an eye
That hath kept watch o'er man's mortality.
Another race hath been, and other palms are won.

All at once, the remembered image of Janet Chisholm materialized, arms open into emptiness as she called a warning across the turbulent gray sea.

Ailsa reached outward, but the image wavered. She wanted to see Janet's diary now, this instant, to hold it in her hands and know that it was real. She rose, rubbing her bloody hand on her wet gown. She had to find that little book. She rifled drawers, left them half open with lace, linen, and corsets trailing over the edges. She searched the floor of the armoire, growing more and more frantic, scratching at the wood with her nails. Finally she found the book at the back of a drawer in the stand beside her bed.

Drawing the lamp close, she sank to the floor and, huddled in the circle of yellow light, began to read. The diary fell open on the final entry.

"Our last day in the hills we love and, we pray, our last

grief, though 'twill haunt us for the rest of our days. We'll no' be forgettin' the Highlands, nor the voices of the past that speak to us here. We'll no' forget the burns, the tumblin' water over stones, the heather, and the swirlin' mist. To forget these things would be to lose all hope, all beauty, all that we hold dear.''

> Thanks to the human heart by which we live,
> Thanks to its tenderness, it joys, and fears,
> To me the meanest flower that blows can give
> Thoughts that do often lie too deep for tears.

How was it that this poet, a Sassenach, another stranger, spoke again and again through the voices from her past? Ailsa shook her head violently. The pain was close and hot now in her throat. A drop ran down her cheek, then another and another until the grief that had been welling inside her spilled out in a rush of tears she could no longer hold back. She sank to the floor, sobbing, grasped her arms, and rocked while she wept—deep, wrenching sobs that drew the pain up from the dark place in her heart. She shuddered and cried out silently until the tears became one with the rain on her gown.

She understood then her strange feeling of empathy for Janet Chisholm, a woman she had never met, the impulse that had made her keep the diary and refuse to give it up, the emptiness she had felt when she last touched the chest in the secret cave.

Ian had been right, just as Mairi had been right, but that knowledge came too late. Somehow, Ailsa had lost control of her fate. She was falling into the center of a whirlpool of silence and grief too great to bear. *Ye haven't ever known the mysteries of that other world, but neither have ye known the sorrow,* Ian had warned her. *Ye haven't ever felt real hurt. Ye don't even know what it means.*

If only Ian could reach her now. But the whirlpool was too strong. It would carry her down into darkness and she would never see the light again. The windows flew open with the force of the wind and the rain poured in, knocking over her lamp, so the flame sputtered and went out.

"Ian!" Ailsa wept. "Ian, *mo-charaid!*" The words were whipped up by the wind and carried, whirling, into the heart of the black, angry storm.

All day Ian had walked the hills with a shadow on his shoulder. When he lay down in bed that night, the shadow settled around him in the folds of his woolen blanket. He fell asleep to the sound of soft rain falling, but his rest was not easy. He tossed and turned, bedeviled by demons without shape or form. As he slept, the shadow grew into a dream.

The rain fell hissing through the wind while Ailsa stood high on her precipice, arms open wide in celebration. She was smiling, her face washed with the cleansing rain. Ian drew nearer at a roar of thunder that forced her closer to the edge.

Then he saw that her mouth, which he had thought was smiling, was twisted in a cry of despair. She was reaching desperately for a branch to cling to. Her face was washed in soot-blackened tears that became one with the rain as they ran down her cheeks. She trembled with the fury of her weeping and rocked, forward and back, backward and forward, moving inch by inch closer to the edge of the steep precipice. Then, without a sound, she fell, her body caught in the darkness of the swirling storm. She cried out, "Ian! Ian, *mo-charaid!*" in a voice so full of anguish that it woke him from his sleep and he lay there covered in sweat and shaking in fear with the chill of night outside his window.

He rose at dawn, the sheep and cattle forgotten, to make his way to Mairi Rose's croft. She met him at the door, her face pale, her eyes shadowed. She did not need to speak for him to know that she had dreamed his dream.

"Ailsa needs ye," she said. "Can ye go to her?"

"I will go, but I don't see how. The coach and train fare—"

She put a finger to his lips. "I have been thinkin'. There is a way." Mairi smiled her bittersweet smile, went to the shelf where Charles Kittridge's miniature sat, and placed her hands on the rosewood box. For a long time she stood silent, lost in her memories. At last she lifted the lid and took something out.

"Ailsa told me once that Janet Chisholm would have wanted me to have this." She held out the brooch of silver and emeralds that Ian and Ailsa had found in the Chisholm chest. "I knew then 'twas so, though I didn't know why."

Ian stared at the brooch, which glistened in the light of the fire like a fistful of stars. "I don't understand."

"Take it," Mairi whispered. "Sell it and use the money for the fares."

"But 'tis so beautiful. How can ye give it up?"

"For Ailsa's sake I would give up even my life, as so would ye. Don't stand here bickerin', Ian Fraser. Go to her quickly, before 'tis too late."

He cupped the brooch in his hands, tenderly, as if it held within it Ailsa's heart and hope. "Thank ye," he said.

When he turned to go, she stopped him. "Are ye certain ye want to do this thing? Do ye know that ye stand now in *Edin-da-hin-Veaul*, the Jeopardy of Baal? His two fires burn on either side of ye. No matter where ye turn, the flames will singe ye. Are ye strong enough to bear the pain?"

"I'll pray to Dagda and Neithe to make me strong," he said. The pain had been with him for a long time now and had not beaten him yet. "Besides, 'twas ye who said—"

Mairi shook her head. "To lose your life is one thing, Ian-*mor-run*, to lose your hope another. There's peace in death, but only unendin' sorrow in hopelessness."

He nodded, though he did not really understand, took the brooch, and left her. When he was gone, she turned to the bed that had once been Ailsa's. Stiffly, she knelt to lay her hand on the clarsach, but there was no music within it today—only silence and stillness without sound or feeling.

For two days, Ailsa lay unmoving. Lizzie had found her mistress on the morning after the storm, huddled on the floor in a pool of rainwater, wet, shaking, and pale as marble. After the maid had tucked her into bed, Ailsa began to burn with fever. She coughed and gasped and muttered in her restless sleep while Lizzie placed cool cloths on her forehead and gave her the tonic the doctor had left behind after his visit.

The maid herself grew pale as she cared for her mistress. Eventually William sent the girl to her own bed and took her place at his wife's side. She tossed and turned, her face flushed, then pale and sallow, then flushed again. William held her damp, cool hand, pressed it now and then to his cheek. Her breathing was harsh and ragged; he would have infused his own breath and blood into her if he could, in order to end her illness. She was more precious to him now than ever, because, for the first time, she needed him. He dried her sweat-covered forehead, pressed the cool cloth to her heated skin, and held her hand until, at last, the warmth began to return to her limp fingers and the furious color to fade from her cheeks.

The doctor returned that afternoon and declared that Mrs. Sinclair was better and would recover most quickly if left alone to rest. For two more days she slept off and on while Lizzie crept in and out of the room so she would not disturb her mistress's sleep.

Ailsa shivered a great deal at first, and felt weak, as if her bones had turned to milk. And she could not force her limbs to move. William visited her on the first morning after she was conscious, sat by her bed, and stared down at his hands. "Why were you sitting on the floor? When the rain came pouring in, why didn't you call for Lizzie or get up to change your gown or sit by the fire?" He did not look at her because he feared her answer.

Ailsa brushed the tangled hair back from her face and felt the unfamiliar roughness of a bandage on her hand. She remembered then that the flying glass had cut her. She fought back the memory of what had followed. "I couldn't move," she said carefully. "I didn't know where to go."

Her husband winced as if she had struck him. He left her soon afterward, telling her to rest, to take care of herself. Never once did he meet her eyes. When he was gone, Ailsa huddled deeper into the heavy covers, pulled them over her head to shut out the image of William's hands spread helplessly on his knees. She wanted to ease his pain but did not know how, any more than she knew how to ease her own.

Her depression had not lifted with the fever. Instead it grew and lingered, like the memory of the night when the storm had invaded her safe and empty room.

On the third morning after her fever disappeared, she awakened and knew that she had to get away from the bed where she had been a prisoner, the room that was filled from edge to edge with the sound and weight of her misery.

It was Lizzie's day off; she had left an hour since. When Ailsa was certain William, too, was gone, she rose and threw on the first gown she could find. She did not bother with undergarments but did slip on the leather shoes Callum Mackensie had made for her.

She darted like a wraith through the house, down the steps, and along Larkspur Crescent, hardly aware of the rows of shade trees, the wrought-iron railings, or neat green lawns. She walked mindlessly, hour after hour, fleeing from a shadow that would not leave her, a fear that she could not escape. As she walked, the sun grew pale beneath a drift of fog that settled downward inexorably. It enveloped the streets in damp, clinging gray.

Ailsa shivered at the ugliness of the alleys she passed—the high, soot-blackened buildings, the starved, ragged children who played at the edges of the filthy squares, the stench of open sewers and old garbage. Her heart grew heavy as the streets became narrower and the unfriendly fog closed around her, covered the sound of her footsteps on the muddy streets. She felt the shadow draw nearer, reach out with grimy fingers to capture her in its grasp. Ailsa began to run.

But she could not find her way in the unfamiliar city cloaked in fog. The heavy moisture blinded her but did not stop the darkness from following at her heels. She tripped on her long skirt as it dragged through the gutters; she cried out for help, but found she could not make a sound.

She felt adrift, alone, enclosed by a ring of strangers with staring, sightless eyes. She ran faster, confused, aware that she had wandered too far from home and had no idea where she was. Then she heard it, soft and distant, like a whisper half remembered—the song of a flute. She stopped still in the middle of an alley. She knew that tune.

She paused to catch her breath, then moved toward the

muffled fragments of song that came to her, then disappeared like an indrawn breath. Slowed and weighed down by the fog, she came up against a wall that blocked her way. Ailsa leaned on it, gasping, while the fog clung in her nostrils, surrounded her until the song of the flute faded into the soot.

The shadow was at her heels; she could feel it crawling up her back. She turned so the music could find her, praying she would reach it before the darkness swept her up and she was lost forever. The notes grew louder, lured her back toward light and warmth and comfort. She recognized at last the tune she had created long ago beside the stream when the song of the lark, the cool breeze, and the rush of the river had enchanted her.

Only one other person on earth had heard that song, could play it back to her now like a promise. She was bent over, choking from lack of air, when she turned at last onto Larkspur Crescent. The trees rose out of the gray moisture and she recognized the houses set neatly one beside the other. She knew when she reached her own steps, for the song of the flute was clear and undiminished by distance or grief or the fog that had become her enemy.

Ailsa raised her head, then stumbled forward, laughing, weeping, tripping on her skirt as she hurried toward the figure seated on the top step, a rosewood flute to his lips.

Ian. The sight of his face was a joy beyond words, the sound of his song a blessing, the smile on his lips a miracle she had never thought to see again.

218

·16·

Ailsa moved in a daze to the step where Ian waited. She did not touch him, did not speak. It seemed like a lifetime since she'd last seen his face, his clear green eyes that saw beyond her smile of greeting to the desperation underneath. Neither spoke as she led him inside to the sitting room. It seemed unfamiliar today, softened by the feeling of unreality that transformed her as the moonlight alters the darkness.

She went to the window and threw the velvet curtains open. She was determined to see, in the fog-tinted sunlight, every line and plane of Ian's face, every smile and frown and lift of his eyebrows. They sat in overstuffed chairs a few feet apart. Instinctively, she did not touch him; the joy she felt at his presence told her that to do so would be to risk too much. She could not betray William in that way, too.

So they sat drinking in each other's breath and laughter and hurried speech, as if they had only an hour in which to share the rest of their lives; for the glen called him back, even now.

"How did ye find the fare to get here?" she asked finally.

"Your mother gave me the Chisholm brooch to sell."

Ailsa thought of Mairi, how she had cradled the brooch in her hand and said, *I'll leave it here till 'tis wanted again.* Then she thought of Janet Chisholm and her dream and knew that all was as it should be. "But how did ye know?" she demanded.

"Mairi and I shared a dream of your grief. So I came."

Ailsa winced. "Why did ye care, after what I did to ye?"

Ian leaned forward. "*Ye* still care, don't ye?" The look

219

in her eyes gave him her answer. "The past doesn't matter," he said. "Ye are in need. There was naught else I could do."

Perhaps only then did she realize fully how much she had lost when she left him behind. She wanted to weep, but the tears would not come. She sank back in the chair and closed her eyes. "I can't bear it anymore. The silence and emptiness and the cold stares of others."

"But ye can. Ye know that, Ailsa, in your heart."

What was it Mairi had said on her daughter's wedding day? *Ye'll find ye can bear a great many things that ye think too cruel, birdeen. Ye are strong. Never forget that.*

"Tell me what troubles ye, *mo-aghray*," Ian said.

She began to describe what her world was like, how little joy it held and how much darkness.

"Mayhap," he said thoughtfully, "ye've no' looked close enough for the happiness. Mayhap ye've cloaked yourself in shadows."

She shook her head. "There's no music here, no magic. 'Tis a cold and unfriendly world. And William blames me because I can't change myself into the image of his aunt."

"Has he told ye so? Has he asked ye to be like other women?"

Do ye think I'll ever make a lady? she had asked her husband once. He had answered, *I sincerely hope not.* Ailsa frowned. "No, but I've seen the look in his eyes. Since the first day in London, he's regretted that he married me."

"Has he now? Are ye certain of that?"

She looked at Ian's dark hair, tangled and dusty from the journey, at his eyes, lit with every thought and feeling that crossed his mind, at his face, touched with sadness, hope, and fear. She need not guess what Ian felt. He told her with every look, every breath.

Not until that moment, when the pain rose crippling and twisted within her, did she realize how deeply she had missed him. She clenched her hands into fists and fought back words that were better unsaid.

Ian saw through her silence and had to look away. He knew how to heal her pain with his hands and his songs and the beat of his heart, but he no longer had the right. This time he would have to use words, and they were poor imitations. "I asked ye a question," he reminded Ailsa gently. "Are ye certain he doesn't want ye still? If he loved ye enough to marry ye—"

"No." She rose to wander restlessly about the room, stopping at the window to gaze at the tidy street with its orderly rows of trees. "Ye don't understand."

Ian went to stand beside her but did not reach out, as every instinct told him to, and take her hand. "Mayhap 'tis ye who doesn't understand. Mayhap ye don't wish to because 'tis really *ye* who blames *him* because he's no' the man ye think your father was. Ye married William Sinclair, no' Charles Kittridge. Remember that and tell your husband what ye feel. Ask him to tell ye what *he* feels. Mayhap words don't come easy for him."

She turned, so close that he could feel her cool breath. Suddenly there was no past, no present, no William, no dark, unfriendly London. There was only the song of the water, and the trees with their shivering leaves, and the mountains, wild and beautiful around them.

"Why should it be so," Ailsa whispered, "when with ye I need no' speak at all?"

He did not say he had warned her of this, pleaded with her, shown her that she belonged to him alone. Though his anger flared hot and bright because he had to heal what she had torn apart through her own blindness, it was not as great as his compassion, his need to see her eyes unshadowed, her smile undimmed by sadness.

"I don't know why 'tis so, Ailsa Rose. What is, the gods have made to be. But I do know that ye'll no' find joy if ye don't seek it out. Put aside your fear, your sorrow, and open your soul to the man who is your husband. If ye don't, if ye break his heart in the end, ye'll never forgive yourself." He wondered where he found the strength to speak those words when all he wanted was to take her in his arms and tell her she belonged beside him always. "And remember this. Ye're good enough for any man. Ye mustn't doubt that, ever."

Mairi had said the same thing once. Ailsa thought of Abigail Fielding's derisive laughter and tried to believe Ian. She could have done it—for she knew the woman's heart was cold as flint—except for the look she had seen so often in William's eyes.

" 'Tis time," Ian said.

She blinked at him, uncomprehending.

"Time to remember what ye've chosen to forget. I mean to show ye that there *is* music here, if ye open your ears and your heart to it. I saw a harp in the room we passed. Come play ye while I play the flute."

She shook her head. "I can't do it. It hurts too much."

"Ye can, and so ye shall. Think back, Ailsa, to the night of Beltaine, when Jenny Mackensie was pale with terror because your skirt had caught afire. Ye laughed and asked her what there was to fear. Surely ye, who were always so brave, can't be afraid of the very thing ye've loved most all your life. Come."

She followed him reluctantly. Though she sat beside the harp and pulled it down to her shoulder, she did not play. Instead she closed her eyes to listen as Ian began to speak. He reminded her of moors that were green seas of grass in the breeze, of the boisterous river Affric that rushed through the dark coolness of the forest, of Torran barking a challenge to every standing stone. He spoke of the fires on Beltaine, of the silver birches swaying in the wind, of the rugged mountains, of sun and moonlight on crumbled rocks in a cave, of the copse beside the river where water tumbled over stones. The rhythm of his voice made a dream in her head of all the things that she had loved and lost. She could not shut them out this time, for Ian had made them real again, so real that she was certain she could reach out and bring her cupped hands to her lips full of water from the burn. At first the sound of his voice, the memories he created, made the pain wash over her like the waves of the loch in a storm. Then, slowly, the waves became fewer until the storm passed and the loch grew still and calm and silver blue.

Ian began to play softly—thin sweet notes that drifted through the pale sunlight to settle on Ailsa's shoulders. With his breath and his clever fingers, he played a stillness upon the ragged beat of her heart, a deep and restful sleep upon her feverish emotions. He played a calmness over her that blocked out the fog, the stifling clutter of the house, and left a cool tranquillity behind.

Eventually, without being aware of it, she too began to play.

"Let the music heal ye," Ian whispered. "Let it soothe your hurt."

All at once, the strings of the harp were like the shuttle under Mairi's hands. Back and forth Ailsa's fingers moved, weaving her despair into shadows that dissipated in the gray afternoon light. At last she looked up at her friend to smile slowly; all the memories of their youth were in that smile. What was it Mairi had said? *Ye go far about, seekin' the nearest.* She had come to London seeking happiness, but it had been there for her in the glen all the time. Why had she let Ian go?

He took a step toward her and her heart began to pound. She could feel the color rise in her cheeks at the thought of his nearness and suddenly she knew. She had turned him away because she was afraid of the feelings he awakened in her—just as Mairi had once turned Charles Kittridge away.

She met Ian's gaze and her eyes told him this: "Ye are more to me, Ian Fraser, than all else in the world that is. This I swear by the sun and by the moon, by flame and wind and water, by the dew and the twilight that is neither night nor day."

She spoke in silence without words, but he heard and understood. Ian turned away—he did not trust himself to answer—and gripped the windowsill until his knuckles were white with pain. But he held the memory of her smile, the message in her eyes, and knew he would carry it with him always.

William stood outside the drawing room and listened to the lilting music. He saw the young man by the window—the one who had held Ailsa's hand and looked into her eyes as if he knew her soul. William wanted to turn away but could not do it. It seemed he was doomed forever to watch from a distance the magic moments in Ailsa's life and never to be part of them himself.

He saw how she played her soft, yearning song, saw the pain and despair leave her eyes and, finally, the shadow. A dull throb began in his head that turned to a pounding which deafened him but did not take away his sight. How he wished it had done so when he saw his wife look up to smile tenderly at the one who shared her music.

William's heart stopped beating, though the pounding in his head went on and the pain inside took his breath away. He had lost her. She had left him behind along with the shadow of her grief. This was the Ailsa he had fallen in love with, the Ailsa he had not seen since a gray morning in Glasgow, the Ailsa who, in one short month, had made his life a paradise and a wasteland.

He turned without a word and left the house.

That night, long after Ian had returned to the hotel where he had booked a room, Ailsa lay silent in her bed. William had not returned for supper. He had never stayed away like this, not even on the first day when he could no longer meet her eyes. Tonight she had been eager to see him, but had sat alone at the table, which groaned under the weight of silver and china and platters of uneaten food. She had waited until everything was cold, then left the room without touching a plate. Was it possible her husband was hurt? That he was wandering somewhere, alone and without help? The longer she was parted from Ian and his reassuring voice, the more uncertain she became.

Ailsa raised her head and sat up against the feather pillows; she sensed a presence on the other side of the door. As she had once before, she called out, "William?"

There was a long, painful silence, then her husband opened the door and entered the room. He was still dressed, though he had discarded his coat. His waistcoat was stained and unbuttoned, his cravat trailed limply over his shirt, as if he had clawed it undone and left it to wilt. His hair was in wild disarray; he must have run his fingers through it until they were numb. His collar was unbuttoned, the studs missing. His eyes were wild and his breathing harsh.

He stopped at the sight of her and gasped as if she had struck him in the stomach. She watched in dismay as he began to pace the floor, his hands clasped behind his back.

William had not been prepared for the sound of Ailsa's voice or the sight of her beloved face. He had thought she would be gone, on her way back to the Highlands. Yet here she was, warm and breathing and far too real, made even more alluring by the soft lamplight. She was too lovely; if he continued to look at her, he would not be able to let her go.

"William, what is't?" Ailsa cried.

He stopped, his back to her. "I saw him here today—with you." It was not what he had meant to say.

Ailsa turned pale. "Nothin' happened between us—"

Her husband shook his head in distress. He had not intended to accuse her. With a heavy sigh, he went to stand beside the bed. "Forgive me, Ailsa. I know you didn't do anything wrong." He closed his eyes and tried to order his thoughts, but could not seem to manage. "It's just that I saw how you looked at him."

"Ye are my husband," she said simply.

He gazed down at her, an anguished question in his eyes. "But you wanted to touch him."

"We don't need to touch."

William turned away, stricken. "Dear God. So I *have* lost you."

Only then did Ailsa realize what she'd said. "Ye must listen to me," she began, choosing her words with care. "I only meant that I've known him since I was a bairn, that we've been friends for many years."

Still her husband would not look at her.

"We understand each other's thoughts, Ian and I, but 'tis no more than that." She knew the gods would forgive her for the lie if it eased a little of the pain that ravaged William's face.

"You should have married Ian. Why in God's name did you marry me?" He had accepted her answer without question when she told him she would be his wife. Now, for the first time, he stopped to wonder why.

Ailsa hesitated, her fingers braided together on the pale blue coverlet. "Because I chose to."

It was not what he wanted to hear. When he saw her expression, he realized that whatever had made her choose him, it had not been love. "Why?" he repeated desperately.

"Because ye seemed to walk out of a vision. To me, ye were a dream made real—a dream of flesh and blood and bone that I could see, touch, and believe in. Because ye said things to me, beautiful things I'd never heard nor thought to hear. And because ye made me understand that though ye wanted me, ye didn't ever think to have me. Don't ye see, William? Ye touched me in a way none had touched me before."

It should have been enough for him, but somehow it was not. His wife reached out to take his hand but William pulled it away and began to pace again. "You should have stayed in the glen where you belong. I should never have married you."

Ailsa felt tears burn behind her eyes. "I'm sorry that I'm no' the wife ye need. I didn't mean to embarrass ye over and over. If ye regret your mistake—"

"No!" He whirled in disbelief. "How could you even think such a thing? You don't understand!"

Ailsa saw the torment in his eyes and began to wonder if Ian were right. "Then make me understand," she said softly.

He knelt at the bedside, head in his hands. "I can't. Don't you see that? I don't know how."

Still afraid that he would draw away, Ailsa gently ran her fingers through his hair. "Don't ye?"

He looked up to see her smiling uncertainly, her lips slightly parted. "Are ye certain of that, my husband?"

The lilt of her Highland voice, the warmth of her fingers on his skin, the rise and fall of her breath were an invitation he could not resist. Without a word he tangled both hands in her hair and drew her toward him. Eyes closed, he breathed in the scent of her; he wanted to inhale her youth, her music, her energy, and make it his.

She raised her head and touched her lips to his, so lightly that it might have been a breath, a whisper. He pulled her closer to kiss her hungrily. There was a new fierceness in his kiss, an urgency in the way his hand moved over her body in a lingering caress.

This time William did not turn off the light, but looked directly into Ailsa's eyes as he cupped her breasts in his open palms. The ruffles of her gown impeded him and he hesitated only briefly, then drew the garment over her head, revealing her naked body to his gaze.

She was more beautiful than he had imagined—white, soft, and perfect. He leaned down to kiss one breast and then the other. For the first time, she trembled at his touch. He found he could not breathe, so intense was his pleasure. He buried his face between her breasts and listened to her heartbeat as if it were a song.

"William," she murmured, "ye're wearin' too many clothes."

He smiled while she removed his cravat and tossed it on the floor. Then she unfastened his shirt and pushed it away, his waistcoat tangled with it. Finally she reached for his pants, but these he removed himself until he was naked. Ailsa rose to stand beside him, ran her hands across his shoulders, down his chest and around his back, then up to his sensitive neck. She shivered with delight when he gasped and kissed her again, her face cupped in his hands.

At last they climbed into bed. With the soft yellow light around and about them, they caressed each other slowly, drawing out the pleasure, the warmth that pulsed between them.

William trailed his fingers down her body, from her throat to her breasts to her belly. Then, tentatively, he touched the place between her thighs. Ailsa moaned, eyes closed, and raised her hips toward him. He lay beside her, one hand wound in her hair, the other moving slowly between her legs.

Ailsa felt the heat rise within her, the colors behind her lids like pale lights hidden in the mist. Then the lights went whirling into darkness, she gasped, stiffened, and called his name. "William!"

His heart was pounding wildly when he entered her. She sighed and drew him closer, moving with him, rocking, thrusting her hips upward. He wrapped his arms around her and pressed into her again and again, until he could hold himself back no longer. He shuddered as ripples of pleasure moved through him like fire through tender grass. Then they cried out together and he fought to catch his breath.

"I love you, Ailsa," he whispered.

It was the first time he had ever spoken those words.

◇   ◇   ◇

When Ailsa awoke in the morning, William lay beside her, one hand caught in her hair, the other resting on her shoulder.

He had never stayed with her for an entire night, never thought it proper to do so. She felt contented with the weight of his body next to hers, the regular beating of his heart. It was good to know he was there, to feel his breath on her cheek.

She lay still, unwilling to move and perhaps wake him. The heat crept through her body at the memory of his love-making the night before. It spread and curled into her belly, where it lingered, soft and warm with promise. Ailsa smiled slowly, with wonder. She rested her hand on her stomach and sensed a movement, not yet felt, but soon, soon. She knew, as surely as if she had felt it kick within her, that she and William had conceived a child last night.

It was a new chance, a beginning. She was suffused, all at once, with joy.

William opened his eyes sleepily, drawing a handful of Ailsa's hair toward his face, rubbing the strands against his cheek. Then he saw her smile, the light in her eyes. "I've never seen you smile like that," he whispered, so grateful that his own eyes burned with tears. "What are you thinking?"

She knew she could not tell him the truth. He did not believe in the Sight, in a knowledge that came from a source he could not see or understand. "I was thinkin' about last night," she said.

"I wonder if you know how happy you make me."

She reached down to touch his cheek. "Ye know I'm no' like your aunt and her friends."

He took her hand and kissed her palm. "You still don't see. I don't want you to be like them. I married you because you're unlike anyone I've ever known. Because you're Ailsa."

"Then ye're no' disappointed in me?"

Suddenly all the words that had been too long pent up inside came tumbling out. "Have you any idea how barren my life was before you? There was no music, no magic, no laughter. In two days you showed me those things, made me feel them and believe in them. I felt trapped in London and didn't know it until I met you. You opened a door I had never imagined existed.''

She stared at him incredulously. ''But ye've been so distant and cold.''

''Because I saw how my aunt and her friends hurt you and I couldn't forgive myself for bringing you here. I thought I'd killed the very thing in you that I most loved. Don't ever change what you are, Ailsa, not for me or anyone else. Treasure the secrets you learned in those Scottish hills and don't ever lose them.''

She slid her arms around him and leaned her head on his shoulder. ''And I thought that I'd failed ye.'' She was silent for a moment, then added, ''Besides, there hasn't been much music and laughter in the past few days. Didn't ye regret your marriage, even a little bit, when ye realized that?''

He made her look at him. ''No, my heart. For once I'd shared those things with you, the thought of life without them was more than I could bear. I would have waited forever if need be, to see you smile like this again.'' He spoke fiercely and she knew he spoke the truth.

She was awed by the love and admiration in his eyes. Like her husband, she had never thought to see those things again. She drew him closer, craving the warmth that had been denied her for so long.

''I have to go now,'' he said with regret. ''Will you be waiting when I get back?''

''I will always be waitin', William,'' she answered.

17

After William had left for his chambers, Ailsa dressed quickly and went down to the drawing room. She paused on the threshold to look at the matching red velvet settees and the brocade sofa, and the red and purple Brussels carpet. She had never noticed how beautiful the colors were, perhaps because it was always so dark in here. She drew back all the brocade curtains, then the filmy lace beneath, so the morning light spilled through the windows.

She liked the room better now that the shadows had disappeared. For the first time, she noticed the marble mantel that glowed as if lit from within. It, too, was lovely, as were the Chinese vases at either end—the pattern was of blue, pale pink, and scarlet, which picked up the color of the rug. Why had she never seen it before? *Mayhap ye haven't looked close enough,* Ian had told her. *Mayhap ye've cloaked yourself in shadows.* She stood in a pale wash of sunlight, gazing at the room intently.

There were heavy gilt-framed mirrors above the mantel and sofa, between each set of windows, and over the sideboard. The mirrors reflected and multiplied the many tables and plant stands and chairs and sculptures, so the true beauty of the room was obscured. Ailsa stood pensively, her face trapped time and again in the gleaming glass around her.

"Why, ma'am," Lizzie gasped, rushing in, hair flying, cap tilted precariously on her head. "I tried to go help you dress this mornin', but I heard voices and thought I'd best stay away. Then later, when I went back, I found you gone. Are you all right? Should you be up so soon after your illness?"

"I'm well," Ailsa answered calmly. "Besides, I didn't need your help this mornin'."

The maid stopped, hand to her mouth, when she saw that her mistress wore the blue and purple gown she had brought with her from Scotland. Lizzie gaped at the skirt, which was less than half as wide as those currently in fashion. But the gown was not the end of it. Ailsa's hair, tied back with a purple ribbon, hung loose down her back.

Now that she looked closer, Lizzie saw that there was color in her mistress's face. This morning her eyes were no longer tinted gray, but a vivid blue-violet that caused the maid to sigh in admiration. She had never noticed how beautiful Mrs. Sinclair's eyes were, and how mysterious. She considered her mistress from head to toe and pronounced firmly, "It suits you, that gown. You look lovely today."

Ailsa smiled and raised the hem of her dress to reveal bare feet. "No boots either, at least no' while I'm in my own house."

Lizzie looked startled, then smiled back. "Good for you. What did you do, lock 'them' in the closet?"

Ailsa was grateful for the girl's acceptance and the glint of humor in her eyes. "I told 'them' they weren't welcome in my home and must find someone else to bother."

Lizzie grinned.

"There's a gentleman to see you, ma'am. At least—well, he sounds like you," Emma announced. Her mouth fell open when she saw Mrs. Sinclair caught in the morning sunlight. When she realized she was staring, the girl blushed and mumbled, "Shall I show him in?"

"Aye," Ailsa told her, "please."

She turned to Lizzie, who wisely declared, "I'd best go see to the bedroom and begin my other chores. If you need me, ma'am, just call."

"I will, and thank ye."

As soon as Ian entered the room Ailsa felt a sinking in her stomach. His eyes were still, his smile only a half smile. When she saw the rigid lines of his face, she knew. "Ye're goin' home," she said without preamble.

"Aye." His voice was low, expressionless.

231

"But why so soon? Ye've come so far for a single day. Can't ye stay yet awhile?"

Ian shook his head and his hair fell over his forehead. She ached to brush it back, but stayed where she was, with half a room between them. "I can't leave my father to do all the work alone. He needs me. Besides," he added, "I've done what I came to do." He had not failed to notice the difference in her today—the flush in her cheeks, the luster in her eyes, the soft curve of her lips. No doubt she had sorted things out with her husband after all. The thought made his head throb dully.

Ailsa nodded. "Aye," she said softly, "and I thank ye for that. I'll always thank ye. I know 'twasn't easy."

Her compassion drew him toward her until they stood a breath apart. He wanted to reach out and draw her close, to hold her so tightly she could never get free. But as she raised her head to look at him, he knew he could not do it.

Ailsa smiled a sad smile that reminded him of Mairi and touched his arm lightly. "If I can learn to be happy, Ian-*mo-ghraidh*, then so can ye. It's been long enough. 'Tis time to stop your mournin' and take yourself a wife."

Carefully, he backed away so her hand slipped from his arm. "What makes ye so wise this mornin'?"

"Ye do," she whispered, "and well ye know it. Ye made me remember the glen I was so determined to forget, ye brought back the magic I had lost and made me see more clearly. I can't ever thank ye enough for that."

" 'Tisn't your gratitude I want."

She did not ask what he did want, for she already knew.

He stared at her long and hard, then glanced down at her stomach. His eyes widened in comprehension. "Somethin' has changed in the night. There will be a bairn." The words came out easily, as if they had not been torn from inside him, as if they did not echo the sound of his bruised, slow-beating heart.

Ailsa smiled, this time without sadness. "Aye," she said.

"Listen to me," Ian insisted. "Don't keep the magic of the glen from her. Play for her, sing to her, tell her the old stories as ye would if ye'd borne her in your mother's croft.

232

Give her your music, *mo-charaid*. 'Twill make ye happy, too.''

"I will."

They stood for a moment, unmoving. Then Ian murmured, " 'Tis time I was away." He swallowed and could not restrain a last, longing look, a silent plea so strong that she leaned forward, drawn by the need in his eyes.

Ailsa's mouth was dry and her heart beat unsteadily. "Don't wait for me, Ian. I'll no' be comin' back."

He nodded, unable to speak. He started for the door, but she called him back.

"Ian!" She made no sound and yet he heard her, felt her grief that was his own, and stopped still. Slowly he turned. She raised her right hand, he his left. They touched gently, palm to palm. Yesterday he had saved her from despair, giving her the courage she had lost, but now it was he who was in need. Her strength flowed through her fingers into his, through his hand and into his blood, giving him the will to turn away without anger or hate or bitterness, but only sorrow—deep and eternal.

For an endless moment, it was as if they stood again in the mist outside Mairi's croft while the wind called out its lovely, keening song. All at once, they were children again, free from care, from pain, from the knowledge of their own weakness.

"What's between us hasn't changed," Ailsa told him when she could speak again. " 'Twill never change."

"Aye." The word was little more than a sigh, a breath of half-remembered breeze.

"Remember, *mo-run*," she murmured, *"Deireadh gach comuin, sgaoileadh—*the end of all meetings, parting—*deireadh gach cogaidh, sith—*the end of all striving, peace."

"I will remember." He reached down to take something from his pocket. "I want ye to keep this."

He held out the rosewood flute he had carved for her years ago. Ailsa took it in trembling fingers. As she looked down at the worn, familiar wood, he slipped away, as silent and swift as a brief summer storm soon lost in the trees. She followed him to the door and stood smiling her good-bye. The smile faded as he moved down the stairs. It was the last time she would know him like this. They had lied to each other a moment since. It could never be the same between them again. He was going and would not return. She felt an ache in the center of her body as he walked away from her, step by step, while the fog swirled about him, enfolding and enveloping, until he disappeared into its clinging folds and she could see him no more.

The hollow beat of Ailsa's heart echoed the rhythm of his retreating footsteps long after the sound itself had faded. She stood in the doorway and stared blindly into the fog, opening her mouth to call out, to bring him back to her, to bind him to her forever. But she did not make a sound while the pain of loss swelled inside her, so deep and all-encompassing that it seeped into her blood. For an instant, her newfound strength began to ebb. Then she felt a rush of hope and her courage returned, stronger, fiercer. She knew that Ian had turned to smile at her, though she could not see his face.

Don't ever despair, Ailsa-aghray, he'd told her once. *I'm here for ye.*

"And I for ye," she whispered, but the words were swallowed by the gray, curling billows of fog.

That night, William took a hansom cab from his chambers near Westminster. Usually he walked, but he was eager to get home tonight. Emma had barely closed the door when Cook swooped down upon him, hands on hips, face flushed, eyes tiny slits of fury.

"Good evening, Cook," he said.

"Good evenin' indeed," the woman snapped, affronted that he should make such an assumption without her acquiescence. "And well it might be if the Mistress hadn't gone and lost her mind."

William frowned in concern. "Is Mrs. Sinclair all right? What do you mean?"

"Ooohh, happy as a lark, she is, turnin' this house upside down and orderin' me to toss out the menus for the month and start again. You wouldn't be believin' what she said, Mr. Sinclair. Near curled my hair with horror, I can tell you."

"Oh?" William's concern changed to amusement and he suppressed a smile. Mrs. O'Neil's wiry gray hair did look more disheveled than usual and her white ruffled hat sat at a dangerous angle on her head. "What's that, Cook?"

The woman glanced around, afraid one of the other servants might overhear. "She said—the saints preserve us from all lunatics—that I'm to serve for dinner nothin' but the leftover mutton from last night, a bit of carrots and potatoes and the rest of the plum pudding. Now what do you think of that?"

She crossed her arms on her plump bosom with a self-righteous harrumph, waiting for him to turn pale with shock.

"Did she?" William replied blandly. "And what else?"

The cook regarded him through narrowed brown eyes. "It set my head spinnin', sure as you're born, but she said"—she glanced around once more—"she told me to be givin' away all the rest to the poor in the Narrows. 'Starvin' half to death, they are,' she told me, plain as plain, 'and us eatin' like royalty and throwin' so much away.' Said there was far too much waste in this house. Called it a sin, she did, right to my face."

William blinked at the large, overbearing woman in disbelief. How often had he watched her send in course after course of food enough for ten, though he was eating alone or with one or two friends? How often had he pitied poor Martha, overburdened by ungainly platters covered with fishes and meats in sauces that made him vaguely queasy? How many times had he pushed his chair back from the table, too full to move, unpleasantly aware of the huge amount he had eaten, not because he wanted it, but merely because it had been set before him? He had heard his aunt's ponderous warning echo in his ears and learned it too well. "Eat what you're given, William, or you'll surely go to hell. Waste is a sin, you know." Yet Abigail Fielding's platters, too, had been filled so high he often wondered how the servants managed to carry them without spilling salmon in lobster sauce over the damask tablecloth.

More than once he had wanted to object, but on every occasion, his courage had failed him and he'd kept silent. Yet his wife had spoken her mind: she had done in a single day what he had feared to do for a lifetime. He smiled and patted the cook soothingly on the shoulder. "It's a bit out of the ordinary," he said, choosing his words with care, "but it does make sense, you know."

She snorted and stepped away from him, as if his touch might contaminate her. "Madness is catchin' now," she muttered under her breath. "So it must be." Then she raised her head, glowering. "But that's not all of it," she said, puffing out her bright red cheeks with the force of her distress. "She's been at Lizzie and Emma, too. Handed over half the gowns your kind aunt had made and told the girls to give them to some worthy ladies. Worthy ladies, indeed," Cook snorted. "When Emma said she'd have nothin' to do with it, and rightly so, if you ask me, the mistress said to give them to the secondhand man. And"— clearly the woman had saved the most horrifying bit of information for last—"Emma says there's not a single proper garment left in that room, if you know what I mean."

William understood at once that she was referring to such things as corsets and crinolines.

"A lady wouldn't mention such a thing," Mrs. O'Neil added, "but I thought you should know. Give the food to the poor! My stars and garters, I'd as soon live on a farm and feed it to the cows and chickens."

William was having difficulty maintaining his grave demeanor. "Speaking of farms," he said judiciously, "didn't you once tell me a story about your brother and his family? I believe they farmed on an estate in Norfolk. I seem to recall something about a year when the crops were bad, and times hard, and the lord of the manor fed and clothed the family until things were better. Or am I mistaken?" he added hurriedly at the look on her face.

"Mistaken or not, 'tisn't the same thing. Those people who live in the Narrows, they court their poverty, and well I know it. Just waitin' for people like us to give them a handout."

William shrugged. "Perhaps they once worked for a master who was not as kind as your brother's when the crops failed."

"Well I never!" she huffed, crossing her arms with such

force that her breath escaped in a rush. "I can see she's turned your mind against us and there's to be no help from you."

"If you ever need my help, Cook, you know you need only ask."

"Hummmph!" In a swish of skirts she turned away, but as she went, the outrage faded from her eyes. By the time she reached the haven of her kitchen, she was looking thoughtful.

William watched her go, no longer able to restrain his smile. Then he heard a sound from the sitting room and stopped, frozen in disbelief. Was it really laughter? He hurried forward, dropping his case and papers onto the table in the hall. They slid to the floor in his wake, but he did not stop to pick them up. He paused in the doorway of the sitting room.

Ailsa and Lizzie were dragging forward a large brass sculpture of cupids draped about a woman's naked body, though wings and leaves and berries carefully placed covered the immodest areas. The leaves were painted vivid green and the berries purple, the cupids' hair was yellow, while the bows in their hands were blood red.

"Oh, how I've always hated this thing. I'm glad to see you gettin' it out of the house at last." Lizzie gasped and blushed scarlet when she saw William in the doorway. "Forgive me, sir. I didn't mean any disrespect, truly."

"No," William said with a wry twist of his lips. "I'm sure you didn't." While the maid crouched on the floor, afraid to move, he looked around him curiously.

The heavy green brocade drapes had been removed along with the light green tassels, leaving only the fringed muslin beneath. The thinner curtains had been looped back and the light they allowed to filter through the windows revealed a room startlingly unfamiliar. The green-papered walls were the same, but the furniture had been moved about and many of the shelves, plant stands, and tables removed completely. The marble mantel, once cluttered with cases and figurines of all shapes and sizes, held only an ormolu clock in the center, a miniature of his dead parents, and a photograph of his Aunt Abigail on one side, on the other a

237

likeness of William on the day he'd been called to the bar. He glanced at the patterned rug of forest green, light green, and yellow leaves twined together. It was quite pretty really, but he'd never noticed it beneath all the objects that filled the room.

Ailsa swallowed nervously. William had told her once to make the house hers, but what would he say now that he realized how far she had gone? "Well?" she asked when she could bear the suspense no longer. "What do ye think?"

"To be scrupulously honest," he said slowly, "I've never liked that statue either. My aunt's taste, while impeccable, does not, unfortunately, always agree with mine." He saw his wife watching him anxiously and grinned at her. "As for the rest of the room, I always thought it rather too close and dark and—well, green. Upon crossing the threshold, one was inclined to feel lost in a gloomy forest out of which a chap might never find his way. I think what you've done is delightful."

"Ye're no' angry, then?" Ailsa asked. Her voice shook, but he noticed her arms were crossed and there was a determined set to her jaw. She was ready to do battle if necessary.

Only then did it strike him that she was wearing her wedding gown with no crinoline beneath. Her bare feet were crossed in front of her on the floor. Her hair hung down her back, but many strands had come loose and strayed over her cheeks and down her slim throat. "You look very lovely," he told her. Then, right in front of Lizzie, he drew his wife to her feet, took her in his arms, and kissed her. "Not only am I not angry, but in point of fact," he murmured, "I have never been happier."

Ailsa smiled back at him. "Your aunt will no' like it and Cook is complainin'."

"Let them suffer for a while. They'll get used to it in the end. They'll have to, won't they?"

"Ye're daft, William Sinclair," Ailsa whispered with affection. "Ye'll be arguin' and explainin' day and night about your wee mad wife."

"I think I shall enjoy that very much," he said. Then, for the first time in twenty-five years, he threw back his head and laughed aloud.

18

The month before Ailsa's child was to be born was cold, cloaked in rain and fog that never seemed to lift. But as William explained, it was January in London and nothing could be done about the ghastly weather.

Ailsa did not mind as much as she might have, for she was busy making clothes for the child. She had finished her own new wardrobe a month earlier, with Lizzie's help and the assistance of a seamstress who came in twice a week. Ailsa had chosen simple colors, blues and lilacs, grays and greens, that complemented her eyes. Though her gowns had wide skirts, there were few ruffles and little lace. She had discarded her corsets and crinolines long since, as well as her button-top boots. At home, she never wore shoes, but when she went out, she would slip on the soft leather boots William had had made for her, or velvet slippers that caressed her feet instead of punishing them.

"I can't get over it," Lizzie said as they worked in the sitting room one morning with the pale light from the window falling between them. "You have the courage of all the simperin' ladies in London put together. I only wish I had half as much."

Ailsa smiled mysteriously. "Ye'd be surprised what ye can do when ye have to." She worked her needle in and out of the tiny cambric gown she was making, humming to herself. A song had been running through her head for the past three days. She'd tried many times to capture it, but knew something was missing. Then she remembered the windblown woods and the poignant cry of the lapwing. She tried the song again, humming with more certainty.

"Why, that's lovely, ma'am!" Lizzie exclaimed. "Did you make it up yourself?"

"Aye," Ailsa answered. The music had come back to her.

That night she sat in bed, a shawl around her shoulders, sewing by the light of an oil lamp while William read beside her. Ailsa closed her eyes and listened to the murmur of night that came when all other sound had ceased. She sensed a movement and looked up to find her husband watching her. "She's restless tonight," she said, hand on her belly.

William frowned. His wife always referred to the unborn child as "she." "How can you be so certain it will be a girl?"

"I just know, 'tis all." She glanced at him in concern as a new thought struck her. "Will ye mind that 'tis no' a boy?"

"You could give me girls one after another for the rest of your life and I'd be happy."

Ailsa went back to her handwork and William to his papers. When her eyes began to droop and the needle fell from her fingers, her husband took the gown and placed it on the bedside table. Then he put aside his own work, turned down the lamp, and drew Ailsa into his arms. She smiled and snuggled closer. In another moment she was asleep.

She was running through the Highland mist, warm, happy, safe, when the mist turned to rain and the rain to a torrent that slashed against the earth, trapping her so she dared not move. She woke up shivering, thinking of Ian.

In the morning, she was more weary than when she had gone to bed, and the following night it was the same. She dreamed that Ian was running, always running from a darkness he could not escape. When he turned, it was before him; when he fled, it was behind. When he climbed, it was above him in the air, in the wind, in the bare woven branches of bleak winter trees.

Ailsa awakened, shaking with cold yet covered in sweat. She tried to lie still, but William woke and bent over her.

"Did you have a bad dream?" he asked. He ran his fingers over her cheek, tucked a stray hair behind her ear.

She shivered and he pulled her close. "It was only a dream. Try to forget it and go back to sleep."

"Aye," she whispered, "I will." But she could not forget.

Several times William awakened to find her shaking. Finally he said, "No doubt the baby is giving you trouble." He put his hand on her belly gently, afraid to disturb her or the child. "Would you sleep more peacefully if I left you alone?"

"Och, no!" she cried. "Just hold me. Your warmth gives me comfort."

William closed his eyes. To hear her say she needed him meant so much. He would never get used to having her beside him, never cease to wonder how it had come to be or to fear that it would end. "I'll stay," he told her, "as long as you want me."

The next morning Dr. Holloway came to call. "I'm concerned about you, don't you know," he said, noticing Ailsa's pallor and the shadows around her eyes. "You may have problems with this birth if you don't take more care. And rest."

Ailsa took a deep breath. "I don't suppose 'twould be wise to travel just now?"

He stared at her in horror. "Good God, young woman, do you want to risk your life and the baby's as well? No, you must stay right here until after the birth. Then perhaps a holiday in the country would not come amiss." His voice was pleasant but there was a thread of steel in his tone that told her he would keep her here by force if it came to that.

She clasped her hands in agitation. She was certain Ian was in trouble but she could not go to him as he had come to her. She paced the floor, aching, afraid, knowing there was nothing she could do. Never in her life had she felt so helpless.

One starless night she turned and turned in her sleep, twisting the blankets until their weight became unbearable. She was walking in the forest with Ian, but he was wrapped in his pain and moved ahead, so she could not see his face.

241

Surprisingly, he began to sing; his voice rose through the trees, through the mist, through the wind to the top of the sky.

> "Look, flowers their lovely petals shed
> At close of day and soon are dead,
> Scattered along the roseate bed
> On wretched stalk that hangs its head.
> O LOVE, MY HEART, choose life instead!"

He looked back pleadingly, but she did not know what he wanted of her. When she did not answer, he stood at the edge of the river and stared at the water that swirled threateningly at his feet. Ian leaned forward, drawn by the force and fury of the torrent. Ailsa cried out, but he did not hear. He fell forward, caught up in a whirlpool of darkness that sucked him down, down, down, until he rose no more.

Ian lay awake, the scent of heather in the air. He could not sleep, had not slept, in fact, for many nights. He could feel the shadow follow him everywhere, feel the desperation growing, the frustration, the uncertainty.

He thought of Ailsa and her husband in their drawing room, Ailsa at the harp, William in the overstuffed chair nearby, listening, eyes closed, while his wife played to him. Ian groaned. Mairi had been right when she said he risked much by going to London. Now that he had seen Ailsa's home, her husband, her world, it had become real to him. Once it had been a nightmare without substance; now it was a certainty, a pain that never left him. He had once thought he feared nothing—nothing but shadows and the memories cloaked within them.

Earlier that day Jenny Mackensie had come by, as she did so often of late. He had watched her talk softly of unimportant things. She bent over her sewing and never looked his way, as if she might surprise a look of sorrow on his face. She did not want to laugh at his pain, but to ease it. Today he had seen a single teardrop fall onto the plaid skirt she was finishing. The expression on her face when she glanced up had hit him like a stone in the chest. He realized then that it was not out of pity that she came each day, listened to his melancholy silence, bore his frowns and his unpleasant moods. It was out of love.

In that instant, he understood—as Ailsa had understood on Beltaine—that Jenny loved him, that she was suffering, too, because she could not find a way to reach him. The knowledge only deepened his despair. He could not go on this way while everyone lived their silent agony for his sake. Poor Jenny, poor Mairi, alone in her empty croft, poor Ian, grown a stranger to himself and to his family.

He rose abruptly. In the half darkness he could see the Chisholm plaid and claymore above the door. Their presence was a pale defiance of an enemy long gone. The men who had owned those things had fought, failed, lost everything for what that plaid and sword represented—their country, their heritage, their families, their homes. Far luckier were those who had died, whose souls had become part of the mountains, whose spirits wandered the glens and burns and hills they loved. Mairi's warning echoed in his head: *To lose your life is one thing, Ian-mo-run, to lose your hope another. There's peace in death, but only unendin' sorrow in hopelessness.* It struck him then with the force of a blow that he was one of the living dead.

All at once, he knew what he had to do.

He went through night and cold and a thin layer of snow to the mountainside he had visited often in the past seven months. He climbed slowly, a step at a time, finding his way by feel instead of sight to the precipice that had been Ailsa's special place. When he reached the ledge, he stood and opened his mind to her. One last time, he let his soul speak for him, remembering the moments they had shared, the magic and the stillness full of wonder. He relived each minute of their youth until he came at last to that night in the cave when he had made love to her. He conjured her image before him—her eyes like the rippled water of the loch, her hair spread all around her, her face, her mouth, her hands that he knew as well as his own. He pulled the image close until it breathed with the rise and fall of his breath. Then he spoke to her softly:

"Lift me unto the topmost boughs of some tall tree,
Sink me into the coldest waves of the deep sea,
Or set me in the clouds, whatever clouds there be;
Make me by far the farthest of all men from thee."

He looked down at the glen he had known since childhood and the stillness enfolded him, clung to him, beckoned
him. His face covered with tears, he surrendered at last to
that silence.

In Ailsa's dream, the darkness passed and she felt Ian's
hand on her cheek. He was with her, closer now than he had
ever been, so real that she could touch him.

They were lying together on the floor of the cave with
the chill of early May upon them. She could feel his warmth,
the pressure of his lips on hers, the moist insistence of his
seeking tongue. He kissed her again and again, gently at
first, then more and more fiercely, so that she trembled and
sighed in her sleep.

She felt the touch of his callused palm on hers, his
fingers on her naked body, saw his secret smile. His passion
burst into flames that consumed her until she threw back her
head and reveled in her blazing body.

Her dream was memory but the memory was sharp and
clear; Ian was real, his hands, his lips, his tousled hair, his
captivating eyes were real. He was so close that she was
certain if she awoke he would be beside her. But she did not
awaken, did not dare open her eyes, as if she knew that
when the dream came to an end, she would lose everything
she held dear. So she slept through the night, reliving each
moment of her life with him from the first time they had
swum together, naked babies tumbling in the water, to their
walks through the glen, to the music they shared, to the
meeting of their palms and their first kiss. Always Ian was
with her, beside her, inside her. He was her.

When Ailsa awoke in the morning, for the first time in
weeks she felt no sense of frustration or despair or pain.
What she felt was not peace, but a lack of turmoil—silence,
nothingness. She felt empty, as if a vital part of her had

slipped away during the night. She rose up on her elbows, terrified. Had she somehow lost her child?

Then she touched her belly and felt the baby move within her. She turned, afraid the bed would be empty, but William lay beside her, sleeping soundly, his breath warm on her shoulder.

At last, closing her eyes, she concentrated, trying to see Ian's face, but the image would not come. Then and only then did she understand the emptiness. She sat up, too stunned to shiver or cry out or weep. This was a stillness that would go on forever, a silence that would never lift from around her heart.

She did not need to see Ian's broken body to know that he was dead.

19

For six days Ailsa moved awkwardly through the house on Larkspur Crescent. She spoke to Cook about the meals, worked with Lizzie to ready the nursery, finished the clothes she was making for the child. She was cold and aching and empty, but she tried to hide that from the others. More than once she started to tell her husband of her grief, but she knew if William saw how deep her sorrow went, it would only hurt him, and she had already hurt him enough. So she carried the secret inside and waited.

"You seem so tired this past week, as if you can hardly lift your feet," Lizzie said one morning. They sat in rocking chairs by the window in the nursery, sewing. The thin muslin curtains were open, revealing a sky half-hidden by fog, though an occasional ray of sunlight penetrated the haze and touched their faces, bent in concentration over their work.

"Aye," Ailsa murmured. "I'm sore tired, 'tis all."

Lizzie frowned. She did not like the glazed look in her mistress's eyes. The maid could not explain why, but she sensed that Ailsa's exhaustion was a weariness of spirit, not of body. "The doctor says it's often that way, especially the first time, and with you so young and all. He said you should sit and rest as much as you can, though I told him he'd sooner see Abigail Fieldin' kickin' up her legs in a Scottish reel."

Ailsa heard what Lizzie said, but with only half her mind. The other half was listening for a strange footstep at the door, an unknown face at the window. She knew her mother would write to tell her what had happened. She needed that letter, that physical proof of what her heart had long been certain.

Lizzie raised her head at the sound of a distant bell. "There's Cook again. Probably needs someone to tie her apron in a proper bow and poor Martha's hands are already worn down to the bone." She grinned wickedly and added under her breath, "Not her job, you know, dressin' herself. 'What's a maid for,' she asks me, 'if not to be seein' to the details that make everyone else more comfortable?' I'd tell her what I think of her, but I'm afraid she'd put a bit of arsenic in my plum puddin'."

The bell jangled again and Ailsa listened, suddenly intent. Her throat grew tight and she started when Lizzie rose.

"I'd best go see to that."

Ailsa sat, hands clasped—still, contained, cold—her heart beating in a slow and labored rhythm. Time stopped, held frozen on the watery January morning like motes of dust that ceased their movement in the single ray of sunlight through the window.

Lizzie reappeared, flushed with excitement, holding an envelope in her hand. "It's a letter all the way from Scotland. Imagine! That's your first, isn't it?"

Her mistress did not hear a word. She held out her hand and Lizzie dropped the envelope into it. Ailsa felt ill. She closed her eyes and swallowed while the letter slid into her lap.

"Are you all right, ma'am?" Lizzie gasped. "You look like you've seen an army of ghosts, indeed you do."

"No," Ailsa said in a strange, distant voice. "Only one."

But she was not looking at the maid. She gazed instead at the carved mantel she'd had done for the child. Along the wide edge were deer, larks and red squirrels, lapwings and rabbits and tiny foxes—all the animals she had known in her own childhood. She stared at the figures, so lifelike and yet so false.

Lizzie gulped. The letter must mean bad news. "Shall I leave you alone, ma'am?" she whispered.

"Aye."

For a long time, Ailsa sat with the folded parchment in her lap. She could not make herself reach for it and break the seal. She realized she did not want to see in black and white the words that would deprive her of half her soul.

Outside, the clouds shifted, allowing a wider shaft of sunlight through. It fell across the floor, making the green-patterned rug glow. Slowly, as if her hands were aged and cramped with pain, she lifted the letter, turned it over, and slipped her finger under the seal. She unfolded the edge, spread it carefully over her knee, afraid a single wrinkle would distort the message, make it somehow incomplete.

She stared at the letters in their untidy rows without comprehending their meaning. Slowly, the words became real.

Ailsa-*mo-aghray*,

When last ye saw Ian Fraser, he told me ye said he should marry. In a month, he will take Jenny Mackensie to wife. She has loved him long and without hope, till now. She will make him a faithful and comfortin' companion. Try to be happy for him. Try to understand as he once tried to do for ye. Ye owe him that much, my birdeen, my heart.

Mairi

Ailsa gasped, unable to understand. Ian to be married? He was not dead? Then why did she feel such emptiness, such overwhelming sorrow, if he still lived?

It came to her slowly, as the fog covered the sun, drifted away and back again, casting her face first in light then in shadow. The turmoil she had felt night after night had been Ian's attempt to make a difficult decision. The silence had come when he made his choice.

Her heart sank, heavy and leaden within her. He was not dead; he had simply closed his mind to her. He had reached out that night in her dream, taken her back through the days of their past, then cut forever the thread that bound them. She clasped her upper arms and leaned forward, keening silently at the pain that assaulted her.

Ailsa sat with the silver drift of fog reflected in her

eyes—pale, empty, utterly alone in a way she had never thought to be. She bent double but the pain would not ease.

Lizzie appeared then out of nowhere. "You look like you need a drink of brandy." She offered a snifter of amber liquid. When Ailsa continued to stare at her blankly, the maid took her mistress's hands and cupped them around the glass. "Drink," Lizzie insisted. "It'll make you feel better."

Ailsa swallowed the liquor, gasped when it burned its way down her throat. But still she did not speak.

Lizzie indicated the letter, which had fallen to the floor at her feet. "Is someone dead?" she asked gently. "Is that it?"

Ailsa looked away, brow furrowed. "No," she said. Odd—and strangely cruel—but the news of Ian's death would have hurt her less than this purposeful breaking of the bond between them. To know that he was alive but beyond her reach was a sorrow without hope, without meaning. In the shadows, in the light, in the mist, in the mountains, even in the soot-sodden London streets, Ian had always been there. She turned to the maid and said stiffly, " 'Tis only that a friend of my heart is to be married."

Lizzie frowned and remembered a tall, Scottish man with black hair and green eyes who had lifted the burden of sorrow form her mistress's shoulders in less than a day. "Married? Then you should be glad for him. Unless—" She broke off, flushing when she realized the implications of her mistress's pallor. "Do you mean he is—was—" She broke off, unable to continue.

"He was my friend," Ailsa repeated. "He knew me all my life, better than anyone ever can. But now he's shut me out. I can't reach him anymore." She cried silently, without words or tears, while darkness descended around and within her.

Lizzie realized she had been wrong to doubt her mistress. Ailsa would never be unfaithful to her husband. It was not in her to betray someone she loved. But still, she looked so pale, so shaken. "I'm sorry," the maid said.

Ailsa nodded and looked into Lizzie's eyes. There were no secrets there, no shadows. No doubt she had loved many people in her life, but never had she shared with another this extraordinary sensitivity, this understanding beyond understanding, so she could not know the pain of losing it. *Ye are me.* Ian had whispered once. *Without me there is no ye and without ye there is no me.*

When she left Scotland, then again when Ian left London, she thought she had felt his loss. But those times had been unreal, half-lived. *Together we are all and everythin'. Apart we are half-finished, nothin' but shadows.* The gods forgive her, but it was true, and the truth was more than she could bear.

Ailsa gripped Lizzie's hand so tightly that the maid winced. She felt she should say something more, something to force a spark of life into those blind and staring eyes. "Why did he have to shut you out?" she asked without thinking.

Ailsa bit her lip. Why *had* he done it? "Because he's a good and honest man," she said at last. " 'Twas the only way he could be fair to his wife. 'Twouldn't have been right to marry her when half his mind and dreams were still with me." Her hands shook when she met Lizzie's gaze and realized what she was saying. Ian would be fair to Jenny as Ailsa had not been to William. She had chosen to marry one man, but had not been willing to give up the other. She looked away to hide her shame.

"Why did you marry Mr. Sinclair?" Lizzie asked curiously.

Ailsa remembered how he had spoken of London and the spell of her music, how he had stood in the hall and turned to her, how his frown had turned to a delighted smile. Then she remembered, brightest and most vivid of all, hearing her father's voice on the ledge: *Come to me, Ailsa. Forgive me and come to me. I need you.* Why? she demanded without making a sound. Why did you bring me here? She saw then, in a cold, clear flash of understanding, that she had not heard her father's voice that day. She had heard the voice of her own dreams, conjured out of her imagination, because she wanted so much for Charles Kittridge to need her. As William needed her now.

"When I married my husband, I was runnin' away from what I knew, from a fear I couldn't even name, runnin'

250

toward a dream I had created in my mind that never really existed." She looked directly into the girl's eyes and squeezed her hand in a kind of plea. "But ye must know this. I wouldn't ever betray William, Lizzie. I care for him very deeply. Can ye understand that?"

"I can try."

"Thank ye," Ailsa said softly.

"It's all I can do for you, ma'am. Believe in you, I mean. And it's not enough."

" 'Tis enough," Ailsa assured her, "to know I have a friend."

When Lizzie had gone, she sat rocking slowly in her chair. Suddenly she leaned forward, crying fiercely, "Damn ye, Ian Fraser. If I'd never known ye, then I wouldn't know such sorrow now." But neither would she have known the joy, which was as deep, as far beyond words as the pain. What was it she had said to William once? *How could ye know what a miracle sunlight on water is if ye hadn't also known the darkness?*

The baby kicked out, making her gasp in surprise. The child was feeling her mother's anguish, sharing her pain; the blood of Ailsa's body pulsed through the baby, too. That blood must not be tainted with grieving as Mairi's had been.

Ailsa caressed her swollen belly, speaking soft Gaelic words full of the sound and rhythm of the hills. *Don't keep the magic of the glen from her,* Ian had said. *Give her your music,* mo-charaid. *'Twill make ye happy, too.* Ailsa closed her eyes and drew a song from her distant memory.

"O lay me by the streams that glide,
With gentle murmurs soft and slow,
Let spreadin' bows my temples hide;
Thou sun, thy kindest beams bestow."

Ailsa was carried back to her childhood when Mairi used to hold her daughter on her lap and croon the familiar song.

"And be a bank of flow'rs my bed,
My feet laved by a wanderin' rill:

Ye winds, breathe gently round my head
Bear balm from wood and vale and hill.''

The child grew still, calmed by the tranquil flow of the music. Ailsa saw that as she sang the fog had burned away completely and the sun reached out to fill a pale blue sky. She felt a strange warmth on her skin and sensed that though she had been desperately alone a moment since, she was not alone now. She looked up, puzzled, and saw the indistinct figures of two young women that wavered in the too bright light. One was dark, a foreigner with straight black hair, the other a mere wisp of a girl with pale hair and blue eyes flecked with gray.

They reached out to her with compassion and tenderness, as if they understood her sorrow because they, too, had suffered. She felt a deep bond with these strangers; in a way she did not understand, she had always known them and been part of them. Then, as quickly as they had appeared, the apparitions were gone. They left behind a fleeting scent of exotic places, a memory too impalpable to grasp, and a comfort that began to lift the shadow of Ailsa's grief from around her heart. She knew then that she had never been truly alone and never would be again, though even that certainty was inexplicable. It came to her in the wake of her vision that, day by day, the light would shine more brightly, diminishing the darkness inside until it was no more. But the emptiness, the sense of loss would never leave her.

She heard a sound and looked up to see that William had come in. With an effort, she smiled, at first tentatively, then with fondness. "What are ye doin' here in the middle of the day?"

Her husband grinned sheepishly. "I thought of how you looked this morning, sleeping with your hair spread on the pillow, and suddenly I couldn't wait to see you again. I'm sorry if I'm disturbing you.''

"No," she said, and meant it. "I'm glad ye came." She winced when the baby kicked again.

"What is it?" he asked in concern.

" 'Tis nothin' to fret about. 'Twas only that the bairn

252

moved within me.'' She took his hand and placed it on her stomach. ''Feel how she leaps like a wild bird cryin' to be free.''

He felt a kick, drew back, startled, then leaning closer, he listened until he swore he could hear the beat of the baby's heart. He looked up at Ailsa with pride and warmth in his eyes.

''Thank ye,'' she murmured.

''For what?''

She touched his temple, then his lips. ''For bein' the man ye are, William Sinclair.''

— ◦ 20 ◦ —

One evening, four months after the birth of Alanna, Ailsa and William's first child, a small group of people gathered in the Sinclair drawing room. Phillip and Anne Kendall, as well as Giles Saunders, had come early for a simple meal of barley soup, roast beef and potatoes, with black buns for dessert.

"Always a pleasure to dine with the Sinclairs," Giles remarked, patting his stomach as he leaned back in his chair. "Nice to be able to see what one's eating, don't you know. Here one doesn't need to fish through oceans of sauce to discover what might be hidden in the depths." He grinned devilishly. "And once a chap does find whatever it is, more often than not he'd just as soon throw it back into the sea."

The small group doubled in size as they moved to the drawing room where they were joined by Anthony and Maude Steel, David Finney, Lau ⸻ ⸺rand. Finally, Robbie Douglas arrived, disheveled, his waistcoat unbuttoned and cravat forgotten, as usual. He sank with a sigh of relief into a wing-backed chair. He took the snifter of brandy William offered and downed it in a swallow. " 'Tis grateful to ye I am," he declared in his ringing voice. "To both of ye. More grateful than ye can know, for makin' a haven in this unfriendly city. Without your house to come to on a cold ni⸺t, where would devils like me find peace?"

Ailsa flushed with pleasure while Anthony Steel nodded his agreement. "He's right, you know. Why just last evening, Maude and I spent a wretched couple of hours at Lady Worthington's. Everyone spoke in whispers, seemed to me. I wanted to laugh aloud, just to see what would happen. But I could practically feel the chill of their disapproval at even

254

thinking such a thing, and I knew I was coming here tonight, so I behaved myself. I shall not be so inclined this evening.''

''Oh dear!'' Maude, with her fair hair and skin, exclaimed. ''I shudder to think of the consequences.'' But she was smiling. They all were. She, like Laura and Anne, had discarded her gloves and fans, so useful for disguising one's expression. Such subterfuge was not necessary here.

The soft light from the candles and a single paraffin lamp—Ailsa rarely lit the chandelier, preferring the intimacy of smaller, flickering lights—gave a mellow glow to the room, emptied now of the paraphernalia that had once disguised its charm. The women in their wide-skirted gowns seemed less rigid, as if the candlelight had melted the stays in their corsets, the bones in their crinolines, so they could laugh and breathe again. The men had discarded their coats, revealing brocade and satin waistcoats; Anthony and David had untied their cravats and leaned back comfortably on the sofa and settee.

Phillip Kendall and Giles Saunders, however, sat across from each other, faces flushed, arguing heatedly, as was their wont. ''I say it can't be done through the factory owners. If we want to help the poor, we've got to legislate! Those greedy bastards—excuse me, Mrs. Sinclair—won't give an inch and well you know it!'' Phillip shouted.

''I don't see that you've given them half a chance,'' Giles sputtered. ''You and your kind haven't got the patience—''

''The poor haven't the patience either,'' Ailsa interrupted. ''No' when they're starvin'. 'Tis hard to wait at such a time.''

William did not interfere. He knew his wife could hold her own in any argument. He was content merely to watch and listen.

''Hoots!'' Robbie Douglas proclaimed, pounding his fist on the nearest table. ''Be damned to your politics. I've come to enjoy myself, no' listen to your blatherin' all the night. Come, Ailsa, birdeen, let's have a little music, shall we?'' He took his fiddle from its case and held it out in invitation.

''Oh yes, let's do!'' Maude agreed. ''I so enjoy the songs you and Robbie play together. Not at all like the stuffy things we listened to at Lady Worthington's.''

"Suffered through is more like it," her husband interjected. "Dreadfully dull. Meant to put one to sleep, I suppose, so one is sure to go home early. Do play, my dear.
We've been so longing to hear you."

Robbie made himself comfortable by the fireplace with
one foot on a low stool while Ailsa took her flute from her
pocket and seated herself on a spindle-legged chair nearby.
They began to play a slow, mellow tune at first, that flickered
with the motion of the candlelight. Laura and Maude sighed
with pleasure and closed their eyes, as did William. Then
Robbie began to tap his foot and move his bow more quickly
over the strings. Ailsa instinctively picked up the new, lively
rhythm.

Before her husband could object, Anne Kendall took
his hand and drew him into the center of the room to dance.
Giles Saunders joined them, dipping and bowing with exag-
gerated courtesy to an imaginary partner. Everyone began
to laugh.

The laughter mingled with the notes of flute and fiddle,
which rose, filling the room, the house, the foggy night
beyond the windows. Anthony and Maude began to dance,
moving with care around Giles's invisible lady friend. "Pardon me, madam," Anthony intoned when he tread on the
lady's nonexistent foot. "If only your partner weren't such
a clod, this might never have happened. Permit me to show
you how real dancing is done." With a humorous glower and
a flourish, Giles relinquished his partner to Anthony and
whirled off with Maude in his arms.

"Oh dear!" Phillip exclaimed in distress to the air
Anthony clutched in his arms as if it were a lovely, fragile
creature. "I believe I've torn the hem of your gown. But
don't concern yourself overmuch. My wife will repair the
damage."

Anne Kendall collapsed on the sofa, laughing, while the
others cavorted like children let out of the nursery for the
first time. William joined in the laughter with enthusiasm.
He glanced at his wife fondly. She had given him much more
than the gift of laughter; she had given him these people as
well. They had come out of curiosity at first, having heard
of her reputation for doing the unexpected and unacceptable.

Once they met her, her warmth and openness had brought them back time and again. She swayed now as she cradled her rosewood flute with graceful fingers. He smiled in gratitude as she played a blessing over himself and their friends.

William awoke later that night to find his wife was not beside him. The covers had been thrown back as if she had hurried from the room. His heart began to beat unsteadily. Perhaps there was something wrong with Alanna. He rose and went down the hall to the nursery. Ailsa had refused to have it on the third floor, no matter that his aunt insisted it was where the nursery was in every good English home. Ailsa had shaken her head firmly, explaining that she would be near her child, not a long narrow staircase away. She had laughed with William later. "If your aunt doesn't know by now that we don't have a 'good English home,' then she hasn't been lookin' very close."

William was breathing heavily by the time he reached the nursery. The door was ajar and he glanced inside. The nurse was nowhere to be seen; no doubt his wife had sent her to bed, as she often did, and seen to the baby's needs herself.

Ailsa was seated on the floor, her legs crossed in front of her, her bare feet peeking from beneath the plain wool nightgown she chose to wear (when she wore one at all, he thought, flushing at his own boldness). Her hair fell loose around her.

She held the baby in her lap and the firelight moved over them caressingly. His wife's head was bent toward Alanna. She spoke softly, changing from the Gaelic to English and back again as if the child could understand the sounds that were part song, part legend, part soft crooning like the sigh of wind in tall silver birch trees.

Inexplicably, William felt tears burn his eyes. He moved into the room and closed the door behind him. Absorbed in her story, Ailsa did not know he was there until she felt the gentle touch of his fingers in her hair.

He folded his legs beneath him and sat next to her on the floor so he could breathe in the scent of her hair and see Alanna's face, flushed and glowing with firelight.

257

Ailsa fell silent and William leaned over to kiss his wife's temple. He brushed her hair away, catching his fingers in the strands. She smiled and moved closer. She was glad he had come.

The birth of her child had done much to ease the slow throb of pain inside her. The baby gave her pleasure merely by sleeping, smiling, listening raptly to her mother's rambling stories. Ailsa loved her with all the fierce devotion that had once belonged to another.

William slid his arms around his wife and she rested her head on his chest. She gazed at the room for a moment, her eyes misted. She had tried to re-create the feeling of her childhood here; the edge of the mantel was carved with lifelike animals and the top covered with tiny glass and porcelain birds, many with wings poised, ready for flight. The furniture—two rocking chairs, a chest by the wall, a crib—was made of natural oak rubbed smooth by many hands. The rug was pale green, like the grass on the moors in springtime, and the soft wool blanket in the crib was the color of heather that covered the hillsides. William had commissioned an artist to paint tall swaying trees, clouds, and gentle rolling hills on the walls. The one thing that was completely English was the harp Ailsa had had moved from the drawing room. She felt it belonged here, somehow.

"This is a lovely room, isn't it?" William murmured.

Ailsa smiled. It was not the first time he had read her thoughts of late. "Aye, lovely."

Suddenly her husband drew away. "Sing to me, Ailsa."

He had never asked that of her before. "What would ye hear?"

"One of the strange Gaelic songs you sing to Alanna."

Ailsa was touched. "Ye'll have to hold the bairn."

"I can manage," he said. Though he was nervous, he took the baby, staring in wonder at her face, her tiny hands that flailed in the air as he cradled her. She is beautiful, he thought, a constriction in his throat. As beautiful as her mother.

Deprived of the warmth of Ailsa's lap, Alanna became restless. She screwed up her face, then blew out her breath in warning. Her father held her closer, spoke to her softly, as he had seen his wife do. He turned when Ailsa took the harp on her shoulder and began to run her fingers over the strings. All at once, the room was filled with soft wisps of song that wove a thin veil of music. Ailsa smiled to herself, recalling how she had once told Ian that the world beyond the glen held beauty and elegance; he had replied that there was nothing but ugliness, filth, and suffering. In a way, they had both been right. Beyond these walls, a few streets away was the suffering Ian had spoken of, the dirt and poverty and hunger. But this room, just now, was full of grace and beauty and warmth. Ailsa began to sing.

> *"O Sweet! Sweet! Sweet!* long-drawn devout delight,
> My ransomed love, condign and recondite!
>
> It dawns. Slowly, that golden gemmuled rose,
> Whose saffron leaves transparently unclose.
> A tree is now, and its wide branches spread,
> In transfused beams, transfigurèd."

William let the music wash over him, reminding him of the first Scottish dawn he had ever seen, when the colors had whirled through the sky to make the landscape brilliant and frightening in its tinted magnificence. Out of that same pearly dawn, he had first seen Ailsa running, a spirit made of pink and lilac mist.

> "Beneath its boughs, like blissful seraphs stand,
> A multitude of lovers hand-in-hand
> And breast-to-breast. Ah me! how sweet! how sweet!
> To fall or kneel or lie before her feet
> As these do."

Alanna had grown quiet, lulled by the soft, flowing sound of her mother's song. Grasping her father's open shirtfront, she closed her eyes.

> "Now hath heaven to earth descended,
> And cloud and clay and stone and star are blended."

Smiling with unshed tears, Ailsa remembered that she had last sung those words on Beltaine when she had leaped the fire and hovered, palm to palm, with Ian over the glorious flames.

"There is no worldly atom but doth glow,
This pavement and th' ungarnished ramparts show
As do the fretted, star-strewn roofs above,
Such luster and transcendency hath LOVE."

She looked up to find William watching, his face full of love. She smiled at him, at the child in his arms. Suddenly Alanna reached up to tug on her father's sideburns.

He laughed without trying to disengage her groping fingers. "You can pull all you like, but it'll take more than that to frighten me away, little one." The baby gurgled in response and William gasped, astonished, as if she had spoken her first word.

At that moment, Ailsa recalled how Mairi had said that Jenny Mackensie would make Ian a faithful and comforting companion. Mairi, so wise, who saw beyond the limited, unbending vision of others. Her mother had been right, as always. Jenny would be a good wife to Ian, just as William was a good husband to Ailsa.

They came back to her then, those words she had whispered to her friend as he turned to leave her for the last time: *The end of all meetings, parting; the end of all striving, peace.* He had listened, he had heard, he had taken her comfort to heart. He had ceased the struggle, the striving that could bring only pain.

Ian had found his peace, as she had found her own.

Epilogue

In the summer of 1878 the letter arrived. The Sinclair family was sitting at breakfast when Lizzie ran in, her hair flying out from under her cap. She cast an apologetic glance at her husband, the butler Harding, before coming to rest at Ailsa's side. "A letter from Scotland, ma'am. I thought you'd like to see it right away."

In the past twenty years there had not been many such letters. Lizzie remembered all too clearly the first of them and never failed to overreact.

Ailsa took the envelope and glanced across the table at William, who was watching her curiously. His light brown hair had long ago turned a thin, silvery gray that curled about his ears in a way that his wife liked. His face was lined, but subtly, and his gray eyes still sparkled when he looked at her. Ailsa only hoped that she had aged as gracefully.

"Well," nineteen-year-old Alanna said, imitating her mother's Scottish brogue as she always did when anxious or excited. "What does it say? Is't from Grandmother Rose?"

Her sixteen-year-old brother Colin shook his head and rolled his blue-gray eyes heavenward. "No one would ever know you're British to listen to you, Alanna. Honestly, I thought you'd outgrown that habit."

"I hope no'," Ailsa said, smiling fondly at her eldest daughter. "I think 'tis charmin'."

"Well, Mama, of course you do," Cynthia, named after William's long-dead mother, interjected. "You'd be happy if we all talked that way, I'm sure." She straightened the collar of her layered lace gown. Since she had begun to choose her own fabrics and styles, her clothes had become more and more elaborate. Her plain brown hair was looped and curled around her face in the latest fashion, a sharp contrast to Ailsa's crown of braids and Alanna's red curls tied back with a single ribbon.

"Never mind them, Mother," Alanna said impatiently. "Tell us what it says."

Ailsa recognized her mother's handwriting on the envelope. She opened it slowly, remembering, as Lizzie was, the first letter she had received so many years ago.

"Ailsa-*a-graidh*," it began.

Ailsa smiled. The sound of the Gaelic, even on paper, was still like music to her.

How can I tell ye what I sometimes can't believe myself? Your father has at long last returned to the glen. He is old, *mo-run*, and ill. I fear he'll no' be with us for long. He has asked for ye, would see ye once, while he still can.

I know how difficult 'twould be for ye to come back, but 'twould mean all in the world to him. There is much to explain and much to understand, but I would have ye remember this: all who would have all, all would forgive. I wouldn't ask this of ye if I didn't believe 'twould ease your heart as well as his.

As always, it was signed simply, "Mairi."

At the bottom was scrawled in a different hand, "Come to me, Ailsa. Forgive me and come to me. I need you. Charles Kittridge."

Ailsa grew pale when she recognized, even after so many years, the exact words she had heard on the precipice, the plea from her father that had brought her to London. She forced herself to breathe regularly, to ignore the rapid beat of her heart.

"What is it?" William asked, half rising from his chair. "Your mother?"

"No," Ailsa replied. "My father. He's ill and has gone to the glen. He wants me to come to him there."

The three children gasped while William sat down, his face drained of color. "You want to go?" he asked softly.

"I don't know—" Ailsa began.

"Of course ye want to go!" Alanna cried. "How could ye no' when he's asked for ye?"

Ailsa looked up at her daughter, at her violet eyes and red hair, so like her grandmother's. "I've never even known him."

"Then learn to know him now. I want ye to go, Mother. And I want to go with ye."

"To Scotland?" Colin asked, aghast. "Surely not. Everyone knows how wild and dangerous it is up there."

Cynthia shivered. "I've heard they don't even wear shoes. Can you imagine?"

"Perhaps you've forgotten that your mother is Scottish," William reminded the two younger children sharply.

Cynthia blushed and glanced at Ailsa apologetically while Colin stared at his plate.

Ailsa sighed. She had described her home to all her children, told them the old legends, sung them the old songs, even tried to teach them the Gaelic. She had wanted each of them to see the glen through her eyes, to love it as she did. But only Alanna had been willing to learn. It seemed the other two had been English from the day they were born. " 'Tis more beautiful than ye can imagine," she said, forcing Colin to meet her eyes. "Ye can't understand how magnificent 'tis till ye see it once. Mayhap I should take ye, too."

William saw her eyes grow luminous as she spoke. Her smile was so sweet that it hurt him inside.

"Oh no!" Cynthia cried. "You wouldn't make us go, would you?"

"I should simply refuse," Colin said. His tone was calm and perfectly polite, as if that would somehow ease the blow of his defiance.

"I'd go with ye, and gladly," Alanna whispered. "I want to see the hills and moors and the storms that are full of magic."

Ailsa smiled with tears in her eyes. "I think that on all

263

the earth there is only one paradise and 'tis in the Scottish Highlands." She gazed intently at Cynthia and Colin. "Would ye really risk missin' a chance to see paradise?"

She looked up in surprise when her husband pushed back his chair, rose without a word, and left the room. She heard the front door slam behind him. For a long moment, she sat staring, bewildered, at the place where he had been, hoping he might reappear at any moment. But William did not return.

"Once you go back, how could you ever leave such a place?" Alanna mused, speaking without an accent now that she was calmer. She seemed unaware of her father's strange behavior.

"I left it once," Ailsa said. But she wondered if she would have the strength to do so again. That was why she had never gone home in the twenty years since she had left the glen. She feared that the moment she touched the soft earth, she would be caught in the spell of the mist and to free herself would be to destroy her spirit.

Ailsa waited for William's return, wandering barefoot through the house, her hair loose around her shoulders, as if she were a girl again. She heard her husband come in at last and go straight to the study, where he closed the door. Usually that meant he had work to do, and she did not disturb him. But this could wait no longer.

She knocked on the door, heard his brusque response, and entered the room. She saw with a sinking in her stomach that he stood staring out the window at the tree-lined avenue. His back was rigid, unbending. "Well," he said before she could speak, "are you going?"

Ailsa wanted him to turn, wanted to see his eyes, his dear, familiar face. But she sensed that he would not, could not look at her just then. "I want to very much. Ye know how I've wished all my life to meet my father. He says he needs me."

"He never seemed to care before."

There was an ache in her throat. She had thought the same thing many times in the dragging hours of this endless day. But she knew Mairi was right; it was time to forgive a great many things. She had waited a long time to make the shadow of her father into a man of flesh and blood. "What's past is long past. I can't change that. I can only change what is to come. I have to try."

William was silent for so long that she thought he had lost his voice. Then he turned to look at her. He saw her flowing hair, her bare feet beneath the hem of her gown. "You've already gone, haven't you?" he said in a choked voice. "You're already lost among those hills."

His hand shook as he reached back to lean against the windowsill for support. He realized then that all along he'd been ignoring what he knew to be true: Ailsa belonged in the Highlands she loved. For years he had suppressed that knowledge, lied to himself, convinced himself that in time she would forget her past. Now at last he had to face the truth. Time would never change how Ailsa felt; there were not enough years in all eternity to alter a spirit born to the glen. "You won't be coming back, will you?"

She saw that there were tears in his eyes. Ailsa moved toward him, arms outstretched. "Of course I'll come back. This is my home."

He shook his head blindly. "No. This was never your home. Not deep inside where the real Ailsa sleeps. That Ailsa has always longed for Glen Affric, grieved for its loss. Don't you think I know why you've never returned? Once you see the mountains again, you're certain you'll never be able to turn away."

She stared at him in astonishment. How was it that he knew her so well? She had always thought her secret soul was beyond his understanding, a part of her he could not see and did not wish to recognize. She had been wrong. He knew her far better than she had ever known him.

"If you go, I've lost you," William murmured, "to a man you've never even met, just because he's chosen to die in a place that speaks to your heart as London never can."

The sight of her husband's pain took Ailsa's voice from her. She had known that he loved her, that she made him happy, but never, until this moment, had she understood how deep that love went. As deep as her love of the hills and the moors and the dream of her childhood. She found that her cheeks were covered with tears. "Ye'll forbid me, then?"

William shrugged and looked away. "Would it matter if I did?"

"Aye," she said. "Ye are my husband. Ye have never been unkind or unfaithful, ye've shown me every day that ye care for me, ye've been a kind and lovin' father to my bairns. Ye've shown me the whole world, taken me to places I never thought to see and wonders I never thought to feel. Ye've given me everything."

"No," he murmured, "not everything." He *had* given her all that was in his power to give, yet he was powerless, just the same. He could never replace what she had lost. William closed his eyes. He did not want Ailsa's obedience, her faithfulness and gratitude. He wanted the words she had not spoken aloud in all the years of their marriage, though she told him she cared with her hands and eyes and body, which she gave only to him. Why was it not enough?

He clenched his hands into fists. Without Ailsa life would be barren, drained of beauty and light. "Go to your father," he said softly. "As you say, you have waited a long time, and he needs you. Go and be happy."

His wife saw how hard it was for him to speak those words. She saw that he loved her enough to let her go, believing he would lose her, because he thought it was what she wanted. She could never leave him, knowing that.

"I am happy here with ye," she said with complete honesty. She reached up to touch his cheek. "I will go to the glen and stay with my father till he dies. And then, my William, I will come back to ye. This I swear by the sun and by the moon, by flame and wind and water, by the dew and by the twilight that is neither day nor night."

He stared at her, afraid to believe. Yet he knew Ailsa well enough to understand that to her such a vow was sacred. "You'll come back?" he repeated as if he had not heard correctly. "But why?"

"*Mo-charaid,*" she said, calling him by the Gaelic endearment for the first time in twenty years, " 'tis simply because I love ye."

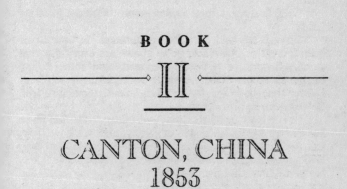

BOOK

II

CANTON, CHINA
1853

Prologue

Slowly, Ke-ming lit the candles, her slender fingers poised for a moment near each flame that rose and wavered in the darkness. As she made her languorous way from sconce to ornate sconce, the lacquered furniture began to gleam until the hidden room seemed less remote from the thriving center of the city. She moved silently, the light shimmering over her embroidered silk gown, and reached out to close the reed curtain. Even in the recesses of these lost corridors, there were prying eyes and lips that spoke heedlessly of things they did not know.

Ke-ming turned, smiled her slow, secret smile, tossed the elaborate hat off her head and, hands extended in a graceful arc, began to glide dreamily, seductively in the ancient courtship dance. There were those, she knew, who did not bother with the enticement, the kindling of the first embers of desire, but to Ke-ming the tantalizing sense of expectation was part of the pleasure of meeting a secret lover.

Charles Kittridge leaned back on the brocade couch, watching the sensuous curves of Ke-ming's body, draped in layers of colored silk that covered but did not conceal the graceful limbs beneath. She swayed and dipped, turned and beckoned with her hands and her legs and her black almond eyes. Her lips were slightly parted with promise, but even that could not make him forget the danger of being discovered where he was forbidden to go. "Have you taken care in coming to meet me?" he asked.

Ke-ming smiled. "You must not concern yourself," she murmured without breaking the rhythm of her dance. "I have lived at the Emperor's court and learned when only a child how to tell the lies they wish to hear." Her voice dipped and turned with the motion of her body. "I have always known how to hide my thoughts and desires from others."

Under the spell of her lilting voice, Charles felt reassured. There was no music, but Ke-ming's garments whispered softly, filled the room with unspoken invitations. Her black hair began to come loose from its confining pins and the long tendrils settled against the golden skin of her neck. She raised her hands before her face so her sleeves fell back; with her fingers she made a pattern in the air, parting them to reveal her half smile, then braiding them together like a woven screen.

She turned and turned again on her tiny bound feet, leaned back so the silk tightened across her chest, emphasizing the swell of her small breasts. Weaving her way over the tiled floor, Ke-ming let her body deliver its intoxicating message to the man who waited breathlessly. She had seen the desire in his eyes and now she sang it back to him, a song without words.

She was a temptress; from the beginning he had been captivated by her beauty and the secrets hidden in her almond eyes. Learned in the arts of love as well as astronomy, politics, and literature, she was a woman unlike any he had ever known. Least of all was she like Mairi, who had been wild and untouched by civilization.

Charles closed his eyes against the image that even Ke-ming's beguiling ritual could not destroy. Why must he always think of Mairi, even after nine long years without her?

"Your thoughts have wandered, my love," Ke-ming whispered. She regarded him pensively. "You are thinking of another who holds you still, though she is far away."

He stared at her in astonishment, though it was not the first time she had read his thoughts. Why was it that she saw so clearly the things he tried to hide?

"But she could not have known the things I know," Ke-ming continued. "She could not have tempted you with the skills I have learned in the Garden of Perfect Brightness.

Therefore, do not leave me for her. Not now when my body calls out for you.''

She pulled the last jade pins from her hair, so it fell over her shoulders, thick, black, and radiant in the fluttering light of the candles. With infinite grace, she knelt and began to stroke his clenched hands. She bent to kiss the sun-browned skin, until the heat of her lips eased the tension and his fingers curled up to cup her face.

"I want you," he murmured. When she smiled, traced his lips with her finger, he pressed her hand to his mouth, breathing into her open palm. His breath caressed her from her fingertips to her slender wrist; she quivered at the feather-light touch. He paused when he felt the cool gleam of the bracelet he had given her. The interwoven bands of white and yellow gold shone like polished moonlight against her burnished skin. She drew in her breath, shivering as he touched his tongue to the tender inside of her elbow, then continued up her arm until the cling of her wide, quilted sleeve stopped his progress.

Ke-ming shook her head so the jade at her ears and throat caught the light and held it captive, just as she held Charles. She had woven a web of desire around him, and although he knew she was using him for some purpose of her own, he did not care. He wanted her because her body and lips and eyes told him she desired him, too. "It is dangerous," she warned teasingly, "to think while your senses are spinning in a whirlpool. Do not wonder, my Charles. Just love me."

She had begun to discard the layers of billowing silk; he reached out to remove the last wispy garment.

Without a word, Ke-ming drew him down beside her as he touched her lips lightly with his. Just as her mouth opened to him, he drew away, trailed his tongue down the line of her throat. Fingers caught in the luxuriant strands of her hair, he circled her shoulders and back until his hands were free of the last silky barrier that kept his fingertips from her naked skin.

She trembled when he drew her closer. Charles flicked his tongue along the hollow in her throat and she moaned at the warmth that spread through her body, reaching even her heart, which once had been unyielding as stone. In the beginning Charles had been only a means to an end; she had come to him to protect those in danger. But that was true no longer. She could not say when the change had come—perhaps that first moment when he had caressed her breasts as he did now, reverently, coaxing a response from deep inside, where no man had touched her before. When he kissed her again, lingeringly this time, he burned away the memory of other hands upon her golden body.

Without the need for words, they rose to make their way to the wide couch. Quickly, he tossed away his clothes; now he lay naked beside her, trailing his fingers over her shoulders, delaying, for a moment more, the meeting of their bodies.

Ke-ming leaned above him, let her hair fall forward so the black hairs twined among the golden, then she reached out to touch the soft curls that covered his chest. He shuddered as her warm breath caressed his face. They kissed, their tongues touching, then entwining.

Ke-ming stretched her body above his and he rolled with her, tangling them in her hair as he cupped her buttocks and entered her fiercely, his control slipping away at last. One hand gripping her shoulder, he rocked with her until she cried out and the darkness inside her fell away for one suspended instant. Then he shuddered, gasping as he crushed her to him. Charles called her name, caressing the sound of the word on his tongue, until his voice was taken from him.

Afterward, they lay silent, while he buried his face in her hair. "You are lovely," he said at last. "I want to—"

"No," she murmured, her voice still husky. "Do not tell me lies. Do not spoil what is already so rare."

Charles shook his head. He had not meant to lie; there was no need. But he was content to hold her, to feel the last trembling of their passion leave her body.

Ke-ming lay with her head on his shoulder, her hand spread on the hair of his chest, and wondered why he should have the power to take her away from this room, this palace, this world of evil.

Then she remembered the other reason that had brought

her here tonight. "Charles," she said, "you must listen to me."

He raised his head but did not move away.

"I heard Governor Kao speak against you yesterday. The Viceroy Yeh will surely listen to him. I believe he will hurt you if he can."

Charles shook his head. "I don't think he would dare."

With a sigh, Ke-ming raised herself on her elbow. "You are a fool, my Charles." She could not hide the hint of fondness in her voice. "But foolish or not, you must take care. It is not only because you are English. There is also trouble for you because of me, is there not?"

"Yes, but it doesn't matter."

Ke-ming smiled, pleased that he had told the truth. It was always so with Charles; there was no pretense between them. He was a man of honor in a court full of deceivers. Sometimes she feared his willingness to believe the best of others would eventually destroy him.

"Don't worry," he told her now. "God will protect me."

"God!" she said, laughing. "I do not believe in God. But I believe in Fate. It is everywhere, shaping the world as it sees fit. Each moment of the future has been ordained long before it comes to pass."

Charles frowned as he wound one finger in a strand of her hair. "You make it sound as if we're helpless puppets," he said. "But we choose our own paths. You of all people must know that."

"I know only that we choose what we must choose, what we are *meant* to choose." A thread of despair ran through her voice.

"You mean it was ordained that I should come to China and fight this battle for England and the Empire?"

Ke-ming looked away to hide her thoughts. "That—and more."

"That I should be here now, with you?"

She smiled at last. "Even that."

Charles laughed and bent to kiss her. She saw there was no shadow of unease to darken his eyes. Was it that which drew her to him? It was certainly not the strength of his body, for she had known many men who could fell him in a single blow. And it could not be his influence with the English king and court, for there were others with much greater power. There were even those who shared his charm, his unfailing ability to choose the right word in an uncomfortable moment. But Charles was not like the others. No man she had ever known had gentler hands—hands that worshiped her and gave her pleasure as he took what he desired. He gave without condition—and without fear.

He had felt deep sorrow, she guessed, but never terror. He still knew nothing of the deceit and cruelty of his fellowman. But Ke-ming knew. And no matter how many times Charles Kittridge held her in his arms, she would never forget. This she had sworn and so it would be, even when, in the soft darkness of the night, she remembered the gentle touch of his hands and the sound of her name, spoken in wonder.

Even when, nine months later, she held his tiny daughter in her arms and knew that, in this single night, he had given her a miracle.

PEKING, CHINA
1872

At dusk when the moon is rippling on the waves,
The cormorant still stands, thinking,
   with one foot in the current . . .
Just so a man, his heart burning with passion
Stares at the undulations of his dream.

—Su Tong Po

1

The sun rose from the lake at the far-eastern edge of the world, rose from the Valley of Light to send a lilac glow through the windows of the House of Wan. Wan Li-an parted the gauze curtains of her rosewood bed and gazed up at the crushed mother-of-pearl that covered the intricate latticework. The light grew brighter, shimmered against the gauze, so the shadows of satin butterflies fluttered over the wrinkled quilt. Li-an loved to watch those shadows, to sit within her curtained world where all was peaceful, safe.

Except, sometimes she felt a restlessness she could not explain. It hovered now at her shoulder, a dragonfly whose wings beat heavily, slowed by the deep chill of winter. A slight breeze rustled the curtains and Li-an felt a change in the air. Perhaps because it was the thirteenth day of the first moon—the first day of the Festival of Lanterns.

Despite the cold, she slipped out of bed and climbed three heavy chests that were placed against the wall. Balanced precariously, she pushed back the latticework that had come loose since the New Year. She could just see the tiny courtyard, drifted with snow that lay like rippled satin on the frozen pond. The bare branches of potted chrysanthemums were covered in thin crystal leaves turned pink by the dawn light. The wind whipped past, rearranging drifts of snow, touching the tips of the dwarf pines with white, swirling through the snowbound garden in pale purple swathes. The feeling of motion and confusion pleased Li-an.

She inhaled the fresh, cold air and remembered the words of the poet Li Po, long dead.

The reed-blind is rolled high and I gaze
  at the beautiful, glittering, primeval snow,
Whitening the distance, confusing the stone steps
  and the courtyard.
The air is filled with its shining; it blows far out
  like the smoke of a furnace.
The grass blades are cold and white,
  like jade girdle pendants.
Surely the Immortals in Heaven must be crazy with wine
  to cause such disorder,
Seizing the white clouds, crumpling them up,
  destroying them.

Li-an let the latticework fall back into place. As she climbed down, she noticed her ivory-backed mirror lying on the lacquered chest beside the bed. Enveloped by pearly light, she picked it up to stare intently at her reflection in the clear, round surface. Her face was pale and oval, her eyebrows like delicate moth wings, her skin smooth and golden. Her black hair, parted in the center and loosely woven down her back, fell heavy and luxuriant to her waist. She could see much of her mother in the mirror, though Wan Ke-ming was more beautiful, her expression more serene. And Li-an's eyes, which should have been soft black, instead were startling blue. Her eyes alone betrayed her English blood, the rest of her face her Chinese heart.

Silently, she cursed Charles Kittridge as she did each time she looked in her mirror and saw the eyes that ruled her fate. Nearly twenty years ago the British diplomat had come to the Middle Kingdom. He had stayed only long enough to woo Ke-ming and plant his English seed in her body. Long enough to mark his daughter as a stranger in her own country, so that she could not forget him, even if she wished. But he had not stayed long enough to keep Li-an and her mother safe.

She frowned. Should she not be glad that another night had passed without the sound of marching feet or the glitter of raised swords to disturb her sleep? Another night of safety. She marked it as she did each one on the calendar of

278

moon months in her mind. Another night of rest, another day of freedom. At least one more.

Lowering her lashes so her eyes were almost closed, she tried to see her image in the moon-shaped glass. She had been told she looked like any other Mandarin lady when her eyes were not visible. She wanted to see for herself that it was true. She wanted to believe, if only for a moment, that it was possible to forget Charles Kittridge, forget that his English blood flowed through her. But she could see nothing besides the fragmented color on the backs of her eyelids. She sighed in frustration.

"She who stares into her mirror with eyes closed, though she linger a whole day, will still be blind."

Li-an blushed and looked up at the familiar shriveled face of Liu Kan, the servant who stood watching with bright, birdlike eyes. Her wrinkled face was expressionless except for her eyebrows, arched in disapproval. "Your bath is ready, Young Mistress, if you can bear to leave your ivory moon behind."

Without a word, Li-an followed the woman into the next room where a shallow tub of hot water stood waiting. She slipped off her long gown of green silk and Liu Kan's daughter, Mei, took it away. Li-an stepped into the tub, where the warm water caressed her ankles as the steam rose in comforting clouds around her. The old servant took a soft cloth and began to clean her mistress's body with soap. Li-an stared at the woman's bony, clawlike hands and noticed that Kan breathed heavily; even so small an effort exhausted her. "You work too hard," Li-an said. "Shall I speak to my mother about lightening your tasks?"

Kan smiled, revealing the gaps between her teeth, and smoothed her gray cotton tunic with her wet hand. "Not if I can seal your lips. What would I do with myself if I did not work? Talk to the chickens in the kitchen courtyard? Or sit under a pine tree and stare at the sky?" The servant shook her head. "Such things are for poets and scholars, not for foolish me. As long as my hands are busy, I am happy.

"But you, Young Mistress," Liu Kan added slyly. "Already you are eighteen years and still alone. You should have been a bride long since. I was married and with child at fifteen."

Li-an stared down at her slender body, untouched by any but women's hands. "It is my mother's choice that I take no husband."

The servant bowed her head. "Then it must be best."

Suddenly Li-an stiffened. "What is that? It sounds like marching."

"I hear nothing," Kan said.

"Did you not know," Liu Mei asked as she slipped into the room with layers of clothes over her arm, "that the soldiers of the Army of the Green Standard are in the streets of Peking today?"

"Amitabha!" Kan exclaimed, rolling her eyes heavenward, "but I swear Young Mistress could hear a needle pass through silk three hundred *li* away."

"What has happened?" Li-an asked.

"The butcher who delivered our meat says that a minor official has been plotting with the foreign devils to harm the Son of Heaven and take the Dragon Throne back from our Manchu rulers." Mei spoke in a whisper, aware that the caned and papered walls in a Chinese house concealed little. "The guards say the traitor fled at dawn from the Meridian Gate of the *Tzu-chin ch'eng*, the Forbidden City, through which only the Son of Heaven himself may pass."

"Or his mother, the Empress Dowager," Kan muttered under her breath.

"Did the official spend the night inside the sacred walls?" Li-an cried in astonishment. It was an ancient law that no man but the Emperor could remain within those walls after dark. "He must be brave indeed, or mad."

"They are searching now because, madman or not, he managed to escape them."

The color drained from Li-an's cheeks.

"You look as if your own brother were in danger," Liu Kan snorted. "And such a one was never born. What has this rebel to do with you?"

"Nothing," Li-an replied. "At least I do not think so."

"Young Mistress is seeing *kuei* in the shadows again," Kan observed. "There are no evil spirits here." When Li-an did not respond, the servant added, " 'Man does not live a hundred years, but worries enough for a thousand.' "

Li-an did not hear her. She was listening to the distant rhythm of marching feet. It was barely discernible in the stillness after dawn, but in her ears the sound grew until it filled her head and she could hear nothing else. Thus she had listened many years ago to the stamping of feet through the streets of Canton for two endless days and nights.

She remembered so clearly how she had lain in bed that last night, shivering, though the summer air was warm. She had heard the chirp of crickets, the song of a lark, but these familiar sounds did not soothe the flicker of fear inside her.

The folding doors between the reception room and her bedroom had been left open to let the sultry air pass through. Peeping around a crack in the curtains, Li-an could see her mother seated on an ebony stool, her cheeks pale in the lantern light.

The fear of two days and nights grew as she watched her mother's averted face. Li-an sensed Ke-ming's apprehension, felt it steal into her own lungs until each breath brought effort and pain. Harsh whispers curled about her head and shadows danced along the walls like silent demons. Why, oh why did her father not come and take them away before those people in the streets came with their swords and sticks and rage?

Li-an froze when she heard the tap of knuckles on the lacquered doorframe. Her mother rose swiftly, opened the door, and closed it. Charles Kittridge stood there, gasping for breath, his hair blown into disorder by the sea wind. When he glanced furtively over his shoulder, Li-an looked, too, expecting the shadows of madmen to rise along the paper walls. But there was nothing.

Her father crouched in the corner with Ke-ming, speaking quickly, urgently. Li-an strained to hear what passed between them, but could not understand. The child was caught up in the alarming rhythm of the words, the dips and panicked rises that turned her flicker of fear into a flame.

She watched her parents' shadows as they fluttered on the walls like puppets dancing on a distant screen. They kissed, clung together, then Charles came to lean over his daughter's bed. He touched her cheek and whispered, "Take care, little one. Don't forget me."

She gasped and locked her arms around his neck. "Do not go, my Father. If you do, they will come and take us away. I know they will come."

"No," he told her. "It's me they want, not you. I'm leaving China and shall not return. You'll be safe now. The people's anger will soon die and they will forget. Go back to sleep and dream of Ma-ku, the kind fairy."

His eyes were strangely misted and his hand shook as he touched her hair, then turned away. He slipped like a specter through the silk-softened light, under the cane mat and into the courtyard as the stamp of feet grew louder and the shadows of strangers loomed outside, twice the size of normal men. The thunder of feet became the pounding of fists on wood. The walls shook with the rage of those men and Li-an winced as if the fists were striking her own body.

Endless seconds passed while her mother delayed, standing frozen in the center of the room. The sound beat its way into the girl's brain until her head began to ache. The pounding, the throbbing, the pain, blended and became one as the men burst into the house.

Li-an crouched in the corner of her bed when the soldiers entered, followed by the poor men who shouted filthy names at Ke-ming. The child heard the crash of breaking glass, the clatter of chairs pushed over, the ripping of paper as scrolls were torn from the walls. The noises came closer until her voice left her and her breath and the beat of her heart. Only the terror remained.

The men drew back the gauze and saw the child hidden there, her eyes lowered as she had been taught.

"Where is the foreign devil?" the soldiers demanded.

"I do not know."

"Tell us where!"

"She speaks the truth. Leave her be!" Ke-ming cried desperately.

The men dragged Li-an from her bed and she stood shivering, her gaze on the floor. She knew if they saw her eyes they would kill her where she stood. Her mother had taught her well. "Where?" they demanded, waving their swords in the air. "Where? Where? Where?"

Beaten down by the harsh rasp of their voices, she fell

to her knees. Her head throbbed with a pain so piercing that she knew she could not bear it. "I do not know." She felt their disbelief, the hatred that circled around her. She bowed her head. "I do not know."

One of the soldiers raised his sword. He was going to kill her because she would not tell him what she did not know. "My Father!" she screamed. "Come back and take me with you! Father!"

There was no answer and the pain splintered inside her head into shards of brilliant light that left her blind.

She was not certain what happened next. She remembered that her mother called out once. Li-an heard the rustle of silk, smelled the fragrance of perfume as Ke-ming bent to protect her child. Then, suddenly, there were new footsteps, curses, a scuffle. Finally the sword was withdrawn.

Li-an kept her eyes lowered, praying to Kwan Yin, Goddess of Mercy, obsessed by the pain behind her eyes. There was more shouting, the clash of swords and sticks until, at last, the men with rage in their hearts were gone. She knew because the stillness fell around her like summer darkness, soft, warm, and clinging. She heard through the pain-wracked silence a footstep she recognized—Ke-ming's other lover, who came late at night with the stealth of a panther and disappeared before dawn. Li-an had never seen his face or heard his voice.

He spoke to her mother in the reception hall, followed her when she returned to her daughter's room. He was standing so close that Li-an could see the hem of his blue gown. Because the pain had blinded her, she forgot that others still had sight. She looked up.

She heard a gasp and lowered her gaze at once. She had done the worst of all forbidden things and let a stranger see her eyes. Now he knew her secret, this man without a name. Li-an cowered on the floor as he stalked from the room. Gently, Ke-ming lifted her daughter and laid her on the bed with the quilt wrapped around her. She lingered for a moment, her cool hand on the child's forehead, then followed the man into the reception hall.

Li-an lay with her hands pressed to her throbbing head. Sometimes, when the pain abated, she heard snatches of angry conversation. "That foreign devil's bastard," "spawn of a demon"—the words rang in her ears. "You knew about him, my lord. You know why it was necessary." "But I did not know—" "Did you think she was yours?" "I did not think of her at all . . . only of you." ". . . should have drowned her." ". . . my daughter . . . sooner drown myself!" "Leave me! I can no longer look at your face!"

At last the furious voices ceased and silence fell, full of uncertainty now instead of fear. If the mysterious man turned them out, they would starve, since Charles Kittridge was gone. Li-an curled into a ball as the old confusion returned. Why were there two men who came and held her mother? Why did neither come to stay? Why were there so many secrets, so many footsteps in the night? Her questions only made the pain greater. She wrapped the quilt around her head to stop her whirling thoughts.

Ke-ming did not speak of confusion or uncertainty as she sat by her daughter's side and made her drink willow-bark tea to ease the pain. She did not speak at all, only played softly on her lute as if the world had not collapsed beneath her feet.

Later, Li-an heard the familiar footsteps again. "The night is too cold without you," the man told Ke-ming. Then his footsteps and her mother's faded and there was stillness and calm. Soon afterward, Ke-ming told her daughter it was too dangerous for them to remain in Canton, so they packed their things and moved to a new house in Peking, where the man came as he had before, shrouded each night by protective darkness.

Only later did Li-an learn of the two Opium Wars against the hated Westerners who took the Middle Kingdom's treasures, made her poor, and worse, brought opium to the people so they were weak and unable to resist. The superior British and French ships had battered the coast, killed the people, and choked off the ports until the Son of Heaven had at last bowed his head and granted the white men all that they asked.

The Treaty of Tientsin had been signed in 1858. When the people of Canton—who had suffered most because the foreigners made their base there—learned of it, they had cried out against the foreign devils who had made the Emperor and his people lose face by betraying their weakness. So, for those few days and nights in Canton, they had roamed the streets, killing every white man they met, seeking out the ones who, like Charles Kittridge, had been part of this final humiliation.

Slowly, Li-an had come to understand, but the fear that had lodged in her heart that night had never left her. She had not forgotten in the fourteen years since, that although her own father had fled, a stranger had protected her. Even though she was only four, she had understood that the mysterious man despised her and had done it only for her mother's sake. For Ke-ming's sake, too, he had procured this house, the silks and satins and jewels she and her daughter wore. Li-an did not love this man, but she thanked him every night and called him secretly by the name of Father Without a Face.

She was hardly aware of Mei and Kan rinsing her body, then rubbing in perfumed oil of dried oranges and musk. She stepped from the tub and they slipped a *p'ao* padded with raw silk over her head. The lilac silk gown fell to her feet; the wide sleeves rustled as she took the three-quarter-length purple satin *kua-erh* and slipped it over her head.

She sat still while they parted her hair, oiled it, and wound it in two coils above her ears. She could still hear the echo of those marching feet, though they had passed the house long ago. She sat frozen, praying they would not return, and so it was—this time. Slowly, while the two women fluttered about her, she suppressed her memories and stared into the mirror at a face free of fear. Ke-ming had taught her to wear this mask of calm no matter how deep the turmoil inside her. "A man who feels fear may be wise to sense danger," her mother had said. "A man who shows his fear is a fool." Li-an knew it to be true, yet her hand would not stay still. When she tried to put in her jade earrings, she dropped one and it rolled beneath her ebony stool.

At last, Liu Mei and Liu Kan left her, taking with them the cloths and the tub full of water. Li-an remained motionless. She had not thought of Canton for a long time. Why had the memory come back now, as sharp and bitter as the day it had happened? There was no answer in the image of her impassive face, the clear blue of her stranger's eyes.

Li-an shook her head, which ached dully. She should not be sitting here wasting time. This was the first day of the Festival of Lanterns and she had much to prepare. Leaving her memories caught like invisible threads in the blank mirror, she hurried down the passage toward the kitchen.

She paused when she reached the reception hall, where the cane mats had been raised to let in the morning light. Quickly, she crossed the room to look out at the far wall of the garden and beyond it, the wide blue sky above the Western Hills. The peaks were swathed in fragile mist, cool, violet, and inviting—so still, so beautiful, yet so uncivilized. They called to her, as they had called to others, offering retreat and solace.

> I stand at the door through which my friends
> no longer come,
> And stare at the distant mountains.
> How I long to find my way up to those lofty peaks,
> cloaked in a fragile stillness,
> Where the sound of voices is not expected
> and so not missed.
> I want to lose myself among the gnarled old pines
> as the Immortals did.
> Perhaps the sight of a single branch,
> A perfect shadow on clear white snow,
> would heal this loneliness for a time.

It was one of Li-an's favorite poems. She had found it years ago in her mother's jewel box and read it aloud in delight. "Who wrote it?" she had asked.

Ke-ming had answered without thinking, "Your grandfather."

The girl had stared in astonishment. Never had she heard mention of a grandfather, a brother, an uncle or aunt. She had begun to think that in all the Middle Kingdom, Ke-ming was the only woman who had no family to speak of with pride and honor. As soon as the words were out, Ke-ming had turned away, refusing to answer Li-an's questions, except to say that the man was dead and best forgotten. Her daughter had been horrified. Ancestors were not forgotten, but worshiped like gods. Yet Ke-ming had remained adamant and had never spoken of her father again.

Li-an narrowed her eyes at the brightness of the sun on snow. Other women were blessed by the three kinds of womanly dependence: to father, husband, son. Yet she was blessed by none. As she breathed in the cold air, she wondered, fleetingly, what it would have been like if her father had stayed. She pushed away the thought before it was fully formed and looked yearningly at the mountains. Someday she would go there and find peace as her grandfather had longed to do. He was a stranger whom she knew only through the scrawled characters of a poem, yet she missed him often. Years ago, she had written her own poem in reply to his. This man that she would never see had touched her as her own father had not.

I will wait for you in the stillness of the mountains,
Where the clatter of cart wheels is not heard,
Nor the sound of running feet.
Where only the wind sighs through the pines—
A whisper of serenity that echoes
    the touch of moonlight on a clear, running stream.

For the second time, Li-an had to shake herself awake and remember her errand. She turned from the hills and made her way to the kitchen. When she pushed aside the reed curtain, she entered another world, where the air was thick with steam and the odors of cabbage and pork, fish and spiced oil. The kitchen was crowded with chopping blocks, a huge earthen stove, and large black caldrons. Here was the noisiest room in the house; the servants ran in and out, shouting curses at the chickens that wandered from the courtyard through the wide open door. Liu Mei stood chopping scallions. The rhythm of her knife mingled with the sound of sizzling meat in oil, the gurgle of water in the cooking pots, and the laughter that rose through the thick, steamy air.

Li-an loved the warmth and chaos of the kitchen. She

let the reed curtain fall so the fragrant air enveloped her. She saw that Liu Kin-shih, Liu Kan's youngest daughter, was plucking a chicken while trying to keep her eye on some sesame toffee. "I will finish plucking, Little Sister," Li-an said, "if you will help me later with the fish and pork for my sacrifice."

Cheeks flushed from the heat, sixteen-year-old Kin-shih nodded gratefully.

"What sacrifice?" Liu Kan demanded as she ducked inside, a squawking chicken in her hand.

"My mother, the thirteenth day of the first moon is the anniversary of Young Mistress's grandfather's death."

"Ah yes." Kan nodded. She knew as well as anyone this was not true, but she said nothing.

Li-an had no idea when her grandfather had left the earth to travel the road to the Yellow Springs. But in other houses on such anniversaries, the families worshiped at the altars of their ancestors to show their reverence. Wishing to show her *hsiao*, Li-an had chosen her own date—the beginning of the Feast of Lanterns, which presaged the coming of spring. Later she would perform the ritual ceremony in secret. She knew her mother would not approve.

For the moment, however, after she threw a cotton tunic over her clothes, Li-an concentrated on plucking the last of the feathers from the bird. She washed it thoroughly, then placed it in an empty caldron on the earthen stove. She went to the coal bin in the courtyard, skirting the piles of grain scattered over the pebbled ground while flapping her arms to keep away the noisy chickens, ducks, and geese that fluttered about her. In a woven bamboo basket, she gathered some fuel, then returned to the kitchen and crouched behind the stove to add coal to the already smoldering pile inside.

Liu Kan grimaced when she saw the Young Mistress, her face and hands black with coal dust coated with a thin film of sweat, a chicken feather clinging to her tunic. "You should be sitting quietly somewhere sewing, not dirtying your hands with servant's work," the old woman scolded.

Li-an smiled. Kan had said the same thing many times. "Someone has to cook the chicken. Kin-shih is busy with the toffee and you and Mei have many other tasks. Besides, is it not good for a woman to know how to prepare a fine meal?"

"To know is one thing, to collect coal in the courtyard, dragging your velvet slippers through chicken dust, is another."

"You are only jealous, my Mother," Mei said with a grin, "because Young Mistress's dumplings are lighter than yours."

Kan snorted with disgust. "So light that when the Venerable Wu Shen ate them, he did not rise from his chair for a week."

"That was only because he was so satisfied that he did not wish to go," Mei insisted. She grinned when she saw her mother's lips twitch in an attempt to restrain a smile.

As they spoke, Li-an had washed her hands and helped Kin-shih to spread the toffee on a soft cheesecloth. Now the two young women were laying out a whole carp in an open pan. They covered it with vinegar, ginger, pepper, and garlic and placed the pan on the hottest portion of the stove. When Kan turned her back to begin the fish broth, Li-an whispered to Kin-shih. "I see that your hands are becoming rough again. Have you used all the mutton fat I gave you?"

The girl nodded surreptitiously; her mother disapproved of such vanity.

"I have a new recipe for softening the skin. It is from India and is made of fresh cream and pounded orange peel. I will leave some for you later," Li-an murmured.

"What is all this whispering?" Liu Kan demanded.

"We were thanking the Kitchen God for the abundance of food in our pots." Li-an pointed to the paper image of the brightly colored god on the wall above the stove. His vivid red and green robes glowed even through the steam; he beamed at the confusion all around him.

Kan was more concerned with the condition of Young Mistress, whose hair had begun to come loose, trailing through the coal dust and the moisture on her face. There was a smudge of soy on her cheek where she had brushed a troublesome tendril away.

"I do not know why your mother allows it," Kan muttered. "Should you not be playing your flute or painting on silk or embroidering a pillow?"

"Those things I have done," Li-an said as she plunged her hands into the dough that would make little pockets of bread filled with meat. "I would do others as well." She did not say that when her mother had first suggested she learn to work in order to make herself strong, Li-an had declared that she would rather study her books. But she soon learned that in the kitchen and the attached courtyard, the servants dropped their masks of formality and became her friends. The Liu family had served hers for generations and knew the secret of her foreign blood, but they did not blame her for what she could not change. She was at ease with them and would not give up these mornings for anything. So, at Ke-ming's insistence, she had learned to lift and carry heavy buckets, to light fires, to buy food in the market, to cook, to help shape the garden, and many other little tasks.

"Your head is full of unwomanly things," Kan said. She turned to regard the Kitchen God through narrowed eyes. "I only hope you gave him enough offerings of honey and sweets to seal his lips before New Year's when he made his report to Heaven. Kwan Yin forbid that he should recount all that happens in this house."

"But there is nothing evil here," Li-an objected.

"Evil no," Liu Kan said thoughtfully, "but much that is against tradition." Hands on hips, she turned back to Li-an. "This afternoon, your honorable mother will be visiting with Chang Jui-chueh and her mother-in-law. Will you be with them?"

Li-an shook her head emphatically. Because of the constant risk that someone should discover her parentage, she stayed in the background much of the time. The women who came to visit her mother did not think it odd, for Chinese women kept to themselves and rarely left the safety of their quarters. Occasionally, Li-an came out for a brief time while the ladies sipped their tea. She sat with eyes lowered, as was proper and modest, spoke quietly, and never raised her head. "I stay away from Chang Jui-chueh," she told Liu Kan now. "Each time she comes I live in terror that a golden pin will work loose from her perfectly coiled hair and she will fall into a faint and have to stay a full moon to recover from the shock."

Kin-shih covered her mouth with her sleeve to hide her laughter.

"Perhaps you could read her poetry or play to her while she lies pale and fragile on the silken quilt," Liu Mei suggested.

"I do not think she would like that," Li-an replied, giggling. "There is no rhythm in her voice, no music—only ice."

Liu Kan shook her finger at Li-an. With an effort, she kept the smile from her lips. "How can you speak of her that way when you have never even seen her face?"

Her mistress grinned. "I have sat watching with my lashes lowered and seen the precise placement of her golden lilies, how properly she folds her soft hands in her lap and holds them as still as white jade. I have learned to know her from her unscuffed satin shoes and the hem of her gown, which shows no hint of dust. She does not allow herself to be soiled by the filth in the world. She is more concerned with the perfection of her body than her spirit."

Kan stared open-mouthed. Everything Li-an said about Chang Jui-chueh was true. "And your mother's other friends? You know them as well?"

"I do. You need not see a person's face to know what is in their soul."

"All this you have observed, yet never have these ladies seen your eyes?"

"I am careful," Li-an replied with a sigh. She grew tired of always taking care and wanted, just once, to look openly into a stranger's face. But she dared not take the risk. She wondered, sometimes, if she would spend the rest of her life, head bent and eyes lowered, seeing only the ground and never, except when she was alone, the wide blue sky. The pain that had hovered in the back of her head began to pulse against her temples; she could not seem to rid herself of the nightmare of Canton today.

Liu Kan's husband Ch'eng came in from the courtyard, wiping the sweat from the shaved front of his head, his gray queue blending with his plain cotton tunic. He stopped when he saw Li-an. "There is a visitor," he said mysteriously. "Young Mistress might like to know her errand. Your honorable mother has received her in the large reception hall."

Intrigued, Li-an started for the door.

"Are you mad?" Kan cried. "You cannot go to your mother looking like a kitchen girl." Quickly, the servant helped Li-an remove her tunic, wash her face, and tuck her hair into place.

"Now go, Young Mistress, before you knead the pastry into rubber."

Li-an half smiled and went on her way.

Wan Ke-ming knelt beside the charcoal brazier in the reception hall. She held a red silk packet sealed with the mark of the House of Chin in red wax. The go-between who had brought the proposition had just left. Ke-ming tapped the packet against her open palm. She knew that Chin Chao, whose family sought her daughter for a bride, was a brilliant and outspoken scholar who made no secret of his admiration for the West or his desire to make China strong with the knowledge of Western technology. She respected him for that and thought he would be a good and loyal husband.

But the packet weighed heavily in her hand, and she felt a stirring of unease. She stared into the brazier and saw writhing snakes within the red coals just visible beneath hot ashes. Ke-ming closed her eyes, but the image grew brighter until, with an effort, she turned away from the brazier. She could not even consider such a marriage. What would the Chin family do when they caught their first glimpse of Li-an's blue eyes?

She knew too well the answer to her own question. They would cast her daughter out, humiliate her, shout her secret to the world. Ke-ming clenched her free hand. She would not let it happen. She had sworn long ago to protect her child from mindless prejudice, from the jealousy and bitter loneliness that had haunted her own life. She looked down in surprise at four half-moons where her nails had pierced her palm.

Ke-ming frowned when she heard Li-an approach. The uneven rhythm of her daughter's footsteps told her the girl had one of her headaches. She did not have to see the tinge of gray in Li-an's eyes to know that it was so. She turned in concern as the girl entered the room.

Li-an stopped to look at her mother in admiration. Ke-ming was wearing a pale green *p'ao* and a forest-green *kua-erh* embroidered with lotus flowers. The colors deepened the glow in her perfectly oval face and reflected the shimmer of white jade in her ornately styled hair. Li-an saw this even through the haze of pain in which she moved. Then she noticed the packet wrapped in silk. It was red, the color of joy and celebration. "What is it?" she asked.

Ke-ming rose gracefully to her feet. "I think you can guess. Another offer of marriage. The go-between has just left me."

Li-an's head throbbed dully. "Marriage? Do you mean that I will be a bride at last?" Even as she spoke, she knew it was a foolish question. There had been many such offers over the years from the families who visited Ke-ming. The women were impressed by what they took to be Li-an's shyness, her demure and proper behavior. Since they never caught a glimpse of her restless spirit or the lively intelligence in her eyes, they thought her the ideal obedient wife for their sons. Sometimes, knowing what they thought of her, Li-an wanted to recite one of the Old One's suggestive poems and watch the ladies recoil from her in horror. But she kept silent. To do otherwise was to risk too much. "Who has asked for me this time?"

"The House of Chin. They want you as wife for their eldest son, Chao."

Li-an paused, trying to remember where she had heard the name before. "What did you say?"

"You know the answer to that, my daughter. I refused."

Li-an sighed. Then she remembered. "Is Chin Chao not the one who went to study in America? I would think you would want him for a son-in-law."

Ke-ming stared intently into the girl's gray misted eyes. "Surely you do not wish to marry a stranger?"

"I wish to marry someone, to have a man who will give me a home."

"It shall not be this man," her mother declared vehemently. "Fate has already decided."

"Fate?" Li-an asked while the pain splintered behind her eyes. "Or you?"

"Would you enjoy serving a mother-in-law who might despise you, who might make of you a slave as might your husband? Is that truly what you wish, to become a possession of others?"

"I no longer know what I wish."

"Then you must believe me when I tell you it would not work," Ke-ming declared. "You could never be a Chinese wife. You would shrivel and die under the weight of their rules and rituals."

Li-an fought back the urge to weep. "I suppose it is so."

"Yes," her mother agreed. She turned to toss the silk packet into the brazier, where it folded in upon itself while the wax seal sizzled. "Come," she said, gentle now that she had won the battle. "Come and let me soothe your pain. It has been long since you suffered one of your headaches. It must be an omen that such a marriage was not to be."

Li-an hardly heard her, for the crackle of burning silk was in her ears, the smell of melted wax in the air. Quietly she crossed the passage, each step jarring her head, so the pain beat against her temples more and more furiously. Ke-ming drew back the satin coverlet on her daughter's bed and the girl slipped under the pale pink quilt.

Li-an lay still while the scent of camphor enfolded her, but above that there was another fragrance that rose from the folds of Ke-ming's gown. Li-an had never smelled it on another: the scent that clung about her mother's body was one of Ke-ming's many secrets.

While Li-an tried to make herself comfortable, Ke-ming went to get her lute and laid it aside. She drew a stool close to the bed and began to massage her daughter's feet, then her wrists, and finally her pounding temples. Now and then Ke-ming's bracelet brushed Li-an's forehead. She welcomed the feel of the cool woven white and yellow gold. It was the only piece of jewelry her mother always wore. Li-an opened her mouth to ask why, but her voice had left her, and with it, her sight.

Rhythmically, Ke-ming continued her massage. When her daughter grew still, she picked up her lute and began to play. She watched the pale, strained face on the pillow and her heart ached. How much her life had changed since she learned that she carried this child in her womb. She had had many lovers, but none who would ever be truly hers. She had lost so much—her home, her family, her father—but Li-an, the child of her body, was something they could not take away. To her, the girl with the blue foreign eyes was a gift beyond price. She saw her daughter relax and brushed a stray hair from her face.

A little at a time, the pain began to ease as the music soothed away Li-an's troubled memories. Just before she fell asleep, the girl was surprised by a thought that formed sharp and clear through the haze in her mind. Why had her mother burnt the offer of marriage from the Chin family? Usually she sent a polite refusal. But Ke-ming had done this fiercely, as if to destroy every trace of the proposal. It seemed to Li-an that her mother had acted out of fear. But that was not possible. Ke-ming feared no one, nothing.

Or so her daughter had come to believe.

2

Li-an awoke to find her headache had gone. She felt stifled by the gauze curtains and wanted to be outside, where the air moved freely and the light was not altered by mother-of-pearl windows. She put on her short padded jacket and velvet slippers to protect her from the winter air, hurried through the reception hall, and escaped into the garden. Keming had refused to bind her daughter's feet, so Li-an moved quickly, easily, while other women walked with care on their tiny "golden lilies."

She ducked beneath the reed curtain and found her way down the stone steps and pebbled paths of the garden. Li-an sighed with relief. Here, at least, she did not have to hide her eyes or bow her head. She paused in the cold air to breathe deeply. She hoped the chill, the soothing silence, would make her forget the marriage that would never be, the family she would never have.

She looked around the garden, her refuge, even in this season. The leaves of the bamboo were still green as were the twisted pines and the plum trees—the Three Friends of Winter, an old poet had called them. She paused next to the wide pond that curved between the strangely shaped rocks whose fissures and crevices held tiny patches of melting snow. Through the thin layer of ice that covered the water she could see the bent stems of lotus that would turn into a sea of white, lilac, and green in summer. The shadows of tall bamboo fell across the pond, blending with the broken stalks under the ice—a poem of Chinese characters beneath the blue-green water. Li-an tried to read it, but the words had no meaning.

She continued down the path into the roofed corridor,

open on one side, that connected this courtyard with the next. The sun shone through the patterned windows, making phoenixes and cranes, peonies and chrysanthemums in patches of light on the tiled floor. Finally Li-an stepped through a moon gate into the far courtyard. She stopped as she often did to admire the two oldest pines in the garden—gnarled, curved, and tortured by age and wind. Their tops had long ago grown together and the strange shape of their trunks made her think of two dragons locked in eternal combat. She reached out fondly to touch the rough bark. She felt a spirit of age and wisdom in the pines, just as she did in the boulders that rose like tiny mountains from the landscape.

Streams murmured around and through the shaped and carved stone, a pleasing contrast to the harsh outlines of the rocks. They stood immobile, unchanging, caressed by the flowing water whose motion never ceased.

She ducked under the bare branches of a willow and made a sharp turn where the waterfall, that rushed like sparkling crystal in the spring, trickled now over the pitted rock. Like the purple Western Hills in the distance, the garden appeared wild, but she knew each rock, tree, and stream had been carefully planned to imitate nature in every aspect—its imperfections as well as its beauty. As she moved deeper among the mountains of imported stone and bare winter trees, she could almost make herself believe that she was lost in the hills far away from the dusty city, the cries of the vendors, the soft-spoken scholars who roamed the streets with abstracted expressions.

She wandered across a bridge, enchanted by the woven shadows of branches, trunks, and bamboo leaves that fell over her face and hands. In some ways she loved the garden better in winter than in springtime when the blossoms burst into brilliant color, filling the air with their heavy scents. The crystal stillness of the snow, the bright morning light, the drifting shadows, the trees in the wind, all called to her, offering comfort in the midst of this charming confusion.

Finally she came to the western wall and climbed the steps to a red and green pagoda, where she leaned on the carved railing. The morning was clear enough that she could see the White Pagoda on Jade Fountain Hill at the foot of the mountains. While she stared at the blue-tinged peaks, she felt a sense of apprehension she could not explain.

"The rivers are the arteries of the earth's body," a man's voice said unexpectedly behind her.

She turned in relief at the sight of her tutor and friend, Wu Shen, an official on the Imperial Board of Astronomy. His gray hair was combed back from his face, his round cap with its pearl button perched on his head. The peacock embroidered on his blue robe and the clear sapphire button at the top of his *p'ao* revealed his position as an official of the third class. Li-an smiled at his familiar wrinkled features. "Good morning, honored guest." She clasped her hands and bowed.

"Good morning, my friend," he replied. "But you have not finished the thought I gave you when first I arrived."

"If the rivers are the arteries of the earth, then the mountains are its skeleton."

"You are pensive today," Wu Shen observed, leaning beside her on the carved red railing. "What you need is to distract yourself from the contemplation of shadows. I have brought enough books to keep you busy from moon to moon."

Together they walked into the pavilion and sat on one of the stone benches where he had left the books. She noticed *Utopia* by Sir Thomas More and the *Poetics* of Aristotle among the many titles. They were in English, not Chinese, for Ke-ming had insisted that her daughter learn both languages. Li-an's mother had met Wu Shen long ago when she spent some time at the imperial court, and when she returned to Peking, she had sought him out and asked him to teach her daughter. He himself spoke English, and as a member of the Board of Astronomers, he had access to the imperial library where he found books that the Jesuits, much favored during the reign of the Ch'ien Lung Emperor, had left behind.

Li-an had studied with him from the time she was seven. The girl learned quickly and was never satisfied; whenever a new book came from the West, the old scholar brought it to her so they could read together. Except to Wu Shen and Ke-ming, Li-an never spoke of her knowledge of philosophy, art, and literature. Long ago she had studied the *Analects of Confucius*, the Four Books and the Five Classics, the *I Ching, Tao-te-Ching*, the *Shih Ching*, as well as Descartes and Socrates. She had studied the great poets and painters of the East as well as the West—Li Po and Yuan Mei, Shakespeare and John Donne, Kuo Hsi and Wang Wei, da Vinci and Botticelli.

Li-an enjoyed these lessons, for Wu was a kind and generous teacher who understood her deep love of books, her reverence for the written word, and her endless desire for knowledge. But today her thoughts would not rest; they fluttered hither and thither like restless birds in a clear sky.

"Your mind has left your body," Shen observed quietly. "But that is just as well. I cannot stay. The Son of Heaven has called for a general audience concerning the scholar official who spent the night in the Forbidden City and threatened harm to the Emperor." He dared not mention the words "kill" or "death" when he spoke of the ruler of China. It was forbidden.

"Did he escape?" Li-an asked.

The old man sighed heavily. "They caught the man, I'm afraid. A brilliant young official named Yuan Tung-li. I expected great things of him, but now he is lost." Wu Shen looked away, his eyes full of sadness. "They say he plotted with the foreign devils, but that I do not believe. Why should the white men try to overthrow the Dragon Throne? They are pleased with the frailty of the Ch'ing government, for it lets their merchants plunder us more freely, and the increasing weakness of the dynasty only makes the Westerners stronger. The Middle Kingdom has not been the same since the Taipings rebelled twenty years ago. We will never recover from the blow they struck at our heart."

Under Wu Shen's direction, Li-an had studied the Taiping Rebellion led by the madman, Hung Hsiu-chuan. He had called himself the Chinese Christ. With a Sword of Flame he had conquered many of the southern provinces and held them for fifteen long years. Already weakened by the two Opium Wars, the Ch'ing Bannermen had been unable to stop the rebellion and scatter the rebels. The dynasty had tottered on its weak legs and nearly fallen until the hated foreigners had joined the imperial forces and destroyed Hung's power at last. The purple dragon of the Ch'ing still fluttered over China, but its colors were faded, its fabric tattered.

Shen looked toward the gray walls of the Imperial City with their parapets and tall, impressive gate towers. The red, yellow, and blue roofs of the city glittered in the sunlight like an ocean of gems with whitecaps of drifted snow. "I have learned much from the English, the French, and the Americans," Shen mused, "but I grow weary of their egos and their arrogance." He shook his head. "Do you know that they place their personal name first, as if a single man matters more than the family from which he comes? They do not respect the proper things—the laws of good behavior, the value of literature, their revered ancestors. They do not understand *hsiao*. To them filial piety is important only so long as it is convenient. They do not follow the *tao*, the moral way, but the *ch'i*, the desire for concrete things, for wealth and possessions."

Li-an frowned. "If these men are evil, why are so many fascinated with them? Why does my mother make me read their books and learn their ways when I want only to be Chinese?"

Wu Shen looked away. "Ke-ming is a wise woman. You must remember that. She knows," he added wistfully, "that the men from the West are young and vigorous. They are making their worlds bigger by the hour while we are old and weak and have already lost much of our power. There are too many scholars who believe they know all, who still think the Middle Kingdom the center of the world."

"And so it is."

He smiled sadly. "No, my child, not for many moons. Our vision is too narrow and self-contained. You know what the ancients said: 'He who sits in a well to observe the sky does not see very much.' I fear we have been sitting in a well for a long time now and cannot find our way out."

His voice was full of bitter resignation, and she reached out to touch his hand in reassurance.

The old man smiled. "How strange this world is," he declared enigmatically as he looked into Li-an's blue eyes.

He was the only one outside the Wan household who had seen those eyes and knew from whom she had inherited them. It was as well, he thought, in spite of the danger. Li-an had the body of a woman, but the mind of a scholar; he was not sorry he had said these things to her. Ke-ming had asked him to tell her daughter only the truth, all the truth, and this he had done. He hoped it would be enough to save the girl in the end.

She saw the shadow of worry on his face. "You are grieving," she murmured. "Can I ease your pain?"

He cupped her face in his age-spotted hands. "If you could, you would be a sorceress, for the sadness goes deep. But I did not come to pass my burden on to you. I will leave these books and hope they distract you," Wu Shen said. "I must go now to the Son of Heaven." Wearily, he rose and wandered away. The graceful shadows of bamboo leaves played over his pale blue robe and his cloth-soled shoes crunched rhythmically on the graveled paths until the sound faded and stillness returned.

Later, after she had shared dinner with Ke-ming, Li-an returned to the kitchen. She wore a lilac silk tunic embroidered with peonies. The wide sleeves and high neck were graceful and went well with the maroon satin *p'ao* she wore underneath. Her golden earrings swayed as she moved. The soft lantern light emphasized the brooch of pearls in the shape of a butterfly that she wore on her breast.

She took the two silver platters Kin-shih laid out and slipped down the corridor, full of whispering shadows from the oiled paper lanterns. She stopped when she reached the long narrow room where the altar to the Wan's ancestors stood at one end, the altar to Confucius at the other. Li-an gazed up at the exposed beams of the ceiling, painted red and green and carved with symbols of luck—the dragon, the phoenix, scattered peach blossoms. The walls were hung with scrolls bearing moral sayings in fine Chinese characters that Li-an knew by heart. There were only two lanterns in the Hall of Ancestors, so the mood of the room was always dark and still. It welcomed Li-an, making her feel that indeed the gods watched over *T'ien-hsia*—all under heaven.

She placed the offerings of food on the altar to her ancestors, then lit the candles that stood on either side of the incense burner. She paused and thought she smelled the lingering scent of sandalwood. One stick of incense had been burned since she last came and there were fresh apricot blossoms among the branches of bamboo she had left yesterday in the porcelain vase. She frowned, perplexed. Had someone been here before her?

Even as she wondered, she took the spirit money from her sleeve, placed it in a copper dish, and set it aflame. The money, along with the offerings of food, would help make her grandfather comfortable on his journey through the heavens. Finally she lit her own incense. The fragrance rose to curl about her shoulders, a graceful wisp of smoke. She knelt before the rectangular altar with a skirt of silk around it and a marble top.

Above it hung the likeness of a stranger her mother had painted to represent the man who had founded the Wan family. When they arrived in Peking, Ke-ming had erected this altar so there would be no talk, no questions about her past. Each time Li-an knelt before it, she grieved because it was a lie. The only truth was the poem by her grandfather which she had copied out in careful strokes after her mother hid the original away. Li-an had hidden it beneath the altar in place of a soul tablet. It was to this man, this stranger revealed through the lines of a single poem, that she prayed for protection and happiness.

There was a soul tablet, too, for Ke-ming's dead husband. She and her lover had created the dead man to explain Li-an's parentage; in Peking no one knew about the foreign devil with the charming blue eyes. The people here thought Ke-ming one of the virtuous *kuei-chieh*, the widows who chose to remain alone rather than remarry. For this they honored her.

"But how can your husband die," the five-year-old Li-an had asked her mother, "when he never lived?"

"That is only what we will tell others," Ke-ming had replied.

"Why, when it is a lie?"

"So that we may survive. Simply that. Here one must

tell the people what they want to hear. Never tell the truth. Never reveal to them the secrets of your heart.''

"Why not?" Li-an persisted. "I do not understand."

"Because," her mother explained with infinite patience, "when they know your secrets, they also know your weakness and it is easy for your enemies to destroy you."

Even though she was so young, Li-an understood the bitterness in her mother's voice. "Have we so many enemies?"

Ke-ming had looked away. "It seems that I was born to make foes instead of friends." She turned back to her daughter and grasped her hand. "That is why, my pale jade, you must always be strong. Stronger than they. Never weaken, not even for a moment. Promise me!"

Mesmerized by the gleam in her mother's obsidian eyes, Li-an had nodded dumbly.

Now the young woman shook the memory away, then kowtowed, hitting her head on her crossed hands three times three to show her respect. As was her custom each time she visited the altar, she whispered a special prayer to her grandfather. "I pray that you found your peace in the hills of the Yellow Springs and that someday you will show me the way to my own mountain solitude."

She felt warmth flow through her as she often did when she knelt here in the cool, dim silence. She knew the gods were all around, hovering with her grandfather's spirit in the incense-fragrant air. When she looked up at the portrait, the face of the stranger seemed to shimmer and change. The eyes became blue, the hair light brown, and the mouth smiled with irresistible charm. Charles Kittridge. Li-an felt a pang of regret before her anger returned. Without the Englishman her life would have been free of fear, free of shadows, free of the thunder of marching feet in the night. Her jaw set in a stubborn line, she stared at the fine silk painting until the image disappeared as abruptly as the man himself had disappeared into the garden that night so many years ago.

Her devotions completed, Li-an rose to make her way down the passage to the large reception hall, feeling oddly restless.

She paused when she saw her mother seated at a rosewood table, her chin in her hands. Her hair, looped and piled on her head, glittered with sapphires and silver filigree. Ke-ming's sleeves fell over the carved edge of the table, a splash of vibrant green against the pale ivory glow of the lanterns. Her *p'ao* brushed the white-tiled floor where no speck of dust remained.

Li-an saw the pensive expression on her mother's face, the shadow of sadness in Ke-ming's veiled eyes. She crossed her arms when a gust of wind escaped through the cane mats that covered the end of the hall usually open to the garden and courtyards. The ornate lanterns swayed on their silken cords, cast dancing shadows over the walls.

Three rows of three tables had been placed down the length of the hall, each with ebony stools or elbow chairs. At the four corners sat tall simple tables; one held a glass globe for the tiny fish whose fins and tails undulated like golden fairy wings through the clear water. Other stands held porcelain vases full of plum blossoms and one an artificial landscape made of precious stones. The walls were hung with long scrolls bearing the sayings of Confucius and Chuang-tzu as well as several landscapes sketched in ink.

The folding doors between this room and the next had been pulled closed, so the light glowed through the upper portion, covered with latticework and painted gauze. Li-an ran her hand over the wall of teak at her back, divided into many sections, each beautifully carved with landscapes and flowers. The largest, her favorite, was a carving of a wu-t'ung tree.

Ke-ming sighed and raised her head. She was part of the perfection in this room. All was still and lovely, nothing out of place. Each chair, table, and fine vase had been arranged to best advantage. Even the lantern light fell in pleasing patterns of light and shadow. There was no confusion, no chaos; here Li-an felt like a stranger, as if this were not really her *lao chia*—the home of her heart.

Ke-ming sensed her daughter's presence and turned.

"There will be visitors tonight?" Li-an asked.

"Yes, and I would have you here with them."

Li-an smiled. "I have always been here, hidden behind

304

the screen." Many times, she had sat with the screen as her shield when the scholars and officials came to call on Ke-ming. She was well known for her hospitality, even to those who were not in high favor with the Son of Heaven or his mother, T'zu Hsi. Many years ago, Wu Shen had brought a friend to visit, knowing Ke-ming would put the man at ease. The next night the friend had brought another, then another. Now once or twice a week the men gathered in this room because they knew that here they could talk more freely than in the teahouses where there were always listening ears and mouths willing to carry tales to the Forbidden City. Over the years, the House of Wan had become a haven for restless young men who had not yet found their place in the Ch'ing bureaucracy.

Li-an had observed many visitors from the safety of her screened corner. She could not see much through the carvings of phoenixes and lotus blossoms, but Ke-ming had encouraged her daughter to learn what she could from these scholars. "Just because your eyes cannot serve you does not mean you must be blind," Ke-ming had said. "You watch and listen with your ears and your mind. You learn to feel a change in the air that means a change in someone's mood. You learn to see expression in sound. You shall become very wise while you listen to things that others ignore." Now Li-an looked around and noticed that the screen was gone.

"I have taken it away," Ke-ming explained, rising without a sound to glide over the gleaming tile. "I have been thinking about what you said this morning. You are right, my daughter. You have become a woman long since and yet still I hide you away. It is time you came out into the light. Tonight I would have you pass among the guests as I do, if this is what you desire."

Li-an felt a surge of excitement. For a moment, she was afraid to believe. But Ke-ming never lied to her.

"They will be arriving soon. Perhaps you would be wise to have a piece of needlework with which to occupy your hands—or at least pretend to do so."

Her daughter smiled and hurried to her room, found an unfinished square of satin, and returned to the hall out of

305

breath. She had just seated herself on a soft cushion when Liu Kan appeared.

"Several gentlemen have arrived, Honorable Mistress."

"Tell them to come." Ke-ming threw a last concerned glance at her daughter, then hurried to greet the guests. Li-an stayed where she was, for still she must take care not to reveal her secret. She kept her eyes on the cloth in her hand, or at least appeared to do so. But she saw the feet of each man as he passed before her, the white bottoms of boots and black felt tops that showed beneath robe after blue robe.

She sensed that each man bowed to Ke-ming with respect, though they knew she was the concubine of a rich and powerful man. No important ministers or officials came to the House of Wan; they could not risk having their names associated with Wan Ke-ming. But many scholars studying for the *hui-shih* exam came and lesser officials and members of the Hanlin Academy.

Li-an recognized many of the men by their footsteps, which she had come to know well over the years. Some of those footsteps she had matched with voices and names, others Ke-ming had revealed to her. She heard several men ask about the girl sitting silently with her eyes downcast.

"She is the daughter of my house," Ke-ming replied in a tone that said clearly that more questions would be unwelcome.

Li-an paid little attention. Tonight she listened for one scholar in particular. She was curious to learn what she could about Chin Chao, whose bride she might have been.

She knew when he came, for Ke-ming greeted him by his full name. Li-an watched him pass with a firm tread and seat himself at the table in the center at the front of the room. She observed the young man from beneath lowered lids. There was a chessboard on the table and he began to rearrange the ivory figures impatiently, his long fingers surprisingly adept. But then, every scholar learned when only a child how to hold a brush and make a delicate line. "Ah! Huang Ta-ch'ing," he cried in relief when another man took the chair across from his. "I was afraid you would not come. We did not finish our game the last time, you remember."

Li-an had heard his deep voice before. She remembered

it because he often became caught up in arguments with the other scholars and ministers.

Wu Shen had said that Chin Chao was a brilliant man, the youngest member of the Hanlin Academy, the youngest man to succeed at all levels of the imperial exams and receive the *chin-shih* degree. Most did not attain that level until they were thirty-five, yet at twenty-five Chin had passed the exam with honor. The young officials whispered that perhaps it was because he had been sent by the Ch'ing government to study in America for two years.

At last everyone was seated. Li-an listened intently; she had trained her ear to pick up conversation from far across the room. Not much passed that she did not hear. She watched her mother move among the tables, her tiny golden lilies making no sound on the tile. Some of her guests played chess, some showed off essays or poems they had written, others read then discussed the *Ching-pao*—the *Peking Gazette*.

Chin Chao fixed his attention on the board in front of him while Huang moved an ivory horse forward, then leaned close to whisper, "Do you not hear what they are saying about your friend Yuan Tung-li? That he plotted against the Dragon Throne and spent the night in the Forbidden City? I've heard that the President of the Censorate himself called for Yuan's arrest."

Chin clenched his hands into fists. "At the instigation of T'zu Hsi, the Empress Dowager, no doubt." His knuckles grew white with the tension in his hands and his eyes blazed with a fury so bright that his friend backed away.

"Do you think he is guilty?" Huang asked.

Chin Chao did not respond. Instead he moved his cannon to a square where Huang's general was threatened. He dared not talk about his friend, even here where free thinkers were welcome. He had learned that it was not safe to trust anyone involved with the court, even if they called themselves your friends. He could not be certain that any man was trustworthy anymore. Except Yuan Tung-li. He had been a true friend, but Chin could not help him now. He could not even manage to see Yuan in prison, though he had tried. He felt sick with sorrow over the loss of his friend, fury at the injustice of the charge against him, frustration that he had no way to vent his rage.

"I suppose you will say this never would have happened in America," Huang observed. Deftly he moved his general out of danger.

Chin looked away in order to compose himself. His gaze fell on Li-an, head bent, fingers busy with needle and thread. Her feet were hidden demurely under her chair. In that moment, it seemed to him that she represented all the repression and false perfection of a country ruled by tradition and ritual instead of by wisdom. "Nor," he said bitterly, "would that."

At Huang's look of surprise, Chin added, "In America, there is no law that men and women must be separated after the age of seven, so they need not break the rules as Wan Ke-ming has done in order to converse with one another. In America the women do not sit in corners with their heads lowered modestly. There they are allowed to think and even to express an opinion. Western women are not like the embroidered pillow over there—pretty but empty-headed. She is like a shadow without substance."

He spoke low but Li-an heard him. She stiffened, though she did not look up. She did not remember Chin Chao being so haughty before. There was something in his voice that made her think his face looked like the Thunderer, the deity of the storm who beat his drums with a hammer until the heavens shook and men hid their faces and covered their ears.

"Are we going to play chess or merely throw hot air at one another?" Chin demanded, scowling. Thoughtlessly, he changed the position of his minister.

His friend shrugged. "I know why you speak so harshly of a stranger. I heard your family sent a go-between to the House of Wan today."

Chao looked up, eyes wide with astonishment. "Here?" He turned to look at Li-an, who had not moved, had not by so much as the flicker of an eyelash revealed that she had heard him. "Her?" It was too much in a day already full of unpleasant surprises. He rested his head in his hands in despair. "Do you not see how she sits without raising her head? She must be a true Mandarin woman, yielding always to others with no life or spirit of her own."

"So long as she yields to you, what do you care?"

Chin Chao raised his head. "I do care. I will not accept such a wife."

Li-an thrust her needle forcefully through the peach satin. She did not miss a stitch, but her heart pounded and her cheeks were flushed with anger that this man who did not know her should dismiss her so easily. Wu Shen was right; the foreigners were arrogant. By living among them, even for so short a time, Chin Chao had become too much like the Westerners he so admired. When she saw Liu Mei approach with a tray of rice wine and porcelain cups, Li-an rose, dropping the fabric onto her chair. "I will serve the wine tonight," she told the surprised servant. "It is my mother's wish."

Mei shrugged and gave up her burden gratefully.

Li-an moved from table to table, eyes lowered, seeing only the tabletops, the hands of those who sat around them. She moved gracefully in spite of the tray she carried, for her arms were strong and she had practiced long and hard to be able to walk, though she could see little through her black, silken lashes.

Finally she stopped at Chin Chao's table. "Rice wine, honored guest?" she asked in her softest voice while she stared intently at the chessboard. He nodded but did not look up, though she felt that his friend was watching her closely. Li-an set the tray on the table, poured the wine from a silver pitcher, and handed Chin Chao a cup. He took it absently, moved his cannon forward.

"Most unwise, Venerable," she said, speaking the term of great respect in a tone sweet as honey. "Now your minister and general can no longer protect their emperor." Quickly she took the tray and moved away.

Chin looked up, astonished. "She is quite mistaken. What can she know about such things?"

"And she no more than an embroidered pillow," his friend said gleefully as he moved his general. "Yet she saw more than you."

Chin Chao stared at the board incredulously. His emperor was trapped by Huang's pieces. He had lost the game. He looked up to see Li-an near the folding doors, where the light through the lattice-work made a maze of shadows on the cool tiled floors.

When she felt him looking her way, she returned to his table at once. "Is there something I have forgotten, Venerable? Do you wish for a little rice-flour dumpling or some sesame toffee?"

Though her tone was respectful, he felt sure she was laughing at him. Chin noticed that her lids were still lowered; suddenly it annoyed him. He wanted to see her eyes. "Why do you not look at me when I speak to you?"

"This unworthy one would not dare raise her gaze to one so high."

This time she could not hide the touch of sarcasm in her tone. In spite of himself, Chao smiled. "How did you know that moving my cannon would make me lose the game?"

"Perhaps you should quote to her the proverb 'He is truly a gentleman who can watch a game of chess in silence,' " Huang suggested with a twinkle in his eye.

Chao glared at his friend, who fell silent.

"It happened thus," Li-an replied as if the other man had not spoken. "I was sitting on my embroidered pillow when I saw the many pieces of ivory, the shadows, the movement of nimble fingers, and I sensed that something was wrong. Kwan Ti bade me come to your rescue. But I suppose you who know the West do not believe in our primitive gods, so you did not listen."

Chin Chao's smile broadened. Kwan Ti was the God of War, patron of Literature and Upholder of Justice, but more than that, in his human life as Kwan Yu, he had also been the protector of women. Chin opened his mouth to reply, but Li-an had already slipped away to take her tray to the kitchen.

When she returned, Fan Fu-ku was calling from the back of the room near the reed blinds, "Will no one try a poem tonight?"

"I will try," Li-an whispered, her hands folded demurely.

Ke-ming raised her eyebrows but did not object. "So be it. Tonight the daughter of my house will begin."

Li-an stood with the magnificent teak wall behind her. One by one the men fell silent, surprised that a woman would join the game scholars and officials often played of creating witty poems on the spot. Her lashes lowered, Li-an said, "I shall call it 'The Imperious Official.'" She bowed slightly toward Chin Chao.

> "He speaks of the flaw in the pale jade
> But does not know its sacred power.
> He knows the moon will rise in the darkness
> But does not feel the light touch his cheek.
> He watches the withered apricot branch
> But does not see its fragile winter blossoms.
> His blindness comes not from the eyes,
>   but from the heart."

There was absolute silence as she resumed her place by the wall and took up her embroidery once more.

Chin Chao's smile turned to a frown. A moment ago the girl had amused him, but now she had brought back his frustrated anger. He knew he was the official in her poem; her bow had told him as much.

"Perhaps Chin Chao, who is so famous for his poetry and wit, would give us a poem now," Ke-ming suggested, her almond eyes on her uncomfortable guest.

Chin rose, his face expressionless. "As you wish it, so it shall be." He cleared his throat.

> "She sits, still and silent in the corner,
> Her shadow moving on the paper wall.
> The shadow in its subtle dance
>   is more alive than she—
> Beautiful as porcelain, cold as jade—
> In the flickering light of the lanterns."

There were murmurs of approval as Chin took his seat, but he did not really hear them. He was ashamed that he had accepted the challenge offered by the daughter of the House of Wan. He had let his anger speak for him and it had been a mistake. It was not this girl who had enraged him but T'zu Hsi and the president of the Censorate who was little more than her spy. Impulsively, he rose and went to sit near Li-an. She stared down at her bit of satin, he straight ahead. "My honorable parents sent a go-between to your house today," he said.

"They did," Li-an replied coldly. She was disconcerted by the timbre of his voice. It was a beautiful voice, she realized. Her anger hardened within her. "My mother received the offer into her own hands."

"And your honorable mother—what did she do with it then?"

Li-an suppressed a smile. His manner was very different now than it had been a few minutes earlier. Was there more than curiosity in his voice? She did not know why the idea pleased her so much. "She burned it," Li-an said matter-of-factly. "Would you like to see the ashes?"

There was a long silence during which she wished for the first time that she could look into his face.

"I see," he said tonelessly. Then he rose and left her.

Ke-ming sat with her sleeves spread on the arms of her chair and missed nothing that passed between Chin Chao and her daughter. Though her face was serene, her heart was not easy. She understood now why she had felt no peace when she destroyed the offer of marriage from the Chin family. Fate had set in motion what she was powerless to stop. Against men and their foolish rules she could fight, but not against Fate. She had learned that bitter lesson long ago, even before her father— She closed her eyes and brushed the thought away. It was madness to think such things. Madness to remember what could only bring danger. Or was the danger here, now, already among them?

When the guests had gone, the lanterns had been put out and the reed curtains closed, Li-an lay in bed and heard the footstep she knew so well. Father Without a Face had come to her mother for the first time in several nights. Li-an heard a whispered greeting, the sway of silk and satin, then the footsteps faded into silence—a stillness that was deep and black. Just before she fell asleep, she remembered Chin Chao's voice. "The shadow in its subtle dance is more alive than she." He was wrong. Surely one who was lifeless would not ache as Li-an ached now with cold and grief and emptiness.

3

On the fifteenth day of the first moon, the third day of the Festival of Lanterns, Li-an rose, her thoughts full of the celebration to come. Yesterday she had been troubled by the memory of Chin Chao and how unwisely she had behaved at the gathering of scholars and officials. Many times she had looked up to find Ke-ming watching; her mother, too, was remembering. Li-an had felt a flutter of unease at those long, pensive looks that seemed to hold a warning without words. But today that did not matter—nothing mattered but the festival.

After her bath, Li-an dressed quickly in a purple *p'ao* embroidered with plum blossoms and a sleeveless gray tunic worked in a bamboo pattern. As she moved through the passage to the dining hall, she glanced out the windows that opened onto the courtyard. The reed curtains were raised and the ground glittered as if Ma-ku, the benevolent sorceress, had sprinkled it with stars. Li-an was mesmerized by the rhythm of bamboo shadows on clean white snow. Already light from the heavens had touched the earth; tonight it would glow through every street and *hu-tung* in Peking as millions of lanterns heralded the coming of spring. Li-an's pulse raced at the thought.

She found her mother in the dining hall, staring, transfixed, at the same shadows that had fascinated her daughter. "You are eager, little bird, to be out and away," Ke-ming said. "Your step is impatient and your wings beat against the sides of your cage."

Li-an smiled. "I suppose it is so. I always want to fly on the Feast of Lanterns, because for a day and a night there is no darkness." She picked up a couple of rice-flour dump-

314

lings and added, "Forgive me, my Mother, if I do not sit with you today. There is much to be done."

Ke-ming smiled for the first time since the gathering two nights before. She could not resist the light in her daughter's eyes. "Even if there were not, I think you would go. When your heart is restless it is difficult not to listen to its call."

"Impossible," Li-an declared. With a smile and a bow, she was gone. She went first to the kitchen, where the steam embraced her.

The servants were busy elsewhere, so she ate her dumplings in silence, then prepared a bowl of rice, an offering to place before the kitchen god as she did at each new and full moon. Tonight the moon would be round, white, and perfect, the brightest of all lanterns. For a moment she lingered, absorbing the fragrances that swirled through the steam, then hurried to the hall where the lanterns were stored. She spent the day with Kin-shih and Mei, hanging horn and silk and paper globes throughout the house and garden. They could hear the revelers filling the streets while firecrackers exploded around them.

When the task was finished, she took the *Poetics* to her favorite pavilion over the water and tried to read. But the laughter, the bursting of firecrackers, the excited tap of footsteps distracted her until she gave up. When the sun began to set, she could pretend no longer. She left the book on the stone bench and made her way to the outer courtyard. Using the red painted screen that hid the entrance as a shield, she glanced beyond the gate. The people were bathed in soft red from the glow of the setting sun. Their faces shone with pleasure and excitement as they held their lanterns high. They turned now and then, their simple robes swinging about them, to watch a firecracker whirl through the street. Men and women alike laughed and shouted greetings to everyone they passed.

Li-an envied them their carefree happiness. She and Ke-ming had wandered the streets on this day many times, but always they wore silk and satin robes and elaborate veils and headdresses that set them apart from the others. Li-an did not want that tonight. She wanted to forget the wealth that was not her own, the status that came from a man she had never seen, the secrets in her mother's eyes and heart. She wanted, for this one evening, to be a child again, full of joy and unafraid.

She ran to the kitchen courtyard where she found Liu Kin-shih shooing away the ducks and geese. "Second Daughter," Li-an whispered, "I would borrow one of your gowns. Just for tonight."

The girl turned, almond eyes wide. "What are you thinking of, Young Mistress?"

Li-an glanced about to make certain they were alone. "You must not tell, but tonight I will join the people in the streets. I will not stand in my gallery of stone and watch the excitement from a distance. Tonight I will be in the center of it all."

The girl looked doubtful, but Li-an was not deterred. "I will wear my veil, so it will be safe enough. No one will know me." When Ke-ming took her into the Imperial City to shop, each wore a veil, cleverly woven so she could see out but no one could see her eyes beneath the clinging gauze. The people assumed Ke-ming and her daughter were too modest to show their faces as they wandered the market streets.

"Are you certain it is wise?" the servant asked in concern.

"It is not at all wise. That is why it will be such fun."

Kin-shih's eyes sparkled. "I will help only if you promise to take care. And then, tomorrow, to tell me everything."

"I promise." Li-an's heart beat with anticipation as she and Kin-shih ran to the servant's small room furnished with a bamboo chair, a chest, and a sleeping pallet on the floor. Kin-shih took a cotton *p'ao* from the trunk, along with a tunic and padded coat. She turned when she heard movement in the kitchen. "My mother comes to finish the evening meal. Hurry or she will see you."

With a whispered "thank you," Li-an took the clothes, which she intended to return with a jar of the cream she had promised the girl. She hid them beneath her *kua-erh* and hurried through the corridors from courtyard to courtyard until she reached the one outside her room. Silently she slipped beneath the cane mat and entered the cool stillness of her sitting room. She drew the curtains closed, removed her clothes and put the others on quickly, took down her hair, combed it out, and secured it in a bun at the back of her neck. Now that she had decided, she could not wait to be out and away from these confining walls. She wore her simplest slippers of dark blue and her veil attached to a plain ring of silver.

She folded her own clothes and put them away. She hoped her mother would assume that she had lost herself in the garden, as she often did, to watch the festivities. Finally she took several strings of cash, pushed them into her wide sleeves, and slipped through the reception hall. She did not stop to admire the lanterns swinging from the ceiling along the hall and the gallery beyond. But once she was in the garden, out of sight of the women's quarters, she paused to look back at the house. Lanterns shone from every inch of curved roof, glowed from the columns along the gallery and through the carved windows. At the two corners of the building there were double painted lanterns of silk with two flames that made them revolve slowly, so they cast a pale pink light among the shadows.

She crossed the bridge, hung with lanterns of transparent horn in the shape of fish. In the trees perched glass lanterns formed into graceful birds. There were even tiny boats on the water lit from within. They swayed, luminous in the breeze. She paused when she saw the last trace of twilight draped around the distant mountains, deep purple in the falling darkness. She could see the silhouettes of pines against the purple sky and longed to seat herself beneath those trees and rest her head on the fragrant bark.

But tonight she did not have time for such fantasies. She heard freedom drift through the laughter outside the gate and smiled secretly to herself. In a moment more, she had opened the twin gates, stepped around the screen, and joined the crowd. She turned toward the Tung Hua Men and Ch'ung Wen Chieh. The lantern market was nearby. She would choose a lantern of her own and join the procession that became a single line of radiant light, winding through the city from end to end.

As she ran, she passed girls giggling into their sleeves,

men who smiled at one another and called blessings across the road. Some of them set off firecrackers as they went. Li-an had to leap aside when someone set off a double-kicking-feet nearby. It exploded on the ground in sparks of colored fire, then shot into the air, where it split apart in a shower of red sparks. Even the vendors paused to watch in admiration. As soon as the colors had faded, the men began to call out, selling dumplings and candy, hands behind their ears while they shouted; they thought if they could hear their voices better, so could the people in the streets. Children in bright robes stopped to buy pieces of candy that one vendor blew and shaped into animals while the children watched, mouths open in wonder.

Li-an smiled when people jostled against her, begged her forgiveness, and stumbled into the next person. Soon they gave up the apologies. Everyone laughed and brushed arms and shoulders as they would never have done on an ordinary day.

Soon Li-an reached the lantern market. Though darkness had fallen, the booths were well lit. She considered the many choices through her veil, unable to decide between a mother-of-pearl shaped like a lotus flower and a silk painted with the story of Meng Chiang Nu, the Pumpkin Girl. Finally, because it was her favorite legend, she took the silk in exchange for one of her strings of cash.

She laughed as she turned away, the lantern held high. It was good to be here, to be free, to be just another face on the crowded street. Mesmerized by the snap of firecrackers and the ribbons of light that streamed through the night, Li-an moved forward. She reached a bridge crowded with people, who sang, shouted, leaned on the marble railings to hold their lanterns so they were reflected in the water beneath. The people flowed like a river of silver through the city, swaying with the breeze, twisting and turning along the cobbled streets, one long mass of color and light, warmth and laughter. From above, Li-an thought, it must have looked like a fairy-tale land or one of the Nine Heavens whose beauty she could only imagine.

All at once she was no longer a stranger, an outcast with bowed head and lowered eyes. She was simply Li-an, a

Chinese girl with a piece of moonlight in her hand. She was part of the celebration, another of the revelers, indistinguishable one from the other. But more than that, as the light flowed around and inside her, she felt that she was living again the glory of the past when the Middle Kingdom had been strong and there had been no foreigners to taint their joy. She was part of the perfect beauty of this clear night scattered with stars, part of the tradition, the ritual, the country she loved.

She felt the spirits of the Ancients all around her. They hovered in the lighted trees, their faces reflected in the water, their hands stretched out to bless the people who made Peking a city full of moving stars. Tonight Li-an was happy as she had not been since the soldiers had knocked at her door in Canton.

She realized she was hungry when she came to the street where the vendors sold food. She bought a hot dumpling filled with pork, some dried apricots and two *yuan hsiao*—little cakes made especially for the Feast of Lanterns. She saw a small child drop his cake; it was crushed by the crowd before he could retrieve it. She gave him one of hers, and he smiled up at her gratefully.

Then, at last, the sound of distant explosions caught her attention. The fireworks had begun in the Forbidden City. Everyone paused to watch in fascination as the sky filled with exploding light and color—ladies who leaned in green and blue pagodas, veils of trailing wisteria, showers of stars and flowers that settled to the earth in glowing fragments. There were "peonies-strung-on-a-thread" that hovered for a moment in the darkness, then disintegrated and fell downward. Even their descent was beautiful.

Li-an gasped with the others at each new splendid display. She had watched them from the high pavilions in her garden, but somehow, out here, they were more brilliant and enchanting. When an explosion of lotus blossoms seemed to fill the sky, Li-an turned with the others to exclaim at its beauty. She did not realize until it was too late that somewhere along the way, she had lost her veil. So drunk was she with exhilaration that she met the gaze of the women beside her. In the brilliant light of the lanterns,

Li-an's blue eyes gleamed like polished lapus and the women backed away, hands to their mouths. They, too, were caught up in the feeling that the past was all around them, that the spirits hovered everywhere, watching and waiting. "Look!" the women cried. "The spirit of a foreign devil lives inside this girl. I can see it in her eyes."

Li-an quickly lowered her lashes, but it was too late. She felt the mood of the crowd shift as they turned toward her, one by one. "A foreign devil," the people whispered to each other, until everyone knew of the stranger in their midst. "She does not belong here." At first they spoke softly, then more and more loudly. "Let us rid ourselves of the evil spirit." Their voices rose as they felt a surge of power that came from the light of their lanterns and the strength of their tradition. They were invincible, or so they believed, as Li-an had believed a moment before. They were not rational, but drunk with pleasure and excitement. They felt, in that moment of madness, that if they defeated this one foreign spirit, they could drive all hated Westerners from their land.

Li-an gasped and turned to run. She had seen the hatred in their eyes. The people followed her, calling out curses. The pounding of feet grew louder until it filled her head. The fear was with her again, beating against her temples. As the crowd ran, she felt the anger swell like poison inside them. Others joined when they heard the shout, "Defeat the foreign devils!"

She ran, head lowered, breathing in sharp gasps. Now the light that had been a miracle was an enemy that betrayed her every movement to the people who stalked her, spitting out their hatred as eagerly as they had shared their joy. Li-an heard a thump beside her and realized they had begun to throw sticks and stones. She was strong and ran faster, unhampered as her pursuers were by women with bound, useless feet and scholars who spent the day in study, not running through the streets. But she knew she was not strong enough. Always when one or two of her pursuers fell behind, there were others to join the group. Others whose voices rose with the sound of their thundering feet to make a living nightmare inside her head.

At last, because she watched the ground and not the way before her, she ran headfirst into a group of men in scholars' robes. She raised her head, but not her eyelids, and cried out for help, though she knew they would not give it.

Then she heard a familiar voice. "Look, it is the daughter of the House of Wan, dressed as a serving maid."

She risked a glance from under her lowered lashes and recognized Chin Chao and his friend Huang Ta-ch'ing as well as some others who had been at her home that night. "Help me!" she said. "They will kill me."

The scholar frowned and watched the crowd approach, lanterns waving, sticks and stones clutched in their hands.

"Exorcise the evil!" they cried. "Kill the foreign spirit."

"Come," Chin Chao said sharply. "This way. No doubt I know the streets better than you."

His friends called after him, but he did not stop. Against all tradition, he took Li-an's elbow and guided her down one street after another until they found the quiet *hu-tungs* that were not lighted with lanterns, where they could slip into the shadows and Li-an could stop to catch her breath.

"You are lucky I recognized you," Chin Chao said. "You look very different tonight."

"I am very different tonight," she rasped unwisely. "At least I was."

He heard the quaver in her voice, saw her stiffen when the sound of footsteps grew louder. The crowd had found them again. Chin Chao put his hand on her shoulder and whispered, "This way. We must not go directly to the house of your mother or they will follow and know where you live. We must make certain we have lost them before we find our way back."

He spoke as they ran. Li-an wondered how he could make a sound when her own breath was painful and her side split by a pain that drained the color from her face. The pounding in her head had splintered into tiny shards of agony that blurred her vision. The fear was everywhere now, in her blood, her dry mouth, her stomach, even in her aching feet.

She began to shake, to move more and more slowly.

Chin tried to help, but she had walked far before the fireworks and her energy was spent.

"Just a little farther and I think you will be safe."

She nodded blindly, stumbling when the pain in her head grew white hot. Then she felt something hit her shoulder—a stone thrown by a strong man at the front of the group. They had struck her, these people who did not know her, attacked her without reason, merely because her eyes were light and theirs dark. Unexpectedly, her anger drowned her fear and she turned.

"Are you mad?" Chao asked. "They will kill you."

"I want to fight, not flee. I want to show them I am strong, that they cannot destroy me with stones and curses."

"No!" Chao hissed. He grabbed her arm and forcibly pulled her with him. "There are times when to stand and fight is foolish beyond words. Foolish to die just so they think you brave. Run!" he said.

Li-an followed his lead out of necessity, for she could see little on her own, but still the anger burned within her, threaded again with traces of fear.

"Amitabha! We have lost them at last."

Li-an heard Chao's sigh of relief and realized that the night had grown quiet, except for the screaming voices in her head.

They stopped to lean against a tree whose branches held many lanterns. Li-an did not look up at Chao's face, for she dared not betray herself a second time. "Thank you," she gasped.

"You are very pale," he said, brushing away her gratitude. "I must get you home. Whatever possessed you to dress like your servant and come into the streets anyway?"

"I wanted to know what it was like to be—" She broke off; it was too difficult to speak above the pain.

"To be what?"

They moved more slowly now, but still her breath was ragged. "To be normal, for just one night to be no one, not friend or enemy, daughter or mistress, but merely Chinese."

Chao's frown deepened. He did not understand, but he heard the desperation in her voice. He had just begun to wonder if he would have to pick her up and carry her when they reached the rear gate of her mother's house. He glanced back once to make certain no one had followed, then opened the gate so they could slip inside.

Li-an found a familiar tree and circled it with her arms, reassured because she knew every knot and branch and strip of bark. She had thought she would be safe lost in the crowd, but it was not true. There was no place where the sound of marching feet would not follow her.

When he saw how tightly she grasped the tree, Chao impulsively put his hand on her shoulder, in spite of the teaching of many years that told him it was wrong. "Weep if you wish. You will feel better," he said.

Li-an stiffened. "I do not wish to weep," she said, forcing her voice to remain steady. "I am safe now. What would be the point of shedding tears once the danger is past?" She knew he must not see her fear; Ke-ming had taught her well.

Chao let his hand drop to his side. "I see that you are very much like your honorable mother. Is that why the people chase you with murder in their eyes?"

Li-an laughed bitterly. "No," she told him, turning. "It is because I am like my father." She raised her lashes and stared him full in the face so the moonlight shone like silver in the heart of her blue eyes.

Chao gasped and took a step backward.

"Now you, too, despise me," she said tonelessly. "Perhaps you wish to destroy me as the others did."

"No." He managed to choke the word out with difficulty. "I am just surprised, that is all. I did not expect—"

"The bastard of a foreign devil," she finished for him, repeating the words she had heard long ago. She raised her chin to show that she would not let his hatred move her, as if a wall of stone surrounded her that he could never breach.

"You are a tiger," Chao said softly, "with a fierce proud heart. That is what I did not expect." He leaned closer, drawn by the rise and fall of her breath, and noticed that as they ran, Li-an's hair had come loose. It flowed around her shoulders, radiant in the light of the lanterns, softening her oval face. But it was not lantern or moonlight that made her blue eyes burn.

323

Li-an was struck speechless. He did not care about her English father. She had expected disgust but could not deny the sincerity in Chao's voice, the admiration in his eyes. For the first time, she noticed his broad forehead and well-favored face, the fierce arcs of eyebrows above his black eyes. Their gazes met and held; neither seemed able to look away while the light settled around them like a cape woven of moon and mist. Finally Li-an shook her head and the cape fell in tatters at their feet. She started to turn, but Chao was not yet willing to let her go.

He was transfixed by the sight of her hair, which fell around her body to her waist. He had never noticed a woman's hair before, never wanted to catch it in his hands and draw her close so he could see more clearly her tiger eyes. He did not understand the impulse that made him reach out to cup her face in his palms.

Li-an froze, too surprised to object. She stared at him coldly, but behind the iced silver in her eyes he recognized a vulnerability that betrayed itself in the slight shaking of her hands, though her face was rigid as stone. He drew her closer, leaned forward, and kissed her.

She gasped at the touch of his warm, moist mouth, the gentle pressure of his hands on her face. The blood rushed through her veins like heated wine and her head felt light, as if she stood among the cloudy heavens and not the coral stones of the garden. She swayed toward him for an instant, then a splinter of pain, a glittering warning sliced through her head and she wrenched herself free. She had behaved like a fool before this man once already. Twice would be madness, twice and she would have no dignity to pull around her like a protective cloak. Li-an took a step backward.

Chao followed, tangled his fingers in her hair. She was appalled by the desire that rose within her when his fingertips brushed her neck. It was the first time she had felt the passion hidden deep inside; it was stronger than her fear, stronger than her anger or any emotion she had ever felt. The touch of his lips left her breathless, defenseless. If he looked into her eyes now, he would see everything—heart, soul, breath, and being. Here, she sensed, was a danger greater than any she had ever known. She drew away abruptly.

"Forgive me," Chin Chao murmured. "Heng-o, Goddess of the Moon, has woven a spell to make me a madman."

Li-an struggled to catch her breath. "There are many madmen in the streets tonight. At least you are not alone." She paused to stare at the ground while Chin stared at the midnight sky. She did not understand the tumult of warmth and fear, desire and pain she felt. "I must go in," she said at last. "I thank you again for your kindness. I would not have made it home without you." She bowed formally, hands pressed together.

"You are welcome," he said with equal formality. Then, because he wanted only to kiss her again, he bowed and slipped through the little gate.

An eternity passed while Li-an remained unmoving, listened to his footsteps disappear into the night. Only when silence had cloaked the garden, except for the sigh of bamboo, did she let the tears fall. She stood, her cheeks covered with liquid moonlight, and leaned against the pine as if its support alone could ease the turmoil inside her. For the second time in her life she had broken the most sacred of rules and let a stranger see her eyes. She had put a deadly weapon into Chin Chao's hand. She wondered, with the memory of his lips on hers, how he would use it.

4

For a long time, Li-an stood alone, then sat on a flat cratered rock while tears spilled over her cheeks. Even now, in the stillness of the night garden, she could not weep with abandon; Ke-ming's lessons had gone too deep. So, one tear at a time, she let her confusion, her fear and loneliness escape.

When at last she turned toward the house, where the lanterns had ceased to glow from within the shell and paper walls, she heard a crackle beneath her feet and looked down to see a scroll rolled and tied with ribbon. She frowned. How could such a thing have gotten here? It could not be one of hers; she would never have been so careless. Perhaps it belonged to Chin Chao. It might have fallen out of his sleeve when he turned to go. She hesitated briefly, then bent to pick it up. Tapping the rice paper against her palm, she stepped beneath the cane mat.

The reception hall was empty and still. Quickly, Li-an slipped into her room and drew the folding doors closed. It took her only a moment to discard Kin-shih's clothes and hide them away in the chest, along with her battered satin slippers. She threw a silk sleeping gown over her head, lit her own lantern, and sat on the satin coverlet with her feet crossed. Slowly, she unrolled the scroll. It was a poem written in a scholar's careful hand, the characters neat and precise. Curious now, she began to read the poem entitled "The Dream of the Dragon."

Surrounded by fish who leap and flail about him,
The Dragon sleeps the sleep of deadly flowers.
His lake boils and spits, splashing on his yellow robe—

A warning—but he snores and does not heed it.
For when he stirs, the women caress him,
Lure him back toward slumber
That he might never awake from his trance
and look about him.

Li-an grew pale and found she could not breathe. Chin Chao must be mad to write such a poem about the dragon Emperor and his frailties, to put into words the dangerous influence the Empress Dowager wielded over her weak son, blinding his eyes to the truth so that she could rule in his place. But for the scholar to carry the scroll with him, to let it fall so easily from his sleeve, was more than mad; it was suicidal. Li-an shivered, though there was no draft, and read on.

Many moons have passed since the faithful
delivered pears to the Vermilion Gates.
Many moons since the tigers entered the lake
And drank of its poisoned waters.
Yet while the poison saps the Dragon's power,
It makes the tigers strong and their claws sharp.
They bring their tiger wisdom, hidden in
their strange blue eyes,
Which see what the Dragon does not wish to see.

Li-an clutched the rice paper in rigid fingers. The tigers could only be the Westerners who inched their way deeper into the Middle Kingdom with each day that passed. Chao had called her a tiger, too. The thought made her uneasy. Even with a "fierce, proud heart," a tiger was still a stranger in this land.

In his sleep the bejeweled Dragon writhes in fear,
For his dream is of a prophecy fulfilled,
When the five tigers with their sticks of flame
Should convulse the Flowery Land,
And the golden-haired barbarians from the Four Seas
Knock at the dragon gates
Until they bring them crashing down.

327

While the butterflies on her bed curtains fluttered around her, Li-an stared at the finely drawn characters that could destroy the man who had created them. She thought of Yuan-Tung-li, who had been arrested by the Bannermen for plotting against the Son of Heaven. Chin Chao was careless and the Empress Dowager was quick to strike at those who did not take care.

She remembered how quickly Chao had assessed the mood of the crowd tonight, how he had helped her flee without awkward questions. She remembered the touch of his hands in her hair. Li-an rolled the scroll, tied it tightly with the ribbon, then placed it in the bottom of a lacquered chest beside her own poems, where she knew no one would find it.

Too exhausted to blow out the lantern, she lay back, the curtains drawn around her. She was certain she would dream of Chao—his eyes in the moonlight, tigers and dragons struggling at his back—but she was wrong.

In the morning, the sun fluttered weakly through the shell-latticed windows; the dawn was dim and cloudy, as if to make up for the spectacle of light and warmth the day before. Li-an stood silently in a tub of steaming water, half listening as Liu Kan chattered, but her thoughts were on a garden at midnight and the first touch of a man's lips on hers.

Dressed in a blue *p'ao* and a long-sleeved tunic embroidered in peacocks, she went to join Ke-ming in the dining hall. Her mother had raised the reed blinds and sat looking out at the garden. The snow was beginning to melt; it dripped over the tortured rocks like a hundred tiny waterfalls. Li-an noticed that the table was laid with their best blue and white porcelain dishes and a lovely *chien lan* orchid had been placed in the center. No doubt the pale green flower with its soft green heart had been raised in the hothouse of Father Without a Face.

Ke-ming turned, slow and graceful as the petals of the orchid. "So the little bird bought its freedom for a night," she said quietly. "Was it worth the cost?"

As Li-an moved closer, the scent of flowers rose to greet

her, and mingled with it, the fragrance of her mother's skin. Li-an met Ke-ming's gaze and whispered, "Yes, it was."

"Well then, I am glad." She pointed to the dishes of quail eggs, pickled cucumber, sweet dumplings, and meat pastries. "Sit and eat. Your adventure must have made you hungry."

Li-an settled herself in an elbow chair and considered her mother's face. "Will you not scold me for the risk I took?"

"Always I have made my own choice, as far as Fate allowed. You too must make yours. I am only glad, my daughter, to see you smile. To see the flush of color in your cheeks."

"But if I was wrong—"

"It is not wrong," Ke-ming interrupted, "to find pleasure where you can, precious jade. To enjoy the few moments in your life when beauty is greater than sorrow or fear. Such moments are as rare as perfect pearls and must be treasured accordingly."

"Is that how you feel when your lover comes to you at night?" Li-an gasped and covered her mouth with her sleeve. She would have withdrawn the words if she could.

"His company is pleasant," Ke-ming replied with care.

Li-an placed her elbows on the table, nearly upsetting a tea saucer. "Do you love him still after all these years?"

For an instant, something luminous moved behind the veil in Ke-ming's black almond eyes. "He loves me still."

"But you—how do you feel?" Li-an was not certain why she must know these things, but suddenly they were important.

Chin in hand, her mother pondered the question.

"If you do not love him, why do you not send him away?"

"Because he has been generous and kind. He is not a kind man by nature, yet to us he has shown only consideration and warmth. As long as he wants me, I will be here for him." Ke-ming turned to find Li-an's disturbing blue gaze fixed upon her. "Do not forget that we owe him our lives. And everything around you he has given freely."

Impulsively, Li-an put her hand on her mother's. "Because of that, he owns your body for as long as you live?"

Ke-ming shook her head and the orchids seemed to tremble. "No man owns my heart or soul or body and none ever shall. But if I share these things, that is my choice. He does not force me. You see, my daughter, I welcome him. Lying night after night in my bed alone is a cold and empty feeling. I give him the warmth of my body and he gives me his. I am content with what we share."

"Contentment is not enough!" her daughter cried, surprising herself with her own vehemence. "If it were, you would not have become involved with my father all those years ago."

Ke-ming heard the unspoken question in Li-an's passionate tone. Perhaps, at last, it was time to give an answer. "In the beginning it was not my choice. You see, I had just been sent from the Imperial Court and Tsai Shen—that is my name for my lover, for even I cannot speak his true name—had followed me. He wanted me and made me his. But he did not wish it known. He was a high official and I had been an Imperial concubine. It was a dangerous situation."

She smiled to herself. "Then Charles Kittridge appeared. He made no secret of his interest in me. Tsai Shen thought Charles would be a good distraction. If I became involved with a foreign devil, all eyes would turn toward us."

"He wanted you to give yourself to another man?" Li-an asked, appalled.

"He did not want it, but thought it wise. And I listened, because the Englishman was charming, handsome, courteous, and most important, a Westerner. I had never met a white man before and was hungry for the knowledge he could give me." She paused and a strange look crossed her face—half shadowed memory, half tender smile. "At first I did not care for him, yet slowly, before I realized it, my feelings changed.

"He was the only man I ever knew who had no secrets in his eyes, and more than that, no trace of fear. There was much he should have feared, but he was blind to his own danger. He gave me everything and did not ask for more than I could give." She met Li-an's gaze directly. "There are few men who ask so little yet give so much." Almond eyes dark and unreadable, she added, "I heard voices in the garden last night."

For a moment, the girl could not find her voice. How much did Ke-ming know? Or had she only guessed? Surely her mother could not know about the kiss or that her daughter had, for the first time in her life, looked a young man full in the face. Li-an blushed and murmured, "Chin Chao helped me home when the night grew ugly."

Leaning forward so her sleeves spread like pink snow over the tabletop, Ke-ming took her daughter's hand. "Remember this, Li-an. Chin Chao is not a kind man either. He is too full of anger." She stared into her teacup at the pattern of leaves and whispered, "Take care that you are not consumed by his rage."

"I do not know what you mean."

"Only this. 'There are two dangers in this world: a dangerous river and a dangerous heart, but the latter is most dangerous of all.' "

"Chao has nothing to do with my heart!" Li-an objected.

Ke-ming smiled sadly. "Remember, little one, that there are blind men who have sight and sighted men who are blind. Fate has chosen your path, and you can only walk it, taking the turnings offered with wisdom and care." At her daughter's look of confusion, Ke-ming waved her hand to dismiss the subject. "Never mind for now. You will see when the time comes for the blindness to be lifted from your eyes. Tell me instead about your dreams."

Li-an tried to understand the thoughts concealed in Ke-ming's gaze, but could not see beyond the veil. She turned, stared out at the snow, and tried to bring back the images that had followed her through the night. Often, in the morning, she and Ke-ming sat at this table and shared their dreams. It was the time when Li-an felt closest to her mother.

She saw a bird flit through the branches of a pine and disappear into the sky. In that instant, her dream returned. "I was flying, my Mother, rising into the sky while my sleeves flowed out behind me. I could feel the wind on my face, see the mountains before me, and I thought, finally I will find peace there. But the wind carried me beyond the sharp peaks, higher and higher until I felt that I was spinning backward. The days went by from sunset to sunrise rather than from dawn to twilight. Many days and moons flew past. The time slipped away like shadows on the snow. I tried to grasp it, but like the shadows, I could not hold it in my hand. Slowly my joy left me, for wherever I was going, sorrow awaited me. This I knew."

Ke-ming listened, stirring her tea with one graceful finger so that the woven gold bracelet on her wrist tapped against her cup. Her eyes were bright with curiosity. "And then?" she prompted when Li-an paused.

"I was in a room, a strange room with thick walls and a gray sky beyond the window. A tiny girl with the yellow hair of a foreign devil hovered beside me. We stood, she and I, watching another, heavy with child, who sat in a chair and wept. I felt her sorrow as if it were my own. I wanted to heal her. After a time, she looked up and I saw her face, her odd blue-violet eyes. She was a stranger, yet she was not. I wanted to help her. I sensed that the girl beside me wanted it, too. We reached out to the woman in the chair until she smiled sadly and was eased."

"There was no more?" Ke-ming turned so the sun caught the golden butterfly pinned in her hair.

"I remember spinning back in time, only now the days went from morning till night. I passed over the mountains and the barren plains and awoke at last in my own bed. For a moment, I felt"— she paused and tried to find the right word—"as if I did not belong here. The gauze curtains were unfamiliar, and the satin coverlet and the dark rosewood. Then I heard footsteps and Liu Kan's admonishing voice and the dream retreated.

"But the image of that woman's face lingered like the scent of perfume after a flower dies. I know her, Mother, though I have never seen her face before. Perhaps she looked like—" She broke off abruptly. She had been about to use Charles Kittridge's name. Like the name of her grandfather, it must never be spoken. Yet Li-an could not forget her father. Always he came back to haunt her, in her dreams and in her waking. "I felt that it was—"

"A dream that was true," her mother finished for her.

"Yes, but more than that, I felt a strange peace and contentment, a calm I do not remember ever feeling."

Ke-ming looked away. "Before the heavens open and pour their rage upon the earth, there is always an unnatural stillness."

"What do you mean?" Li-an grew apprehensive when her mother would not meet her eyes. "Did you dream, too?"

Ke-ming rose, moved into the corridor that led to the front courtyard. She paused at a window carved like an owl and looked up at the blue sky. Li-an followed, waiting.

"I dreamed of the weeks I spent in the *Yuan Ming Yuan*, the Garden of Perfect Brightness where the Son of Heaven spent his languid summer days. When the blossoms of peach and cherry trees fell from the branches into my hands, onto my hair and gown."

Out in the street, someone let off a firecracker, a straggler from yesterday's celebration. It rose into the cloudy sky, barely visible in the dull morning light. Pale colors exploded into a hundred fragments; the sparks fell to the earth to sizzle on the cold, wet ground. Though the roof of the corridor protected her, Li-an felt that the glowing embers fell on her shoulders and smoldered there, drawing her back in time to a day when the ashes had fallen from the sky as if Ch'ih Sung-tzu, Lord of the Rain, had gone mad.

On that day, columns of black smoke had risen in the sky. The wind had blown them toward the city, where they hovered like a pall over the colored tile roofs. The people ran into the streets like children, weeping in terror, screaming that the soldiers were on the way. But everyone grew silent when they saw the columns of flame, saw noon turn to night so quickly that breath and fear were taken from them and all that remained was horror.

Li-an had felt their fear, made it her own as ashes fell around her like black rain. It had been less than two years since she fled Canton. The memory was still bright within her, easily awakened by the sound of marching soldiers or the panic that possessed the people now. While pieces of charred wood fell from the sky and hot cinders settled in the streets of the capital, the people spoke low in voices of doom.

"The city is burning!" Li-an cried to her mother.

"No." Ke-ming's quiet voice rose above the sound of madness. "The smoke came from far away. I do not think Peking burns."

"Then are not the Nine Heavens on fire?"

"No," her mother said, "but I fear paradise is burning."

"I do not understand." Li-an grasped Ke-ming's hand.

"Two years ago the representatives of the Son of Heaven signed a treaty with the English and gave them many rights that they had demanded for years. Ever since, at the Empress Dowager's insistence, the Emperor has delayed making the treaty final. We have lied to the white men and attacked their ambassadors, who thought they came to settle the peace. At last the patience of the English is at an end. I heard they came a few days ago to meet the Son of Heaven at the *Yuan Ming Yuan*, but he had already fled. I think, in desperation, they have set fire to the Garden of Perfect Brightness."

The acrid smell of burning timber clung in Li-an's nostrils as her mother motioned for the servants. She guided her daughter into a sedan chair and instructed the carriers to take her to the Western Gate. While others fled from the smoke and cinders, Ke-ming sat calmly and was carried toward them. Li-an cowered in the corner of the chair, afraid to look out and find that a wall of flame had engulfed them. The sedan went beyond the Western Gate, over the Jade Canal, down the stone road toward the palace. Hidden by protective shadows, Ke-ming spoke as though in a trance of how these roads had once been frequented by jugglers and men on stilts, actors, singers, and brilliantly colored processions, but now they were silent and covered with soot.

The farther they went, the more dense the smoke became until Li-an began to cough. She looked out the window and for the first time saw the flames that rose in fury toward the blackened skies, the columns of smoke that lay like a nightmare over the pavilions and gardens.

"Enough!" Ke-ming called to the carriers. Gracefully, she got down from the chair and stared into the blazing distance. "There were housed here all the great treasures of art and literature—so many beautiful things, so much of China's history and her glory. I spent a full moon here once, met the Son of Heaven, was rowed across jade lakes, and stopped to drink rice wine on flowering islands.'' Her cheeks grew pale and her eyes moist. ''The white men have destroyed it all,'' she murmured when she felt her daughter press close to her side. ''They are too powerful; we cannot win in this battle against them. They will destroy us, too, in the end.''

Ke-ming closed her eyes and the child saw images flickering behind her lids. For the first time in her life, Li-an felt her mother's deep sorrow in the tears that Ke-ming did not shed.

The sight of her mother's glistening eyes terrified the girl even more than the flames that turned the water orange like the rage of spewing dragons. Silently she cursed the foreign devils who had left their seed in her. ''My father's people did this!'' Li-an cried wildly. ''He did this to make us pay!''

Ke-ming had turned, cold fury in her eyes. ''Your father had nothing to do with it. He was not like the other British, not like other men. He did not come, like the others, to destroy. He came to China to build.''

''But he failed and he fled!'' the child shouted over the sound of her furiously beating heart and the pain in her head.

''He failed to change the Son of Heaven's mind. Do you know why? Because he was too kind, too forgiving. He did not know that Chinese do not yield because they will not recognize that anyone on earth is stronger than they. He did not know they will cling to the glories of the past while the present falls to ruins at their feet.

''He did not know as Confucius did that 'It is easier to move mountains than to change the hearts of men.' Yet your father tried. He did not know our hearts were stone, our eyes blind, and our ears deaf. He did not know that only guns and fury will make the Manchus change. Even now.'' She knelt beside her daughter on the ash-strewn road. ''He succeeded in other things, and his success caused his danger. For he made friends of men he should have hated, and he made you—and loved you.''

"He did not love me! He ran away. He escaped the danger and left it for us to suffer! I hate him for that!"

She had run back to the sedan chair and curled into a corner. When Ke-ming joined her, she said softly in her normal voice, "You will not speak your father's name until you speak it with love, Li-an."

The girl had raised her head in astonishment. Her mother had said her name as one foreign-sounding word, the way her father used to do, not in the lilting two-syllable manner of the Chinese. From that day on, it had been the same. Ke-ming had called her the strange and unnatural form of her name and her mother's obsession with the West had begun. She had insisted that her daughter learn English, that she study Western books, Western inventions, Western artists and philosophers. Young as she was, Li-an had understood that something fundamental had changed in Ke-ming as she stood mourning the destruction of the palace. By the time the skies had cleared and the smoke and ashes disappeared, Ke-ming had been a different woman— a stranger to her daughter, to everyone. Except perhaps Father Without a Face, who came in the night as he always had. Perhaps only in the light was her mother cold, beautiful, and intent on a purpose the child could not understand.

Long afterward, Li-an had written a poem about that day. The words came sailing toward her now on the back of a breeze.

> She stood alone, hands buried in her graceful sleeves,
> Ashes in her hair and in her heart,
> While all around her, Heaven burned.
> When at last she turned away,
> The smoke curled about her head
> Like a veil of shadows or the coils of a snake.
> She could not see me anymore.

Now, as Li-an stood in the corridor with the gray-cast sky above her, she saw that her mother, too, was looking into the past. Ke-ming's eyes were empty like the blank, clean snow—as if her spirit had left her for a time. "My Mother?"

The woman turned. Slowly, her eyes began to clear. "It is sad to dream of being happy again," she said. Then she slipped away.

into the paper. Its corners were nearly like the pillow brocade — as if that spot had torn his dreams. "His Mother—"

The woman turned slowly and wiped her eyes open to clear. "Go to the—" She nodded slowly, his eyes shining. Then the turned away.

5

Li-an sat in the study with the window opened to the courtyard behind her. She loved this room—the wide rosewood desktop, the ink sticks and stones and brushes laid out neatly, the blank rice paper that fell over the back of the desk. She loved the rose-colored tiles that covered half the wall and turned deep purple when the light of sunset fell upon them. Most of all, she loved the shelves filled with books that covered the two inner walls. She often ran her fingers over the bindings, wondering at the secrets the books held.

Now she held a brush in her hand with the ink stone before her. She had mixed water with a stick of ink and placed the crystal weight in the shape of a crane to hold the paper still.

Usually when she worked here, she was content. She loved to feel the brush in her hand, to see the ink curve gracefully over the paper. The characters she shaped so carefully gave form to her thoughts and feelings—grace and balance, symbol and meaning. Often the ink flowed effortlessly, but today her fingers were stiff. She was troubled by the memory of a pair of lips that had brushed hers briefly, an unwise poem from Chin Chao's pen.

Strangers, we ran through the streets,
Fleeing the glow of lanterns, seeking darkness.
Silent, we moved down shadowed alleys;
The touch of a hand, a soft-spoken whisper—
   impersonal, only a necessity.
Winded, we reached the safety of the courtyard
Where we spoke and touched, became more than ever—
   Strangers.

Li-an heard footsteps and quickly tore the paper to fragments which scattered at her feet like windblown petals. She recognized the sound of Wu Shen's breathing long before he paused in the doorway.

She rose to bow, hands clasped. "Good morning, Venerable."

"And to you, my daughter." The old scholar smiled, but his heart was heavy. His sorrow showed in his eyes.

"May I bring you tea or red sugar cakes?"

"No," he replied, brushing the thin white hair back from his face. "I find my appetite grows weaker with the days."

Li-an was at his side in a moment. "Are you ill?"

He shook his head. "My body is well enough, but there is more to a man than his body."

"Come and sit." She led him to the bamboo couch, where he sank down gratefully.

When he was comfortable, she sat in one of the elbow chairs.

"You have been reading the books I brought?" Shen asked, though his eyes spoke of other things.

"I have not gotten far," she admitted with regret. "My mind has been caught up with inconsequentials."

"You are not alone in that. The scholar Yuan Tung-li remains silent and those within the Forbidden City can speak of nothing else."

Li-an felt a cold draft that raised chills along her arms. "What will happen to him?"

"The Son of Heaven will listen when the Empress Dowager says the man is guilty and then—" Wu Shen had been staring out the window as he spoke, but now he turned to meet Li-an's gaze.

She twined her fingers tightly together. When she thought of Chin Chao's poem hidden away under layers of satin, the characters burned before her eyes.

"You must tell your mother to take care," Shen continued. "I have tried, but she does not listen."

For a moment Li-an stared at him blankly. This was not what she had expected. "What has my mother to do with Yuan Tung-li?"

The tutor shook his head. When his hat fell into his lap, he did not bother to replace it. "Nothing, as far as I know. But there is a dangerous wind in the Forbidden City that creates fantasies in frightened minds. Everyone knows of the entertainments your honorable mother holds here weekly. Even the Empress Dowager has heard. She is not pleased."

Perplexed, Li-an considered the furrows in her old friend's face. "Why does one so powerful care what my mother does?"

Wu Shen rubbed his chin thoughtfully, caught his fingers in the thin strands of his beard. "T'zu Hsi has reasons of her own—a woman's reasons. I have seen her cheeks turn angry red when Wan Ke-ming is mentioned in her presence. She has been told that your mother welcomes all to her home—frustrated scholars, officials and ministers with loose tongues, even troublemakers like Chin Chao who have studied in the West."

Li-an's heart paused then began, slowly, to beat again.

The old man did not appear to notice. "T'zu Hsi says Ke-ming would probably welcome foreign devils, too, if they came to her for shelter. You know how much the Empress Dowager hates the men of the West, who have held up a great mirror in the sky to show her her own weakness and the weakness of her country."

The draft lingered, a chill of melted snow on Li-an's skin.

Wu Shen leaned forward, eyes narrowed. "I heard there was a girl—half Chinese, half foreign devil—chased through the streets of Peking last night. She was not very wise." He paused. "She who rules the Middle Kingdom can never learn your secret. Ke-ming must think before she opens her doors to all who wander near them. She must learn to turn people away."

Li-an laughed bitterly. She had seen her mother turn away many. Chinese ministers and foreign princes, self-important officials and Manchu Bannermen, women who would criticize her ways or her child. "My mother is as she is. She will not change, not even for the Empress Dowager."

"Have you forgotten the wisdom of Lao T'zu, who said, 'Of all the dangers, the greatest is to think light of the foe.'"

By now the chill had settled in Li-an's chest. "Is T'zu Hsi really our foe?"

"In her heart, yes."

"But why?"

"This is a question you must ask your mother. And please, my treasure, make her more cautious, like a shadow whose image fades at noon and disappears with the coming of night. Let her keep her name from T'zu Hsi's ears."

Li-an shook her head. "I will do what I can, but—"

"It is enough," Wu Shen replied. "It will have to be."

"Young Mistress?"

Li-an crouched closer to the brazier. She had held her hands toward the pale ashes that covered the glowing coals for a long time, but could not seem to get warm. Now she looked up to see that Liu Kin-shih stood anxiously in the doorway. "Yes?"

"There is a man to see you. Your honorable mother says you may speak to him in the garden."

Li-an cried out when her fingers touched the red-hot coals. Quickly, she folded her hands in her lap. The visitor must be Chin Chao. No other man had ever asked for her. No doubt he had discovered the loss of his poem and come in search of it. "Thank you, Kin-shih. Thank you as well for the use of your clothes."

"It was wonderful?" the servant asked eagerly.

"More than wonderful." Li-an frowned. That was not what she had meant to say. Yet she realized as the sound of Kin-shih's footsteps faded that it was true. In her memory, the joy of last night was greater than the fear. How odd that it should be so.

She rose, brushed off her tunic, shook out her sleeves, and went to her room. Removing the scroll from the chest, she tucked it into her sleeve and went out to the garden.

Chao stood where he had the night before, surrounded by a silence so deep that the rustle of pine needles only made it seem greater. He stared into the stream that cut its way through jagged rocks as if some answer he could not grasp were hidden in the murmuring water. His round hat with the brim slanted upward was askew, revealing part of the shaved front of his head as well as the thick queue that fell down his back. His hands were clasped behind him— scholar's hands with long narrow fingers and moon-shaped nails. Li-an felt that he had drawn the garden around him like a robe, creating this strange stillness, this moment of frozen time, by the power of his will.

She stopped, unwilling to break the silence, but Chao turned and the stillness fled. The two stood staring, blue eyes into black, recreating the sway of lanterns, the magic of moonlight, the instant of communion that neither could forget.

Somehow, Li-an found the strength to break the invisible thread that bound them. "You have lost something, I think." She removed the scroll from her sleeve and handed it to him.

He breathed a sigh of relief. "You read it?"

"I did."

"And what did you think?"

She motioned toward a bench, where they sat with a width of stone between them. "I think you are foolish to carry it around with you. There is much danger in these words."

"I am not talking about the danger. What of the poem?"

She looked up at him, eyes narrowed against the sun. "It is well written, the characters beautifully drawn. I thought it most clever and very frightening."

Chao's steady gaze did not waver, though his lips grew pinched and white. "Do not tell me that, like the others, you are frightened of the truth."

"No," she said thoughtfully. "Frightened for you."

Startled, Chao looked at her more closely, at the pearls in her hair, the green satin that rippled when she moved, the shadow in her vivid eyes. "Shall we walk for a while?" he suggested.

Li-an saw that his hand shook and he hid it quickly in his sleeve. That single glimpse of his unease made her feel safe, though she could not explain why. "Yes," she said.

So they walked among twisted pines, the bare branches of date and peach and cherry trees, followed the stream until they reached a bridge with a carved marble balustrade. Li-an stopped to gaze pensively into the distance until he asked softly, "What are you thinking of?"

"The tigers in your poem. You seem to admire the foreign devils who are bent on destroying us."

He stared at her in surprise. "Even *you* can say that?"

Li-an stiffened. "It was not my choice that my father should be one of the enemy." She heard the bitterness in her voice, saw that he had heard it, too. Only once before had she revealed her feelings for her father—when she stood beside her mother and watched the *Yuan Ming Yuan* burn. She did not know why she had let it slip now.

Chao sensed her unease and asked no further questions. "There is much to admire in the men from the West. I saw wonderful things when I was in America—clocks that put our water clocks to shame and books on every subject because none are forbidden. Their ships are strong and invincible, their weapons so advanced that they make us look like schoolboys wielding sticks against a horde of wild and angry beasts."

Li-an whirled. "There, you have hit upon it—they are little more than beasts. We govern through tradition, ritual, ethics, shape our lives upon moral values while the foreigners, out of greed, make war to make money. Death and silver is all they know. They are truly barbarians. At least we are civilized."

"Are we?" Chao said. "I wonder." He glared into the water that flowed over smooth stones. "Then why does my father have the right to sell my youngest sister to Wen Hsi as a concubine?"

Li-an gasped. "Everyone knows the minister is corrupt, that he has many women and does not care from where they came, so full is he of opium and false pride. Your sister cannot want this."

"You are not like other women," Chao said, "who do not ever speak their thoughts aloud. Even most scholar-officials would not dare speak of Wen Hsi in that way." He scowled darkly. "The worst part is, everything you say is true. I hear from my sister's woman that each night after her bed curtains are drawn, she weeps till there are no tears left."

"Why does she not tell your father how she feels?"

He gave her a little half smile. "Because she has not a mother like yours. To her, duty and *hsiao* are more important than happiness. She bows her head and waits in silence for my father's decision. She would not have it said that she is disobedient and unfilial."

Li-an shuddered at the thought of a young, innocent girl sent into Wen Hsi's house of corruption. For the first time, she was grateful that Ke-ming had refused all offers for her daughter.

"Do you not see," Chao declared passionately, "that we are clinging to the dream of an ancient past, listening for a whisper from a voice long dead? At least in the West they do not silence those who speak against their fantasies."

Li-an felt the cold wind again and pushed her hands deeper into her wide sleeves. "You are thinking of your friend, Yuan Tung-li."

Chao leaned on the cold marble to stare at the mountains, veiled in a light blue mist. He was silent for so long that Li-an thought his spirit had left her. Then he murmured, "They tell me I should deny him, denounce him as a traitor, but I cannot. He did nothing more than speak the truth. He asked what would happen to the Middle Kingdom if the corruption of the Son of Heaven was not put to an end. He spoke of midnight visits with the Ministers Kuei Pao and Wen Hsi to Willow Lane, where there are many women and much opium to be had. He said that the Emperor will soon kill himself with the surfeit he enjoys of every pleasure at his command. Yesterday that truth made the Empress Dowager tremble with fear that it might be so, and today my friend is called a traitor." He began to pace, his face so dark that he might have been touched by Yu-ch'iang, the violent God of the Ocean Wind.

"They say Yuan plotted against the Son of Heaven, that he spent the night in the Forbidden City," Li-an offered.

Chao groaned. "How often have I heard the same? They say, too, that he escaped through the Meridian Gate.

Only a madman would attempt such a thing and surely he would fail. You must have seen the place."

Li-an nodded.

"Did you not notice the number of Bannermen who guard it? Did you not see how strong they are, how intent upon their task?"

"I have seen."

"How is it possible then that a single man, a scholar who has no training with a sword, should have slipped by them unharmed?" he demanded.

Li-an had no answer.

"The plot exists only in the Empress Dowager's head and the mind of Tso Ch'eng-ta, the President of the Censorate." As he spoke, he clutched the marble railing as if it were an enemy to be crushed with the strength of his palms. Li-an met his gaze and saw rage and frustration at his own helplessness. But behind the fury there was something more—the vehemence of his beliefs, his faith in his friend, and a nameless passion that smoldered like the sun at noon.

Li-an stood hypnotized by the look in those eyes. She did not see such things when she met her mother's gaze; Keming's eyes were lovely, cool, alluring, but her secret heart was veiled. And Wu Shen's gaze was wise, warm, sad, but never brilliant with emotion. The Lius' eyes revealed humor, anger, resignation, but never, never passion.

Once Li-an had said she could know a person without looking at his face; she saw now she had been wrong. It was Chao's eyes that betrayed him, his eyes that showed the spirit of his soul. She stared at him, into him, as a distant memory hovered at the edge of her mind. She had seen this passion once before, but she could not remember where. Her heartbeat slowed and her mouth grew dry as she thought back in time. Then it came to her like a burst of cold rain on her upturned cheeks; she had seen the same look in Charles Kittridge's eyes.

She wanted to turn away, but Chao touched her arm. "It is pleasant for once to look into someone's eyes and see no secrets, no blank, careful stare. Your eyes are so alive, so radiant. I have never known another with so powerful a gaze."

Her body turned to jade beneath his hand and she found she could not look away. "You should not speak so to a stranger." She forced the words through dry lips.

"But you are not a stranger," he said, surprising himself as much as her.

He reached out to grasp her other arm, held her apart from him and looked directly into her eyes, giving her the gift she had yearned for above all others through the endless years of her half-blindness. She did not shrink from his gaze, but drank from it, absorbing all she saw there, every flicker of thought and warmth and passion. He drew her closer and she knew that when he drank from *her* gaze, he saw the mirror image of his feelings. It was true; they were not strangers. No matter that they had spoken only thrice. Somehow, in a way she could not understand, they knew each other in their hearts and where their spirits lingered. She swallowed dryly.

As he leaned toward her, she fell into the well of thought and need and memory in his eyes. She saw his golden skin, still smooth with youth and health, his lips, parted, inviting. For an instant, she closed her eyes, then shook her head and backed away. "No matter what our souls tell us, we are still strangers, Chin Chao."

"How can we be strangers after last night?"

" 'A single filament does not make a thread, nor a solitary tree a forest,' " she replied, her voice surprisingly steady.

"Why do you speak to me in proverbs? Is it safer that way?"

"As safe as you hiding behind your politics and anger."

His eyes glittered and she thought she had gone too far. Then slowly, he smiled. "If you say we have only a single filament, then let us begin now to weave a cloth. When it is done, we will no longer be strangers."

She smiled when she should have glowered in disapproval, moved closer when she should have turned away. The blood pounded dully in her ears as Li-an reached out for the first time in her life to touch a man's face. She ran her fingertips over his cheek as if only her hands could see. "We can begin and see what we create, I suppose," she whispered. What was she saying? Had she gone mad?

She trembled and dropped her hand to her side. "Let us walk," she said.

In silence now, but companions, not enemies, not strangers, they walked the paths of the garden, ducked beneath bent and burdened trees, crossed narrow bridges, paused to watch the fish in the water. Finally, they stopped on a hill of stone, where the view of the Western Mountains was unobstructed.

"Do you not wish to go there?" she asked, breaking the silence at last. "To find peace in the mountains that the gods created instead of these rocks and hills made by man?"

Chin Chao heard the longing in her voice, and behind it the loneliness. "I have longed for them since I was a child and first saw them rise into the cloudless sky. But I cannot leave this place, my *lao chia*. I could not bear exile, even amidst such peace and beauty. I must be here, where perhaps, if I struggle long and hard enough, I might bring a little change."

"You are a brave man," Li-an said.

"Perhaps only a stubborn one." Smiling, astonished that he should have reason to smile, he touched her hand. "So we know what I am, but what about you?"

"You have said already that I am not like other women."

"I have said it, though when I see you in your unicorn gown with jade in your ears and pearls in your hair, I forget that there lives the spirit of a tiger within your woman's body." Chao took a step closer. The shadows of bamboo leaves fell on his face and pine needles drifted on the snow at his feet.

"Is that not enough to know?"

Chao shook his head. " 'You may sketch a tiger's skin but find it hard to sketch his bones; you may know a man's face but not know his heart.' "

"Now it is you who speaks in proverbs," she said, laughing.

"Could it be that now it is I who am afraid?"

Her laughter faded and they stood in silence, content with the stillness broken only by the murmur of the water and the sigh of the dying winter wind.

That night, Li-an sat alone in her room with the folding doors closed. As the shadows grew and multiplied around her, she thought of Chao and shivered, whether with delight or apprehension, she could not tell. She only knew that tonight she was filled with a warmth she had never known before and the world was soft, seen through a frail gauze curtain. The shadows fell like feathers to the ground where they trembled beneath her feet. The words of a poem by Tung Tun-ling ran through her head and would, she knew, follow her into her dreams.

Alone in her chamber
A young girl is embroidering some silken flowers.
Suddenly she hears a distant flute . . .
She trembles.
She believes that a young man
   is speaking to her of love.

Li-an listened to the sound of moonlight on shifting leaves and imagined the place where she and Chao had leaned against the wall to gaze at the mountains beyond their reach.

Through the paper in the window,
The shadow of an orange leaf
Comes to rest upon her lap . . .
She closes her eyes.
She believes that a hand is tearing her robe.

With a sigh, with hope, a smile and secret dread, Li-an sank back on her bed. Though she was certain she would not sleep, her lids fell closed. Gradually, she slipped away from sight and sound and memory, into the comfort of her dreams.

6

Several weeks later, Li-an sat at breakfast with her mother
in the dining hall. The wind howled outside, shaking the
walls with its fury, carrying on its back the fine yellow dust
of the northern plains. The dust lay like a filmy shroud on
tables and chairs, drifted like fine gold in the corners. The
wind that crept beneath the latticed door was cold and
unpleasant; it stirred in Li-an a feeling of uneasiness that
lingered even in the rare moments when the blowing ceased
and there was calm. Spring had come to Peking.

Li-an drank her Dragon Well tea in a few sips and ate
some millet broth and flat wheat cakes before the sand could
ruin her meal. When Ke-ming cleared her throat delicately,
her daughter looked up and saw that her mother had something to say. Her heart beat faster.

Mother and daughter had spoken little in the past few
weeks; both knew Li-an had been meeting Chin Chao in her
courtyard early in the morning. Ke-ming said nothing, but
Li-an knew from her mother's furrowed brow that she did
not approve. Her almond eyes, usually so placid, were
troubled when they rested on her daughter. But she did not
speak and did not criticize. It was she, after all, who had
taught Li-an to think for herself.

"You should read the *Peking Gazette* this morning, my
daughter. There is a memorial to the Son of Heaven that I
think will interest you." She reached across the table to
point with her long nails at the characters of Chin Chao's
name.

Li-an took the rice paper, crinkled the edges in her
hands, smoothed them carefully before she began to read.
She gasped at the stark black characters that cried out his

349

rage and frustration more loudly than his voice, which only a few could hear; this memorial would be read by many. He must be mad to object so openly to the corruption of the court, the life of dissipation the T'ung Chih Emperor led, the manipulations of the Empress Dowager to steal money from the depleted treasury in order to build herself a palace. He implied that the Mandate of Heaven, which the gods bestowed on a virtuous ruler to give him strength and power, had been withdrawn. The gods were angry at the Manchu government and the Ch'ing must fall if these abuses were not stopped. Finally, Chao had quoted the poet Po Chu-i: "A Dragon by itself remains a dragon, but man makes it a god."

Now Li-an understood the feeling of dread that had assailed her when she awakened to the wailing wind. She ached for Chao, for his visions of the future that would never come to be, for the sorrow and despair that had already carved lines deeply in his face, though he was so young. But she was afraid, too.

"Would you not say that this man courts death?" Ke-ming inquired. "It is as if he dares the Empress Dowager to force him to be silent."

Li-an dropped the *Gazette* from nerveless fingers. "It seems so," she said hollowly. She stared at her hands but did not see the slender fingers and moon-shaped nails. She saw only the bold strokes of Chao's characters on a pure white page.

"My daughter," Ke-ming said at last, "I have kept my silence until now, but I must speak. You have forgotten in the rise of your new passion the wisdom of the Ancients. 'Curses and blessings do not come through gates; man himself invites their arrival. The reward of good and evil is like the shadow accompanying the body.' "

Li-an's heartbeat grew slow and labored. "Chin Chao makes me happy. Can you not rejoice that we have found each other?"

Ke-ming bowed her head. "I wish I could. But I am not certain you realize how deeply he could hurt you."

"I realize it." Often at night, she awoke with the pain like a warning at her temples and wondered if Chao's virtue would not someday destroy him. The thought made her cold with fear. She knew what it meant to have enemies who sought you day and night. She knew the terror of being alone with no defense against the cruelty of other men.

As the days had gone by and she walked with Chao in the garden, spoke to him of poetry, history, and the stars, she grew to care for him as she had never cared for another. The touch of his hand was a spark that set her blood afire, the brush of his lips a miracle and a blessing. But most important, he was her friend—the first she had ever known. The fear that she would lose him made her heart, which had only begun to open, shrivel and die as the splendid lotus died with the approach of autumn.

"I know the risk, my Mother. But I cannot give him up. He is in my thoughts both day and night. When he withdraws his hand, I feel only cold and emptiness. Now that I have known this warmth, I cannot live without it."

"I did not know it would go so deep," Ke-ming said sadly. "But you are mistaken. You will live, just as I lived when my heart was torn from me. You are strong enough to stand against the wind; like the bamboo you will bend, but never break."

For a moment the veil was lifted from Ke-ming's eyes and Li-an saw a reflection of Charles Kittridge's face. She looked away as the old anger rose within her. That her mother could have loved and trusted a man without a heart or a conscience—

"Do not make the same mistake that I made, pale jade."

"No," Li-an said, pushing her chair away from the table. "That I swear I will never do."

Chao was waiting in the courtyard outside her room. His face was obscured by the eddies of dust that whirled at his feet, then rose to paint the sky pale gold. His black eyes were fierce with pride and anger. At the sight of him, Li-an felt light-headed with joy. Always, when he touched her hand as he did now, there was an instant when the world around them ceased to exist, when her fear and uncertainty were consumed by the happiness that made her cold fingers grow warm in his grasp. He held her tightly, she heard the

351

murmur of his breath in her ear; the wind seemed to cease and the sand to settle in harmless drifts at her feet.

"You are a fool," she said, "but I am glad you have come."

He touched her cheek. "You know I could not stay away."

She smiled and he drew her hand through his arm as they walked the narrow courtyard. She preferred the huge garden, but it was safer here. They moved over the tiny footbridge of stone toward the pond that undulated like a think golden quilt. The orange carp beneath the surface were still; the crickets and even the pheasants had hidden themselves from the dust and wind. Chao and Li-an were alone in the world.

"Why did you do it?" she asked when they stopped to watch the bamboo scatter shadows on the surface of the water.

He did not ask what she meant. "I could hold my silence no longer. Tso Ch'eng-ta, the President of the Censorate, is more stubborn even than the Empress Dowager. He refuses to release Yuan Tung-li, so I decided to show them that there are others like him who are not afraid."

"Does it help your friend to destroy yourself along with him?"

"Perhaps it helps him to know that he is not alone, that not all run from the power of a woman who would crush honest men in her palm like dragonflies. She would save only those who bow their heads to her in fear and adoration."

Li-an looked in admiration tinged with dread at Chao's strong face, his black eyes that glowed like onyx with the vehemence of his beliefs. She felt a constriction in her throat. He was a man to be proud of and therefore a man to fear for. She thought of the broken dragon wings T'zu Hsi had cast into the wind and could not help but tremble.

"But I do not wish to speak of politics, my blue-eyed tiger. I wish only to breathe the scent of your perfumed hair and golden skin. I want only to touch your face with my fingertips and see for myself that you are not a dream."

She heard a quaver in his voice that had not been there

before and understood that he too was afraid. An ache began at the back of her head that moved slowly forward as he took her in his arms. He held her too tightly, afraid that she would crumble like the yellow dust and fly away.

Finally he leaned down to kiss her. This kiss was not like the others, the brush of a bird's wing, the caress of a butterfly, but the demanding pressure of a man starved for the things only her body could give. His lips moved against hers, warm and moist, and she felt her heart flutter, her pulse begin to race. He ran his hands down her back; she could feel the heat of his palms, the enticing movement of his fingers on her spine. He kissed her throat, flicking his tongue over her skin until she quivered with desire while her fear spiraled upward until it became one with the pounding in her heart and head.

Then he touched her breast and the nipple hardened under his gentle fingers. She gasped with a pleasure so intense that it stopped the breath in her throat. In that instant, Chao held her heart and soul in his hands. Li-an tried to catch her breath, but the dust filled her nostrils and lay like sawdust on her tongue.

Chao shook at the madness inside him, the heat that flared in his blood when he felt her body pressed to his, the roundness of her breasts beneath his hands, the way her breath caressed his cheek and her fingertips his back. He wanted to do more than hold her; he wanted to absorb her into himself so that his spirit, alone and adrift, would never again feel the emptiness that lay like a weight of lead in his heart. He knocked a pin from her hair, twirled his finger in the tendril that came loose. He saw the look of wonder on her face and suddenly the fear was upon him, so dark and all-encompassing that he shuddered and released her. He turned away so the budding branches made a tracery of woven shadows on his pale blue robe.

"What is it?" she asked.

For a long time he was silent, then he murmured, "I thought to lie to you, to tell you I have only just remembered what the Ancients taught with such diligence: 'Earthly passions are the thieves of life.' " He frowned at his reflection in the dusty water. "But I have looked into your eyes and

353

know you would not accept such a lie." He sighed and turned to face her. "The truth then is that I have chosen a path that is narrow and dangerous and I will not turn back."

"Do you think I did not know it?" Li-an demanded. "Do you think me so foolish that I cannot see the rage like poison in your eyes? It is true that I am afraid for you—for us—but that does not erase your image from my mind or the touch of your hands from my body. I would not give up the radiant light just because I fear the darkness."

He smiled and reached for her, but the sound of Wu Shen's voice carried through the house in a cry that froze Li-an and Chao where they stood.

Shen reached the courtyard, hands pressed to his breast to calm his racing heart. "You must go, Chin Chao, and you, my daughter, must come inside and make yourself composed before it is too late!"

"Too late?" Li-an repeated blankly.

"I have hurried from the Forbidden City to warn you." He leaned against the carved doorframe, his face pale and haggard, the lines full of fine yellow dust. His blue robe was wrinkled and he had lost his hat along the way. While he struggled to continue, Li-an gripped Chao's hand. The pain throbbed in her head. "The Empress Dowager has said that when Yuan Tung-li escaped, he took with him some of the Imperial jewels. Since they were not found when he was arrested, she claims they must be hidden somewhere else."

"But what has that to do with us?"

Shen's white beard quivered. "Simply this. The Most High claims that since your mother welcomes rabble-rousers and those who love the foreign devils, she might well have welcomed Yuan Tung-li. Perhaps even kept something for him that he did not wish to be found on his person. She has sent the Imperial guard to search your home." He paused, hands on knees, head lowered.

Li-an felt cold as stone, as if she had flown back in time to a distant nightmare. "But—" she protested feebly.

Wu Shen raised his head and she fell silent. He fixed his gaze on Chin Chao. "It is not really the jewels they seek. I believe they wish to know if you are here. Your memorial has set them talking and they are afraid. They want to connect you with Ke-ming and thereby stain her name with your crime."

"My crime, which was only to tell the truth." Chao laughed bitterly but stopped when he saw how pale Li-an had become. "I told you I would not turn back, but neither will I take you with me." He squeezed her hand once, so tightly that she winced, then released her and started away. "You need not worry," Chao called over his shoulder to Wu Shen. "I am going and will not return."

Li-an stared in disbelief as he climbed over the courtyard wall and disappeared from view. She opened her mouth to call him back, but no words came. Her mind and heart were as empty as her open arms.

Wu Shen touched her sleeve. She stared, uncomprehending, at the crabbed hand she knew so well. "You may not believe it now, but it is best," he said softly. "Come, we must appear to be at ease when they arrive. The Army of the Green Banner believes as the Ancients did that 'A man with a clear conscience is not frightened by a midnight knock on his door.' "

Li-an followed him numbly, her head pounding and her eyes blind.

Ke-ming, her daughter, and Shen sat in the study, while Liu Kan went to answer the knock at the outer gate. Li-an had a book open on her lap, but the words were meaningless. All she could hear was the sound of marching feet. An echo, she told herself, just an echo from a night long past. Though she could see only a blurred image of her mother, she knew Ke-ming sat rigid and regal on her lacquered chair with the brocade seat while Wu Shen bent over her desk.

Li-an imagined how the door would slide back, revealing the soldiers in their armor, how they would step over the threshold in spite of the *Men Shen*—the guardians of the door whose painted images she had placed on either side of the main entrance at New Year's. The *Men Shen*, armed with painted halberds, arrows, and magic symbols, guarded the house against vicious spirits, but could not keep away angry soldiers. The guardians frightened the *kuei*, but were powerless against human evil.

Li-an lowered her eyes as a row of figures, dark and indistinct, appeared in the doorway. Mouth dry and tongue swollen, she forced her body to be still.

"We come in the name of the Most High Empress Dowager to search for that which belongs to the Son of Heaven."

Ke-ming nodded. "Search," she said calmly. "We have nothing to hide."

"That we shall see for ourselves."

Li-an struggled to breathe through the weight in her chest. She heard the strangers move through the house, turning over coffers, emptying vases, spilling the contents of rosewood and lacquered chests on the floor. She heard the ripping of bed curtains and rose, propelled by anger, which eclipsed even her fear. There could be nothing hidden in the gauze bed curtains, but that did not stop these men. She had barely risen when Wu Shen touched her arm and shook his head in warning. "Let them vent their fury on the house and not on us. Vases can be restored and torn cloth mended, but a heart, once pierced by their swords, will never beat again."

Wearily, knowing he was right, she sank back into her chair. The soldiers took a long time. They searched every room, every courtyard, every corner of the garden. Li-an was amazed at how loudly their felt boots thumped against the tile in an uneven rhythm until her own heart beat in that unsteady meter. She pressed her fingers to her temples but the pain would not ease. Then the men stood in the doorway where the sunlight could not reach them to stare threateningly at Ke-ming, Wu Shen, and Li-an. "We found nothing, but it does not mean we will stop looking. The eyes of the Forbidden City see all that passes through your garden gate. Do not forget."

Finally they went away, leaving chaos behind.

Still the three sat with books open and unread before them. When the sound of stamping feet had died away, when the pain in Li-an's head grew muted and, at last, bearable, she looked up at Ke-ming. She could not see her mother's sculptured face in the tinted yellow sunlight, only the dark blur of her looped and coiled hair. With an effort, Li-an spoke steadily. "I do not believe the Most High sent those men only because of Chin Chao. She wanted to hurt you, my Mother. Why is this so?"

Ke-ming turned to look out the window at the whirling, clinging sand. "It is time you know," she said, "about the cruelty and pettiness of those in power." She glanced at Shen, who nodded slowly.

"It happened many years ago," the old man began, "when your mother was taken to the *Yuan Ming Yuan* at the time when T'zu Hsi also came. The Empress Dowager's name was Yehonala then and she had not yet made herself the H'sien Feng Emperor's favorite. Wan Ke-ming was brought with the Manchu virgins among whom the Son of Heaven was to choose his concubines. She was the only Chinese there; the eunuchs whispered that it was because she was renowned for her beauty and grace over all the Middle Kingdom."

The pain in Li-an's head receded as she listened and tried to understand.

"When your mother was brought into the audience chamber, she stood before the Emperor and prepared to make her obeisance, but he rose and stopped her, held her hand, and let her gaze directly on his face, though all know this was forbidden. 'So beautiful a creature should not bow to god or man,' he said."

"What did you do then?" Li-an asked eagerly. Her mother did not answer. She gazed into the sunlight as if it were a lantern guiding her back in time. She was smiling a little, because her memories pleased her.

"Ke-ming bowed her head and replied, 'She who builds a life on external beauty will end in sorrow. So, if that be your only reason, I would kneel before you just the same.' But he refused. For days afterward he spoke of Wan Ke-ming's wit and beauty."

Li-an frowned. "I do not understand what that has to do with T'zu Hsi."

She smiled knowingly. "Yehonala was among the other concubines chosen and she heard how a mere Chinese woman had so charmed the Son of Heaven. When her turn came, she, too, looked upon the face of the Emperor, and in time he loved her so much that he made her Empress along with her cousin Sakota. But she was reminded always of the Chinese lady who had not knelt, who had first earned the Son of Heaven's respect. She convinced her cousin, then the first concubine, to have Ke-ming sent away."

"Then T'zu Hsi won. Why does she hate my mother still?"

Wu Shen ran his fingers through his wispy beard. "Had she been merely beautiful, Ke-ming would have been forgotten. But she was also wise. And that T'zu Hsi could not bear. She would have everyone believe that of all the women in the world, only she is wise as well as beautiful, only she is strong. Later, the troubles in Canton and your mother's relationship with a foreigner only added to the anger that had simmered in the Empress's heart for so long. Now she cannot bear to hear Ke-ming's name mentioned any more than she can Lord Elgin's—he who burned the Garden of Perfect Brightness to the ground."

Ke-ming crossed her arms and spoke at last. "All is foolishness and lies and deceit. It has no meaning anymore, except to that woman who cannot forget. She would have me pay the price for her unpleasant memories."

Unconsciously, Li-an shook her head. "There is something more, some unspoken thing. I have felt it many times."

Ke-ming rose to look out at the courtyard where soldiers had slashed the budding branches from the peach and willow trees and uprooted potted chrysanthemums and dwarfed pines. The spilled earth had muddied the stream and the footprints of strangers stained the simple wooden bridge. "What is unspoken," she said firmly, "is often unspeakable. It is safer that you do not know." Slowly, she lowered the blind; then, sheltered by the dim grayness of the room, she slipped away.

Li-an felt suddenly cold, as if she had lost something precious beyond words. She started to follow her mother, but the sight of Wu Shen's face stopped her. He looked old, suddenly, and without hope. "What is it, Venerable?" she asked, dropping to her knees beside him.

"It is only that I am human," he told her, "and my body grows weak while my mind grows strong. I am nearly eighty and I have learned that what they say is true: 'A man at seventy is like frost on the roof tile; a man of eighty is like a candle before the wind.' Sometimes my flame is weak."

"You are not old," Li-an cried. She took his chilled hands in hers, to warm him, and thought of Chao. Would she ever see this look of resignation in his eyes? Would she hold his cold, wrinkled hands in hers when he grew old? Then she remembered that he had gone, had sworn never to return. Her heart stopped beating, tears filled her eyes, and she raised Wu Shen's hand to her cheek. Whatever warmth was left in him, she needed to diminish the cold grief inside her. "I am glad you're here," she told her teacher fervently. "It seems you alone are a true friend. Like the gnarled pine that is always green, you do not abandon your friends in adversity. Remember, it is the old trees which have weathered wind and rain and drifting sand that are most beautiful."

Shen smiled and patted her hand. "Even in your fear and sorrow you have time to comfort an old man. You are kind, my daughter, because your heart speaks and you listen. Do not ever silence that voice, but do not forget that there are other voices, wiser ones. To these you must listen as well."

"I have listened. I have heard. But wisdom is not enough to fill the emptiness inside me."

Wu Shen paused thoughtfully. "Chin Chao is gone," he said, "but he will return."

"No."

"It is so," Shen insisted. "And when he does, First Daughter, I would have you remember that 'He who rides the tiger finds it difficult to dismount.' You are flirting with great powers, pale jade, not gnats and moths. Do not forget it."

"I will not forget." She could not, even if she tried.

7

Ke-ming lay awake in her rosewood bed, though her lover slept peacefully beside her. In the passage, a lantern burned, making circles of shadow on the paper walls. Quietly, she moved away from the man she called Tsai Shen, after the god of wealth. She dared not speak his real name, not even in her own house.

She rose, then paused with the shredded bed curtains in her hands. She remembered Tsai Shen's expression when he saw what the soldiers had done. He had said nothing, for they did not speak of such things, but his eyes had burned with a spark of anger quickly suppressed. He had had this silk worked in phoenixes especially for her. She ran her hands over the fine needlework and felt cold and very much alone. Beautiful things she had in plenty, but they did not give her peace.

Ke-ming moved down the passage, stopping outside Li-an's door. She gazed at her daughter and smiled with infinite tenderness. It was an expression Li-an had never seen and probably never would. Ke-ming ached at the innocence of her daughter's face, her half smile—a reflection of some pleasant dream. She was not yet ready, this child with a woman's need, though Ke-ming had done her best. Slowly, reluctantly, she crossed the passage toward the Hall of Ancestors.

Ke-ming went to the altar with the painting of a stranger above it, but she did not see a stranger's face. She saw instead her father's kind eyes, his furrowed brow, the beard he had often curled with restless fingers. She remembered the smile he had worn on the night she had last seen him, laid out in unfamiliar Buddhist robes, hands folded on his chest, eyes staring sightlessly into the night sky.

Grief welled within her as painful as on the night when she had sat beside him and held his lifeless hand. He had left her a very small legacy: his wisdom, his divination box, full of the little sticks painted with characters that foretold the future, a vial of liquid with the power of visionaries inside, a poem about the peaceful mountains, and a note in which he told her to change her name to Wan, the word for ten thousand: then she would be part of the ten thousand stars, the ten thousand books, the ten thousand beauties of nature, and the ten thousand wise men who wandered the earth. He had told her to leave behind with his body the memory of her past, her grief, even her happiness. The note and the poem he had told her to burn, but the poem had been too precious and she had kept it with her—the only link to the man whose blood flowed through her veins.

Ke-ming lit the candles on the altar, then two sticks of sandlewood incense, whose fragrance mingled with the smell of melting wax. With great care, she removed her father's vial from under the altar, drank three drops, and replaced it. Finally, when the candle flames began to fly like comets through the darkness, circling, always circling until the light seemed to rise from the center of the earth, she reached for the divination box. She sat on the floor with her feet crossed, her satin gown spread around her, her hair loose down her back, and shook the carved wooden box until two sticks fell out.

Ke-ming was confused by the moving lights, the incense, and the tiny sticks that lay like broken twigs on the tile floor. She leaned down to read the characters. The lights spun faster, carried her beyond this room into the void, the silence without sound or meaning. The future rose before her so clearly that she had to close her eyes against the light. She saw it all—the joy, the life, the loss, the horror beyond words or memory. She gasped and the blood drained from her face while evil *kuei* cavorted in the shadows. It was too much for anyone to see. She covered her eyes, but the image would not go.

Shaking, her face pale and waxlike, Ke-ming replaced

the vial and divination box, then drew the satin curtains closed. She rose in a trance, bewitched by the mad, flaring light until the face above the altar became that of a stranger and the incense ceased to burn its way into her brain. When she could move again, when the fear was less like lead and more like flame, she left the room and went to her daughter.

Li-an tossed and turned, her half smile gone, as if somehow she had sensed her mother's distress. The girl moaned, grimaced in pain, and Ke-ming understood. She had guessed that the headache would come tonight in the wake of the soldiers. She had prepared the willow-bark tea earlier; now it must be heated and brought still warm to Li-an's waiting lips. Ke-ming hurried to the kitchen, found the teapot, and started a flame from a glowing coal. Her eyes were dry with tears she could not shed, her heart heavy with a knowledge too great to bear.

Li-an was dreaming of the beat of her heart when Chao touched her hand, the swirl of her green satin robe that mingled with his blue one like the colors of the sea. Then, abruptly, he turned away and her heartbeat became the sound of his footsteps as he left her behind. Soon the footsteps became a drumbeat, the drumbeat the stamping of soldiers' feet that swelled inside her head until she thought it would burst with the sound. The noise grew and lingered until it became the image of Charles Kittridge's haggard face. "Take care, little one," he whispered and left her with a sword above her head. All the while the feet were marching, moving inexorably closer, until she awoke in a sweat, grasping the coverlet with bloodless fingers.

Slowly, she became aware of a breath of cool air, the light, soothing motion of a hand on her hot skin. A soft voice sang meaningless little words whose rhythm calmed the beat of her heart. Blind with pain, she raised her head to drink while cool fingers, magic, gentle fingers continued to circle, slowly, tenderly. Her mother's fingers, the sound of her music, drew Li-an away from the nightmare, away from the darkness, away from the pain, and into the safe and certain world where Ke-ming sat with the gauze curtain like a shawl around her shoulders. Ke-ming leaned forward, sang and hid behind her smile the sight, the sound, the rhythm of her own breaking heart.

◇ ◇ ◇

A week later, Li-an sat in a pavilion with a gaily painted green and red roof. On one side she could see the peach trees bursting into bloom, on the other the mist-blue mountains. Her mind was empty, except for a single line, a scrawled group of characters Chin Chao had sent her in a blue silk packet two days before. "A heart that is distant creates a wilderness around it." In the midst of the rumors that trickled down the *hu-tungs* of the city, the cries of discontent as the officials took sides concerning the affair of Yuan Tung-li, the watching, waiting eyes of the Bannermen, Chao had sent this line to tell her—what? Try as she might, she could not understand.

Li-an had grown pale and silent during the past several days. Her head was full of echoes and whispers, memories and warnings that made a chaos of sound and feeling in which she could not find a pattern. Chao was foremost in her thoughts, the heart of her sorrow. She carried always in her sleeve a poem he had written about the Feast of Lanterns—a fragment of the moments they had shared before the soldiers came.

In the light of the lanterns
Her eyes, cold blue like a lake in the chill of winter
Stared blindly into the shadows
As she laughed and turned away.
    Beneath the stillness of the lake,
        Tears.

Her face in the mirror is like golden marble,
But the chill has not yet reached her heart.
    Beneath her silence,
        Songs of joy.

Li-an sighed, inhaled the new fragrances of spring, let the garden enfold her, now that willow leaves, peach blossoms, splashes of color and greenery hid the stark shadows of winter. All at once, she longed for Chao fiercely and his image filled her mind. Then she heard a soft footstep, looked

363

up, and he was there. She rose, smiling, hands outstretched, but when she saw his expression, the smile disappeared.

"Forgive me for breaking my vow," he said in an unnatural voice, "but today I am in need of a friend."

"What is it?" she asked, dismayed.

"They have executed Yuan Tung-li as a traitor."

Li-an gasped and grew pale. "His family?" she asked.

"They were luckier than he. They had gone into hiding and were not taken." Chao spoke mechanically, as if reciting a lesson he had learned by heart, except that since the learning, his heart had grown hollow and cold.

Li-an took his chilled hands and drew him inside the pavilion where no eyes but hers would see his grief.

He stood for a moment, holding her tightly, afraid to let her go, as if she, too, might be snatched away.

"I am here," she said softly. "I will always be here."

The sound of her voice, the compassion in her eyes made the pain rise like a torrent inside him. He began to pace the marble floor, unable to stay still, unable to express the sorrow too deep for words. He stood and stared at the mountains, leaning on the balustrade until the unevenness of the wood was pressed into his palms. "It looked the same last spring," he said, "the city, the mountains shrouded in mist, the peach trees and willows and the tall green bamboo. The birds and crickets sing the same songs. Every year the same—but it is not the same. It cannot ever be the same again.

" 'The Four Seasons go on forever and ever:
In all Nature nothing stops to rest
Even for a moment. Only the sick man's heart—
Deep down, still ashes as of old.' "

Li-an stood beside him. She did not touch him, but rested her hand on the railing where he could see it, know that it was there.

Chao swallowed dryly and covered her fingers with his. "I have lost more than a friend today. I have lost hope. All around me I see men close their eyes against the truth, lower their heads so they need not see the omens in the sky."

Chao released her to cross and recross the floor, his fierce eyebrows a dark slash across his forehead. "The Manchu government has chosen blindness," he muttered. "When they open their eyes and see the heavens whirling toward destruction, the fear is too great. Because of them we have gone backward to the time before time when the gods Shu and Hu came together to bring an end to chaos so the world could be born."

He stopped, breathing heavily, and met Li-an's gaze. "The lightning of Hu and Shu will not destroy the darkness again. We are alone now, ruled by weaklings, thieves, and fools. Each day another rebellion arises. Soon there will come an army like the Sword of Flame whose rage will give them the strength to topple the Manchus with their tight closed eyes. The Ch'ing think if they silence the voices that cry out against them, if they kill us one by one, they will be safe. But they are wrong!"

Li-an listened in silence to the ranting and stamping of feet, which was the only way Chao could begin to heal himself.

"No one stood up for Tung-li. No one fought to save the life of a brilliant scholar. They all turned away, so that he died without even the small comfort of knowing he would be mourned."

"Did you not try to see him?"

"Many times, but I was not allowed. And now, because of that, they watch me."

"Did even you turn away from him in the end?"

"Never," he said. "I was there when he died, but he did not see me in the crowd. To die is one thing. To die alone, abandoned, betrayed, is another." He shuddered.

"He was not alone," she whispered. "You at least were with him. He will have known that in his heart."

He shook his head violently and paced up and down, forward and back, his face twisted in rage, grief, and frustration. Again and again, he struck the wall with his fists until both hands were covered with blood.

Li-an gasped at the sight of his red-stained skin.

Chao turned, stopped still, remembering suddenly that she was there. He stared at her pale, shadowed skin and the hollows in her cheeks. "Forgive me," he said. "I should not talk so to you of all people. You should not be the one to bear my anger."

"You are grieving," she replied. "You do not realize what you say. I only wish I could do more than listen. But I do not know how to help you."

"You help me by staying beside me, even in the face of my madness." He took her hands in his. "Why did the gods see fit to bless me with a friend like you?"

Li-an wanted to weep, though she wasn't certain why. "Perhaps because they knew I, too, was in need of a friend."

Chao's hands trembled as he drew her close. He craved the touch of her golden skin, the comfort of her beating heart. Li-an slid her arms around him and they stood without speaking. Chao gripped her so tightly that her ribs ached, but she rested her head on his chest and felt unaccountably safe. He trembled now and then as if his grief would overwhelm him, but each time he looked into her eyes, he saw in them the endless blue sky and was calmed. After a long moment, he drew away.

"You know what we do is wrong, Li-an, but do you know why?"

"I do not care why," she said firmly.

"But I do. It is wrong because we have made our own choice, because we are giving in to our own desires, our own feelings. It is forbidden to follow your heart. You must bow down like the others when the voice of tradition speaks and never break the rituals that hold our Chinese lives together by narrow threads. You are a rebel, my tiger, because you do not yield to the forces that would shape you into a woman like all women."

Li-an smiled. "Then let us be rebels together and yield only to each other." He started to protest, but she shook her head. "If you looked into my moon mirror, you would see your face instead of mine. We are the same."

He grasped both her hands. "Today I saw a dear friend die. He is gone and will soon be forgotten by everyone but me. I know now how few are the hours we have to find our own happiness. I need you, Li-an. I would have you for my wife. I do not wish to die without ever knowing joy."

"Nor do I." She felt a desperate urge to make Chao hers, as if it were her last chance. "Your wish is also mine."

Her face grew flushed and the blood sang in her veins. She did not wonder if this were right; she knew. Her hands and heart and spirit told her so. She did not think of practicalities—what his family would say when they learned of her heritage, the impossibility of hiding her eyes from a whole house of new servants, the danger. She thought only of Chao and the warmth of his arms around her.

When he kissed her, she closed her eyes and felt his rage and grief turn to passion. She opened her mouth to his warm tongue, to the movement of his lips on hers. Slowly, he drew away. "Let us go to your mother and ask her permission."

Li-an hesitated for an instant; she remembered the cool warning in Ke-ming's almond eyes. She would not let that stop her, she decided. This time she would fight for what she wanted, even against her mother's will of iron.

Chao and Li-an left the garden and went down the broad passage through the center of the house. They found Ke-ming in the Hall of Ancestors, replacing the peach blossoms in a tall porcelain vase on the altar to the dead.

Li-an stared in astonishment. Many times when she came to worship, she had found a stick of incense burnt in her absence or fresh greenery or blossoms, but it had never occurred to her that Ke-ming had done these things. Her mother touched the branches carefully, reverently, until the arrangement was perfect.

Ke-ming's fingers grew still when she heard her daughter's footsteps, the whisper of robes that meant she was not alone. The older woman did not turn; she did not wish to see the light in their eyes or the hope. Nor did she want them to see the despair she was afraid she could not hide. "What is it?" she asked, though she knew the answer, had known it since she sat last night with the scent of incense all around her.

"Honorable mother of the House of Wan, I, Chin Chao, want to make your daughter my wife."

Ke-ming raised her head slowly, but did not turn. "I gave the go-between my answer many weeks ago. You accepted it then."

"But then I did not know this woman as I know her now."

Ke-ming shook her head. "It does not matter now. It is already too late." She would not lose Li-an as she had lost the others, Ke-ming swore to herself. Her daughter would not go down into darkness. She alone would find her way to the light.

Chao saw how Ke-ming stood as if carved from jade, cold, her voice expressionless; she would not even look at his face. He felt rage at such discourtesy. "I will have her in spite of what you say," he declared unwisely. "If you will not listen—"

Now she turned so he could see her eyes, black and hard as obsidian in her lovely face. "I will listen when you act from your heart instead of your fury. 'One who is willing to restrain a moment's anger will avoid a hundred days' sorrow.' But you have not yet learned that lesson."

"This action is from my heart."

Ke-ming shook her head. "I will not wed my daughter to a man who daily endangers himself and all who care about him."

For the first time, Li-an spoke. "It is not your decision, my Mother. You taught me always to think for myself, told me that I had a choice as you did not. I have made that choice."

When Ke-ming met her daughter's gaze, she grew rigid. The girl was right; there was nothing her mother could do. Except forbid the marriage. Then perhaps Li-an would be saved from the fate that awaited Chin Chao. "I ask you, Chin Chao, to leave us. I will discuss this no further."

Li-an was appalled. This cold and distant woman—was she the one who had massaged Li-an's head, who had sung and played and lingered until the headache disappeared? No, this was the woman who had stood and watched the *Yuan Ming Yuan* burn.

Chao was breathing heavily, clenching and unclenching his hands. "I will go," he said. "I do not wish to endanger you or your daughter further." He whirled and left the room.

Li-an stared at her mother, so their eyes met and held, clear blue and cold black. For a long moment, neither moved, until, without a word, Li-an followed Chao. She caught up with him at the far end of the passage. When she touched his arm, he paused.

"If you send to tell me where and when, I will come to you."

He stared in disbelief.

"This choice I have made," Li-an said. "I will keep my vow."

"You would come to me, not yet a wife? You would risk your mother's displeasure, the shame if she should know?"

"I would."

He smiled sadly and took her hand. "Are you certain?"

"Yes," she said without hesitation. "I am certain."

· 8 ·

Li-an heard nothing from Chin Chao for a week and began to think he had changed his mind. Then, one evening when the garden was heavy with the scent of lilac, Liu Kin-shih brought a package wrapped in red silk. Li-an took the packet to her courtyard, hung a lantern from the branch of a plum tree, and sat on the low marble railing of the bridge. Carefully, she broke the seal and unfolded the silk. A shower of peach petals fell into her lap. One she caught in her open palm. It lay against her skin, fragile as a snowflake, yet strong enough to survive the bright spring sun. She closed her fingers over it and unfolded the rice paper inside. "To Li-an, First Daughter of the House of Wan," it began.

> I, Chin Chao, aged twenty-five years, First Son of the House of Chin, born in the fifth month of the Year of the Phoenix, healthy of body and adventurous of spirit, scholar and member of the Hanlin Academy, send to you my name and other particulars and ask most humbly for the honor of your reply in regard to our exchanging names and gifts.

Smiling at his formality, Li-an sent her response, including her own name, age, date of birth, and accomplishments. Into the folded square of silk, she put a willow leaf. Kin-shih took the packet directly to Chao. Two days later, Li-an received another silk-wrapped package, larger than the first and heavier. Again she took it into her courtyard where the fragrance of orchids clung to her robe and the cackle of peacocks and bantam hens filled her ears. Eagerly, she

370

unfolded the silk to find a beautiful silver-backed mirror whose surface was a crescent moon. The note read:

> Having received your reply (and the healing willow
> leaf), with this gift, I signify my intention to make
> you the wife of my body as well as my heart.

Li-an's throat tightened and she ran her fingers over the characters as though she could still feel the sweep of Chao's brush on the page.

> Each time you look into this glass, know that it is
> not your own face you see, but my image reflected
> in the image of she who shares my soul.

She understood then that, in his own way, Chao was fulfilling the six steps that must be taken before a marriage could occur. Already there had been the asking of names, and now the exchange of gifts. She would have to send him one—something special, so that each time he looked at it, he would think of her. Finally she read the poem by Chiang Che-kin that followed the note.

> That maiden, dreaming at her window ledge,
> Leaning on her soft white arms . . .
> I do not love her for her great house
>   on the shore of the Yellow River.
> I love her because she has let fall,
>   floating down the stream,
> A little willow leaf.

Li-an found it difficult to breathe; the scent of the orchids was too heady.

> I do not love the east wind because it
>   carries to me the scent of blossoming peach trees,
> That are like snow on the mountain.
> I love it because it has carried
>   the little willow leaf to my boat.

The words grew soft and blurred.

> The little willow leaf—I do not love it because
>   it reminds me that delicate spring
>   has come into flower again.
> I love it because the maiden
>   has pricked a name on it with her needle,
> And because that name is mine.

Li-an smiled and tried to think of what she could send Chao in return. Then she remembered a man's girdle ornament of kingfisher feathers and silver that she had bought at the jade shop on the street of markets. She had thought it beautiful and picked it up, though she had no one to give it to. She found it buried in a chest and sent it to Chao through Kin-shih, who had begun to sleep on a pallet in Li-an's sitting room. When Li-an had asked this favor of her mother, she had expected trouble, but Ke-ming had agreed, tonelessly, without meeting her daughter's gaze.

Kin-shih smiled now as she took the silk packet. She was thrilled by the romance of this secret courtship and proud of her mistress's trust.

Finally, Chao sent a note to inform Li-an that he had gone to a Buddhist temple and the priest had determined a propitious day—the eighth moon of the third month. He would send a sedan for her. She must be discreet and wear plain clothes, and she would be brought safely to him where he waited.

On the eighth moon, Li-an walked in the garden all day, stared longingly at the mountains. Surely among those gray-blue peaks, the murmuring streams would flow through her blood and still the sense of anticipation that left her frightened by the power of her longing.

After dark, when all had retired for the night, Li-an lay waiting. She heard the familiar footsteps of her mother's lover and was grateful that Father Without a Face would claim Ke-ming's attention through the long hours of darkness. Soon, Kin-shih appeared, offering her own clothes for

Li-an to wear a second time. When her mistress began to draw her hair back from her face, Kin-shih objected.

"Your clothes can be plain, but your hair will be beautiful to show off your glowing face, Young Mistress." Quickly, the servant coiled Li-an's hair above her ears and inserted golden lotus blossoms into each coil. Finally she declared that her mistress was ready, and while Li-an sat, hands cold and still on her knees, Kin-shih slipped out to wait for the sedan that would come to the hidden gate.

Soon she was back, motioning to her mistress. Li-an rose, outwardly calm, but inside she quivered with apprehension and expectation. She ducked through the little gate, squeezed Kin-shih's hand, and stepped into the sedan chair, face veiled so no one would recognize her.

As soon as the chair was in motion, she sniffed curiously. Surely the scent of flowers drifted through the small dark enclosure. She brushed the seat and discovered a single peony. It was early for the reddish-purple blooms, but somehow Chao had found one. She knew the *moutan* was a symbol of many things, but most important, of lasting affection. She fought back tears, though her vision was blurred in the darkness. There were those who called this "the blinding herb." She thought that they were right.

She did not know how long the chair jounced over the streets, for her thoughts were with Chao. What if she did not know what to do, how to please him? What if she made a fool of herself? She clasped her hands in her lap so tightly that the blood left her fingers. Suddenly the sedan came to a stop. The door was opened and she stepped out, expecting to find Chao waiting, but there was only a servant girl.

"Come," she whispered. "We must hurry if you are to be ready in time."

"In time for what?"

Already the girl was hurrying forward. Li-an could do nothing but follow. She crossed a tiled courtyard, stepped beneath a cane mat, and found herself in a room full of chests, a few chairs, and a table. There were beautiful red lanterns of horn and silk, gold foil symbols of double happiness on each side of the door, and the walls were hung with red scrolls. Red—the color of joy; this room must be full to bursting with happiness. She gasped when she saw the scarlet gown laid across a chest. It was made of layers and layers of brocade and satin, embroidered with butterflies and peonies in gold and silver. "What—" she began.

"It is your wedding gown," the servant explained, dimpling in delight at Li-an's astonishment. "It belonged to the groom's mother. He had it brought for you. Come quickly. He awaits you in the reception hall."

A strange calm filled Li-an when the servant helped her slip the gown over her head. She revolved once to make the red skirts swirl about her ankles.

"A bride cannot meet her groom without a bridal head-dress," the servant said with a grin. From one of the chests she lifted the most unusual headpiece Li-an had ever seen. It was a peacock made entirely from mother-of-pearl, except for the eye of each tail feather where a circle of lapus lazuli gleamed.

"I could not wear a thing of such value."

"This, too, was the groom's mother's. It was a gift long ago from the Ch'ien Lung Emperor to a young bride of Chin. The girls have worn it on their wedding day for nearly a hundred years. It would break my master's heart if you refused."

Li-an touched gently the peacock feathers that turned to rainbows in the shifting light. How much trouble Chao had taken to make this marriage seem real, instead of a game between forbidden lovers. Her heart was full of gratitude and love for such a man. She sat on a stool while the servant lowered first the red bridal veil, then the headdress over her hair. She could see only her feet and the plain slippers of the servant, but she had learned long ago to move gracefully while half-blind. She rose and turned for the young girl's inspection.

"Now you are ready!" the servant exclaimed. She tapped softly on the latticework door. Immediately Li-an heard a flute, a lute, and drum begin to play in the next room. The musicians played three songs in the traditional test of the bride's patience. Under her veil, Li-an smiled. It seemed Chao had forgotten nothing.

When the third song was over, the servant threw the

door open and Li-an moved forward. She saw a pair of cloth-soled shoes and felt Chao take her arm. She knew it was he; she recognized his touch even through heavy brocade and satin.

"Let the ceremony begin," he called, and the room rang with the rhythm of cymbals and drums. Regally, the groom led his bride forward. "Here," he said, pointing to two empty chairs, "we must bow before my honorable second aunt and her husband."

Li-an and Chao knelt, touched their foreheads to their hands as reverently as if his relatives sat judging the bride whose face they could not see. Thus they moved about the room to bow before his mother, his father, his sisters, uncles, aunts, and finally, the Matriarch. In front of her ornate empty chair the couple kowtowed, hitting their foreheads three times three against their folded hands. All the while the rhythm of cymbal and drum pulsed through the room. When Chao and his bride rose from making obeisance to the absent Matriarch, Li-an whispered, "I would bow before my grandfather's spirit so that he, too, may bless this marriage."

"So it will be." Chao led her to an altar flanked by two vases of lilacs where bride and groom bowed one last time.

Head lowered, Li-an prayed silently, "Look down upon us from the Yellow Springs, my grandfather without a name, and do not blame us for what we do. Our hearts have called as the mountains called to you and like you, we must listen."

A soft breeze rustled the blossoms and the candles flared for an instant, as if disturbed by a gentle voice. It was enough. Tears of pure happiness burned behind Li-an's lids when, with the musicians and servants following, she and Chao walked through the house from courtyard to courtyard until a curtain fell behind them and they were left alone. Chao guided Li-an to a chair and sat across from her. "I never thought to see a woman wear that headdress and not resent her for binding me in the chains of another's choosing. But tonight I am content."

"I, too." Li-an spoke in a hushed voice, for she knew that on the other side of the paper wall was the bedroom. Her heart began to race.

Chao saw her hands shake and covered them with his. "Be at peace, for I will not harm you."

"I know. I was only thinking how odd that you who mock all ritual should do this for me, when I would have come to you in silence and secrecy, wearing my servant's clothes."

Chao smiled tenderly, though she did not see it. "Such a meeting is not worthy of you. Even if the world will scorn our ceremony, I know in my heart as you know in yours that we are now husband and wife." Carefully he lifted the headdress and took off the red veil to reveal her flushed face.

"I do not think I have ever told you that I love you," Li-an whispered.

"You have done so many times with your eyes, which can conceal nothing, and with your hands and lips. But it is good to hear the words, just the same." Chao leaned forward, suddenly intent. "This I would have you know. I love you as I have never loved another. You have brought me happiness that I did not know could exist. It is true I did not miss it before. How could I when I have never felt it until you?

"Come," he said, embarrassed that he had said so much, "we must eat our wedding feast." He pointed to a table laden with delicacies—brown duck, eggs with grated almond and sugar, smoked chicken, pork-stuffed dumplings, preserved plums, pecan cakes, as well as red sugar cakes and heated rice wine.

Li-an turned gratefully to the distraction the food offered; her heart was too full, just now, to let her speak. She had not eaten much all day; now she tried a little of everything while Chao ate heartily. "How did you do all this?" she asked at last.

"There are a few servants I trust. We managed."

"Whose—" Li-an began.

Chao put his finger to her lips. "No questions tonight. We are here to get to know each other. The place does not matter, except that we will not be disturbed."

She nodded and rose. Chao rose with her; they had agreed without words that it was time. Her pulse beating in her ears, Li-an went to the wooden screen and folded it back. She saw that a huge rosewood bed dominated the other room. The red satin wedding curtains were embroidered in gold with symbols of happiness and good wishes. The quilt was red silk and scattered with hundreds of rose petals. Li-an drew in her breath. "Thank you," she said.

He smiled and reached out to remove the gold pins from her hair. He cradled the lotus ornaments in his palm for a moment, then set them on a low table nearby. When he had removed the last pins, her thick black hair fell around her shoulders to her knees. Chao's mouth went dry and his heart began to pound. When he looked into her eyes, he saw the sky there, wide, endless, beautiful beyond words. Slowly, caressingly, he drew his hands through her hair. He bent to kiss her and she leaned closer. She opened her mouth under his, sliding her hands up his blue silk robe.

When at last he drew away, she was breathing heavily, shivering with pleasure.

"Shall I leave you now?"

"No," she murmured. "Not even for a moment."

Chao saw the trust in her eyes, the glow that had transformed her face. Again he wondered why the gods should have given him such a miracle.

Carefully, he lifted the tunic over her head, then her red brocade gown, and finally her silken undervest. She stood naked, smiling, while he caught his breath in wonder. Her body was long, slim, and perfect. He did not want to touch her for fear she would shatter in his hands and he would hold no more than fragments of a dream he had created.

"I am not a ghost who will disappear at a touch," Li-an said. She took his hand and guided it to her naked throat. Gently, he ran his fingers over the soft skin, pausing at the pulse in the hollow where he felt her heartbeat. With his warm hand he caressed her shoulder, her back. Finally, he cupped one breast in his open palm.

Li-an gasped and pressed closer. He kissed her lightly, then left her for a moment to draw back the quilt, scattering rose petals everywhere. Suddenly shy, Li-an climbed into bed to cover herself with the silken quilt. Chao removed his clothes and joined her, drawing the curtains behind him.

They were enclosed in a world that glowed soft red from

the lanterns in the room beyond. Chao drew Li-an near, kissing her until she sighed with pleasure. She wanted to feel him everywhere, the pressure of his body, the touch of his lips, the gentle movement of his hands. The yearning was strong within her; she rubbed her hands along his back and felt the texture of his skin, the muscles beneath, the rhythm of his breathing. Colors spun through her head when she lay back and he caressed her, beginning at her ear, where he traced the curve with a fingertip, then moved down her throat to her chest. He cupped her breasts, circled the nipples enticingly with his thumbs. She gasped at sensations she had never felt before—and never thought to feel.

Li-an quivered, eyes closed, delighted by the tiny paths of liquid fire that burned along her skin wherever Chao's fingers rested. She rose to hold his face in her hands, kissed him fiercely, astonished at the desire that shook her body from head to toe. She ran her hands over Chao's back and down to his buttocks. Li-an saw that he was hungry for her, felt the unfamiliar pressure on her thigh.

Enveloped in her red cocoon of happiness, she traced new paths over his skin, learning to know him as she had never known a man. Her breasts rubbed against the smoothness of his chest and he held her closer, tangling his legs with hers, kissing her hair, her eyes, her lips, her cheeks.

She laughed aloud when he tickled her throat with the tip of his tongue. Chao laughed with her, recklessly, while they clung together, bound by the strands of her hair, caressing each other until both trembled and the laughter turned to gasps of pleasure.

Slowly, Chao turned so Li-an lay beneath him. He looked down at her face, made mysterious by the lantern light through the red curtains, and felt that he held in his hands a treasure beyond price. He leaned down to kiss her again, circling his tongue between her moist lips. Then, with great care, he parted her legs and entered her.

She stiffened, surprised at the pain, and bit her lip to keep from crying out. Chao whispered reassurance in her ear as he rocked against her gently, teaching her body to welcome him. Soon her rigid arms grew slack and the spinning grew wild and bright within. She rocked with him, then slowly, slowly, thrust upward to meet him. Her heart was pounding, her pulse so rapid that it painted rainbows behind her closed lids. The vibrating colors enwrapped her as Chao's arms enwrapped her. His body clung to hers and they moved together, skin to skin and mouth to mouth. The colors grew hot and bright until they exploded in shimmering fragments as she cried out Chao's name.

He clutched her so tightly that it hurt, but she did not care. They lay immobile, breathing in each other's breath.

Li-an closed her eyes to savor the moment; for the first time in her life she was truly happy. Chao drew her into the curve of his arm and she laid her cheek on his heaving chest. It was thus, smiling, that they fell asleep.

Li-an awoke with a start to the sight of Chao asleep beside her, his features oddly young in the red-tinted light. There was no rage in his face now, only peace and contentment. He was smiling slightly and she smiled, too, surprised at the joy she felt at such a little thing. Tonight there were no shadows, no fear, no memories of the past, no future. There was no reality beyond this bed, this man who loved her and the newly awakened hunger in her body. She felt that she could fly, raise her arms and rise into the midnight sky, holding her joy on widespread wings. Like the hawk, she would move among the stars, gaze down on the mountains she loved, caress the clouds as she passed them by.

Chao stirred and awakened to find Li-an looking down at him. "Are you happy?" he said.

"I am." She could find no other words to tell him what she felt, but she knew he understood.

Chao grinned, his eyes glistening with mischief. "Do you know what we have done tonight?"

"What?"

"We have taken the fine threads that bound us in the beginning; one at a time, we have made them into a cloth. A cloth of ten thousand threads for the daughter of Wan." He laughed at the pun on the name of Wan. Li-an bent to kiss him but he rolled away.

"What is it?" she whispered, afraid to disturb the fragile contentment between them.

"A poem has come to me in my sleep. Would you hear it?"

"You know I would."

> "This happiness is like a piece
>   of pale green jade—
>   rare, beautiful, and indestructible.
> Like the jade it can be hidden away
>   in a rosewood box for years,
> Yet lose none of its magic.
> Once the jade is carved, shaped, perfected,
> It will never change.
> Someday a woman will open the box and hold
>   in her soft white hands—
> The jade, the stone, the memory of this night."

Li-an smiled up at him and he held her face in his hands. "You are incredible. I have never seen such courage even in a man's eyes."

"I am not brave," she said. "I am haunted always by nightmares." As they lay together on the wrinkled quilt, she told him what had happened in Canton. He listened gravely, stroked her hair while she spoke, as if to soothe the young child she had been. When she mentioned her father, Chao frowned. "He could not have saved you by staying behind. If the people found him there, it would only have endangered you further. They had suspicions but his presence would have been proof. They would have killed all three of you."

Li-an looked away. "It does not matter. It was long ago. I only told you so you would understand that I am a coward."

Chao shook his head. "You are indeed blind, my pale jade. Would a coward have challenged the chess move I made or recited that poem before all those scholars? Would a coward have gone out alone on the Feast of Lanterns or wanted to turn and fight though the crowd was huge and mad with anger?"

Li-an looked thoughtful. It had not occurred to her before to wonder at these things.

"One more thing," Chao continued. "Would a coward have come to me tonight and given so much?" He gazed at her pensively. "I have often wondered why it is that you are so strong."

Li-an stared down at her hands, brow furrowed. "If I am strong, it is because my mother taught me to be."

Chao pulled her close. "So it was Wan Ke-ming who made you into a tiger."

Before she could answer, he kissed her, then lay down beside her. They made love again, more slowly this time, tenderly, now that the madness had eased a little, yet in the end, the wonder was the same. When they lay waiting for their hearts to still and their breath to come more easily, Chao whispered, "Do not ever leave me. I need your strength, my tiger."

Li-an kissed him into silence.

Later, she awakened for the second time to find Chao watching her. He noticed how her hair lay around her like a fine, thin veil, how her lips parted in a half smile, even in sleep, how flushed her cheeks looked in the warm red light.

She grinned at him and took his hand. "I am hungry. Is there more food?"

"Yes." He rose to throw on his outer robe while she did the same. Half clothed, they went into the next room. When her hunger was satisfied, Li-an leaned back, at peace, and looked around the room for the first time. One wall was teak carved with flowers and dragons; one panel told the legend of how the god Wu, son of Shen-hung, had controlled the floods and saved the earth. Octagonal lanterns of crushed shell swayed at the corners of the room and the tile floor was cool light blue. A rosewood table held a profusion of flowers in a huge porcelain vase and there was another full of branches of coral. On one tabletop there was a little landscape made of amber and ivory, crystal, pearls, and other stones.

"This house is lovely," she said. "Whose is it that you dare to bring me here and know we will not be interrupted?"

Chao hesitated and looked away.

Li-an felt a flicker of unease. "Tell me," she said.

"It belonged to Kuei Ch'ing."

The flicker grew and spread. "The official who was banished to Mukden?"

Chao nodded but did not speak. All at once there was a shadow on Li-an's happiness. She remembered that there was indeed a world beyond these narrow walls. Those who lived in that world would not share their joy, but would ridicule and try to destroy it. Out there, in the streets beyond this little paradise, was a city full of enemies. Her heart turned cold and she closed her eyes but the image would not go, the sudden certainty that danger awaited them—a danger beyond words or description, beyond, even, the flame of her fear.

Chao took her hands and forced her to look at him. "Do not think of anything but me, my heart, as I think of nothing but you. Let us make to one another Li Po's pledge from long ago. 'We shall grow old together. Together at the same time, your hair and mine will turn white as the snow on the mountains, white as the summer moon.' Swear that it is so," he said.

She met his eyes, so bright and black, her own eyes full with tears of joy and sorrow. "I swear it," she said. "I will be as faithful as Meng Chiang Nu, the Pumpkin Girl."

Chao slid an arm around her and drew her head onto his shoulder. "Tell me the legend of the Pumpkin Girl."

"You must have heard it many times before."

"But not from your lips. Tell me."

With Chao's fingers tangled in her hair, Li-an gave in. "Long ago, in the reign of Emperor Huang Ti, a giant pumpkin grew on the boundary line between the House of Chiang and the House of Meng. One day the two families opened the pumpkin and discovered a lovely girl inside. They named her Meng Chiang after both families, since neither could claim her as their own."

Li-an paused to glance up at Chao, who was listening intently. Shaking her head with affection, she continued. "Meng Chiang Nu grew into a lovely woman, unaware that in the far north, the Emperor Huang Ti was building the Great Wall to keep out the barbarian invaders. He was told by his astrologers that the Wall would not stand unless ten thousand men were sacrificed to the gods. But the people heard and were afraid, so the astrologers chose one man named Wan and claimed that since his name meant ten thousand, the gods would be satisfied."

"I see now why you have chosen this story," Chao said.

Li-an ignored him. "Wan was no fool; he ran to hide in the south where he met and fell in love with Meng Chiang Nu and made her his wife. But soon the Emperor's soldiers found him and took him back to the Wall, where they put him to death." Her voice faltered, but she went on. "Meng Chiang followed, searching for her husband's body along the huge Wall that wound like a snake through many *li* of hills and valleys. At last, in desperation, she sat down to weep because she could not even give her husband a proper burial and send him to the Yellow Springs. The gods were moved by her grief and the Wall crumbled behind her, revealing her husband's bones."

For a long time, Li-an listened to the beat of Chao's heart before she continued. "When the Huang Ti Emperor heard of Meng's faithfulness, he was intrigued and asked to see her. One look at her beauty and he was enchanted. He offered to make her his empress. Before she would agree, Meng insisted on a large funeral for her husband and a high tower to be built in his memory. When all was done, she climbed to the top of the tower, reviled the Emperor, and threw herself to her death.

"Enraged, Huang Ti ordered that her body should be ground to dust and thrown into the river. The dust became a thousand silver fishes in which Meng Chiang Nu's soul continues to live. When the sun hits the water, the silver scales gleam more brightly than moon or stars or the Emperor's empty palace of gold."

"But not," Chao said softly, "more brightly than your eyes."

◦ 9 ◦

For the next two months, Li-an was happy as she had never thought to be; the stars seemed more brilliant, the flowers more fragrant, and the moon became a changing mirror of her reflected joy. Yet she was haunted by an impalpable shadow that hovered at her shoulder, and when she lay in bed at night, curled around her beating heart. Often, she slipped out to meet Chao; when she lay in the circle of his arms the shadow faded and disappeared.

"Why should I have been granted such happiness?" she asked one night as they sat in the garden of Kuei Ch'ing's house. The leaves rustled above them, the sound of water on cratered stones below. Li-an closed her eyes, waiting for the moment to reveal the secret she carried with her—the other reason for her joy.

"Do not wonder or doubt, just believe that it was meant to be."

Li-an tilted her head at the eerie hooting of an owl. The half-moon shone on the ghostlike garden, making dragons and unicorns of the twisted trees. Chao drew her close and kissed her until she gasped for breath.

"Wait!" she cried, holding him away with her hands on his chest. "There is something I would have you know."

"I know already that I love you more than heaven and earth and that you love me, too. What else is there to learn?"

For a long moment she stared into his eyes—endless wells of darkness and anger, passion and honesty. Then she said quietly, "That I carry your seed within me and will bear your child."

The worry lines around his mouth eased and his face was suddenly young again. "Truly?"

She nodded.

Chao rose, unable to stay still, lifting his arms to the sky to proclaim his happiness. Then, abruptly, his smile faded. "Forgive me. For a moment I thought only of my own joy and not what you will suffer. A mother who is not also a wife—this will bring you ridicule and sorrow. What will you do?"

She smiled, for once undisturbed by his fear. "I will have our child, and thank the gods each day for this miracle. The people do not love me anyway; their ridicule will do me no harm. I do not care what they say or think of me," she told him fiercely. "I will love the baby because it comes from the mingling of our blood. Such a child is worth any price. The hatred of strangers will never change that."

Chao knelt and took her hands. "You, my heart, are a tiger indeed, and every one of us a coward."

Li-an did not understand, but the words echoed in her mind through the days that followed when Chao sent messages but did not ask her to come to him. On the third morning, she stood in a steaming tub of hot water while Liu Kan washed and perfumed her body. The servant kept her eyes lowered and her hands were rough on Li-an's skin. "Something troubles you?" her mistress asked.

The servant did not raise her head. "I have seen that for two full moons you have had no flow of blood. Do you know what this means?"

"I know."

Kan eyed her narrowly. "There are ways—"

"No!"

"You and your mother," the servant whispered. "Two of a kind." She scrubbed in silence for a while, then stopped, wet hands on hips. "You have not been to the kitchen for many moons and I fear we shall float away to the Nine Heavens without your leaden dumplings to keep us on earth."

Li-an flushed. It was true that she had not lost herself in the steam and smells of the noisy kitchen for some time. She missed those moments of laughter and ease with the Lius, but her mind had been absorbed with other thoughts.

Now she smiled apologetically at Kan. "I will come today. Kin-shih says you are making pecan cakes this morning. Perhaps I will try with my clumsy hands to make some as sweet as yours."

Kan snorted in disbelief, but a smile lurked at the corners of her mouth. "You can always try, Young Mistress. They tell me failure builds character."

Li-an grinned. "I have always thought your face full of character. Now I know why."

"That, Oh Foolish One, is wisdom," the servant said wagging a finger in Li-an's face. "You must learn to know the difference."

When her mistress was dressed in a green *p'ao* and tunic, the woman stomped off, the tub in her hands, muttering under her breath. Li-an pressed her hand to her belly and smiled tenderly.

Ke-ming sat at the table in the dining hall, the *Peking Gazette* in her lap. She stared out at the spring garden, vibrant with purple and white peonies, wisteria that swayed like lithe dancers in the breeze. Graceful willows circled the clear water, and the leaves of the catalpa tree, guarding clusters of pale bell-shaped flowers, fluttered and whispered among themselves. But the garden splashed with vivid color might as well have been covered with snow. Ke-ming's eyes, turned inward, saw only the stark white of winter.

She knew Li-an had been slipping out to meet Chin Chao for some time. She had watched her daughter bloom in the past two months, seen her hold her head higher, move more confidently, smile into empty air as if it held a prism of rainbow light. Li-an's blue eyes had lost their shadows and her touch had grown gentle, her heart whole and healthy, though the fear had not left her completely. All these things Ke-ming had seen and each sight brought more pain, because she knew what was to come. How much would she not give to forget the images that had whirled before her one night in the Hall of Ancestors? How much to share her daughter's joy as Li-an had once asked her to do?

Her hand brushed the rice paper that made a stain of white on her purple tunic. She wanted to crumple it and throw it among the ashes; for the first time, she wanted to hide the truth so she need not see the joy fade from her daughter's face to be replaced by cold, stark fear. Then she heard the sound of Li-an's footsteps, light, effortless, free of dread. Ke-ming found she could not breathe.

Li-an stopped in the doorway to admire her mother in the morning light. Ke-ming sat, her robes flowing around her like a tapestry of purple spring blossoms that swirled into foam at her feet. Her hair was piled on her head in a simple style without adornment that emphasized her almond eyes. Then her mother turned, and Li-an felt that a gust of winter air had invaded the spring fragrance of the house.

She hurried to the table. "What is it, my Mother?"

"First, drink your chrysanthemum tea. You must keep yourself healthy and strong, especially now."

Li-an paused with her hand outstretched toward the half-filled saucer. Could her mother have guessed her secret?

"I know of the child to come, yes," Ke-ming said in answer to the unspoken question.

"But how?"

"By the glow in your eyes and the burnished color of your cheeks. And I have seen you touch your stomach sometimes with a look of wonder. It was not so very long ago that I saw those things in my own moon mirror."

Li-an straightened her shoulders, ready to do battle. "You will not tell me to rid myself of this baby?"

Smiling with infinite sadness, Ke-ming whispered, "No. This miracle is yours alone. No one can take it from you." She looked away because she could not bear the radiant smile on her daughter's face.

Impulsively, Li-an reached out to touch her mother's hand. "Thank you," she said.

This time, Ke-ming could not answer. She stared intently at the shadows of flowered branches on the paper wall.

"Something is very wrong," Li-an declared at her mother's continued silence. "What is it?"

Ke-ming reached for the paper in her lap. Her daughter took it from her, and it was too late; the choice had been made.

Li-an held the *Gazette* gingerly. She did not need to ask what new disaster it held; in the center of the first page in large, confident characters, was the poem Chin Chao had dropped in her garden on the Feast of Lanterns. She read with growing horror the lines:

> Many moons have passed since the faithful
>   delivered pears to the Vermilion Gates.
> Many moons since the tigers entered the lake
> And drank of its poisoned waters.
> Yet while the poison saps the Dragon's power,
> It makes the tigers strong and their claws sharp.
> They bring their tiger wisdom, hidden in
>   their strange blue eyes,
> Which see what the Dragon does not wish to see.

There was more, but she knew the words too well. Beneath the poem, Chao had written, "Perhaps it is time we listen to the tigers, follow their example, learn from their strength, for our own is waning by the minute. Without them we will turn backward until Phan-ku closes himself once more inside his egg of chaos and the world is in turmoil."

The paper fell from Li-an's hand. Now, at last, she understood what Chao had meant in the garden. Because of his love for her, he had ceased to write his memorials that brought danger without reward. For her sake he had kept silent and therefore safe. In the days and months when they made themselves a paradise, he had come to believe that because he no longer fought the battle, he had become a coward. Her courage, her fearless love for the child within her had unmanned him somehow. Li-an started to rise, but Ke-ming stopped her.

"Where are you going?"

"To the House of Chin. He has done this thing because of me and I must go to him."

"It is too dangerous. He has pushed them too far," Ke-ming said quietly.

"Yes." Li-an did not know where she found the strength to speak even that simple word; she only knew that today the shadow which haunted her had taken on the shape of the Empress Dowager and her stubborn ministers. She sank back into her chair as if struck by a powerful wind. "You think they will arrest him?"

"If they do not, the people will stone him," Ke-ming replied. "They do not love the foreign devils any more than T'zu Hsi."

"You have given up on him already. We do not yet know his fate. Perhaps we can change it, save him somehow from himself."

"It is far too late for that, my daughter."

Gazing at her hands, which might have belonged to a stranger, Li-an said softly, "I must go to him just the same."

Ke-ming rose. "That is madness. I forbid it." She did not raise her voice; she spoke quietly, for her strength came from within. Every angle of her body, every plane of her face spoke of that power that would not bend.

This time, Li-an did not fall under her mother's spell. She, too, rose, placed her hands on the table, and met Ke-ming's eyes steadily. "It was you who taught me to be strong, my Mother. You who instructed me in the ways of the West. Why? So that you could lock me away in this house forever where danger dares not cross the threshold? Yet already it has done so. The soldiers have come once; they will come again. You know it as well as I." She paused to take a deep breath. "Do not make me a prisoner now that you have had me taste freedom. Let me go, my Mother. It is time."

"So be it, Li-an." Ke-ming stood rigid, her face a mask of clay.

Li-an's courage wavered at the sound of her name on her mother's lips. Ke-ming still said it as though it were a Western word and not a Chinese one. Li-an had never become accustomed to it; the foreign sound startled her and made her pause. "Why do you not argue, shake me, scream your anger to the skies? Why are there never feelings in your eyes, even when I break the thread you have woven so carefully to bind me?" Her voice shook as if each word had been torn from inside where it had lain, unspoken, for years.

Slowly, Ke-ming raised her head. "There is much to

read in my eyes—fears and sorrows, joys and pain. But you are not yet ready to see these things. You have learned too well how to make yourself blind."

Li-an opened her mouth, but no words came. Her heart cried out in silence and in silence she turned away.

Ke-ming stood motionless, watched her daughter go while behind her eyes burned tears so dry and bright and painful that she closed her lids to block the harsh glare of the sun. But the tears did not fall, nor would they, even in the bleak stillness Li-an left behind.

Li-an ran, stopping when she reached the Hall of Ancestors. She would pray to her grandfather to make her journey safe, to help protect Chin Chao from the force of his own rage. She knelt before the altar with her head on her crossed hands. "Help me," she prayed, "so that my courage does not fail me."

The light of many candles flickered over her face, the carved teak walls, the reed curtain, the cool tiled floor. The shadows became voices, one inside another, crying, "hide yourself away in safety"; "go to him, he needs you"; "wait and see, wait and see." One said, "protect yourself" and one, "think of your mother." One said, "you made a vow and must not break it." "Run to him," "hide from him," "go before it is too late." The voices that were shadows fluttered and danced, mesmerizing her. In a trance she rose to blow out the candles until the room was in darkness, except for the light that came through the reed curtain in strips like threads of woven silk.

We will begin with a single thread and weave a piece of cloth, Chao had told her once. Li-an turned back to the altar and whispered, "Tell me that my heart speaks the truth. Tell me I am right to do this thing." She looked up at the altar, at the drift of incense that rose toward the ceiling like a breath expelled in the chill of winter. Then, unexpectedly, a gust of wind whipped through the room; it set the branches of peach blossoms swaying, so a few petals came loose and drifted downward, coming to rest in Li-an's open palms. She closed her eyes. "I understand," she said.

◇　◇　◇

Wearing her simplest *p'ao,* with a veil to cover her face, Li-an went into the street and waited for a sedan chair. The strings of cash jingled in her sleeve as she felt the rocking motion of the chair, smelled the dust of the streets, heard the shouts of vendors and the laughter of children. To her these things were only a blur; reality was her beating heart and the heart of her child beneath it. She motioned to the carriers to stop several *hu-tungs* from the House of Chin, then made her way carefully along the alleys, head lowered. At last she reached the green carved screen that blocked the entrance. She slipped inside and stopped the first servant she saw, a bent old man with a hoe in his hand.

"I would see Chin Chao."

The man eyed her warily, for everyone was wary in this house today.

"Tell him Li-an is here and he will come," she cried in desperation.

The gardener shrugged and muttered, "Go and wait in the women's quarters at the back. If he wishes to see you, he will meet you there."

She bowed gratefully and made her way through court-yard after blooming courtyard until she reached a reception hall open to the garden, where she stood at the end of a marble bridge.

The women were gathered around a brazier of hot coals, though the day was warm. No doubt the chill of fear was in their blood. A table covered with mah-jongg tiles stood nearby, forgotten. No one spoke and no one raised her eyes until the Matriarch on her high teak chair sensed Li-an's presence.

"What do you wish?" the old woman asked, hands spread like narrow claws on the arms of her chair.

All the women turned to stare and Li-an struggled to remain calm. "I wish to see Chin Chao."

The woman's birdlike eyes grew bright. "Are you then the one of whom my grandson speaks so often?"

"I believe I am she."

The silence grew as heavy as the heat that rose from the smoldering brazier.

At last, the Matriarch spoke. "These are Chao's rela-tives. There used to be many more, but now only his mother, his First and Second Aunts, his two sisters, and myself." The old woman paused to stare intently at Li-an's concealing veil. "Is it true that there was a ceremony to make you my grandson's wife?"

"There was."

"Is it also true that there will be a child?"

Li-an raised her head, answered without hesitation. "It is true."

The other women looked away, but the Matriarch saw how Li-an stood unbowed by her sin, proud that she carried such a child. The old woman's heart softened, for she had once known love and understood the strength and weakness it created. "Then you must take off your veil. It is not necessary to hide your face when you are with your family."

Li-an moved slowly forward, too stunned to reply. She had never expected this. Quietly, she knelt beside the others. Before she tossed aside her veil, she saw that Chao's mother's cheeks were covered with tears. Li-an kept her eyes lowered while the woman spoke.

"May Kwan Yin bless you and keep you safe," she said quietly. "Such a child means much to us. Especially today."

The Matriarch reached out with a clawlike hand and squeezed Li-an's fingers. "I am glad you came, my almost daughter-in-law. We had need of cheerful news. Yesterday Chin's father sold Third Granddaughter to Wen Hsi for his concubine."

"And she went?"

"How could she not? She is only a woman with no choice but to yield. She did as she was told."

"She will stay with this man who all know to be cruel, corrupt, and free with the women in Willow Lane?" Li-an demanded.

"She will stay. It is her fate. Who can change Fate?"

All at once, Chao was there. He knelt beside Li-an, who sighed in relief; even now the sight of his face brought joy.

"Are you mad to come here like this?" he demanded. "Do you not know what I have done?"

"I know and I have come."

He was pale and haggard, but he smiled at that. "I should have guessed. Still you must go. They are watching me as vultures watch a moldering carcass, waiting for their chance."

Li-an's mouth went dry, but her resolve did not waver. "I think you have forgotten your own wisdom, my husband. Was it not you who said, 'There are times when to stand and fight is foolish beyond words. Foolish to die just so they think you brave.'"

"You remember too well," he told her, "but turning my own words against me will not change my mind. I do not care what 'they' think of me, only what I think of myself. This you have taught me. I heard a voice inside that would not be silenced anymore. I could not live in paradise forever; that would have been to live a lie. Forgive me and try to understand."

"I do understand," she told him with a sad smile.

He looked at her in admiration and in fear—fear that he would never see her face again, and worse, that somehow, in the barren days of his future, he would cease to believe in the dream they had made one night in a moonlit garden. "I love you," he said.

"And I you."

"Enough of this foolishness!" the Matriarch declared with a crooked smile. Before she could say more, she stiffened at the distant cry of a servant. "They come! They come! The Bannermen have knocked down the outer gate and blow like a winter wind through the houses."

The women rose, cackling and screaming their terror, but Li-an stayed where she was, frozen for the third time in the heart of an old nightmare.

"Let us run through the back!" Chao's mother cried.

"No," Chao whispered. "It is too late. They will have sent soldiers to all the gates."

Li-an stared at an imperfection in the pink floor tile as if it were her only hope. Then she heard it—the marching of feet, which sent a pain through her head like a bolt of lightning through a midnight sky. The women gathered in the far corner of the room behind a lacquered chest while Chao went out to meet the soldiers in the courtyard.

The stamping feet grew louder, mingled with the sound of harsh voices that called for Chin Chao. Li-an sat alone by the brazier and heard Chao's voice cut off, his cry of surprise as the Bannermen grasped him brutally by both arms.

But the soldiers were not finished. They came farther, forced their way into the women's quarters and began to harass the frightened ladies, shouting questions the women could not possibly answer.

"What do you want with them?" Chao demanded. He struggled to free himself from the arms that held him like bands of iron.

"The charge is high treason. If you are guilty, your whole family pays the price. We will take everyone."

Li-an knew, although she could not see him, that the blood drained from Chao's face. It had never occurred to him that T'zu Hsi would go this far. He had thought he endangered only himself. In her mind she saw his shoulders bowed in despair, and through the pain in her head, through the images that scattered and whirled within her, she tried to send him comfort, but her heart had turned to stone and she had no warmth to share.

Only she, crouched silent by the brazier, saw one soldier cross the room stealthily to drop a packet wrapped in yellow silk behind a pile of pillows. Her sight was growing dim, but she understood from muttered curses that the Bannermen were searching for something. When a man passed beside her, he brushed her robe and asked a question she could not hear. The agony increased and she rocked forward, trying to ease the pain.

She heard a man toss the pillows about and realized that someone stood beside her, waiting for her to move. Then she heard a shout of triumph and saw a flash of yellow—the packet the soldier had dropped a moment ago.

"I have found the Imperial jewels stolen by the traitor Yuan Tung-li. See how this coward hides the proof of his crime in the women's quarters so that they, too, will be stained by his sin?"

Li-an gasped and raised her head, staring with her blind eyes. "No!" she rasped. "It is not so." She heard a movement beside her and quickly lowered her lids. Had the man seen her eyes? Her heart thundered in her ears while the soldiers dragged the weeping ladies from the room. Li-an remained silent, frozen, praying to Kwan Yin.

"I will see to this one myself," the man said when all the others had been taken. "The Empress Dowager has many questions for Chin Chao and wants him as soon as possible. Tell the head of the Imperial Guard that I shall join him soon."

Li-an's stone heart stopped the blood in her veins. It was too late. He had seen too much. She felt a hand close around her arm in a grip that made her wince. As she rose, she swayed at the shattering pain in her head. She was dragged to a nearby gate and pushed unceremoniously into a sedan chair. She dared not look again at the official who was taking her—where? To the prison in the Imperial City? Her skin grew so cold that sweat broke out upon it. This time she had sealed her death warrant. She held her head in her hands, jumped at every bounce of the chair, which sent pains shooting through her eyes. Then the official spoke sharply to the carriers and the chair stopped.

The man pulled Li-an into the street so abruptly that she nearly fell. The bright light burned against her lids and her head ached so badly that she thought she would be ill.

"Walk, damn you!" he hissed.

She walked, not knowing where she went, except that each step brought her closer to the shadow of the Forbidden City, the cold, brilliant glare of the Empress Dowager. She felt that death was near, so near that she could smell the stink of it in her nostrils. Then, through the beating of her heart, the rasping of her breath, and the splintered pain within her head, a noise caught her attention. A footstep— one she had heard before. The man walked beside her, grim, determined. Her heart raced even faster and her breath would not come. This was not just any footstep, but the one she heard so often in the middle of the night, the one she had memorized when she was only four years old. This was Father Without a Face.

She risked a look upward at the blur of his face and below that, the ruby button of his rank. There was a white crane embroidered on the breast of his blue robe and he wore a girdle clasped with jade. She swallowed convulsively. This man was an official of the highest rank. "It is you," she said in a strangled whisper. His features were indistinct, yet she was certain she had seen him before.

He did not reply, but led her on in silence. Where was he taking her? Would he pay her back now for the hatred she had heard in his voice so many years ago? Would he kill her himself to avenge his pride, stung by the blood of an Englishman that ran in her veins?

When she stumbled again, he took her arm and led her through a maze of streets until she heard a gate open and close and smelled pine and peach blossoms, plum and lilacs. Then, without warning, he drew her beneath a low doorway and spoke at last. "Take her and hide her. Only I know who she is. If she does not appear, all will forget her. But I warn you, bind her with chain and lock and key, for the anger is great and the madness of the people will grow until it consumes this city."

He thrust Li-an forward and she fell to her knees while the pain filled her body until it was everything and she was nothing. Then she heard the footsteps retreat, those familiar footsteps from the dark of night. She felt hands on her shoulders, around her waist, lifting her gently. She sniffed at a scent she surely knew, a fragrance that belonged to one woman on earth. "My Mother?" Li-an said in a cracked, hollow voice.

"You are home, my heart. Be at peace. Lie still and I will ease your pain."

Li-an collapsed into Ke-ming's arms as darkness fell inside her and without.

10

Li-an awoke and lay for a moment, trying to remember where she was. She heard the murmur of voices outside her room, her memory came rushing back, and with it the gnawing fear for Chao and his family. She shivered; she could not seem to get warm, though the sun shone through the windows, making pleasant shadows of the latticework on the floor. It seemed to her that when she lay down the shadows had come from the other side. It must be morning then; she had slept the whole night through. She stiffened when she heard Chao's name mentioned. She listened more intently, grateful that the folding doors between her room and the reception hall had been left open. She could just see her mother and Wu Shen seated in elbow chairs, talking together.

"They have taken him to the prison in the Forbidden City and the charge is to be high treason."

"Because of his memorial?"

"That is not the reason they gave. They say the discovery of the jewels proves he was involved in Yuan Tung-li's plot. Now the President of the Censorate is saying Chin himself conceived it. I'm afraid the Most High will use him as an example to show that the Son of Heaven destroys his enemies from within and so makes the Middle Kingdom strong again."

Li-an shuddered.

"We must keep this from my daughter," Ke-ming said even lower. "I fear she will not be wise."

"You have always told her the truth before."

Li-an blessed Wu Shen for his faith in her, but knew he would not change her mother's mind. She waited until the two adults left the room, then climbed out of bed, found a gown and girdle, and slipped them on. She was going to try to see Chao. On an impulse, she took from a lacquered chest the mother-of-pearl headdress he had given her on their wedding night. It would hide her face. Her head still ached dully, but she did not pause even to drink the willow-bark tea beside her bed.

Picking up several strings of cash, she crept into the courtyard and made her way to the side gate. She put the headdress on, then swung the gate open soundlessly. Once in the street, she hailed a sedan chair. "The Vermilion Gates of *Tzu-chin ch'eng*."

The carriers stared at her. "You would go to the Forbidden City?"

"It is what I have said." Once the chair was in motion and she had time to think, Li-an wondered what madness had brought her on this futile errand. She would never get in to see Chao; none but the chosen—the concubines, the ministers, officials, and messengers—were allowed inside the Vermilion Gates. But she had to try. Her empty stomach rumbled, but not with hunger, as she approached her destination.

The door was opened from without; she alighted and handed the carrier two strings of cash. He bowed low, but she did not see him. All she saw were the high red walls, the ornate red gates, the guards in red fur hats and yellow tunics who stood with gleaming swords at their sides. The sight made her freeze; her feet would not move one step farther. She wanted to turn away, but then she remembered Chao's face, the shout of triumph when the soldier had "discovered" the jewels his associate had hidden behind the pillows. She walked up to a guard and said, "I wish to go in."

He glowered at the woman in the strange headdress. "It is forbidden. You know that. Be on your way."

Li-an did not move.

The guard leaned closer to hiss, "What do you want?"

"I wish to see a prisoner."

Intrigued because she did not shrink back at his glower, which made most men tremble, he asked, "Who?"

"Chin Chao."

The Bannerman stiffened. "He is a traitor." He glared at Li-an. "Why would you want to see a traitor, unless you, too—"

"Because," she interrupted quickly, "Confucius taught us to look with compassion on all men, even our enemies. Is that not so?"

Frowning, the man observed her through narrowed eyes, as if to penetrate the veil so he could see her face. "I do not see what that has to do with the traitor housed within these walls."

"Do you not?" Li-an noticed his fingers had tightened around his sword. "Then I will give you time to think on it. If you change your mind, I will be waiting." She clasped her hands and bowed, then backed across the dusty street and stood in the shade of a willow tree. From there she could see the gate clearly. Though the guards could see her, too, she knew they could not guess who she was. She remained unmoving, hands folded modestly before her, and watched the gates. For two hours she stood. Her heart pounded in her ears, her hands shook, though she hid their trembling by clasping them tighter. The Bannermen came and went, their swords swinging at their sides. Each time a soldier looked her way, her heart paused in its normal rhythm.

As the pain in her head increased, she was grateful for Ke-ming's teaching; it was that which helped her to hide her distress, to appear calm and regal as she stood with the shadows of willow leaves on her robe. To distract herself, she thought of Chao as she had last seen him in the garden of their private paradise. She realized now that in the past two moons, the house of Kuei Ch'ing had become her *lao chia*, her home.

She wanted to weep for the loss of Chao's touch, for the things his family suffered now, for the uncertainty of his future. Instead she focused her attention on the soldiers. They spoke to each other and looked her way, turned their backs and murmured low, deciding what to do. But what could they do? She merely stood, silent and unthreatening, to watch the gate in the shadow of a tree. When the head-dress began to weigh upon her, she returned to the first guard. "Have you considered?"

"I have not changed my mind. You may not see those you are forbidden to see in a place you are forbidden to go. Leave us in peace."

"I will go," she said softly, "but I will return."

When Li-an entered the reception hall with her head-dress under her arm, Ke-ming and Wu Shen were waiting. She told them bluntly what she had done. "I will do the same tomorrow."

"Do you not realize you are calling attention to yourself?" Wu Shen asked softly. "Is that what you want?"

"I am drawing attention to a strange woman in a head-dress like no other. That is what I want. There are those who I hope will hear of it and understand." It occurred to her that if she were discovered, she would also bring disaster to Ke-ming. She could only pray that such a thing would not happen.

Ke-ming remained silent. She remembered that once she, too, had felt the despair of helplessness, inaction, waiting endlessly to know if Fate had swept her life away in one cold burst of wind.

"It is all I can do for him, my Mother, and so I must try. Can you not understand?"

Ke-ming looked at her daughter's pale cheeks, the dark circles beneath her eyes, and felt she was staring at her own image in an old and clouded mirror. She knew then that this small, futile hope was Li-an's only defense against the desperation that hovered at her back, gripping her shoulder with a dark hand. "I understand." Deep in her heart, though she feared for her daughter's safety, Ke-ming was proud of her. Without a word, she treated the four nail-shaped wounds on each of Li-an's palms, the only sign of the agony it had been for her to stand and watch those soldiers—the enemies of her lifelong nightmares—and yet show them no fear.

"I will go again," Li-an insisted. "You will not try to stop me?"

Ke-ming shook her head. "I will only pray that Kwan Yin goes with you."

◊   ◊   ◊

So it was that Li-an returned to the Vermilion Gates day after day and asked to see Chin Chao. Each time she was refused; each time she went to stand beneath the willow, waiting for the guards to change their minds. Soldiers began to pass the gates on purpose to see the mysterious woman in a peacock headdress of mother-of-pearl. They stared openly while her heartbeat slowed and each breath caused pain, but she did not flinch or look away.

Eventually, the guard she had spoken to on the first day began to answer softly, rather than in anger. He came to admire her; he knew of no other woman so brave—none but the Empress Dowager herself.

Courteously, he told Li-an she was disrupting the order of things; courteously, she replied that she would stop if she could see Chin Chao. The Bannerman shook his head. The order had come from Tso Ch'eng-ta, the President of the Censorate himself. This traitor was special and no one would see him.

Day by day, Li-an grew paler. She ate less and less, though she felt the changes in her body and knew that, for the child's sake, she should eat more. But everything tasted like dust in her mouth, no matter what delicacy Ke-ming had Liu Kan prepare. She moved without thought or feeling, numbed by the disbelief that was her only comfort.

Finally, one afternoon, she arrived home, removed her headdress, and collapsed on a dragon couch.

"My daughter," Ke-ming murmured, "you are not strong enough to continue this way. They will never let you in."

"But I must know what is happening to him."

"I can tell you that."

She looked up to see Wu Shen in the doorway, his hair as white as snow, his shoulders more stooped than ever. He carried a dragon-headed cane as he moved forward over what seemed to him an endless sea of tile.

Ke-ming drew up a chair and he sank into it with a sigh. He stared at his gnarled hands for a moment, then looked Li-an in the face. "I will tell you the truth, because you deserve no less, but it will cause you pain."

She reached out to grasp Shen's hands. "Is he . . . ?" She could not say the words.

"Chin Chao and his father have been tortured. The Empress Dowager and Tso Ch'eng-ta were hoping for a confession of treason, but neither man will give them the lie they seek."

Ke-ming rose abruptly to stand facing the garden, arms spread, hands pressed to the narrow beams between the cane mats. She looked like an angry goddess waiting to wreak havoc on the heavens. What had changed her so quickly? Then Li-an stiffened. Tso Ch'eng-ta. Could he be the man who had taken her from Chin Chao's house? Suddenly the blurred face became painfully clear in her mind; everyone had seen the image of so high an official. The man with the familiar footsteps, her Father Without a Face, was the president of the Censorate, the Emperor's private army of spies. Her pale cheeks grew ashen.

No wonder it had been so important to keep his relationship with Ke-ming a secret. The president of the Censorate must be above reproach. Yet it was he who had ordered Chao's arrest. She looked up at her mother, and for the first time, Ke-ming would not meet her eyes. It was true then. "Could you not ask—" Li-an began.

"No," her mother whispered. "I have sworn to him never to interfere."

"But for Chao—"

"I fear it could only hurt him further."

Wu Shen stared, bewildered, from mother to daughter, then, slowly, he began to understand. "Tso Ch'eng-ta!" he muttered under his breath. "Amitabha!"

"You have not finished," Ke-ming said, her eyes on the arbor of the dragon-clawed pagoda. "What else have you heard?"

The scholar-official bowed his head. "Even without a confession, Chin has been convicted. He and his whole family will be executed in one week's time in the marketplace."

Li-an gasped and cradled her stomach where Chao's baby had begun to grow. "No!" she cried. "No!"

Shen put his dry cool hand on hers. "There is nothing you can do, my friend. I'm sorry."

"Did no one argue for him? Did all bow down to T'zu Hsi's lie?" she cried bitterly.

"There were those who fought to save Chin Chao's life, the same who fought to save his friend. I remonstrated, as did Li Wen-t'ien, Li Hing-mu, even Prince Kung, the uncle of the Son of Heaven himself. But in the end they were not powerful enough to defy the Empress Dowager. I do not think there is a man in all the world with that kind of power."

"Except for Tso Ch'eng-ta."

"Not even he," Ke-ming said softly. "He is as fearful as the others, perhaps even more, because he is so high."

Li-an clutched her teacher's hand with shaking fingers. "I cannot save him."

"No. You cannot."

She felt the numbness slip away and in its place rose darkness, desolation, and cold terror. Li-an felt her stomach contract and stood abruptly. "I think I am going to be ill."

In an instant her mother had brought her a basin. When Li-an had done and lay shaking on the couch, Ke-ming wiped the film of sweat from her daughter's forehead with a cool cloth. Li-an started to rise, though her body quivered with spasms of heat and cold, but Ke-ming stopped her. "You must take care or you will harm the child. You do not want that, do you?"

Li-an looked down at her slightly swollen belly and cupped it tenderly with her hands. Tears came to her eyes but she fought them back. "No. I must keep the child safe. It is all I shall have left."

For a week, in every street and *hu-tung* of Peking, there had been talk of the executions to come. Li-an did not understand why she continued to live and breathe when her heart had stopped beating long since. In the morning, the jubilant voices of the people haunted her; at night fear and shadows lingered in the folds of her satin quilt. She lived in a tortured state halfway between dream and waking, hoping for a miracle, knowing none would happen. She prayed to Kwan Yin, to Kwan Ti, God of War and Justice, but the skies were silent.

On the day of the executions, Ke-ming closed the doors to her daughter's room and for the first time locked them. But Li-an did not intend to abandon Chao, even now. When she asked for Kin-shih's help, the servant stared at her in disbelief.

"Are you mad, Young Mistress, to seek such pain? They say that all who see the executions are haunted by the ghosts of the dead men at night. Surely, in your condition, you should not take such a risk."

"I am already haunted by Chao's spirit, for it is mine," Li-an said. "Spirit, heart, soul—we have shared everything. I must go to him now."

Unnerved by the wild gleam in her mistress's eyes, Kin-shih agreed at last. It was not long before Li-an had slipped out through the courtyard and climbed the locked gate, her headdress under her arm. She did not need to ask the way; it seemed that everyone in Peking was headed for the marketplace.

Once outside, she felt an intense weariness, so she hailed a sedan chair to carry her. She did not want to collapse before Chao's eyes and she knew she had not eaten enough to give her strength; only enough to keep the baby alive.

When she arrived at the marketplace, she saw at once the raised dais in the center of the square. She sank back into her chair and listened to the people who awaited the spectacle to come.

". . . say there's to be five beheaded today. I have never seen so many at once."

The note of anticipation in the woman's voice made Li-an ill.

". . . not the Matriarch. They strangled her quietly in her cell this morning. They were afraid to start a riot. The people revere old age too much to watch such a woman die in violence."

Li-an thought of the Matriarch's crooked smile and her body went cold. There was a sudden silence, then the swell of voices told her the prisoners must be coming. From a long way away, she heard the bounce of the cart wheels over the uneven roads and her throat grew dry and tight. She could not do it. She could not stand and watch while the man she loved died because of the web of lies an angry woman had woven around him.

Drawing several deep breaths, Li-an forced herself to put the headdress on. She felt a surge of energy; once Chao's own hands had removed this from her head. He had touched it and cherished it. The thought gave her the strength she needed. He would not die like Yuan Tung-li, alone and without friends. Slowly, she stepped from the chair and stood on a nearby box. From there she saw the carts arrive, one for the women, one for Chao and his father. All had their hands bound behind them and the women were a pitiful sight. Their clothes were little more than rags, their hair was uncombed and fell around them like tortured snakes, their eyes were hollow; there was no pain there—only emptiness. Their souls had already left them.

Yet they trembled when they saw the executioner. Li-an did not look at him, but kept her eyes fixed on the cart that held Chao. She saw how, as he passed, the men who had been his friends looked away and would not meet his eyes. He raised his head higher, determined that they would not beat him down. Li-an raised her head, too, and focused all her thoughts on Chao. I am here for you, she thought. I have not abandoned you. I am here and I love you. She stared at the man across a crowd of shouting people until at last he looked her way. He froze when he saw her and she knew he had recognized the headdress. There was a flicker of gratitude in his eyes, but it quickly turned to fear and he looked away. She understood he was not afraid for himself, but for her. To be his friend was to be the enemy of the Son of Heaven. She knew that as well as he, but did not care.

The voices around her swelled like thunder, though she was not certain why, for under the heavy headdress, she kept her eyes on Chao, memorizing every detail of his face for the long cold nights to come. She heard a hush fall and guessed that one of the girls had been taken to the block. That was the way in the Middle Kingdom—a traitor's family died with him and the officials made him watch until it was his turn. What was it she had said to him once? *The foreigners are barbarians. At least we are civilized. Are we?* Chao had murmured. *I wonder.* Li-an bent double at a pain in her chest. This ritualized murder was not an act of justice, but an act of fear.

She flinched when she heard the first blade fall and Chao went gray. He stared as if hypnotized at the block where the first of his sisters had died. There was silence for a moment, then a low murmur of approval when the guard shouted, "May all enemies of the Son of Heaven suffer the same fate."

Then the blade fell again and Chao closed his eyes. This time the crowd shouted more loudly. Li-an glanced away from Chao only long enough to see that they held a girl's head up by the hair with the dust of the ground on her face, while her body lay unmoving at their feet.

Li-an gasped and looked away. She had not imagined it would be like this. She was frozen with shock, rigid with horror when she turned back to Chao. The blade fell again and the crowd called out curses to all enemies of the Emperor. She saw by Chao's eyes that he wanted to weep, but dared not; the crowd would never understand that his tears were of grief and pain for his mother and sisters, not the weakness of a coward. He could not die a coward. That would only hurt his cause. But his skin was so pallid, his eyes so empty. She could see now the bruises where they had tortured him and she felt the blows on her own body. Then the guards came to drag his father forward and Chao clenched his hands to keep from reaching out to stop them. They had won. He could not fight them anymore.

Li-an stood still, her eyes dry and painful with unshed tears. I am here, she thought to Chao. I carry our child. I will teach him about you—the truth, not the lie. I am here and I love you.

He nodded slowly, though she was not certain he had understood. She knew he dared not look at her again. When the blade fell this time, the crowd roared without ceasing as the guards approached Chao. The sound rose through the sky like thunder, like a great cry of jubilation, like joy unrestrained; it rang in Li-an's ears like a hollow bell of doom. She saw that since he had seen his family die, Chao wanted to go. He did not want to live with the burden of their deaths upon his shoulders. He moved forward eagerly when the guard touched his arm and she felt a pain that split her heart in two.

Without thinking, propelled by an instinct deeper than feeling, she got down from the box and started forward. But something stopped her. A hand gripped her shoulder brutally, so she could not move. A man in official robes came close and hissed, "What do you think you are doing?"

It was Tso Ch'eng-ta. "I am going to save him."

"You're mad. You will only die with him."

"Then so it shall be." She wrenched free and started to run, but he caught her.

His hand closed around her arm, and when she tried to break away, he struck her across the jaw with his fist. The last thing she heard as she slumped into his arms was the fall of the blade and the reverberating triumphant shout of the crowd.

11

When Li-an awoke, she was in her own bed. She rubbed her bruised jaw, then stopped, hands frozen in midair as the scene at the marketplace came back to her. She found a porcelain bowl near the bed and vomited again and again. Unable to move, she crouched, shivering, on the floor. She might as well have died with Chao. This stillness inside was not living; it was empty, meaningless.

"Come into the courtyard and breathe some fresh air."

Li-an jumped at the sound of Wu Shen's voice. She had not known he was here. Numbly, she took his arm and they went through the sitting room and into the courtyard. The sun had begun to set. Li-an wondered if the smell of blood lingered in the dust of the marketplace.

She turned to Wu Shen, who caught her in his arms and held her as she shuddered. "He is dead," she whispered.

Her friend gently brushed the hair from her face. "Yes."

Li-an closed her eyes against the image of that dust-filled square, the sound of those triumphant voices; nevertheless, the horror rushed over her in waves. "I did not forsake him," she said. "I wish he knew—"

Shen raised her chin with his thumb and forefinger. "He knew, my daughter. There are many voices to whisper through the walls of a prison. Voices that spoke of a woman who wore a strange headdress, who came daily to ask for Chin Chao, and who stood for hours across the way, trying to make a chance where there was none. He knew what you did for him. If you do not believe me, then perhaps you should read this."

He drew a ragged scroll from his sleeve and slipped off

the ribbon that bound it. Guiding Li-an toward the light of a lantern, he indicated a bench. She sat awkwardly, smoothing the rice paper again and again over her satin gown. She knew at first glance that these characters had been drawn by Chao; his bold strokes and fine curves had become as familiar as her own calligraphy. The sight only made her fingers grow stiff and her vision blurred.

"Read it," Shen said, "and know that you did not fail."
Li-an took a deep, ragged breath and began to read.

> She stands beneath the willow,
> Her face white and still.
> Like fine carved jade she stands,
>   —beautiful and indestructible,
> Like the ancient gnarled pine
>   —steadfast and loyal,
> Like bamboo in a summer breeze,
>   —bending but never broken,
> A tiger with her courage wrapped about her
>   like a silk cape of ten thousand threads.
> She stands in silence,
> Watching for he who never comes,
> Though the sun grows hot and bitter
> And the leaves fall around her
>   —shadows grasping at her feet.
> She stands forever unmoving,
> Her eyes reflecting the wide, empty sky.

Li-an's face was covered with tears as sorrow entered her blood and coursed through every vein. The bright hot agony throbbed in her eyes, from which the tears flowed endlessly. She gasped at the overwhelming pain. But it was not her head that hurt. Something was wrong. Only when Wu Shen reached down to help and she fell to her knees with a moan did she realize that the pain was her child crying out in a torment so great that she could not bear it.

In the hours that followed, she slipped in and out of consciousness, racked with pain when she awoke, her head full of a dark mist that would not leave her. More than once, when the agony became unbearable, she saw Ke-ming's face, felt her long cool fingers on Li-an's fevered forehead, and there was a momentary cessation of pain. The agony came, her mother's face appeared, the pain faded. She heard voices, saw faces come and go. She cried out and bent her body double, but the contractions went on, and the voices and the endless watching faces. She drank when cups were held to her lips, then slept again, though not in peace. She turned and tossed and always a new twinge of pain awoke her. Shivering, her body covered with sweat, she reached out for her mother's hand.

At last she awoke and there was no more pain—only the taste of willow-bark tea in her mouth and the fog that dimmed the room around her like drifts of smoke that lingered after the fire had gone. She felt light-headed, as if her body had no weight, no substance. Within her, where there had been turmoil, there was nothingness. She clutched her stomach, praying to all the gods of the Nine Heavens, but she knew it was too late. She had lost the child, the precious child that would have been her hope and consolation.

There was nothing for her now—Chao was dead and his family and his child. No trace of him remained. She was alone while his soul drifted in some dark half-world where the *kuei*—the spirits of those who had died by violence—wandered in solitude and loneliness. She began to weep, but no tears came, just dry, racking sobs that shook her body as she turned toward the wall to escape the light. She wanted only darkness, forgetfulness. Curled under the satin cover, she slept again and dreamed.

She was reaching out to her baby, but her arms were not long enough—always the child was just beyond her reach. She began to weep as she tried to touch the baby she would never hold. Then someone grasped her cold hand. Strong, warm fingers closed around hers. "Don't grieve," a voice said softly.

She glanced up at a face she knew, and yet this was a stranger. A woman with chestnut hair and blue-violet eyes full of understanding and a depth of knowledge that had not come from books.

"Hold my hand," the woman said. "Close your eyes and see through mine what your daughter's life would have been. Look with me and see beyond today and tomorrow. Look long and hard."

Li-an looked. She squeezed the woman's hand and felt as if her warm blood entered Li-an's cold veins. Then her blurred vision grew clear and she saw a child, hiding, running, ducking behind bushes, eyes wide with fear. She saw a little girl who was pale and ill with uncertainty. Then she saw, far in the distance, among the mountains with the pine trees all around, the birds fleeing from a house engulfed by flames. In the center of those flames she heard a child's desperate cries. "My Mother! Help me!"

Li-an tried to run but could not move; her feet were caught in a tangled root.

"Mother!" the child screamed again before the flames spread over the roof and it crashed inward. The girl's cries disappeared under the rush and roar of the consuming flames.

"No!" Li-an screamed while the tears streamed down her cheeks. "No!"

"No," the strange woman whispered, her face dim and soft around the edges. " 'Twill never be. Ye have lost much, and ye should grieve, but remember always what would have been. Remember and be grateful that there was no sufferin' for this child, no pain, no loss, no grief. Remember."

As she spoke, her voice faded. For a moment, the image of her brilliant eyes lingered until that, too, was gone.

Li-an awoke drenched in sweat, tired and thirsty, her body aching. She gazed around her familiar room, blinking to make certain that the branches of trees were not above her or the tangled roots below. That the fire nearby was nothing more than the glow of a lantern. That the shadows on the walls were not the wings of fleeing birds. "It was only a dream," she murmured. The grief welled within her again.

"What did you say, my daughter?"

She turned her head and saw Wu Shen's face. Shakily, she touched his withered cheek to assure herself that he was real. When he took her hand, she began to weep.

"I have lost the child."

411

"Yes," he said softly. "The gods did not think the time was right for you."

"But I wanted her so much. I needed her."

Shen frowned at her vehemence. "Why?"

"So I would have someone who needed me."

"You are much needed now. Do you not know that?"

Wincing at the pain, Li-an raised herself on one elbow. "Who?" she demanded. "Who needs me?"

"I do."

She stared in disbelief. "You are strong and wise and kind. Why should you need me?"

"Do you not realize how much it has meant to have a student like you to teach—one who is willing, eager to learn more than just the ancient traditions? With your questions and your curiosity, you made me think and wonder about things that would never have entered my mind."

He touched her tangled hair. "But more precious than that, far more precious, was the knowledge that always I could come to you and say what I felt without fear of betrayal. Li-an, my precious jade, do you know how many officials have not one true friend who will stay by them, no matter what? To know that we share such a friendship is more to me than gold or fame or even wisdom. If you think because you need me that I do not need you, then you are blind."

Still the tears fell. "But there is no one else. Now that Chao is—" she stopped, swallowed dryly, then forced herself to say the word "dead."

Shen leaned closer. "You taught him much."

Li-an shook her head and a teardrop stained the satin coverlet. "He was a brilliant scholar—"

"But you gave him poetry."

"No." She looked away, remembering the first of Chao's poems, the one that, in the end, had cost him his life. "He wrote poetry long before he met me, since he was a child."

"In a way," Shen said. "But that was poetry of the mind, not of the heart. He did not know he had a heart until he met you. You taught him how to love."

"I saw him with his family. He loved them deeply."

The old man sighed. "*Hsiao*—filial piety—is not the same. You gave him a different kind of love, and joy, Li-an. If not for you, he would never have known those things before he died. No other woman would have had the courage to show him."

Li-an smiled bitterly. "I told him once that I am always afraid."

Wu Shen turned so the shadows of the lanterns played across his face. "Strange, is it not, to live in a world where she who is most afraid is braver than all the rest of us together?"

A cold breeze crept over her skin. Chao had said the same too often. She could hear his voice now. . . . "If not for me, he would not have died at all."

"You are wrong." Shen met her eyes, his dark gaze steady. "Chin Chao had to die, because he was an honest man in a court full of deceivers. He could not keep his opinions silent; he had to try to change the world. It was his integrity that killed him, because he was not willing to live a lie."

"But you are an honest man and you have lived long and happily."

"Long," Shen agreed, "though not always happily. But you see, that is because I am a coward. I abhor the corruption of the court as much as Chao did, but I do not try to change what I abhor. I have kept my silence all these years, so I have lived and flourished."

Li-an shook her head, but she had no strength left to argue. After a long time, she whispered, "But my mother does not need me. She does not need anyone."

" 'Such sorrow blinds the eyes,' my daughter, for your mother needs you most of all."

"Wan Ke-ming needs no one."

Shen smiled sadly. "That is what she would have you believe. But it is not true. She is a woman with feelings like any other." The old man's eyes were full of regret. "It is sad that your mother has let you know her so little. You really do not see how much she cares for you—so much that she has spent all her effort in teaching you to be strong, to survive. It was the only thing of value she could give you.

413

She is not a soft woman, but a soft woman would have let you die long since."

Li-an opened her mouth to reply, but a pain sliced through her body and she gasped and doubled over.

Wu Shen tilted her head and offered her a cup of tea that tasted strange and bitter. "Sleep now to regain your strength, but hear what I have said. Do you hear?"

She gripped his hand once before her fingers lost their strength and his face began to blur. "I hear."

She awoke in darkness. As the healing mists of sleep retreated, her heart stopped and her throat grew dry and painful. She heard voices in another room and concentrated on the rhythmic sound instead of her own sorrow.

"I fear they followed her from the marketplace. If that is so, then they know who she is."

The voice of Tso Ch'eng-ta.

Ke-ming murmured something unintelligible.

"The Empress Dowager has long been waiting for a reason to do you harm," Tso continued. "Your daughter's connection with Chin Chao is a ripe plum fallen into her lap."

"She has turned the ministers and officials against us," Ke-ming offered tonelessly.

"It is more than that. You see, the people themselves are calling for blood."

"Did they not have enough of it today?"

Tso sighed. "Perhaps you do not realize that the people feel the weakness of the Middle Kingdom. They feel the very earth crumble beneath their feet, see the palaces falling, and do not understand. Then someone like Chin raises his voice and they are happy to hate him, to blame him for all their ills. They convince themselves, in times like these, that to destroy him—all he believes, those he loves, his values and integrity—will rid them of the poison in the air, the earth will grow firm again beneath their feet and the palaces cease to totter."

"Is that why you persecuted Yuan and Chin so furiously, though you knew they were not traitors? Because the people are afraid? It is not enough, Tsai Shen."

Even now she would not speak his real name.

"It is not enough that twice I saved your daughter's life?"

"No," Ke-ming said deliberately. "Not anymore."

There was a silence that stretched into eternity while Li-an drifted back to sleep. This time she slept deeply, without dreams. When she awoke, the pressure in her chest was greater and every breath an effort. She turned at an unfamiliar sound to find Kin-shih scrambling about the room from chest to chest, Li-an's clothes over her arms and around her neck.

"What are you doing?" Li-an asked.

Kin-shih spun, wide-eyed. "Thanks to the gods you are awake at last, Young Mistress. We have been warned by a high official that the Most High will send the Bannermen after you. The official said he would delay the order as long as possible, but in the end, he must let them come."

Li-an blinked the mists of sleep away, trying to understand.

"You must go away before it is too late!" the servant cried. "Wu Shen says he knows of a place in the Western Mountains where you will be safe."

Her mistress rose on her elbow, rigid as polished stone. The nightmare that had haunted her all her life would finally come to pass. The soldiers were coming, not for her father or her lover, but this time for *her*. She forced herself to breathe evenly and rise slowly from the curtained bed. Now that the moment was finally here, she felt strangely calm, numbed by the weight of grief and emptiness inside her.

She stood for a moment, waiting for her legs to grow steady, watching the servant fold and pack away a satin *kua-erh* embroidered in silver thread. "Do not bother with that one," Li-an said. "I will have no use for such robes in the hills. Pack only the simple *p'aos* and tunics, my cloth shoes and padded jackets." She bit her lip and tried to think. "We shall need the jewels to sell off now and then, so wrap them carefully." Pausing to catch her breath, she looked around the comfortable room and felt no sense of loss. "Is someone seeing to my mother's things?"

"Mei has begun to pack—" Kin-shih began, astonished at her mistress's strength of will.

"Tell her, please, what I have told you. We will take only what is necessary and practical except for that which we can sell." She frowned. "What about the kitchen?"

"My honorable mother is packing pots and pans away."

Li-an nodded, glad to have something to occupy her mind. She felt the need to hurry; it crackled in the air like unseen sparks. She realized then that she was listening for the sound of soldiers' boots on the cobbled streets. "I must speak to my mother."

"You will find her in the Hall of Ancestors."

Li-an bowed before moving down the passage to the hall. The reed curtains had been lowered and the room was dark, except for a single candle that burned on the Altar of Ancestors. The fragrance of sandalwood met her at the door and she saw that Ke-ming knelt before the altar with her head on her hands.

Her daughter stopped in the doorway, astonished by Ke-ming's simple robe, her long, flowing hair, which she had not even tried to contain. She had never seen her mother kneel before, not to god or man. Yet here she was, her arms stretched out in supplication toward the altar of a stranger.

Ke-ming sensed her daughter's presence and raised her head. Her eyes were no longer veiled, but full of grief, and more than that, remorse.

Your mother needs you most of all, Wu Shen had said. Li-an came forward to kneel beside Ke-ming.

Her mother gazed at the portrait above the altar and murmured, "Chin Chao was a good man. I knew that from the beginning. But I knew, too, what the end would be." She stared at the painting as if afraid to turn and meet her daughter's gaze. "I wanted to keep you from suffering, and now I cannot even share your grief." Her voice shook a little and Li-an touched her hand, the cool gleam of her gold bracelet against her pale skin.

"Perhaps you have felt enough of your own. Besides, we have no time for grief, my Mother."

"I know." Still Ke-ming did not move, mesmerized by the wavering candle flame. "We will run now for the rest of our lives," she said. She could not stop the desolation from creeping into her tone.

Li-an clasped her mother's hand more tightly. "We have been running for as long as I can remember, hiding from the sight of others." Li-an gazed at the portrait that was a lie and smiled sadly. "We have hidden our eyes, our thoughts, our secrets, our dreams. In the hills there will be no need to hide these things. Always, I have known that in the mountains we would find peace."

Ke-ming turned. "After all that has happened, do you really believe such a thing is possible?"

"I do not know. I know only that my spirit belongs high among the pines and mountain peaks, not here, under gold-tiled roofs and the threat of a soldier's sword." She tilted her head, listening, listening. . . .

Ke-ming rose and straightened. She could see the infinite sorrow in her daughter's eyes, feel it in the cool touch of her hand, yet she spoke of hope and peace. A miracle indeed, this child of her heart who had so quickly and brutally become a woman. For the first time, Ke-ming felt Li-an's strength flow into her, renewing her.

"Come," her daughter said briskly. "You must see that Mei is packing the proper things for you. I will go to the kitchen and help Liu Kan." She drew her mother up and released her hand. "Come," Li-an repeated, "there is little time."

Ke-ming stood and watched her go. She knew Li-an's drive to prepare things for their departure was only a shield. She had built a wall around her grief so that it could not touch her, much as her mother had done years ago. Ke-ming closed her eyes against dry, burning tears. Li-an would survive, as her mother had survived, but at what cost?

In an hour the trunks and bamboo baskets full of food had been loaded on an old cart Wu Shen had bought in one of the narrow *hu-tungs* nearby. For the last time, Li-an had donned Kin-shih's clothes so she would fade into the landscape, like all the other travelers on the road. Ke-ming wore Mei's simple cotton tunic and trousers and her hair, like her daughter's, was pulled back in a neat bun.

Everyone stood beside the cart in silence. There was much to say and much that could never be expressed. Shen had promised to find a place for the Liu family where they

417

would be well treated; Liu Kan had offered to go with the two women, but Ke-ming had refused. She would not put someone else in danger. Tso Ch'eng-ta would see to the house. In the meantime, the fire in the stove had been put out and the braziers had grown cold. There was nothing left to do but say good-bye.

Ke-ming and her daughter bowed to each of the servants in turn, thanked them for years of faithful service. Twice Li-an reached out, once to take Liu Kan's hand and then to take Kin-shih's. They had become her friends; she would miss them. The block of ice around her heart began to melt and she turned away to find herself staring into Wu Shen's soft black eyes. She blinked back tears and took his hands, but he drew her close to whisper, "You have been daughter, friend, and confidante to me. There will never be another like you."

The frozen tears began to break free, one by one. "Nor like you," she said, resting her head on his shoulder.

Her weeping made a circle of moisture on his robe and he smiled. "I will carry with me always the stain of your tears, and so I will remember."

Purposefully, he guided her toward the wagon. Brushing his wrinkled cheek once more, she climbed into the cart and watched Ke-ming give Shen her hand.

"I thank the gods daily for sending me a teacher and friend such as you." Quickly, she joined her daughter in the back of the wagon. The driver, an old and trustworthy friend of Shen's, started the horses in motion and at last they were on their way.

The dust that rose in the street behind them mingled with Wu Shen's parting words.

> " 'Friend, I have watched you down the mountain
> 'Til now in the dark I close my thatch door. . . .
> Grasses return again, green in the Spring,
> But oh, my Prince of Friends, do you?' "

As Shen's voice faded, Li-an heard, far in the distance, the sound of marching feet. This time the soldiers would be too late.

Epilogue

Six years later, in the summer of 1878, Li-an perched on a rock beside a lake of blooming *lien*—lotus. She had watched the leaves and blossoms struggle up from the water through spring and summer until the translucent petals and huge leaves covered the lake in a billowing sea of green and lilac. Li-an lay stretched out, lulled by the heat, her gaze fixed on the leaves; waxen and blue green, they caught a drift of afternoon rain, swaying in the wind so the sun flashed off the drops of moisture like blue lightning in a jade-green sky.

With her eyes nearly closed, she listened to the stillness while the words of a Li Po poem ran through her head.

> Summer, too lazy
> To wave my feather fan.
> Out by the green woods,
> Naked I lie,
> In rest complete,
> Looking at my hat hanging
> on a rock.
> The sweet wind sighing
> through the pines,
> Gently caressing me.

She smiled and did not know this was the last peace she would feel for a long time. She heard the crackle of twigs and sat up, peered through the pines until she saw the bent figure of a man. He picked his way with a gnarled stick over the uneven ground. Li-an leaned forward. The figure was familiar, as was the wizened face with the wispy white beard.

In an instant, she was up and running in her cloth-soled shoes. She ducked beneath the twisted branches, her hair, drawn back in a simple queue, swaying as she hurried toward the traveler who had stopped to catch his breath.

"Wu Shen!" she cried in joy. "My friend!"

He raised his head and she saw his eyes, full of despair and a resignation that had not been there before. She paused while he stared at her as if she were an apparition. Then he hurried forward. For a moment, when they met and bowed and she reached out to clasp his hand, he smiled. "You cannot know what the sight of your face means to me," he said. "At first I did not know you, so glowing are your cheeks, so clear your eyes. The hills have welcomed you, I see."

"We are happy here," Li-an replied. "We did not ever think to be so happy."

Shen frowned and a shadow crossed his face. "I am glad to hear it." But there was no gladness in his voice.

"You have ill news," Li-an guessed. "Come. My mother will be weaving on the porch, no doubt."

Wu Shen's breathing was still labored, so Li-an took his arm and led him up the hill, through rows of tortured pines to the simple house made of wood and stone with reed curtains on the doors.

"My Mother," she called, "see who has come."

Ke-ming looked up with a smile, but when she saw Wu Shen's face, the smile disappeared. As he approached and sat on the step, leaning heavily on his stick, she said softly, "The time has come, has it not?"

"It has."

Li-an stilled her questions for the moment. Shen looked pale, and her mother, too, so she went inside to brew some chrysanthemum tea. In a few minutes she returned with a melon and a plate of rice-flour dumplings. It was good that she had learned how to cook, for she lived alone with her mother and had to gather what food she could and prepare it herself. She enjoyed it, just as she enjoyed planting her vegetable garden and sewing their clothes. She had felt at home the moment she arrived in the hills. No task was too small or too difficult to bring her satisfaction. She set the lacquer tray on a bamboo stool and offered first Shen, then her mother a saucer of tea.

Their faces were grim as they sipped the tea and ate a bit of melon. Li-an sat on a stool near the loom. "Tell me what has happened."

Shen stared at the trees whipped by the wind of approaching evening, his brow furrowed. "The court grows more corrupt by the day, the Empress Dowager more grasping, the West more demanding. So many men have been banished and executed that the gutters in the Forbidden City run with blood and tears. Even Tso Ch'eng-ta, the President of the Censorate, was arrested."

Ke-ming dropped the shuttle and sat upright. "That is why you have come?"

Shen nodded sadly. "He tried to bargain with She Who Would Rule the World, but T'zu Hsi is stubborn and would not listen. So, in the end, to save himself, Ch'eng-ta told the truth about you and Hung Hsiu-chuan."

Li-an stared, open-mouthed. "He was the leader of the Taiping Rebellion, was he not? Did you know him, my Mother?"

Ke-ming was silent for so long that her daughter thought she would not answer. Then she whispered, "He was my brother."

Too shocked to speak, Li-an sat still as stone on her bamboo seat.

"They said he was the son of a farmer, an ignorant man from the Hakka province, but it was not so," Ke-ming continued. "Before she became that poor farmer's wife, Hung's mother, Yi-ma, was my father's concubine. The child she bore after her marriage was the seed of my father, but this her husband did not know. Only we knew, or so I believed. For Yi-ma's sake, we kept our silence. Then one day my half-brother Hsiu-chuan saw the gleam of swords reflected in the midnight sky and believed it was a sign from the gods. He knew of the powerful swords full of virtue that the ancient ruler Chao Tho, King of Yueh, had buried in the hills to help him rule his kingdom. Hsiu-chuan believed they had appeared to show him he was born to save the Middle Kingdom from destruction.''

She paused, toying with the gold bracelet on her wrist. "Then we were glad, my father and I, that we had kept our silence. The Son of Heaven believes treason is born in the heart, that it flows like poison through the veins of all who share the traitor's blood. Hung Hsiu-chuan's relatives died in the end, paying one and all for his crime.''

Just as Chao's family had paid with him for his, Li-an thought. The grief welled within her, as strong as the day when he had died. "Is that why you never mentioned your father?'' she asked when she could speak. "If no one knew—''

Ke-ming stared down at her hands. "Someone did know. My father was prefect in the province of Kwantung where I lived with him. Then I was sent for by the Emperor, and while I enjoyed myself at the *Yuan Ming Yuan*, someone sent my father a silken rope.''

Li-an knew that often, when a corrupt official had been caught, the Emperor would show him mercy by sending a silken cord. It was a sign that the official should take his life quietly, without disgrace, so his family need not lose his fortune and die with him. "But—'' Li-an began.

Ke-ming did not seem to hear. Her thoughts were somewhere in the past. "One day my father received a note that read, 'Your blood is tainted by the stink of rebellion. Which is worse, death or disgrace? Death by the sword or death by the rope? The truth will die with you and those you love will be free. Remember that.' ''

"Did he—use the rope?'' Li-an asked haltingly.

Gaze locked on a distant, painful memory, her mother replied, "Not at once. Instead he retreated to a Buddhist monastery in the hills, where he hoped no one would find him. There he learned to meditate, so the ugliness of the world did not exist, but only the peaceful silence in his mind. Eventually, I discovered where he had gone, but by the time I arrived, he was dead.'' Her voice shook and she felt again the disbelief, the cold, piercing sorrow. "He left me a new name, his divination box, and a poem. But more than that, a strange stillness within my grief. The monks there had respected him and told me he was a good man, an honest man, who loved me enough to free me from his shadow.''

"It seems it is always the honest men who have to die.'' Li-an wandered to the edge of the porch to stare at the sun as it settled behind the mountains. "So for all those years, you never spoke his name or told his story?''

"No. He had chosen that it should be so.'' Ke-ming went to stand beside her daughter. "I could not betray his trust and thereby endanger us all. But I wish you had known him, my daughter.''

"I did in a way,'' Li-an murmured. She had built a new altar to her ancestors here, smaller and simpler than the other. In it she had placed the precious poem she had found in her mother's drawer so long ago. Each night she knelt and thanked the stranger who was her grandfather for leading her here, where she was finally at peace. She smiled sadly and hoped that, at his monastery in the mountains, he, too, had found contentment before he died.

Pensively, Ke-ming contemplated the misted twilight. "I have always wondered who sent that silken rope.''

"You need not wonder anymore,'' Wu Shen muttered. "Tso Ch'eng-ta admitted he sent it, for he had seen you at the *Yuan Ming Yuan* and desired you. But he knew you were strong-willed and so wanted something to bind you to him. He looked into your past, talked to a woman who had served Yi-ma, and coaxed the truth from her. He thought if he did this terrible thing, you would be afraid of discovery and would let him protect you always. He did not merely want you to love him, he wanted you to need him so you could never turn away.''

Ke-ming shook her head incredulously. "He was always so kind.''

"He could afford to be. He had you in his power. He did not recover from your loss, you know. These past six years he has grown pale and thin and at the same time unwise. He spoke too often and too loudly of things he knew. But he paid for it as have many others before him.''

Ke-ming looked up, her face drained of color. "You mean—''

"I mean that T'zu Hsi was delighted to learn your

secret. She will send out soldiers to find you, now that she knows. This time she can destroy you with reason and no one can object. But that was not enough to save Tso. In the end. he, too, hung himself by a silken cord.''

They sat in silence while darkness fell around them, and with it a slow, creeping fear.

"We cannot stay here," Li-an said at last. "She will certainly find us.''

"She is very determined," Wu Shen agreed.

"Come," Ke-ming said. "Let us go inside and eat while we think what to do. My friend, you must rest after your long journey. I thank you for coming to warn us. It cannot have been easy to climb these hills.''

"There is one thing more," he said, and drew from his sleeve an envelope, folded and sealed with wax. "This letter was a long time in finding you. It went first to Canton and then to Peking, where it fell into my hands because someone remembered that I was your friend. It is from England.''

Li-an stiffened. England? She rose at once and went inside, returning with a wick in a saucer of bean oil. They saved their candles for festival days or storms so dark that the rage of the Thunderer crept inside the thin walls of the hut. Li-an set down the saucer and watched Ke-ming open the packet, take out several folded sheets and an inner packet. Slowly, she spread the first sheet on her lap and leaned close to the wick to read.

Ke-ming,

I remember well the things you told me on the night I left Canton. Thus I have not tried to contact you or our daughter since. But I remember, too, the secrets in your eyes, the curve of your cheek, the play of lantern light over your face. I know I will never see these things again; you made your feelings all too clear. I will not insult you by asking again. But if I could see our daughter, just once, it would mean a great deal to me. I have never asked anything of you but this. I hope you are well and safe from the hatred that poisons your country. I hope your veins still run clear and free, if not of bitterness, then at least of fear.

Yours Ever,
Charles

Ke-ming remained motionless by the flickering light of the wick while shadows danced like ghosts over her face. Her eyes, for the first time since Li-an could remember, were soft with warm memories. Gracefully, as if charmed by the music of a distant lute, she picked up another packet and handed it to her daughter. Now it was Li-an who leaned close to the flame, she who hesitated with the paper spread on her lap and stared at the strange English characters. For a moment they swam before her eyes—a senseless chaos of black marks that fell, one by one, into a pattern. "To my daughter Li-an," she read.

I am breaking my long silence and my promise to your mother in writing to you. I would not have done so, except that I am ill and know I will not recover. I have a very great favor to ask. I am now in the hills of Scotland where the clear Highland air does me good. I would like for you to join me here so I may see you once more before I die. I have enclosed the money for your fare, if you should choose to use it. If not, please keep it to do with as you wish.

I have not been much of a father to you and can give you no reason why you should do this thing for me, except that it would ease my heart to hear your voice and see your face, not pale and full of terror as it was on that last night, to know that you are alive and well.

Yours Most Sincerely,
Charles Kittridge

Without a word, Ke-ming handed her daughter the other two packets. In one, Li-an found a pile of British pounds. She frowned and touched the paper curiously. This was money, that did not clink or fall on a string or weigh like a tael of silver? Then she unfolded the last page and found herself looking at a sketch of her own face when she was four years old. She was smiling and there was no fear in her wide-open eyes. She dropped the paper from numb fingers.

"He could not have chosen a better time," Ke-ming said, breaking the stillness that hummed with fireflies. "Now you have somewhere to go."

Li-an did not reply. She placed the pages on the bamboo table and without a word went down the steps and into the woods.

Ke-ming watched her with concern. "You are tired, my friend," she said when she heard Shen sigh. "Come and rest."

She held his arm while he rose awkwardly and leaned upon her as they ducked beneath the cane mat. "There is not much time," he said as he lay down on the *kang*—the bed of bricks in the center of the room heated from within and covered by a braided mat of soft bamboo. Many times, Li-an and Ke-ming had sat there, painting on lanterns or silk, talking long into the night.

"You must convince her soon."

"I know. But you must forget our problems for now. Already they have brought too many gray hairs to your head and too many wrinkles to your face."

Wu Shen smiled. "It is of those gray hairs and wrinkles that I am most proud."

He turned his head and was soon asleep. When she heard his even breathing, Ke-ming went back to the porch and sat on the top step to wait. It was not long before her daughter returned and sat beside her. Li-an would not meet her mother's eyes. Ke-ming had much to say, but she waited for her daughter to speak; she felt Li-an's rage and frustration building as surely as if she had touched her shaking hand.

"Why has he never written before? How dare he send for us only now, when he is dying?"

The anger was good, Ke-ming thought, for it meant Li-an still cared. "I made him promise not to contact us in any way. It would have been too dangerous."

There was a long, strained silence, then Li-an cried, "Why didn't he take us with him? Why?"

"He could not have done so, my pale jade. He was a man alone, running for his life. He had no choice."

Li-an shook her head, unconvinced.

"Nevertheless, you must go to him," Ke-ming said.

"No. I do not wish to see his face again."

Softly, her mother murmured, "You are not even curious about the man he has become?"

"I know too well the man he was."

"It is true that more than once I have told you about the man he was, but you did not hear. It has been twenty years since you last saw your father. It is time to let go of your anger. What happened in Canton was not his fault. If you must blame someone, then it should be me."

"I want only to forget him."

"But you cannot forget him. Do you not see that? You cannot escape your destiny."

"Which is?" Li-an asked, her voice full of bitterness.

"To be Charles Kittridge's daughter. The part of him that is in your blood has kept you alive until now. Any other girl would have crumbled under the weight of fear and uncertainty that you have borne with unbowed shoulders and a straight back. His blood, his history, his energy have made you strong. How many women from Peking could have come to this wild place and so easily made us a comfortable home?"

Li-an turned. "You could have done it."

"No, my daughter. Not without you."

In her heart, Li-an knew it was true. It was she who had cleaned, cleared the land, made a garden, grew their food, and cooked. And there was something else. Here in the hills, Li-an was happy, but when she looked down on the roads and cities, she felt like a stranger who did not belong—and had not, since she stood and watched Chao's family die. All at once, she wanted to weep.

"Listen to me," Ke-ming insisted. "No matter what you believe, no matter what childish hatred you have carried with you all these years, Charles Kittridge is a good man."

"Chin Chao was a good man, and Yuan Tung-li, and

your father. Such men do not last long in the Middle King-dom.''

"They do not," Ke-ming agreed sadly. "The fear of change is too great. That is why your father had to leave us, why you must leave now."

Li-an ran her palm over the gnarled pine that curved toward the porch. She thought that she would like to see her father once, ill and vulnerable, lying in his bed as she had lain one night and begged him not to leave her. Then her fingers grew rigid on the bark and she half turned. It struck her for the first time that Ke-ming had said, "you must go," not "we." "If I go, *if*, you will come, too." It was not a question.

"No." Ke-ming spoke softly but firmly. "I cannot leave this place. I am too old and tired to run. I have found peace here and I will stay." When Li-an stared at her in disbelief, Ke-ming added, "Do you not see that to turn my back on the beauty, the history, the tradition would break my heart?"

"I thought you hated this place. All my life you taught me how destructive were the laws and rituals, how weak the government, how pervasive the oppression."

Ke-ming lowered her head. "That was because I knew that, much as I loved it, this country would betray us both in the end. So I taught you that there are other ways, better ways than the ancient, well-trodden paths of our ancestors. I showed you the decay, the corruption, the injustice, but I see now that was not enough." She looked up, her eyes misted. "I spoke only of the bad and never the good. It was wrong." She paused, then said wistfully, "There is much that is beautiful here, much to cherish and be proud of—the splendid palaces unique in all the world, the gardens where so many souls have found rest and peace. The poetry, the painting that is ingrained into each child from birth, the scholarship, the will to achieve perfection. And the sky full of clouds or a lake of lotus like blue fire with the sun upon them. These things are miracles that you will find nowhere else. I should have taught you that."

"Then how can I leave it? How can I leave you, my Mother?"

428

"Because I am a captive of my own history, but I have raised you to be free, to move toward the future—and the future is in the West. Here we have only shadows of the past and I was meant to die among them, weeping inside as the world crumbles around me. I have seen the future, Li-an. I know that a day will come when the good will disappear with the bad, and the Middle Kingdom will become a ruin. You must be far away by then, where people look forward instead of always behind them."

"I cannot go. I will not leave you here alone."

Ke-ming rose, as regal in her plain cotton *p'ao* and *kua-erh* as she had been in satin and silk. "You must. If not for your father's sake or your own, then for mine. I could not bear to see you destroyed along with all the rest. You are my hope."

Li-an thought she saw tears in her mother's eyes, but could not be sure in the uncertain light.

Ke-ming took her daughter's hands. "Promise me you will survive."

Mesmerized as she had so often been before, Li-an whispered, "I promise."

"Tomorrow you must leave with Wu Shen." Reluctantly, Ke-ming released Li-an's hands and climbed the steps. Her daughter turned away from the house, too restless to sleep. She walked through the forest, drifted now with mist and moonlight. The wind in the trees spoke to her, and the rippling of the water in the breeze. She thought what it would mean to leave this place and felt a pain inside that left her hollow. Here was everything she had ever loved—here, too, everything she had ever feared. Perhaps, after all, her mother was right. She returned to the hut to find Ke-ming and Shen asleep. Taking a brush, an ink stone, a stick of ink, and a tiny candle, she sat on the porch and wrote until the first streaks of dawn lit the sky.

Li-an stood on the porch, memorizing the bent bamboo couch, the stools with battered legs, the lacquered table with its pitted surface. She would miss these things that had become so familiar. She lifted her bag over her shoulder. She was taking little with her, just enough to get by, as well as Charles Kittridge's letter and his sketch of her. Wu Shen carried a small bag with her ink stone, brushes, and rice paper. He was waiting for her at the bottom of the hill. He had explained that he knew the way to the closest river where she could find a boat to carry her down to the eastern ocean. At the port of Tientsin, she would catch a ship to London. She carried a basket full of dumplings, rice cakes, and smoked meat to keep away hunger. There was nothing left to do but say good-bye to Ke-ming.

Her mother stood tall in a pale lilac gown, her hair, uncombed or braided, hung around her shoulders. To her daughter, she looked as young and beautiful as she must have been the first time the Emperor saw her.

"My mother—" she began.

Ke-ming raised her hands and Li-an fell silent. "I will pray nightly to Yu-ch'iang to keep you safe on your journey over many seas." She slipped off the gold bracelet she always wore. "This may help, for it came safely one way and may take you safely back another."

Li-an shook her head. "I could not take that. I have not seen you without it since I can remember."

"It was a gift from your father," Ke-ming explained. "Take it back to him, show him that I treasured it all these years. It will please him, I think. And I want you to have it."

Li-an slipped the cool bright metal over her wrist and felt the warmth of her mother's fingers on the white and yellow threads of gold. Tears sprang to her eyes, but she dared not let them fall. Her mother's face was strangely calm, devoid of emotion. "Take care, my daughter, and go quickly before it is too late."

Ke-ming covered Li-an's hand with hers. "I will miss you, pale jade. You do not know how much."

For the second time, Li-an thought she saw the shimmer of tears in her mother's eyes, but she could not be sure. Then Ke-ming stepped back and she knew she must go. The constriction in her throat stopped her breath, and her heartbeat was painfully slow. "Good-bye," she whispered in a choked voice. Why, just once, could her mother not pull her close and weep? Just once, could she not let her feelings overcome her caution? Li-an remembered that the night before Ke-ming had murmured brokenly, *You are my hope*. That was all she would ever have, for her mother did not cry, not even when her daughter was torn from her grasp and she stood, finally and always, alone.

Li-an turned to join Wu Shen, who waved once, then started away. She wanted to look back, but fought the impulse. Her mother had told her to look only forward, and this she had sworn to do. But with each step her heart ached more until she wept silently and the tears fell onto her gown.

Ke-ming stayed on the porch long after the two travelers had disappeared. She stood, rigid as jade, her eyes dry and aching, her body empty. The last of her heart had just left her behind. Then slowly, awkwardly, as if she had aged ten years in a few minutes, she went back into the hut. There on the table was a sheet of paper covered with the firm graceful strokes of her daughter's hand.

Ke-ming lifted it, blinking twice before she could read the characters.

Often I have feared the darkness,
The sound of autumn leaves like marching feet;
The flash of lightning like the stroke of
    gleaming swords;
The whispers of ghosts and shadows in the night.
I have shivered in my bed with terror
And in my loneliness, wept
    that there should be no comfort.

But among those days and nights there have been
    moments:
A peach blossom that fell into my palm—
    a flake of snow that would not melt;
The sigh of wind on still blue water
    that shaped the reflection of the lotus
    into a magic dragon swaying in the breeze;
The glow of a hundred lanterns whose
    butterfly shadows dance over a marble bridge
    like puppets on a carved and molded screen;
The touch of my mother's cool fingers on my forehead,

the sound of her voice
bringing peace to my haunted dreams.

Tears, loneliness, fear
I will leave behind in time,
    as memory fades.
But these moments of perfection—
        fleeting, intangible—
I will carry with me
                        Always

The characters faded, the graceful strokes became blurred and softened by the tears that fell down Ke-ming's cheeks and onto the fragile paper in her hand.

BOOK

III

DELHI, INDIA
1859

Prologue

Dusk was falling, so Emily Townsend hurried her step, pulling the sari over her face to hide her features from the stares of passersby. Although there were several British and a few Indians along the Calcutta street, no one looked her way. Still, she was grateful for the draped Indian garment, which made her look like a native to eyes deceived by the fading light. Besides, it was much cooler than her English gowns and petticoats, which hung about her like meaningless rituals in the cloying heat.

She kept close to the stone wall that separated the cantonment from the native section of the city until she passed the gate, which hung open on its creaking hinges. In spite of herself, she stopped to stare in fascination at the scene beyond. The scent of strange perfumes, of sandalwood, incense, and crushed jasmine petals, mingled with the smell of animal dung and billowing dirt to clog the air. The babble of voices rose toward the purple sky, chanting, crying, shouting, each louder and more demanding than the other. So great was the cacophony that it nearly drowned the clatter of carts and bullocks over the muddy streets. The narrow alleyways were crowded with people—peddlers, dark-skinned beggars, bearers, Muslims, Hindus, Sikhs in white robes, women in bright saris. One glimpse brought rushing back the clutter, the filth, the chaos that was India.

Emily shuddered and turned away. It frightened her, that teeming confusion of sound and smell and color beyond the narrow wall. It was too much like the whirling nightmares that plagued her in the light as well as the darkness. She thought she would choke on the odor of the city, even after

435

she had left it behind. She gasped with relief when she saw the pink bungalow surrounded, like the others, with its long, low veranda.

She glanced over her shoulder to make certain no one had seen her approach the walkway, flanked by frangipani bushes. Their heavy fragrance clung to her, reminding her too piercingly of exotic Indian perfumes. Fear pounded a warning in her head, but Emily ignored it as she moved toward Charles Kittridge's front door. For him she would risk everything.

She knocked so lightly that she was certain no one could have heard, but a slender Hindu woman opened the door. She glowered with obvious disapproval when she saw the European's blond hair beneath the edge of her sari. Emily fingered the silk nervously.

"Who is it, Jalana?" Charles called from inside.

Before the servant could answer, Emily slipped past her. "It's me," she said. "I had to come."

He was there in an instant, as astonished at the sight of her garment as was the Hindu. "Why are you dressed like that?"

"So no one will know I've come. So no one will see." She was grateful when Jalana slipped away, silent except for the jangle of bracelets and anklets.

Charles blinked at Emily, too startled to speak. Even in the gloomy light of the hall, he saw how she wavered, ready to turn and flee. As always, he was touched by her uncertainty. Taking her hands, he drew her inside. "Forgive me. It's just that I was surprised to see you. But you must know how lovely you look in blue silk. You should wear it always." A thought struck him and he frowned. "Won't Edward miss you?"

"My husband is with his friends at the club. He won't even know I've gone. Besides, I wanted to see you. To see if you had changed." He had not, she realized with a little shock, though she had not seen him for several days. When he was out of her sight, she convinced herself that he had become a different man, a stranger who did not care for her anymore. But she had been wrong again. His light brown hair was slightly touched with gray, just as it had been the last time—when he had taken her in his arms beneath the insubstantial shade of a tamarind tree and kissed her into forgetfulness. And his blue eyes still sparkled with pleasure only slightly tinged with sadness. At forty-one, he had begun to age gracefully. Emily envied him that. "You haven't forgotten me after all, then?"

"Of course I haven't forgotten."

With a tremulous smile, she rested one hand on the wide lapel of his coat. "Do you think anyone saw me?"

Shaking his head, Charles traced the wisps of pale blond hair that lay against her cheek. She was so small and vulnerable with her white English skin, not yet parched and aged by the pitiless Indian sun. As she clutched his arm, he felt that she might slip out of his fingers at any moment to shatter against the unforgiving earth. He could not let that happen. "No one saw," he assured her. "You're safe here, Emily."

Gazing up at him in wonder, she said, "Make me believe it, Charles. I want to feel safe."

He felt the rush of compassion that the sight of her frailty always caused. "As long as you're with me, no one can hurt you." Charles looked into her strange, vague eyes of pale blue ringed in gray and marveled again at how young she seemed, despite her twenty-seven years. Her youth, her fragile beauty made him want to protect her from all the ugliness she imagined in her world.

Through the thin silk of her sari, he could feel Emily tremble, though the night was heavy with the lingering heat of day. "Why did you come?" he asked softly.

She looked up, eyes cloudy and bewildered. "Because I've missed you. And I had to get away from that house." She shivered, thinking of the swarms of bugs that crawled along the floors and over the heavy English furniture despite her efforts to shut them out. And the winged night intruders which all the screens and netting in the world could not keep away. Then there were the servants who skulked at the edges of the room with their dark, watching eyes and mysterious smiles. She could not even tell them to go away, because they did not understand her language. But worst of all was the boredom and the horrible, enveloping silence, broken only by the sound of the punkah, which stirred the dank air but did not cool it.

Emily shrank back when Jalana and a young Indian girl appeared as if summoned from her troubled memory. Heads lowered, they worked quickly to clear the remains of Charles's supper of *chupattis* and curried rice. They did not speak or raise their eyes from their task. As they glided soundlessly toward the door, Charles spoke a few words of Hindi, telling them he did not need them further, that they might return to their quarters in back of the house.

"Dear God!" Emily cried when they had gone. "Did you see how they stared? They're laughing at me again. I know it."

For a moment he was too surprised to reply. He had never heard his Indian servants laugh. He had seen shared looks and secret smiles, but their laughter was something he could not imagine. And he knew they had not once looked at Emily. It was their way to keep their eyes lowered, in order to avoid contamination from their British masters. Even with several servants in the room, Charles often felt he was alone.

"They always laugh at me," Emily continued, twining her fingers together while she paced the floor. "They talk about me, too. They know I can't understand. But I see how they look at me. As if they know—" She broke off to stare through the slatted blinds at the settling darkness.

Charles hesitated, then put his hands on her shoulders. "Know what, Emily?"

"How frightened I am," she muttered so low that he had to bend forward to hear.

She *was* frightened; he could feel her shaking. It was important, suddenly, that he see her face. He turned her so the lamplight touched her hollow cheeks. Charles stared as though he had never seen her before, for indeed, he had not. In the past they had come together with few words, carried away by the force of their passion. They had talked in whispers and broken phrases, letting their bodies speak for them. But now he heard the apprehension in her voice, saw the wild look in her eyes, the way she twisted and untwisted her fingers endlessly.

When she noticed the lamp burning on a low table nearby, a look of stark terror flashed over Emily's face. "Put it out, Charles, please."

438

"How can I see you if I turn out the light?"

"Please," she repeated.

Moved by the desperation in her tone, he did as she asked. Even now, her vulnerability touched him. Yet he felt that something was very wrong. He wanted to turn away, to give himself time to think, but Emily sensed his withdrawal. She pulled him closer, her fingers digging into his arms. "Don't leave me. Just hold me and help me forget their laughter. Help me forget everything but you."

Charles closed his eyes. She needed him, more now than ever, and because of that, he could not let her go. Perhaps, for a while, he could even comfort her. He wondered, all at once, if that would ever be enough.

"Charles," she murmured, now that her fears had been lulled by the comfort of the darkness, "let me dance for you." She wound her fingers in the cool fabric of her sari and began to draw the garment away from her body, circle upon widening circle.

Then it came to Charles again, clear, bright, and bitter—the memory of Mairi and her red woolen plaid.

The image still had the power to hurt him, to make him wonder what had brought him here, to this country, this woman. The darkness gave no answer but the rise and fall of Emily's breath.

Leaving the sari in a tangled heap, she glided toward him, weaving a sensuous path across the bare wood floor, moving her naked body in unspoken yearning. In a flash of lightened shadow, he saw the glistening whiteness of her skin, filmed with the liquid heat that lingered long after the sun had disappeared.

She found her way easily through the scantily furnished room, unburdened by the absence of light. She touched his hand hesitantly and her breath was warm on his cheek.

Emily leaned into him so her body pressed against the rough barrier his clothes made between them. Slowly, she undid his shirt buttons to slide her hand beneath the damp fabric, searching, exploring, caressing the golden hairs that curled beneath her fingers. She began to sway against him, describing her longing with the measured rhythm of her hips. She was not really aware of the power she had over him; she

439

only knew she had to make him desire her or he might send her away. And she wanted him so much. Tonight especially, she needed to feel his touch.

Despite his doubts, Charles felt his body respond to the gentle torture of Emily's hands. Her head rested on his shoulder and her eyes were closed, her lips slightly parted. When he bent down, brushing her mouth with his, her eyelids opened in pleased surprise. Catching her face in his hands, he drew her up until they stood hip to hip with her naked breasts pressed to his chest. He could feel her nipples rise as he released her lips and traced a long, tantalizing path across her shoulder, between her breasts to the taut white curve of her stomach.

She moaned and buried her nails in the soft wool of his coat. Then, with infinite tenderness, he guided her to the bed. He pushed back the netting so Emily could slide onto the cool white sheets, where she waited impatiently as he took off his clothes and stretched out beside her.

With one foot, Charles kicked the sheet away and began to kiss Emily's eyes, her forehead, her throat. When she reached up to draw him closer, he sought the warm moistness of her lips, her tongue, the smooth edges of her teeth. Then he trailed his hand down the silver sheen of her body, finding the hidden hollows until she trembled beneath him.

Emily wound her fingers in his hair as he entered her and began to move in the slow, intoxicating rhythm that echoed the pulse of her blood. Her body, starved of love for so long, seemed to move beyond her control to a place where only sensation mattered. She twined her legs with his, reveled in the rough texture of the hair that grazed her soft thighs and calves, uncaring of the dampness that fused their skin together.

Arms locked around his back, she rubbed against him, absorbing the heat of his body. The hair on his chest brushed her sensitive nipples until she wanted to scream with pleasure. She loved the solid feeling of his weight upon her, holding her down so she need not fly away into the suffocating darkness. The rhythm of his body as he rocked with her, the heavy rasp of his breath in her ear, the smell of his sweat—these things told her he was real and that he would not leave her. She sensed when Charles was ready and she shuddered as the light fragmented in her head, blinding her with its brightness.

He opened his eyes to look into hers, wild with an emotion he could not understand. He felt that she did not see him, that she was staring at a vision somewhere in the shadows beyond.

It was that look which had first drawn him to her. Her gray-ringed eyes had reminded him of Mairi's—misted with visions of things he could not see or understand. Ke-ming had shared that vision, that wisdom. He had believed that Emily shared it, too. But now he saw the truth; slowly, inevitably, Emily's vision had become clouded, twisted by her fear until all she saw was her own distorted reality. He was frightened by the feeling of helplessness that overwhelmed him in that instant.

"Charles," she murmured when her eyes were focused again and her breathing had settled into its normal rhythm, "tell me that you love me."

He stared at the shimmer of the woven gold necklace that rested against her throat—the necklace he had given her the first time he had said those words. He found he could not repeat them now. Pushing back the damp hair that clung to her forehead, he ran his finger over her flushed cheek. "Of course I do. I've told you so many times." He knew as he spoke that he was clinging to a shadow, a ghost he had created out of some lost dream. He was foundering in the past while Emily was lost in her own dark future. He would never find Mairi again; he knew that now. But Emily did not know it. He prayed to God she never would.

God! Ke-ming had said once, laughing. *I do not believe in God. But I believe in Fate. It is everywhere, shaping the world as it sees fit. Each moment of the future has been ordained long before it comes to pass.*

Even this moment, when the ache of loss and regret caught in his throat and stopped the words he would have spoken. Charles looked down into the blurred, trusting gaze of the woman beside him, and for the first time in his life, he wanted to weep. He had finally opened his eyes and understood at last why he had kept them closed so long. The reality of the world that had made Emily Townsend was not a pleasant one. He wanted nothing more than to shut his eyes again and have that knowledge leave as unexpectedly as it had come.

But he knew it was a vain hope. Ke-ming had known it, too, many years ago, as had his young wife with the all-seeing violet eyes. It was too late for him, and had been, ever since young Mairi had chosen to give her life to the hills of Scotland instead of the man who loved her.

Too late for Charles, too late for Emily, too late, though neither knew it, for the child they had conceived that night— in fear and pity and yearning and sorrow.

CALCUTTA, INDIA
1878

Stars gleam, lamps flicker, friends foretell of Fate;
The fated sees, knows, hears them—all too late.

—INDIAN PROVERB

1

Paintbrush in hand, Genevra Townsend leaned forward to stare at a single cloud in the endless sky above the plains near Delhi, India. That cloud, tiny and distant though it was, promised relief from the cloying humidity that left a sheen of sweat on her skin even so soon after dawn. The puff of gray was the only hint of coolness in the overwhelming white-yellow heat; Genevra had raised the matted blinds on the veranda to give herself better light in which to paint. Behind the row of adobe bungalows, the wind howled over the plains, raising dust that mingled with the distant blue mist in whorls of gray. Behind her the spires, domes, and minarets of Delhi gleamed, restored to glory by the power of the sun.

When a breeze whipped the last pin from her pale blond hair, Genevra sighed. The long tendrils already clung to her neck and fell down her back; they never remained neatly in a roll on top of her head, where her stern Aunt Helen said they should be. But her aunt did not understand that the wrath of Indra, God of Wind and Air, was stronger than an eighteen-year-old girl. Genevra did not even attempt to repair the damage. She had learned long ago that there was no point in struggling against the environment of India. Better to give in, to give yourself up to wind and dust and the ever-present sun.

She squinted at the sky where Devendra, master of the Hindu deities, ruled; already the sun had burned away the vibrant blue of early morning. The sun god Surya would win this battle as he always did, enveloping the earth in his blaze of light that left no corner dark or safe or hidden. It did not fall in streams or beams or splintered fragments, but in one huge blaze across the sky—melting, blending everything into a brilliant image of desolation. Like the netting that hung from the English rosewood beds, it dimmed. Like the sweat that ran down flushed and breathless bodies, it slipped in drops of pallid heat. It drained the color from the sky and the life from the English.

It was everything and nothing, more than light and heat; it was the whole universe, all-encompassing, everywhere. It was part of the moisture, the dryness, the river, the plains. It was the dust and the languor of the people, the god before whom they were helpless. Genevra loved it, for all its discomfort, because it was free of shadows and lies. You could not misunderstand it; it simply was, as India was. But the date was June 28, and soon the rains would come to make a different India.

She turned from the brilliant light and concentrated on the self-portrait before her until the details became clear. She could see the blue silk of the sari with its black and gold border, the blond hair on her bare white shoulder. She knew she had captured the curve of her high cheekbones, the half smile on her parted lips, the skin once fragile and pale, turned warm brown by the sun. She reached out to paint a highlight into her hair and became aware of Gur, the *methur,* sweeping the dust from the walks around the bungalow. There was also movement below; Pachari, the water carrier, was returning from the well. Genevra could see by the native woman's glistening skin that she had already been to the river Jumna to bathe.

The thought of water made Genevra's mouth feel dry, but she did not go for a drink. Instead she returned to her painting. She must finish before the others arose. She thought she saw a tiny movement on the canvas, a flicker of light in the blue eyes flecked with gray. She shifted on her cane chair and stared into those eyes until they engulfed her and she recognized the distant image of her mother's face. She saw Emily Townsend's blue eyes ringed in gray, staring into her daughter's that last night before the world of pink bows and laughter had crumbled at their feet. Genevra remembered vividly that her mother had opened her mouth to speak—a promise, a lullaby, an endearment?—but no words came. Only silence like the blankness in Emily's eyes. But within that blankness there had been pain.

Genevra had reached up to reassure her mother, but Emily had flinched and turned away. The child had never minded the darkness before, but suddenly she was alone and the room full of sounds and movement, shadows and color that swirled about her shoulders. She fought her way out of the mosquito netting, struggled against the vivid, threatening colors. Barefoot, foolishly risking a meeting with a lizard or scorpion, she went down the hall, drawn by the sound of voices raised in anger.

She crouched in the doorway of the drawing room. The furniture was familiar—the chintz sofas and huge piano, the overstuffed chairs, Oriental rugs, shelves and tables and cabinets crowded with photographs, clocks, vases, and porcelain figurines. Even the whine of the punkah overhead, the soft breeze that stirred the heat from side to side, was the same. But the people were strangers. Her mother, who had always been soft blue and gray, was encircled by a ring of fear, black as obsidian, while her other colors swirled, darkened, grew pale around her until all was chaos and nothing was clear. Edward Townsend, who had been to his daughter a comfortable rust brown, was rage red and the midnight blue of anguish and grief.

The child wanted to make things right, to shift the colors back to normal. Then she heard her mother say that Genevra was not her father's child, but the seed of Charles Kittridge. The girl closed her eyes as her chest grew tight and full of pain. She knew the man; he came often with gifts and drawings for her. He was her father's friend. She shrank back against the wall, shaking her head. It could not be true.

"You've destroyed my home!" Edward Townsend shouted. "Destroyed everything."

The raw pain in his voice only made Genevra hurt more.

"You don't love me," Emily whispered. "You never loved me! Never!"

There was a moment of silence so profound that Genevra's grief curled in her chest like a snake whose poison seeped into her heart.

"I loved you," Edward replied too softly. "So much.

And I loved Genevra. You were all that mattered. But now you are filth—you and your bastard child. I want you out of my house. You defile it with your presence."

"Can you give me no pity, no compassion?"

Silence. Then, at last, "How can I feel pity when I have just been torn in two? Get out."

Emily whimpered in disbelief. "I have nowhere to go. What are you doing to me?"

"Charles Kittridge did this to you. He did it and you let him. You're ruined now in Anglo-Indian society. No one will accept you or that child."

Genevra winced. This man who had always called her "Genny," or "luv," or "angel" could speak of her only as "that child." She thought her heart would break, prayed that it would simply cease to beat and then the pain would go away. But it did not cease. She saw Emily kneel on the floor, her gown a tumbled sea around her, a silent plea in her eyes. Her hands bled as she wrung them, scratching her nails cruelly over the translucent skin. She needed help. Didn't her husband realize that?

Genevra looked up to see Edward Townsend turn his back. He knew, he had seen, but he didn't care. He refused to look at his wife again. Emily rose and began to throw vases, tiny figurines that smashed into fragments at her husband's feet. "Look at me!" she cried. "Please, look at me!" He did not even turn his head.

Genevra crept down the hall. She heard the servants whisper in their sibilant Hindu voices that spoke the name of Charles Kittridge over and over. They stared at the child with hostile eyes, then looked away. These women, crouched in their dark corner, had loved her that afternoon, had laughed with her, called her *larla*, played games with colored blocks. Now they would not meet her eyes. But their voices, the sound of Charles Kittridge's name on their lips, followed her to her room that night. They had followed her ever since. She would never escape those cold, disapproving whispers—or the memory of her mother's eyes, wild and gray-ringed, full of anguish.

Genevra heard a voice through dust and sun and mist. Was it real, or just another of the phantom murmurs that haunted her in the light as well as the darkness?

Then the words became clear and she recognized the soft, musical chant she had come to know so well.

"Nasmeeeha-namama-naham!"

It was Narain's morning prayer, repeated in a rhythm that never varied. The chant faded into sun-drenched air and the English girl saw Narain approach on silent feet. The past receded; the whispers became the rustle of the native girl's sari, the jingle of her bracelets as she crossed the veranda.

Genevra looked at the portrait to find she had painted the gray cloud into her eyes—those eyes that held the past locked in their gray-flecked depths. She was glad to turn away. She welcomed the sight of her friend with the cool brown eyes and dark, soft skin. Narain moved with quiet grace, her head high, self-contained and self-assured. To Genevra she was shimmering silver; there was no flame or ice in her eyes, no pain or secrets, only peace. She touched Genevra's shoulder with a cool hand that brought calm in the midst of raging heat.

"Come, Genniji," Narain said in her lyrical voice. "My mother would have a *chotee boli*, a little talk with you."

"I shall have to put my paints away first," Genevra replied, "and change my clothes. My aunt and uncle would not approve." She indicated the sari she wore, the one in the painting. She only dared put it on while they slept.

Narain nodded knowingly. "Ah yes, you must trap yourself in those foolish *feringhi* clothes, even now that the Hot Weather has come and the monsoon follows on the wind." She stared into the sky, past the Red Fort and the British Cantonment, down along the river to the ridge. "They will never learn, the *feringhi* from Belait, that India is not like your England."

"Not *my* England!" Genevra denied hotly. "I've never even seen it, nor do I care to."

Narain smiled. "Ah, but you are different, *larla*, altogether different from the others. You belong here."

Genevra smiled and drew cheesecloth over her painting, then picked up her brushes and paint to follow the Indian inside. She paused in the middle of the drawing room. The blinds were down and the room was shadowed, empty. She felt that it had been this way, not just for a moment, but

449

forever. It was drained of life and spirit, like that other bungalow—the one that had belonged to Edward Townsend. She and her mother had left the house the next morning and gone to Emily's sister, but Genevra had slipped away; she wanted to see her home once more.

It had not been the same. Already her father's things were gone. The furniture remained, but it was lifeless. No color moved in the corners. There were no dancing shadows. Only dust—dry, brittle, lifted on the breeze, so it caught in her nose and throat and hair. The emptiness had reached out with long arms to take her, but she had turned and fled.

She started to do so now, as if *bhootams*—evil spirits— were behind her. But Narain touched her arm and for the second time the past retreated. Genevra saw the question in Narain's eyes and tried to explain. "My memories are too real today."

"Come," Narain said. "We will put remembering behind you."

Genevra followed her to the tiny room at the back of the house, where, because she was the ayah, Narain's mother Radha was allowed to sleep on a simple charpoy. The older woman sat cross-legged on the floor scattered with bright cushions. The wall behind her was hung with blue and green, red and yellow cloth. Radha's thick black hair was rolled at the back of her head, her bright green sari a touch of spring in the midst of the heat. Like her daughter, she wore a bodice of lighter green in deference to the British distaste for the sight of native skin. The color was her only ornament, except for the sacred stone around her neck and her plain silver hoop earrings. As a widow, she could wear nothing more. She had given up the pure white she should have worn in mourning for the rest of her life, because Helen Bishop thought it inappropriate, but the ayah had not forgotten her husband. His saber hung on the wall behind the netting; sometimes Radha gazed at it as if she would caress it like the body of the man who had died long ago.

Genevra sat beside the ayah. In spite of Radha's widowhood, to the English girl she emanated yellow and red, the colors of Hindu ritual and celebration. This woman had raised the girl since her uncle and aunt had brought her to

Delhi; Radha had been mother, teacher, everything. She and her daughter alone had shown the seven-year-old Genevra affection.

The girl gazed at Radha's familiar dark face with its broad forehead and curved cheekbones. Today the ayah was thoughtful and her black eyes wary. Genevra placed her hands palm to palm in greeting. "You wished to see me?"

Radha returned the gesture. "I went to the Red Fort yesterday to move among the soldiers as I sometimes do."

Genevra had often wondered why Radha did this, since she clearly hated the British. Her eyes burned when she spoke of them and her dark cheeks grew pale. But the girl did not ask; she knew that there were questions without answers, questions that were dangerous and would intrude on Radha's past. "Yes?"

"A Jemadar told me of a new English officer in Shahje-hanabad." She refused to refer to the city of Delhi by its newer name.

"There are many officers," Genevra said.

Radha raised her eyebrows. "But this one is no ordinary soldier. He is here for a purpose. And I do not like it."

Genevra was confused. "Why?"

"Because I dreamed of him last night." Radha placed her fingers at her temples as if to ease a pain there. "And in my dream he cast a shadow on this house. Such a shadow from such a dream does not lift, Genniji. I wish to stop it from falling."

"How?"

"By your knowing what we cannot know. You are British. You can become acquainted with this man, charm him into giving up his secrets as no Indian could." The ayah leaned forward. "You need not worry that what you do is wrong. Why else have I taught you to understand, as the Hindus do, that all this"—she swept her hand around the room to make it into the world—"is mere *maya*, illusion. It does not really exist. This soldier, Captain Alexander Kendall, does not really exist. How can he hurt you if this is so?"

"Why would he want to hurt me?"

Radha frowned. "I do not know. 'Only the sea knows

451

the depth of the sea, only the firmament the expanse of the firmament.' I know only that you must beware. I have told you this is no ordinary man. He is more than just a soldier with a purpose. He is a shadow from the past. And you know that you are always chasing shadows.''

Slightly disturbed, Genevra went to her room, where the blinds were closed tight and the punkah moved slowly back and forth through the already stifling air. Before she dressed, she knelt in front of the jolly figure of the Hindu god Ganesha beneath the window. His head, in the shape of an elephant with one tusk, rested on a short, rotund body with four arms. Ganesha was the God of Good Luck, he who removed obstacles and made all things possible, and Genevra prayed to him each morning. Unlike most of the other Hindu deities, there was no dark side to his nature; he was of the earth and the people, not the mysterious heavens. The idol had been a gift from Radha and the girl treasured it.

Reluctantly, she rose, turned from the clay figure to put on her chemise and petticoat, gathered in ruffles at the back to give the effect of a bustle. The horsehair bustle itself, along with a confining whalebone corset and uncomfortable stockings, she refused to wear in the cold weather as well as the hot. She slipped a simple blue-gray cotton gown over her head with a single ruffle about her throat and darker blue piping down the bodice. She combed out her hair and rewound it, pinning it securely, though she knew it would not stay. Then she started for the drawing room, where she could hear voices. The ladies of Delhi were making their calls before the heat became unbearable.

She paused when she passed the little sitting room. Though she tried to go on, her feet would not move. Narain came up behind her. "What is it, Genniji? You seem troubled today."

Genevra barely heard her. "This is like the room where she left me in Calcutta. I was seven years old. There was the same ormolu clock ticking on the shelf, the spindle-legged chairs, the writing table with its stiff bench where I sat for so long."

"Who left you?"

"My mother. She dressed me in my best white dress and petticoats, rumpled hat and dusty gloves and told me to wait for a moment. But she didn't come back." Genevra could not understand why the memory should hurt so much after all this time. She turned to find Narain staring at her quizzically, unflustered as always. She wished she could absorb some of that calm. "How do you do it?" she asked.

Narain tilted her head curiously. "Do . . .?"

"I've never seen you the least bit perturbed, even when your pet monkey died or your mother was ill. Why?"

"Because, as my mother said, it is all *maya,* this life. There will always be another. You know the words of my prayer:

"I exist not in any thing!
Nothing exists in me!
I myself exist not!"

She touched her friend's cheek. "Perhaps someday you will learn to feel the words in your heart, as I have. Then you will see that none of this matters, these dark memories, this pain you will not release."

Genevra shook her head. It mattered to her, very much. She went into the room to sit on the bench where she had sat when her mother took her hands. Genevra had sensed even then that something was wrong; Emily's face had been strange and distant.

"I hate Charles Kittridge!" the girl had cried.

Wispy hair falling in loose curls from beneath her hat, Emily had gaped at her daughter in horror. "You must never say that, Genevra, never. He is a wonderful man—so strong, so handsome, so kind. And he knows many wonderful things, magical things, things I could not understand. I could see them in his eyes. Incredible eyes, my child, blue like the sea where no sand mars its surface, warm like the sky of an Indian winter. He is a man who can do anything, anything."

Genevra was mesmerized by the rhythm of her mother's voice, the look in her eyes, the grip of her frail fingers. These things filled the room with the presence of Charles Kittridge to make him more than a memory. The child felt a prickle at the back of her neck. Emily had conjured the man out of the shadows; he stood staring at Genevra through clear blue eyes. He wore the sad half smile she had seen so often when he came to visit the Townsend house. She had always thought of him as the Golden Man. He alone had been able to make her forget her troubles and laugh aloud. He had only to look at a shadow to make it disappear. But now her life was full of shadows—all because of him. She caught Emily's sleeve, uneasy at the feeling that he stood so near yet was far, far away. "But he left us."

Emily tilted her head awkwardly, like a vulnerable sparrow. "Yes," she said. "He was the only man strong enough to save me, but he left me behind." She forced herself to focus on the child, forced a reassuring smile to her lips. "But he will come back for us. He'll find us and everything will be all right. He can make it right."

Genevra knew it was not true by the expression of dismay on her specter father's face. He would never come back.

Emily had gripped her daughter's arm tightly. "You see him, don't you? I've made him real for you. That's all that matters. Remember that, little one." Her fingers dug into Genevra's skin, then she rose abruptly and fled. The girl was left alone. The image of her father had disappeared, too.

She sat for a long time in that tiny room, while the clock ticked above her and the silence lay heavily on her shoulders. When her aunt Helen Bishop entered the room, Genevra jumped up. "Where is she? Where's my mother?"

Behind her aunt, her uncle stood stiffly in his padded smoking jacket.

"She's gone, Genevra. She left you with us," Aunt Helen explained. "She thought you would be happier living a more stable life." Her tone lacked conviction, and though she tried to smile in a kindly way, she did not succeed.

Genevra knew her aunt did not believe what she said. Tears burned behind the child's lids and the pain in her chest spread. "But my mother needs me. She hurts inside and she needs me."

"Balderdash!" Gilbert Bishop snorted. "Fully grown

woman, you know. And you only a child. Emily can jolly well take care of herself."

Genevra saw the look in Helen Bishop's eyes and realized that her aunt knew the truth: Emily Townsend *did* need her daughter, now more than ever. Then her aunt blinked and the knowledge disappeared like a candle suddenly snuffed out. She did not want to admit the truth; she preferred the comfortable lie.

"You have lost yourself often today," Narain observed, drawing Genevra back to the present. "What is it that troubles you?"

The other girl shook her head. It was true that she could not seem to escape her memories today. Perhaps it was the humidity that made her clothes cling to her body, or the waiting, the constant silent prayer that the monsoon would come, and with it, long-awaited relief from the searing heat.

"Do not worry about your mother," Narain soothed. "No doubt she found her place, just as you have found yours."

"What? Here?" Genevra laughed. The British Raj was not her place, this false little kingdom created by men like Charles Kittridge. The English world in India was cruel, cold and heartless, without warmth or laughter or real pain. No one dared feel the pain that welled inside them daily, or it would wash them away in a storm of tears that never stopped.

"Genevra!" Her aunt's voice reached her from the drawing room. "*Are* you coming in or will you stand in that hall till the floods come?"

Narain winked reassuringly, and with a deep breath, Genevra moved down the hall. She passed the dining room and saw the bearer clear away the dishes from the huge mahogany table. Her uncle and aunt had not waited for her; they had already consumed their cold mutton, eggs, and bread. Genevra did not mind. She had eaten *chupattis*, nuts, and figs much earlier with great pleasure, unencumbered by the oppression of the cluttered dining room and her relatives' grim faces. She paused in the doorway of the room where her aunt and several guests had gathered.

Despite their gay cottons and calicoes—ruched,

pleated, ruffled, and ribboned—despite their flowered bonnets with elegant feathers and colored brims, to Genevra these ladies seemed a pale collection of dull pastels without depth or warmth. Aunt Helen sat nearest the punkah on a leather chair. Ranged on the horsehair sofa and brocade overstuffed chair were Maude Butler, Elizabeth Browne, and Mary Wellesley. Normally there would have been others, but most of the women who could afford the expense had gone to Simla in the nearby mountains for the Hot Weather.

The ladies heard the rustle of Genevra's skirts, crossed their lace-gloved hands primly, and looked up as one with a frown of displeasure.

"Whatever possessed you?" Aunt Helen demanded.

Genevra shook her head. "I don't—"

"That portrait you left on the veranda. Dressed in a native costume with your shoulder bare—"

"Quite utterly shocking, as if you were a savage like *them!*" Elizabeth interjected.

"Repellent really. How can you bring yourself down to their level? I think—" Maude added with a sniff.

"Well really," Mary interrupted, "wherever do you get your ideas? I know it's not from your charming aunt. Such a good, proper sort of woman. The sort one can admire and look up to."

Genevra ignored what they said; she had heard it all before. "You looked at it?" she asked, just able to control the anger in her voice. Nothing was private or sacred to these women. In their perpetual boredom and physical unease, they felt compelled to probe every mystery and indiscretion.

"I'm sure we had no intention of prying," Maude said, deeply offended.

"But a breeze came up just as we crossed the veranda," Elizabeth continued.

"And we couldn't help but notice that—rendering," Mary finished. "You can't wrap a thing like that up in clean linen. Naturally, we came to speak to Helen straightaway."

"Must put a stop to this sort of thing before it goes too far," Elizabeth added with a pious purse of her lips. "I've

456

seen it happen too often. First it's a painting and the next thing you know, some perfectly white Englishwoman is rolling about in the mud with the coolies.''

"It's the sun that does it,'' Maude intoned. "Damages the brain, you know. Nothing to be done, I'm afraid.''

"Or perhaps it's in the blood,'' Mary suggested, lowering her voice, but not far enough. "You know what I mean.'' She raised her eyebrows suggestively.

Genevra did not shrink away. She looked directly at the three women, but did not really see them. She was used to the taunting, the whispers, the haughty, curious glances tossed her way. She had simply learned to shut them out. There were colors and patterns enough in her head to keep her occupied.

Helen peered at her niece uneasily. Genevra was so stubborn; she did not even try to fit in. No wonder men never showed any interest in her. Who would dare to be seen with such a girl? Still, she must get lonely. Her aunt felt a stirring of compassion that she dared not express. Yet when the three women leaned together and began to list the girl's faults, Helen remained upright and apart, her lips pressed into a thin line. She felt the oddest impulse to cry, "Foolish tongues talk by the dozen!" But, of course, she said nothing.

Genevra stood in the doorway only long enough to hear fragments of the ladies' conversation. "Mother mad, you know . . . Charles Kittridge . . . adventurer . . . shocking stories about him . . . and what about her . . . may not be true, but make no fire, raise no smoke, I always say.''

The sound of the voices faded as, smiling to herself, she whispered a Hindu prayer:

> "Lead me from the unreal to the real.
> ➤Lead me from darkness to light.
> Lead me from death to immortality.''

She was soothed by the rhythm, the power she felt in the ancient words, and most of all by the knowledge that to hear those words on her lips would shock these already pale matrons so badly that the last of their color would fade, leaving them as bleached and white as marble.

Down the dim corridor, Genevra saw Radha motion to her. Aware that the ladies in the drawing room were too busy berating her to note her departure, the girl slipped away.

"You had better hurry," the ayah whispered. "Your Uncle Sahib has ordered Hazari to destroy the portrait. You must not allow him such a victory."

For a moment, Genevra was frozen where she stood. Would even Gilbert Bishop go that far? Then she remembered how his nostrils flared in disgust when he spoke of the "natives," how he struck the table until china and crystal were in danger of complete destruction. With a muttered, "Hanuman will bless you," Genevra hurried toward the door, closed tight to keep the light out and the darkness cool. With one wrench, she opened it wide and let the morning sun pour in.

2

Genevra found Hazari, the *mali* who kept up the garden, lifting the painting from the easel.

"Please!" she cried.

Hazari raised his head, topped by a round red hat. "Ah, Memsahib, do not worry. Hazari hears very badly. 'Take the painting,' they say. They add something more, but he does not hear." He shrugged. "So, I think I am to take it someplace safe for when the monsoons come." He winked and pointed to the sky, where lightning flashed occasionally. "It will be soon, so Hazari will hurry."

Genevra smiled in relief while the Indian placed the canvas under his white cotton sleeve. "Besides," he added, "I see how you painted the cloud in your eyes. That cloud is beautiful because it is part of the land of Hind. Too beautiful to set aflame. 'In the lightning, in the light of an eye, the light belongs to the spirit.'

"It is evil to destroy such light, such beauty. It is bad kharma. Vishnu, the Preserver, would not like it." He leaned close to whisper, "I might be reborn as a frog or a snake. For Bishop Sahib I would not risk such a thing." His tone was serious, but his round brown face, sun-cracked lips, and black eyes sparkled with mischief.

"Thank you," Genevra said fervently. "But where will you take it?"

The gardener grew pensive. "I thought to deliver it to Tamarsha Begum. She will protect it for you."

Genevra nodded in agreement. "But why do you call her that? Her name is Phoebe Quartermaine."

The *mali* shuddered. "Such a name. It is far too cold and stiff, like the *feringhi* themselves." He winked again.

459

"You know what I mean." He put the painting down, threw his shoulders back and his chin out, pursed his lips, and stared haughtily down his nose. "I think their limbs are made of sticks that do not bend. That is why they move as they do." To demonstrate, he marched up and down, arms straight at his sides, legs swinging out in a rigid line. Even his white cotton jacket and dhoti, already damp with sweat, did not detract from his portrayal.

Genevra knew she should not encourage him, but she could not help laughing.

Hazari was delighted and began to tap the veranda imperiously with an imaginary cane.

The girl pushed a hairpin back into place and tried to hide her smile. "You forget that I am British."

Hazari abandoned his pose and melted back into a graceful Indian. "But are you? Are you truly, in your heart?" he asked. "You, *Asparaji,* my pale fairy, have a soul like ours that listens to the music of life. Thus was it written on your forehead by Brahma at your birth. You cannot change it any more than the *feringhi* can take new souls. Pah!" He spat red betel juice onto the dry ground. "They hear nothing. They are made of stone so they cannot be hurt by the Indian sun and rain."

He leaned on the cane rail. "But because of that, they also cannot see the beauty of the sun or the magic of the rain. They do not know these things are the heart and soul of India. They do not feel it here and so they are unhappy." He beat his fist against his chest, frowned, and added, "Or perhaps it is only that their collars are always too tight."

Genevra smiled at the image of row upon row of Englishmen with faces turned beet red from their tight starched collars.

All at once, Hazari became impatient to be on his way. He turned to pick up the painting again. "Tamarsha Begum feels it," he murmured. "To her everything is a celebration, a joke, a glory, a wonder." He grinned. "It is why we call her *tamarsha*—festival. I have never heard a woman laugh so much. And you must admit, Memsahib, she is very handsome when she laughs."

"Of whom do you speak in such intimate terms?"

Gilbert Bishop demanded, stepping out reluctantly from the cool protection of the bungalow. He drew his shoulders back, puffed out his chest, and looked down his nose at the *mali*. It did not occur to him to speak to Genevra or wish her good morning. "Hope you're not referring to an English-woman. Shocking impropriety if you were. I should have to take action." He pounded his cane on the wooden floor for emphasis.

Genevra clenched her teeth to keep from smiling. Her uncle's mustache quivered with his indignation.

"Certainly not, Sahib," Hazari lied smoothly. "I would never consider such a thing. The gods would not allow it."

"He was talking about Radha," Genevra interjected.

"Hummph," Gilbert Bishop grunted. "Radha indeed." His hazel eyes narrowed when he noticed the covered paint-ing. "Trying to distract me, that's what you're doing. What about that, that—" He waved his hand limply toward the canvas. "I never want to see it again." He started down the steps, muttering to himself. In spite of his hat, a modified pith helmet that cast a shadow over his brow, within seconds the wind and dust had wreaked havoc with his perfectly combed gray hair. He ran his hand through it futilely, then sighed in resignation. "Still, what can you expect from these coolies. Radha handsome!" He chuckled once, then frowned and continued to mutter until he had disappeared down the neat path flanked by frangipani bushes whose blossoms had long ago dried in the heat.

The *mali* started after the Englishman. "Another day of toil for poor Bishop Sahib." There was a touch of irony in Hazari's tone. "You will also come to see Tamarsha Begum, will you not?"

"I'll come," Genevra replied. She picked up her plain straw hat from the wicker chair where she had dropped it yesterday and followed Hazari. As they turned into Alipur Road, she saw the retreating, rotund shape of her uncle. She had no idea what his job entailed; she only knew he went daily to the town hall to work for the Indian Civil Service. From the stains on his silk waistcoat when he came home each evening, she could only imagine that he spent his day at the European Club, which was also in the town hall. She pictured him seated at the table eating roasts of beef while he spilled port down his chest and over the white damask tablecloth.

Hazari was singing under his breath by the time they reached the river, where, by silent consent, they had chosen to walk. Surreptitiously, Genevra watched the Hindus who bathed in the Jumna each morning. She had always been fascinated by the need that drove them to the water to wash away all defilement and purify themselves. Each day the Brahmins, the highest Hindu caste called the Twiceborn, came to perform their ablutions. They bathed, caressed their sacred threads, murmured their prayers for the rains to come and save the crops. Around them, the people submerged themselves, rose, and submerged themselves again in endless repetition of an ancient ritual.

Genevra envied the Hindus the feel of the water sliding down their brown burning skin. To her it looked like a moment of heaven in India's beguiling hell of incandescent sunlight.

"Too bad," Hazari muttered. "Too, too bad."

Genevra looked up to see him scowl at the crumbling red sandstone wall that surrounded Delhi.

"After the Mutiny, the Sahiblog tore at our wall with their fingernails until it came away in their hands," the *mali* mused.

Genevra knew he was exaggerating only slightly. She had learned from Radha how, in 1857, the Indian Sepoys in the British army had risen in rebellion, killing not only the English soldiers, but also civilians, even women and children.

Hazari shook his head mournfully. "The Sepoys should not have gone so far, but when there is a fire in your body it is difficult to be reasonable. 'There are seven tongues of fire,' " he quoted, " 'the ruinous, the terrible, the swift, the smoky, the red, the bright, the flickering.' The Sepoys burned with all seven tongues and so they let themselves be taken by the Devil's Wind that sought to destroy the *feringhi* intruders."

Genevra glanced at the ridge where the British had stood—and fallen—against the maddened Indians, and thought she saw Charles Kittridge poised there, rifle in hand. She looked away. The British retribution had been a horror worse than the Mutiny itself. Radha had told her such stories that she had awakened sobbing for weeks. In her dreams, her father had raged through India to wreak revenge on Sepoys and innocent Indians alike.

Ahead they could see the walls of the Red Fort, once the Mogul palace—the center of grace, culture, and art in northern India. Its beautiful tile walls were now obscured by ugly yellow British barracks. Her countrymen had looted and torn down ancient buildings to make a wide swath for their cantonment so Delhi would be protected, and never be taken by surprise again.

Hazari followed her gaze. "The killing I can understand," he murmured. "Who does not know that violent death begets more death? But this—" He waved his hand to indicate the once magnificent palace. "This is the ultimate punishment of the Sahiblog, Genniji, to destroy the beauty of our city. It is that which we cannot forgive."

Genevra started to reply, but gasped instead when her button-top boots sank into the silver-white sands of the Jumna. Her feet were already swollen, chafed, and hot.

With a frown, the *mali* looked down at the skirt twisted about her awkward black shoes. "This cannot be," he said firmly. "Those shoes were made for Belait, not Hind."

Genevra nodded. "They are a bit ridiculous, aren't they?"

Hazari merely raised his eyebrows. "But I have something much better. I had forgotten altogether. The clouds of confusion must have gathered in my head." From the voluminous pockets of his pajama-like pants, he took a pair of leather shoes with thin leather straps to tie up the legs. "Here. For you."

"But how—where . . . ?"

"Unrao the shoemaker made them in gratitude for the very beautiful picture you drew of his very beautiful wife. His heart will break if you do not cherish them as he cherishes your gift."

"I can't break Unrao's heart. His wife would never forgive me." Genevra sat down on the burning sand—grate-

463

ful, now, for her petticoats and heavy gown—removed her own shoes, and replaced them with the fine, soft leather. It felt delightful on her hot, swollen feet. She rose to walk with the lap of the water beside her, smiling. Now she could feel the shifting sand beneath her feet, the movement of earth and water, wind and sun—the music of life as Hazari called it. She threw out her arms and chanted a verse from the *Upanishads*. "Life burns in the fire, shines in the sun. Rain, cloud, air, and earth are life."

Hazari nodded solemnly. He liked to hear the girl repeat lines from the Indian literature Radha had taught her. He knew Genevra had read the *Mahabaratha,* the *Ramayana,* and the *Bhagavadgita.* She had told him she loved the musical flow of the words, the rhythm and enchantment of the magical stories. To her, she said, British books seemed tame by comparison and British poets dull and uninspired.

"You see," the *mali* exclaimed, white teeth gleaming against his dark skin, "you are one of us! You feel it in your soul." He waved his arms and whispered in his native Hindi, "*Tat twam assii*—thou art that."

Genevra wondered if right now, this moment, her mother felt the same rapture, if she had ever experienced such exhilaration. The girl had finally stopped looking for Emily Townsend, accepted that her mother had chosen to disappear into the huge, pulsing heart of India. But that did not end Genevra's questions.

At a rumble of thunder, she looked up to see the pariah dogs lying in the curves of the dusty street, the jackals racing across the plain. Did they mean to outrun the heavy dark clouds that covered the sky and shot lightning toward the earth? A garuda, the sacred bird of the Brahmins, circled in the clouds. Was it a good omen? she wondered. The wind whipped her straw hat from her head. She watched it spin away into the distance to land on the water, where it twirled and leaped with the current. When thunder ripped across the sky like the furious pounding of copper drums, she turned to Hazari in alarm.

"Do not worry, the monsoon is not yet." He cupped his hand over his eyes. "But soon. Any day, the rain will come."

Nevertheless, they hurried toward the Bridge of Boats and the gate in the red wall. In silence they passed the ugly barracks, the few British soldiers, their pith helmets pulled low on their heads to protect them from the sun. The members of Gordon's 92nd were scattered among the Indian regiments in their mufti and turbans. All were grim and unsmiling today.

Hazari and Genevra made their way around the fort to the Chandni Chowk, the main thoroughfare of Delhi. Down the center ran an avenue of trees that would have offered shade, except that the June sun had shriveled the leaves to black wisps of memory. Both sides of the street were lined with shops and modern buildings raised by the Raj; among them, the town hall and the spacious grounds of the Company *Bagh*—the gardens where British met with Muslim and Hindu businessmen. Near the tidy marble benches and stark, leafless trees crouched naked children, watching all who passed with huge, hungry eyes.

Genevra had seen many such children and knew that they and their parents were starving slowly to death. The burden of taxation the Raj had put on its poverty-stricken people had been too great, while the East India Company had taken over the trade and profits, making themselves wealthy on Indian misery. In her mind, she saw Charles with a moneybag in his hand; he smiled his charming smile as he collected money from thin, brown outstretched hands. The natives gave to him willingly, hypnotized by his smile and his clear blue eyes. Just as Emily had been hypnotized. Because he was so pleasant outside, they did not see that inside he was cold as stone, without a soul. Yet in all Genevra's visions, he was still the Golden Man. Even she could not deny him his vivid color.

To her, he had become the symbol of Anglo-Indian power and arrogance, the source of all the evil and suffering caused by the Raj. Just as he had filled her life with shadows, so he and his Empire had crisscrossed with false shadows a land whose essence was the infinite sun. The Raj had made the natives outcasts in their own home, as Charles had made Genevra an outcast in British society. For eleven years, in the back of her mind, she had heard her mother's fragile voice: *He can do anything—anything!* Somehow, Genevra had come to believe it.

She forced her thoughts back to the crowded gardens, the streets filled with carriages, soldiers, and beggars, all swallowed by columns of dust. There were shops with moderate displays of grain and plain cloth in the windows, the town hall with its out-of-place classical façade. Everywhere people watched the skies, waiting for the rains that would break this terrible heat. Captain Governor Montgomery had once called Delhi "a city on which there is a curse." Sometimes, when the shadows muted the sound of voices and the filth covered everything of beauty, Genevra agreed.

Hazari and the girl turned off the Chandni Chowk to the street where Phoebe Quartermaine lived. Here they passed into another world of splendid spires and domes and minarets that the great Mogul princes had built long ago. Men like Akbar, Jahangir, and Shah Jehan would not be forgotten; it was they who had left behind this evidence of a glorious past. Here were the tiled buildings of fretted marble and fine white stone, of colorful mosaics and magnificent gateways that still stood radiant in the sun. Many of the gates led into gardens astonishingly cool and lovely.

Genevra and the *mali* passed through the outer gate of Phoebe's house, curved and pointed at the crown, with colorful tiles that faced the inner gate of intricate wrought iron. They crossed the flagged courtyard and at last reached the front of the house, ornamented by marble fretwork and many arches that curved gracefully around the ancient building.

To Genevra's surprise, Hazari said he had an errand, gave her the painting, and left her to stare after him, bewildered. She was soon distracted by the colored tile around the doorframe. Phoebe and her now-dead husband had bought the house from a minor Indian prince years ago. They had not changed it, except to repair what had begun to fall. Genevra would have touched the tile lovingly, but she knew it would burn her fingers, so she raised the wooden door knocker instead and let it fall.

Phoebe Quartermaine opened the door and threw her arms around Genevra. "Thank God you've come! I was in desperate need of relief today." She drew away to fan herself with a woven grass fan that stirred the edges of the indigo-blue and yellow sari she wore as a top above her gray cotton English skirt.

Used as she was to Phoebe's eccentricities, Genevra hardly glanced at the clothes as she carried her painting inside. The door closed behind her, shutting out the sun, and the coolness of colonnaded rooms and Persian-rug-covered marble floors enfolded her. She noticed that Phoebe, who was at least forty-five, though her sun-browned face and lively green eyes made her look much younger, wore a single reddish-brown braid down her back. To Genevra her friend was bright blue, green, and turquoise with a little splash of dangerous red.

Phoebe led the way down many corridors into the main room, scattered with bright pillows as well as three English settees. The punkah whirred, and the huge tatties were kept constantly wet in case a wind arose to blow a breath of cool air through the screens woven of grass.

Phoebe whirled, eyes bright. "What's this, demanded the cat of the king?" She pointed to the covered painting.

Genevra rested it on the nearest settee, since there were no tables, and drew back the cheesecloth.

"My dear!" Phoebe exclaimed. "It's lovely. But why have you brought it here?"

"Hazari brought it, actually, to keep my uncle from destroying it."

Phoebe nodded, finger beneath her chin. "The sari?"

"The sari."

"It's too bad of them to be so judgmental. Let he who is without sin cast the first stone, I always say. But really, to hurt you so much just because of a perfectly harmless garment—"

Genevra shook her head. "They don't like any of my work."

"That's because it makes you happy to create it, I'm afraid to say. Besides, it's an Englishman's privilege to grumble." She considered the painting, brow furrowed. "It's more than that, though. You do tend to paint that native girl and little brown children a lot. I think your uncle and aunt don't understand. There's something in your work that threatens their tidy little world of tea parties and carriage rides to the gardens. No dreams or shadows allowed in the India they've created. And you're full to the brim of dreams and shadows. It makes them terribly nervous, that's all. They're so narrow-minded they think *you're* the one who's not normal. But I'm afraid you'll have to make the best of a bad bargain. And just remember this: 'They that burn you for a witch shall lose their coals.' " She broke off when she saw the girl's horrified expression.

"It's just an old saying, my heart. You know how dreadfully fond of them I am. The point is, I'll have the enjoyment of the picture for a while, and that will make me very happy. Just leave it. You look ghastly and overheated. Lost your hat again, I see. Come cool yourself in the garden. Hazari brought you, you say? Oh dear. That man. Bit potty, if you know what I mean."

She left the room in a swirl of yellow, blue, and gray with Genevra close behind. "Maybe the British don't like your work because they're so unhappy here," Phoebe suggested, continuing the previous conversation as if there had been no break. "How could they be, poor things, when so many of their children die soon after birth and then, if they live, they're sent off to England to grow up and the mother never knows them after all. Very sad. Very sad indeed. I prefer potty Hazari, thank you very much. Better the head of an ass than the tail of a horse.

"And speaking of Hazari, he has become rather a nuisance. You remember the monkey he brought me a month ago?" Phoebe did not wait for an answer. "He came back a week past, assured me the animal was lonely, and brought a female to keep it company. They chatter incessantly—not unlike Hazari—in the trees in the garden. I'm on tenterhooks to see what he'll bring next."

Genevra was not really listening. She was thinking about Aunt Helen and Uncle Gilbert, who had lost a son and daughter on a P&O bound for England that had sunk on the treacherous sand reefs outside Calcutta. By sending them away to keep them safe, her aunt and uncle had sent their only children to their deaths. No wonder they had resented

Genevra when Emily dropped her daughter so carelessly on their doorstep.

She pushed her uneasy thoughts away as she approached the dining room, smiling, as always, at the huge oak table that had no chairs. Instead there were thick cushions in every color on the floor. The table was high, far too high to be reached by anyone sitting on the cushions, but Phoebe always ate in the summerhouse, so she didn't mind.

Finally they walked through the tiled archway that led to the garden. At first glance, it always took Genevra's breath away. The house had a traditional Mogul garden with narrow coral paths between carefully laid-out flower beds, a *baradari* or summerhouse with thin, graceful pillars, a curved roof, and white wicker furniture covered with pillows. There were rows of cypress and acacia, tamarinds and date palms, as well as large plots of lemon, mango, orange, and cherry trees, all kept fresh by underground wells. There were shaded arbors, climbing roses, and magnificent bougainvillea that blanketed the white walls with vivid red. But the secret of this garden was the water.

Stone chutes in the walls sent water, taken from wells outside, rushing down in showers of clear crystal. The chutes were curved and twisted so the water fell in angles, was thrown into the air, fragmented into waves and strange rippled designs. These beautiful creations had been called by the Moguls *chadars*—white shawls of water.

There were huge pools, the sides and bottoms covered with tile, where water glimmered, cool and inviting, protected from the heat by the roofs and trees. Waterfalls gushed over stone, one above another, landing at last in the blue-tiled pools where they splintered the stillness into prismed light. Finally there were copper fountains that flowed with fresh water.

Phoebe sighed with delight and quoted the Song of Songs: " 'It is a garden enclosed, a garden of living waters.' "

Genevra removed her new leather shoes and sat at the edge of the nearest pool, dipping her feet with a sigh into the water. She loved this place more than any other and wanted to cry as Shah Jehan had in the palace garden:

469

"If there be a paradise on earth,
It is here, it is here, it is here!"

"What would I do without you, Phoebe?" She sighed.
"So often you have given me heaven."

"What a lovely way to put it."

Genevra opened her eyes in consternation at the sound
of a strange voice. A British officer stood across the pool
from her, his long, wavering image reflected in the water.
She could tell he had just arrived in Delhi by the gleam of
his tall boots, the whiteness of his starched gloves that flared
almost to his elbow, the pure, undimmed red of his coat, and
by the gold braid and the saber at his side. His pale skin was
unmarred yet by sand and dust, unburnt by the pitiless sun
of the plains. Strange that he should be here; Phoebe allowed
few English into her home. When she did they were always
the ones who understood the land of Hind, not strangers
with fine black boots and unshadowed eyes.

"Captain Alex Kendall, may I present Miss Genevra
Townsend," Phoebe said in her most formal tone, pleased
by her little surprise.

Genevra found that her tongue was dry and she could
not speak. That was the name Radha had spoken in fear.
The ayah's warning rang in the girl's ears. *Beware of this
man. He is more than just a soldier with a purpose. He is
also a shadow from the past.* His bright blond hair, a little
too long, stirred in the scented breeze, revealing his aristocratic cheekbones and clear blue eyes. She was transfixed
by the look of admiration in those eyes. She stared at his
image in the water while it blurred and changed. His face
became older, his hair touched with brown. Around his blue
eyes were wrinkles of sorrow and merriment. Those eyes—
those familiar, laughing eyes. *You know that you are always
chasing shadows.*

The man also seemed to have lost his voice in the rush
and murmur of the water.

"Well," Phoebe said, "I realize this is a house where
tradition is not often maintained, but I do think you might
speak a word or two of greeting to one another. It's the thing

to do, you know. I find silence so depressing." She laughed, the man laughed, and in spite of herself, Genevra smiled.

"Terribly sorry," Alex Kendall said, his pith helmet in his hand. "It's just that you took me by surprise."

He meant it; Genevra could see that. Perhaps he was not like other British soldiers who said what they thought you wanted to hear. "I was rather taken by surprise myself. I expected Akbar or Shah Jehan, certainly not an English soldier." She was not easy; shadows and colors shifted in her mind, but she forced her vision to remain clear.

"Alas, I am only what you see," Alex replied. "But then, I am alive and that does give me a certain advantage."

"If you're sufficiently recovered from your mutual surprise," Phoebe interjected, "let's sit in the *baradari* and Ameera will bring us refreshment."

Genevra rose, her wet petticoat and gown clinging to her ankles. The Captain looked discreetly away and followed Phoebe. Soon the three were seated in the summerhouse shadowed by plantain and *aswatta* trees. The large green leaves of the *aswatta* shifted in the breeze, so thin they seemed to whisper cool promises overhead. Among the branches, the monkeys chattered, swinging in and out of view. Genevra sat on a tiled bench while the other two chose white wicker chairs with bright embroidered pillows. Ameera came with a platter of dried dates, almonds, and musk melon and a pitcher of fresh water.

"Thank you," Alex Kendall said as she poured him a glass. He spoke directly to her, not to the air above her head, smiled at her, and met her gaze. "You're most kind." His voice was pleasant, but he did not look at her young body, wrapped enticingly in a red sari with a black border. The girl smiled back, pleased and unafraid.

This was not an ordinary Englishman, Genevra thought, not graceless and ineffective like her uncle and his friends. No, with his straightforward gaze and pleasant, honest smile, this Captain Alex Kendall was far more dangerous.

"When I decided to come to India," he said, after taking a sip of water from his hand-painted earthenware cup, "I never thought to find paradise. Yet here it is." He spread his hands to indicate the garden.

471

Genevra blinked at him. He had echoed her thought of a few minutes before so closely. She was intrigued against her will, drawn by his delight in the garden she loved. Then she remembered Radha's eyes that had burned like coals when she said, *You can know what we cannot. Become acquainted with this man. Charm him into giving up his secrets.*

"This is how it must have been when Shah Jehan lived." Alex turned to Phoebe. "But this isn't the real India, is it? Or even the real Delhi?"

Phoebe laughed her warm, throaty laugh, which was so hard to resist. "No, my dear captain. This is where people come to escape the real India, to forget for a moment the curse of Delhi." She leaned close to add in a conspiratorial whisper, "Except those, of course, who say I am part of that curse."

Alex started to object, but Phoebe interrupted him. "If we don't let Genevra ask the question fizzling like a hot coal in her mouth, it will burn a hole in the tip of her tongue. Then we will bear a heavy burden of guilt the rest of our days. Genevra?" The woman turned, head tilted, her braid falling over her thin silk sari.

"I was wondering why you *had* come to India," Genevra said.

Alex paused and stared at the shadows the leaves made on the ground. "Like all good soldiers, I came for my country. There are things to be attended to," he informed the shadows vaguely.

He obviously did not want to answer her question. Perhaps Radha was right.

"Tamarsha Begum! Tamarsha Begum! To where have you disappeared? Hazari the *mali* has brought you a gift."

The man appeared under a date palm, cap awry, hair blown into tangles, his white clothes covered with dust and debris. Phoebe exchanged a resigned look with Genevra. "I'm here, Hazari."

"What name is it he calls you?" Alex asked, smiling again, now that their attention was no longer fixed on him.

"He speaks as if I am an Indian married lady and a celebration both combined," she told the Captain with a

472

grin. "He does make me laugh and I can't stop him from behaving like a lunatic. It would break his heart. He'd probably moon around until he'd made me miserable as well. I couldn't bear it, you know. One had as well be nibbled to death by ducks as worn away by a Hindu's sorrow. Oh dear me, *not* a minah!"

"Yes, a minah, a sleek black talking minah with a golden-yellow beak. A treasure indeed. Speak for the lady."

"Nasmeeha-namama-naham!"

"You see," he said, "it is not just any bird. He has belonged only to the Children of the Sun, the descendants of the Mogul princes who ruled Shahjehanabad with wisdom long before it was called Delhi and the Company came to steal its heart."

Genevra glanced at Alex, expecting to see shock or anger. Perhaps he would even reach for his sword. Instead he merely held back a smile.

The bird spoke again, more loudly. *"Dhrtarastra uvaca."*

"Dear God, it's going to recite the *Bhagavadgita*. Stop it Hazari, I beg you."

"For you, anything." The *mali* bowed deeply. "Instead I will tell you how I acquired such a treasure." He did not wait for Phoebe's acquiescence. "I chanced to be passing the Mori Gate where the dispossessed from the palace live, and I came upon one of the Sunborn who had fallen into poverty and depression." He pressed his hand to his heart and closed his eyes, his expression mournful. "He begged me to purchase the last of his pets so he and his family could eat tonight. This I have done." He paused to look anxiously at the group in the *baradari*.

"Does it not make you happy, Tamarsha Begum, that because my heart burns only for you, this prince and his family will eat well tonight?"

"Goddamned boxwallah!" the minah cried shrilly. 'Blackguard cheated me blind, that's what he did."

Phoebe laughed uproariously. "The Sunborn have grown shockingly English in their use of language, it seems."

Hazari shifted from one foot to the other. "Perhaps he did live in one sahib's home, but not for long."

"I'm sorry, dear," the bird replied. "So dreadfully sorry. I hope the thugs strangle him on his next journey south and offer his soul to Kali."

Genevra, Alex, and Phoebe laughed so hard that Hazari hung his head. "I will go. I am not appreciated here."

"Of course you are," Phoebe called. "I adore people who make me laugh. But you must stop bringing these gifts. People will notice and tongues will wag."

"Be blasted quiet, you bloody nag," the bird interjected.

With an effort, Hazari suppressed a smile of his own. "People always talk of you. If they did not discuss the shocking things you do, they would have nothing to say to one another. Besides, the monkeys are comfortable in your wonderful garden, are they not?

"And the bird will be as well. So, the animals are happy. It makes me happy to give them to you, and they make you laugh. If I bring no more, you might stop laughing, and that would anger Parvati, who would bless all the earth with joy. I would certainly be unhappy if you were so, and the animals would weep bitter tears. To create sorrow when there could be pleasure is foolishness, is it not?"

"Foolishness indeed!" Phoebe declared. "You are very wise, my Hazari of the burning heart. Now come and sit with us."

For a while the four listened to the songs of the water, the chatter of monkeys, and the harsh voice of the minah. Genevra found herself staring at the Captain, remembering how his image had altered in the water. At last, she noticed that the shadows had grown long and narrow across the tiled floor. "I must go," she said quickly. She rose to smooth her blue-gray skirt.

"I will call a palanquin for you," Hazari cried. He leaped up at once. "The sun is far too bright for you to walk."

She turned to thank him but he was gone.

"It's been a lovely visit," Phoebe said. "You must come back during the rains. The water does such lovely things when the monsoons stir them with madness."

Then, to Genevra's dismay, she hurried away. Alex

Kendall rose to reach for her hand. She felt his warm fingers close around hers, felt his grip drawing her into—into what? His colors swam before her. He was golden, this man, and warm rust and the bright orange of a flame. She stared, mesmerized by the buttons on his uniform. They seemed to multiply until she was faced with every other uniform in the British-Indian army. She was swallowed by the reaching hands, blinded by the grim, gleaming perfection of thousands of polished buttons.

She forced her gaze upward to see Alex's lips curve in a smile so like Charles Kittridge's that it stopped her heart. His brilliant smile, his sparkling blue eyes sucked her into the soul of the Empire, consuming her as India had been consumed.

Alex felt Genevra's hand tremble in his. He saw the color leave her cheeks until, finally, she looked away. He sensed that it was not out of shyness or false modesty or a game of flirtation; it was something deeper. The gray flecks in her eyes covered the blue like a mist and her hand was cold—too cold in this overbearing heat. "What do you see that disturbs you so much?" he asked softly.

"See?" Genevra repeated in a hollow voice. "Only the army that stands behind you, feet buried in the soil of Hind, the Indian Civil Service that shelters in ancient Mogul palaces, and every brutal thing the British have ever done to a foreign land."

Alex gaped at her, appalled. "But you're British."

"No." She shook her head firmly. "I am an outcast."

She sounded glad of that, he noticed. He noticed, too, that he still held her hand. He released her and she sighed with relief.

"The palanquin has come!" Hazari announced. "You must hurry, Genniji, or the coolie will go. He does not like to stand in the street and wait for the clouds to burst open above him."

Just then Phoebe reappeared with a covered basket in her hand. "Special mangoes and almonds and oranges. Give them to your uncle and aunt, my dear. Though I must say it seems a bit like casting pearls before swine. Tell them the mad Englishwoman sends her compliments." She smiled and added with a wink, "Her mind might be gone, but her heart is still in working order."

Genevra thanked Phoebe, nodded to Alex, then followed the *mali* through the house. As the heavy carved door closed behind her, she felt unexpectedly that she was being shut away from some treasure whose value she could not understand, and so might never find again.

3

Reluctantly, Genevra closed the latch of Phoebe's gate and stepped into the waiting palanquin. She left the curtains open, though the sun poured in, soaking her body in sweat and blurring her thoughts. She looked out at the Jumna River, abandoned now by Hindu bathers, to watch the water lap and swell on the sand. Thus she had watched the water of the Ganges caress the shore as she traveled from Calcutta to Delhi with her aunt and uncle eleven years ago. The small steamer had crept up the river while the passengers sat on a barge attached by long chains from behind. Her relatives had looked at her rarely, as if their neglect would somehow make her disappear. The whispers, first heard in a dark hallway, had followed her like threatening shadows.

From daybreak to evening, the barge moved slowly with the sway of the river. Sometimes Genevra got out with other passengers tired of being cramped and bored, to walk along the shore. She moved in a trance, listening to the voice of the water, while her raw grief came to echo the ebb and flow of the sacred Ganges. She walked until dark, then sat on the deck, surrounded by people but deeply alone, rocking, her arms crossed to hold her sorrow in. Sometimes the others would sing while the smoke from the steamer blew back in their faces, full of sparks.

Then the steamer reached sacred Benares, with its burning ghats. The steps that led down to the water were crowded with women in colorful saris, men in white dhotis, Brahmins and *sannyasis* in loincloths. The people submerged themselves in the water until the river purified them, healed them; she could tell by the look of peace on their faces when they stood, dripping, to mount the steps once more.

Genevra's face was blackened with soot; she had not bothered to wash it. As she stood on the shore, the river called to her. "Come heal and purify yourself. I will take you just as you are," the ripples whispered on the sand. "I will take you in and hold you like a child."

One of the Brahmins saw her standing in her dirty pink-and-white-checked gingham dress, torn stockings, and uncomfortable button-top boots, her pale blond hair turned dingy and stringy by neglect. He saw, too, the pain in her eyes. "The *Upanishads* say," he murmured kindly, "that 'When rivers mingle with the sea, they lose their names and shapes and people speak of the sea only.' " He smiled the blind, all-seeing smile of the holy man and added, "So your sorrow, once given to the river, will flow to the sea and mingle with the sorrows of others, until there is no more sorrow, but only the waves of the sea, guided by the power of the god Varuna."

Drawn by his softly spoken promise, Genevra plunged into the river, clothes and all, to wash away the grime, the stain of her mother's sin, and the whispers that faded at last into the radiant silver water.

She felt hands grasp her roughly, voices hiss in her ear, "Are you mad? Mad like your mother?"

Genevra looked into her uncle and aunt's horrified faces. She knew they would not chide her further; they would not speak to her at all, but only sit in rigid, disapproving silence. They would never know how deeply their silence hurt her.

The chatter of the *satht-bai* drew her from the past to the discomfort of the present. The little birds hopped about at the edge of the river, seeking the coolness of water-dampened sand. They were called "seven sisters," because they went about in groups of seven and twittered like care-free girls.

Genevra watched until she could not see them anymore. Even then the river murmured in her ears until the palanquin drew up before the Bishop bungalow on Alipur Road.

The mats had been lowered on the veranda and the

house was closed up tight to keep out the afternoon heat. Genevra paused for a moment while the lightning played above her, sliced through the lowering clouds with the white-hot voices of the gods. " 'Wind has no body,' " she whispered to herself, " 'cloud, lightning, thunder have no body; but when they conjoin in the light and rise in the air, they show in their own shapes.' " Their shapes were bright and heavy today. The monsoons would come soon. Surely they would come and then the waiting would be over.

Genevra sat at the dining-room table with its heavy damask cloth, covered from end to end with Wedgwood china, silver-plated tureens, salvers, a silver tea and coffee service, and enough silverware to feed the entire Delhi Civil Service. The glassware, carved with leaves and flowers supported by thick curved stems, gleamed in the light of the candelabra at the center of the table. For dinner there was soup, tea, roast beef, vegetables, boiled mutton, and barley cakes. Genevra longed for curry, but did not say so.

As usual, no one spoke during the meal. The girl watched her relatives covertly. She could not get Phoebe's words out of her mind: *They must be terribly unhappy, you know*. For the first time, she saw the weary lines around her aunt's brown eyes. Her gray hair should have been lustrous brown, but the sun and sorrow of India had bleached the color from Helen Bishop's hair as it had the life from her face. Genevra saw the woman's hollow cheeks, the empty look in her eyes, and realized Phoebe was right. Even Uncle Gilbert with his blustery laughter, red cheeks, and graceful white mustache, had a strained look to his smile, a dull, lifeless sheen in his hazel eyes.

To Genevra her uncle and aunt had always been gray, without color to make them warm and real. It occurred to her now that they might be lonely. Perhaps as lonely as she, or even more so; at least she had Radha and Narain, Hazari and Phoebe to call her friends.

The *khidmutgar* brought course after course while the lightning played outside the covered windows and the Bishops sat in the false yellow light of the candles. It illumined with a strange sheen the buffet, whose shelves were filled with cut glass, china, and silver. There were photographs along the top shelf, but none of Genevra. So planned, so contained was the English perfection of this room that there might have been no India beyond it, except for the blinds that closed out the heat and the murmur of the punkah overhead.

The silence began to weigh on Genevra. The English roasts of beef, mutton stew, and little cakes helped in the pretense that there was no all-consuming sun beyond the windows, no dust or dark-skinned natives or vast, endless plains. But the food gave no comfort to the exiles who consumed it. In an effort to lighten the mood, Genevra pointed to the basket of fruit Phoebe had sent. "Won't you have a mango?" she asked her aunt.

Helen screwed up her mouth in distaste. "I shouldn't want to do that. The juice runs all over one, so disgustingly sticky. It makes one feel like, like—"

"A swine?" her niece offered with a glimmer of a smile. She had long ago taken to eating the succulent fruit in the claw-footed tub at the back of the house, where the servants crept in with buckets of warm water to cleanse the juice away.

Her aunt's cheeks grew pale, then flushed. "I don't know why you must speak so indelicately. You know how it displeases me."

"Must be those dashed natives she hangs about with. You know how *they* are."

Genevra's face grew pink with anger. "How exactly are they?"

Uncle Gilbert looked up from his beef for the first time. "Sly as a pack of foxes if you ask me. And stubborn—why, most of them won't even be bothered to learn the Queen's English. Might civilize them if they did." He pointed his fork at her, jabbing the air to punctuate each word.

"But we're in *their* country. Why should they learn English when you don't speak Hindi?"

Uncle Gilbert dropped his fork. "What in the Lord's name would I want to do that for? Speak Hindi, indeed!" He rolled his eyes toward the adobe ceiling.

Genevra took a deep breath. "Radha and Narain and many others have learned our language. What about them?"

"Probably trying to impress us," her uncle blustered. "Ingratiate themselves by pretending to learn our ways. But they don't fool me. Not for a minute, they don't."

Swallowing the cry of frustration that rose in her throat, Genevra looked down at her plate.

"Do you know what galls me most?" Gilbert continued, his chest puffed up with indignation, his red cheeks blowing in and out as he warmed to his topic. "It's their damned ingratitude for all we've done for them."

His niece choked on a drift of air.

Gilbert did not notice. "We've united the whole country, don't you know. Brought in the telegraph and postal service, and what's more, created a legal system where criminals aren't executed by having an elephant crush their heads on the block." His face was as dark as the port in his glass. "Bloody savages, they are. Burning their widows like yesterday's rubbish."

"Gilbert Bishop!" his wife cried, deeply shocked.

He sputtered on, unaware that she had spoken. "I was in the army when those blackguard Sepoys mutinied. I saw the things those barbarians did to God-loving white women and children who'd never done them a bit of harm. Makes my stomach turn to think about it. After that, I got out of the military fast, I did. Got me a civil job. Much safer, don't you know." He wiped the port from his chin and his cheeks faded to dusty rose. "Where was I?" he muttered, brow furrowed. "Oh yes, the railroad. What about the railroad? You can't deny what a boon that's been to this city."

Genevra could keep silent no longer. "There wouldn't even *be* a railroad in Delhi if the Hindu and Muslim merchants hadn't invested so much money in it!"

Her uncle opened and closed his mouth soundlessly. How dare she challenge him that way? But then, she'd always been difficult. Just like her mother, she was. "About time those coolies did something useful with their money for a change, instead of wasting it on offerings and festivals and all that other religious claptrap."

His niece did not see Helen's rare look of compassion; she knew what Gilbert was thinking. She sighed wearily. It was too bad about Emily's tainted blood. Too bad Genevra

481

could never escape her sordid birth. Her future could hardly be a happy one. Facts were facts, after all.

The girl would have argued with her uncle further, but before she could get a word out, she heard the plop of a raindrop in the dirt outside. Then there was another and another. Gilbert and Helen turned to the covered windows as the rain began to fall faster until it came in torrents that filled the whole of the wide, dark sky. The monsoons were here at last.

Gilbert Bishop spilled another drop of gravy on his white shirt and managed a half smile. "Well, it seems we've managed to survive one more year in this Godforsaken hellhole."

"If that's what you think of India," Genevra muttered, "then why did you come here?"

"Because," he said succinctly, as if speaking to an idiot, "there was nothing else."

Later, Genevra glanced into the drawing room where her aunt sewed on a slipcover for a pillow and her uncle smoked his fine silver hookah—an Indian innovation he did not reject, because it gave him pleasure. The two adults sat silent, too absorbed in their tasks to see their niece on the threshold. She slipped past the cheerless room and went instead to Radha's, where she felt at ease among the scattered pillows and bright wall hangings.

When Genevra appeared, the ayah looked up and smiled a strange, disturbing smile. "I see you could not bear to stay and watch the sahib pig puff on his pipe while his large belly wobbled with each sigh of pleasure."

Oddly, Genevra felt she should defend her uncle. She had heard this bitterness in Radha's voice before when she spoke of Gilbert Bishop. "Why do you hate him so much?"

"Because he is one of them. He who is a fool is also my master. Because he would destroy the fire and beauty of my country if he could and turn it into another Belait. He has not the right even to want such a thing."

Narain had crept in as her mother spoke and now sat cross-legged on an indigo-blue cushion. "It is so," she said simply. "The *feringhi* love only themselves and their own comfort. This you know, my friend."

Genevra could not deny it. They were silent for a moment while the rain struck the roof like the frenzied beat of a thousand *tabla* drums, demanding their attention and their worship.

Radha put Gilbert Bishop from her mind. She let the sound of the rain beat against her, enter her, and flow through her parched and aching body. She closed her eyes and swayed a little, in gratitude that the dry, killing heat was at an end. Then she stiffened, opened her eyes wide, and turned a troubled gaze on Genevra. "You are deeper in the past now than you were this morning. You have met the man, have you not?"

The girl wanted to look away, but could not. "I met him."

The ayah waited. The questions she would have asked hovered in the air, unspoken; she knew Genevra understood without words.

"I could learn nothing. Except that he was kind to the servants and he laughed most charmingly. I do not see how such a man could bring a shadow to this house." Yet she felt uneasy when she thought of him.

"I see what you feel," Narain observed. "If, in my mother's dream, he brought a shadow, then so it will be." She covered Genevra's hand with her cool brown one. "You need not lie to us. You know that."

Genevra looked into Narain's eyes, full of peace, and knew it was true. She turned when Radha rose to stand before her husband's saber mounted on the wall. He, like so many others, had been a Sepoy in the British-Indian army. Genevra wondered if that were how he had died.

Radha began to chant to herself; the words were indistinguishable, but within them was the sound of mourning, of grief long held in darkness. Slowly, performing a familiar ritual, the Indian reached out to touch the handle of the saber, run her fingertip down the colored tassel, then slide her hand through the grip. She closed her eyes and felt the coldness of steel; with her other hand, she caressed the long, curved blade. All the while she chanted rhythmically, singing a low and bitter song. She wept with her voice and the motion of her hands, though no tears came.

Then she turned, the fire in her eyes once more, and sat cross-legged on the floor. "Tonight I will not tell you of the mountains from which I came. The mountains which, through my memories, you have grown to love, though you have never seen them. I will not speak of the blue, green, and silver peaks rising into a sky full of brilliant stars," she said softly in her musical voice. "Nor of the trees that never lose their greenness or the flowers their scent. Nor of the wind in the leaves that murmurs softly, nor the sound of the water that swirls with air and wind about your shoulders, becoming part of you as heat and sun never will. Tonight I will send you away from me to think, to remember the new sahib with the eyes of a Cold Weather sky and hair like wheat that dries in the sun. Remember him, remember my dream, and remember the words of the *Bhagavadgita*:

> " 'Man should discover his own reality
> and not thwart himself.
> For he has the self as his only friend,
> or as his only enemy.' "

She fell silent and, in the flickering candlelight, blended into the colors of the room.

"We must go," Narain said over the sound of the ceaseless, sunless rain.

"Yes." Genevra was exhausted and surprised by her exhaustion. She rose shakily, her eyes already half-closed with sleep. When she swayed for an instant, her friend took her hand.

"Come," Narain said softly, leading Genevra to the room they shared. The Indian girl's charpoy had been placed there because, as a child, Genevra had been troubled by nightmares and Narain seemed the only one able to soothe her. Reluctantly, after much pleading and tears from her niece, Helen Bishop had agreed to let the native sleep in the bedroom. It was the only real gift she had ever given her sister's child.

That night, twisted among the sheets on her rosewood bed, the mosquito netting a thin, protective veil around her, Genevra lay with the moisture on her body and dreamed.

She was in Phoebe's house, going from room to room, drawn deeper and deeper into the marble corridors by a force she could not resist. Through the matted blinds she saw the trees sway, the rise of the mountain peaks, the whisper of wind that promised peace. The vision of the distant mountains was part of the voice that called her, yet it was not.

She came to a thick oak door and pressed herself against it. She felt sorrow on the other side—deep sorrow that had no expression in words. She wanted to ease that sorrow; there was already too much pain in her world. She opened the door to enter a strange room.

It had pale green walls painted with unfamiliar trees and a white carved mantel covered with animals. The room felt cool and comfortable, like a garden in the midst of a dark, grimy city. There was a woman poised by the fireplace. A woman with golden skin, a fine silk embroidered robe, long black hair, and slanted eyes of startling blue. Genevra did not know her, yet she looked familiar.

Genevra moved toward the stranger, then turned to see a woman with long chestnut hair loose about her shoulders. She was sitting by a window where the watery light fell over her as she cried out silently. The woman looked up and Genevra was hypnotized by the pain in her extraordinary blue-violet eyes. Behind the sorrow was a plea for release. Genevra had seen that pain, that plea in her mother's eyes before she left Calcutta—the kind of grief that ate at a person from within until they were empty and cold and forever alone.

Genevra knew she must ease this woman's sorrow as she had not eased her mother's. The thought had haunted her since Emily left, alone, bereft, so many years ago. Genevra felt the golden-skinned woman move beside her and a bond seemed to form between them—without words, without touch, they knew what to do. Together, they reached for the other woman and she half smiled in recognition. Her pain seemed to ease a little, to drift away like smoke in the thin, gray light from the window.

It was not enough. Genevra moved closer, drawn by the woman's eyes, her tremulous smile. She touched the stranger's shoulder and the woman reached up to take her hand. They pressed their palms together for an instant, then their fingers locked. Genevra knew the touch of that hand. Somehow she had always known it.

She opened her eyes to moist, clinging darkness. The chill was gone, but in the choking heat, she still felt the pressure of that hand. She squeezed the fingers tighter as the pale green room retreated, and with it the image of the two blue-eyed women. She saw at last that the hand she held was damp and brown, smooth and cool. The mists of her dream turned to rain. "Narain?" she murmured.

The other girl shifted so her naked body lay closer to Genevra's. She offered the coolness of her own dark skin to ease the heat that lay like a film on her friend's body. "You wept in your sleep," Narain said, "and I thought you needed me."

Genevra reached up to touch her cheek and found it was covered with tears. Slowly, as she wiped the tears away, she became aware of Narain's body through the thin fabric of her nightrail. The Indian's skin was damp but always cool, even on the hottest night. Yet Genevra's body burned with the fever of a sun that had set long since. Narain had come to her like this before to hold her, calm her, cool her. But the Indian girl could not make the dream disappear.

Genevra could not rid herself of the memory of those faces—the Oriental beauty and the chestnut-haired woman with the pain in her eyes. She had never seen them before. Yet she was certain she knew them as she had never known another—beyond memory, beyond loss, beyond the shadows, colors, and whispers that haunted her. She knew in those women the light and peace she had never found for herself.

When she moved restlessly, Narain began to chant low in her musical voice that echoed the steady rhythm of the rain. "Remember, *larla,* 'The dreaming mind enjoys its greatness. What it has seen, it sees again; what it has heard, it hears again.' "

Strange, Genevra thought, how easily the other girl understood her thoughts. Stranger still that she should find those words, that lilting voice so soothing.

" 'Whatever is seen, unseen, heard, unheard, real, unreal, here and there, the dreaming mind knows. It knows everything.' "

Genevra's lids grew heavy and the faces began to fade.

" 'When man is asleep . . . no harm can touch him, for he is filled with light.' "

With Narain's cool breath against her neck, Genevra fell asleep.

4

When she awoke, Narain had gone, the rain had stopped, and Charles Kittridge was in her mind. She did not understand why the vivid image of his face—that golden familiar face—should haunt her now when the memory of the dream was still so strong. She summoned her anger and bitterness against his inquisitive smile that gleamed against his sunburned skin, but the vision would not leave her in peace. Restlessly, she dressed and gazed out the slatted blinds. The sky was clear for the moment; she knew there would be half a day of calm and then the storm would come again. She decided that in a few hours, after the water had had time to soak into the earth, she would have herself carried to the Company *Bagh*. Its name had been changed to the Queen's Gardens since Victoria's coronation as Empress of India, but Genevra preferred the old title, which used the native word for garden.

She stopped in the hallway, dark and dim as usual, when she heard low-pitched voices. Hand pressed to the doorframe, she stared in astonishment at Radha and Uncle Gilbert, who stood in the shadows speaking together. Radha had obviously been out already, though it must have been before the rain stopped. Her cloak was soaked; it dripped monotonously on the wooden floor. She held a brown bag clutched to her chest. Gilbert reached for it, but she seemed reluctant to give it up.

What surprised Genevra most was that her uncle listened closely to every word the servant said and the blank look had left his gray eyes. His niece felt they had not met here by accident; their manner was too intense.

Odd, but there were colors between them where it had

been dull gray before. Genevra saw red, which she sensed meant danger—blue, which was cold and hard—silver, which she could not understand. Something in the position of their bodies, the wariness in their eyes made her uneasy. Last night Radha had called Gilbert Bishop a pig; now she was sharing secrets with him. For some reason, Genevra thought of Charles Kittridge and his betrayal. He, too, had had his secrets. He and Emily. Agitated and disturbed, the girl turned silently away.

Genevra sat on a camp stool before her easel in the Company *Bagh*. The ground was still wet and her boots sank into the grass, but she did not care. She was grateful to be out and away from the dark, dank bungalow. The branches of tamarinds, palms, and plane trees that dotted the large expanse of grass had ceased to drip, but in the clouds and the marshy earth, she sensed the sound of moving water. Some Hindu and Muslim businessmen were seated on damp benches near the town hall, but they did not interest her. It was the children—the English in their proper little suits and checked gingham calf-length dresses, the Indians in their saris or simple dhotis—that fascinated her.

She noticed that the *Sudras*, the Untouchables, the lowest Hindu caste, huddled at the edges of the grounds, and that Hindu, Muslim, and British alike made a wide path around the figures dressed in filthy rags. Even she dared not approach, though she pitied them and wanted to help. The tradition was too ingrained that the *Sudras* were no better than pariah dogs and their touch a defilement. She could not change the beliefs of centuries.

She looked away and began intently to sketch the park. Now and then, she added a splash of color to her drawing.

"Memsahib! You must help me or my heart will break!"

A young Indian boy, wearing only pajamalike white pants and a round cap, rushed up to her, his bare feet covered with mud. "Your name is Rammi, isn't it?" she asked. She had seen him here before, spoken briefly with him as he admired her pictures.

"Yes, Memsahib, it is so. But that is not why I came."

"No." Genevra suppressed a smile. "I don't imagine it is. How is it that I can keep your heart from breaking?"

He took off his cap to thrust it toward her. "You can paint a monkey on the top of my hat."

"I don't understand."

The boy patted her arm in compassion. Of course a *feringhi* could not understand even so simple a matter. "I had a pet monkey, you see, and he was the joy of my life." Rammi looked up at her mournfully. "One day I fell asleep here in the *Bagh*, and when I woke up, he was gone. He had run away." He sighed heavily. "But if you paint the monkey on my hat, then I will have him always on my head, so he cannot run away again."

Genevra choked on her laughter. "What if you lose your hat?"

Rammi stared at her in great seriousness. "I wouldn't dare do that. The sun would crawl into my ears and burn away the inside of my head. So, if you would just——" He offered his cap a second time.

"Of course." She took her brush and with a few deft strokes created the face of a monkey on the round surface. "There."

"May Vishnu bless you, and Agni and Indra and Brahma himself." Rammi took his cap with reverence. "Your kindness is so great that I cannot find the words to tell you. It is too bad you are a *feringhi*." He grinned at her and skipped away, admiring his prize.

When he was gone, Genevra quickly sketched Rammi in the corner of her drawing. She added a real monkey clinging to his shoulders, its chin propped on his red hat. Now, whenever she saw the boy, she would also see the imaginary monkey, winking at her above the round cap.

"Look at her! Her hat's blown off and she hasn't bothered to pick it up," Ava Cunningham said snippily, patting her own velvet bonnet with its graceful peacock feather.

"But my dear, her hair! Honestly, it looks as though it's going to fall loose round her shoulders any minute. Ah-ha!" As Laura Bayley spoke, a gust of wind took the last pin from Genevra's hair and the blond waves fell down her back.

"She looks like a . . . well, you know. Why I wouldn't be surprised—" She broke off when the officer fresh from England approached. "Good morning, Captain Kendall," she said.

He nodded politely at both women, but stopped to look at Genevra perched on her stool in the marshy grass, her plain straw hat a few feet away, her hair loose and free. "You were talking about Miss Townsend, I believe," he said to the two ladies in gaily colored cotton print gowns, decorated with lace and ruffles from throat to hem and bustles heavily draped with bows in back.

"We should pity her, I know," Ava murmured. She disliked the way the young officer had looked at Genevra and intended to see that it did not happen again.

When she raised her lace parasol, Alex Kendall smiled to himself. The contraption was so fragile, it wouldn't keep out the morning sun, let alone the Indian rain that seemed to shake the earth beneath his feet. Then he realized what she had said. "What do you mean, you should pity her?"

"Oh, I couldn't repeat such a thing. Laura will have to tell you." She smiled coquettishly.

Alex frowned. "Tell me what?"

Laura brushed a dark curl from her damp forehead. "That she's not—well"—she looked demurely downward— "legitimate. She only lives with her uncle and aunt because her 'father' threw her out and her mother abandoned her. Too shocking, I'm sure. Perhaps that's why she behaves so unnaturally."

"Of course," Ava added, not to be outdone, "she's not received anywhere."

With a conscious effort, Alex forced his anger down. He had heard enough of this kind of thing in England. It was part of the reason he had agreed to come here; to escape gossips like Ava Cunningham and Laura Bayley, to find a society less strangled by tradition, rules, and the suffocating presence of a "they" who judged everyone and generally found them lacking. He had been in Delhi less than a week, but already he could see that these people were more British than the ones at home, more rigid, more tight-lipped, and even less forgiving.

Ava was becoming annoyed at the captain's inattention. "Did you know she befriends the natives?" she persisted.

"And that mad Englishwoman who lives in the house of some Indian prince," Laura contributed. "We all find Miss Townsend's behavior quite appalling."

"Do you?" Alex inquired mildly, though his eyes were narrowed and his fists clenched. "How interesting." Without another word, he turned on his heel to cross the wet lawn toward Genevra.

The two young women in their fashionable gowns and bonnets stared after him, their mouths quite unbecomingly agape.

Genevra felt a familiar prickle at the back of her neck. She looked up, expecting to see the image of Charles Kittridge staring at her across the lawn, but instead found Alex Kendall gazing over her shoulder.

"I didn't realize you were an artist, Miss Townsend."

Her hands went cold and she was so shaken that she could not find her voice. "I tried not to be," she managed at last. "They told me it was impractical and self-indulgent. But I couldn't help myself. The colors are in my blood. 'Orange, blue, yellow, red are not less in man's arteries than in the sun.' "

"Only some men's arteries, I believe. I've known one or two rather colorless chaps myself." He was occupied with his own thoughts and did not see Genevra's eyes widen in surprise. How was it possible that such a woman was Gilbert Bishop's niece? Could it be that he was wrong about the man after all? He would have to take care or he would make a mistake that Genevra Townsend might come to regret, and if he weren't mistaken, she had suffered enough already.

He stood, brow furrowed for some time, then shook himself awake. "If you don't mind, I think I'll find a camp stool myself so I can watch you for a while." He did not make the excuse that he only wanted to find out what she knew. Alex Kendall was not in the habit of lying to himself. This girl interested him, with her fragile features that even her sun-browned skin could not hide, her gray-blue eyes and enigmatic smile.

Genevra had not yet recovered her composure and felt a shiver of apprehension at the thought of Alex joining her. But Radha had asked her for something, and the girl did not wish to fail the ayah. "Of course."

The captain went away, but returned quickly to sit beside her. Once there, he was not certain how to begin. He felt ill-at-ease and that was not like him. "How long do you suppose we have before the rain begins?"

Genevra looked at the cloud-laden sky, then turned back to her easel. "At least an hour, I should think. Perhaps even two. You can't predict things here, you know, especially not the weather. You'd best learn that straightaway."

"There must be patterns one can trace," he objected. "Surely, if one takes the time to understand—"

"There are always patterns, thousands of patterns, followed for thousands of years. How do you make sense of so many? You can't *understand* India either. It's too much of a muddle all round. But a wonderful muddle that's always surprising and"—she frowned, tried to think of the word— "disturbing as well. It's the contradictions I like best. The mountains and the plains, the sun and the shadows, the sacred rivers and choking dust."

"You seem to understand the country," Alex said challengingly.

Genevra smiled for the first time. "Not in the slightest. I admire it, but I don't really understand. It's beyond me. I think I like it that way. But the other British don't."

"You mean they despise anything they can't identify, give a name to, and catalog tidily in a little pigeonhole?"

Genevra stared at him in astonishment. "That's exactly what I mean."

"You needn't look so shocked. You aren't the only one who thinks like that, you know."

"I always thought I was." She leaned forward, drawn by the familiar look in his eyes, his winning smile. With an effort, she broke away. It was Charles Kittridge's eyes she was smiling into, slipping into as if they were a deep ravine where she could fall and fall and never touch the earth again.

"For he has himself as his only friend
and as his only enemy."

493

Radha's warning hovered before her, caught in the wavering heat. Genevra clutched her pencil tight until the falling stopped.

Alex felt her retreat and did not understand. "What are you drawing?" he asked, hoping to distract her.

"You."

She tore off the sheet and handed it to him.

He had not expected that. "It's a wonderful likeness. I don't see how you did it, when you weren't even looking at me."

"I saw you yesterday," she said. "My fingers remember."

Alex was shaken, not by the accuracy of her memory, but by the background in the sketch. There were rolling fields, the hint of a church long crumbled into ruin, and an old, ivy-covered well. The top of the well was draped in flowers and the leaves of ivy formed a woman's face. He had grown up among those familiar things. She had drawn part of the estate where he'd been born. "This looks like my home," he said when he could find his voice. "How did you know?"

Genevra examined the portrait, as surprised by the background as he was. "Sometimes I draw things without realizing it, things I sense in the back of my mind. My charcoal just seems to take over for my fingertips." She touched the face above the well. "Tell me about the woman in the well."

Alex went pale. "How did you know about her?"

"I told you before," she answered patiently, "I sense things sometimes. Tell me."

"During the Reformation, a Catholic ancestor heard that King Henry was coming to visit. The family priest urged the man to hide a figure of the Virgin Mary that was made of gold and very precious," Alex explained. "My ancestor tossed it into the well. Later, when the danger was past, he could not find the statue again. But sometimes her face appears in the water. Catholics from all over England come to worship her. Often, they leave gifts of flowers like the ones you've drawn."

Genevra shivered, unnerved, as she always was, by her inexplicable talent. But she noticed that after his initial shock, Alex Kendall had not shrunk away from her as others had before him. She watched as he ran his fingers over the sketch with admiration, touching gently the things he had loved in his youth. She was transfixed by the gold and orange haze around him. "Why did you come to India?" she said unexpectedly.

She had asked him before, with the same intensity that he saw now in the pressure of her fingers on the pencil she held.

"Because I'd read about it and thought I'd like it here. I was told that the land speaks in an ancient voice. You have to pause and concentrate; you can't hurry by like you do on a London street. If you wait long enough, they say, you can actually hear the voice of the past."

"But it's not only the land that speaks." In her excitement over his understanding, Genevra forgot who he was. "You should listen to the wind. It sings and cries and moans, and its voice is so familiar, as if I'd heard it before." She paused, her gaze distant. "Perhaps in my dreams." Then she realized what she'd said and stiffened. "That's not really why you came."

"You don't believe me?" He did not assume a look of false hurt or accuse her of being rude. He liked her honesty and was ashamed of his own deception.

Regarding him closely, Genevra replied, "The British Army does not send men to India for that. The English don't know how to listen to the earth and they don't care about the voice of the past—except their own."

Alex was taken aback by the bitterness in her tone, even though he had heard it before. A drop fell on the paper in his hand and he quickly folded it to place it in his tunic.

Genevra watched it disappear with regret. She did not want to give it up. It was as if she were giving away part of her soul for anyone to look at.

Alex saw her look of hesitation. "It's only fair," he declared as another drop fell. "You've put a part of my past, my secret heart on this paper. It's not for strange eyes to see."

Drawing a deep breath, she looked away. It was not the first time he had echoed her thoughts. By now the drops were falling faster and she knew she had to get home before the storm began in earnest. "I told you you couldn't predict things in India," she murmured as she gathered her paper, easel, brushes, and pencils to start toward the street, where she could get a palanquin.

Alex followed, made certain she was safely enclosed inside the heavy curtains, then told her, "You're wrong about the British, you know. Someday I'll prove it to you." That, at least was not a lie.

That afternoon, while the relentless rain fell, Genevra sat in her room, the door closed. She did not want even Narain to disturb her.

The image of the Golden Man had followed her home, merging at last with the memory of her father's face. It was then that she'd remembered the drawings she'd done of Charles Kittridge and others—the sketches she didn't show people because she drew them blindly, seeing through her fingers. She had not done one for a long time, until today, and those she'd kept, she'd put away in her bureau. Now she wanted to see them again.

She found them in a thick paper wrapper at the back of a drawer. Moving close to the lamp, she settled herself in the yellow pool of light.

With a sense of anticipation she did not understand, she opened the wrapper and took out what lay inside. The first sketch she turned upside down. It was the only one she had done of her mother after Emily left her. The woman's face, so fragile and lovely, was distorted beyond recognition and the background so disturbing that Genevra had stopped in the middle and hidden it away. But she could not bring herself to destroy it.

Next there was a drawing of Radha that still confused her, though she'd examined it many times. Behind the ayah's face were flames, turmoil, and, in clear pools of standing water, reflections of bitterness and hatred that frightened Genevra. She dropped it on top of her sketch of Emily.

With a sigh of relief, Genevra picked up the drawing of Narain. The Indian girl was lovely, her face smooth and free of distressing emotion. The background was sweeping white—pure and unstained. This was Genevra's favorite. She had painted Narain many times because of it. She wanted to capture the infinite calm in her friend's eyes. This sketch, too, she put aside.

There were many drawings of Charles Kittridge, most half-finished, all done in an effort to discover something about the man who was her father. In one sketch a jagged purple mountain towered behind him. A waterfall rushed down the side with the face of a woman just discernible in the white, foaming water. Another drawing showed Charles's face transformed by grief and fear while behind him men with curved sabers ran through a garden of rocks and trees. There were so many backgrounds—one with Indian palaces rising majestically, one with the ever-changing sea all around. She squinted at the sketch of a barren plain that stretched behind him and made her hurt inside. Why should she hurt for him?

One of the drawings revealed Emily's shadow in Charles's eyes, but Genevra did not appear on a single page. Her fingers, which saw what she could not, knew that to Charles Kittridge she was not a memory, not even a shadow. She pushed the drawing away in anger.

Finally she came to the last sketch, drawn long ago and forgotten. She froze, the paper clutched in her hand. Behind Charles Kittridge's head were the faces of two women—one Oriental, with slanted blue eyes, another with chestnut hair and the blue-violet eyes that still burned in Genevra's memory. There was no doubt. These were the faces from her dream.

5

Through July the monsoons came, making day into twilight, twilight into night. Often there was a ring of red between storm clouds and earth where the light broke through. The Hindus pointed to the vibrant circle and whispered that the gods were at work. The wind rose with a roar through the slashing rain until the sound was everywhere, above and below. Lightning shot from massive clouds, trees bent to the earth with the force of the wind, and the sky roiled and spat, aflame.

The macadam roads in the city were dangerous courses of rock and rushing water, while the ground itself was a sea of mud. The streams were full, and the rivers and lakes; even the dry *nullahs* ran with water. Bugs and snakes came by the hundreds to find shelter in houses and bungalows, so that verandas and walls were riddled with scorpions, toads, centipedes, lizards, and cockroaches. The long-sought release from the heat became a burden and a trial of endurance.

Helen and Gilbert Bishop suffered horribly from prickly heat every year at this time, but Genevra had never been afflicted. That was because Radha rubbed the girl's skin with a special salve and fed her teas brewed with herbs to keep away the cholera. Genevra did not understand how her relatives could become so ill with someone like Radha in the house. When she asked, the ayah merely shrugged and did not mention that she kept her salves and teas a secret from the Bishops, who deserved their suffering as Genevra did not.

Each day there was a brief reprieve from the ravages of the storm. The rain would stop, the clouds dissipate, and a

498

blue sky appear, touched by a golden sun. White clouds drifted above as if the savagery of the monsoon had never been. The British breathed with relief the air washed clean by the rain. In these moments of calm, the heat abated and the temperature never rose above ninety. Yet even then the feel of rain was in the air and water circled in the heavens.

During these idyllic hours, the British crept from their bungalows, the soldiers from their barracks, and the Indians from their houses. No minute of dry clean air was wasted.

One afternoon, when the rains stopped for a while, Alex Kendall went to call at the bungalow on Alipur Road.

Helen heard the bearer open the door and offer his most respectful greeting. Then a strange voice inquired, "Is Mr. Gilbert Bishop at home?"

"Bishop Sahib no here. Go to monstrosity called Town Hall. Mutter about much work to do."

Alex, who had already been by the Town Hall and found it practically deserted—the storm that morning had been particularly fierce—narrowed his eyes. But then, he had expected as much. When he saw Helen hovering uncertainly at the end of the hall, he smiled. "Would you be Mrs. Bishop? I'm Captain Alexander Kendall, Life Guards, Household Cavalry. I don't mean to intrude, but I was calling round for your husband and find him not at home. I wonder, is your niece about?"

The sun shone on his red coat, the epaulets and gold braid across his left shoulder. His white pants were spotlessly clean as were his high black boots, and how he managed that, she'd like to know. He certainly looked official, and his smile was warm, though there was an expression in his eyes she did not like. A flicker of—what? Curiosity? No, more than that; he was assessing her. "Genevra!" she exclaimed when she realized what he'd said. "You wish to see my niece?"

"It's really all right, you know. We've been introduced. I met her at the Queen's Gardens. We chatted about her painting. Since I'm here with a bit of time on my hands, I thought she might like some company."

Helen twisted her fingers nervously. Her ruffled and bustled beige gown seemed to fade into the adobe wall, while her gray hair was pulled back so severely that Alex was certain she must be suffering from a headache.

"I suppose it's all right," she said at last.

Before she could call out, Genevra appeared in the doorway. She came forward in a soft gray printed muslin gown with a blue underskirt and piping around the square neck.

Her eyes seemed to glow with a strange light, Alex thought, but then, everything in India glowed with a strange light. "I wondered if we could talk for a bit. I called round for your uncle, but he's not at home."

"Oh. Aunt Helen?" She asked politely for her aunt's approval, though that was not her habit.

Suddenly Genevra felt Radha's eyes upon her, though she knew the woman was not in the room. The ayah saw all that went on in this house, if not with her eyes, then in her dreams. Genevra felt the power of those dark eyes and remembered that she had not yet "charmed Alex's secrets from him." She did not yet know "what the Indians could not know." She was not at all certain she wanted to know his secrets, however.

"Tell the young man to come in," Helen declared. "We can't leave him standing about on the veranda all afternoon."

"Won't you come into the drawing room and have a cup of tea?" Genevra offered.

Alex grinned with relief and stepped inside.

When the Captain passed her, Helen could not resist one more look into his vivid eyes. The curiosity had gone; now there was only compassion. For her? She stared after him as he turned the corner and disappeared with her niece. No one had shown her compassion in a very long time. She felt unsettled by the thought, and slightly apprehensive.

Genevra stopped just inside the drawing room with Radha's gaze upon her, Radha's questions in her head. Alex seemed hardly aware of her; he was looking closely at everything around him, examining each piece of furniture, each picture frame, candelabra, and cut-glass bowl. He stopped to stare intently at an ebony table with a white marble top. The legs were carved in an intricate design of leaves and exotic flowers.

"Remarkable piece," he observed. "Quite expensive, too."

Genevra could not see his expression; suddenly she wanted very much to do so. She watched, perplexed, when he stopped at the rosewood cabinet full of figurines and Chinese vases to peer at the objects inside. Then he noticed her uncle's hookah. The stand was embossed silver, as was the cup that held the tobacco, which was hung with silver chains. There was a snakelike pipe, quite long, with a mouthpiece in exquisitely wrought silver. He took a deep breath and his eyes narrowed dangerously.

"What is it?" Genevra asked, alarmed.

"An item to be treasured by collectors if I'm not mistaken," he replied stiffly. "I wonder how it came into the hands of a man like your uncle?"

She heard a hiss behind her and then silence. Shaking herself free of the power of Radha's gaze, Genevra regarded Alex, her cheeks flushed with anger. Had he come here to examine every possession her uncle owned?

Before she could speak, he said, "You think I'm dreadfully rude and are wondering, besides all that, why I've such an inordinate interest in your uncle's possessions." He gave her no chance to respond. "It's because your uncle possesses such inordinately interesting objects to observe."

Genevra turned pale. Why was it so easy for him to guess what she was thinking?

"I see," Alex said quietly. "I'm not allowed to read your thoughts, though it's perfectly all right for you to see my deepest secrets and put them down on paper, as well."

At her expression of dismay, he relented. "I was only joking, you know. And as for the rudeness, that was unforgivable."

She smiled bitterly. He could not know how often she had been ignored, stared at, giggled over, how many disparaging whispers—spoken a little too loudly—she had overheard in the last eleven years.

Startled by the pain in her eyes, Alex moved closer. "I truly meant no offense. It's just that, for a moment, the British officer in me overshadowed the man. I'll try not to let it happen again."

She knew it would happen again; he had no power to stop it. The Army, the Empire would always win in the end. She could not fight such strength and neither could Alex. She did not imagine he wanted to. "Why should a British officer be so interested in all this?" She indicated the cluttered room around them.

Alex sighed. "I'll never lie to you, Genevra, I swear, but there are things I simply cannot tell you. Please trust me."

"Why should I, when the English are so good at lying? Especially to themselves."

Hands clasped behind him, Alex began to pace, reminding himself that she had reasons for her bitterness. "I do not lie to others. I dislike intensely those who do. As for deluding myself, well, I try not to do so. I don't suppose I always succeed. But then, I don't suppose you do either."

Genevra winced and moved out of the range of his perceptive gaze. She stared at the shadow patterns the half-open blinds made on the floor. "When I hold a paintbrush or piece of charcoal in my hand I cannot lie, even if I wish to. My fingers always tell the truth, perhaps the only truth there is." She wanted to take back the words the moment they were spoken. She had not admitted this before, not even to Phoebe.

"Show me," Alex said unexpectedly. "I want to see your work."

She whirled, astonished. "You don't know what you're saying. You don't understand—"

"Then make me understand."

He touched her shoulder gently. The weight of his hand, so slight, so tender, made her hurt inside. No man had touched her that way since she was a child. She was used to laughter and derision, even cold neglect, but tenderness she could not bear. "Why have you come here?" she cried.

Surprised by her anguish, he told the simple truth. "Because I find your company agreeable."

"Don't you know about my mother, my past?"

Alex frowned. "I've heard things. One can hardly avoid doing so. But gossip means nothing to me. I could no more pretend to dislike you than you could pretend you love your countrymen. I dislike hypocrisy, Genevra. That's why I left England. I hoped to find more honesty here."

She laughed harshly.

"I was mistaken. I know that now. Except about Phoebe Quartermaine, and you. Show me your work, please. Show me a little of the honesty I seek."

"I keep my paintings at Phoebe's now, where they're safe."

"Then we'll meet at Phoebe's. Tomorrow."

Biting her lip, she looked into his clear blue eyes. "I don't think that would be wise."

"Sometimes," he said softly, "wisdom means following your heart and not your mind. You know that."

Genevra opened her mouth to object, but the words of the lie would not form on her tongue. "Sometimes that kind of wisdom is the most foolish of all."

"That sort of thing usually matters to me," he murmured, "but not, I think, to you. I envy you that." Then he turned and was gone.

Genevra did not visit Phoebe for the next few days. When she did go, Alex was there.

"He just appeared, utterly by coincidence," Phoebe said, a wicked gleam in her eye, "and quite a delightful one, I'm sure."

There were many more such coincidences. "I just called round to enjoy the waters," Alex would say with an innocent smile.

Occasionally he called at the Bishop bungalow. "Merely attempting to be polite," he explained unconvincingly.

Still Genevra did not show him her paintings. Instead they talked or recited poetry—she Hindu and he English—to one another until gradually Alex began to gain her trust. One day a few weeks later, while the thunder drums beat fire into the sky, they sat in Phoebe's *baradari* and Genevra brought out her work at last. She showed Alex paintings of the bright, barren plains and glittering water gardens of Delhi, of Hindus who crouched, lithe and brown, in the grass or worshiped beside the flowing river.

With each canvas, Alex was more impressed by the

vivid colors, the life, the feeling in the paintings. When he came to one of the *Sudras*—thin and ravaged Hindu outcasts with huge eyes full of suffering, he felt their pain as if it were his own. Genevra left several canvases untouched in the corner, but Phoebe would not allow it.

"Don't, I pray you, be such a stubborn old stick, Genny. You know those are your best. If you don't share them, you shall spoil our fun altogether and I shall never forgive you. Never."

Reluctantly, Genevra brought out her paintings of Narain—praying, mixing curry, staring at the midnight sky, surrounded always by a profound sense of peace and beauty. Alex drew in his breath, delighted and astonished.

When he turned the last canvas toward the sky, Genevra gasped and tried to snatch it back. This one, of all the others, she had not meant to let him see.

Alex raised his hand to stop her. It was not the gesture that made her pause, but the expression on his face. His eyes widened in wonder at the image of Narain rising in a rush of sun-touched crystal from the river Jumna, her dark hair shimmering with beads of water, her skin sleek, soft, and cool. Alex was speechless at the mood of jubilation Genevra had captured.

He touched the canvas, expecting to feel the coolness of sparkling water, surprised to find only dry, ridged paint.

"I did that, too, the first time I saw it," Phoebe interjected. "The water lives in your hands and your eyes, doesn't it? It takes great talent to endow not only flesh and blood but even clear water with such light and life."

Alex could only nod, gaze at Genevra as if he had never seen her before—or if he had, he had not understood. "This is miraculous," he whispered.

Genevra clasped her hands until her fingers ached. She had not expected him to understand, nor had she expected the turmoil of pleasure and fear his understanding caused inside her. She rose abruptly. "It's time to go, I think. It's quite late."

Perplexed, Alex followed her away from Phoebe's house. She walked a few steps ahead of him as they crossed the Chandni Chowk, moved through the cantonment, and across the bridge of boats.

Moment by moment, she regained some measure of control as her delight in his response to her paintings slowly eclipsed her fear. Glancing up at the sky, she said softly, "It's a beautiful day for listening to the sounds of the earth, don't you agree?"

"A better day still for walking with friends," Alex replied. "Phoebe has told me that in the *Mahabaratha*, 'The sages teach that to walk seven steps one with another, maketh good men friends.' I should like to think it's true. Shall we stop at the Nicholson gardens to take the air?"

"You mean the *Qudsiya-Bagh*?" she asked, smiling obliquely.

Alex concentrated on the forming gray clouds against a background of endless blue. "Do you do that on purpose? Show your knowledge of Hindi when you're uncomfortable? Does it make you feel better?"

She considered, unpleasantly aware of the weight of her skirt and petticoats about her ankles. "It makes me feel less British, if that's what you mean." She stopped when she saw Ava Cunningham and Laura Bayley coming toward them, their gowns held up delicately to avoid mud that could not be avoided.

Alex smiled stiffly, inclined his head toward the two women, who greeted him warmly but only glanced at Genevra, then away.

When they were gone, she hurried her step, seeking the cool shade of the lush green trees of the *Bagh*. Her throat burned. Even after all this time, even from women as small-hearted as Ava and Laura, it hurt.

Following close behind, Alex held in his anger at the two empty-headed women. He ached for Genevra; all he could think of was soothing her pain. When he reached the copse of palms, acacias, and *aswatta* figs where she had taken refuge, he cupped her face in his hand. "Try to forget them. I know it doesn't help, but Ava and Laura and many others are so very unhappy in India. They're exiles, you know, uncomfortable, misplaced, longing for home. Perhaps that's why they're so unforgiving."

Genevra took a deep breath. "Perhaps. But I can't help thinking they're exiles because they choose to be. They don't even try to understand the ways of the Hindus—the magic, the history, the music and rhythm of life. They prefer to cling to their Britishness, to be narrow, petty, rigid, arrogant, cold and unforgiving, bigoted and blind, blind, *blind*!"

Her cheeks were flushed and her body quivered with the force of her rage. Alex was appalled. He had never guessed that her pain went so deep. "You aren't being fair, really. You should try to see the good as well."

Genevra shook her head. "No. I want only to lose myself in India, forget the British, forget I ever heard an English word."

Pointing beyond their shelter of trees, Alex demanded, "You want to be part of that? The filth, the disease, the mothers who let their children starve because they refuse to hurt a cow? All you see is the beauty. You've been hypnotized by music and ritual. But there is much more here than that. India is full of a savage cruelty you can't even imagine."

"Surely it's no more cruel than the English in their make-believe world that has no room for imagination or for those who are different in any way."

Alex shook his head. He did not know how to fight such determination. "What about the dust and the heat, the disorder, the beggars, the shouting, the drums, the confusion in the city, the absolute *chaos* of this country you love so much?"

"Far better to be caught up in chaos, color, movement, life and dust, creation and change than to be a prisoner in a cold, empty house, dying a slow death from hidden pain you pretend not to feel, boredom that eats away at your sanity, and loneliness." She turned, with the shadows of the leaves on her face, and reached out to embrace all of India. "There's so much out there that we miss. The British look at the vibrant chaos and see criminal disorder. They look at the beautiful temples full of music, history, and ritual and see only a refuge for heathens. They look at fascinating ancient ruins and see only crumbled stones. But most of all, they look at hundreds of thousands of Indians with souls and culture and history and emotions and the self-important

British see only hordes of servants and soldiers." She turned to him again. Her eyes glowed a brilliant gray-blue, even in the shaded light. "The British have no heart, no spirit, no fire in their souls."

Alex was mesmerized—by the lilt of her voice, the passion in her eyes, the way she moved her hands to make him understand. She, who had great reason, had molded no careful mask to hide her true feelings from others. He thought of his mother, of the flicker of hurt he had seen in her eyes when he told her he was going to India. She had hidden it quickly, raised her own delicate mask so her eyes became blank and her smile falsely pleasant. He had wanted to smash that mask, that hollow smile, to see the tears that had no doubt fallen onto her pillow that night. But the mask was her protection; he had no right to rip it away and leave her exposed, vulnerable.

Yet here Genevra stood, maskless—snubbed by society, an outcast judged and rejected out of jealousy and fear of her extraordinary talent as much as her past. She made no attempt to hide her pain or her passion or the depth of her fury. "Do you know how easily I could love you?" Alex murmured.

Genevra stiffened. "No," she cried. "Don't say that. Don't ever say that." People had told her they loved her once; she'd believed they would love her forever. But one day, without a word of regret or compassion, they'd simply gone away and left her to struggle alone in the darkness. She would not let it happen again. She backed away, turned to stare up at the huge, soft leaves of the *aswatta* rustling overhead. While she watched the green movement of light thin leaves, listened to the sound of their voices in the breeze, her heart slowed and the warmth faded from her cheeks. The leaves met and parted, sang like the *veena*, offering peace, refreshment, and infinite coolness. "The Indians believe the *aswatta* leaf can cure any ailment," she whispered painfully. "Even the pangs of passion."

"What about love?" Alex demanded. "Will your leaves cure that?"

Genevra turned to look at him and time was caught, unchanging, frozen forever in the cave of leaves and shifting shadows. He stood tall and golden, like the vision whose sparkling eyes and sad smile had haunted her for so long. In that moment, his image wavered, grew clear, wavered in the speckled sunlight. When the seconds began to tick by once more, Alex had become woven into that vision of Charles Kittridge—a shadow from the past. Genevra closed her eyes. "Some people don't believe in love. It's not that they don't want to; it's just that they can't. They know too much, have seen too much suffering. Those people won't ever fall in love. They wouldn't dare." She spoke in a monotone, repeating a lesson learned by heart, as if there were no feeling behind it, no nights of tears that had lasted until dawn crept in at the windows.

For the first time in his life, Alex Kendall wanted to weep.

That night, Radha called Genevra into her little room of candlelight and colored silk. The ayah sat beneath the saber of her dead husband, her hands folded in her lap. The shadows danced over her face and the face of her daughter, who sat in silence at her side.

For a long time Radha regarded Genevra in her clean white wrapper, as if she could see inside the girl's mind to that moment with Alex among the trees. "Tonight," the ayah said at last, "I will tell you a fable. You would be wise to hear me and remember, for I know the evils of this world as you do not."

She stared down at her brown, cracked hands, examining each line as if it held some message only she could understand. "There was a morning," she began in a low, rhythmic voice, "when a Brahmin started on a journey—a pilgrimage to the sacred river Ganges where he hoped to gather merit and make himself more pure.

"One day he stopped to bathe in a river, and when he stepped into the water, a crocodile approached him. The animal soon learned where the holy man was going and begged to be taken along. He told the Brahmin sadly how the river in which he now lived often ran dry and how much the crocodiles suffered because of it. Perhaps, the animal suggested, he could live more comfortably in the Ganges.

"The Brahmin was a man of compassion and charity, so he put the crocodile in his bag, lifted it to his shoulder, and carried the animal the rest of the way. When they arrived at last on the shore of the most sacred of rivers, the Brahmin took the animal from his bag and showed him the inviting water.

509

"The crocodile moaned that he was exhausted from the long journey and begged the Brahmin to carry him to the water; he did not think he was strong enough to reach it himself. The Brahmin, who was a trusting if foolish man, did what the animal asked. As soon as they reached a certain depth, the holy man released the crocodile and turned to go, but the animal grabbed him and determined to eat him.

" 'What?' the Brahmin cried. 'Is that how you show your gratitude for my kindness? You have dealt dishonestly with me.'

" 'Do not be ridiculous,' the crocodile told him. 'Do not shout at me about honesty and gratitude. The only honesty of our days is to ruin those who cherish us.' "

Radha stared through Genevra and beyond her to the shadows at the edge of the room. "It is only a fable, but it is true, Genniji, sadly true."

"I don't see—"

The ayah rolled her eyes heavenward. " 'Must I tell you a tale and find you ears, too?' You cannot trust all who call themselves your friends."

Genevra knew Radha was speaking of Alex, and her own fears made her shrink from the woman's gaze.

"Do not turn away, but hear me. The *Bhagavadgita* says, 'Ignorance veils wisdom and misleads people.' You can see gold, touch it, hold it in your hand, but only when it is too late do you find it is not gold at all, but worthless glittering dust."

A gust of wind crept under the door and Genevra shivered. She knew too well that the Golden Man, like Charles Kittridge before him, was only an illusion, that the feelings he stirred in her were dangerous—as dangerous as those that had destroyed Emily Townsend. Nor could she forget his strange behavior on that first day at the bungalow, the unanswered questions that lay between them like a fine mesh screen, a wash of gray that could not be painted bright and clear. Genevra bowed her head, weighed down by fleeting shadows, glimpses of a truth she did not seek, the threatening hues that filled the room.

"Do you hear?" Radha demanded. "Do you hear me in your mind and your beating heart where all foolish passions lie? Do you feel the truth in the power of the storm, in the pulse of your blood through your thousand veins? Do you hear?"

"I hear." Genevra rose but could not move. Her feet, her heart, her soul were made of lead.

Then Narain was beside her. "You have understood. That is all that matters. Come to bed. Sleep will heal you."

Unable to resist, Genevra followed her friend. As she crawled into bed, she heard Narain whisper, "The *Bhagavadgita* says more and other things. Things just as true, *larla*." Softly, she began to sing.

> "Again and again, the whole multitude
> of creatures is born, and when night falls,
> Is dissolved, without their will,
> and at daybreak, born again."

Her sweet voice carried through the darkness, rose and fell with Genevra's breath.

"You will be reborn tomorrow; tomorrow all things will be new. Perhaps this man will go and you will be free."

Genevra did not answer.

That night, in the steamy darkness of cruel and beautiful India, Genevra dreamed herself into the mountains of Radha's childhood. She gazed in delight at the blue-green trees, the rocky hills, the clear azure sky. As she stood among the voices of water and wind that swirled about her, the caress of a cool breeze ruffled her hair. Rain drifted like a blessing over her face. She heard the wind sighing to her in the leaves.

There were other voices that beckoned to her. "Come, wee one, do not grieve. We're here for ye. We'll keep ye safe. Come." Another spoke, more softly. "Sorrow goes, but the mountains remain. Come where the sound of the wind in the trees is as cool as the touch of a hand on your cheek. Come." She yearned toward the voices, toward silence in the midst of sound, peace in the midst of wind and rain. She reached out blindly and found nothing; her hands were full of mist.

She awoke to darkness that no light could break, to the beat of rain that drowned all sound, to the sweat on her skin no sun could dry. She longed to return to her dream, to disappear into the hills where she was certain peace awaited her.

The next day when the rain had stopped, the ground ran rivers of mud and the sun reigned brilliant in a clear blue sky, Genevra went to Phoebe's house. It was the only place where she was certain to find a moment of calm in the heart of the sunstorm.

The woman greeted her at the door, red-brown hair wound in a single braid twined with purple ribbon. "Ah, Genevra," Phoebe said with a strange look in her eyes. "I knew I need not send for you, that you would come on your own. The truth is so alluring, is it not? And yet so painful once it's known."

"What—" Genevra began.

Phoebe did not reply. "No shilly-shallying about. Straight to the garden today." Her tone was abrupt—not at all like Phoebe, who spent her life shilly-shallying about.

The first thing Genevra saw when they reached the garden was a peacock, magnificent tail feathers spread, strutting in the shade of an acacia tree.

"You'll never guess," Phoebe said with a roll of her eyes.

"Another gift from Hazari?"

"Indeed. Poor man. He was meant for a gentleman, but spoiled in the making, I'm afraid. I told him if he didn't stop, I would have to hire a zoo keeper and that I simply *could* not afford it."

Genevra smiled. "What did he say?"

With a dramatic sigh, Phoebe threw her arms out. "He pointed to the carved marble and tile and mosaics and merely looked at me as if to say, 'If you lie to me, Tamarsha Begum, you will lose my respect and then I will bring you no more presents.'" She paused, frowning. "Which is, of course, exactly what I had in mind, but once I thought about the loss of his grinning brown face, I began to feel rather depressed. Then I realized he wouldn't listen to me anyway. The moon, after all, does not heed the barking of wolves."

Phoebe became pensive as they went to the *baradari*, where Ameera brought them lemonade, figs, almonds, and oranges, which the monkeys came to beg for. The older woman glanced at Genevra. "It never stops, you know. I really should show them the door. Still, they are poor but honest, so I forgive them for begging."

The minah bird, seated on the back of an empty chair, croaked, "Forgive them again or show them the door. Poor but honest, begging but poor."

Phoebe scowled at him. "As for you, you should remember that a poet is born not made."

Genevra laughed but Phoebe fell silent, folded her hands in her lap, and contemplated the rushing waters. "I have something to tell you."

"Yes?" Genevra felt the same chill that had touched her in the wind the night before.

Phoebe took her hand. "About your mother."

Genevra refused to understand her friend's grim expression. "She's been found?"

"I know where she is, yes. I've been looking all along, as it happens, but kept it a secret. Least said, soonest mended, you know. Now I've located her at last."

"You did that for me?"

"But of course. I'd do anything for you. You know that." Phoebe's normally vibrant eyes were dimmed by a gray, formless shadow. "I'm afraid Emily is dead."

For a moment, the girl felt deeply cold—as though her body had been turned to marble and her heart to ice. "Dead?" The word was dry and unfamiliar on her tongue.

Phoebe nodded. "She breathed her last on the twenty-eighth of June, the day the monsoons began." She touched Genevra's cheek. "Remember what your beloved Indians say: 'Temporal blessings pass like a dream, beauty fades like a flower, the longest life disappears like a flash. Our existence may be likened to the bubble that forms on the surface of the water.' "

Genevra turned to stare at the waterfalls that leaped and splashed and glittered in the sunlight. She would like to think of Emily fading into the water like a bubble—rainbow-colored, fragile, beautiful, and fleeting. But instinct told her that was not how it had been. "Where is she? I must go to her."

"Genny, she's dead."

"But I must go just the same, to put flowers on her grave. To see that she was real."

With a sigh, Phoebe frowned. "This should tell you she was real." She took from her pocket a necklace woven of white and yellow gold. "Your mother told the matron it was a gift from a man of gold. She wanted you to have it. You can touch this chain and hold it in your hand; you cannot deny that it exists. But where Emily Townsend has been you cannot ever go."

Genevra reached for the necklace, which was cold and lifeless, though exquisitely beautiful. She felt a strange hollowness inside, as if her grief for her mother were deep and painful, but formless, just as her love for the woman who abandoned her had been. "Why can't I go? Was it so awful?"

Phoebe nodded. "I've never lied to you before, nor will I now. I think you should know the truth, that you *need* to know. Do you want to hear it, no matter how disturbing?"

Running her fingers over the fine gold chain, Genevra considered. Could anything be worse than the things she had imagined over the years? "Yes."

"Your mother died in a native asylum for the insane. She found the place and chose it herself. No one forced her, no one advised her. She told the English nun who ran it that she felt it was where she belonged."

When the girl began to shake, Phoebe took the necklace and grasped her hands. "Emily was a woman in pain all her life. But she didn't have a disease a doctor could treat. All she had was the terror in her own mind. I don't think anyone understood that 'the wound that bleedeth inwardly is the most dangerous.' No one ever really knew her."

"I never did," Genevra murmured. "I wanted to, but I never got the chance."

"You have the chance now, if you've the courage to take it."

"I don't understand. You said she's dead."

"She's been dead to you for a long time. Ever since she

left you in Calcutta. Your father was more alive to you than she."

Genevra looked up in astonishment. "That's not true!"

"Isn't it?"

The girl felt a prickle on her neck and looked up to see Charles with his blue eyes and sad smile. Phoebe was right. Somehow, for a reason she could not explain, her father had always been with her, but her mother had disappeared completely. Genevra had looked for Emily, wondered about her, but the image of her mother's face had slowly faded. She felt like crying, but her eyes were achingly dry. "Then how can I know her now?"

"Because she kept a diary. I think she wrote there all the things she dared not say aloud. Perhaps it helped her. The matron said she seemed unafraid at the end, almost peaceful. I have the diary for you." She took it from the wicker table and handed it to Genevra. "As I said, it will take courage to read this little book. The truth can be very ugly, very painful."

"I know." The girl stared for a long time at the worn leather cover, the edges of the smudged and bent pages. This was all that was left of Emily Townsend. "Will this make me understand her?"

Her friend's expression was infinitely sad. "You know what the sages say: 'The meaning of a dream, the effects of clouds in autumn, and the heart of a woman are beyond anyone's understanding.' "

Genevra looked away. "Thank you for all you've done."

"Shed your tears, my dear," Phoebe murmured. "If you hold them inside, you'll only damage yourself. Weep for her."

"I can't. There's a cold, hard core inside me and the tears are frozen there." She touched the leather and felt a jolt like the ones she remembered from the erratic caress of her mother's fluttering hands. She closed her eyes and summoned the colors, but they would not come. All she saw was black, and behind it, dingy gray. She was afraid, suddenly, to open the book. She was not certain she had the courage Phoebe had spoken of. At last, slowly, she lifted the battered cover and read the verse from the *Bhagavadgita* her mother had copied onto the flyleaf.

> "It is desire, and it is anger, and arises
> from the state being known as passion.
> It devours much and is a great evil.
> That is the enemy.
>
> This enemy covers the world
> as smoke conceals fire,
> As dirt clouds a mirror,
> or a membrane envelops an embryo."

At the bottom of the page Emily had written, "This Edward told me and Charles taught me. It is true! It is true! It is true!"

7

Genevra sat motionless while the leaves of the *aswatta* swayed, casting thin shadows over the colored tile. The book weighed heavily in her hands.

"No doubt you'd like to be alone," Phoebe murmured. "Stay as long as you like. I'll see that no one disturbs you, unless of course—" She broke off in mid-sentence but her friend did not notice.

"She was mad," Genevra whispered.

It was not a question and Phoebe did not deny it.

"And I am just like her."

Phoebe was on her knees in an instant, holding Genevra's hands so tightly that they ached. "You are not 'just' like her. You share the magic of the images in her head, but not the terror. She had no way to express the things she saw; you have your painting. Haven't you learned yet to measure yourself by your own foot? It was her unreasonable fear that destroyed her, not her sensitivity, the colors and shadows that you see, too."

"I *am* afraid."

Phoebe shook her head. "It's not the same. Emily Townsend ruined her own life as well as her husband's. She almost ruined yours. But you—you create instead of destroying. You're a good, loyal friend with a too-soft heart. You're willing to give more than you take. Your paintings are wonderful, especially for one so young. You should be proud, my dear. Proud that Emily had the strength to let you go, and proud that you took that gift and made yourself into the woman you are."

Before Genevra could object, before she could open her mouth to speak, her friend was gone. She was alone. She smoothed the draped skirt of her lilac gown, then, with great care, as if each page were spun glass that might shatter at a touch, she began to read.

March 15, 1858

I am frightened of the shadows, the queer, reaching shadows that tug at my skirt. They come from the pit where darkness waits to close around me. Now that we are here in Calcutta where the heat beats at my temples and boredom stifles me, there are more shadows than ever. They breed like mosquitoes and like that tiny insect, suck slowly at my blood and my courage and my strength.

I don't dare tell Edward. He would only laugh. I need him to hold me, but he does not believe in darkness and so will not protect me. Sometimes when he's gone, I sit in the corner, covered in sweat, yearning for the light outside the window, but afraid to move toward it. I wish Edward would show me the way.

There were many similar entries, many cries for help that went unanswered. Even in the ninety-degree heat, Genevra shivered. She had always believed Charles Kittridge had caused her mother's madness, but Emily had not met him until 1859. That much the girl had learned from her aunt. All these years, Genevra had blamed him for the wild look in Emily's eyes, the blankness, the cold, transparent texture of her skin. It seemed she had been wrong. She flipped through the pages until she came to May of 1859.

May 1, 1859

The Golden Man will keep me safe. He says he loves me, so I know. Charles touches me with magic fingers, watches me with clear blue eyes and I am healed and whole again. He is strong and unafraid and will make a light in the darkness so I need not fear it ever again. When it's done, he'll hold my naked body next to his and I'll run my fingers through his fine, soft hair and all will be light and goodness and the shadows will not haunt me anymore.

Genevra took a deep breath. No wonder Emily had believed Charles Kittridge could do anything. She had made herself believe it in order to survive. But it had been too late for her, even then.

August 12, 1859

There will be a child, Charles's child, and I am afraid. Voices in my head tell me I have sinned, that I will pay, while the shadows grow in the black watching eyes of the Indian servants. The pit of darkness is near—too near. Charles could save me and our child, but he avoids me now. I don't understand and I'm more afraid than ever in my life. Edward is happy. He thinks the baby is his. But I know. I know too much. Someday he'll see the sin in my eyes and he'll spit on me and the blackness will engulf me.

Genevra wanted to close the book, to ease the ache in her chest that stopped her breath, the pity she felt for this woman who had closed herself alone into her own little world of terror. But something made the girl go on.

January 25, 1860

I knew it! My daughter was born today. This golden child with sad blue-gray eyes could only belong to the Golden Man. Only he could have made such a miracle. But I see the eyes watching me, the ears listening. I hear the whispers. The shadows know my sin, and the sunlight and the endless sky. I drink, but the water doesn't cool me. My sin burns like fire in my veins and I know Edward will find it there. I read a poem once called

"Sonnet to Genevra." It made me cry, so Genevra
is the name that I will give my daughter.

In the years that followed, Emily lived in terror that
Edward would discover her secret. Slowly, Genevra pieced
together the story. Emily could not believe her husband
loved the child, spoiled her, brought her presents. Then
Charles began to come to their bungalow in Calcutta and he
did know the truth. He sensed it as Edward could not.
Charles came to make Genevra laugh until Emily loved him
all over again. As her love deepened, so did her fear. Finally
the fear consumed her; she could see nothing else.

April [She no longer put the dates or years, as if
they had no meaning for her anymore].

He knows. I'm sure he knows. I see how he
looks at me, stares at me with hatred in his eyes
when he thinks that I don't see. He watches me,
judging, planning for the right time to punish me.
He is playing a game, a cruel, cruel game. Every
morning I wake up and wonder, Will it be today
that he lets the darkness take me? I can't bear the
waiting any longer. I'll tell him tonight that I know
and the sin won't burn in me anymore. The pit
can't be worse than this living hell. I used to hope
that Charles, my Golden Man, would come and
take me away. I know now that hope is but the
dream of those who wake.

I just went to look at Genevra—my child. The
child that Charles and I created. To me she is a
stranger. I looked for her soul but could not see it.
I *will* love her someday, I swear it, when she is as
strong as her father. When her hands are as gentle
and full of magic. When she can heal me, as he
promised to heal me, *then* I will love her, worship
her, cling to her. Because Charles let me go and I
have no one else.

Genevra flung the book aside and lay unmoving, cold as
stone, her face buried in a pillow. Charles Kittridge had

been the reason for Emily's destruction, but he had not destroyed her. That had been Emily's choice. The girl felt a prickle of skin on her neck and glanced up to see her father nearby, his eyes dark with misery. She looked away.

She had been right when she told her aunt that Emily needed her. Yet her mother had called her a stranger and left her behind. The dark, chilly emptiness that came before grief filled her head, her chest, her stomach. She curled her body into a ball and lay still, shivering. Then the murmur of *aswatta* leaves spoke softly while their shadows danced above her: "You cannot lie here forever. You cannot become stone or marble, which alone survive for years under the blazing Indian sun. Go heal yourself. Go." Her heart heavy with years of sorrow, she turned to gaze at the lush green garden.

The bougainvillea climbed the walls, altered the light through the marble filigree, the patterns of shadow lace that fell on the grass and the cool interiors of the pavilions. The heavy bushes spilled over paths that meandered through the garden, leading to shady rows of cypress and tamarind, fruit trees and mimosa. Compared to the bleakness of what she had just read, the beauty only made her grief more intense. *I will love her someday, I swear it.*

Genevra bent forward, listening for the wind, for the warmth of the sun that was the god of India, for the movement of dust against the blue sky, but it was the water that drew her—the music of falling waters that filled the courtyard with cool promise.

"May peace and peace and peace be everywhere," the *aswatta* leaves murmured.

Genevra rose, removed her stockings and shoes, and sat at the edge of a pool made from luminous blue tiles. The sun burned her eyes, the leaves above her shifted, changed, became the sacred water of the Ganges. All at once, she was back at Benares, standing on the riverbank to watch the people bathe and go away with a peaceful smile. The old bewildered pain and loneliness welled within her. She stared, hypnotized, at the pool, the movement of light on the undulating water, the caress of the water on the cool tile. The silver light on the crystal water, the water on the gleaming tile, the light, the water, the water, the light. Out of those images came the voice from Benares like the gentle movement of leaves overhead. *Your sorrow, once given to the river, will flow to the sea and mingle with the sorrows of others, until there is no more sorrow, but only the waves of the sea.*

She could not resist the call of that long-ago voice. She would slip into the pure, clear water and wash away the smell of Emily's terror, the stain of her sin. Quickly, Genevra removed her gown, tossed it aside, stood motionless at the edge of the pool. She saw the Brahmin's face clearly in her memory. She let him draw her forward until the water closed around her.

She sank through the waves of glimmering coolness, moved her arms slowly, drew herself along the bottom where mosaics of bright flowers had been set in stone by a craftsman long dead. She ran her hand over the stylized bits of gem and tile, absorbed the color, the pattern, the beauty that a strange hand had created. For an instant she laid her cheek on the mosaic, pressing so the design remained briefly on her skin.

When her lungs began to ache, she rose to the surface. She swayed with the lap of the water, let the motion carry her, but it was not enough. She wanted more. Carefully, she untied the ribbons of her chemise and drawers and let them drift away. Now, at last, she was unburdened. There was no past, no shadows or whispers—only the water, the coolness, the peace of soundlessness beneath the surface.

Genevra moved toward the far end where the water fell in shell-like patterns—the *chadars*, white shawls of water that glittered in the air, then disappeared into the pool. Supporting herself with one hand on the side, she let the water rush over her. It caressed her breasts, her thighs, the place where her slender legs met.

She closed her eyes as her body came awake and made her forget the emptiness within. Her skin tingled and a flush spread over her, through her, inside her, so it mingled with the colors in her mind. She had never known her arms could feel so heavy and sensuous, her legs so graceful, her blood so warm. She drank the clear water and cried into the sparkling cascade,

"The finest quality of the water we swallow
   rises up as life.

The finest quality of the light we swallow
   rises up as speech."

Yet there was something missing. Lips and hands to
caress her, legs and arms to intertwine with hers. Eyes so
blue they reflected the Indian sky, hair that was golden even
damp with sweat. Alex. She wanted him to hold her, to ease
the pain. Somehow, in that moment, she knew that it was
possible. The passions of her body, which had slept for so
long, had awakened at last. Then she remembered her mother's pitiful cry: *The Golden Man will keep me safe*.

Suddenly Genevra was cold. She swam from one end of
the pool to the other and back again, up and back, her hair
flowing behind her, caught between her lips, tangled on her
cheek. She stroked until her arms were too heavy to lift and
her body ached and her breath refused to come. Only then,
gasping, did she find her way to the side and cling there.

When she felt that her legs would support her, she drew
herself out of the pool and looked for her gown. She found
instead an Oriental robe draped over a bush of hollyhocks.
She slipped it on, wordlessly thanking Phoebe for her
thoughtfulness. Then she saw her gown laid over a chair,
beside it her chemise and drawers. How silent her friend
must have been, how blind Genevra herself, not to have
noticed.

"You're very lovely, you know."

She drew her robe tighter at the sound of that voice. It
was too enticing, too full of subtle music, and she wanted so
much to hear it—too much. For a long time she did not look
up, but stared at the tiles where the water dripped from her
body and lay in a pool at her feet.

Alex watched her, struggled to breathe around the pressure in his chest. Genevra's hair fell in twisted strands to
her waist, woven with water that caught the sunlight and
held it fast. Her eyes glowed with a look he had never seen
before, a strange mingling of pleasure and sorrow. The silk
robe clung, outlining her damp body, as slender and fragile

as he had suspected. To him she was beautiful, but so vulnerable that he feared she might crumble at his touch.

He saw, in that instant, what he had begun, dimly, to recognize before. There was no woman like Genevra. None who had eyes that turned to gray mist when her thoughts began to drift. None who saw in colors, who sensed the secrets in people's minds and gave them back as gifts in charcoal. Who understood wind and sun, earth and rain, knew the voice of the past and loved India because of it. No woman like Genevra, no woman *but* Genevra.

"Please," he said softly, "I didn't mean to intrude."

She looked up, blue eyes flecked with gray like a sky scattered with clouds full of rain, and smiled a smile so sad it made him ache. She glanced at the clothes folded carefully over the chairs, at her own bright blue silk robe. Her heart began to beat in warning. "You didn't—"

"No," he reassured her. "Phoebe did all of that and sent me here, too. She thought you might like a friend."

She nodded and without a word he drew her close and held her. Genevra looked up, her lips slightly parted. Alex closed his eyes, leaned down to kiss her. For a moment, their lips met and clung before she drew away.

There was danger here; she felt it in the urge to touch his body, to let him fill the emptiness inside her. But Emily's voice would not be silenced. *The shadows know my sin, and the sunlight and the endless sky. It burns inside me like fire in my veins.* "I won't be like my mother," Genevra said. She prayed that he would understand, that he would never know he stood in the shadow of another golden man with magic hands and lips and eyes to drown in.

Alex took a step back. "No," he said, "never."

"I won't do what she did, be the cause of so much pain."

He swallowed dryly, nodded. "I wouldn't want to hurt you that way."

His kindness touched something brittle inside her— brittle and ugly with twisted pain and grief. "Will you stay, just the same," she asked, "and hold me for a little while?"

He did not answer, only pulled her back into his arms. As she leaned her cheek on his shoulder, felt his hand in her hair, the tears held inside for eleven long years began to fall at last.

That night, when the rest of the Bishop house was dark, Genevra drew the lamp near her bed and closed herself inside the netting so the light made fine, woven shadows on the sheet. She had put the gold necklace away in her drawer; she could not bring herself to look at it. Now she was glad that Narain sat close by, silent, still, within reach if her friend should need her.

Something had happened today that had changed Genevra forever. It was not just the glimpse she had had inside her mother's disturbed mind, though the images she had seen would never leave her. She had also felt the first real yearnings of her woman's body and could not forget how gently Alex had held her, asking nothing in return. Somehow, while the water rushed and whispered around them, Alex had made his way into her heart. The thought brought a fear she had never known. To care so much for a shadow— surely that was madness and could only bring more sorrow.

Emily had known all about such sorrow; perhaps it was that which had killed her in the end. Genevra said a silent prayer, opened the diary, and turned to the last entry, which she had not read earlier.

> I have found my home at last. They call it an asylum, but it's no more so than the world outside these blessed doors. Blessed because they close me in and keep me safe, because the world cannot find me here, not the laughter or the whispers or the horrible glare of the Indian sun. I have nothing to fear anymore. All my worst terrors are here within these walls. The shadows, the darkness are with me always, day and night. This is the final punishment for my sin.
>
> But the shadows do not bother me. They don't look at me or judge me or whisper behind my back. They haven't time for me, sitting silent in the corner, gathering my colors around me like warm

blankets, for the shadows all have nightmares of their own to fear.

I have only one thing more to say to my daughter if she should ever read these words.

The wise in heart,
    mourn not for those that live, nor those
        that die.
Nor I, nor thou, nor any one of these
    ever was not, nor ever will not be,
Forever and ever afterwards.

A Brahmin read me that once from an ancient book and it gave me comfort. May it comfort you, too, Genevra. I can offer you nothing more.

Emily's daughter wept. Narain slid her arms around her friend and rocked her until the tears had stopped.

"What is it that draws this pain from you?" the Indian asked.

Genevra found to her surprise that she wanted to talk. "My mother died not long ago. In an asylum full of madmen. She said—" Her voice broke and she fought to steady it. "She said she had finally found her home."

Narain, who did not believe in the wild passion that had shaped Emily Townsend's life, looked puzzled. "I am sorry that it has hurt you so much."

She did not really understand, Genevra realized. "You must swear to tell no one else," she said in agitation. "You know how cruel they can be. You must swear on our friendship."

Narain raised her hand and Genevra pressed her white palm to it. "This I swear by Indra, God of Air and Wind, Devendra, Master of the Deities and Lord of the Sky, and by Surya, God of the Sun."

They sat unmoving while the netting settled and the shadows grew still. Genevra gazed at Narain, mesmerized by her dark eyes. In the English girl's mind, Narain glowed pure white—an absence of color that echoed her absence of turmoil and pain.

The Indian smiled a knowing smile and spoke softly:

> "A man is of firm judgment
>   when he has abandoned all inner desires
> And the self is content,
>   at peace with itself."

She drew out each word like a musical note. The sound of her voice filled the tiny world of the netted bed.

> "When unpleasant things do not perturb him,
>   nor pleasures beguile him,
> When longing, fear, and anger have left,
>   he is a sage of firm mind."

Was it true? Genevra wondered. To have no pain, no fear, no passion would be to find peace—the place in the mountains of her dreams. Yet even in the midst of her grief and shock, there was the memory of something splendid that made her understand why Emily had given herself to Charles. Genevra had felt it more than once: when she lost herself in a painting, when Alex had held her today, in the moment when she paused beneath the *chadars*, naked, and let the water take her.

As the punkah murmured soothingly above them, the two girls twined their fingers together.

"You're a good friend," Genevra said.

With her free hand, Narain touched the other girl's face. She explored the pale skin with her fingertips as if learning to know it for the first time. "I see your soul in your eyes, *larla*, your troubled, aching soul. You are not like the others. You alone are not a stranger."

They stared at each other, fingers locked, for a long time. So long that Genevra began to feel uneasy. There was something in Narain's touch, something strange and hungry that turned her dark skin warm. Then, with a sigh, Narain drew her hand away. Her bracelets and bangles jingled, breaking the spell of silence, of motionless communion that had held them in its grip.

527

"Good night, my friend," the Indian murmured in her musical voice. "May your dreams be of the mountains you long for, but may never reach."

Gracefully, she slipped from the bed and the thin woven curtains fell closed behind her.

8

August raged into September. The heavens roared with the fury of fire and rain and fierce, beating drums. But as the weeks passed, the sound faded, the light grew dim, and the rain grew less and less frequent. Still the water would not sink into the earth; everywhere on the roads, in *nullahs* and fields stood puddles and ponds where insects bred, then carried their diseases to the exiles—white and brown alike. The soft earth gave beneath the passing of many feet and the rivers overflowed their banks, swollen with the power the monsoons had given them.

In the gardens and on the plains, the grass was green and healthy; it swayed with breezes that no longer whirled like the wings of wild birds through the sky. Slowly, day by day, the standing water evaporated and the yearly danger of cholera passed. As September became October, the sun turned gentle golden, the nights cool, and the madness left the people. A pervading calm took its place.

Genevra saw Alex often, but they did not touch. She had begun to realize what the meeting of their hands, their lips would mean; what had once been a formless fear now had substance and reality. Yet her affection for him grew until it, too, was strong and bright and real. Night after night she dreamed of the cool mountains where soft voices called to offer her peace. She could not have both, she knew. One day soon she must choose.

Then came November and the day of Depavali, the Festival of Lights, to celebrate the passing of the rain, the appearance of the sun from behind its shroud of clouds. Narain awoke smiling, thinking of the festivities that night. She must purify herself, be without stain for the celebration of all celebrations. She rose, took a simple white cloth to wrap around her body, then picked up several copper vessels and brushes. With these in a basket on her head, she started for the river. The sun was not yet up, but she knew many Hindus would be there before her.

While the first pink light of dawn curled itself into the blue haze over the plains, she found an isolated spot in the river. She tossed the white cloth aside and walked naked into the chilly water. She welcomed the cold, which awakened her sleeping blood. In her hands she held a *chembu*—copper vessel—which she filled with water, then retreated to the silver-white sands. Shivering, her legs folded beneath her, she cleansed her teeth, rinsed out her mouth twelve times, and finally splashed water over her hands and feet to rub them clean.

She lifted her head when she felt the warmth of the sun on her hair, then rose once more to enter the river. She moved over the silty bottom, spread her arms above her head, and plunged into the water so it covered and caressed her. She surfaced, raised her arms, and submerged herself eleven times. Each time her head came up glimmering, the heat radiated over her face.

Twice more she left the river to rub herself—first with a paste of cow dung, *tulasi,* and earth, which she washed away, then with saffron. Finally she dipped herself three times in the water. She crouched on the bank to paint a red spot in the center of her forehead before she rose to face the sun proudly, now that she was pure, free, unstained. She stood, her eyes closed in silent communion with the sun god while the heat dried her brown naked skin.

Genevra opened her eyes and looked around the sparsely furnished bedroom. Through the netting, she saw that Narain had already gone. She felt the stirrings of excitement—silver and bright yellow—within her. Today was Depavali, the Festival of Lights.

Tossing the covers aside, she called for Jarita to bring warm water for her bath. She swung her legs over the bed, but the netting clung, holding her back. She pushed it away in annoyance, rose quickly, put on her wrapper and slippers, pinned up her hair, and started for the chilly little room where the bathtub was kept.

She stood, shivering, while Jarita emptied buckets of water until the tub was half-full. Genevra closed the door and latched it before removing her wrapper and nightrail. She slid into the tub, sighing with pleasure despite the lukewarm water covered already with a thin layer of dust. She took soap scented with lilac, turned it around and around in her hands until the lather spilled over into the water. Slowly, she massaged the soap into her skin, achingly aware of her tender breasts and thighs. Reluctantly, she rose, dripping soapsuds, to pick up the full bucket left by the tub. She raised it to her shoulder and spilled it over her body until the last trace of soap was gone. Then she reached for a huge linen towel, stepped from the tub, and rubbed herself dry, shaking free the damp tendrils of hair that had slipped from her combs.

When she felt clean and dry and warm, she threw her nightrail over her arm and slipped on a fresh white wrapper.

Narain got out her gold earrings—huge circles that nearly touched her shoulders—her bangles and bracelets and lapus beads. Then she picked her anklets of thin silver, brass, and copper. She knelt beside the chest where her clothes were folded away, chose her yellow sari and a yellow bodice with gold embroidery. She laid these out on her charpoy, then went to her mother's room and sat on the floor beside the pots of cream and perfume.

Carefully, she removed every tangle from her still-damp hair, using a twig she had picked up on the way home. When she had finished, and her hair swung free to her waist, she took oil scented with sandalwood to comb into the long, dark strands to make them more silky and shiny. Then, deftly, she parted her hair in the middle before rolling it again and again, until she created a thick knot behind her left ear. This she secured with a single comb. She would add the flowers later. She painted kohl heavy and dark around her eyes, making them deeper wells of endless stillness. After all else was done, she rubbed the scent of jasmine at the base of her throat, under her arms and breasts, across her shoulders. At last she smiled, satisfied.

◊ ◊ ◊

Genevra had only one fine dress of silk and lace, which she removed from her armoire and laid lovingly on the bed. Beside it she placed the full satin petticoat gathered at the back. She slipped on her thinnest chemise tied with satin ribbons, as well as a pair of fine lawn drawers, and sat at the small vanity table where her brush and combs were laid out. From a small rosewood box, she took her only cameo; she would put it on last, when her toilet was finished. Finally she released her hair from the combs and stared at it in dismay.

It fell about her shoulders in a tangle of fine blond curls that she knew would not stay confined for a whole day and night, no matter what she did. In desperation, she brushed it vigorously, swept it to one side, fastened it with combs, and let it fall free on the other side. She frowned into the large oval mirror. It would have to do.

Narain put on her bodice, enjoying the feel of silk against her cool skin. She fastened the hooks with nimble fingers before she put on the sari. She ran her hand over the yellow silk, turning in a graceful dance as she tucked the long, straight piece of fabric around her waist so it fell to her feet like a skirt. With a flick of her wrist, she wrapped the garment around her body and flung it over her shoulder. Then, lingeringly, she slipped the bracelets over her arms. Her feet bare, she put on the anklets, one on top of another, and shook each foot to hear herself jingle. As a last touch, she put the string of lapus beads around her neck. She was ready.

Genevra struggled with the ties of the petticoat, the ruffle in back that would not stay in place, the hooks that were always just beyond her reach. Other English girls had maids or ayahs to dress them, but Genevra believed a girl should be able to dress herself. She had refused both Radha and Narain's help over the years. She grinned in triumph when the petticoat was secure, then slipped the gown over her head, twisting and turning to fasten the hooks and ties. The gown was deep rose, a bright contrast to her usual gray or blue, but she wondered more than once if even such a flattering dress were worth all the trouble. She was out of breath by the time she finished; the gown was so thoroughly fixed on her body that she wondered if it would ever come off. She tossed aside her uncomfortable button-top boots and silk stockings, wearing instead the leather slippers Unrao had made for her. When she was dressed, she placed the cameo carefully in the center of the rows of lace and dabbed a little rosewater behind her ears. Finally, she was ready.

"No," Narain said, examining her friend with a shake of her head. "Tonight you must forget that you are English. You must be one of us. You shall wear the blue sari."

Genevra collapsed on the bed with a rustle of silk and a heartfelt sigh. No doubt Narain was right, but she would wear this for the rest of the day. Her aunt and uncle would surely lock her in her room if she appeared at breakfast in a sari. As Narain jingled from the room, Genevra rose. She meant to go to the dining room, but the sight of Radha and Uncle Gilbert in the hall stopped her.

The ayah motioned wildly with her arms while Gilbert crossed his and glared. Both were angry and neither tried to hide it, but more than that, she realized, they were afraid. The colors between them had changed. The icy blue had gone, and the silver. Now there was only vivid red and a pale ugly green.

"You look lovely this morning!" Aunt Helen exclaimed when she passed her niece in the doorway. "I don't know what's happened to change you. I only hope it continues."

By the time Helen was gone, Radha, too, had disappeared.

Breakfast was silent, as usual, though today Gilbert frowned into his eggs and beefsteak, twirling his white mustache until the ends were dangerously pointed. His wife watched him in distress. She shifted in her chair and asked far too often if her husband wanted more tea. He did not seem to hear her.

Genevra was preoccupied with the memory of the fear and anger that had flashed between her uncle and the ayah.

For the first time, she awoke from her grief for Emily, her uneasy dream of Alex, to realize that something was wrong in this house. It struck her that her uncle had been behaving strangely for weeks and Radha's eyes were always still, unreadable. Yet behind the cool blackness, there was a bright hot flare of accusation. The ayah no longer spoke of the mountains she loved, but only of warnings and betrayal. Genevra had been foolish. She had thought the warnings were Radha's attempt to protect her charge from hurt; she realized it was not so. Somehow the ayah herself was in danger.

Genevra raised her head to look out the window. Thank goodness the blinds were up to let in the sun and the sight of a blue sky scattered with clouds. She was relieved when she saw Hazari slip off the veranda with more stealth than usual. Abandoning her half-full plate, she said, "I'm not really hungry. I think I'll take a bit of fresh air."

Her uncle grunted, her aunt nodded, but neither really noticed their niece's departure. She hurried outside, pausing only to pick up her hat.

She found Hazari crouched beneath an orange tree, a cloth spread on his lap. He tried to fold it up when she approached, but she stopped him. "We have no secrets, Hazari, you and I. What have you got that is so precious you must bring it here to look at it?"

The *mali* grinned widely. "A present for Tamarsha Begum."

Genevra rolled her eyes. "Not another! She told you to stop, didn't she?"

"How can I, when the fumes in my heart rise to my head and tell me I must never give up? I would worship at her feet, give the clothes from my back to call her and her garden mine."

"So!" Genevra cried in triumph. "It's her garden you really covet. Perhaps you don't care for her at all."

Hazari gazed mournfully at the ground. "This is not so, I swear by Hanuman, the Monkey God. I would serve her in all ways. My belly burns with fire from thoughts of her. Only such a woman would have such a garden. Besides," he said, returning to the original subject without the slightest repen-

534

tance, "this time my gift is not an animal. It will not beg or drive my *larla* mad reciting poetry. It will not strut about like a king. This gift will only add to her beauty. I do not think I am touching the skies with my chin"—at Genevra's blank look, he considered, then corrected himself—" 'bragging,' I think the *feringhi* would call it, when I say she has never received another like it."

Genevra was decidedly curious. "What is it this time?" Oblivious of her fine skirts, she crouched to see what he cradled in his lap. She gasped at the sight of a necklace of gold set with emeralds and pearls. There was an intricate circlet of worked-gold filigree set with stones, then at least fifty pearls that hung from tiny gold fingers. It looked to be very old. "Where on earth did you get such a thing?" She felt a chill of apprehension that made her reluctant to touch the necklace.

The *mali* scratched his hook nose. "Hazari is very clever. He finds pearls and gold where others find only filth. It was in the shed where I store the dung for the garden."

"But it looks as if it's worth a fortune." She regarded him through narrowed eyes. If he were lying, if he had stolen it, he would be in a great deal of trouble, which she doubted even Tamarsha Begum would be able to get him out of.

"Hazari—" she began.

The *mali* grinned. "You worry your head with too many things and your mind will become a hopeless tangle that even your aunt the seamstress could never unwind." He looked down at the prize in his lap, smiled with delight, and rocked back and forth on his heels. "Have you never heard Tamarsha Begum say, 'Do not look at the teeth of a gift cow'?"

Genevra could not help smiling. "I don't think she would have phrased it quite that way. But that's not the point. Don't you understand that something of such value could bring danger?"

"This way, that way, what does it matter? When you hold a star from the sky in your hand, you are a fool not to enjoy it."

"You, who are so full of proverbs, should listen to one of your own," Genevra admonished the Indian. " 'It is easier to snatch a pearl from the jaws of a crocodile or to twist an angry serpent round one's head like a garland of flowers without incurring danger, than to make an ignorant and obstinate person change his mind.' "

With a crooked smile, Hazari shrugged. "But Genniji, it is true. How can I change what was written on my forehead?"

Genevra was glad to escape from the house that night. All day tension had hovered in the air like the moisture before a monsoon. Alex had come by briefly. He had been distracted and left after half an hour. Genevra had felt bereft, and angry that she should feel so. She knew that each desire that bound her to him was another thread in the many-colored fabric Emily had woven of her life. Now the pattern, the weave, the heartache were being repeated in her daughter. She tried to think of other things as Narain finished the sari around her shoulders and draped it over her head.

The Indian girl stood back to consider her friend, whose eyes were ringed in kohl, her wrists jingling with bracelets, glass beads around her throat. Her hair was hidden by the gold-patterned border of the sari. "You are almost as lovely as an Indian princess," Narain said in approval.

Genevra felt a prickle at the back of her neck and saw Charles watching in disapproval. Behind him now stood Alex, always Alex with his blue perceptive gaze.

"I said that you are lovely," Narain repeated.

Genevra looked away from the twin golden images and shook her head.

Narain frowned, took Genevra's arm, and led her to the mirror. "When I look in my glass, I see that my face is good to look upon, my features pleasing. You should see the same."

Genevra stared at her blue-gray eyes, made huge by the kohl Narain had skillfully applied, at her cheeks, flushed with excitement, her aristocratic nose and parted lips. Again she shook her head.

"You only choose to be blind," the Indian insisted.

"It's safer that way," Genevra whispered.

◇　◇　◇

536

While Helen and Gilbert sat in the drawing room, wrapped in their mutual silence, Narain, Radha, and Genevra slipped out the back door and down the steps of the veranda. They could hear the procession forming and hurried along in the twilight.

"Now," Radha said to Genevra, "you will see the gods and they will make you one of us." For the first time in weeks, the ayah smiled as the three women crossed Alipur Road. She knew the power of the *Rasa Lila*—the moonlight dance in honor of Krishna. She knew the power of music and firelight. These things would win Genevra back to her; the girl would not have the strength to resist.

People had already gathered by the hundreds, dressed in their finest; their cheap jewelry made a jangling music all its own. The Hindus fell silent when the sacred cows came, their necks hung with garlands of leaves twined with flowers. The animals were followed by the temple musicians, who plucked the stringed instruments—the sitar, the *bin*, the *rahab*—blew the thin, reedy song of the flute, and beat the noisy drums whose intoxicating rhythm rose from beneath their dexterous hands. *Kirtans*, *tabla*, and *tavil* were pounded by eager drummers while the temple nautch-girls shook the *khanjara*, or tambourine. The noise of lowing cattle, music, drums, the stamp of feet and the jingle of bracelets seemed to fill the night.

Behind the dancing girls came the Brahmins, carrying the idols from the temple. The bright painted faces of the gods glowed in the torchlight and the people bowed as they passed, then opened their arms toward the sky to welcome the return of the sun.

Last came women bearing wooden platters of food—plantain leaves laid out with every fruit and vegetable imaginable and one or two platters of fish. Genevra wondered where it had all come from. These people were so poor that often they had nothing to eat for days together.

When they passed the shrine where the margosa and the fig tree had been ritually married with full ceremony, Genevra paused, amazed that Hindus should endow even trees with soul and spirit and life. Her attention was caught by the nautch-girls, who had stopped to sway and twirl in

537

their rose-colored garments and long braided hair. The drums beat out a sensual rhythm and the women gyrated, turning their bodies suggestively.

At last the procession reached a huge field far down the river. The cows were sent to graze in the next pasture while the musicians settled themselves on the ground with the dancing girls before them. Each girl grasped a torch that she held above her head; each twirled the fire as if it were water, as if she had no fear of the flames.

When the Brahmins arranged the idols, the people fell silent. First came Brahma, the Creator, with his four heads and four hands, and his wife, Saraswati, the Goddess of Wisdom. Next was Vishnu, the Preserver, sitting on a lotus with Lakshmi, his consort, the Goddess of Good Fortune. Then there were a host of other gods—Ganesha with his elephant's head, Indra and Agni, Gods of Wind and Fire, Varuna and Surya, who were Sea and Sun. Two Brahmins placed Kali, the Avenger, at the base of a huge torch, where the bright light honored her. She was a frightening image with her many arms and weapons, the human head she carried in one hand, and the lion she rode upon, who devoured a man as she watched. Last of all, on a little hilltop, the holy men put Siva, the Destroyer, in his pose as Nataraja, Lord of the Dance. He was carved within a circle of flame, one foot raised in the rhythm of the dance, the other balanced on the dwarf of ignorance. He held a drum in one hand and a ball of flame in the other. The goddess Ganga and the moon were tangled in his hair and serpents curled about his body. To Genevra he looked more like a devil than a god.

The people raised their hands, palms pressed together, then fell down in worship, noses to the earth.

"We come to honor Earth, Water, and Fire, to sing our praises to Brahma, Vishnu, and Siva, Lord of the Dance!"

"*Namah Sivaya!*" the people cried in a single voice.

" 'On what is the wind woven, warp and woof?' " the Brahmins chanted.

" 'On the sky,' " the people answered.

They spoke in Hindi, but since Genevra was a child, Radha had taught her by translating, then repeating the ceremonial chants until the girl understood the sacred words. Genevra listened, breathless. Finally she was part of the magic.

" 'On what is the sun woven, warp and woof?' " the Twiceborn continued in their hypnotic voices.

" 'On the moon.' "

" 'On what is the moon woven, warp and woof?' "

" 'On the stars,' " came the resounding reply.

" 'On what are the stars woven, warp and woof?' " Each Brahmin, his sacred thread over his shoulder, stood in the torchlight, his face raised to the heavens.

" 'On the region of the gods.' "

" 'On what is the region of the gods woven, warp and woof?' "

The people raised their heads to stare into the fires in a circle around them, into the torches of yellow-orange flame. " 'On the region of light.' "

They laid their sacrifices before the idols—sacred *darbha* grass, food, wine, silver, and copper. The Brahmins stood tall, chanting in the voices of the gods themselves:

> "I am the rite, I am the sacrifice,
> the libation for the ancestors,
> and juice for the gods,
> The priest's verse and the sacrificial butter.
> I take the offering, I am the offering."

The people began to sing strange, incoherent words, grateful that their offerings had been accepted.

" 'May peace and peace and peace be everywhere!' " the Brahmins cried.

In reply, the Hindus closed their eyes and swayed, heads thrown back, hands weaving intricate shapes in the air. Narain had disappeared into the crowd long since, drawn by the pulse of the music, but Radha stayed by Genevra's side. "You must dance," she said. "Forget the rules that bind your heart and mind. Forget and let your soul soar above you into the light."

She twirled away and back again, held up her arms in silent invitation. Unable to ignore the intricate rhythm, the notes that wept and laughed, called softly, cried out in rage, Genevra responded. All around her, the music enfolded, enveloped, until no one was free from its spell. Genevra began to dance, turning easily in the unfamiliar comfort of the sari, swaying like the reeds in the wind by the river. Within her, she felt a change, a murmur of longing that became a cry of passion. She flung her arms out toward the fire-lit night. She leaped and spun, twirled and dipped, while the star-streaked sky swirled madly above her.

She began to gasp and fell onto the cool grass to rest for a moment, but her heart would not cease its furious pounding. She leaned back on her elbows to watch the other dancers, distorted by the light of the flames. She saw the rapture on their faces, the sense of celebration; yet there were other things besides. There was rage, stamped out in rhythm with the beat of the drums. There was madness in the black eyes that glowed like water and wind tossed in a storm. There was desire that burned in the sensual movements of bodies caught in the spell of the light and the music.

Genevra saw the platters of food stepped upon, broken, and with them, one after another of the idols were taken up, spun around, and sent earthward again to protect the mad ones who worshiped them through destruction. Some survived the fall, many did not. In the glare of the torches, Genevra could see gems in the eyes of some of the idols, detailed enamelwork, and ancient molded clay. These whirling dancers, come to celebrate the light after the rain, these people so poor that often they starved, were destroying all that they valued. They cared only for themselves, for their pleasure, for the meeting of their bodies. Many sank into the grass where they tumbled, half-naked, drunk with wine and the flicker of flame and song. Genevra heard the cry, "*Namah Sivaya!*" until it echoed in her head.

She shuddered when she realized how many people were making love—frantic love, grasping, panting love that had more violence in it than caring. She looked away, unable to bear the sight.

Then Narain came up beside her, eyes glowing, face flushed. "Is it not wonderful?" she asked. She swayed even as she spoke; her body could not stay still. She stamped, cried out, and her face, too, was full of rage and desire and the wish to destroy. She was possessed, as were they all, by the dark side of her nature that was hidden away all year and now came spilling out.

"Is it not the most wonderful night you have ever spent?" Narain did not see the horror in her friend's eyes. She saw only the light, the music, the feeling of sweat on her naked skin. *"Namah Sivaya!* 'May peace and peace and peace be everywhere!' "

This was not peace; this was some kind of hell. Genevra felt she had stepped into the heart of Emily's nightmare, where people danced at the edge of the pit and dared the darkness to take them. The girl stumbled past Narain, who barely noticed, so mesmerized was she by her own passionate frenzy, and tried to find her way out of the circle of fires and torches and spinning bodies.

With a sigh of relief, she saw Radha kneeling alone outside the circle. As Genevra approached, she heard a strange low keening coming from the ayah's throat. Her face was lit with a weird orange glow; her eyes glittered and her lips were parted in a kind of prayer. She seemed to be praying to the vessel in her hands.

Genevra understood why when she saw the perfectly round white jade with a molded spout and rim of green jade. It was latticed by gold set with emeralds, rubies, and sapphires. The vessel was exquisite. Radha held it close to her breast, cherished it as if it were a child. Genevra spoke to the ayah, but Radha did not respond. She rocked, clasped the vessel, and cried a single high-pitched plea that had no meaning.

Genevra might as well have been a shadow given substance by the movement of the light. When a man grasped her arm to pull her toward him, so she smelled his wine-soaked breath, she screamed, broke away, and ran. She did not care where she went, so long as it was far from the light of the fires that seemed to burn in a single, all-consuming flame—searing, incandescent, inescapable. It seeped into the blood of the revelers, fell from their foreheads in glistening drops of sweat, shone in the feverish gleam of their eyes. They could not free themselves from the heat of the blaze, nor did they wish to. The fire was their god; it was everything and nothing—coiled violence and beauty, hunger and passion, power and rage, the obliteration of darkness and darkness itself. It was the false sun they had created, and in creating it, they believed that for a single night, they had made themselves into gods.

9

Genevra ran but the madness followed in the weird, pulsating music, the hollow chants of the Hindus, the distorted shadows cast by the flames. The scent of sandalwood and crushed jasmine clung in her nostrils, confused her thoughts as thoroughly as potent wine. The darkness closed around her, swirled with the memory of undulating bodies, the dust that rose in choking waves from beneath the dancers' feet, the blank look of rapture in their eyes—the chaos, the passion, the confusion of color and shadow, light and darkness that was India.

She ran instinctively, south toward the river, where the lap of the water on the shore drew her forward. She stumbled more than once, but did not stop. Some instinct deeper than sight or sound guided her, for her ears and eyes were deaf and blind.

Lights rose before her out of the night. She moved toward them with relief, running through dark alleys and serpentine streets until a glow in a window brought her up short. She stared, breathing raggedly, hypnotized by that single yellow flame as she had not been by the blazing fires. With a gasp, she doubled over; she could not force the breath through her body. But eventually, while the lamp in the window flickered and flared, the sounds of the festival faded and she began to breathe again, to recognize the things around her.

She saw a walkway flanked by frangipani, a low, yellow bungalow with bougainvillea climbing over the veranda, a row of windows with the blinds lowered. Behind those blinds burned the beckoning lamp. She knew this place. It was Alex's bungalow.

Genevra bit her lip. What had brought her here? Why did the light in the window call so she could not resist its summons? Perhaps it was the sudden silence, the cessation of sound and color and chaos. Or was it something else? Something more dangerous altogether?

She hovered uncertainly at the end of the walk. The whispers rose in the darkness, warning her away, but her heartbeat increased in contradiction—a voice of its own, a power beyond memory. She moved forward slowly to knock at the door.

When she heard the latch click, she thought of turning back. Then Alex appeared and she could not move.

"Genevra!" he cried in astonishment. For a moment he was assaulted by a confusion of feelings that left him speechless—stunned surprise at finding her on his doorstep dressed like a native, the constriction in his throat at her beauty in the Indian sari, concern at her pale skin, alarm at the strange glow of Hindu fires that still burned in her eyes. Alex saw how her hands shook, took a deep breath, and collected his thoughts. "Come in," he said softly. He drew her into the hall without hesitation or thought of propriety.

Genevra opened her mouth but no words came. He shook his head as he took her hands. There was no need to speak. Not yet.

They stood for a long time in the friendly darkness of the hall. Warmth and strength flowed from Alex's hands into hers so that her trembling ceased. She felt his calmness and absorbed it. Odd, she thought, when her mind had cleared. Usually his touch brought turmoil, uncertainty, but now he brought her peace.

Still without a word, Alex led her to the light in the drawing room. Genevra looked up, full of curiosity, to see that he had not changed after all. Though he wore no formal coat or epaulets or braid or gloves, his blond hair was the same and the look in his blue eyes. His English face, the cheeks burned red by the Indian sun, was familiar, not distorted by fire or madness or uncontrolled desire.

"Where have you been?" he asked in a whisper. He did not mention the sari, nor did she sense his disapproval.

As her own panic eased, she began to recognize his

nervousness. "At the Festival of Lights. I wanted to see it, just once." She looked away. "Once was enough."

Alex tightened his grasp until her hands ached. "You're all right? No one hurt you? You looked so frightened."

"I'm not hurt." Genevra pulled herself free and turned to stare at the tightly closed blind. "It was just so—it seemed that everyone went mad. Even the people I knew became strangers with wild, staring eyes. I had to get away."

He turned her to face him. "I'm glad you came to me."

She knew he meant it, but there was something else on his mind as well. She remembered that he had behaved oddly today; even now he was not quite himself. "Something's wrong," she said. "Tell me."

Shaking his head, Alex ran a fingertip over her cheek. "You've just escaped from one danger. You need not run headfirst into another."

Before she could reply, she heard a moan from the other room. Genevra frowned. "Someone's in pain."

He wanted to deny it but knew it was useless. She would find out eventually anyway. Still, when she turned in the direction of the groaning voice, Alex reached out to stop her.

Genevra shook off his hand and found her way to the bedroom. It was dim, lit by a single lamp turned low; even so, she noticed how sparsely furnished it was. There was a wicker chair, a chest, a night table, and the bed, hung with the inevitable mosquito netting.

"Watch out! the *bhootams* are coming. They will tear out your heart if you let them."

"Hazari!" Genevra exclaimed. "Is that you?"

"Hazari thought it was only a garuda bearing prey, but no, it was a flock of hungry vultures." His words were slurred and his eyes glazed with pain.

"You've been hurt." Genevra moved closer, though Alex grasped her arm tightly.

"You shouldn't look."

"What happened?" she asked, ignoring the warning. She picked up the lamp and held it over the *mali,* whose dark skin was covered with sweat, though the night was chilly. His chest was wrapped awkwardly in bandages soaked in blood.

"He was shot," Alex said. "I did manage to get the bullet out."

Genevra jumped at the sound of his voice. With an effort, she regained her composure. "I'm afraid for an army man you don't know much about patching wounds." She had many questions, but she would ask them later. Just now, Hazari needed help. "If you'll get me a few things, I can make him more comfortable." Carefully, she opened the bandage and examined the wound just below Hazari's shoulder. The flesh was red and swollen and he had obviously lost a great deal of blood. Genevra's heartbeat slowed to a labored throb. She leaned on the edge of the bed and tried to steady her breathing.

She felt Alex's hand on her shoulder and was grateful. "I need some kerosene in a big bowl, lots of cool water, and as many clean rags as you can find." Her voice shook when she looked at Hazari's face, pale and gray-tinged against the pillow. She had never seen him when he was not animated— smiling or grimacing or winking slyly. All at once she was afraid. "Hurry!" she cried to Alex, who had not moved.

"What do you know about bullet wounds?" he asked, too stunned to do as she asked.

"Radha taught me many things," she replied. "Now go. And bring some whiskey."

While he was gone, she used part of the sheet to wipe Hazari's forehead. The man opened his eyes, stared at her blankly for a moment, then rasped through dry lips, "You were right, Genniji. He who practices somersaults over spikes or thorns is bound to slip someday."

"Hush," she said. "You need to rest, not talk."

When Alex returned, she gave the *mali* a drink of water, then a large tumbler of whiskey. "For the pain," she explained at his perplexed expression. He had been trying to steal whiskey from the pantry at the Bishop bungalow for years, but she had always stopped him.

Genevra removed the rest of the blood-soaked bandages and gave them to Alex.

"It's not good, is it?" he whispered.

She shook her head without looking up. When she placed a cool cloth on Hazari's burning forehead, he grabbed her arm. "I hear what the *feringhi* says. I understand. If I am lucky, I will go to paradise by means of a thread, yes?" He tried to smile, but only managed a scowl.

"Yes," Genevra replied, "if there is a thread that strong in all the world." Somehow she kept her voice calm. She bathed the wound first with water, then with kerosene to stop the bleeding. Hazari gritted his teeth and clutched the sheet with fingers gone white at the knuckles.

"Ha!" the *mali* grunted while she padded the wound with rags. "I have poked my nose into one too many holes, it seems."

Frightened as she was, Genevra smiled. "I think you'd better lie still and be quiet." Gently, she began to fix the new bandage in place, motioning for Alex to help her lift Hazari so she could wrap the cloth around his shoulder and under his arm. When she was finished, she turned, a bowl in one hand. "What happened? Do you know?"

"Him?" the *mali* scoffed. "A damned *feringhi*? 'He knows nothing except the road to the market.' " But he spoke with affection. "I went looking for treasure, that is all, and found a nest of serpents instead."

"Treasure like the necklace you showed me this morning?"

The Indian nodded reluctantly. "Someone did not want me to look and so shot me." Even in his pain and fever, he sounded more offended than frightened.

For some reason, Genevra remembered Radha cradling a jade vessel set with gems. That she should see two such objects in one day seemed unlikely. "Who shot you?" she demanded.

"Do I know? The coward came up behind me and—" He broke off with a groan.

"Forgive me," Genevra murmured. She dipped the rag from his forehead in fresh water and replaced it before offering him another drink of whiskey, which he swallowed with difficulty. "You should try to sleep." She did not like the shadows in his hollow cheeks or the way his skin grew hot, then cold. She closed her eyes and said a silent prayer.

Hazari nodded. " 'Better to remain sleeping than to run after mountains,' as the sages will tell you."

Genevra changed the cloth on his forehead—it was already warm from the heat of his skin—then motioned to Alex that they should leave the room.

"Do not worry for this *badmash,* this rascal," Hazari croaked after them. "It does not matter if the dawn comes or the night goes on forever. The *Upanishads* say:

> " 'A man is never born
> He never dies.
> You cannot say of him,
> He came to be
> And will be no more.
> Primeval, he is
> Unborn,
> Changeless,
> Everlasting.
> The body will be slain,
> But he will not.' "

Quietly, Alex and Genevra collected bowls, rags, and bandages as they prepared to leave.

"I know what you say to yourself, Genniji," the *mali* called with one last burst of breath. "Even when Hazari is dying, he chatters like fried rice in the pan. So it has always been. I am afraid that charcoal cannot be washed white."

They had paused in the doorway to listen. When he fell silent, gasping, Genevra went back, set her bowl on the table, and took his hand. Hazari motioned for her to lean closer. "You have heard, have you not, the wisdom of the Hindus who say, 'If there is much sound, there is little pain'?"

"Yes."

"Do not believe it, *Asparaji*. Those wise men are fools." Then his grip on her hand grew slack as he slipped into unconsciousness. Genevra swallowed dryly; she wanted so much to see Hazari's whimsical smile and hear him call himself clever once more. She turned and picked up the bowl to find Alex staring at her oddly.

"You didn't even flinch when you saw that wound. Yet when you came here, you were terrified."

She was too weary to lie. "I'm afraid of shadows, voices in the darkness, confusion and madness, but not of blood or death."

"Not even of death?" he repeated in disbelief.

Genevra followed him from the room. "There is peace in death," she said wistfully.

They went to the kitchen where, for a while, they were too busy to speak. Alex collected all the bloody rags while Genevra used the pump to rinse out the bowls and wash her hands.

"I'll have these burned tomorrow," he said.

"They burn everything in India," Genevra observed tonelessly. "Or else the jackals come, and the pariah dogs and, worst of all, the vultures."

Alex crossed the room to take her in his arms. She trembled and her skin was cold. "He may pull through, you know. I've seen men with worse wounds persevere."

Genevra nodded without understanding. There had been too much to feel tonight, too much to fear. Confusion filled her head in a burst of sound like the deafening monsoons. "If only the cacophony would end and leave me silence!" she cried.

Startled by her vehemence, Alex asked, "You want peace that much?"

She struggled to find words to describe the turmoil she had lived with all her life, but there *were* no words. "If ever I could know one moment of peace, one single moment, I would treasure it, try to make it last forever."

She spoke so fervently that he could not help but believe her. For the first time, he began to understand fully the storm inside her, the scars her suffering had caused. He drew her close so her head rested on his shoulder. "You mean you would choose nothingness?"

" 'A lamp in a windless place still has a flame.' "

He shook his head, uncomprehending. "Peace without passion would be like silence—pleasing for a moment, calming, but in the end it would drive one mad."

"What do you know of madness?" she demanded.

"I know that you are not your mother and never will be. Believe it, Genevra. Let go of her nightmare."

549

She felt a chill and saw a flash of Charles Kittridge's face, but it was gone before she could discern his expression.

"Do you believe it?"

She gazed up at Alex in the flickering light. "I believe *you*," she said.

The look in her eyes made him hurt inside. "Let's sit in the drawing room." Just now they were surrounded by the evidence of violence and he wanted to take her away.

"You go," Genevra said. "I want to look in on Hazari."

Alex nodded. He understood that she needed some time alone.

Genevra stood at the bedside, wrung out the damp cloth again, and placed it on the *mali*'s head. "My friend," she whispered, "I am with you." Then, with an unsteady breath, she went to join Alex in the drawing room.

"Now," she said, "what happened to him?"

Alex regarded her intently. "Are you sure you want to know?"

"I have to."

As always, he seemed to understand. "I'm not entirely sure. I assume whoever shot him must have wanted the necklace, since it wasn't there when I arrived."

For the second time, an image of Radha with the priceless vessel rose in Genevra's mind. But the ayah had been at the festival tonight. She could not have attacked Hazari. "You don't know who it was?"

Alex glanced away uneasily. "No."

"But you can guess, can't you?"

He would not meet her eyes. "I have suspicions, but it wouldn't be fair to voice them just yet. Not until I can prove what I say."

"Then tell me this," she said. "How is it that Hazari came to be here?"

"I was out walking and happened to find him lying wounded. Naturally, I brought him back to tend to him."

"You were walking so far away in the middle of the night?"

"I've been restless of late. Can't sleep, all that sort of thing. So I walk."

550

Suddenly she understood, at least part of it. "And watch."

He hesitated, then sighed heavily. It was time to tell her the truth. "Yes, I watch. I was sent here to find someone."

"Who?"

"Someone who's been smuggling ancient artifacts out of Delhi, then selling them overseas to private collectors for their own profit. No matter what you think of the British, they don't approve of such activities. I'm working with Colonel Maclean to find whoever's responsible and stop him."

Genevra knew there was something she should ask, something he did not wish to tell her, but she couldn't think clearly. Instead she murmured, "You don't mind having a native in your bed?"

He rose and began to pace the floor. "I'm fully aware that there are Englishmen who would shoot themselves rather than allow such a thing, but I'm not one of them. You should know that by now. The man needed me. I did all I could to help him. It's as simple as that."

It was not at all simple, Genevra thought. With each passing moment she admired Alex more and the tumult of emotions inside her increased. He was so like her father. Could he also be so different? She wanted fiercely to believe in Alex, but then, Emily had wanted fiercely to believe in Charles. "We should stay by Hazari," she said at last. "He should not be alone."

For hours they sat in chairs beside the bed, replacing the water when it grew warm, cooling Hazari's overheated body as best they could. When the wound began to bleed again, Genevra reapplied kerosene, then put on a clean bandage. All the while, the *mali* tossed and turned, muttering incoherent phrases, forming meaningless patterns in the air with his hands.

At one point, Genevra thought Alex had dozed off. She began to chant the Hindu prayer she knew best.

> "Lead me from the unreal to the real!
> Lead me from the darkness to the light!
> Lead me from death to immortality!"

She repeated it softly, again and again, let the rhythm overtake the meaning, praying with her mind and soul and body.

Alex heard a murmur in his dream that he could not understand and fought his way toward the distant light. When he opened his eyes, he saw Genevra bent forward, speaking in Hindu.

"What—" he began.

She raised a hand and he fell silent. "I'm giving him the only gift I can—'of speech, the one supreme, subtle sound of sacrifice—the offering of whispered chants.' "

The top of her sari had fallen away and her hair had slipped free of its pins. In the light of the single lamp, with her eyes on her friend, her lips moving in sound almost without sound, she was so lovely that Alex had to look away.

Genevra touched Hazari's forehead. "Alex!" she cried. "His temperature is lower and his breathing seems easier."

Alex leaned closer. To his surprise, he saw that the color was creeping back into Hazari's cheeks. "I believe you're right." He turned. "It's all because of you, you know."

She smiled for the first time, then fell forward into his arms.

Alex sat on the sofa in the drawing room, Genevra's head in his lap while she slept. He felt a rush of tenderness at the pale curve of her cheek, the whiteness of her hand against the deep blue of her sari. She had seemed so strong, so self-assured as she bound Hazari's ugly wound. Yet now, asleep, she looked as vulnerable as the candle flame that wavered with the rhythm of his breathing.

Genevra dreamed of the cool green mountains and the wind on the water. As always, the voices called her to safety and warmth and peace; the sound was irresistible. She started toward the hidden voices, but the sun came out from behind a tree, so bright it made her blind. She ignored the call of the voices and welcomed the sun's heat, gave herself up gladly to the orange-gold flame she knew would consume her in the end.

She opened her eyes to the sight of Alex's face made golden by the lamplight. Panic nearly overcame her, despite the reassuring warmth of his arms. She should not be here alone with him, bewitched by the look in his eyes, his parted lips, the slow, hypnotic beat of his heart. Her mind, her memory, and her mother's troubled voice told her to get away, but her arms and legs were heavy with the weight of her dream and would not obey.

" 'Wonder grew,' " he whispered,

" 'in the darkness—as the moon among the stars
Grows from a ring of silver to a round
In the month's waxing days.' "

Genevra shivered at the sound of his voice in the hushed, waiting stillness.

"You're so beautiful," he said as he lowered his head to kiss her. Against her will, she rose to meet him. Their mouths met and clung, though her heart beat out a ragged warning. Deliberately, seductively, Alex circled her lips with the tip of his tongue. When he drew back, she reached up, trembling, to touch the mustache that curled above his mouth. With her fingertips, she explored his face—his forehead, nose, and sunburned cheeks. How could she turn away when she wanted him so much?

Genevra felt his arms close around her; when he touched her breast through the thin silk fabric, she gasped and silenced the droning voices in her head. Tentatively, she pressed closer, seeking the fire and passion that had only begun to grow inside her. Alex kissed her again, on the forehead, the cheek, the tip of her ear. Her heart pounded erratically as he reached beneath the sari to caress her shoulder, then, gently, her naked breast.

When she sighed with pleasure, Alex felt his control slip away. Fiercely, he drew her to him, sliding his hands around to her soft, white back.

She reached out to unbutton his tunic and run her hand over the blond hairs on his chest. How soft they were, how like finely woven silk that caught at her fingers and held

553

them as surely as his arms held her body. She touched her mouth to his.

Her uncertainty, the look of wonder in her eyes, the yearning she could no longer hide made her more alluring to him than any woman he had touched before. He groaned, stretched out, and pulled her closer.

Genevra could feel the tension of his body, see the hunger in his eyes. She shivered, afraid of the whirling colors, the heat like the sun in her veins. Yet when he cupped her breasts with both hands, the sensitive nipples tightened in his palms.

She moaned, but whether in delight or denial he could not tell. He moved one hand downward to where the silk wound at her waist stopped his searching fingers. Alex paused, then drew his hand over the blue fabric, so cold and gleaming compared to Genevra's warm, bare skin. He kissed her, cradling her head with one hand, while with the other he explored the curves of her thighs beneath the silk. Slowly, tenderly, he rested his fingers over the V where her legs met. He could feel her warmth, even through the sari; he shuddered at the need that sliced like shards of hot, bright diamonds through his body.

Genevra began to shake and could not stop. She wanted—something she did not understand. Something to ease the ache of longing, the fire of the sun that shimmered in her head. Only Alex could do it with his gentle hands and his body, tensed now and waiting for her acquiescence. But the Hindu fires still burned in her memory, the panting madness of intertwined brown bodies, the desire that they had turned to rage. She opened her eyes where her fear glowed in silver flecks that absorbed the blue, concealed it.

Alex looked into those eyes and knew. He moved his hand away and fought to catch his breath. "You don't want this," he panted as the fragments scattered and fell, leaving scars in his blood like the white trails of stars.

Genevra felt a wrenching inside, a tearing away of all that was vibrant and alive, but she knew he was right. "I want it," she whispered, "but I can't."

Alex nodded while he struggled for control. His heart,

his body, his blood told him he dared not let her go, that his need was greater than her fear. He knew that with a single touch he could banish her apprehension and make her body his. But he wanted more than her body. When he could bear to, when the pain and frustration had eased enough, he caressed the tangled hair around her face.

Tears came to her eyes and the beat of her heart was a silent agony. She wanted to weep wildly for her mother, who had never known joy, as Genevra herself might never know it, because she hadn't the strength to take the risk. Not when Emily Townsend had taken it and lost, become part of that rage and madness, the nightmare that her daughter had seen tonight.

Genevra started away, but Alex followed.

"I want you to marry me," he said.

She stopped where she was, unable to take another step. Without turning to look at him, she said, "That won't change anything. It won't change me."

"Don't you understand yet? I don't want to change you. I love you as you are—just exactly as you are. I love you, Genevra."

"Don't," she implored him. "I've told you before—"

"I know what you told me." He took a deep breath, his gaze fixed on the unbending line of her back. "But things are different now."

She turned then, finally, to meet his eyes. "How?"

Alex Kendall had taken many risks in his life. He decided to take one more, and this the biggest one of all. "Because I think you love me, too."

Genevra wanted to cry out that he was wrong, that she would never love anyone again, but she could not speak.

Her silence hurt Alex deeply. "Say it," he murmured at last. "Tell me that you love me."

There was a plea in his eyes that broke her slow-beating heart. "I can't," she said. "I can't." She clenched her fists, dug her fingernails into her skin, feeling hollow inside.

Alex sighed, his mouth set in a rigid line. "You're lucky, Genevra. You can express your feelings on canvas, make swathes and swirls of the brilliant colors and desires that flare inside you. I have no way to express those things except through my hands and my body and my lips. I wish it were otherwise. I wish I could share your ability to create beauty in paint, but I can't. I can only see it through your eyes and feel it through your pulse and your skin and the beat of your heart." He paused, then added tiredly, "How long before you put the past behind you, admit that you are well and whole, that your mother is only a shadow you cling to for protection, that you have as much passion inside you as I have? How long before you see that your painting is only a reflection of that passion?"

"I don't know," she rasped. "I just don't know." This time, when she moved toward the bedroom, Alex did not follow.

Hazari was awake, his face strained and pale, but his wound was less swollen and the fever had abated. "You'll be all right," she reassured him.

"*I* will," he said with difficulty, "but will you?"

"I don't understand."

"Hazari thinks perhaps you do. I speak of Captain Alex Kendall, the *feringhi* who does not have a soul of stone, who looks at you with tenderness in his eyes. He wants you, *Asparaji*, and for this you should praise the stars and the sun.

" 'The sea gathers the waters,
It fills and fills itself.'

"So will this man fill you with passion, with wonder, with many children. He knows, as I have always known, that you are one of the Sunborn, the most blessed of all races. How else would you have brought life to this empty shell of a worthless *mali*? How else would you paint such beautiful pictures unless you were touched with the golden light? Few are so touched. Do not deny what you are, what you were meant to be."

Genevra shook her head firmly.

"You did not listen when Radha told you: 'They that deny the Self, return after death to a godless birth, blind, enveloped in darkness,' " Hazari said. "I, who have seen the edge of that darkness, know it, and you who live always in a darkness full of whispers, know it, too."

He shifted, moaned, and closed his eyes. "Do not be like Rama, who lost his beloved Sita more than once because he had no faith in his heart. Believe for once, *Moti*. You have borne punishment long enough for a sin that is not your own. Believe and be happy. The time has come."

10

Alex asked Genevra to stay at his bungalow for the rest of the night, claiming it was dangerous for her to be out so late. He said he would sleep on a charpoy in the bedroom so he'd hear Hazari if the *mali* awoke. Genevra could have the drawing room all to herself. "I'll leave you in peace, I swear," he told her.

She did not understand why he was so adamant; she would be perfectly safe if he escorted her. With great reluctance, delaying as much as he could, he found a carriage and took her to the Bishop bungalow.

Alex walked her to the door. "Take great care," he said. His eyes shone with an intensity that alarmed her. "It's important. Will you at least promise me that?"

She winced at the bitterness in his tone. "Of course."

He left her and she stood in the dark hallway with her hand on the adobe until every imperfection was pressed into her palm. When she heard the rhythmic crunch of wheels on dirt, a deep sense of loss washed over her. This was not the gentle lap of the river on the shore, but the turbulent rush of the sea in a storm. Why, in God's name, had she let him go?

Her head throbbed dully as she became aware of the silence that had fallen on the house—a stillness so complete that each breath echoed upward. Yet this calm was not a pleasant one. Genevra shivered at a gust of wind and made her way to her empty room. She sat on the bed in the darkness with the memory of Alex's voice. *I love you as you are—just exactly as you are*. To be a wife, to have a man want her, to want him so much that she ached with it—these were things she had thought would never be. She had not been born to be happy; her aunt had drilled that into her head until Genevra believed it. Yet the Golden Man, the man of dream and shadow, had asked her to marry him. She rubbed her temples when the throb in her head grew worse.

How long, he had demanded, *before you put the past behind you and admit that you have as much passion inside you as I have?* Did he really want her, or had he spoken thoughtlessly in a moment of frustrated desire? She remembered Hazari's admonition. *Believe for once. Believe and be happy.* Did she dare? How could she when she knew so much?

Yet she knew nothing. Now that she was free of the spell of Alex's eyes, the questions she should have asked about the attack on Hazari came back to haunt her. Why hadn't she pressed him to tell her why he had walked so far from the cantonment? And if Alex had found the *mali* near this house, why hadn't he brought the man here to care for him? Why put him through the agony of going all the way back to the Red Fort?

Alex had said he suspected someone. Genevra sat up sharply when she remembered how he had examined her uncle's possessions, wondered how a man in Gilbert Bishop's position could afford them. And Radha had watched it all, cursing Alex with her eyes. Why? Genevra did not like the answers that came to mind. She tried to shut out the questions, the doubts that would not let her rest. *To choose to be blind is foolish,* Narain had murmured.

I love you, Genevra. She clung to the memory of those words as if they could save her from the disaster she felt moving closer in each cry of the wind over the dusty plains. She closed her eyes and saw Alex clearly. *I think you love me, too.* His voice whirled in her head, then Hazari's: *Do not deny what you are, what you were meant to be.* She heard Emily's plaintive warning: *It is desire and it arises from passion. That is the enemy,* and Radha's: *Beware of this man. Beware!* Alex again and Emily, Radha and Hazari, until Genevra's thoughts spun like a whirlpool sinking into sand. She had to get away from the sound of those voices before they drove her mad.

She found a small lantern and lit it, then crept through the house and out the back where she could breathe fresh air. But the voices were still with her. *Man has the Self as his only friend or as his only enemy.* She went further, toward the old servants' quarters. She thought even then that she had not escaped her memories until she realized the murmur of voices she heard now was real. They were low-pitched, conspiratorial, coming from the long, low building that had housed the Indian servants before the Mutiny.

She saw a tiny crack of light through a blind that had not been closed properly. Her stomach contracted with a sense of foreboding. Perhaps she should turn back. But she had to know.

She put out her lantern and went forward in the darkness. Her soft leather slippers made no sound as she moved closer, leaving damp imprints in the grass. The voices rose and fell, faded and crackled with fear and rage. At last she put her hand on the old, battered door and stood, her pulse so slow she thought it might cease altogether. Her hand shook as she reached for the latch and pushed the door open a crack.

Genevra stifled a gasp at the scene lit by the faint glow of a lantern. The interior was full of packing cases with a matting of woven grass thrown over them. Radha stood in the center of the room, holding the jade vessel. The light flashed off the gems in sparks of green and blue. Beside the ayah stood Gilbert Bishop with Hazari's necklace in his hands. A red haze hovered between the two that was more than anger or fear; it was blind terror.

Though Genevra wanted to deny it, she knew in her heart that these were the smugglers Alex had described. She wanted to get away, to absorb the shock in private, but her feet would not move. She was frozen with her hand on the door, her fingers numb. Not Radha, she cried silently, who taught me everything, who was always kind when the others were cruel. Not Radha, my friend, born of the cool mountains. But the ayah herself had said, *You cannot trust all who call themselves your friends.*

The dull pain in Genevra's head grew bright and hot. As she swayed, the door creaked on its ancient hinges. She heard a gasp, looked up, and saw Radha's eyes fixed on her. They were the eyes of a stranger, a woman obsessed. Uncle

Gilbert had turned away; he did not appear to have heard. For what seemed like forever, the two women stood unmoving, their gazes locked. "What will you do?" the ayah seemed to say. "Will you betray me, after all I've given you?"

Genevra blinked, paralyzed by the pain in her temples. She knew she had to get away before her uncle saw her, to escape from the shadows that reached threateningly outward. She released the door, her fingers stiff. It took all her strength of will to make herself look away from the woman who had been her friend, companion, mother. As she turned to run, the black gaze followed, luminous, cold, and hard as obsidian.

Genevra lay in bed, eyes open, curled inward upon herself. At least it had not been Radha who shot Hazari, she thought. The ayah had been at the festival. But that meant— She could not quite make herself believe that her uncle had done such a thing. Not he who was so blustery and ineffective. Yet what other answer was there?

None.

Why hadn't Alex told her the truth? Why hadn't he warned her? She was certain he had known. She shivered, colder than she'd ever been. She felt numb all over, afraid that, once she allowed herself to feel the pain, the wound would never heal.

Just before dawn, Narain slipped into Genevra's bed. "Do not grieve," the Indian whispered hypnotically. "There is much you do not understand. This thing you have discovered is not your worry, *larla*, not your grief or your burden. We will carry it. You sleep. Go to sleep and forget." All the time she spoke, she ran her fingers through Genevra's disheveled hair, touched her cheek, her eyelids, her silent lips.

"Do not hate her, Genniji. Do not be unforgiving. It does not matter in the end, you know. Remember, 'Life falls from Self as shadow falls from man.' What you saw tonight is only a shadow that will disappear with the light."

She held her friend closer, so that Genevra felt Narain's supple, dark body pressed to hers. She felt the rise and fall of the Indian's breath, the lyrical sound of her voice, the gentle touch of her fingers.

561

"Tomorrow we will tell you what you wish to know. Tomorrow in the sunlight. Treasure that sunlight that erases all shadow, believe in it. Listen to the ancients, who cried, 'Protector, seer, fountain of life, do not waste light; gather light.' " She fell silent for a moment, circling her fingers over Genevra's tense shoulders. "But now you must sleep. Sleep and tomorrow we will gather light together."

The dream was so real, so vivid, so necessary that Genevra knew she would never awaken. The rugged peaks rose, tall and breathtaking, the water murmured, and the wind swept past like comfortable old friends. The voices called, familiar, inviting. "Don't grieve for your loss. Ye've come home now, *mo-graidh*. Ye've found your peace." "Peace," the other voice added, "and beauty and comfort. This we will share with you. Come."

When she awoke, the voices were still with her, but the sun streamed through the window, painted patterns of netting on her arms and legs. When she realized where she was, the voices faded and disappeared. She rose, weary and aching, to dress in a plain dark gown. It was a gray day, she thought, despite the glow of the sun beyond her window. She paced the floor, unable to stay still, unable to silence the turmoil of emotions inside her. She prayed for the numbness to return, but it had slipped away in the night. The colors in her head had gone mad; they spun in a frenzy of red, black, and orange that blended one into the other until nothing remained clear.

She could not stay in her room forever, hiding from the truth as Emily had done all her life. She would have to face it—now.

When Genevra entered the dining room, her uncle and aunt fell silent. Gilbert stared down at his plate while Helen busied herself with the silver tea service. Genevra could understand her uncle's reticence, but why would her aunt not meet her eyes?

Then the bearer entered with a message for the sahib. He was followed by the *khidmutgar*. Neither looked at Genevra. They made wide circles around her and left the room as soon as possible. Her already heavy heart grew leaden and the red and black spun faster, made her pulse race. The whispers seemed to rise from the shadows to echo threateningly in her ears. Her uncle was a criminal, yet *she* was being treated like a *Sudra*, an Untouchable who would defile any who came too close.

She took a deep breath and faced her aunt. "What is it?" she demanded. "Why won't you look at me?"

Helen's hand shook and she spilled some drops of tea on the damask cloth. Quickly, she set the teapot down. Her cheeks pinched and pale, she stared at her plate. "It's unspeakable, that's why. Unspeakable and intolerable."

Genevra was more and more bewildered. She saw that her uncle shifted about, his face unusually flushed. "What do you mean?"

"I know. I've heard the rumors. This time you've pushed me beyond the limits of my patience."

The rumors again, the whispers. "Tell me what I've done."

Helen cleared her throat, shook out her napkin with a quivering hand, and murmured at last, "You and that Narain, that native, have—" She broke off, blushing furiously.

Genevra felt a presence behind her and saw that Narain had paused on the threshold.

The color drained from Helen's face. "That you have been—together." She pressed her hand to her chest and looked away. "I cannot bear it."

Genevra's heart stopped beating. "It's not true!" she cried. "Narain, tell them it's not true."

The Indian girl said nothing. When she lowered her head as if in shame, Genevra's blood turned cold. "It's not true," she repeated, but no one heard her. All they could hear were the hostile accusations. It was all they had ever heard, all they ever wished to hear.

"Well, after all," her uncle muttered, "what can you expect from a girl whose mother died in an Indian madhouse? All those vermin crawling over her and she crawling with them, crawling in the darkness with the other fools and lunatics."

The colors exploded in Genevra's head—the dark, ugly colors of horror and shock and searing pain. She thought she had felt the pangs of betrayal last night when she saw what Radha had done. But this was more than betrayal; there was no word by which to call it. She turned to look at Narain, whom she had trusted above all others, the only one to whom she had confessed her mother's secret. The girl stared at her with blank eyes, which said, as Radha had once said, *The only honesty of our days is to ruin those who cherish us.*

It came to Genevra then, as she sat speechless with disbelief, that what she saw in Narain's eyes was not peace, but emptiness. The girl had taken her own counsel and killed every emotion. No fear or love or joy, loyalty or regret remained inside her—nothing.

Genevra rose, stumbled past Narain, who had been her friend, and left the house. She ran instinctively toward the cantonment, to Alex's bungalow, where she leaned against the doorframe, gasping for breath. Dimly she heard him inside; he stomped about and cursed with violence. She started to turn away, but the door was wrenched open and she found she hadn't the strength to run.

Alex stood in the murky light of the hall, his face flushed, his hair in disarray. He stared at her as he would an apparition.

"You've heard what they're saying about me?"

He drew her inside and slammed the door. "Everyone in Delhi has heard."

"And you want me to go away so your name won't be sullied."

Alex gaped at her in disbelief, then disappointment. "Have you so little faith in me?"

"I don't understand."

"I don't believe the rumors. I know you too well, Genevra."

"But you saw the paintings." Only as she said it did she realize how damning those paintings must look.

"I saw an artist's renderings of her beautiful friend. I saw an appreciation for that beauty, a need to capture it on paper. That's all." He regarded her intently, saw that she had heard him but did not understand. "I believe in you. Is that really so difficult for you to accept?"

"No one's ever had faith in me before. How *can* I believe you?"

Alex swung away from her to hit the wall with his balled fist. "Damn those hypocritical sanctimonious prigs!" he shouted. "Damn them all to hell for what they've done to you." Then he turned, his eyes wild with fury. "But for God's sake, Genny, can't you see that they have nothing to do with me? I'm Alex, just myself, and I love you. No matter what they say or do, no matter what lies they tell or what truths, for that matter. *I love you!* Can't you get that through your head?"

She stared at him mutely. She saw his face, so like another image, his eyes, so clear and blue and free of lies. For the first time, she did not see Charles's shadow over his shoulder. Her heart began to beat again, slowly. "Even though—" she began.

"Even though you're stubborn and afraid, though you choose to remain blind when you need only open your eyes to see, though you won't admit what you feel and how deeply you feel it. Yes, I love you."

Genevra burst into tears. She did not remember that Alex moved, yet she was in his arms, weeping on his red coat. All the sorrow and passion and pain of the last two days came welling up from the darkness inside; she could not stop it. She wept for a long time, and when she had done, the hollowness inside her had begun to fill, the blackness to dim a little.

At last she looked up, her eyes more gray than blue. Alex cupped her face in his hands, but a knock at the door made him release her. "Forgive me," he said, "but this can't wait. Are you all right now?"

She nodded, noticing for the first time that he wore full-dress uniform, as he had the day she met him. When he opened the door, she saw a group of soldiers outside. One stood on the threshold, saluting. "Private Ross of the Ninety-second Gordon's, sir. Colonel Maclean's waiting, sir."

Alex frowned. "I'll be with you in half a moment." He closed the door and turned back to Genevra. With a sigh, he took her hands. "The last thing you need is more bad news,

565

I know. But there's something I have to tell you about your uncle and the ayah, Radha—'' His voice was full of regret.

"I know," Genevra interrupted. "I saw them." She let her hand fall as a sickening suspicion struck her.

"Did they see you?" Alex was thinking the same thing.

"Only Radha." She licked her dry lips. "She must have been afraid I'd tell you. She didn't know you already suspected them. Narain must have started the rumors to protect her mother."

"I don't see how that would help."

Genevra looked at him sadly. "Don't you? The English in Delhi already disapprove of me, because of my mother, my illegitimacy, my friends. Narain wanted to make certain they despised me so much that they wouldn't believe a word I said."

She collapsed on the sofa, head in her hands. "Why didn't you warn me? Why?"

"I tried, if you'll remember. You promised to take care."

Of all the voices that had guided her, prodded her, echoed in her head last night, that one alone she had not heeded. "If you'd told me everything—"

Alex shook his head. "I explained that. I didn't want to accuse anyone until I had proof of their guilt."

"Apparently you've found what you needed." She did not know why her heart sank, even now.

"Yes. This morning at dawn I discovered crates full of relics hidden behind your bungalow. The necklace Hazari described was there as well as a gun. It's enough to allow me to make some arrests."

There was another knock on the door. "I have to go," Alex told her reluctantly. "But I think you should stay here. If you come with us—"

"The British will think I betrayed my uncle out of spite." She looked up in despair. "Don't you understand that there's no point in protecting me? They'll blame me anyway. They'll always think the worst. They have nothing better to do."

Alex could hardly argue with her now. He put his hand on her shoulder, pressed it reassuringly, and went to join the other men.

After he had gone, Genevra sat thinking of the many nights when Narain had come to comfort her. It had not been out of friendship. She had only wanted to ensure that Genevra was theirs, that she would owe them everything and never betray them. She crossed her hands over her stomach and bent double. She thought she might be ill.

"Hah!" came a cry from the other room. "I hope he catches the jackals before they become cowards and run."

Hazari. Genevra had forgotten him. She rose and went into the bedroom. His color was a little better this morning, his fever down. "How do you feel?" Her concern was genuine, but in the back of her mind, one word repeated itself in a monotonous litany. Why? Why? Why? Her uncle she could understand; he must have done it for the silver it brought flowing like bright water into his pocket. But Radha would have spit on the sahibs' money. Genevra was certain of that, in spite of everything.

The *mali* managed a smile that was only half grimace. "I will be as useless as ever soon enough, spitting at the skies so it falls on my face."

She checked the bandage, but it was fresh. Why had Radha done it? What had she gained?

"Your man, the *feringhi* learned a few things from watching you last night," Hazari explained. "But he has not your gentle hands." He broke off when he saw her distracted expression. The *mali* reached out to touch her hand. "You have questions, Genniji. I see it in your eyes. Go and ask them. If you do not, they will burn within you like a serpent's venom until your blood turns to poison. Go."

Genevra flushed. Now even Hazari could read her mind. Her face must be very transparent today. "You'll be all right?"

The *mali* nodded. "An army of elephants could not hurt me now. Go."

By the time Genevra reached her uncle's house, he had been taken away. Aunt Helen had followed her husband to see what could be done. Genevra went directly to the drawing room, where she heard voices. Radha and Narain sat on the English horsehair sofa, looking out of place in their

bright saris; this was a room for dimness and restraint. Both
Indians were paler than usual and silent. The soldiers
watched them closely, but Genevra knew they would cause
no trouble. She could see the resignation in their eyes.

Alex came up beside her. "Was it wise to come back?"

"No," she told him, "it was foolish beyond words. But
I have to speak to them, at least for a moment."

He frowned in disapproval, though he knew she was
determined. "You're sure?"

"I'm not afraid they'll hurt me, if that's what you
mean." She did not mention that no physical wound could
be deeper than the ones they had already inflicted. "Nor will
they try to escape. Hindus are fatalists, you see. They fought
the battle and lost; they've given up. And there are things I
must know."

Alex considered the two women on the sofa through
narrowed eyes. Their shoulders were slumped, their heads
lowered; every line in their bodies spoke of defeat. "All
right," he agreed without enthusiasm. "I'll be just outside if
you need me."

"Thank you," she said, and meant it. Genevra was
hardly aware that the door slammed shut behind her, so
awed was she by the quality of stillness in the room. It was
as if not only the Hindu women, but the air itself had
evaporated, leaving the room empty of color, light, or sound.
Their defeat, like Narain's eyes, held nothingness.

In the vacuum of their own making, Genevra turned to
face the ayah and her daughter.

"Narain was never involved," Radha said unexpectedly. "They say they will not take her. The *feringhi* think I
did it to make us rich, to give my daughter jewels and myself
the house of an Indian princess. Pah!" She spat on the
Persian rug at her feet. "I do not want their silver. To me
water is more precious."

Without thinking, Genevra sat at the ayah's feet as she
used to do. "Why did you do it, then? Why work with a man
you pretended to hate so much?"

Radha smiled bitterly. "I do hate him. And because my
hands are idle and that is dangerous, for the serpent watches
and never sleeps, I will tell you how it came to be so."

"Make me understand." Why did she care? Genevra wondered. Why did she not simply turn her back? Because she couldn't. Their friendship had been false, but hers was not.

The ayah shook her head. "This kind of hatred you could never understand. You were not here when the Devil's Wind, the Mutiny of 1857, blew down from the sky like a black cloud of sorrow that hovered long after the wind had died."

Her eyes were veiled with memory. "Before the Mutiny, my husband Syed had been a Sepoy in the army for many years, but he was wounded in 1855, so they sent him home to me in the mountains. Great was my joy on that day, for Syed was a good man. Even with his trouble, he did not beat me. He loved his home, and when he knew I carried a child, he loved me, but still he longed to return to the army he loved best of all."

Her voice took on a keening, piercing quality and she chanted under her breath the words she had spoken as she touched her husband's saber. "Then came the Mutiny and Syed did not understand, because he was a loyal man, how his companions could have killed so many British officers and soldiers, women and children. He refused to think his friends would do such horrible things." She glanced down at Genevra. "Like you, he was a fool with a too soft heart.

"Then we heard the Sahiblog had risen all over India, bringing death for death, suffering for suffering. They sought out traitors and murderers, and created them where none existed. I was afraid the army would come to our little shack in the mountains, but Syed said no, they would never climb so far. If they did come, he said he would tell them how it was and they would leave us in peace. I listened and believed, for I had not yet seen how black the hearts of men can be.

"Then one day the soldiers came. We could have been blind, yet known they were British from the imperious stamp of their boots. Syed, who claimed he was not afraid, told me to crawl beneath the charpoy where the soldiers would not see me. I did not wish to go, but the lord of my house had spoken." She closed her eyes and swayed, remembering. "I watched from my hiding place, my hand on the heartbeat of my child, as a single soldier entered the house.''

While her mother spoke, Narain remained stiff and silent, her eyes on the sky beyond the window. It seemed the story had nothing to do with her.

Radha did not notice; she was too far lost in the past. "The *feringhi* came with his saber drawn and saw the Sepoy uniform my husband would not give up, the saber of which he was so proud. The soldier turned his weapon toward Syed, who cried out, 'Stop! I have not been in the army for two years now, since my injury. My soul was not touched by the Devil's Wind and I killed no British, nor did I wish to.'

"But the sahib did not listen. He raised his sword and my husband did not flinch. 'Are you so much a coward,' the soldier cried, 'that you won't even fight?' '' Radha paused. "My Syed placed his hands together, palm to palm, moved them up and down in a blessing and said, 'A virtuous man ought to be like the sandal tree, which perfumes the ax that destroys it.' ''

The ayah bowed her head, unable to face the light. "The soldier only became more angry because he could not understand. He raised his saber and ran it through my husband's chest. There was much blood, but Syed made no sound as he died. Still, in spite of what he had said, I saw the disbelief in his eyes, the feeling of betrayal." Radha laughed bitterly. "You see, the *feringhi* soldier cut my Syed's heart, but he broke it, too.''

She rocked and rocked, her hands clenched so tightly that her nails pierced the skin.

"Then that man, who had entered my house without asking for the right, who had killed a man as he sat unarmed in his chair, noticed the crutches carved of wood that leaned against a nearby wall. He pulled back the shawl on Syed's lap, though his lips curled with distaste that he should have to touch a native, and he saw where the bullet had passed through both legs, shattering my husband's knees. The wound was clearly old, healed over with many scars. I could see by the stranger's expression that he knew Syed had spoken the truth. Can you guess what he did then?''

Genevra shook her head mutely.

"The *feringhi* did not turn away in shame, or fear of reprisal, or regret. He replaced the shawl soaked in blood, repeated his name and rank proudly, as if reporting a brave deed to his superior. Finally he raised his saber in a salute and smiled.

"I saw in his smile that it did not matter to him if my husband had been a traitor or not. Syed was an Indian; that's why he died, the only reason. I saw the hatred in that bastard's eyes and I knew. That soldier—the image of his face has haunted my dreams for twenty years. His rank I do not remember, but his name I could never forget. It was Gilbert Bishop."

Genevra, who had not even been born when Syed died, could not meet Radha's eyes. "What happened then?" she whispered.

The ayah opened her hands and laid them on her knees, staring at her bloody palms in surprise. "I left the mountains where I had been happy, for I knew my happiness was at an end. Your uncle had killed my only joy and gone away laughing. He left me bitterness and a Devil Wind of my own that blew always in my heart and blood. I wandered with my baby on my hip, working here and there to keep us alive. Each place I stopped I asked about the sahib Gilbert Bishop.

"Great was the day when I heard he had gone to Calcutta to work in the Indian Civil Service. I followed him there, and after many months, I found him. I became his wife's ayah and soon I learned that he was shipping out little artifacts now and then for extra money. I made myself necessary to him over the years. When we came to Delhi, I told him I knew of a place in the Red Fort—once the greatest of Mogul palaces—where many precious things had been hidden when the *feringhi* came. I brought them to him, one by one, made him more and more a thief, more and more guilty, even in the eyes of the other *feringhi*, so that one day I could betray him. The fire, the hot wind in my blood kept me alive until that day."

For the first time, Narain spoke.

" 'Anger leads to a state of delusion;
delusion distorts one's memory.

Distortion of memory distorts consciousness,
and then a man perishes.'

"This I told my mother but she did not hear. I knew she
would destroy herself in time. It was her foolish choice. We
live in *Kali-Yuga,* the Age of Misery. It is to be expected."

Genevra felt a cold rage that surprised her. "Yet you
protected her."

The Indian girl rose, her face smooth and lovely, her
limbs brown and lithe as a dancer's. "I had no choice. To let
her fall would have meant dishonor, and you know well that
dishonor is worse than death."

With an effort, Genevra found her voice. "What about
the dishonor you caused me?"

Narain turned to her with still, empty eyes. "It is
different for you. You are *feringhi.* Besides, as I have told
you so often, nothing matters in this life that is only the
momentary dream of a sleeping god."

The ayah smiled in pity at Genevra's stricken expression. "She is cruel, but in some things, my daughter is right.
It is not important that I will go to prison to pay for my
revenge. I knew always that if *he* must fall, I would fall with
him. But it does not matter, not if I starve or am attacked by
rats or fall ill with cholera and die. Nothing matters except
that your uncle will suffer for the rest of his life. I have
learned to know the British well. They do not forgive."

"Or perhaps," Narain interjected, "you secretly hoped
you would escape the web you had woven for your enemy."

Genevra did not hear her. "If you already knew you
would suffer, why did you try to stop Alex from discovering
the truth?"

Radha leaned forward, eyes glittering. "It was to be *my*
revenge, not some *feringhi* who did not understand Gilbert
Bishop's black cold heart."

"But Hazari suffered, too," Genevra said accusingly.

"In his fear, your uncle lost his head." The ayah spat
out the words. "I would never have hurt Hazari; he is one
of us."

"And me?" Genevra whispered. "Why were you kind
to me?"

Radha smiled, her eyes empty, like Narain's. "In the beginning, it was because Gilbert Bishop hated you. There was no other reason." She turned to hide a flicker of emotion. "But later, when I began to understand that you were not one of them, when I saw how much you needed me, how eagerly you learned, what lovely things you had in your mind that flowed into your fingertips and onto paper, I no longer thought of you as his. For a few years only, you were mine. You may believe what I say or spit in my face, but I cared for you, Genniji. And now I have lost you, too."

11

When Alex had taken Radha away, Narain slipped into the shadows. Genevra let her go. Drained of energy and warmth, she wandered through the house, which had been bleached of every color; all that remained were shades of gray. The rooms that had always seemed dreary had now become stifling. She wondered, as she closed one door after another, what would happen to her aunt and herself, now that Uncle Gilbert had been arrested. She had no doubt that he would be convicted. Alex would see to that.

Alex—whose golden hue was the only color that lingered in the dull haze around her.

Finally she made her way to the veranda. From there, at least, she could see the blue sky, the plains stretching toward the distant mountains.

She was surprised to find that her aunt had returned. Helen sat on the porch, a cold cup of tea on the wicker table at her elbow, rocking slowly back and forth in her old rocking chair. A piece of embroidery lay in her lap, but she did not reach for the colored threads. Now and then she heard a sound and looked up eagerly at the empty walkway.

Genevra's heart contracted with pity for the woman who had caused her so much pain. No doubt her aunt was watching for friends to call and comfort her. Friends who would never come, now that the house was tainted by the rumors of Genevra's sin as well as the stain of Gilbert's crime. Aunt Helen might even be waiting for the familiar footstep of her husband—a sound from the past that she would not hear again.

Genevra went to sit beside her. Silently, she took the woman's hands in hers. They were cold and rigid; Helen had not moved them for a long time. Genevra massaged the chilled fingers gently, until the blood began to flow again.

The older woman looked up, bewildered. "Why are you here?" she asked blankly.

"I think you need me."

Aunt Helen frowned. "Just this morning I was dreadfully cruel to you. How can you bear to touch me now?"

"Because I understand how you feel."

Helen's eyes grew damp with unshed tears. "Do you?" She shook her head at the absurdity of her own question. "Of course you do. And it's my fault. Mine and Gilbert's. We didn't even think you might be hurting, too." Her hands began to tremble. "I didn't understand what it was to be alone. Maybe if I had—"

"You're not alone," Genevra said, though it took her last ounce of charity to speak the words.

Helen closed her eyes and the tears she had held back with such effort began to fall. Her whole body shook with the force of her grief, which was not just of a moment, but of a lifetime. Her aunt was not an enemy anymore; she was unhappy, abandoned, desperately afraid—not only because her husband had been arrested. The sorrow she sobbed out on her niece's shoulder came from yesterday, the day before, all the years and months and days of the past. Helen Gilbert had been careful to hide her pain, as a good Victorian lady should. She had pretended to be strong, but underneath she was as human, as frail as her poor mad sister.

Genevra held her aunt while she wept, while pain and frustration and years of silent agony flowed free. She gave to Aunt Helen what she herself had prayed her aunt would one day give to her. Ironically, that moment of communion healed a tiny corner of Genevra's scarred and battered heart.

When the walls began to close around her, Genevra knew she had to get away. She headed up the river to the city and Phoebe's house. Her friend would know how to sort out the tangle of anger, bitterness, and grief from so many deceptions and betrayals. Phoebe would know how to bring back the colors. Without them, Genevra was empty and lost.

She turned with relief into the street of marble walls

until she came to the familiar wrought-iron gate. The instant she raised the door knocker, Phoebe was there, green eyes full of compassion.

"I knew you'd come," she cried. "I've heard everything, my dear. All of Delhi has heard. It seems to be the only topic they find worthy of discussion." As she spoke, she drew Genevra inside the cool marble corridor. "But you must try to forgive them and pay them no mind. There is so little of interest in their lives, so little magic. They don't believe in it, you know. 'Damned lot of nonsense!' they'd tell you if you asked them. That's why they don't understand about you and your paintings and that girl Narain. They don't want to understand." She collapsed on a huge wicker chair when she ran out of breath.

"But your uncle!" she continued before Genevra could open her mouth. "Now that *was* quite a shock. It seems Gilbert Bishop didn't believe that 'he who steals honey should beware of the sting.' Imagine him making pots and pots of money for all those years and no one the wiser. 'Though thy enemy seem a mouse, yet watch him like a lion.' I wonder if it occurred to him that he never could have done it if it weren't for the brilliance of Indian artisans who'd never even heard of British superiority and wouldn't have believed in it if they had? By the way, Hazari is comfortably installed in the garden, allowing Ameera to wait on him hand and foot. Now *he* can deal with those dreadful animals for a change."

At Genevra's look of surprise, Phoebe explained, "I told you I'd miss his ugly face if I never saw it again. How could I possibly turn him out?" She tossed her braid over her shoulder. "Haven't you anything to say? I rather thought you'd want to rant until your voice echoed off the walls."

With a crooked smile, Genevra murmured, "I did want to, but the desire seems to have left me. I'm glad about Hazari."

Phoebe narrowed her eyes. "You've a strange expression on your face which I suspect has nothing to do with vicious rumors or stolen Indian art. Has something else happened of which I am not yet aware?" Her eyebrows rose at the unlikelihood of such a possibility.

"I don't suppose you've heard that Alex has asked me to marry him?"

Phoebe rose like a whirlwind from her chair. "Did he now? Well, that puts a different light on things altogether." She paced in a wash of sunlight, muttering to herself. Then she spun to face Genevra. "I needn't ask what your answer was, need I?"

"I rather think it was 'no.'" The girl felt the familiar slowing of her heartbeat.

"You 'rather think'? Isn't this generally the sort of thing one *knows*?"

Genevra shook her head. "That's just it. I *don't* know. We've only just met, really. He's not much more than a stranger. He's an army man and that means a certain kind of life, and I can't be sure—I mean . . ." she trailed off in confusion.

Brow furrowed, Phoebe approached her friend. "A lot of balderdash if you ask me. You're thinking of your mother and Charles Kittridge and trying not to repeat their mistake. Don't try to fool me, my dear. I know you too well. There's only one question that matters here. Do you love him?"

Genevra shifted uneasily under her friend's discerning gaze. "I care about him, but—"

Phoebe noticed the dark circles under Genevra's eyes, how pale she was beneath her tan. "Ah, my poor child. You've had too much to accept in the past two days, haven't you? It's not a good time for clear thinking, I'm afraid. The worst part is, what I'm about to do will only muddle things further." She put her arm around the girl's shoulder. "Come, I've something to show you."

They stopped in a room with bright pillows on the floor and silk hangings on the walls.

"I'd take you to the garden, but Hazari and his menagerie would only drive you mad. Now, where did I put it? It came only a few days past."

"What did?"

"The letter from your father, of course."

For a long moment, Genevra was speechless. Then she gasped, "My father? Charles Kittridge?"

"Certainly Charles Kittridge. How many fathers do you

577

think you have?'' Phoebe paused, eyes wide with dismay. "I'm sorry, my dear. I forgot you didn't know." She sat on a green cushion with her ankles crossed. "I found him quite recently, or he found me, in much the same way I found your mother. He'd been looking for you for years, you know. But I told him the time was not yet right to try to see you. I've received a few letters and sent him a few, to keep him apprised of how you were. He was very grateful for every scrap of information."

Genevra stared at her, astounded. "I don't believe you." She knew Phoebe would not lie, but—the colors returned in a rush. "He doesn't care about me, just as he didn't care about my mother. He left us and went on with his life as if we didn't exist. I hate him for that." She had never spoken the words aloud, not to Phoebe, not even to Narain, but they had festered inside her for eleven long years.

Phoebe took Genevra's hands. "My dear, don't you know that 'hatred is blind as well as love'? I think, because of your mother's obsession, you've never seen your father clearly; he's always been a shadow to which *she* gave color and form. Use your own eyes now to make him real. It broke his heart when he lost you. I don't think you can imagine how greatly he cares for you, even though you're as much a shadow to him as he is to you."

Genevra frowned and shook her head. "You said there've been letters before. Why is this one so important?"

"Let me find it so your father can tell you himself."

She left the room to return with a battered envelope postmarked Dundreggan, Scotland. Phoebe sat quietly while Genevra unfolded the paper inside and held it in trembling hands.

Dear Genevra,

I know it's unforgivable that I have never written before, but perhaps Phoebe will explain. I may have been wrong to listen to her; my heart told me I was, but my head would speak more loudly. So I left you to her kind graces, knowing you were lucky to have such a friend. There are few enough of those in a lifetime.

Now, however, my heart has begun to drown out the voices in my head, because I am ill and fear I won't live out another year. I tell you this because I would like to see you before I die and did not think you would come otherwise. There is so much I want to know, so much I want to tell you. I have seen you in dreams, but it is not enough.

If you can forgive me for my silence all these years, for the horror that Edward Townsend created because of me, and most of all, for my own cowardice, I would ask you to come to Scotland. I have chosen a beautiful place in which to breathe my last. If there is a paradise on earth, I'm sure it must be here. Please come and share it with me for as long as I have to share such things.

I will certainly understand if you refuse my request. You owe me nothing, I fear, but derision. But if you should decide to come, I have enclosed the fare. Phoebe will help see to your passage. Listen only to your heart and do as you think is right.

> Yours Most Sincerely,
> Charles Kittridge

Genevra let the letter fall from nerveless fingers. She had seen his face many times—his smile, his eyes, his every expression—but never thought to hear his voice again. She swallowed dryly, her heart pounding. "I don't want to go." Her anger, resentment, grief were still red and bright within her. One letter could not change years of neglect. "He's right when he says he's been a coward," she said.

"My dear, foolish friend, 'many would be cowards if they had the courage.' " Phoebe frowned and toyed with the tassel on a pillow. "I suppose I didn't realize how deeply he had hurt you. But 'it's never too late to mend,' you know. Don't you think you should give him a chance?"

"I don't know if I can. It's too much of a chance. Too

far to go for a stranger." Her hands continued to shake as she folded the letter into a tiny square and put it in her bodice. "I don't know what to do—about anything. I don't know what to feel or think or see," she cried. "There's too much—too many shadows, too much light."

Phoebe gazed down at her hands. "I felt like that once. So sunk in despair and lost dreams that I almost gave up."

"I can't imagine you in despair."

The woman smiled a bittersweet smile. "But you never knew my husband, Arthur." She leaned back with a faraway look in her eyes. "You would have liked him. He spent a great deal of effort in trying to shock his compatriots so those stiff British upper lips would bend, just a little. He used to say, 'Phoebe, my darling, life lieth not in the living, but in the liking. Don't ever forget it. Don't let those stuffy old bastards knock it out of your beautiful head.' "

Her smile was so sweet and full of memory that Genevra ached for her.

"He was delighted when we bought this house, couldn't wait to brag about it to the others. 'You should have seen their pasty faces turn fuchsia when I told them!' Arthur crowed. 'Too stupefied to speak, they were. It was really too marvelous!' He laughed aloud and handed me a glass of sherry. 'A toast,' he cried, 'to the blessed fact that we have a sense of adventure as well as a sense of humor!' " Phoebe touched the wedding band that still circled her finger, though her husband had been dead for many years. "Do you know what his favorite saying was?"

"What?" As she listened to Phoebe, Genevra had managed to suppress her own troubles, at least for a while.

" 'You may if you list, but do if you dare!' I believe he would have dared anything. And I with him." She sat up, her eyes full of grief. "You may wonder why I never told you about him before. It's because I find it so difficult. Each time I speak of him, he becomes alive again in my mind. Then, when I lose him . . . well."

"I'm sorry," her friend said inadequately. "You needn't go on, you know."

Phoebe looked up. "But don't you see, I must. For your sake—and for mine. Come." She rose and offered her hand. "There's something you should see."

Genevra followed her from the room. Phoebe's turquoise sari and yellow skirt, her red-brown braid and easy gait were the same, but there was a difference. This was a woman with a purpose.

They went outside, crossed the courtyard, and followed the dusty road to where a stone gate curved above the street. Phoebe stopped with Genevra beside her. "When Arthur died of cholera, I told the undertaker to burn his body. That shocked the Brits, I can tell you. Heathen, they called it. Unchristian. But I called it practical. Arthur and I had discussed it, you see, and decided the Indians were wise to burn their dead in this climate where heat and jackals and vultures hover about waiting for new flesh. We both wanted to be burned rather than join the stuffy rows of stuffy English dead in their tidy, stuffy graves."

She paused, her eyes glazed with tears. "When the day came for the funeral I left the house and passed this gate. It's a Suttee Gate, you know, where the widows to be burned on their husband's funeral pyres stopped to place their handprints in red paint."

Genevra looked at the scattered handprints that made her shudder.

"I didn't mean to stop," Phoebe continued, "but suddenly the handprints fascinated me—the red paint on white burning stone. And the size of those hands. Just look." She put her palm over one of the prints and covered it completely. "Children they were, so many of those widows. I stood here, my hand pressed to the stone, unable to move. It was hot. So hot that my palm blistered and I thought, I know one way to shock those English out of their complacency. I'll do what these brave children did out of love and loyalty and a religious fervor I can never understand. I'll throw myself on Arthur's pyre and burn with him. Otherwise I'll be alone and how will I be able to bear that? Alone among heartless, humorless crows without Arthur's laughter to make it all right."

Genevra wept silent tears. She understood too well.

"I thought I'd find some red paint and put my palm print next to these. I thought that would make me part of India and nothing to do with Britain anymore. Then a cloud covered the sun, a shadow fell on the wall, and it woke me from my daze. I realized Arthur would hate it if I did that. It would be giving up. He would never have given up, nor forgiven me if *I* did. So I went to the funeral and came home to my empty house and went from room to room, wondering what on earth to do with the rest of my life."

Abruptly, Phoebe turned for home. Genevra followed. She did not speak, was afraid to interrupt, and knew besides that her friend would not hear her.

They entered the dim hall where Phoebe tossed her straw hat on a table. "At first I thought I'd go home to England and get away from these people. After all, Arthur always used to say, 'He that is afraid of wagging feathers must keep from among wild fowl.' Then I realized that in England it would be the same. Only there I wouldn't have the sun and the mountains and the endless plains. I wouldn't have the raging heat and the wonderful madness of the monsoons. All I'd have would be soft rolling hills and gentle English mist and dreary gray rain. You may be on land, I told myself, and not be in a garden.

"Then suddenly, it came to me. My greatest revenge against the unforgiving British—my greatest tribute to Arthur—would be to enjoy myself no end, laugh whenever I liked and live every moment as if it might never come again. I knew I had made the right decision, because I thought I heard Arthur laugh, that deep wonderful laughter that rumbled through his whole body.

"I've kept that vow to this day." Her gaze was distant for a moment more, then she turned to Genevra. "Do you understand why I've told you all this?"

The girl started, forced from the wisps of a dream to the harshness of reality. "No."

"Because I wanted you to see that sometimes one has to take a risk. Arthur took his chance and I took mine. It was worth it, Genny. If I'd given in when I wanted to, I would have missed so much. And you—you could sit here painting pictures of Charles Kittridge in your mind and never really know the truth."

"But this is my home, too. I love the raging heat and the madness of the monsoon just as you do. Would you have me lost among the very rolling hills and dreary rain you disparaged?"

Phoebe considered, lips pursed. "For one thing, the Highlands of Scotland are not England, my dear. I've been there and I know you'd find them irresistible. For another, you've never lived anywhere but here. Haven't you dreamed of mountains not engulfed in choking dust? You've never even seen a winter. Don't you think you should, just once? There's another world out there, a world with a different pace and rhythm.

"I'd seen that world, felt that rhythm, when I settled here. I knew what else there was and made my choice. You want to make yours blindly, without knowledge." She took Genevra's hands and squeezed them. "Besides, one thing I learned quickly when I tried to find my Indian soul was that I had English blood not only in my veins but in my bones. I couldn't have it removed or ignore it or send it back in a parcel to where it came from. I had to learn to live with it.

"I suspect you've discovered for yourself how wide the chasm between the Anglo and Indian races is," she said perceptively. "You cannot ever become one of them. Much as you may hate to admit it, you're British to the end. But believe me, that doesn't have to cripple you. It can give you more scope to view the world if you let it. You think you're rooted in this sunbaked soil, but you're not. Spread your wings, my little bird, learn to fly."

When she saw Genevra's hesitation, Phoebe added softly, "I wonder if you really have a choice. Surely you've heard the Hindu saying: 'We may throw ourselves into the depths of the sea, ascend to the summit of the highest mountain, bury ourselves in the bowels of the earth, sojourn in the midst of venomous reptiles, or take up our abode on the moon; yet our destiny will nonetheless be accomplished.' "

Genevra clenched her hands into fists. "I don't think I'm brave enough to meet that destiny yet."

Phoebe stared in dismay. "You're one of the most courageous women I know. Just look at what you've survived, the things you've done in spite of everything and everyone. You refuse to follow the petty rules and traditions in which you don't believe, you dress as you like, make friends with the Indians, and never echo the bigotry and arrogance of those around you. Most important, you paint what you choose and not what they approve. You've lived with rumors and disapproval for years, yet in spite of all they could do to hurt you, you're not hard or cold or bitter. Instead you're kind and sensitive and you know how to laugh. I admire you deeply, and I mean that with all my heart. I will miss you if you go." She did not try to hide her sorrow. "Remember, 'Oaks may fall when the reeds stand the storm.' You're a reed, Genevra, slender, flexible, young, and strong. Don't be afraid of anyone, least of all a dying man who needs your forgiveness so badly."

"You really believe that?"

"I believe he needs to know you even more than you need to know him, and that is a very great deal." She saw the doubt in her friend's eyes. "If you don't go, you've chosen never to know the truth about your father. Don't be blind as your mother was. Open your eyes; there's so very much to see."

Staring at her hands, Genevra murmured, "What about Alex?"

Phoebe tilted her head thoughtfully. "You seem so uncertain about him that I thought some time away might help you decide. If I'm not mistaken, Alex will wait for you. He can't help himself, you see."

Genevra knelt in her room, the blinds rolled up to let in the morning sun. Around her were scattered her clothes, her paints, her few possessions, and her pictures. She was packing them away in a single trunk to take with her to Scotland. She had delayed for nearly a month, telling herself she could not leave her aunt alone, but now, at last, she realized Phoebe was right. She had to meet her father, not only to exorcise the ghost who had haunted her for so long, to turn the specter into a man. She *did* need time to sort out her feelings for Alex. Her body cried out for him, and her soul, but her uncertainty was always there.

She would have a long time to consider on the voyage to Britain, a long time to leave behind the sorrows that bound her to India. She began to pack, quickly, efficiently, to keep her hands and thoughts occupied. When she came across the necklace her mother had left her, she held the gold chain loosely in her hand, then tucked it into a corner. The thought of wearing it was still too painful.

Suddenly the wind swept through the open window, scattering her drawings. She picked them up to find the sketch of Radha on top. She remembered how confused and frightened she had been by the turmoil, the flames in the background, but now she understood. The fire that burned in Radha's eyes had burned also in her soul, until it was devoured, and there was nothing left but the bitterness and anger reflected in the clear standing pools. For Genevra, the fear and confusion were gone, but the sorrow remained. It would not leave her so long as she remembered how Radha had stood touching her husband's saber with reverence, and wept, tearless, from the well of grief inside her.

Genevra put aside the drawing and picked up Narain's portrait. The sight of her face brought a dry ache to the English girl's eyes. She had thought this lovely face—smooth, untouched by care—and the pure whiteness of the background were an image of the peace that she herself sought. But she saw now that the white was a wasteland of passions never experienced—not joy or wonder or even love. Perhaps there had been no pain either, but Genevra did not think it had been worth the cost.

Her eyes grew damp as she packed the sketches away. She had loved Radha and Narain. She loved them now, even knowing they had betrayed her. Because, in spite of everything, they had given her India, made her understand its rhythms and colors and history. They had given her something to care about when she had nothing, and for that she would always be grateful.

"Genniji?"

Narain stood just inside the door, her body half revealed by the light from the window. "Will you really return to Belait?"

"Yes," Genevra replied stiffly.

On silent feet, Narain came closer. "Stay," she murmured. "Do not go." For her it was a plea, though her voice was without inflection.

Shocked into rising, Genevra said, "I have to. There are many reasons why."

"But I will be alone."

For the first time, Genevra saw a flicker of need in the blankness of the Indian's eyes. It was not much to fill a hollow soul. The girl pitied Narain and was surprised by the feeling.

Narain read her friend's thoughts and glowered.

"Many people, freed of passion, fear and anger,
Have been purified by the fire of wisdom,"

she cried defensively.

Genevra shook her head. "You don't believe that anymore, and I never did." She was stunned when Narain reached out to grasp her hands.

"I have cared for you in spite of all the wisdom of the gods. I have shared your shadows and cooled your dreams. You love me. You cannot leave me."

She spoke with a certainty that made Genevra gasp. Narain did not mention betrayal or loss or dishonor; she had nothing to say about how much she had hurt her friend. Genevra looked into the mirror of Narain's eyes and saw her own distorted face, but nothing more. The mirror was only cold glass after all. Slowly she disengaged her hands. "I'm going, but you won't be alone. You can care for my Aunt Helen. She needs you. She'll listen gratefully to your stories, and perhaps you to hers." She took a deep breath, then turned away. "I have to finish packing. Alex will be here soon."

When she looked around, Narain was gone, though the pain in Genevra's chest lingered.

While Alex loaded the trunk into the carriage, Genevra stopped to say good-bye to her aunt.

Helen Bishop looked up, infinitely older than she had been a week before. Her hair was pure white, thin and fragile. In spite of herself, Genevra wanted to touch that hair, to offer her aunt comfort. She sat on a petit-point stool near the sofa.

Her aunt stared out the window at the brilliant red of the bougainvillea and said softly, "It will seem strange and empty here without you. Especially with Gilbert gone." She frowned in concentration, choosing her words with care. "I didn't love him, you know, but I was used to him. The funny thing is, I never really knew him, even after thirty years of marriage." Unexpectedly, tears filled her eyes. "Can you believe me when I say I'll miss you?"

Genevra took the woman's frail, age-spotted hand and held it gently. "I'm sorry. I know it will be lonely here."

Helen Bishop covered her niece's hand with hers. "I was wrong about you, to treat you that way. But I thought I could stamp out that part of Emily that was in your blood and save you from following her path. I'm sorry."

Genevra remained silent, trying to understand.

"An apology doesn't make up for all the suffering we caused you, I suppose."

"No," her niece replied, "but it makes the memories easier to bear."

Helen squeezed the hand she held and realized she had never touched Genevra in this way before. Had she done so, it might have been different. She might have had a child, a companion, a friend, if she'd only tried a little harder to reach the troubled girl Emily had left behind. "Can you ever forgive me?"

Her niece had to gather her thoughts, to push back the rumors, the cruelties, the aching loneliness of eleven years. "Not yet," she whispered, "but someday when the pain is further in the past."

Helen nodded. She had learned to accept a great deal in the last week with a nod of her head and a tightening of her lips. But she could not stop the moisture from misting her eyes. "Will you ever come back?"

Genevra had asked herself that question many times. "I don't know. I wish I did. I only hope you'll be all right."

Helen Gilbert looked at her with colorless eyes and

murmured, "Hope, my dear, is but the dream of those who wake."

For a while there was silence in the carriage as Alex and Genevra rode to the station. Then he turned to take her hand. He regarded her in the bright midday light that filtered through the tiny window. Her pale hair shone in the Indian sun, her eyes were luminous with her secret thoughts. How in God's name could he let her go? "Are you sure you want to do this?"

She nodded. "I need to."

"Because of your father or because of us?" he asked, surprised that his voice remained steady.

Brow furrowed, Genevra considered the question. "Because," she said slowly, "until I've seen him, I won't understand us."

"How can that be? He has nothing to do with me, with what I feel for you."

Genevra smiled a strange little smile. "He has much to do with you in my eyes, and with what *I* feel for you." She reached up to push the hair back from his face and felt a constriction in her chest. "You're so very like him, you see. I thought for a while I had created you out of my dreams—and nightmares—of him." His look of hurt made her want to put her arms out and draw him close, but she was afraid if she did, she would never let go. "I have to think, to untangle things in my head. To make certain that the colors are true."

He tried to understand, but could not deny the overwhelming need to keep her beside him—her fey spirit, her mind filled with colors he might never see, her compassion, her love of sun and wind and dust that only annoyed those who had not the insight to understand. "I wish I could come with you."

Genevra brightened. "Why not?"

Alex shook his head with regret. "Your uncle was only one of many who smuggle Indian artifacts. I'm to find as many as I can in Delhi, then go on to other cities and do what I've done here."

"But—" Genevra began in agitation.

"Phoebe will always know where I am," he said, reading her thoughts on her flushed face. "You can find me when you want to." He did not ask if she were coming back; he might not want to hear the answer. Glancing out the window, he saw they would soon reach the railroad station. Without thinking, he drew Genevra close to kiss her.

She felt the heat of his lips all through her body, which had been still and cold until that moment. She cupped his face in her hands and opened her mouth to his. The storm that rose inside her was a bright whirlwind of passion—wind, rain, and thunder roaring all together—that frightened her with its intensity. Yet within the passion, sorrow struck her heart and stilled it. She was leaving him behind.

Alex kissed her harder and she clung to him in desperation. If he let her go, if he took his lips from hers and his fingertips from her skin, if he left her on the platform and turned to walk away, she feared her heart would never beat again. The colors rose and spun—fuchsia and gold, orange and red, brilliant blue—until they filled her sight and she knew.

"Say it, Genevra," he whispered against her parted lips. "Just once, say it."

"I love you, Alex." She touched her fingertips to his eyelids, drawing them closed. "Perhaps too much."

"It can never be too much. If you learn nothing else in Scotland, the trip will have been worth it."

They arrived at the station and a native opened the door. Reluctantly, they parted. Genevra stepped onto the platform in her dove-gray traveling suit with pale blue lace at the throat and wrists. It had been a gift from her aunt—an offering, a plea, an acknowledgment that the girl in the pink-checked pinafore had grown into a woman with her own life to make.

Genevra concentrated on smoothing her skirt while Alex saw to the trunk, but the fabric might as well have been spun glass. The ache inside her grew into a gray-blue melancholy. Then she saw Phoebe rushing down the platform, straw hat askew, thick braid flying, her skirt swirling like *chadars* about her ankles. It struck Genevra then that

Phoebe and not Radha had been most like a mother to her—a mother *and* a friend.

Genevra threw her arms around the woman as she heard the train pull into the station. "Oh, Phoebe! Whatever will I do without you?"

"Very well, I'm sure. No monkeys to beg for your food, no minahs to shriek obscenities in your ear, no dining room tables that can't be sat around."

"No Tamarsha Begum to talk to by the hour, no friend who's always there when I need her, no one to share my laughter with."

Phoebe cupped Genevra's face in her hands. "There will always be others, especially for you. Have a little faith, my dear." When she saw the tears in the girl's eyes, she added quickly, "I've just popped round to wish you farewell and weep copious tears on your shoulder and wave my handkerchief madly as the train spews dust and grime upon it. Don't forget that the Bakers will be waiting for you at the hotel in Calcutta. They'll take care of you on the voyage."

"You mean they'll be my chaperons to keep me out of trouble," the girl said with a smile.

Phoebe wasn't listening. "I want you to know that those things I said the other day have nothing to do with Alex Kendall, not precisely anyway. But you mustn't forget him, you know. There are few enough good men in the world to waste one as fine as he is." She paused to hug her friend tightly. When Alex approached, she murmured in Genevra's ear, "Don't ever forget, my little bird, to save something for the man who rides the white horse."

Alex joined them and Phoebe backed away. The conductor was calling out for the passengers to climb aboard. For a moment, Alex and Genevra stood frozen, unable to move. Finally Phoebe gave a ferocious cough and the young people took a step closer. Genevra held her breath and memorized each detail of his face so she would not forget it in the long cold nights to come.

"My dears," Phoebe called, "I'm afraid you'll have to move sometime. Trains are machines, after all, and not known for their patience."

Briefly, Alex leaned down to touch his lips to Genevra's.

Just before she turned away, she murmured, "The Indians are very wise. At a time like this, they touch palms once." She raised her hand; he placed his palm against it. "Then they say, 'When all is at an end, the memory of our parting will be but a dream.' "

Before the sound of her voice had faded, she was gone.

BOOK

IV

ROSSHIRE,
SCOTLAND
1878

Prologue

"It is only a wee bittie farther to Mairi Rose's croft. Just across the burn and down yon hill." The old man pointed to a narrow path that wound away into the woods.

Before Charles Kittridge could nod his thanks, the man had gone. Perplexed, Charles turned to follow the path which, even after thirty-seven years was still familiar. He'd asked directions only to reassure himself that his memory had not failed him.

It had not. When he moved forward, the woods closed around him, cool, dark, and mysterious. The leaves interlocked in a maze of shifting greenery that made dancing shadows on the ground at his feet. He had seen those shadows before. He seemed to remember every pine needle and hawthorn leaf, each heather-draped hillock and clod of rich earth. That surprised him, for he had disliked the Highlands the last time he was here. He had never felt at ease among these forbidding hills. But today they seemed to welcome him, to speak to him wistfully of Mairi.

He crossed the sparkling shallows of the stream, hopped from the bank to a boulder to the far shore, where he paused to catch his breath. He looked into the water as if he might see Mairi's face reflected there. His heart beat faster at the thought.

Charles shook his head. He was sixty-one, too old to be indulging in such fanciful notions. He thought he'd lost that ability years ago, somewhere in India where the sun could so easily burn away the poetry in a man's soul.

He forgot India and the sad truths he had learned there

when he saw the mountains, silver purple in their mysterious magnificence, scarred with rock and slashing waterfalls. The scene was lovely in an unsettling way—wild, dark, and enchanting.

Charles was reluctant to leave the woods, the fragrance that spoke of Mairi as certainly as wind and water. He could smell peat and pine and soft morning mist—the scents that used to cling to her when she came in, cheeks flushed from the cold, a basket of roots and flowers in her hand.

The picture was so vivid that Charles stopped, breathless, certain he had conjured her out of his thoughts. Then the image changed; though vibrant in the center, it became blurred around the edges like a fondly remembered dream, a fleeting vision, a wisp of smoke that curled around his shoulders, then disappeared, leaving him oddly apprehensive.

In that moment, his sense of unreality was so intense he could almost believe that it *had* been a dream—those few short months he had spent with Mairi. A dream he had created out of the emptiness and need within him. Only then did he realize he was afraid to see his wife again.

A bird sang piercingly, freeing Charles from his thoughts. Closing his mind against the images—sharp, bitter-sweet, and strangely clear among the jumble of memories from the lives he had lived since he left these hills—he continued to the edge of the woods. He glanced across the clearing and saw the croft built into the side of a hill. It looked the same, with its white stone walls and thatched reed roof. Smoke curled from the stone chimney.

He knew then that it had not been a dream. Every moment he had spent with her had been real—as real as the larch he leaned against now, gasping to catch his breath.

The autumn chill that threaded the air made his chest ache and he found it difficult to breathe. The exertion had been too much for him. He coughed violently into his handkerchief, waited for the uncomfortable pounding of his heart to ease. Even as his vision blurred, the image of the croft did not disappear. It had filled his dreams, beckoning, since his last visit to London. He had suffered no inner struggle, made no painful decision to return to these hills; he had simply known that he must come.

Now the picture of the croft changed to include Mairi as he had last seen her, standing in the doorway with the glow of the fire at her back. He had kissed her, held her briefly, then turned to find his way through the woods into town. He had known she watched while the distance between them grew, felt her eyes upon him like a thread binding him to this place. She had called him back without word or gesture, but with a silent, anguished cry directly from her heart.

He had not understood her grief that night. Not until he returned to find the doorway empty and the croft silent, now that Mairi and her fabrics, threads, and loom had gone. There had been a note, he remembered, explaining that he could never be happy in the Highlands and she could never be happy anywhere else. It was best, she had said, if they parted now before any more damage was done. "I love ye," it had ended. "Ye must believe that. Mairi." It was all she had left him.

Resentment rose within him, flared into anger so intense that he shook with it. He dug his fingers into the bark of the tree, so overwhelmed by his unexpected fury that he hardly noticed the pain. How could Mairi have been so cruel? What had given her the right to decide? He was surprised by his own response; he had not realized how deeply he still felt her betrayal. Even after all these years, he could not quite forgive her.

For the first time, he wondered if he had made a mistake in coming back. Did he really want to see her again? But he knew the answer to that; the woods had told him how much he'd missed her. What if she didn't want to see *him*? What if Mairi had found another man?

As if in answer to his doubts, the oak door opened and a woman stood on the threshold, half concealed by shadows. He knew her at once, though her red hair was streaked with gray and gathered into a bun at the back of her head. He remembered it falling untidily, gloriously, down her back. He knew her in spite of the brown linsey-woolsey gown she wore, so unlike the bright colors she used to choose. Her skin was weathered, aged by years in sun and wind, and wrinkles had appeared at the corners of her eyes and mouth. But he knew it was Mairi by her clear violet eyes which had not dimmed.

She glanced around curiously. When she saw Charles, she paused, eyes narrowed. A flash of recognition crossed her face, changed it subtly, softening the harsh lines, so she looked far younger than her fifty-six years.

She took a step forward, her red plaid wrapped loosely around her shoulders. The wind caught it up, whipped it about her head, creating the illusion that her hair was vivid red again and free of gray. Mairi stopped as another emotion flickered in her eyes—a brilliant flash of something deep, raw, and angry. But it vanished as quickly as it had come when she smiled slowly in welcome and held out her hands to him.

For an instant, he saw nothing but the gleam of his wide wedding ring, which still circled her finger. Her gesture and that single glint of gold told him he had been right to come. Still, he stood motionless, frozen by the joy that rushed through him. Eventually his heart began to beat again and he moved forward to take Mairi's outstretched hands. Only then did he notice he was trembling. Before she could grasp his hands more tightly, he drew her near so her arms closed around him. He felt her shake a little, smelled the scent of peat in her hair, felt the slightness of her body in his arms. For that moment, before either spoke a word, they were young again and free, as if all the years of hurt and loneliness had never come between them.

Slowly, reluctantly, they parted. Charles winced when he saw Mairi's sad, knowing smile. It was the one thing about her he had forgotten—how that smile could make him desperate to understand, to ease her sadness, to bring her out of the mists of her world and back to the reality of his.

She reached out, sleeves pushed back to the elbow, running her fingers gently over his face to reacquaint herself with the lines and curves and planes of his beloved features.

The touch of her palms, callused from years of labor at the loom and in the hills, brought a constriction to his throat. Still without a word, she let her hands fall and he dared to break the silence at last. "You don't seem surprised to see me."

"I dreamed of ye for three nights, one after t'other. On the third mornin', I knew ye'd come."

"Were you glad or sorry?"

"Glad doesn't describe my joy," she told him. Before he could respond, she added, "Nor sorry my doubts."

Smiling ruefully, he nodded his understanding.

Mairi leaned forward to look at him more closely. She knew Charles must be sixty-one, but he looked older. His hair was completely white, without a trace of brown. His bright blue eyes had dulled to gray, but whether with age or pain she could not tell. His face was pallid, his breathing uneasy.

"We've much to talk about," Charles murmured, keeping his voice steady with an effort.

" 'Twill come in time," Mairi said softly. "But now ye're weary. Come inside and rest while I bring ye oat cakes and ale."

He did not have the strength to argue. Slowly, he followed her inside, remembering with pain and pleasure the afternoons they had spent sharing oat cakes and ale in front of the fire.

Then he bent his head to step inside the croft. For a long time he stood, inhaled the familiar scent of peat from the basket near the hearth and the flames that burned in the round fireplace. The house seemed larger than before, but thirty-seven years ago it had been a kind of prison. Now it was a haven.

It was as dark as he remembered, and as cozy and warm. He could see the loom in the corner and the spinning wheel with the thread still wound around the spindle. There was the simple table and two oak chairs and the rough-hewn bed with the sweet-smelling heather mattress.

"Sit," Mairi said, "or your legs will no' hold ye anymore."

"Not yet," he told her in a voice not quite his own. He was eager to see and touch every piece of wood and stone and thread and iron, to reassure himself that he had once been here, that Mairi had once loved him. He stopped with his hand on her loom, too choked by the emotions it aroused in him to speak.

Mairi knew that Charles was right; there was much they had to say to one another. But just now the yellow pallor of his skin concerned her most.

"Drink," she insisted, handing him a mug of warm ale.

He did so without thinking, his mind lost in the past. As she watched him, Mairi had to fight to keep her tears in check. How often had she imagined him standing just there, talking as she wove her vibrant threads together, admiring her colorful patterns, leaning over to kiss her cheek. Her stomach began to churn as the pain of his loss hit her afresh. Even after all these years, she felt it throughout her body.

"Don't you want to know why I've come back?" Charles asked at last. He did not turn from the loom, but clutched the frame until his knuckles were white with the strain.

It was an effort, but she answered calmly. "I think I can guess. Besides, I can wait. I know ye'll tell me, in time."

He drew a deep breath, reminded of the patience that had let Mairi sit at the loom hour after hour, sending the shuttle back and forth, back and forth. He had never been able to watch more than a few minutes before he felt the need to be gone.

Charles turned back to Mairi, but when he saw her face, words deserted him. Their eyes met for an instant, full of questions and answers, entreaties and accusations. He found he had to look away. He was relieved when he noticed an ancient hand harp on the wall. He reached up to touch the beautiful wood, to run his fingers over the strings.

"I didn't know you played the harp," he said.

" 'Tisn't mine." Mairi considered for a moment, then added in a whisper, "it belongs to Ailsa."

"Ailsa?"

She hesitated, clenching her hands into fists, as if that might give her the strength she needed. "Your daughter," she told him, surprised that her voice did not quaver.

Charles froze with his hand in midair. "My daughter?"

For a long moment, he did not understand. "My *daughter?*" he repeated incredulously. He took a deep breath as a rush of pure joy set his heart pounding. Mairi, whom he loved more than any other, had borne his child. He wanted to shout, to dance, to sing in celebration. In spite of his previous weariness, he lifted his wife in his arms and swung her around twice before he had to stop, breathing heavily. He coughed and tried to find the words to ask what he wanted to know. "Tell me about her."

Mairi took a step backward, intimidated by the ferocity of his joy. "She's a lovely girl, really a woman long since, with your chestnut hair and blue eyes. Thirty-six, she is, and ye'd be proud of her." She stopped when his expression changed.

"All this time I've had a child and never knew it?" His joy evaporated as the shock of realization hit him. Mairi had kept the truth from him. A truth so important that it might have changed his life—and hers. For an instant he was blinded by anger and a sense of betrayal for which he could not find the words. He felt as if his wife had struck him a blow with her tightly closed fist.

For thirty-six years his daughter had been growing, laughing, weeping, and he had never known she existed. A terrible sense of loss overwhelmed him—an emptiness so profound that he knew it would never leave him. He felt the world tilt madly beneath his feet; it would not support him much longer. "Why didn't you tell me?" he demanded when he could speak again.

"Why didn't ye come back to find out for yourself?" Mairi cried with equal fury.

Charles was appalled by the raw pain in her voice, the accusation in her eyes. For a moment, he was too stunned by her anguish to reply. He closed his eyes against the familiar sense of guilt that overwhelmed him each time he thought of the other two girls he had left behind, abandoned, lost. Why *hadn't* he come back? "You sent me away," he told Mairi at last.

"Aye, that I did, and I don't think ye can understand how much it cost me." Her lips were suddenly dry. "But still ye could have come back, even once to see—'' She broke off, unable to continue.

Now it was as if he had struck *her*. He saw in her eyes the same feeling of betrayal, the same aching loneliness that had followed him like an illness for thirty-seven years.

"No," he said softly, "I couldn't have come back."

She met his gaze squarely. "Why?"

He considered his answer, unwilling to speak the truth, but weary beyond endurance of the lie. In the last instant, he chose the truth. "Because I was afraid. It would have been too painful to see you, knowing I would only lose you again."

They stood unmoving, staring at each other like strangers with nothing more to say. After a painful silence broken only by the crackle of the flames between them, Charles said quietly, "Will you tell me about Ailsa?"

Mairi took a deep breath, grateful he had chosen a subject they could speak of without hurting each other further. "She's a sensitive lass—or was, when I knew her. She loved to play the hand harp and even created music of her own. She liked to pretend her notes echoed the sound of the burn in spring."

Each word brought to him more clearly the full sense of what he had lost. "What do you mean, 'when you knew her'?"

"At seventeen, she married a Sassenach barrister and went to live in London. She hasn't been back to the glen since."

"Is she happy?"

Mairi frowned. "Ailsa belongs in the hills, just as I do, but she didn't listen to the voices that bid her stay. Ye see, she also had a touch of ye in her, so she had to go."

There was no trace of accusation in her voice, but Charles could not help wondering if Mairi blamed him for that loss, too. "She never came back?"

Mairi smiled the bittersweet smile that sent a sharp pain through his chest. "I think she couldn't bear to return any more than ye could. She loved these hills too much, ye see."

"She was afraid," Charles said wearily. He understood

more about his daughter in those few moments than he might have in a lifetime. How, he wondered, could he feel so bereft from the loss of a girl he had never even seen?

Mairi recognized his bewilderment, even through her own pain. "I did try to tell ye, Charles. I wrote to your parents in London soon after Ailsa was born."

Charles swallowed dryly. "I told them about you, you know. I'm afraid they didn't approve. They must have destroyed your letter; they never sent it to me." He began to pace, unable to stay still, until a new thought struck him. "But I wrote to you all those years. Didn't you get the letters?"

She placed her hand on a rosewood box on the dresser. "I've kept every one, even the note ye wrote when ye last left the glen. I have them still."

"Then you knew where I was. You could have traced me. Why didn't you try again?"

She looked away. "I wrote once more, when Ailsa was seventeen. I sent it to India, to the city ye'd last written me from. Calcutta, I think 'twas. But again ye didn't answer."

Charles frowned, trying to remember. "That must have been 1860. I'd gone on to Bombay or somewhere else. They didn't leave me anywhere for long. It would have been difficult to reach me then, I suppose." But still something disturbed him. "And after that? Did you write again?"

"After that 'twas too late. She'd already gone."

Charles stopped still. "You mean *you* had lost her, so you decided I shouldn't have her either?"

"Mayhap 'tis true!" Mairi cried. She stood with her back to him and added, "And mayhap I was afraid just like ye."

She turned, reached for his hands, and Charles saw she was weeping. His anger dimmed a little at the sight of her distress. She had no doubt suffered as much as he, in her own way. With a sigh, he drew her close so her tears fell on his morning coat. He had always thought Mairi strong and indestructible, like the mountains all around. Yet here she stood, shattered, vulnerable, turning to him for comfort. The sight tore at his heart as nothing in his life before.

He wanted to heal her but did not know how. He was helpless in the face of his own debilitating pain. It seemed every one of them had let their fear rule their lives, keeping them from the people and places they loved most.

"We're such fools, Mairi," he groaned. "You and Ailsa and I. Such damned stubborn fools." He stepped back to look at her tear-streaked face. He felt he had never seen it before. He knew then that he had to get away. His emotions were in turmoil. He needed time to make some sense of all that he had learned.

"Go," Mairi said through her tears, reading his thoughts as she had so often in the past. "I understand."

The simple kindness of those words was more than he could bear. He left the cottage, but could not escape the memory of Mairi's pain-filled eyes. He hurried, hoping to outrun the truth. In his confusion, he did not realize where he was going.

Oddly, he did notice the dark thunderous clouds that had begun to gather in the sky. He saw how the mountains became more threatening in the fading light, how the wind howled above him, cried out his despair, and carried it over the moors draped in heather and eerie mist. The land seemed to answer his mood as if it understood what he suffered. He began at last to see why Mairi loved these hills.

There was about this place a savagery of feeling that he understood. Yet the hills had beauty, too. A beauty so intense it became pain and lingered, colored a person's blood. Finally there was despair like the gnawing emptiness he felt when he thought of Ailsa and her mother alone amidst this terrifying glory for all those endless years.

He knew now that Mairi had been right to send him away. They could never have stayed happy together; one would have torn himself apart trying to please the other. But to have known he had a child as well as the warm memory of a woman, to have been with them now and then for a day, a week, a month would have changed everything. It would have given him a family to come back to. It was not only Ailsa he had lost, but Li-an and Genevra and the other women he loved. He shook with fury at the cruelty of so much barrenness in one short life.

If only he had not been such a coward.

He began to run while the wind roared in his ears. But it was not the wind at all, only the rasp of his own ragged breath. He had to rest or he would collapse. He was relieved to see a cleft in the rock ahead. He stumbled through, his body shaken with spasms of numbness and fits of coughing.

He had made a mistake; there was no refuge here. This circle of jagged rocks was full of shadows that wavered into insubstantial ghosts whose voices were the wind keening through the maze of cracks and broken boulders. Charles sank to his knees in a bed of bracken, holding his head in his hands. He choked and gasped but could not catch his breath. He was surrounded by the restless spirits of dead men. He could not breathe, would never be able to breathe again.

Then the wind grew still and the shadows ceased their mad dance as a warmth spread slowly from his shoulders to his aching chest. His heartbeat slowed, the spasms became less frequent and he felt the color return to his cheeks.

It was a long moment before he realized what had wrought this change. There were warm hands on his shoulders, circling, soothing, kneading. They moved up and down his back, cupped his neck and massaged gently, destroyed the chill as they ordered his fragmented thoughts and calmed him slowly, patiently. Mairi's hands—her magic hands that sent the wind spinning into the void and bade the ghosts return to their dark hollows. After what seemed like hours of circling, warming, circling, his cough ceased altogether and he found it did not hurt to breathe.

"I was worried about ye, so I followed," she murmured into the sudden stillness. "Ye're very ill, are ye no'?"

He could not lie to her. "Yes."

Mairi had suspected as much from the first moment she saw him, yet she was surprised at the grief she felt now. She had never really had Charles to herself, but always she had known he was out there somewhere, that there was a Charles Kittridge whom she loved and who had loved her. "How long?" she asked softly.

"Long enough to regret—"

She stopped him with her fingers on his lips. "The past is past. Think of the future."

He shook his head, uncomprehending. "What future?"

Mairi laid her palm against his cheek. "Ailsa would come back, my Charles—for ye. I will write to her tomorrow."

Charles's throat was suddenly dry. How it must hurt his wife to admit that though Ailsa had never returned to the mother who loved her, she would come back for Charles, a stranger. His hand tightened on Mairi's and she returned the pressure.

" 'Tis time Ailsa took the chance." Mairi paused, brow furrowed. "In your letters, ye told me there were others. Lian, I think, and Genevra? We could write to them, too."

Charles felt the burning of tears against his lids. "You would do that for me?"

"Aye," she said simply.

He did not know how to tell her what it meant to him, but he thought she understood. "Do you think they would come?"

"We'll make them come."

"Thank you," Charles said, but the words said more.

They did not speak for a long time, but sat and listened to the distant thunder, the laughter of the wind that whipped into the valley, over the three large cairns and out again. Mairi began to sing a Gaelic song, softly, so it mingled with the breeze. Charles did not understand the words, but it did not matter; the song was part of the mystery of the hills. Humming softly, his wife moved closer, until her hair brushed his neck. The rhythm of her heartbeat soothed him, lulled him into stillness. His despair and grief began to ebb. With the warmth of her hands on his back and her face next to his, even the hollow emptiness began to fill a little at a time.

Charles looked at the purple mountains surrounded by a stormy violet sky, then turned to see those things reflected in Mairi's vivid eyes. Mountains, sky, and eyes—so beautiful and so disturbing. Yet somehow he found comfort in them all. "Mairi," he said, linking his fingers with hers, "it's taken a long time, but I've finally come back where I belong."

She rested her cheek on his hair. "We have an old sayin', *mo-charaid, mo-run*, that the gloamin' brings all home again."

ROSSHIRE,
SCOTLAND
1879

Charmed by another's purpose, I attain my own desire.

—Kuo Hsi

1

It was late March by the time Ailsa and Alanna Sinclair left London for Glen Affric. First Ailsa's son Colin had fallen ill and she had remained to see him through the illness. Then Cynthia, Ailsa's second daughter, had insisted on having her coming-out before her mother left. Ailsa had received word from Mairi that Charles was improving in the healthy atmosphere of the Highlands; she need not hurry if her family needed her. So she had remained in the dreary gray rain of London to help with the preparations, though she thought the event itself somewhat ridiculous. She had attended while the ladies and gentlemen in London—who had long since given up gossiping about her odd behavior and manner of dress—complimented her, and the young gentlemen fawned over Cynthia in her Ottoman silk gown with imported French lace.

As she watched Cynthia move around the room, careful of her gown and conscious of her carriage, her pride evident in the way she held her head, Ailsa felt that her daughter was a stranger whose heart she could not understand. But beside her stood Alanna, who was nearly twenty, never a stranger, always a friend, almost from the day of her birth. She had felt as out of place as her mother among the sweep of bustled silk, satin, and velvet skirts, the high, chattering voices of the women, the brilliant light of the crystal chandeliers. If not for the wit and understanding of the friends Ailsa and William had made over the years, among them the Kendalls, the Steels, Laura Durand, and most particularly, the displaced Scotsman, Robbie Douglas, the night would have been dismal indeed.

At last, having completed their many duties, Ailsa and

her oldest daughter had bidden farewell to the other members of the family. Now the two women had completed the final part of the journey to the glen in the back of an open wagon where the wind blew their hair and stung their cheeks. Ailsa had remained silent while Alanna exclaimed over the lush scenery.

The wagon pulled to a stop and the women stepped down while the driver put their bags on the muddy road beside them. "We'll have someone get them later," Ailsa said as the wagon rumbled off. She stood at the edge of the woods and her heart pounded dully in her chest. Her cheeks were flushed with more than cold.

"Whatever ye say," Alanna murmured in the Scottish brogue that had become more and more pronounced as they traveled through Scotland. The lilting words came more naturally to her than the London voices of her youth. She saw that her mother's eyes were closed, her head thrown back while she listened to sounds heard only in memory for over twenty years. Ailsa moved forward, hands extended, running her fingers over the bark of a Caledonian pine. The mist swirled about her and she raised her head to breathe it in, but did not open her eyes. It was as though she wanted to reacquaint herself with the beauty of the glen through sound and taste and touch; the addition of sight would be too much, would make her senses spin out of control. "Why—" Alanna began.

"Because," her mother interrupted, "I'm afraid 'twill no' be as lovely as I remember, and that would break my heart."

Alanna shook her head. "Ye're afraid 'twill be as lovely."

Alisa turned to look at her daughter in surprise. "Ye're so like your grandmother, *mo-run.* So wise and so young." Eyes open wide, the two women continued into the forest.

Ailsa felt her pulse slow, then begin to race as she saw the shadows on the soft earth, the bracken that had begun to run riot, now that the snows were melting away. She saw the hills wrapped in cloaks of new heather and beyond them the snow-covered mountains—as powerful and brooding as she remembered. She heard the leaves whisper above her, felt cool, damp air touch her cheek. The darkness, fragrant, inviting, fell around her as the murmur of the river reached her at last and she knew that finally, truly, she was home.

Alanna gazed about in wonder, delighted to see with her own eyes what she had imagined through her mother's stories for so many years. It was magnificent—the whispering woods, the wild grass and snow-spotted moors, the huge purple mountains, ruggedly beautiful and somehow dearly familiar. She turned to find that Ailsa's cheeks were covered with tears. "Mother?" she murmured, but the sound of her voice was lost in the wind.

Instinctively, Ailsa reached for her daughter's hand. The two stood side by side while the glen wove its alluring spell around them.

Ailsa felt uncomfortable in her beige wool traveling dress with its high collar and brown piping, though she wore no bustle and her hair was a simple crown of braids. The embroidered hem of her skirt hid soft leather boots. Alanna was equally overdressed for a walk in the woods; her red hair was pulled back into a chignon and she wore her mother's wedding dress of wool shot with silk. She, too, wore leather slippers.

"Come," Ailsa said unexpectedly. "I want to show ye somethin'." Her tone was vibrant with excitement.

Alanna had never heard that note in her mother's voice; she felt tears burn her own eyes. "I'll come with ye, of course, but what about Grandmother?"

"She doesn't know what day we'll be arrivin'. We'll go to her soon. But first, I want to take ye to my special place."

Her daughter gaped. "Your secret place where no one else has ever been?"

No one but Ian, Ailsa thought. "Aye," she murmured. "Come." It felt strange to walk over the familiar ground in shoes and Ailsa stopped at the edge of the woods to remove hers. "Ye must feel the bracken and grasses beneath your feet or ye haven't really known the glen," she explained.

Alanna followed her mother's example. She suspected that Ailsa was delaying the meeting with her mother and father a little longer; the shock of seeing the hills again had been so great, she was not quite ready for another. Alanna did not argue, but tossed her slippers aside and squealed when her toes first touched the cold grass. As Ailsa ran ahead, threading her way through bracken and heather, Alanna forgot her chilled feet in her attempt to keep up. She had not thought her mother could run so fast. The exertion, along with the wind, had whipped some pins from Ailsa's hair and her braid had begun to come loose. Alanna laughed into the white, swirling moisture when her mother shrugged and smiled, her blue-violet eyes full of mischief. She had grown young again so quickly. There were no tears now; she flung her arms outward to embrace the whole of the glen and threw back her head toward the cloudy sky.

When they reached the nearest mountain, Ailsa paused to catch her breath. She leaned against a hawthorn, gasping. Her daughter collapsed beside her. "I didn't realize how soft I had become," Ailsa murmured.

Alanna rested her head on her knees, staring down at her cold, bruised feet. She did not care about the physical discomfort. How could she when her mother was so happy, when she herself had discovered paradise? "It'll come back to ye slowly, Mother. Ye've been a long time away."

"Aye," Ailsa whispered. "A long, long time." She turned abruptly to start up the side of the hill.

"Surely ye don't mean to climb without your shoes? How do ye dare?" the girl asked, appalled.

"I once said I'd dare anythin'," Ailsa told her with an odd, distant smile. "And I've never turned down a challenge, except for one." Her eyes grew shadowed and she looked away. "Are ye comin' or will ye wait down here?"

"I'm comin'," Alanna declared. "Just try to leave me behind."

They climbed slowly, hand over hand, tearing their feet and palms on the gorse and protruding rocks, but both went doggedly on. Finally, panting, bleeding, bruised, they reached the top. Ailsa moved eagerly forward despite her sore feet to stand at the edge where she could look out over the glen to which she had been born and had never really left behind.

It was the same—the sweeping moor, dotted with patches of snow and vivid grass, the river like glittering silver threads among the trees, the woods full of tall, swaying birches, pines, and hawthorns with their mystical pattern of leaves in the wind. She knew that the mountains rose behind her, broken by rushing waters and jagged, scarred rock. By Dagda, God of Earth, she loved this place. She had not known how much until this moment. Ailsa breathed it in, spread out her hands, and saw in the mist that settled on her palms reflections of all she could not reach. Oddly, the fierce beauty no longer had the power to break her heart. She saw it, embraced it, but there was no pain.

Alanna hung back, sensing that her mother needed to be alone. When she could wait no longer, she moved to the edge, then stopped, dumbfounded by the scene below her. She had not expected this—to stand at the top of the world and see so much, to feel it in her bones and blood, to hear it in the wind that circled her shoulders then fled into the blue-violet sky. She touched her mother's arm, in case it was all a dream, but Ailsa was there; she was warm and real. Because there were no words for what Alanna felt, she spoke the first that came to mind. "The view must be wonderful at dawn."

Ailsa turned. "Ye've never heard the Dawn Song, have ye? Tomorrow before daylight, we should come."

Before she could stop herself, Alanna said softly, "Ye look so young, Mother. 'Twas always too dark in London to see how beautiful ye are."

Ailsa smiled a bittersweet smile that made Alanna want to weep. "Come," her mother said. "We should go down."

Jenny Fraser walked through the forest with a creel full of peats over her arm. When she moved from the shadows into the afternoon light, she saw a movement on the mountain and stopped, her hand raised to shield her eyes. She saw a woman lift her arms and tilt back her head as the wind whipped her skirts about her ankles. Jenny's heart contracted and the breath caught in her throat. Quickly, she followed the well-worn path toward her croft, ducked under the low doorframe.

Ian was seated by the fire, carving a piece of wood into a bird for their youngest child, Erlinna, who sat beside him, watching with awe. Their oldest, Gavin, was away somewhere. Brenna and Glenyss were at the oak table chopping carrots and potatoes for the barley broth they'd have for supper. The scene was so comfortable, so familiar that she sighed with relief.

Ian looked up, sensed his wife's unease and asked, "What is it, *mo-aghray?*"

Jenny looked into his green eyes that she loved so much, at his dark curly hair that had not changed in the last twenty years, though his face had grown more leathered from the sun. "She's back," Jenny said simply.

He knew at once whom his wife meant. For an instant, for a flash that might not have been at all, Ian tensed, then relaxed on the oak stool he straddled. Odd that he had not felt Ailsa's presence, he thought. But then he had chosen it should be so.

"Ian?" Jenny asked anxiously.

He smiled at the woman who had made him comfortable and happy over the years. "Don't fret, Jenny. It'll be makin' no difference to ye or to me."

His steady gaze told her he spoke the truth. Ian had never lied to her, not once in all the years they'd been together. Jenny smiled tenderly. "Aye," she murmured. "Just as ye say."

Ailsa and her daughter reached the bottom of the hill as winded as they had arrived at the top. With difficulty, they made their way back to the river, where they washed their sore feet, drank handfuls of the clear water, then collapsed on the bracken to gaze up at the shifting leaves. For a long while, they lay in companionable silence.

Suddenly Alanna raised her head. "Someone's comin'."

Ailsa looked up, saw a movement in the distance that became a shadow, then more than a shadow—the figure of a woman. She knew who it was long before she could see the woman's face. She rose, hardly aware that Alanna did so as well, then moved back, almost out of sight. Ailsa felt cold, and her heartbeat increased. Finally the woman was close enough for Ailsa to see her breath in the air, her gray-streaked red hair and simple wool gown.

Mairi stopped a few feet away and the two stood, uncertain, frozen by the well of emotions inside—by hope and affection, regret and despair, love and, most of all, the fear that they would find each other strangers. Mairi had thought she would be shocked by Ailsa's appearance, in spite of letters home that had been full of warm contentment. She had expected a ghost of the girl she had known, but this was not a ghost. Ailsa was paler, it was true, for the London sun rarely touched her face. But her smile was natural, her movement graceful, her gaze as perceptive as it had always been.

Ailsa looked at her mother's face, so familiar, so long unseen, and felt a tearing inside as great as the day she had left the glen. But then there came a healing warmth when she saw that Mairi's violet eyes had not changed and that they brimmed with tears of joy and recognition. Mairi hung back, so Ailsa moved forward to take her mother in her arms.

This was not a dream; they were here, touching, together at last. For a long, long time they held each other in silence. There was everything to say and no need to say it. All the days and months each had lived since Ailsa's marriage passed through their minds until the images met and melded and each knew what the other had done and felt and seen in those lost years.

At last, Mairi raised her head. " 'Tis glad to see ye again, I am, Ailsa-*aghray*," she murmured. She paused, head tilted when she saw a movement among the leaves, a figure coming forward. The shadows hid the girl's red hair, making it appear chestnut, and Mairi recognized the gown that shimmered, deep blue shot with purple in the clearing light. She knew that gown with its low neckline and narrow waist, the wide skirt that rustled, weighed down though it was with dirt and grime. For a moment, she thought it was the ghost of her daughter at seventeen, come back to stand beside her. Then Ailsa reached out to draw Alanna forward.

"Alanna Sinclair, meet your grandmother, Mairi Rose."

Mairi took the girl's hands and looked into her violet eyes.

Alanna felt at once that she had known this woman all

her life. She saw the face so like her own; she had seen it each time she glanced in a mirror. She looked beyond the eyes to Mairi's soul and understood at once. In all her life, she had only known her mother better.

Mairi turned, beaming, to Ailsa. "She has the secrets in her eyes, does your daughter. Just like ye."

"Aye," Ailsa said fondly. "Of my bairns, only Alanna has the soul of the glen and the heart of the mountains. For she has *your* eyes, Mother, and your understandin', too."

"Come," Mairi said, her cheeks flushed with pleasure and the color of remembered pain, "come ye both home with me, for 'tis long past time."

As they approached the croft, Mairi noticed her daughter was breathing unsteadily, caught up in the feelings that overcame her in a rush when she saw the house where she had been born.

Ailsa stopped a few feet from the door to stare at the dark, weathered wood, the warped frame that had seemed as high as heaven when she was a child. Mairi touched Alanna's arm and they went inside, leaving Ailsa to her thoughts, which were not true thoughts, but only shocks of memory and pain and all the dreams she had ever dreamed. Was he inside now, her father who had drawn her back to the place of her heart? Was he waiting?

She shook herself, stepped inside, and saw that only Alanna sat on a polished birch chair beside the peat fire. Ailsa's disappointment was so sharp it took her breath away.

"He's out sketchin'," Mairi said, though her back was to her daughter. "I'll go and fetch him home soon."

She busied herself with packets of herbs while Ailsa looked about her at the familiar table, the chairs, the dresser and press. The blackened stone walls had not changed. They welcomed her as the wind had welcomed her—like an old friend. She saw the miniature of Charles Kittridge beside the rosewood box, where it had always been, and felt a sense of unreality. Though her mind told her differently, in her heart she could not really believe in her father's existence; she had ceased to do so twenty years ago in London. She looked away. There, beneath the window covered with leather, was her kist, where she had knelt on her wedding day and wept. Because of Ian. For the second time she allowed herself to think his name and the dull ache throbbed, more intense this time because he was so near.

"Ye'd best take off your shoes like your wise daughter and sit ye down by the fire," Mairi said quickly, as if she sensed the dangerous direction of her daughter's thoughts. "I'm brewin' up somethin' to soothe the cuts and bruises on your feet. Whatever made ye climb barefoot when ye knew what the mountainside was like?"

"Because I'm a great blitherin' fool, that's why." Ailsa smiled and sat down while Mairi poured warm water mixed with herbs into two large bowls, then placed the bowls at their feet.

"This should soothe ye and harden up your soles so ye'll no' limp home to your husband, feet bleedin' and head hangin'."

Ailsa smiled fondly. "He wouldn't mind. He would sit me in the parlor and have Lizzie see to my wounds while he held my hands and asked me all about the glen."

" 'Tis true," Alanna said. "He'd enjoy takin' care of her. Usually she's so strong, Father doesn't get to make much of her." As she slipped her feet into the herb-scented water, Alanna sighed with relief. "Grandmother," she asked eagerly, "will ye teach me about the herbs?"

Mairi smiled, pleased that the girl should want to know. "Aye," she replied, "I'll teach ye more than ye care to learn."

"Ye couldn't do that, for I want to know everything about the plants and roots and healin' leaves as well as the dyes my mother has talked of."

"Do ye now?" Mairi crouched by the fire, her hands extended toward the flames. "Well, ye put me in mind of a bairn I used to know long ago, who was never satisfied with what she knew but always must know more." She turned to Ailsa with a fond, sad smile. "Tell me about your family, *mo-ghray*."

Ailsa did so. As she spoke, she watched her mother move about the croft and noticed for the first time the changes years of suffering had made behind Mairi's new glow of happiness. Sorrow and loneliness had etched wrinkles around her eyes and between her nose and mouth. The startling violet of her eyes had darkened to the color of purple mountains at gloaming. Even now, when she smiled, the shadows were there—beneath her eyes, along her cheeks, in the curve of her lips. She seemed so small and fragile suddenly. Ailsa had always thought her mother strong, tall, all-knowing and unchanging. But she *had* changed, as had her daughter. Mairi was more of this world now; her eyes reflected the hills instead of the endless sky.

Then Ailsa noticed the harp on the wall. Her eyes darkened and memories hovered about her in shapes that she could nearly touch, yet they eluded her. She rose, wet feet and all, to go to where the clarsach hung. Gently, she touched the wood that glowed against the rough white stone. She ran her fingers over the strings.

She felt the vibration of the lilting notes all through her body, closed her eyes against the pain they brought. She let her hand drop and turned away, her face full of anguish.

Her mother felt the echo of that pain in her own blood. "In time, mayhap," Mairi said, "ye'll find ye want to play again. 'Tis too much a part of ye to give up forever."

"She didn't give it up," Alanna interjected. She wondered why no one had yet spoken the name of Charles Kittridge, the reason they had come here, the only force strong enough to make her mother face the past. Somehow she sensed that he was there among them as surely as if he stood leaning with his pipe against a wall. "She plays the harp at home often. She says it gives her peace. I say just that 'tis beautiful and I'd have her play forever." Why didn't she ask the questions about her grandfather that hovered on the tip of her tongue? Because she sensed that it was her mother's place to ask, her mother's place to know.

For the next two hours they soaked their sore feet and talked of the time apart. Mostly Alanna listened, delighted by the lyrical flow of the words, the occasional Gaelic phrases, the magic sound of their speech. She had thought her mother would be a different person once they reached the glen, but she was Ailsa still, only a little more touched with sadness, lost in the beauty of her surroundings.

Eventually, the shadows began to move across the floor and Mairi noticed a chill in the air. " 'Tis time to fetch my Charlie home. I'd best go alone and bring him to ye here."

Ailsa bit her lip. Her mother had spoken the name with such affection. There was no trace of fear, coldness, or anger. Obviously the time spent with her husband had rid her of those burdensome feelings. But Ailsa had a fear of her own, an old, dry anger, as well as excitement that made her pulse race. She would see him at last, the man who had been the focus of her dreams for so long.

Ailsa sat still as Mairi took down her plaid and covered her head, then wrapped it tight about her shoulders. Her mother paused in the doorway to murmur, "He's an old man, Ailsanean, and ill. Try no' to blame him too much for your dreams that weren't real. Try to love him if ye can, even a little."

"I've always loved him!" Ailsa exclaimed. "Ye know how much."

Mairi shook her head. "I know ye worshiped the man ye created out of your fantasies and a few faded words he'd written to me. Ye longed for him and dreamed of him and made images of him in your mind. But that was no' real. That was no' love. All I ask is that ye try." She slipped away.

Ailsa stared after her in disbelief, but as the cold evening wind whipped through the door, raising chills along her neck, she wondered if her mother were right. What would she say to him? What *could* she say? Had she been wrong to come? Until this moment, the thought of meeting her father had been a fantasy. Now, suddenly, it had become real.

Alanna covered her mother's cold hand with her warm one. "Don't fret, as ye've said to me many a time. 'Twill be all right. I feel it here."

She pressed her hand to her heart as Ian used to do and Ailsa winced.

After a few minutes, Alanna rose, dried her feet, and replaced her shoes, found a plaid hanging on the hook by the door, and draped it around her. She glanced out often, her excitement building as time dragged on. "What will he be like, do ye think?" she asked. "Will he be old and sour

621

or distinguished and brave? Will he be handsome still, or shriveled like the apple Colin dropped under the piano that we didn't find for months?''

She chattered on while Ailsa stared into the flames— the quavering golden flames where the past lay and the future, if one looked hard enough, but not the present. She was hardly aware of Alanna flitting about, unable to stay still in her anticipation.

"I see them!" Alanna cried at last.

Ailsa was up in a moment, poised in the doorway to peer through the blue twilight at the couple who moved slowly among the trees. She saw they had their arms about each other and leaned together, Mairi supporting Charles a little over the hilly ground. Ailsa felt resentment rise within her. It should always have been like this. Her mother should not have been alone for so many years; she should have had this man beside her, his arm about her waist.

Like Ailsa she should have had her husband sit nearby when she held her children and told them stories, sang Celtic chansons while the fire flickered around them like a warm, safe shield. She, too, should have smiled and laughed as her husband began to try stories of his own and even a song or two. She should have known the joy of watching the children grow until they listened, enraptured, and begged for more. She should have had a man beside her who turned each night with adoration in his eyes to take her in his arms.

Ailsa's compassion for all Mairi had missed turned to anger at the man who had not come back to share it with her. Then she shook her head at her own foolishness. Mairi had made that choice, not Charles.

When they approached, Ailsa ducked inside. She did not want to see his face through the purple gloaming, as she had always seen it—a shadow in the mist, a phantom. She wanted to see the real Charles facing her in the firelight.

"Alanna!"

Mairi's voice floated in from outside. "Bring a plaid, birdeen, and come walk with me. I'll show ye the glen at gloamin', when there's magic in the air."

Alanna smiled reassuringly, then did as her grandmother had bidden her. She ducked under the door and disappeared. After she'd gone, there was a stillness so complete that it slowed the beat of Ailsa's heart. He was not coming in. He would go with Mairi and Alanna. He was not there at all. She had imagined the two of them walking through the twilight that made things appear to be what they were not. Then the door creaked on its hinges and a tall man bent to step over the threshold.

He was chilled and damp and pushed the door to so the warmth inside would dissolve the moisture. Then he straightened to regard his daughter from across the room while the fire blazed between them.

Ailsa saw a man with pure white hair and blue eyes that had dulled over the years from the portrait she had memorized. Even beneath his aged and weathered skin, burned brown by the Highland sun, she recognized the cheekbones that she shared, the aristocratic nose. But that smile, full of peace yet uncertainty, fear yet hope, was something she had never imagined.

"Ailsa?" he murmured. He shrugged off his greatcoat, hung it on a chair near the fire where it would dry. "I'm Charles Kittridge, your father."

She opened her mouth, but no words came. She had always thought him an incredible man who could set her world to rights with a wave of his hand, but one look into his eyes, dimmed by pain and loss and grief, one sight of his crooked smile told her he did not have that power. He was not a magician, ever young and ever strong. He was Charles Kittridge and nothing more. He had known as much pain as she, perhaps even more. She saw a great deal of turmoil and very little peace in his eyes. At least she had known comfort, warmth, affection all these years. But this man had not; she knew that as surely as she knew her own past. "I didn't realize," she said softly. "I'm sorry, but I didn't know how hard your life had been."

His eyes shone with what might have been the glimmer of tears. "How can you apologize to me? I'm the one who never dared come back and discover he had a child."

She regarded him intently, curiously. "Why didn't ye?"

Charles turned away, began to pace before the door, afraid that if he chose the wrong word he would lose her before he ever had a chance to know her. Yet now, when he needed it most, his facility with words had left him. He could not think while his daughter—the child of his and Mairi's blood—stood just across the room, waiting for his answer. He coughed, grasped the back of a chair to try to catch his breath. "I was sure I couldn't have Mairi, not forever," he began haltingly. "And I thought to see her again, knowing that, would break my heart."

Ailsa wanted to touch him in compassion, but she was not yet ready. There was still too much confusion. "I think our hearts are stronger than we believe." She paused, frowning. "Before ye came back to the glen, did ye ever wish ye'd never met my mother, never had to suffer all the pain she gave ye?"

Charles considered. "Sometimes, but only for a moment, when the loneliness seemed too much to take. Meeting Mairi—it was the best part of my life. Those months with her have stretched into a lifetime for me."

Brow furrowed, Ailsa said softly, "Don't ye see that joy, laughter, love that is a flame which never grows dim are rare in this world? Isn't it worth havin' for a day, a week, a month, even just an hour, no matter what comes later?"

Charles took a step closer. "If you believe that, why did you stay away for over twenty years?"

"Because I *didn't* believe it. No' till I saw the glen again." She remembered the wonderful agony of standing on her precipice, the world at her feet—all the world she ever wanted, all the world she'd ever loved. "Till I felt the mist on my face and the wind in my hair, I was too afraid to take the chance. I realized only then that 'twas worth any cost to lose myself among the hills I love, even the cost of leavin' them behind again."

Her father fought to find his voice. "That's how it was for me, as well. When I saw Mairi standing in the doorway last spring, waiting, I knew nothing else mattered."

"Then how can I blame ye, when my fear was as great?"

He smiled Mairi's bittersweet smile. "You could. Anger isn't rational, you know. It burns just as strongly in those who are wrong as in those who are right. I know because of the rage I felt when I realized your mother had not told me about you.''

''Would it have made a difference?''

They had spoken so far with the fire between them, casting wavering shadows over their faces. Now he stepped around the blaze until he could touch her if he put out his hand. ''It would, Ailsa. That I swear. You would have brought me back in spite of my doubts.''

Ailsa reached out blindly to find herself in her father's arms. They were warm and firm. He was real, not a dream, not a nightmare or a vision. He was a man, flesh and blood, nervous and full of hope, just like her. Like her he had wept and felt alone, bereft. Like her he had been an exile. He was the father she had never had. *That* was the miracle.

She flung her arms around him, buried her head on his shoulder, and even though he was a stranger, she knew him. She had known him all her life, through Mairi's eyes, not her own, which had been blinded by childish hopes. Somehow, in spite of her own stubbornness, she had absorbed a sense of the man he really was. She held him while he ran his hand over her windblown hair, tentatively, as if she might pull away.

''My father,'' she said at last, ''I'm glad we've both come home.''

2

Ailsa lay in her box bed enfolded by the scent of heather. Too exhausted to think about all that had happened, she fell asleep and dreamed.

She was trapped inside a rolling ship surrounded by waves that rose higher and higher. Eventually, they would close forever over her head. She would never be free of the treacherous waves, never be still and warm and at peace again. She wanted to be away from this place, yet she did not wish to reach her destination.

At last the pitching stopped, the waves grew calm, and she left the ship that had been her home for far too long. She stood on a wharf, swaying, until a hand reached out to steady her. She stared about her, horrified by the filth, the noise and squalor that was London. It trapped her as closely as the storm-ravaged waves; she choked on the fetid gray air.

As she walked through the streets, people stopped to stare and point at her golden skin and black braided hair. They called out names she did not understand. Her head began to ache dully. There were friends on either side of her, but they could not protect her from the sneering, angry crowd. There had been another crowd in Peking, she remembered, more dangerous than this. She forced the memory away and concentrated on stepping around piles of filth in the street. The calls became louder, the shouting, the anger. The pain in her head throbbed and she pressed her hands to her temples.

"Bloody foreigners!" the people shouted. "We don't want the likes of you here. Go back where you came from." She refused to bow her head before the wrath of these strangers but looked them straight in the eyes. That only made them hate her more.

She saw a young boy raise his arm, then fling something. She tried to duck the heavy stone, but it hit her squarely on the side of the head. The pain splintered, the light fragmented, and then . . . darkness.

"Mother! Mother! Remember ye promised to take me to the mountainside to hear the Dawn Song. I've been awake for near an hour waitin' for ye."

Blinded by pain, Ailsa stared blankly at her daughter. She reached up to touch the wound on the side of her head, but it wasn't there. She rubbed her eyes, and slowly, Alanna's face came into focus.

"Are ye all right, Mother? Ye look so pale. Does your head ache? I'll wake Grandmother and ask her for an herb to take the pain away."

"No," Ailsa managed to whisper. "Never mind, birdeen. 'Twas only a dream." Yet it had seemed so real. She was certain she'd felt the stone hit her temple.

Ailsa took a long time to get out of bed; her head still rang and spun when she moved. The last remnants of the dream retreated as she recognized the familiar objects in the croft. She saw that Alanna was already dressed and waiting. Still troubled by a feeling of unease, Ailsa threw on a shift and a plain lilac linsey-woolsey gown.

Silently, the two women moved toward the door, so they would not awaken Mairi and her husband. Before they slipped out, Charles lifted himself on his elbow to whisper, "Would you mind if I came along?"

"No, please come. I want Alanna to go up alone. Ye can keep me company till she returns." Strange, she thought, to be doing such normal things with a man she had never met until yesterday.

Ailsa and her daughter stepped outside while Charles dressed, then the three set out well wrapped in red plaids. Ailsa refused to wear her shoes and Alanna was too proud to say she wanted desperately to put on her own; she, too, went barefoot. They moved slowly through the silver-white mist, inhaling the scent of heather and fresh grass.

"I used to hate this place," Charles said when Alanna had begun her climb up the mountain. Ailsa and her father settled into a crevice protected by rock from the weeping wind.

"How could anyone hate it?" Ailsa cried, truly shocked.

"I think because Mairi loved it so much. Perhaps I sensed that it held her more tightly than I ever could."

Ailsa looked at him intently. "Is that really why ye think she sent ye away, because she didn't wish to leave the glen?"

He nodded. Even now there was a trace of bitterness in his eyes.

Ailsa fell silent, listening to the voices all around her. Then she took her father's hand, spotted with age and illness, the skin nearly transparent. " 'Twas much more than that. An Englishman had killed her father and brother before her eyes and spit on them. She killed him for it. Because of her guilt and the things she saw in that soldier's eyes, she was afraid of the hatred your people felt for ours, afraid they would destroy her, too."

Charles frowned. "Why didn't she tell me?"

"She was young and there were many things she couldn't say, didn't know *how* to say. She loved ye too much, ye see. Ye stole her tongue away."

Her father leaned forward. "But you weren't afraid of that hatred?"

"No' enough. I wanted to see the world, the wonders I had missed, livin' here all my life. No fear on earth could have held me back."

"Why?"

She smiled, remembering. "Because of ye. I read all your letters, saw the treasures ye sent to lure my mother away from the glen. They touched me as they didn't touch her; they made me burn to know more. I hadn't seen the hatred then and didn't know how deep it went. All I saw was your excitement, the wonder I felt as I held those letters in my hand. 'Twas that which made me marry William and go to London."

"Are you sorry you did?"

"How could I be sorry? William is a fine and rare man, who loves me as few ever love. I have two other bairns—and Alanna. When I look in her eyes I see a mirror image of myself. She's my friend as well as my daughter. And I have music." She smiled. "No, I'm no' sorry. I thought for a time I should have stayed in the glen with the boy I had known here. But I was wrong." *There are things ye believe and things that are true,* Mairi had told her once. *Someday, mayhap, ye'll learn to know the difference.* Ailsa had learned, not because of, but in spite of her mother's warning. She had learned so much. She took Charles's hand.

"Do ye realize even though ye were lost in distant lands as I grew up, ye were here for me, in your own way? Your letters changed my life. So ye see, ye were always my father, seein' to my needs, though neither of us knew it."

Charles covered her hand with his. "You're sure of that?"

"As sure as I am that the sky is above me and the soft earth below." They stopped to listen as the Dawn Song began—the poignant cry of the lapwing, the larks, the vibrant notes of the mavis. Ailsa closed her eyes. To her the songs of the birds were like heaven put to music. It had been so long. When she glanced up, her father was watching her sadly.

"I never had a family, not really," he said unexpectedly. "There were times—" He broke off. He wanted to tell her about the other two girls, but could not bring himself to do it. He felt so close to her just then, so comfortable. He did not want to destroy that unfamiliar feeling. She would have to know soon, but not yet. "Most of my life I've been alone."

"I'm sorry," Ailsa said softly, with compassion. "But I'm glad ye've found my mother again."

He squeezed her hands. "This time I've spent with her was worth all the loneliness. She has a powerful ability to heal."

"Aye."

Just then, Alanna came down the hillside, cheeks flushed and violet eyes sparkling. " 'Twas beautiful, Mother. Why didn't ye tell me such a thing existed? I felt like the wind lifted me into the sky and the notes curled around and inside me. I can't tell ye—"

"Then don't try," Ailsa said. "Some things don't need words. The look on your face is explanation enough."

They went back to the cottage where Charles sat down to rest. He was tired and pale from even so short a walk. Mairi had already prepared a basket with cheese and milk and black buns for her daughter. She knew Ailsa wanted to show the glen to Alanna today. Quickly, she pointed to the basket, folded a wool blanket over Charles's legs, and moved his chair closer to the fire. As the other two left, Mairi sat at his side with her hand in his.

Ailsa watched her parents for an instant, then slipped a few things from her leather bag into her pocket and started off in the cool morning with her daughter at her side.

"Where are we goin'?" Alanna asked.

"Around and about. Eventually, we'll come to a cave where I've stories to tell," Ailsa said mysteriously.

Alanna nodded. No matter how old she grew, she would never tire of her mother's stories of the glen. "I want to see all your favorite places," she announced.

Ailsa thought of a copse by the river where a hawthorn tree spread its branches and the grass and bracken were soft with welcome, where water raced over tumbled rocks and the song of the river was irresistible. She would not take Alanna there. Not yet.

Instead, they headed for the loch. Alanna stood on the shore to watch the sun on the vibrant blue water, fascinated by the shadows of clouds overhead and the wind that whipped the water into rippled waves. Then they climbed to the Hill o' the Hounds, where Ailsa told the story she had told William as they stood at the window many years ago.

"That house doesn't belong here," Alanna said. "It belongs in a park outside of London."

They crossed the moors to the foot of the mountains and stopped among the outcroppings of rock that made strange patterns on the ground. Here they ate their lunch. While Alanna looked about, enthralled, Ailsa remembered another day when she had stood atop these rocks and thought she could fly with the wind. She closed her eyes at a twinge of long-forgotten pain.

"When do we get to the cave?" Alanna demanded.

Ailsa wondered now how wise it would be to return to a place where the damp walls surely echoed with memories. "Soon," her mother said. "Soon enough."

They rose with the basket between them, weaving their way around clumps of gorse and heather and patches of snow. When they approached the granite incline, Ailsa stopped still. All at once she was on the deck of a boat. The rain poured around her, wild, thunderous, slashing through waves swept into fury by the wind. She tilted her head back to let the rain hit her face and stream through her pale blond hair. It was like home, she thought longingly. Like the madness of the monsoon after the long, sun-blinded days of the Hot Weather. Suddenly arms grasped her to drag her inside and a man cried, "Are you mad?" "Mad like your mother," she thought he added, but it was only the echo of long-ago voices.

"Mother, ye look awful, just like ye did this mornin' when I woke ye."

Ailsa turned, certain she would not be able to move because of the arms that held her back. She found she was free and stumbled forward, catching herself before she fell. It took a moment for her eyes to focus on the wall of stone, then the girl beside her. "Alanna?" she said uncertainly.

"Of course 'tis!" the girl cried. "What ails ye that ye don't know your own daughter?"

Ailsa shook away the memory of rain and thunder and violent waves. The uneasiness that had plagued her dreams had returned; this time it would not go. With an effort, she forced a smile. " 'Tis nothin', *mo-run*, just your poor daft mother lettin' the wind take her mind to the land behind the dew and the moonshine where the fairies live." Odd that as she climbed the incline with Alanna behind her, it was not Ian she thought of, but a girl with pale blond hair and another with golden skin and slanted blue eyes.

She came to the ridge and looked into the dell, circled by jagged rocks. The wind rose, moaning, around the three graves piled high with stones. This time she felt sorrow, but there was no chill in her blood, because she understood what had happened here.

Alanna stood beside her, pale and trembling. " 'Tis so dark and eerie," she muttered. "I want to weep but I don't know why. I'm cold, Mother, cold to my bones." The shadows seemed to move with the wind, the stones to cry out in anguished voices. Alanna paused when she saw a shadow that did not belong. The wind whirled away and the darkness retreated as she leaned forward to see better. Yes, she was right. She glanced at Ailsa but said nothing. It would be her secret, at least for a while. "These are cairns, are they no'? Where the dead are buried?" she asked in a whisper.

"Aye," Ailsa replied. "Sometime when your grandmother is in a rememberin' mood, ask her about the Valley of the Dead. 'Tis her story, her grief, her choice whether to tell ye or no'. But try no' to mourn yourself, birdeen. 'Twas all over long ago."

Alanna nodded but did not seem reassured. Ailsa took her hand to guide her into the cave; the girl's fingers were chilled. It seemed Alanna was as sensitive to the feelings in the air as her mother and grandmother had always been. She did indeed have the secrets in her eyes.

The two women ducked beneath the stone overhang and moved toward the distant light where the stones had fallen from the roof of the cave. The chest lay where it always had, coated with dust from long neglect.

"What is't?" Alanna asked.

Ailsa did not hear. She was remembering the first time she had seen that chest and touched the aged carved wood. The memory of Ian was strong within her. She knelt to lay her hands on the lid, over the words "Chisholm, 1746."

"Tell me about it," her daughter whispered.

Ailsa turned to sit with her back against the chest while she told her daughter the story of the Chisholm family's involvement in the '45, how they had fled when the Battle of Culloden Moor was lost.

"Ye sound as if ye knew them," Alanna said.

"I did in a way." She drew Janet Chisholm's diary out of her pocket. " 'Twas from this woman that I learned the story. She even appeared in a dream to warn me."

"Against what?" Alanna asked. She leaned forward, mesmerized.

"Goin' away from the glen, I'm thinkin'. I don't know anymore. I only know we shared a bond because, for a while, we were both strangers lost in an unforgivin' world. But I made London my home in time and found my happiness there. I hope Janet Chisholm found her own peace in the end."

"Why have ye brought the diary here?"

Ailsa touched the worn leather cover. "Because it served its purpose long since by tellin' me there were others who had shared my grief, that I wasn't alone. 'Tis time to return it where it belongs. Mayhap someone else will find it one day and it will touch them, too." She reached into her pocket and took out the purple ribbons she had worn on her wedding day. "These also were hers. She shared them with me, without knowin', 'tis true, but I think she would have wanted it that way." As she spoke she lifted the lid, then stopped, her throat raw and dry.

On top lay the claymore that had once hung above Ian's door, and with it the Chisholm plaid he had displayed so proudly. Now the tartan was carefully folded and put away. She sensed that it had not been disturbed for a very long time. But there was more. There were little gifts she had given him over the years—a doe she had carved when she was seven and presented to him with pride, though all four legs were different lengths; the wreath she had worn on the last Beltaine she had spent in the Highlands; a chanter she had bought him with carefully saved money, which, when it wore out, he'd kept by his bed so he'd think of her when he turned his head in the morning.

Every last trace of the Ailsa Rose Ian had known was packed away like a treasure too precious to look upon. Or a memory too painful to recall. She closed her eyes and saw Ian's face as it had looked the instant before she left him standing alone on the ledge. *Do ye hate me?* she'd asked. *Aye,* he'd replied. *Almost as much as I love ye.*

Her heartbeat slowed to a labored rhythm and she wondered where he was now. He must have heard she was back in the glen, but he had not sought her out. Nor she him. Yet she expected to see his face everywhere she turned. Perhaps he knew, as she did, that to meet him as a stranger would be more than she could bear. To see his lively eyes still and empty as glass would break her heart.

Alanna drew a sharp breath, her hand on her mother's arm. "Someone's comin'," she whispered.

Ailsa listened but heard nothing. "Ye must be mistaken. Still, 'tis time to go. 'Twill be gloamin' soon and your grandmother will wonder where we've gone to." Carefully, she closed the lid of the chest, knowing it was for the last time, while her eyes burned with unshed tears.

Alanna rose to follow her mother, half listening for the sound of footsteps. She was certain she had heard someone. But no—she hadn't heard anything. She simply *knew* as she had sometimes sensed things in London. There were even times when she'd had dreams that came true. Perhaps this was like that, like the feeling she had had when she looked into the dell. The thought both excited and frightened her.

Then Alanna and her mother stepped into the sunlight. Both stopped when they saw a man retreat down the hill of stone. He had obviously been on the ledge, perhaps near the mouth of the cave.

Ailsa drew her breath in slowly. Even from this distance, she knew it was Ian.

"I told ye someone was comin'," Alanna cried triumphantly.

Ailsa could not speak. She had heard nothing, sensed nothing, though Ian had been so close. In the old days she would have known he was approaching long before he reached the hill. But that communion was gone. He had killed it years ago. The emptiness echoed within her, and the pain like a wound that had half healed over time, but now lay open, bleeding afresh.

◦ 3 ◦

Ailsa sensed something was wrong when she pushed open the door of the croft. Charles sat at the pitted oak table, an oil lamp nearby, an envelope in his hands. His skin was pale, the shadows dark beneath his eyes. Mairi stood with her hands on his shoulders, her hair, released from its usual crown of braids, falling to her waist. "Ye don't know for sure that 'tis bad news," she murmured.

Alanna burst in, cheeks flushed with excitement. "We had such a wonderful day—" She broke off when her mother touched her arm, though the warning was not necessary. She felt the tension surround her like a woven web the instant she entered.

While her daughter hung back, uncertain what to do, Ailsa went to stand beside Charles. She was drawn by his sadness; she could see it in the way he leaned forward as if under the weight of a heavy burden. She touched one bent shoulder. "What is't, Papa, that has taken the light from your eyes tonight?"

She glanced at the envelope, saw it was addressed to Wan Li-an, care of Charles Kittridge. " 'Tis an odd name," Ailsa observed. "Why should such a letter come here?"

Charles exchanged a meaningful look with his wife. "I think it's time to tell her."

Mairi nodded. "Sit down, *mo-aghray*."

"Shall I leave ye alone?" Alanna asked in a whisper.

"No," Charles said. "This concerns you as well."

Ailsa and her daughter slid into chairs while Mairi stood by the fire, her hands thrust toward the crackling flames.

Troubled, Charles took Ailsa's hand, struggled to find the words he needed. "I told you I never had a real family, and that's true. But it's also true that you're not my only daughter."

Her instinct was to withdraw her hand, but his fingers tightened around it. "I had a child by a Chinese woman when I was in Canton. The girl"—he paused, smiled sadly—"but she's a woman now. I keep forgetting that. Her name is Li-an Wan, though in China they reverse the names. It was sent here because she, too, is coming to the glen, for the same reason that you've come."

Ailsa stared, speechless at a wave of bitter jealousy. At last she had found the father she'd sought all her life, and now she would have to share him with a stranger, a foreigner, a woman in whose veins his vital blood flowed. Ailsa swallowed dryly, closed her eyes to try to conquer the feeling. She was being selfish and unfair. Then it struck her that Charles had been unfaithful to Mairi. She glanced up in distress at her mother.

Mairi was smiling slightly, her eyes unshadowed. She had known about the other woman, then. She must have felt jealousy and rage once, but now those feelings had disappeared. Perhaps because, for the first time, she had her husband to herself. In his hour of need, he had come to her and her alone.

Ailsa attempted her own smile, but was not very successful.

"Ye mean I have an aunt?" Alanna asked, to fill the uneasy silence. "I never had an aunt before. There's my father's Aunt Abigail, but she isn't exactly—" She broke off, blushing.

"Ye mean to say she's a horrid old thing with no heart or soul in her stiff gray body," Ailsa finished for her daughter.

Charles smiled and she squeezed his hand. If Mairi could forgive him, Ailsa could try.

"There's one thing more." Her father stared at the well-worn tabletop.

"Aye?" Ailsa said warily.

"I have yet another daughter, Genevra Townsend. I met her mother in India while she was married to another. I knew the child was mine, though; I could see it in her eyes."

His face was shadowed with memory. "Through the interference of others, I lost both mother and child, and have only just found Genevra again. She, too, is coming to the glen." He looked at Ailsa with a silent plea. "I wanted so much to see you all, to know you a little before—" He broke off, his forehead filmed in sweat. "I understand this isn't easy for you."

Ailsa rose abruptly to pace beside the fire. "No, 'tisn't easy to find ye have two sisters when ye thought ye were alone. To learn that I must share your hours with women I've never met." She stopped and turned to meet his gaze. "But 'tis excitin', too. Sometimes as I watched my bairns play together, I wondered what 'twould have been like to have sisters and brothers of my own. Mayhap now I'll find out. And as ye heard, Alanna will be delighted with two new aunts." She smiled tentatively and took the hand he extended. "I'll do my best to behave, Papa, but I can't promise I'll no' be jealous now and then. I care too much to share ye easily."

His hand shook. "Do you really care, even after all those years without me?"

"*Because* of all those years without ye. I'll never take ye for granted as some children do." She saw his relief, but her attention had been caught by the letter again. "May I?" She indicated the smudged parchment.

He nodded.

Ailsa took the packet and felt a rush of sorrow so deep that she shook with it. Whatever news these pages held was not happy. She started to drop the letter, but something stopped her—the image of a girl with long black hair, golden skin, and eyes so blue they reflected the sky. The one she had seen in her dream this morning. There had been other dreams, other visions. She remembered a pale girl with wispy blond hair and gray-flecked blue eyes. Li-an and Genevra. She repeated the names in her mind until they became as familiar as the faces from her dreams. Her sisters. She realized then that she had known them long before tonight; some part of her had always known. She had felt their fear, their anguish, their desire for peace. It was they who had come to her when she was in need and touched her until the pain became bearable.

Li-an and Genevra had always been with her, and she with them, in ways she could not understand. Just that day she had seen them both, on their journey to the glen, no doubt. Perhaps that was why the visions had been brighter, more intense. She smiled enigmatically and tears came to her eyes. She would see her sisters now. She would speak to them, touch them, learn to know their thoughts as she had always known their hearts. Her pulse raced with anticipation.

The letter in her hand grew heavy. Whatever news this envelope contained could well destroy Wan Li-an. That much she sensed, though the nature of the grief eluded her. Somehow she must make it easier for her sister. She must be there for her, this time in the flesh. Before her bond with these strangers had been instinctive, unconscious. This would be harder because it was real.

That night the people from the glen gathered at Mairi Rose's croft. Alanna helped Ailsa prepare food while Mairi and Charles sat by the fire in companionable silence. Alanna put out butter, cheese, black buns, and oatcakes, and Ailsa started the *bannoch claiche* to be cooked over the fire.

As usual, Angus Fraser was the first to arrive. His wife Flora was close behind him. "Well, Ailsa," he called gruffly, "so ye've come back at last." He slapped her soundly on the back, then turned to Alanna. "And this must be your tiny bairn of whom I've heard so much. Just like our Mairi, she looks, with that blindin' red hair and those eyes the color of the sky at gloamin'." He was grizzled and bent with age, but he had not changed in other ways. "Lass, deem warily, for the devil's eye is for the bonny."

Alanna smiled. "Well," she replied, "if I meet the devil, I have to hope he's blind."

Angus put his hand to ear. "What's that ye say?"

"She said," Flora interjected, "that there's no fool like an old fool. Leave the lass be and see to greetin' your hostess."

"Hoots! Charlie," Angus shouted cheerfully, "have ye no' broken away from Mairi's spell the while? She'll be weavin' your clothes to her loom soon and then ye'll never get free!" He laughed uproariously at his own joke.

"You'd better put down that fiddle," Charles said, a glint of mischief in his eyes. "A man your age shouldn't carry such a heavy burden. You might drop it on your toe."

"Keep your wisdom to yourself, old man. I've no' the time to listen to your blatherin'." But there was affection in Angus's voice. "Och!" he added, "are ye no' at your spinnin' tonight, Mairi Rose? I'll have nothin' to say to ye if ye join the rest of us."

"Ye'll find somethin', no doubt," his wife Flora assured him. "Or ye can always talk to Charles about your sheep and your hay, knowin' he's too polite to tell ye to stop *yer* jabberin'."

"Hoots, woman, leave me in peace. I'm an old man, am I, and entitled to my little pleasures."

Flora's mother had died long since, so Flora herself took the rocking chair, a challenge in her eyes that dared anyone to argue. As she sat down, Ian's sisters Megan and Kirstie burst in with their husbands and children. There was a flurry of introductions while the girls and boys settled themselves on the floor with their rag dolls and rowan berries and jumping jacks. Next Callum Mackensie arrived, lit his pipe from the fire, and took his place in the doorway, where his father Geordie used to stand. He seemed undisturbed when several children brushed past him, laughing.

Alistair Mackensie, his wife Janet and their young ones had arrived. Then it was Ian's brother Duncan, his wife, and three offspring. Finally, the other Fraser grandchildren tumbled through the door—Ian's Brenna, Gavin, and Glenyss. Last of all came Jenny and Ian. Their youngest child, Erlinna, held her father's hand and clutched to her chest the wooden bird he had carved for her.

Alanna recognized the man she had seen at the cave, but when she turned to say so to her mother, she found that Ailsa had stiffened and grown pale. Alanna looked back at Ian, who greeted his parents, then Mairi and Charles, before he turned to Ailsa and her daughter. Jenny stood beside him, her straight brown hair pulled back in a tight braid wound at the back of her neck. Her plaid fell off one shoulder and her cheeks were flushed from the cold.

Ailsa hugged Jenny and kissed her cheek, while Erlinna

looked on curiously. Then Ailsa took Ian's extended hand. "Welcome home," he said warmly, as if to an old friend. His green eyes held no secrets, no special understanding. He looked much the same, with his curling dark hair made more striking by occasional streaks of gray, but this was not the Ian she had known. He was at ease, content, his mouth curved in a soft smile.

"Thank ye," Ailsa said. " 'Tis good to be back." She wondered if he felt as cold as she, or as empty. The feeling had nothing to do with her family or William, whom she loved; this was Ian who had shared her childhood and known her thoughts as even Mairi could not. She had become accustomed to the pain of his loss over the years. But it was one thing to know from afar the bond was broken, another to see Ian seated with his wife, her hand in his, their children at his feet.

Everyone fell silent for a moment. Angus Fraser noticed the lull—and guessed its cause. "What are we all grievin' for?" he demanded loudly. "We've every blessin' ye could ask for and an old friend has come home. We should rejoice tonight, no' weep."

The children began to chatter again and the adults followed their lead. Soon the boys and girls were drinking milk from cups Ian had carved, the men had ale from the *quachs* they had brought and the women tea from the wooden cups in the press. Because there were so many children, the croft seemed crowded, warmer, and more full of life. The children eagerly consumed black buns and cheese and *bannoch claiche* until Flora cried out, "Here, there'll be none left for us if ye don't have a care. Ye'd think they'd been starved for a year."

"No, Grandmother," one of Duncan's children explained. " 'Tis just that Mairi Rose makes the best black buns in the glen."

Flora folded her arms in a pretended huff. "So ye say, and ye too young to know such things. There's many that cooks as well as Mairi. Ye'd be wise to remember it."

"Enough of this bickerin'," Mairi called at last. "Tell us a story, Callum."

"Well now, which should it be?" he asked, tapping the

stem of his pipe on his teeth. Glennys, who was crawling between his legs to find some berries that had rolled out of her grasp, looked up. "A ghost story, please! We've no' had one for ever so long."

While Callum puffed, Charles and Angus moved to the corner to play a game of draughts, which Duncan Fraser joined. They had heard ghost stories enough.

"I don't see the harm in tellin' a tale or two," Callum said as a ring of smoke popped from his mouth and dissipated in the air. "Mayhap I'll tell ye about the poor minister of Kiltarlity who had more than a sinful congregation to deal with, I'll be bound."

Alanna moved her chair closer. She had always loved Ailsa's tales about ghosts and was eager to hear another.

"It seems," Callum began, "that the Kirk of Kiltarlity was near the river, which on this particular year ran high with meltin' snow and overflowed its banks. 'Twas a sight to see that water rushin' across moor and brae."

He paused, eyed his audience narrowly to make sure they were listening, then continued. "Now the graveyard was beside the kirk next to the water, and when the river overflowed, it washed away some of the earth and carried it down the moor.

"As it happens, one night an old man was on his way to visit a friend. When he passed the kirk, he thought he saw the friend waitin' in the shadows, greatly upset. The man hurried forward, but each time he got close, his friend retreated, while the wind moaned and cried out overhead. The visitor looked behind him, and there was the figure—on his left and his right and before him all at once. He felt chills rise on his neck and knew 'twas a ghost he'd been followin' through the dark, cold night. He ran so fast to his friend's house that he couldn't catch his breath for near an hour once he arrived."

While Callum spoke, Ailsa looked up to find Ian's eyes upon her, curious, warm, but strangely empty. She looked away, waited a moment longer, then rose to wander outside. She breathed deeply, but the sorrow would not leave her.

She moved away from the house until the sound of Callum's voice faded and she could hear only the wind whistling among the scattered stars. Then she felt someone beside her. She turned in surprise to find Jenny Fraser waiting to be noticed.

Jenny touched Ailsa's arm. "I want ye to know that I became Ian's wife because he told me things were different between ye, that ye weren't comin' back and the threads that bound ye were no more. I wouldn't have married him else."

Ailsa blinked in astonishment. "Why are ye tellin' me this?"

Jenny looked at the ground. "Everyone knew he was yours."

Everyone knew . . . Ailsa closed her eyes. " 'Twas my choice to go to London with another man."

"Why did ye do it? How could ye leave Ian behind?"

Ailsa was silent for so long that the other woman thought she would not answer. Then she said softly, "In some of us there's a fire that burns too brightly. It makes us feel things differently, painfully—even great joy. To feed that fire too often, to make the flames too strong is to destroy yourself. Ye burn and burn and burn. 'Tis too painful to live that kind of life. Yet 'tis beautiful, too. Too beautiful for words or thought, too beautiful to look upon. Ye can climb to the heavens on the colors of those flames, but ye can also fall into the darkness without end." She paused, exhausted. "Do ye understand?"

Jenny stared at her blankly. "I've tried. I tried when Ian was lost in his own darkness, when the pain in him was eatin' away at his insides. I could see it, but I couldn't understand it. I don't think I ever will."

"It doesn't matter," Ailsa said. " 'Tis exactly why ye've made him so happy."

"Do ye really think I have?"

"I need only see his smile when he touches ye or turns to your bairns with love in his eyes to know it, Jenny Fraser."

Jenny smiled. "Bless ye," she said. "And thank the Lord the fire inside didn't burn away your kindness."

Then she was gone and Ailsa was left alone with the voices of the glen and the ache of emptiness inside, where radiant flames used to rise and flicker, flicker and blaze.

◇ ◇ ◇

Callum did not notice Ailsa and Jenny's departure. He was caught up in his story. "The old man wasn't the only one who saw the ghostly figure beckonin', flittin' from here to there and back again in the wink of an eye. Others saw the man, and sometimes a child and a woman. The minister began to worry at the stories whispered through the town when the light was bright and no shadows hovered in dark corners. One cold night, with the mist thick around him, he waited in the churchyard till midnight. Then, from out of the blackness, he saw a movement. He went forward, tremblin', to find three figures wailin' and groanin' and wringin' their hands. Bein' a brave man in his heart, he asked what was wrong and told 'em he would help if 'twere in his power."

Alanna watched the old man, eyes glowing, fingers twined together tightly.

"The figure of the old man glided to the river and pointed to the water, steel gray and flowin' so fast it rumbled and spat like the bitter tears that the ghost-bairn wept. Just at that instant, the cock crew. The three figures faded slowly into the water and the minister watched, brow furrowed, long after they were gone. Then it struck him. Much excited, he went back to the kirk and found the records of the dead. He found there had been three graves in the earth washed away by the flood—of an old man, a mother, and her young daughter."

At this point Ailsa returned to sit quietly next to Alanna.

"So the man began to search along the banks of the angry river, and all the people of the town with him, till they had collected many bones, which they placed on the porch of the kirk. The minister held a funeral service, had a new grave dug, and buried the bones. He even erected a fine headstone above it. And none ever saw the mysterious figures again."

There was silence while the children sat wide-eyed, unconvinced that the ghosts had been laid to rest. Finally Alanna whispered, "What do ye do if ye meet a ghost? Should ye run?"

"No," Ailsa told her. " 'Tis likely he wants somethin' from ye, no' to do ye harm. If he walks the night, 'tis

643

because he can't rest, no' because he's evil. Mayhap if ye do as he wishes, he can lie down in peace and walk no more."

"A ghost would no' dare approach me!" Gavin, Ian's son, cried.

"No doubt ye're right," Jenny said with a fond smile. "He'd be too frightened of you with that dark hair all wild about your head and your strange green eyes. I wouldn't be surprised if *he* turned to run."

Everyone laughed, but the laughter ceased abruptly when Charles began to cough. He clutched his chest and gasped, bending forward, eyes closed. Mairi was up in a moment, opening the cupboard where she kept her herbs. She added some to a hot cup of tea and held it to her husband's lips. " 'Twill have to do till I heat some of the lamb broth with shunnish in it. That'll take your cough away and ease your chest." A space was cleared for her beside the fire. Ailsa held Charles's hand and spoke to him soothingly while Mairi worked.

Alanna watched helplessly when her grandfather rose, leaning on Mairi's arm, and settled close to the heat, his face pale in the firelight. He wore his wife's plaid about his shoulders. "Don't stop because of me," he said. "Sing. It will distract me and perhaps you as well."

They sang for a while, quietly, without their usual enthusiasm. Everyone could see that Charles was tired and weak, so it was early when Flora Fraser rose, gathered her family about her, and bade her hosts good night. The others followed quickly, until only Alanna, Ailsa, Mairi and her husband were huddled in the warmth of the dying peat fire.

Ailsa was weary with concern for her father. She stood behind him, massaged his shoulders, listened for the sound of his rasping breath. Each painful rise and fall of his chest made her wince as if it were she who struggled for air. She stared into the low-burning flames, concentrated on the orange, dancing light until her vision blurred and she saw a woman with long black hair who stared out a window but saw nothing. There was a raw wound on her temple where the pulse throbbed dully. Li-an. She was looking inward, wondering. Her eyes brimmed with pain and the sheen of moonlight reflected in her tears. The Chinese woman released her breath in a rush, shivered, and bowed her head, but did not weep. Ailsa realized her own eyes were wet and blinked away the tears that were not her own, yet somehow they were. Just as her father's pain belonged to him alone, but she shared it, sorrowed wordlessly for his suffering and the suffering of his daughters who had not yet found their way home.

---◆4◆---

When she had been in the glen nearly a week, Ailsa dreamed she was sitting stiffly in unfamiliar clothes, ill at ease, while memories flickered behind her eyes—of mother-of-pearl windows, the smell of frying fish, the shadows of butterflies on a satin quilt. Softly, she murmured to herself:

" 'Her lute in her hand, she carelessly pushed aside
     the curtain of pearls,
So the breath of spring might flow into her room;
But she saw the moon,
     and it was sorrow that entered in.

" 'Her face hidden in her folded arms,
     she remembers a garden, all blue in the moonlight,
Where once she listened to words of love.' "

She sat rigid, her eyes dry, her heart cold. She ached for the sight of a blooming chrysanthemum, a lake of purple lotus, their jade leaves undulating with the swell of water. She imagined the touch of her lover's hand, pretended that if she turned, she would catch a glimpse of her mother's face.

Ailsa reached up to brush her black hair from her face, but found only her chestnut braid. She pushed the dream aside, but the chill would not go. The dreams of the two other girls had come to her more often as the week progressed until she was certain her sisters were very near. She felt an unusual tension this morning and rose quickly to dress.

Charles and Alanna were already gone, as usual. Alanna

went daily to wander the glen and learn of all its hidden places. Sometimes Ailsa or Mairi went with her, but often the girl chose to go alone. Ailsa was glad that her daughter had slipped into the rhythm of this place so naturally, though the thought also brought pain. She could guess where it would lead. But today she was glad. She had to be alone.

As she ate her breakfast of porridge with milk and cream, she wondered about her father, who also disappeared every morning at dawn and returned late in the afternoon, often with Mairi's help.

"Where does he go?" Ailsa had asked the second day she found him gone when she awoke.

Mairi looked wistfully out the door her husband had left ajar. "He's found a place where the light is good and he stays there to paint by the hour. He never seems to tire of it, though sometimes his body grows weary. He doesn't wish for anyone to know where he is. He'll no' even let me see what he's doin'."

Ailsa had been amazed. "He goes to paint?"

" 'Tis what he's wanted since he was a bairn, but his family wouldn't have it. Now he's free and can do as he likes."

A shadow fell between them that did not need words to give it shape. He was free because he was dying. They did not say as day passed into twilight and twilight into night that with each dawn he was a little weaker.

This morning, as she helped her mother rinse the dishes in the bucket by the door, Ailsa asked a question that had been in her mind since her first day here. "Mother," she said, "there's somethin' I don't understand."

Mairi raised her head so the sun touched her hair with gold.

"My father is just an ordinary man."

Mairi managed not to smile. "In some ways, aye."

"Yet ye loved him so much for so long. Why?"

Her mother stared thoughtfully toward the trees. "Because he was Charles," she said, "and because I was meant to love him, just as ye were meant to love Ian."

Ailsa stiffened and the dreamy look left Mairi's face. They had not yet spoken of Ian, nor had she seen him since the night of the gathering. She had explored the hills and moors and mountains and knew she would have met him sometime unless he were avoiding her. She felt in her heart that it was so. He was as afraid as she of what would happen if they met again.

"Good mornin', Mother, Grandmother!" Alanna called as she came up, cheeks red from the morning air. She saw the two women were upset, but did not speak of it. "Ye said ye'd teach me about the herbs. Will it be today?" she asked Mairi eagerly. Her grandmother had already begun to show her how to spin wool into thread and to use the loom. Alanna understood instinctively, as if her fingers had always curled around the shuttle that flew among those colored threads. "The sun shines clear, and the mist will burn away soon."

"How is it that ye're so certain?" Mairi demanded fondly.

"I've been watchin' and listenin' and learnin'."

"Aye, ye've done well, lass. Ye even speak now like ye were born in the glen. Come, and I'll show ye where to find 'em. But after that, there's much to know."

"I'm ready," Alanna replied.

"Will ye be comin'?" Mairi asked her daughter.

"No' this mornin', when the restlessness is upon me."

"Good-bye, Mother, and don't fret. 'Twill be a lovely day."

Ailsa smiled fondly after her daughter as she crossed the clearing with Mairi beside her. "Will ye tell me the story of the Valley of the Dead, as ye promised?" Alanna asked. Her mother did not hear Mairi's reply.

Finally Ailsa went inside, found the letter to Wan Li-an in the rosewood box, and slipped it into her pocket. She was not certain why she did so; her fingers had a will of their own. Then she left the cottage. While she moved barefoot toward the woods, her restlessness grew.

Her feet were still tender, not yet inured to the uneven ground, but she was determined to make them hard and strong again. From within the tangle of trees and bracken and whispering shadows, she heard Mairi singing to Alanna. The words lingered and Ailsa sang them quietly to herself.

"Everything there is, has bein',
Mountains have a voice,
Stars and comets are foreseein',
The little hills rejoice."

The day was cool; as she walked, she unwound her hair, then unbraided it so it fell to her waist. It brushed her neck lightly, felt thick and good around her shoulders.

"And thou, wilt thou no' sing,
Who bearest in thy throat
The Rapture of the Spring,
The Resurrection Note?"

Ian had sung those words to her once. Ailsa paused on the riverbank, filled with an intense longing for William and the comfort of his arms. She took a deep breath, gathered her skirt in her hands, backed up a few paces, and jumped, landing on the far marshy bank. She smiled in triumph while the leaves rustled their approval. She had not become a stranger to the glen; she was part of it still. She had feared most of all that she would be only a visitor here, that she had hardened her heart too long against this wild beauty and it would touch her no more.

She went on her way, wandering wherever her feet led her. She was surprised to find herself at the parting in the trees where the muddy rutted road curved by. She sat on a boulder, head tilted back, her hair lifted by the breeze. A face from her dream hovered in the air; the image was very bright, and so real that she reached out to touch it, but there was nothing. She knew then, as if the wind had whispered the news in her ear, that today her sister would arrive.

Her heartbeat increased with expectation, fear, hope, and anxious longing. The rapid rhythm blended with the sound of an approaching wagon; it was a long time until she recognized the clop of horse hooves, the turning of heavy wheels. Then the wagon came into sight and she stood waiting while the blue-eyed, golden-skinned woman, dressed in a dark wool gown, stepped from the seat of the wagon. Her hair was braided and caught tightly at the back of her neck. Her only adornments were tiny jade earrings and a bracelet woven of white and yellow gold.

As the woman refused the driver's help and took her own trunk from the wagon, Ailsa stared at the gold made brilliant by sunlight. That circle of precious metal reminded her of her mother's wedding ring. She took a step closer, mesmerized by the yellow gleam. Then the woman turned and saw her.

Li-an felt a jolt of recognition that slowed the pulse of her blood. She stood, shaken, pale, her hands clasped tightly together. "Who would you be?" she asked in a strange, singsong accent.

Ailsa, who was equally shaken, though she had known this moment would come, replied unsteadily, "I'm here to greet ye."

There was silence while the two women gazed at one another. Li-an frowned, brow furrowed as she looked at Ailsa's sun-touched face and long, flowing hair. These things were familiar to her—more than familiar. "I am Wan Li-an. I know you, do I not?" Even as she said it, she knew it was impossible.

Ailsa had begun to regain her composure. "As well as I know ye. As well as one can know another from dreams across many violent seas."

Li-an's frown deepened. She remembered that a long time ago she had had a dream where she'd flown backward through time. At the end of her journey, this woman had been there, and someone else. There was another memory hovering at the edge of her mind, but it was too painful. She pushed the thought aside. "Then my dream was real." She felt a flicker of warmth in her cold veins, a feeling that had been absent for many months. She felt, too, an inexplicable fondness for this woman—a stranger.

"Didn't ye know that long ago?"

"Perhaps. My mother said it was so." She put her hand to her chest to protect the hollow place inside, to disguise her pain, which was not for other eyes to see. "How is it that we know each other, yet are strangers?"

Ailsa touched Li-an's free hand. "I think 'tis because we share Charles Kittridge's blood. He is my father, too, ye see."

Bitterness rose like an unfriendly wind inside Li-an, but the pressure of Ailsa's fingers made the wind grow quiet, at least for the moment. With an effort, she tried to think clearly, as Ke-ming would have done. "There should be another," she said at last. "A girl with the pale hair of the for—" She broke off and said instead, "—of the white men." She spoke from instinct, to give herself time. Her thoughts were spinning and she shivered at a rush of emotion she had kept carefully in check until now.

Ailsa nodded. "Her name is Genevra. She's on her way." She sensed Li-an's discomfort. "Come," she murmured. "Ye must be aye weary from your journey. We'll see to your trunk later, after gloamin' when the men are in from the fields and hills."

Ailsa led Li-an among the trees, through the cool darkness to a boulder by the river. She knelt on the bank, cupped her hands in the bright rushing water that scattered silver foam into the air. "Like this," she said, and took a drink.

Li-an nodded. This was a familiar sight—the cool shelter of the trees, the wind sighing in the leaves, the water, clear as crystal in the patches of sunlight that struck it now and then. Many times she had knelt at a stream in the Western Hills and drunk from the water as Ailsa did now. She smiled at the memory and crouched to follow her sister's example. The taste was clean and refreshing. She looked up with a smile as the two women held their hands, dripping, over the water. Their eyes met and held. Each had done this before, but sharing what had once been habit made this moment precious. "This *shan shui* . . . ," Li-an struggled to find the English word, gave up and pointed at the mountains, the river, the encircling trees. "This—place—reminds me of my *lao chia* in the hills of the Middle Kingdom. It should have been the home of my family, but I have no family. Only my mother. Still, it was the home of my heart."

They fell back into the bracken to gaze up at the leaves in their constant dance overhead. Finally Li-an spoke. "Why was it you who came and not *him?*"

Ailsa leaned up on her elbow, shocked by the bitterness with which Li-an had spoken the last word. "He doesn't know ye've come. I only knew because my heart led me

651

before my mind knew what it was about." She saw that Li-an listened intently; she seemed to have difficulty making out the words. Of course, the accent must be strange to her, whose language was not words but sounds. Ailsa remembered that from her dreams. "Besides, I wanted to see ye first."

Li-an stiffened. She had seen the shadow in her sister's eyes. "Why?"

With a sigh, Ailsa took out the letter, smudged and battered as it was, with the strange writing in one corner of the envelope. "Because of this. It came for ye a week since."

"You know what news it contains?" Li-an kept her hands folded carefully in her lap.

"No," Ailsa said. "I only know 'tisn't happy. I didn't want ye to read it before those at the croft, though none would ever hurt ye. But I thought ye needed to be alone."

Li-an nodded. If it were bad news, she did not want all to know, to watch her face for signs of sorrow, to wait for her tears. Yet she did not ask Ailsa to go. She looked down at the Chinese characters that stood for Wu Shen's name, ran her fingers over the carefully inked strokes as if smoothing her old friend's silver hair. She missed him almost as much as she missed Ke-ming. She stopped with the envelope halfway open, certain now of the news it contained, though she could not say why. Her hands began to shake.

"Go on," Ailsa said quietly. "I'm here. Ye're no' alone."

Her face impassive, Li-an opened the seal and slipped the folded rice paper out. She began to read, oddly aware of the murmur of water at her side, the purple mountains that loomed in the distance, the soft bracken in which she lay, and the shadows—the screens around and within her, the mask behind which she hid her fear and the cold, labored beat of her heart.

Dear Friend,

I write to you in English because that must be your language now that you have left the Middle

Kingdom behind. Do not cling blindly to what is lost. If only I could listen to my own wise counsel.

How often have I thought of you when the fragrance of the lotus drifted toward me on the wind, when I saw a delicate stroke of ink on paper, a poem of wit and beauty, a cloudless sky as blue as your eyes, as full of possibilities. Because of these daily reminders, I miss you more than I thought possible.

But you know that is not why I have written to you in a world I cannot even imagine, from a world I can no longer bear. When I left you at the sea, I returned to the hills to try to convince Ke-ming to come with me to safety. I was dreaming, and in a dream I went, knowing the truth before I saw it with my tight-shut eyes. I was too late. Perhaps you can guess what I found.

The hut had been burned to the ground. Around it there were the footprints of many soldiers, and their fingerprints, too; they had sifted through the ashes, looking for valuables to take away with them. Your mother's body was among those cold, gray ashes, undisturbed. The soldiers had long since returned to the Evil One, who had ordered this thing done.

I stood and wept for Ke-ming, an extraordinary woman, a woman like no other. I told myself, as I tell you now, that this is what she chose. She knew when she sent you to safety that she would die; you knew it, too, whether or not you chose to admit the truth. I listened for a long time to the silence that had settled in that place which had once been full with the sound of her lute. To comfort myself, I repeated the words of Yen Yu:

"Like an echo in the void, and color in form,
The moon reflected in water,
   and an image in a mirror,
The words come to an end,
   but the meaning is inexhaustible."

So it is with Ke-ming. Many lives have been changed because of her, many minds made to think harder, many hands touched with a gentleness that belied her calm exterior. Remember that, my pale jade. Remember that you were her future, that because of you she died, perhaps not happy, but full of hope. I know these things will not ease your grief now. But someday, when the wound begins to heal, you will see that to choose one's own death, to leave behind a legacy as precious as a daughter such as you, to die with pride and honor—these things are worth more than a barren, lonely life. Do not let your grief turn to bitterness, for it will poison your blood and kill all joy that you might know. And that would break your spirit mother's heart.

> Your Faithful Friend,
> Wu Shen

Li-an let the letter fall. She shed no tears; her face might have been carved from stone. She stared before her, seeing nothing. But when Ailsa reached for the letter, Li-an nodded.

The other woman read it with tears in her eyes, looked up in disbelief at Li-an's rigid features. "I'm sorry, my sister. Would it help if we prayed and sang for her? Surely even so far away, the gods would hear us."

"My father should never have left us in Canton," Li-an said as if her half-sister had not spoken. "And I should not have left my mother in that hut."

"Ye had to!" Ailsa exclaimed. "Or ye would have died with her. Surely ye didn't want that?"

Far in the back of Li-an's mind, a memory stirred for the second time. Out of the black emptiness came pain, grief, the taste of willow-bark tea. The night she had lost her child. A voice had whispered to her in a dream, a hand had taken hers. *Don't grieve*, the voice had said. Then she had seen a child, loneliness, fear, a fire, the crackling of timbers, and the crash of a roof. The cries of the child had echoed in her ears.

"Ye have lost your mother," Ailsa murmured, "and ye should grieve. But ye should also be grateful that there'll be no more sufferin' for her, no pain, no loss, no sorrow. Remember."

Li-an had heard those words before. They had given her comfort when she knew her child was dead. She met Ailsa's gaze and some of the ice melted from her cold blue eyes. "It was you who came to me. How did you know? You must be a *shen*—one who is of the spirit, who understands the ways of *T'ien*, heaven."

"To me, this is heaven, and this alone I understand. I can't explain what happened. Somehow I knew. Just as ye knew when I was grievin' and in need of friends." She regarded her half-sister pensively. "Ye hate our father, don't ye? The poison is already in your blood, and has been for a long, long time."

"Yes," Li-an admitted, though she had meant to deny it. She could not lie to Ailsa. "When he went away, he left nothing behind but fear. He betrayed us, abandoned us."

"Mayhap ye should have some compassion, try to understand."

What happened in Canton was not his fault, Ke-ming had told her that last night in China. *He was a man alone, running for his life. He had no choice.* Even now Li-an could not believe it. Or did not wish to. Her hatred of her father was a core of steel inside her; it kept her back straight, her determination unwavering. In its own way, that hatred made her stronger and she would not give it up.

The women rose in unspoken agreement and began to walk. Li-an moved faster and faster to escape the knowledge that lay coiled and dangerous in her heart. Her mother was dead. She could not bear it; she did not have the strength. It had taken all she had to get here. The pain began to throb in her head. She had traveled so far. There had been so many storms, so much waiting while one boat sank and another was found, while her chaperons, friends of Shen's whom he'd asked to care for her, had stopped in several ports to do their business. So much hatred from the people she passed in the streets who had called her names and thrown stones, shouting at her to go back where she'd come from.

She had fought every inch of the way from the Western Hills to this place called Glen Affric. And for what? A man she did not want to see and the knowledge that Ke-ming had burned to death. She had no feeling left. No strength, no will, no compassion—nothing but emptiness, deep and black and cold.

She stumbled and started to fall, but Ailsa caught her. For a moment they stood immobile while the warmth from Ailsa's hands flowed into Li-an, but it was more than warmth, more than friendship, more than courage or strength. It was a tiny flicker of hope that lodged in her cold, hard heart and smoldered there.

Li-an shivered and began to run. She ran to the moor where the heather glowed in the sunlight, to the shadows that reached out to her at the foot of the mountains. Finally she collapsed at the base of the jutting boulders that rose around her like a shield, slab after slab of immovable stone. To protect her from what? The turmoil inside her? The landscape blurred and her head whirled with images—of Ke-ming kneeling beside her daughter's bed, playing her lute until the pain subsided; touching Li-an's hand that last night as she murmured, *You are my hope. Promise me you will survive;* her mother standing straight and tall on the porch as her only child walked away for the last time; the morning when Ke-ming had whispered, *It is sad to dream of being happy again.*

"She stood and watched Heaven burn,
Ashes in her hair and in her heart,
Until the flames surrounded her,
Filling the sky with smoke that swirled
   and danced but could not match her willowy beauty,
With the smell of burning wood
   that covered the inimitable fragrance
   of her golden body.
The soldiers stood by, leaning on their swords,
And did not guess what they had taken
   from a world—cold, evil, full of shadows—
A world which once she had made warm with light."

The echo of Li-an's voice rose from stone to grim, gray stone. Only then did she realize she had spoken aloud. The pain was back, more piercing than ever.

Ailsa had let her sister run ahead, sensing her need to be completely alone, at least for a few moments. She had nearly reached the place where Li-an sat huddled among the boulders when she stopped, head tilted, listening. She felt a weight in her chest and thought she heard Mairi call her name. Something was wrong. She had to go back. She stared at Li-an, rigid as the tilted stones at her back, and knew she could not leave her.

"Ye can't run from your pain forever," Ailsa said, as her mother had once said to her. She touched Li-an's arm and knew she felt more than grief, but physical pain as well.

Suddenly the spinning in Li-an's head stopped and the images grew clear, as did the sloping moor and the distant woods. "My thoughts are in *luan*—disorder, but your touch brings *chih*—order. I do not understand."

Ailsa felt a sense of urgency that made her heartbeat ragged. "It doesn't matter now. Only that ye stop your runnin' and come home with me."

Li-an leaned with her hands on her knees. Her braid had come free of its jade pins and fell over her shoulders, which heaved from sorrow and the exertion of her run. "I will not stop until the pain goes, until there is oblivion and comfort."

"There can't be comfort, and the pain can't go, till ye free it from the stone prison inside ye. Pretendin' it doesn't exist will no' make it go. Only feelin' it with all your heart, lettin' the pain tear ye apart will ease it. Ye must weep the tears ye've kept inside, let them flow as they will." Ailsa was more desperate, more torn with each moment that passed. She knew she was needed elsewhere, but Li-an needed her, too.

"That I cannot do." *Never let them see inside your heart, for when they know your secrets, they also know your weakness,* Ke-ming had warned Li-an. *You must always be strong. Stronger than they.* Her mother had been strong to the end; she had not shed a tear even as her daughter left her behind to die alone in a burst of flame. Li-an closed her eyes against the confusion of anger and grief, hatred and sorrow that filled her head. "At the beginning of the world," she whispered, "there was *hun-tun,* chaos, and Phan-ku came to rescue the world from this disorder. But now the *hun-tun* is inside me and there is no Phan-ku to come, bringing light to the darkness."

"I don't know who Phan-ku is, but I know this. Ye have me and my mother and my daughter and most of all your father. Among us, surely we can bring ye from the darkness?" Ailsa did not know how she kept her voice steady, so intense was her desire to run back to the croft. Except that was not where she ought to be. She did not know where to turn any more than Li-an did.

"What makes you so wise, I wonder?"

Ailsa smiled her mother's smile. "The things my mother taught me, and my husband. The people I've lost and the things I have fought for and won." She touched her half-sister's arm. "I want ye to come home with me, meet our father, learn to know him and forgive him. Then, mayhap, your wounds will heal."

Li-an pressed her fingers to her temples as Ailsa's face became a dim white blur. "You do not know what he did—"

"It doesn't matter. I know what kind of man he is. And I know that your anger is hurtin' *ye,* no' him."

It is time to let go of your anger, Ke-ming had said. *Your father was not like the other British, not like other men. He did not come here to destroy; he came to build.*

"Mother, ye must come at once!"

Ailsa turned at the sound of her daughter's voice. The girl was pale and her eyes had a cast of gray upon them. Her mother shivered with apprehension. "What is't, lass?"

"Grandfather's in trouble. Don't ye feel it? Grandmother has gone to him, but he needs us, too, to bring him home."

Ailsa's panic throbbed in her head. She felt helpless, suddenly, and not at all wise.

Alanna grasped her mother's hand. "I know where 'tis. Come. We must hurry." She nodded at Li-an but did not ask questions. Questions would come later, when her grandfather was safe.

Ailsa turned to Li-an. "Will ye come?"

In the face of her half-sister's distress, Li-an's pain had retreated just enough to let her speak. "I will come."

They found Charles on a knoll of grass inside the Valley of the Dead. He was choking, breathing with difficulty, his skin pale and covered in sweat. Now and then he coughed up blood into his wife's apron. "Thank Saint Brigit ye've come. I can't manage him on my own," Mairi cried when she saw her daughter and granddaughter. She stopped, her hand on her husband's burning forehead. There was a stranger who followed Alanna reluctantly. A stranger like none Mairi had ever seen. "Are ye Wan Li-an?" she managed to ask.

Li-an stood frozen at the sight of her father, old, silver-haired, frail, and ill. It was not possible that this was the same man who had promised her once: *You'll be safe now.* The wind moaned among the rocks, screamed in her ears, and she felt her mother's presence on her shoulder, weighing her down. For a long time she did not realize the woman with the gray-streaked red hair had spoken. "I am she," she answered stiffly when the question penetrated her clouded thoughts.

"Can ye help us then? We'll have to carry him."

"I will do what I can." The sight of Charles's pain and discomfort only increased the agony in Li-an's head. This must be a game, a cruel joke the *kuei* were playing on her. Mechanically, she knelt next to Ailsa and took her father's legs.

With Mairi and Alanna on one side, Ailsa and Li-an on the other, they began, step by careful step, to move out of the valley. Slowly, the cry of the wind faded as they left the wavering shadows behind. Li-an sighed in relief.

They followed an uneven path while Charles grew heavier in their arms by the moment. The four women acted together without thought, turning, bending to avoid low branches, stepping across the stream where it was narrow and slow. Li-an watched her father's face in disbelief. It was flushed now; the sweat rolled down his cheeks and into his hair. His eyes were glazed and she knew he did not recognize

659

her. Her own vision blurred. Each step became an effort of will so great that she thought she could not manage one more. Yet she went on.

After what seemed like hours, they reached the croft and laid Charles on Mairi's heather bed. Alanna ran for a bowl and cloth, dipped cool water from the bucket by the door while Ailsa heated the broth her mother always kept on hand. Mairi herself loosened Charles's neckcloth and his shirt, removed his coat, and drew the quilt over him. Then, while Alanna bathed his hot forehead, Mairi made a foul-smelling poultice to put on his chest.

Li-an stood unmoving as slowly, slowly, it came to her that this was not a joke or a nightmare. It was real. This man who thrashed about shouting incoherent words, this old, sick, broken man was her father. She had always thought him strong—strong enough to save them from all that threatened them. But this man was helpless. He did not even know who he was.

The pain splintered in her head and she collapsed into a chair, staring sightlessly at the roaring fire. She prayed to Kwan Yin, Goddess of Mercy, but for whom? Ke-ming? Herself? The three women who clearly loved her father? Or for Charles Kittridge? She did not know. She no longer knew anything. The world had fallen from under her feet and she was being sucked into the gaping mouth of Yu-ch'iang, God of the Ocean Wind.

When Li-an awoke, the smell of herbs filled the air. She stared through the haze and thought she was in her bed with the gauze curtains that dimmed and softened everything around her. Then she realized she lay in a bed of wood with wooden walls, except on one side. A face came into focus, hands holding a cup. The steam rose from the cup; Li-an looked into Ailsa's blue-violet eyes and remembered.

"Drink this before ye rise," her half-sister told her. "It may just keep the pain from comin' back."

Li-an realized in astonishment that the ache in her temples had disappeared. Someone had undressed her and put her in a soft wool gown that felt warm against her cold skin. "Why have you done all this for me, when it is my father who is ill?" She saw that Alanna was working in the kitchen and Mairi sat on the floor beside Charles Kittridge's bed, her head on his pillow. She must have fallen asleep while keeping watch.

"He sleeps now," Ailsa said. "We must check the fever and give him the herbs he needs, but one of us can easily do that. When ye fell from your chair, I realized we had been neglectin' ye. I'm sorry for that." Li-an took the offered teacup and her fingers curled around it, welcoming the warmth. "We haven't given ye much of a welcome, I'm afraid."

Li-an drew a deep breath. "It does not matter. Is my father out of danger?" she inquired stiffly.

Ailsa was perplexed. If her sister did not care about Charles's condition, why did she ask? "No' yet. His fever is high and he was gey chilled yesterday. When he wakes, he coughs so that your heart would break to hear him. I don't know." She looked toward his bed, her eyes full of concern.

"You care for him a great deal, it seems."

Ailsa turned back to the stranger she knew so well, yet not at all. "I love him. He's my father."

"Was he ever there when you were in need of him?" Li-an could not keep the bitterness from her voice.

"He's here now. 'Tis all that matters to me." Ailsa turned abruptly when Charles began to cough.

Mairi awoke, calling, "Ailsa, the broth."

Li-an was out of bed in an instant. "I will get it." Before the blindness took her, she had seen them ladle broth from the pot over the fire. She headed toward it.

Alanna was already there with a bowl and horn spoon in her hand. Ailsa touched Li-an's arm. "There's no need," she said. "Those of us who care for him will tend to him."

"No," Li-an said stubbornly, her voice as cold as new morning air. "I must do it." She watched in frustration as Mairi pressed a cool cloth to Charles's head and Alanna fed him broth and strong, herbed tea between coughing fits.

"Why, when he's a stranger and ye dislike him so?"

Li-an stared at her half-sister incredulously. "My feelings do not matter. He is my father. I must show my *hsiao*, my filial loyalty, even if the sight of his face is unfamiliar to me, even if, now that my virtuous mother is dead, his face is the last I wish to see. This is *kuei-chu*, and it must be followed."

Ailsa did not understand.

"It is the—proper—thing to do. To behave properly is to maintain order, to keep away chaos and confusion."

Her sister nodded. If Li-an could maintain the customs of home, pretend that this was China, do all things correctly, then she could also pretend her mother's death had never happened. She could continue to ignore the grief building inside her. Ailsa saw the cast of gray on her clear blue eyes and knew the shadow was creeping closer, but Li-an refused to recognize it.

Charles opened his eyes, confused by the strong fragrances that filled the air, the steam that rose in opaque clouds, the warmth of the quilt around his body. He began to cough, doubled up, arms pressed to his chest. He felt soft hands, and when the spasm passed, he found Mairi watching him in concern—and fear. She did not wish him to see it, but he knew her too well.

Alanna leaned down to give him a sip of tea, a spoonful of broth, which he struggled to swallow. "The painting?" he asked hoarsely when he could speak.

His granddaughter leaned close to whisper in his ear, "I hid it before they came. Where ye've always left it. Ye've no cause to worry. 'Tis safe, Grandfather."

He reached up to clasp her hand weakly. "Thank you, birdeen. I suppose it's a blessing you discovered my secret—" He broke off and began to cough again.

Alanna backed away so Mairi could hold a mug of steaming mixture beneath his nose. He breathed it in a little at a time until slowly, slowly, the coughing stopped. He shivered with cold, though he was covered with wool blankets and a quilt.

"Another blanket!" Mairi cried.

"I will get it," Li-an insisted, and rose a second time.

"Ye don't even know where we keep 'em," Ailsa called over her shoulder. She knelt before her kist and raised the lid. The smell of fresh herbs rose to greet her. Mairi must have replaced them often. Quickly, Ailsa sorted through the linens to find a finely woven wool blanket. She did not have time now to think of the past. She handed her mother the blanket and helped tuck it around Charles's trembling body.

When Ailsa left her, Li-an found her clothes and put them on, then joined Alanna in the kitchen. "I am Wan Li-an," she said formally. "And you?"

"Alanna. 'Twas my mother who met ye at the wagon. That's my grandmother, Mairi Rose, by the bed. I'm sorry we couldn't be there to greet ye, but my mother didn't tell us. And now we must care for him. 'Tisn't what ye expected, no doubt. I only wish we'd had the chance to welcome ye as we should."

She meant it; Li-an could see that. "It does not matter," she repeated. "Since they will not let me see to my father, will you allow me to help with the food?"

Alanna shook her head. " 'Tisn't necessary."

"I want to. It will be best if my hands are busy."

Alanna stopped to look into Li-an's blue eyes. Like her mother, she sensed the pain held back, the grief hidden and unrecognized. "Well then, I'd be grateful," she said softly.

The kindness in her voice, the compassion in her eyes made a little crack in Li-an's protective wall. She turned away and began to chop carrots until she regained control. She dared not let the pain out. If she did, it would destroy her. She knew that as certainly as she knew that her father lay ill and broken on the bed across the room. He could not save her, even now.

During the days that followed, the four women became acquainted with one another. Eventually Li-an grew less rigid in their presence. It was only when she approached her father that her face turned to carved marble and her eyes to the ice blue of the loch before a storm. Mairi watched the young woman become part of the household, sleeping without complaint on a heather mattress on the floor while Ailsa and Alanna shared the box bed. Li-an helped with the cooking and the gathering of peats, she tended the fire, sat beside it at night with her hands stretched toward the golden warmth. A little at a time, she began to tell them about China, to recite poems and stories to distract them while they worried and wondered if Charles would live or die.

When all three of the others fell exhausted into sleep, Li-an took over, caring for Charles as patiently, as carefully as they had. But when she touched him, her hands were not warm and her eyes were dim and gray.

Mairi saw all this and wondered; she had never known a woman like Li-an. But Ailsa understood. She had seen many in London—women who never showed their true feelings because they thought it improper, or more likely, because they were afraid of what those feelings, once unleashed, would do. She watched and waited and prayed to the Celtic gods that her father would recover, not only for herself and her mother, but for Li-an, who had demons in her soul that only he could free.

Daily, the neighbors came with a hot loaf of bread, a

mutton stew, some brose or bannoch cakes. They brought milk and tea and precious sherry, whatever they could think of to help, then slipped away without waiting for thanks. They knew their offerings would be appreciated. One day Ian came with a side of lamb he'd slaughtered.

Ailsa saw his shadow on the floor and knew it was he. The knot in her throat grew tighter and more painful.

"May I see him?" Ian asked quietly.

She nodded without speaking, aware that both Li-an and her daughter were watching with curiosity.

Ian knelt next to the bed and put his hand on Charles's damp forehead. "Don't leave Mairi yet," he murmured. "She needs ye. She and Ailsa and Alannean."

Ailsa winced when he used the familiar form of her daughter's name.

"Don't go just when we've become used to ye at last, to your strange English voice and your Sassenach clothes. Who knows who Mairi might take in next? Mayhap even a *Treubh-Siubhail*, a Gypsy of the wanderin' race. Ye don't want such a thing, do ye?"

Charles opened his eyes a little and tried to smile. "No," he croaked. "That I do not want."

"Good," Ian replied. "Then ye'll no' be stayin' in this bed much longer. There's sunshine waitin' for ye, and mist to make it friendly. I expect ye'll be seein' for yourself soon."

"Soon," Charles said, and closed his eyes.

Ian rose in silence. Alanna and Mairi were already busy with the lamb in the kitchen, so Ailsa walked him to the door. "Thank ye," she said.

He smiled crookedly. "Ye're welcome, lass." Then he was gone, a part of the falling fog that made the glen a fairyland of silver and shimmering white.

Charles began to improve gradually. Once, when he was awake and coherent, Ailsa decided to take Li-an to him. Maybe the knowledge that she was there would help him recover.

Reluctantly, Li-an agreed. Until now she had cared for Charles while he was unaware of her presence. When he woke, she drifted away or became busy in the kitchen where he could not see her face. The turmoil inside had not abated; when she saw the love and concern with which these women cared for her father, the kindness they showed her, she only grew more confused. She did not know what to believe anymore, and it frightened her. She did not wish to admit that the bitterness that had kept her strong was slipping away, and with it the hatred. She could not admit it, for the thought made her pain pulse and swell until she thought she would choke on it.

Ailsa had told her, " 'Tis time ye spoke to him. Ye came all this way to see him. And 'twill make his day much brighter."

"How do you know that?" Li-an had demanded.

"I saw his face when he looked at the letter with your name on it, heard the tone in which he spoke of ye. No matter what ye feel for him, he feels only tenderness for ye."

Unconvinced, Li-an nevertheless followed her half-sister inside the croft, which had become familiar, even comfortable, over the past week. It was not just the warmth of the fire, but the warmth of the women who gathered around it to share their thoughts and weariness and worry.

Her father was lying in bed while Mairi untangled the covers around him. His eyes were open—those eyes Li-an remembered as bright, irresistible blue—but they were dim and faded now.

"Father, I brought ye a visitor. Ye've been waitin' a long time to see her."

Charles turned at the sound of his daughter's voice. Her face was little more than a blur. Only her blue-violet eyes were clear. "Who—is—it?" he managed to ask.

" 'Tis your daughter Wan Li-an, come all the way from China. She arrived near a week ago."

Dimly, Charles had been aware of the presence of a stranger, of cool hands on his forehead that he did not recognize, of slanted blue eyes and long, dark hair. But he had had no strength for wondering. "Li-an?" he said in disbelief. "Is it really?" His voice trembled and he touched her skirt to assure himself that she was real.

Li-an moved closer and bowed formally. "Yes, my Father, it is I. I have come here, as you asked, to see you. It was my mother's wish." She kept her hands pressed tightly together, even when he reached up to try and grasp them.

"I can't believe it's you. It's been so long." He saw that she would not take his hand and let it fall to his side. He frowned. There was a chill in the air, despite his many blankets. Something was amiss, but he could not think clearly enough to decide what it was.

"It has been many years, my Father, and much has happened since you went away. Someday I will tell you these things, when you are stronger." She could not quite hide her hostility, nor the quaver in her voice that betrayed her instinctive compassion for a man so weak that already his eyes had closed in weariness.

"Aye," he murmured. "When I'm stronger."

With a last rigid bow, Li-an turned away.

Ailsa found her outside, seated on the grass, using a boulder as a table. Li-an had set out a brush, ink stone, water, and a piece of rice paper that she had brought with her from home. Alanna sat beside her, watching in fascination.

"What're ye doin'?" Ailsa asked.

"I am writing a poem."

"Look at her paper, Mother. Just hold it in your fingers. 'Tis so light and thin. And she doesn't write with a pen or charcoal pencil, but with a brush."

Ailsa leaned forward, as fascinated as her daughter. She saw the strange marks Li-an was making, like the ones on the envelope that had come from China. "Those are words ye're paintin' with your brush?" Ailsa asked, puzzled. "What do they mean?"

"They are like words, I suppose. But one character can have many meanings. It would be difficult to say what each stood for." Li-an did not look up. She let her hair fall over her face to hide her expression from the others.

"Well, if 'tis a poem, surely ye can read it to us," Alanna declared. "My mother and I would love to hear it."

667

Ailsa sat cross-legged on the grass. "Aye, that we would."

Li-an hesitated, though she knew there was no secret reason for the request, that if she looked into their eyes she would find only curiosity, perhaps even affection. It was hard to remember that these people she had known so briefly were not her enemies, harder still to learn to trust when all her life she had been taught to doubt, question, and fear. At last she picked up the rice paper and began to read.

"The man—stranger, father, he of dreams and nightmare—
   lay still and thin upon his heather bed,
   calling my name in a broken voice
   as he reached for my hand.
He is not the one I have remembered in bitterness:
   through spring peonies and summer lotus,
   lantern light and midnight shadow;
So I did not dare to touch him,
   though his fingers stretched to take my hand.
I stood, immobile as stone, watching him with eyes
   that were his, and yet not his,
   for he had made them mine—
   these eyes like glittering ice above a winter lake.
I stood until his hand fell and his eyes closed,
   hiding the mirror that revealed my cold moon face,
   until the thin silk thread between us snapped,
   leaving empty air."

"If ye feel that way," Alanna said, "then why did ye come?"

"I came because I had no choice, to escape the soldiers who have followed me, swords raised and eyes full of hatred, ever since my father left China. It took them many years, but they caught up with me at last."

Ailsa touched Li-an's linen sleeve. "Ye did have a choice. Ye could have chosen to die with your mother. But ye chose to live. Now ye must choose once more—to live in the present and no' the past, to know the stranger ye call your father, and to grieve for the mother ye lost, who is more real to ye just now, even dead, than the man who lies alive in my mother's croft. Ye've always had a choice. Ye just don't want to see it.''

Another tiny crack appeared in Li-an's stone armor. She sealed it with the memory of her fear on that night when the sword had hung above her head and her life had seemed as fleeting as the *wu-t'ung* leaf carried into the autumn sky by a chilly wind.

Li-an curled on the makeshift heather bed and dreamed. She was lying again in the dark, creaking ship, with the sound of the sea in her ears. The rhythm of the waves made its way into her thoughts and dreams. Besides the crash of the violent sea, there were shadows all around, and whispers in every corner.

She tossed on her tiny bed, pushed her blond hair away from her cold cheek, turned her face to the wall, and covered her ears with her hands, but the whispers would not cease. The creak of the ship became the hiss of hostile voices calling, ''Bastard! Charles Kittridge did this to you. You defile my house, you and that child! Bastard, impure, tainted, mad!''

She began to murmur fervently, the only soothing words that came to mind:

''Lead me from the unreal to the real!
Lead me from the darkness to the light!
Lead me from death to immortality!''

She repeated the prayer until it became part of her breath and the pulse of her blood and the angry rise and fall of the sea. Then she felt a hand on her shoulder, heard a voice crying, ''We've arrived, Genevra! We're in London at last.''

Li-an sat up abruptly. She saw that across the room, Ailsa had done the same. They turned to each other and their eyes met in a long look that probed beyond the shape and color of their sleep-dimmed faces to the thoughts beneath.

Ailsa began to move her lips silently. ''Lead me from the unreal to the real!''

Li-an replied without a sound, "Lead me from the darkness to the light!"

Together they formed the phrase "Lead me from death to immortality!"

"It'll no' be long now," Ailsa whispered.

"Soon," her half-sister replied.

"So you're finally awake. I'd begun to think you two would spend the rest of the day tossing and muttering in your sleep."

Ailsa turned in astonishment at the sound of her father's voice. It was strong and sure again; there was even a glint of humor in his eyes. She saw that Mairi and Alanna were up and dressed; all three had already eaten. She grinned in relief and delight, but the dream lingered.

When she saw her father turn to Li-an, Ailsa drew a deep breath, rose quickly, and threw a plaid about her shoulders.

"Li-an?" Charles murmured. "I thought I'd only dreamed you." He gazed at her, unable to believe what his eyes told him so clearly. "So far to come, and yet here you are."

"As I told you, it was my mother's wish," his daughter said. Now his eyes were clear blue and she saw in his smile the man she had once known. The man her mother had come as close to loving as she had any other human being. The darkness whirled within her and she looked away while she found a simple *p'ao* to throw over her head.

Then, because she could no longer avoid it, she went to him and bowed, palms pressed together.

"You can't imagine what it means to see your face," Charles whispered. "It's so like your mother's, except for your eyes and perhaps the shape of your nose."

Li-an stiffened. "You remember her features so well?"

"I remember everything about her." As his daughter approached, he reached up to grasp her wrist, on which she wore the bracelet of white and yellow gold. "I even remember the day I gave her this."

"She sent it with me," Li-an explained. "She said she wanted you to see that she had treasured it all these years, and that she wanted me to have it."

Charles bowed his head to hide the moisture in his eyes. "I must thank her for that."

"You cannot, my Father. She is dead." Li-an heard the stillness all around and noticed the other three had slipped outside. They had left her alone with this man, her father, whom she pitied but did not wish to see.

Charles's skin turned ashen. Looking away for a moment, he coughed into his clenched fist, then turned to face his daughter again. "I always thought Ke-ming was indestructible. When did it happen? How?"

Li-an looked down at her hands held properly, palm to palm. "The soldiers of T'zu Hsi burned her hut to the ground not so long ago." She spoke slowly, with no spark of sorrow in her voice or eyes. She guessed how easily a spark would start a blaze that would burn forever. Li, Governor of Fire, crouched in her heart, his torch raised and waiting. "It was just after I left her and gave myself into the hands of Yu-ch'iang, God of the Ocean Wind. I do not know whose hands she gave herself into, but they were not strong enough to hold her."

Charles considered his daughter closely. She spoke of her mother's death without emotion, but he knew her indifference was false. He himself wanted to weep openly for the death of a woman he had thought stronger and wiser than her enemies. A woman too beautiful to die in flames, alone. "You say she lived in a hut? Why was that? She belonged in palaces that never lost their glitter, in gardens where flowers never ceased to bloom."

Li-an pressed her lips into a thin line so he would not see her thoughts. "Such a place was our small home in the Western Hills. Like this house, it was surrounded by beauty—peaceful, safe. Seven years ago, we went there to escape the soldiers sent from the Forbidden City."

Charles frowned. "They were after her even then? And why don't you sit beside me? Surely you're tired of standing."

"I will stand before my father, as is correct." Her eyes were a clear blue that told him nothing. "It was not my mother they sought, though T'zu Hsi hated her always. It was me."

671

Her father sat forward, swallowing with difficulty. "Because you were my daughter, a foreigner?"

She smiled, this time with bitterness. "No. That the Army of the Green Banner and the Son of Heaven and his mother did not know. They knew only that I loved a man who they feared enough to kill, though he had done nothing. And I refused to let him die alone, abandoned. Without words, I spoke my allegiance to him for all to see, so I, too, became a danger to their secret world of lies and corruption and palaces that stood on earth about to turn to dust. They came for me, but I was gone." Without being aware of it, she straightened her shoulders and stood proudly, her head raised.

She is magnificent, Charles thought, just as her mother was. He felt a pain in his chest and bent forward, but it was sorrow that sapped his strength this time and not the consumption that was killing him slowly. They had destroyed Ke-ming, those savages with hatred in their eyes—their blind eyes that would not see what already lay in ruins at their feet. But at the same time, they had made Li-an an unbending tower of strength, a beautiful sculpture of grace and pride with a heart frozen in ice. She looked at him and every moment of anger she had ever felt was in her eyes. "You blame me for everything, don't you?" he asked sadly.

"I do not. That would be foolish and a waste of time. You were not even there."

"Yet even so, you blame me!" His cheeks were flushed and a sheen of sweat covered his forehead.

"No, my Father. You have been ill. You are seeing *kuei* in the shadows. Please, do not excite yourself." She drew the blanket carefully around him, brought him a cup of tea, and when he had drunk it, a cup of broth. She held his hand when it shook, steadied the cup so he could drink, touched a cloth to his head to cool the heat. Each movement was graceful, efficient, and completely without tenderness.

Charles lay back among the pillows when the weight in his chest became a pain that he could bear no longer. His eyes filled with tears that fell over his hollow cheeks—tears for the woman who had died, for the grief he had felt when he left her behind, for the years he had lost with his daughter, now a stranger with cool blue eyes and clever hands and hatred like bitter herbs in her blood.

"Why do you weep?" she asked, shocked for the first time out of her composure.

"Because Ke-ming is gone, and though you're here, your soul is many thousand miles away. You've brought nothing but anger to keep you company, to show me how much you suffered because I loved your mother. But I did love her. Nothing will change that. And I love you. Nor will that change, no matter how long you stare at me with your eyes of ice and your heart of stone."

Li-an turned to go, but he held her back with his hand on her sleeve. "If you loved me," she said slowly, "or her, you would have taken us with you. You would have kept us safe."

Charles's grip tightened on her arm. "I couldn't have kept you safe. Ke-ming told me as much when I begged her to bring you and come with me. I argued, bitterly, but she wouldn't listen. She told me I must go alone or all three of us would die."

Li-an was shaking inside. With an effort of will, she kept her body still. "I do not believe you." Yet somewhere in the back of her mind, she heard the sound of her mother's voice: *If you must continue to blame someone, then it should be me.*

Charles released his daughter's arm. "Ke-ming was right. I hated her for that, for sending me away alone. But I couldn't have made it through the lines of soldiers if I hadn't hidden in the sewers, in stables that had not been cleaned in days, among bushes full of thorns that tore my skin and left me bleeding. I almost didn't make it. Had you and your mother been with me, we all would have been killed. As I lay shivering on the ship that finally took me away, I remembered the light of the lantern on Ke-ming's face. Not until that moment did I recall the look of sadness in her eyes. I wept then, weak and tired and starving as I was, for all of us."

Li-an stood with her back to him, her face averted so he could not see her eyes. "I wept because now I could not deny that the world Ke-ming saw was the real world and my

673

own a fantasy I had created. She understood the ugliness, the corruption of men's souls that I didn't wish to face. She saw it all and knew. It took me a long time to understand fully. It wasn't until one night in India . . ." His voice trailed off. "But that's not what I wish to tell you."

His daughter stared at the light coming through the open door and the emptiness within her grew darker and more hollow. Her father's grief for Ke-ming had made a crack from the top to the bottom of her stone barrier and the echo of her mother's voice was loud in her ears. *I knew that, much as I loved it, this country would betray us both in the end.* "She sent me away also. I asked her to come but she refused." *I am a captive of my own history,* Ke-ming had said. "She sent me away so I would be safe while she chose to give up." *Here we have only shadows of the past and I was meant to die among them.*

"And now you expect me to watch you die, too. It is too much to ask, too great a burden. I have seen so many lose their lives and souls while I stood helpless. I will stand helpless no more." She straightened her back, drew the mask of indifference over her face, and left him.

Midnight lay upon the croft like a thin haze, broken only by the breathing of those who slept, unaware that the moon had risen and set beyond the window. Mairi lay in Charles's arms, her head on his shoulder. She thought he, too, slept and she listened with relief to the rhythm of his breath, unlabored now, with no rasp of congestion, no gasps that woke him suddenly, choking for breath. Though she could hear his heartbeat in her ear, she put her hand on his chest to feel the reassuring pulse with her palm.

"Mairi," he whispered, covering her hand with his.

It was the tone in which he spoke her name and not his touch that gave her pleasure, though had he taken his hand away, she would have felt colder inside. "Ye should be sleepin'," she whispered back. She did not wish to wake the others.

"I've been thinking. There's something I want to talk to you about."

He spoke so low that only she, with her cheek pressed

to his chin, could hear him. Mairi recognized the strain in his voice. "Aye?" she said warily.

"When the time comes," he hesitated, "when I die—"

"I'll have no talk of dyin'!" she hissed, raising herself on her elbow. "Alive ye be now and 'tis all I care about." In the violet darkness, his eyes gleamed as blue as the day when she had met him. "May such thoughts leave ye, *morun*, just as a dream slips away with the comin' of dawn."

"We both know it's coming. Not today or tomorrow, but not so long away, either." She closed her eyes to shut out the sound of his voice. "You've always faced the truth before," he said. "Why turn from it now? I'm happy here with the mountains to protect me, the wind to sing me to sleep, and the mist to soften the harsh edges of the life I once knew. I have my daughters around me." He frowned, thinking of Li-an and the cool distance she kept between them, though he had tried often to bridge it since that first morning. But he would not think of that now. "And my granddaughter—and you. Where else would I wish to breathe my last but where I have been happiest on this earth?"

Mairi lowered her head so he would not see her tears.

"Talk to me, Mairi," he whispered urgently. "I need to say this. Will you talk to me?"

"Aye," she said, running her finger along the stubble on his chin. "Ye know I will."

"Where do you think you'll bury me? In the kirkyard?"

She looked up. "No' if I have anythin' to say about it. In the kirkyard ye don't belong, among a lot of strangers and their stiff, pious bones." She heard his sigh of relief and leaned closer. "Ye've thought about this a great deal, haven't ye?"

"Aye, and I know where I would choose to rest, if I could."

"Where, *mo-charaid*, my *leannan?*"

"Next to your brother and father."

Mairi froze. "But your family—" she protested weakly.

"You're my family. You know that. I want to lie with the others in the valley ringed with stones, where I see your love for them in every pebble on those cairns."

"Ye see my guilt, my grief, my penance, but—"

"I see your love," he interrupted. "Every day I sit and think how you've chosen each stone, how your fingers have placed it on the cairn for years without end. It would please me to think you would do that for me."

"Och, Charlie, my Charlie!" she cried as she slipped her arms around him to pull him close. "Of course I would. 'Tis only that I wonder why ye choose to go to such a place."

He caressed her hair, comfortingly, as if she were a child. "Because you came to me there when I thought I'd lost everything and gave me all I'd ever wished for. Because when I sit among those rocks I think of the touch of your hands on my shoulders, the brush of your hair against my neck, the sound of your voice as you sang. I love that place, Mairi, for that alone."

"But there are evil memories, too."

Charles shook his head. "Those memories are yours, not mine. There's no evil there, only the wind that cries through the rocks, but there's nothing to fear in that. And, Mairi, at dawn, the sun rises above those standing stones and sends down showers of light that gather in the dell and linger until gloaming. I couldn't have created a more perfect place to paint, where the light is everywhere—clear, brilliant, gleaming on every blade of grass until each drop of dew is a prism of all colors."

Mairi closed her eyes. "What of the shadows and the ghosts?"

Smiling to himself, Charles said softly, "What is light without shadow to give it shape and form, to dim it when it grows too bright, to make you understand how precious that light is? If I'd never seen a shadow, I'd take the light for granted. But having lived in darkness, I know and won't forget. As for the ghosts, they're yours as well. Oh, I feel them now and then, hear them crying among the stones, but if you pay them no mind, they see that you don't fear them. They're part of the shadows, the past. They don't disturb me. I only pray that someday they'll not disturb you either."

Mairi turned so her lips were a breath away from his. " 'Tis truly what ye wish, *mo-aghraidh*, to lie among the tilted stones?"

"Truly."

"Then I will make it come to pass. But long from now, I pray, when daffodils and roses bloom no more and Mena, Goddess of the Moon, has turned from silver to dim gray." She kissed him and his arms closed tight around her.

"Ah! if I get to heaven,
    will my love dance with me?"

Charles whispered the words of a Celtic chanson he had learned from Ian Fraser.

"Shall I stand where she stands,
    In some clean filtered sphere,
And touch ethereal hands,
    And sing to spiritual ear?"

"Aye," Mairi replied, "so ye shall."

6

The first morning Charles ventured outside, Alanna found a spot where he would feel the most sun on his face. He leaned on Mairi's shoulder while Ailsa brought a piece of plaid and Li-an carried the rocking chair. She placed it on the patch of springy turf beneath a rowan tree where the shade would protect her father when the sun grew too warm. Charles settled himself comfortably, the plaid wrapped around his legs. Mairi sat at his side with a basket of herbs to sort. Li-an bowed and moved away.

Charles watched her go sadly, but did not yet have the strength to try and bring her back.

"Ye can see how much she's suffered, *mo-charaid,*" Mairi whispered. "She's chosen to hold her bitter memories close to her heart so she won't care for ye and it'll no' hurt her when ye go." Mairi gazed into the woods where primroses and wood anemone had begun to bloom. " 'Twill no' help her in the end." She turned to her husband, eyes painfully dry. "But ye must give her time to realize that for herself."

"I'd best go," Ailsa said. "I don't want her to be alone."

"Go," her father told her. "I'll wait for a better moment, though it'll be difficult, with nothing to occupy my hands."

"What of your paintin'?" Alanna cried.

Charles looked wistfully toward the distant valley. "I'd love to work on it, but the dell is too far away. I can't so easily make that journey now."

"Isn't there another place ye can go?" Ailsa asked.

Alanna leaned forward. Her hair fell over her shoulder

678

and her eyes sparkled. "Aye, 'tis a spot just around the hill behind the croft that I found. There's a little cave in the rocks to protect the canvas and your paints and 'tis close enough that I can take ye there each day."

"I don't know," Mairi said in concern.

"Don't fret, Grandmother. Ye could hear him if he called. And ye know how important the paintin' is to him."

"Aye, well, if ye're certain 'tis safe."

"I wouldn't suggest it else," Alanna insisted. "Shall I get the things for ye today and show ye where tomorrow?"

He smiled at her enthusiasm. "I'd be grateful, birdeen."

"Don't bother to be grateful," she cried, rising to her bare feet gracefully. " 'Tis a great pleasure for me."

She smiled and hurried away. Ailsa watched her daughter go, felt a painful tug at her heart that she did not try—or did not wish—to understand. Remembering Li-an, she rose abruptly, bade her father and mother good-bye, and left them, brow furrowed.

That night Alanna dreamed of the Valley of the Dead. She heard the wind among the stones and within the wind a voice that called her name. "Alanna! Come to me, for I have need of ye." In her dream she followed the voice, flew up toward the stars, her nightrail like pale wings that carried her into the circling clouds above the dell. She looked down at the standing stones, gray and mysterious beneath her.

Shadows flickered in the moonlight, touched her hand, and drew her downward. From out of the shadows came a figure. It pointed to the cairns; there were five now instead of three, one covered with a single layer of stones, the other with barely a few among sprouts of new grass. Silently, the shadow drifted to the tiny pebbles cast among the larger boulders, motioned from the small stones to the graves to the stones and back again.

Alanna moved forward weightlessly to pick up five pebbles and place one reverently on each cairn. The shadow nodded, satisfied, and pointed to the breaking dawn, the dawn beyond it and all the dawns that were to come.

The girl looked up at stars that glimmered like tiny silver flames against a black velvet sky. Each flickering light spoke to her in a different voice; she heard them all and recognized each one, as if she had always known them. Then she was flying again while the wind caressed her with the touch of an old friend, the leaves of the trees made a walkway below, and the mountains rose like a promise of strength and changelessness in the darkness. She rejoiced as she flew back to her little heather bed but could not explain the sadness in her heart.

When she awoke before dawn, Alanna threw on her plaid and went barefoot toward the valley. She did not consider which direction she would take; she followed an instinct deeper than thought. She moved through the woods that had become so familiar in the past few weeks. She knew each bend in the pathway, each fold in the earth, each tree and brae and cluster of bracken that led her to the tall parted stones, where she slipped into the valley.

The voices of the dead howled in the wind, whirled among the shadowed boulders, but she was not afraid. The sorrow she had felt the first time she saw this place had disappeared long ago. She bent to choose pebbles to put on each cairn. As she did so, the voices changed, diminished. She saw fleeting faces in the clefts of rock like the shadows of birds as they passed before the moon.

Alanna knelt with her feet against the cold stones of the cairns, her hands on the dew-wet grass. The wind grew quiet and the first hint of dawn rimmed the valley in pearl gray that quickly turned to rose. The light followed, burst into the sky like pink and lilac tongues of flame that tinted the clouds deep purple and mauve. The darkness paled as the colors grew brighter until the sun appeared and moved upward slowly, blazing.

The girl held her breath, unwilling to break the spell of the sunrise. The lilac-misted world was so beautiful it caused an ache in her chest that would not ease. She wanted to prolong this moment, make it last forever, as brilliant as the instant when the sun first topped the standing stones. She stared at the grass, wet with dew that caught the light in prisms of fragmented color. Her vision blurred, and mesmerized by those tiny drops of tinted light, she saw moments—

splintered, fleeting, but with the clarity of crystal. She saw the past and the future, all that had been and all that was meant to be, until the present vanished and only the dream remained against her violet eyes.

Alanna was enwrapped by a stillness that isolated her from the world beyond the valley. Within the stillness, she felt a deep, vibrant joy. She knew then that this place—the river Affric, the moors, the loch, the mountains, and every sheltered valley of the glen—was her true home. Somewhere in her hidden heart, it had always been so.

By the time Alanna returned to the croft, the sun had climbed high in the sky and all were awake. While Mairi fixed porridge, Ailsa and Li-an dressed and moved restlessly about the room, their expressions distant. Alanna's heart sank.

"What ails you?" Charles asked when he saw how his two daughters gazed inward toward some vision he could not see.

Ailsa smiled enigmatically. "I don't know for certain, but the last time I felt this way, Li-an arrived in the glen."

Charles swung his feet out of bed and clutched the worn oak post to hold himself upright. "Genevra?" he asked in a whisper.

Li-an felt a stab of pain at the excitement in her father's eyes. She berated herself for her foolishness. She had given him no reason to look at her that way. She had given him nothing, not one moment of affection, and so deserved none from him. That was how she wanted it, how it must ever be.

"I'll dress," Charles said, "and come with you to meet her."

Ailsa pushed him gently back against the pillows. "We're no' even sure. 'Tis only that we've both been dreamin' of her again, and I feel strange, as if I'm no' just myself anymore, but part of someone else."

She knelt beside Charles and twined her fingers with his. "Besides, 'tis too far for ye to go. And I think 'twould be better if she comes indeed, that we meet her alone. To give her time to get used to the glen. 'Twill be a gey strange world for her. Can ye understand that?"

681

He nodded, but could not hide his disappointment.

"Ye've waited this long," Mairi said, running her fingers through Charles's silver hair. "Ye can wait a few hours longer. In the meantime, ye've work to do, haven't ye?" He still had not let her see the painting. Only Alanna had done so. He said it was because he had not worked in so long and was unsure of his talent, but Mairi knew him too well to believe that. She did not argue, however. Let him have his secret, for this one would not hurt her.

"I'll help ye set it up," Alanna said. She stood near the fire with her damp plaid about her shoulders. "And I'll sit with ye to keep ye company."

"Thank ye, *mo-run,*" Ailsa said, ruffling her daughter's hair. "I don't know what we would have done without ye these past weeks." She met Alanna's gaze, recognized the joy and sadness there; her own heart paused. "I'm sorry we must go, but we'll be back soon. We can walk then, if ye like, just ye and me."

Alanna nodded. Her mother understood her well. She always had. That was what made this so difficult. Hands gripping the top of a chair, she watched Ailsa and Li-an ready themselves, then slip through the door without a word. Alanna would have to wait, but perhaps it was better that way.

Genevra Townsend had been traveling for months by boat, for days by train and coach. She was so weary that her body felt like lead and her limbs ached from being cramped and inactive. But none of these discomforts compared to the nervous flutter in her stomach that had become her sole obsession. Soon she would see her father, perhaps even today.

She was not ready.

The splashes of green, blue, and rust beyond the wind blurred until a gray haze enveloped her. Oddly, she had not seen Charles Kittridge's face on the journey across India to Calcutta and from there to London. She had dreamed of Alex again and again, of Phoebe and Radha's beautiful mountains, but never once had she looked up to find her father watching with his sad smile or twinkling blue eyes.

The Golden Man had disappeared. In his place was a shadow that frightened her because it was strange and unfamiliar.

As the coach jerked to a halt, she clutched the seat to keep from falling. The driver's face appeared at the window. "Here ye are, lass. Ye'll find the Rose croft just through the woods and across the moor."

Genevra nodded mutely. The blood drained from her face as she climbed from the coach to find herself surrounded by a blur of color, motion, and sound. She stood immobile while the young man lifted down her trunk. She was blind and deaf except to the shadows and whispers that had followed her from India and would not leave her now.

"Good mornin', lass." The driver tipped his hat, shrugged at her blank stare, and mounted the seat on the front of the coach. As he drove away, the dust rose behind him in a cloud that choked her, settled on her clothes and in her throat, adding another layer to the filth that already covered her.

Genevra did not want to move. She had been wrong to come. She should turn right now and shout after the retreating coach that she wished to return to London. The sound of Phoebe's voice stopped her. *You're one of the most courageous women I know*. It was true that Genevra had fought to survive ever since Edward Townsend and her mother had abandoned her. She had grown up fighting with every breath and would not give up now.

She summoned the image of the laughing Ganesha, God of Good Luck, with his elephant's head and rotund body, and prayed for his good wishes. He would protect her—he and Vishnu, the Preserver. Setting her jaw in determination, she left the muddy road and entered the woods.

The trees closed around her, cool and dark, with a sigh of wind through the fluttering leaves. The scene was so familiar that she felt she had been here before. She looked into the blue-green stillness swathed in fragile white, listened to the wind and the murmur of unseen water, stared at the dark, jagged mountains in the distance. The mist drifted like a blessing over her face. She stared in astonishment and wonder.

Haven't you ever dreamed of mountains not engulfed

in choking dust? So she had. These were the hills she had imagined so often, the mountains of her dreams that had offered her peace, stillness, comfort. She had thought, as she lay damp with sweat in the stifling Delhi heat, that it was Radha's beloved Indian hills she longed for, but she had been wrong. "Strange is the course of Fate," the Hindus murmured when the wild magnificence of the monsoons turned to the calm blue skies of fall. Strange indeed.

Genevra's heart began to beat erratically. She had stepped from the nightmare of her journey to the beauty of her dream and could not understand how it had happened. It was too sudden, too incredible to be true. Trembling at the confusion of relief and perplexity, delight and disbelief that shook her, she took a deep, steadying breath. Oddly, she felt that she belonged here, as if she had been meant to come. *Thus it was written on your forehead by the hand of Brahma himself,* Hazari had told her once. It struck her, as she closed her eyes to absorb the feel of the glen, that the whispers had faded into silence and the shadows into swirling light. Phoebe's warning came to her on the wisp of a breeze. *Don't choose to be blind like your mother did. Open your eyes. There's so very much to see.*

Genevra opened her eyes as if for the first time, as if they had been closed tight all her life and every moment until now had been a drama played by shadows on the background of her blue-veined lids. This was a world she had never known, a sense of wonder she had never thought to feel. Not even when Alex held her in his arms and the colors spun inside her. She paused at the echo of his name. She had missed him so much that it frightened her. She forced the thought to the back of her mind.

Instinctively, to escape her pain, she moved toward the water, then followed the river toward the sound of a small waterfall. She stood in a copse where the water poured over tumbled rocks then widened into a pond. She stared, hypnotized by the white foam, the clear, sparkling pond sprinkled with light that danced across the surface as the leaves moved overhead. She felt out of place in these fresh, natural surroundings. She was dirty—covered with the sweat, dust, and soot of her journey. The water called to her. "Come cleanse yourself. I will take you in and wash away the bitterness, the doubt, the uncertainty.''

The water poured over stones, splintered into fragments in the wide, clear pond. She threw aside her hat. Phoebe had told her to listen to her instincts. All Genevra could hear was the music of the river and the voices inside that told her she was safe from observation. Besides, at this moment, the desire for the touch of water on her naked skin was more important even than the risk of discovery.

Quickly, she discarded the jacket of her traveling suit, slid the skirt down her legs. Then she removed her blouse, even her chemise and drawers. She had found the haven of her dreams; she wanted it to take her fully, absorb her into its spell—the spell of wind and murmuring water.

She waded into the cold pond, shivering, and splashed water over her body, washing away grime and memories until nothing remained but the crisp clear images of her newly opened eyes. She took the pins from her hair and let it fall. The pale strands drifted on the surface and the dust disappeared in the flickering sunlight. Slowly, she moved toward the waterfall. She floated while the water flowed over her like a cool, caressing hand. Out of the river rose a voice that called her name.

"Genevra!"

She glanced up. There were two voices and they had not come from the water but out of the shadowy woods. She crouched beside the rocks, listening intently. The voices were familiar.

Suddenly two women stood in the copse gazing at her clothes tossed carelessly on the bank. Then the women turned to look at her. The one with chestnut hair smiled and Genevra felt a shock of recognition. Those blue-violet eyes had filled her dream one night and her thoughts for many days after. Beside her stood the golden-skinned woman with the sky-blue eyes. Genevra felt a chill that had nothing to do with the cold.

A moment ago, these two had been a memory from a long-ago dream, a fleeting image that had once promised her comfort. Now, suddenly, they were real. She found it difficult to breathe. The water splashed her face and she shrank back when she realized she stood naked in the pond. "Who . . . ?" she began.

"Don't be afraid," the older woman murmured. "We've no' come to judge ye. I used to do this often when I was a lass in these hills. 'Tis the loveliest feelin', isn't it? To let the water take ye in and soothe ye. 'Tis what ye came here for, I think."

Genevra shook her head. "I came to meet you." She did not know where her certainty sprang from; she only knew she spoke the truth. "Who are you?" She turned to the Chinese woman who had not yet spoken.

"I am Li-an and this is Ailsa. We, too, are the daughters of Charles Kittridge, your father," Li-an said slowly. "Like you, we have come at his summons."

Stiffening, Genevra looked away. These women were her sisters. Charles Kittridge's daughters. She had forgotten her father in the past few minutes, forgotten it was he who had brought her here, his shadow that had haunted her for so long. The miracle of the mountains had made her forget. Unaccountably, she crouched lower in the water, feeling like a fool.

Ailsa sensed her half-sister's unease and smiled in reassurance. "I think I'll join ye. It's been so many years since I swam here." Without hesitation, she removed her gown and underthings and plunged into the water. "Come," she called to Li-an. " 'Twill ease a little of your pain. The water is healin' and free of human sufferin'."

Li-an glanced at the disheveled pile of clothes with longing. In China one did not behave so. From the time she was a child, she had had to beware always, to be proper, to be careful.

Ailsa turned unselfconsciously onto her back and floated while her crown of braids came loose to trail over her shoulders. She swam toward Genevra and let the spray splash around her, then reached for the younger woman's hand. "I'm glad ye're finally here. We've been waitin' for ye."

Genevra hesitated, glancing at Li-an, who still stood on the bank. Ailsa turned to her half-sister and called again, "Ye're no' in China now, *mo-run*. Do as ye wish, no' as ye've learned. Come. We have need of ye, Genny and I."

Li-an stared at the waterfall and thought it looked like tears pouring down the smooth face of the boulders. Thousands and thousands of tears. Tears beyond counting. The tears that she had never shed for her mother. She had wept for Chin Chao, curled in her gauze-shrouded world of grief and horror; she had wept for their child who was dead; but she had never wept for Ke-ming. Before the stone within began to crumble, before her dry and aching eyes grew damp, she threw off her clothes and laid them next to Ailsa's. Li-an entered the water slowly, let it stream over her skin, her hair. The tears flowed over and around her, not warm and salty, but cool and somehow comforting. She dropped to her knees and the wall rose strong and firm as shining marble to enclose the pain she dared not feel.

She swam across to join the others. The three sisters stood silent, without the need for words, while the water crashed and sang and caught the fleeting light. Li-an took Genevra's other hand, looked into her eyes, and saw her own bitterness and grief reflected there. The grip of their fingers tightened.

Somehow, Genevra managed to whisper, " 'A day passes, but a moment does not.' " This moment—when she read Li-an's past in the clear blue of her eyes, when she felt the touch of Ailsa's hand on hers—would not.

"Nor does the water change with the years or the weight of your sorrow and fear," Ailsa said softly, "nor the mountains nor the wind that rushes through the trees. These things are unchangin'. Ye can believe in them, just as we can believe in each other."

Later, after they had found a patch of sunlight where they dried their naked bodies, after Ailsa and Li-an had told their half-sister about Mairi and Charles and his illness, they dressed and returned to the croft. Mairi was alone, sitting at the table with her elbows on the pitted oak, her chin in her hands. She rose as the sisters entered.

"Ye must be Genevra," she murmured. "Welcome to the glen, lass." She took both the girl's hands in hers and held them for a moment. " 'Tis glad I am ye've come." She did not add "in time," but the unspoken words hung in the air between them.

Genevra was shocked at Mairi's obvious sincerity.
When Ailsa pulled out a chair for her, the young woman sat
near the fire to warm her hands, still chilled from the cold
water. She felt strangely at ease, more so than she had ever
felt in Helen Bishop's house, or even Edward Townsend's,
though she had thought herself happy there. Had she imagined this place, these people who smiled as if she were a
welcome friend?

"Your father will be back soon," Mairi said. She spoke
softly, with affection.

Genevra turned. "You must hate us," she said, pointing
to Li-an and herself—the bastards, children of other lands
and other women.

Mairi smiled her sweet, sad smile. "Never ye," she said
softly, "though I can't say I didn't blame my Charles for a
time. I can't tell ye that the knowledge didn't hurt me."

"So you hated him?" Genevra persisted.

Mairi shook her head. "Never quite that."

"Why?" Li-an demanded harshly. "Why forgive him
so easily?"

Mairi faced the Chinese woman. "Ye mean when ye
can't? Or won't?" She saw that Li-an would not answer and
added, "I forgave him because I loved him. Because I knew
he wasn't a man meant to be alone. How could I expect him
to be true to the memory of the woman who had turned
him away, who had no' even the courage to face him and tell
him it was over?"

"But still," Ailsa insisted, "ye were hurt and angry."

Mairi stared into the fire. "Aye, so I was. But anger
passes, *mo-aghraidh*. Love doesn't."

Genevra did not hear the last words. She was staring at
Li-an's bracelet of white and yellow gold. It was so like
Mairi's wedding ring. And there was something else—the
woven gold necklace Emily had bequeathed to her daughter.
So Charles Kittridge had left his mark on all of them. Before
she could speak, the door swung open and a man stepped
over the threshold. Behind him was a girl of about Genevra's
age who looked very much like Mairi. She carried a creel
full of herbs she had gathered during the day.

Genevra tensed, rose without thinking. Her voice
seemed to have left her.

688

"Charles, Alanna," Mairi said, "this is Genevra, and a long way she's come to see ye. Genevra, your father and Ailsa's daughter."

Charles stood where he was, taking in the sight of his youngest daughter—the pale blond hair and blue eyes flecked with gray, the soft, sun-browned curves of her face. She was very like Emily, and yet not like her. "Genevra," he said in a voice that quavered. Then he took her hand.

She slipped her fingers out of his grasp, shivering as if touched by a ghost. The cool feel of his hand had been real enough, but she could not believe he was Charles Kittridge. This was not the man she remembered. Her memories had not grown pale over the years but sharper and brighter. She had thought she would see light brown hair bleached blond by the Indian sun, vivid blue eyes, a penetrating look, an enigmatic smile. And a uniform perhaps—a red coat, polished saber, and two rows of gleaming buttons to reflect the faces of an endless army, the power of a grasping empire.

But this was a single frail man, dressed in trousers and a plain shirt, without even a waistcoat or cravat. He wore a long red plaid draped loosely about his shoulders. His cheeks were pallid and his hair glimmered shiny gray in the firelight. The vivid blue of his eyes was shaded now, dimmer, yet full of light all the same. The Golden Man had turned to silver.

She saw by the shadows in his eyes, the trembling of his hand, the hope and fear in his gaze, that he had suffered, though she did not wish to see these things. *Because of your mother's obsession, you've never seen your father clearly,* Phoebe had warned. *He's always been a shadow to which she gave color and form. Use your own eyes now to make him real.* His daughter stared at him, into him, and tried to do just that, but the memory of her own past rose like bile in her throat.

"I've waited a long time for this moment," Charles said. "To have my family here around me—every one of you." His voice shook and he sat down abruptly in a polished birch chair.

"I've waited, too," Genevra replied without inflection.

"I think ye'll all be wantin' your supper," Mairi interrupted, "Afterward, ye can talk."

"Aye, I'm half starved," Alanna said a little too loudly. "Grandfather *would* eat all the black buns and leave me no' a single one." She smiled at him affectionately.

Everyone gathered around the table, eating their brose and mutton from wooden bowls. Mairi got out the sherry and each had a glass to celebrate the safe arrival of all three daughters. "Ye must eat," she told Genevra when she saw that the girl sat, her horn spoon motionless in her hand. "Believe me, 'twill warm ye both inside and out. After your long journey, ye need a little warmth, I'm thinkin'."

Ailsa touched her half-sister's hand. "She's right, ye ken. My mother is very wise, Genny. Ye should heed her well."

Genevra gazed about her, startled by the soft tone of their voices, the smiles on every face—for her. To her astonishment, these people made her feel that she belonged here. They welcomed her as Phoebe had, without condition, and more than that, with pleasure. How easily each could have disliked or mistrusted her, with far more reason than the British who had turned from her in disgust. But it was not so. All at once she wanted to weep.

After dinner, the other women went out to look at the stars, leaving her alone with her father.

Charles sat in a rocking chair pulled near the fire, while the cold crept under the door. Genevra sat nearby, silent, too stunned by all that had happened, too confused by her own tumultuous feelings to know what to say.

Finally Charles spoke. "I tried to find you, you know, when I heard what Edward Townsend had done." He did not look at her, but stared into the flames as if drawing his memories from the red-hot center of the fire.

"You mustn't have tried very hard."

With a heavy sigh, her father closed his eyes. "You can't know that. You see, at first I was looking for both you and Emily. I didn't learn for a long time that she had left you with relatives who'd taken you away from Calcutta. 'What relatives?' I asked over and over. 'What are their names? Where did they go?' But no one seemed to know. Or else they wouldn't tell me. They said I'd already hurt you enough.

"I didn't believe them, and it didn't stop me from looking, but in all the cities where the British lived I found the same determined silence. It was as if everyone knew about Emily and Edward and me." He frowned, leaning forward. "They say the Indians know things without speaking, that news spreads among them, even over the entire continent, without words—so quickly that it seems to fly on the back of the wind. The ones who say that do not know the British in India."

Genevra knew it was true, had lived with its bitter consequences all her life. But her heart had been poisoned by too many years without a family, too many nightmares, too many shadows.

"Then the government transferred me home." He did not look up, afraid of what he might find. "And later to Canada, America. It seems I was sent everyplace but where I wanted to be."

"Then how did you ever find me?" She jumped at the sound of her own voice, pressed her hands to her throat to stop the pulse that throbbed there.

"Recently, when I was back in London, a friend who'd just returned from Delhi said there was a woman looking for me. Her name was Phoebe Quartermaine. My friend gave me her address. I contacted her at once. When I got her reply, I wanted to take the next boat and come to you, but she said no." He clenched his fists in frustration.

Genevra regarded her father incredulously. "You wanted to see me that much?"

Charles rested his hand on the arm of her chair but did not quite touch her. "You can't imagine how much. I had no one else. I'd lost Mairi when I was just a boy, then Li-an and Ke-ming when the Chinese turned on me. Then Emily and you." The flames leaped and glimmered in his eyes.

I don't think you can imagine how much he cares for you, Phoebe had said. *Even though you're as much a shadow to him as he is to you.* It was Genevra's turn to stare into the flames. She saw now that her father was just a man like any other—a lonely man who'd lost everyone he ever loved. "Why did you come back here?" she asked at last. "How did you dare, when you knew your wife might turn you away?"

Charles smiled his echo of Mairi's smile. "I had to take the chance. I had to tell myself that she might let me stay this time. Because if she did, it was worth any risk to be near her again, even so late, even knowing . . ." He trailed off.

Sometimes one has to take a risk. You're a reed, Genevra, slender, flexible, strong. Don't be afraid of anyone, least of all a dying man who needs your forgiveness so badly. "Was it the same when you asked us to come, knowing we might refuse?"

Charles nodded. "I had no idea whether you knew my name, if you'd forgotten me or learned to hate me, but I had to try."

Genevra met his questioning gaze. "I hadn't forgotten." She did not know if it was anger or pity that stuck in her throat. Abruptly, she rose, went to the trunk the three women had carried from the roadside, and opened it. She rummaged through the contents, knocking out several pieces of paper, until she found the gold necklace. She was not sure what she planned to do with it.

Charles gaped at the drawings scattered on the floor. "You're an artist?" he asked eagerly.

"Yes."

His eyes lit up as if his daughter had handed him a priceless gift. "It's what I always wanted to be," Charles explained, "but my family had other ideas. I was weak and young; I let them make me into a diplomat. You must have been much stronger than I."

Genevra felt as if he had struck her and was not certain why.

"May I see your work?"

She could not deny him; his voice was so full of pleased surprise. The necklace forgotten, she rose, gathered the drawings, and handed them to her father.

Charles leaned closer to the firelight and examined the charcoal sketches in fascination. They made him want to weep and laugh and weep again at their beauty, their sensitivity. He saw in the faces and landscapes and bodies curved in prayer the talent of a spirit wise beyond even her own knowledge.

Charles looked at his daughter in awe—and gratitude. Out of his own weakness and Emily's dark dread had come Genevra. He knew she shared her mother's fear; he had seen the shadows in her eyes. But she had not allowed it to cloud her vision. She saw clearly, vividly, the beauty to which Emily had been blind, and made that beauty into art. "You hadn't forgotten me," he managed to say at last.

"I told you that."

Her father stared at the drawings to hide the moisture in his eyes. "Here's Ailsa and Li-an. This must be Mairi, and Emily. You've even sketched Ke-ming. But there's nothing of yourself."

"No, nothing."

They sat in silence while she took the drawings in her lap. She looked at the faces of her sisters, their mothers, all the women Charles Kittridge had ever loved. Somehow, he had wrought a miracle and brought them to be with him in his illness. He had not given up or listened to the voice of fear or sat alone to grieve over those he had lost. He had simply set out to find them again.

Unexpectedly, her father took her hand. "I searched for so long. Can't you forgive me for what I couldn't help?"

She pulled away and rose, slipped into the shadows beyond the firelight. The drawings fell in whispers to the floor. "It isn't that. I suppose it was, for a while, but not now. It's the things you *could* have helped that I can't forget."

"What things?"

She whirled, her eyes wintry gray. "You didn't have to lie with my mother."

Charles opened his mouth, but made no sound. "I thought I could help her," he said at last, foolishly. "She was lonely."

"And so were you." The simple words were an accusation.

Her father clasped his age-spotted hands. "Aye, it's true. I needed Emily as much as she needed me. I just didn't see where it would lead. And for that I'm sorry. But out of what we shared we created you. I will not be sorry that you were born, especially now that I've seen your face." He gathered up the drawings and held them out to her. "And these."

Genevra looked up, struck by the look on his face, the way he clutched her sketches in his hands. But there was nothing she could say.

7

For several days, the three sisters walked the glen from end to end, talking of their separate lives, the dreams they had shared, the fears, the shadow of happiness that had followed each. Ailsa showed them, as she had shown her daughter, all the places of her childhood until her sisters came to feel that they had always known the secrets of the hills.

Each morning, Genevra sat beside her father, talking to him quietly, as the others did. She spoke of Alex and India, of Radha and Narain, of Phoebe and her beautiful gardens—but never of Emily or the shadows and whispers. And never of forgiveness.

Every day she saw Charles grow weaker, saw the pain he could no longer hide and the fits of coughing that became more frequent and more violent. Yet as his suffering increased, he became kinder, gentler, rather than withdrawn and moody, as she would have expected. But then nothing was as she had expected.

In the evening, Ailsa played the flute and sang while Genevra sat at the table and, in the light of an oil lamp, taught Li-an how to use a pen to write her poems in words rather than Chinese characters. For hours the fair head and the dark were bent over paper and inkwell. The scratching of the pen never ceased. Because she already knew how to read and speak English, Li-an learned quickly. She fixed her full attention on the task; by listening closely to Genevra, imitating the motions of her dexterous fingers, Li-an could block out all thoughts, all feelings but the sense of her own accomplishment.

Genevra did not know how many days had passed when

she and her sisters prepared for a long walk one clear spring morning. She had forgotten quickly how to measure time and did not care. Like the others, she had discarded her heavy English cloak in favor of a length of plaid that left her free to move. She was tossing it over her shoulder when Charles came in from outside and leaned against the door-jamb to catch his breath.

"Good morning, Genevra," he said.

"Good morning."

Charles rubbed his arms, chilled from air not yet warmed by the sun. "Won't you call me 'Father'? Ailsa does, and even Li-an."

Out of the corner of her eye, Genevra saw Li-an turn away. The English girl had watched her sister speak to Charles in a cool, firm voice, had seen the careful deference with which Li-an approached him. The sight made Genevra hurt inside, though she couldn't explain the feeling. She hesitated, then turned back to Charles. "Good morning, Father," she said.

He smiled and brushed her cheek with his fingertips. To her surprise, she smiled back.

Abruptly, Li-an left the croft.

" 'Tis time to go, I'm thinkin'," Ailsa suggested softly. "Alanna, birdeen, will ye be joinin' us?"

Alanna shook her head. "I'd rather stay by today." She looked meaningfully after Li-an.

"Well, then, shall we be off?" As Ailsa passed the gray stone wall where her hand harp hung, she paused.

"Why don't you bring it?" Genevra cried. "We've so longed to hear it, Li-an and I. Just once."

"Aye," Mairi agreed. " 'Tis time, don't ye think?" She watched while Ailsa hesitated, then lifted the clarsach from the rusted hooks that had held it for so long. Smiling, her eyes damp with relief, Mairi met her husband's gaze as the half-sisters bade them farewell and went to join Li-an.

"Take care," Mairi called after them.

Genevra paused. She knew Mairi included all three women in her concern, not only Ailsa. She had seen Charles's wife watching Li-an often, troubled, helpless, aching as if the stranger were her own daughter and not Charles

Kittridge's bastard child. There had been regret in her father's eyes, too, as they left. Genevra looked back, suddenly uncertain.

"It is easy for him to give affection now, when he has never had to give anything else," Li-an said in her ear.

Ailsa clutched the harp tightly and turned away to hide her anger.

As Genevra followed, an Indian proverb came back to her. "He worships those whom he speaks ill of." She did not say the words aloud. She did not wish to break the thread that bound the sisters closer every day. Besides, how could Genevra speak when her own bitter memories were so strong? She took Li-an's arm and drew her over the dew-wet grass.

Inside the croft, Charles and his wife took their accustomed places by the fire while Alanna slipped outside to wait. Mairi laid her hand on the arm of her chair and her husband covered it with his. Charles looked at his wife's averted profile with an affection that made his breathing painful. This morning she had not bound up her graying hair; the fire gleamed off the loose strands and flared in her strange, all-seeing eyes. The sight of her face was as familiar as his own, yet he was always amazed to look up and find her beside him. Still, after all these years, there were secrets in those eyes that he could not begin to guess, knowledge that was greater than he would ever share. It was part of what made him love her so much.

Softly, he began to sing a song his daughter had taught him.

> "Oh that I were a wood, a stream,
> A flower, a leaf, a tide,
> A thought, a word, a passing dream
> Wherein she might abide."

Mairi turned, her expression tinged with ineffable sadness and joy. Strange how her face could hold so many emotions at once, yet none seemed to contradict the other.

"A freshet where the silver bream
    Adown the currents glide;
I were the stream and she the bream,
    Love link'd us side by side."

He paused to catch his breath. His forehead was beaded with moisture and his hand overly warm on Mairi's cool skin. "I must go paint today," he said.

"Must ye, then? I'd hoped ye'd stay with me a bit."

"A bit," he said, "but no more. It may be the last time I *can* go, and I'm so nearly done."

Mairi struggled to speak but could not find the words.

Charles cupped her face in his hands. "I'll be back, my Mairi. You know that. We've accomplished much since I came to you a year since, but this one more thing I have to do." He thought of Li-an, no closer to him now than she had been on the day of her arrival, of Genevra, who was fighting hard to keep hold of her anger. Those things he could not change. He had tried many times in many ways, but his two youngest daughters remained beyond his reach. Only when he held the brush in his hand and painted light onto canvas did he have the control he had always sought but never found. "I'll be going now, and back before gloaming. And don't worry, Mairi. Alanna will be with me."

His wife nodded, kissed him, and let him go. Then, as she had every day since he'd returned, she went to her loom. She craved the familiar comfort of the motion of the shuttle, the interchange of warp and weft, the weaving of separate threads into a fabric that was whole and beautiful and could never be unraveled, except by the passage of years beyond her knowing.

Ailsa, Li-an, and Genevra made their way to the copse where they had first met. They sat on the grass, the bracken curled at their feet, the mountains rising like purple shadows into the blue, cloud-laden sky. Ailsa leaned against a boulder, Li-an chose a sturdy hawthorn and Genevra a fragrant cedar. For a long time they did not speak, but only listened to the sound of wind on the water. Genevra raised her face to the sky; it was an unusually warm day and she welcomed the touch of the sun. With it came memories and nearly forgotten dreams.

" 'The sun's rays pass between this world and the world beyond,' " she murmured. " 'They flow from the sun, enter into the arteries, flow back from the arteries, enter into the sun.' " She spoke the words from the *Mahabaratha* instinctively. Odd that they did not seem out of place, even in this hidden glen that had never known cruel summer heat.

" 'Tis so," Ailsa agreed. "I've felt the sun in my own blood on many a mornin'."

"It's from an Indian poem I memorized years ago. I'm surprised I remembered it."

" 'Tis hard to forget what's beautiful to ye. Such things linger even when ye think they've slipped away long since." Ailsa closed her eyes and began to strum her harp. She gasped at the first poignant notes, so sweet, clear, and true. She had forgotten how beautiful the music of the clarsach could be.

She remembered the first day she had sat in this very spot and touched the strings of the harp Ian had readied for her with such care. She had been a fool to avoid the clarsach for so long; the sound of its fragile notes brought comfort from the knowledge of her father's worsening illness and the dull ache that had become the memory of Ian. She began to sing, without thinking of the words she chose.

"In the Blue Garden, the Blue Night,
Beholds the Rapture of Delight
          Oy Dieus.

Beholds my Friend, whom most I love,
Singin' his coryphée of Love
          Oy Dieus."

Genevra picked up the sketch pad she carried with her and began to draw, her eyes on the shadow of leaves on the water, the sunlight that made a vivid pattern on the rippled pond. The music flowed from Ailsa's fingers into her sister's and Genevra drew blindly, hypnotized by the place, the music, the rush of water over stones. She felt warm and at peace. She was not reluctant to speak any thought, for she knew Ailsa and Li-an would understand. If nothing else, by bringing her here, Charles had granted Genevra's fondest wish: for the first time in her life, she had become part of a family.

"As the Trees in the tranced Dark,
The sad Bulbul's high notes hark
Oy Dieus.

As the woods in the Middle Noon
In the Sun's Brilliance softly swoon
Oy Dieus."

Like her sisters, Li-an fell under the spell of the music. She forced the image of her father's face into shadow, took paper and pen from her pocket, and began to write a poem. She felt some confidence now when she formed the letters that had once seemed so alien to her. She had forgotten how exciting it could be to learn something new, to master a difficult task and feel silent pride in her own success.

"So I to my Friend's joyous Lay
Until the Dawn comes, bringin' Day
Oy Dieus.

Oh, stay, our love continuin',
When the Dawn comes and the Birdis sing
Oy Dieus."

"What is it?" Genevra asked.

Ailsa raised her head. "A Celtic chanson I learned when I was a bairn, long before I understood the meanin' of the words." She turned to Li-an. "We've both given of our childhood memories. Haven't ye one to share?"

Li-an leaned her head against the rough bark of the tree and tried to think. "I will tell you a story Liu Kan used to repeat each time we passed the Ha-ta-men Gate in the city of Peking," she said at last. Brow furrowed in concentration, she began, "Long, long ago the people who lived in the city with Nine Gates were very much afraid of the gods who ruled in *Ti'en*—heaven—and on earth. It is said that near one of the gates there was a deep, dark well. It was the kind of place where *kuei* or evil spirits make their homes and the people knew that a shiny-scaled dragon lived in this well. It was foretold by the astrologers that one day the beast would rise and flood the city so that all would die in the rushing, churning waters.

"The people listened, trembled, and believed. They shivered with fear and whispered among themselves. 'How are we to stop this evil thing from happening?' Finally a young boy spoke up. 'Why do you not simply cover the well?' The people were astounded that one so young should be so wise. 'But with what shall we cover it?' they asked. 'I have heard,' the boy told them, 'of a stone tortoise so large that only nine times nine men can move it. Surely, if such a thing were found, it would keep the dragon hidden deep within the well.' " Li-an paused.

"Don't be cruel," Genevra said. "What happened then?"

"The people went in search of the tortoise. They left the city from the eight other gates to look over the country-side, in the hills, even in the wide rivers. At last they found the thing of which the boy had spoken at a small temple in the Western Hills. Working together, with horses, carts, and oxen, they brought the tortoise to Peking. It took four days to lift the heavy stone above the gaping black hole of the well, but at last it was done.

"But the tortoise was not happy. They knew this, for Tung-yo, the principal God of the Skies, had spoken from among the clouds to tell them so. 'What shall we do now?' they asked each other in despair. To upset so great a stone beast would surely bring disaster upon them all. Once again, the small voice of the boy was heard above the others. He spoke to the tortoise, saying, 'We will send someone to relieve you of this burdensome watch when the gong strikes to proclaim that day is at an end and the city must close its gates and sleep once more.'

" 'You fool!' the people shouted. 'Do you not under-stand that that will set the dragon free?' The boy smiled, drew the others away from the gate, and said, 'We will place a bell above the gate instead of the gongs that hang above the other eight.' The people laughed and slapped the boy on the back for his cleverness. And so the great stone tortoise sits, century after century, waiting patiently, saving the city from flood and the people from death while he listens for the sound of a gong and hears nothing but the ringing of a bell. There are those who say he is soothed by the music of the bell, and those who say no, but whatever the truth, upon the well he sits to this day."

Ailsa and Genevra laughed. The sound seemed overly loud to their sensitive ears. There had not been much laughter among them and somehow they sensed that this might be the last.

When the sun began to slide behind the mountains, the sisters returned to the croft. When she ducked beneath the warped doorframe, Ailsa found Alanna and Mairi bent over the bed where Charles lay, his bloodless fingers grasping the wool blankets as if to cling to life. Her heart stopped, began to beat again, slowly. She knew then—with a certainty that came, not from the look on her father's face or the fever in his eyes, not even from the despair in her mother's bent shoulders—that this time he would not rise again from Mairi's heather bed.

Li-an saw it, too, as she entered and stood in the warm glow of the fire, the mist at her back. She clutched the doorframe with rigid fingers and the blood left her burnished cheeks until her skin was white and cold.

After dinner, of which no one ate much, Genevra and Alanna cleared away the dishes and rinsed them in the bucket while Ailsa, Mairi, and Li-an sat around the bed. Charles held his wife's cold hand in his feverish one; he was still conscious of everything around him.

When the dishes were done, Ian, Jenny, and their children arrived. They had sensed that tonight all were in need of distraction. Ailsa ached at the sight of Ian's compassionate face, the kindness when he bent to speak to Charles, who was propped up on the pillows. Then she saw that Gavin carried his father's pipes under his arm.

Charles nodded with pleasure. "Will you play, Ian? I'd like to hear the Son o' the Wind tonight. 'Tis the only sound on this earth that can make you forget your own fears and pain and lift you into the sky." His voice was hoarse and his breath rasped in his chest.

Ailsa winced whenever he turned his head to cough into his handkerchief. Then Ian began to play the high, wailing notes of the pipes that whirled through the room and into the heavens. The poignancy of the sound she had not heard for so long only made her sorrow deeper. When Charles began to cough again, she found she had to get away. Taking her plaid, she wrapped it about her shoulders and went outside. The weeping song of the pipes followed and would not set her free.

Ailsa stared at the sky scattered with stars. Her vision blurred as she remembered another night long past when the stars had gleamed above bonfires set to celebrate Beltaine. A night when she had leaped across the flames and hovered in the air, her palm pressed to Ian's, when she had learned how great her strength and determination were. She needed that strength now, and more than that, the touch of Ian's hand on hers. Ailsa shook her head in denial. She felt someone come up beside her and knew without looking that it was Jenny, who did not offer sympathetic words; she knew they would not ease this kind of pain.

Then the girls, Erlinna and Glenyss, ran outside with Brenna close behind.

"Where are ye goin'?" Jenny called after them.

Erlinna, the youngest, turned back. "Up to the hilltop to watch the moon rise. 'Twill be lovely tonight, Mother."

Jenny smiled at her daughter with affection. "Aye, well, take care."

"As ye say," the child replied as she disappeared into the darkness.

Ailsa stared at her friend in surprise. There had been no apprehension in Jenny's tone; she seemed to have given the warning out of habit. "Ye're no' afraid anymore, are ye?"

"No," Jenny said softly. "Over the years the fear just left me, so slowly that I didn't notice till 'twas gone."

"I'm glad."

"Are ye really? Ye don't hate me, then?"

"No," Ailsa murmured, "nor myself, nor Ian. 'Tis all as it should be, I'm thinkin'."

Jenny blinked incredulously. "Do ye really believe that?"

"So I do." Ailsa looked away. "Only sometimes—" She broke off, unable to disguise her sorrow.

"I understand," Jenny said. " 'Twas many years that I watched ye with Ian while I stood in the shadows. I loved ye both and blamed ye neither, but I grieved just the same that he wasn't mine."

Ailsa's eyes burned with tears that she did not wish to weep, even with the Son o' the Wind to cover the sound of her grief. She squeezed Jenny's hand in wordless communion and turned toward the river.

Soon after Ailsa was out of sight, the pipes fell silent. Ian came in the darkness to stand beside his wife. "She's gone?" he said.

"Aye, and I've a feelin' she needs ye tonight even more than I. Go to her, Ian."

He tilted Jenny's chin so he could see her eyes. "Ye're certain?"

She reached out to touch his lips with a fingertip. "I am, Ian Fraser."

" 'Tis a wonderful woman ye are, and I love ye."

"I know ye do," she said softly. "But what I ask of ye isn't so noble. Many was the time when we were young that she sent ye to me and the two of ye together eased my pain. I'd have ye do the same for her, is all."

Ian smiled, kissed her once, and turned toward the woods, following the path he had known by heart since he was a child with Ailsa at his side.

When Charles began to tire, he nodded at Mairi. She took Alanna's arm and drew her away from the bed. Genevra followed reluctantly. Jenny joined them in the kitchen with Gavin while Mairi poured them each a cup of tea.

Li-an was left standing alone at her father's side. She shifted uncomfortably.

"I wanted to talk to you," Charles rasped. "I can't

704

delay any longer. It's time to look at me, Li-an, and truly see me. You can't keep pretending that the truth is not the truth.''

You cannot escape your destiny—to be Charles Kittridge's daughter, Ke-ming had warned in a time so long ago that it seemed years had passed since then.

When Li-an did not answer, Charles said gently, "I've been worried about you, wondering what you'll do when you leave the glen. It doesn't seem that you wish to stay.''

His eyes, gray and clouded, were full of kindness. Why would he not show his anger, rail at her, shake her until the wall of stone crumbled inside her? Because, she thought, Charles Kittridge was not that kind of man. She heard the people at the table speaking in low tones, but they seemed far away, surrounded by a haze that cut her off from them.

Charles reached out to take Li-an's hand. She felt his skin grow hot, then cold, and the blood in her veins seemed to do the same.

"Well," he persisted, "will you leave us all behind you, Li-an? And where will you find another place where there is no war, no public executions, no soldiers to come after you with gleaming swords?''

She stiffened and tried to draw her hand from his grasp, but he held her too tightly. "How did you know?'' she demanded. She struggled to force the anger up through her body to warm her cold heart, but tonight her bitterness was less real, less reassuring.

"Ailsa told me of your past while you wandered alone among the hills. Forgive her for that; she thought I should know.''

Li-an inclined her head but did not respond. The words stuck in her throat.

"I ask you again, *mo-ghraidh,* what will you do when you leave the glen? You aren't a prisoner here, you know.''

I am a captive of my own history, Ke-ming had told her that last night, *but I have raised you to be free, to move toward the future—and the future is in the West.* Li-an frowned and remembered all Chin Chao had said about America—the freedom, the books, the new ideas that were spoken of without fear of reprisal, the women who did not bow their heads in terror of meeting a strange man's eyes. "Perhaps I will go to America," she said thoughtfully. "There I might have a chance to survive."

"You'll have a chance wherever you go. You're a rare, strong woman, like your mother. You'll survive because she taught you how."

The part of him that is in your blood has kept you alive until now. His blood, his history, and his energy have made you strong. Li-an choked down a hysterical laugh. "Ke-ming *was* rare, a woman like no other. But why was she so distant except when I was helpless and in pain? Why did she make herself a stranger to me?" She covered her mouth with her hand, appalled at what she had said. She had not even known the thought was in her mind until the words came tumbling out.

"Because she was afraid. Like you."

Li-an shook her head. "My mother did not fear anything."

"Then why did she protect herself with such determination? Why did she change her name and never tell you the truth about her father? Why did she spend so long weaving the careful tissue of lies that became her whole life—and yours?" Charles asked.

His daughter stared at him blankly.

"Because," he continued, "she did not wish to die."

Li-an opened her mouth to object, but as she did so, fleeting memories came like flickers of lightning in a black night sky. She remembered how often her mother's jaw would tighten when she began to speak or smile or even weep—which she had never done. She remembered every one of the lies, the fabric that Ke-ming had woven and rewoven time and again. She remembered that always her mother had been looking over her shoulder, waiting for a blow she knew would fall no matter how far she ran.

Bowing her head to hide her pale cheeks, Li-an fought to keep her hands from shaking. She had always believed the fear that haunted her had begun on the night when her father abandoned her to the wrath of his enemies. She had lied to herself. The dread had been with her since the first time she saw Ke-ming stiffen at a little sound, her face still as marble but far more fragile. The sense of impending fear had come from China itself—the turmoil and violence that had risen like a slow, devastating storm as the Middle Kingdom began to disintegrate from within. And Ke-ming had seen it all. Li-an's terror had grown and lingered because of her mother's fear, which had fed it like peat fed the fire at their backs. It had not been Charles Kittridge's fault.

More than once, I have told you about the man he was, but you would not listen. He did not know as Confucius did that "It is easier to move mountains than to change the hearts of men." And yet your father tried. He did not know that our hearts were stone, our eyes blind, and our ears deaf. Li-an's protective wall shattered and the rough edges made her bleed. "My Father," she whispered, "I have not been fair to you." *You will not speak your father's name until you speak it with love.*

Tears filled his eyes and he kissed the hands he held in his. "It doesn't matter. Can't you see that?"

She drew back at the sight of his tears. "You do not fear anything, do you?" Not even letting others see your sorrow and weakness, she added silently.

Charles shook his head. "Not anymore."

His daughter examined his face intently and saw that he spoke the truth. Death hovered very near, yet there was no struggle, no violence in Charles Kittridge, in spite of his physical pain. His smile was soft, his eyes full of peace—an acceptance of something she could never accept. Her father had fought for most of his life; he was tired of the struggle and wanted to rest. It struck her then like a blow in the chest that she would grieve for him when he was gone. Though she had tried to keep herself apart, untouched by his penetrating gaze and age-spotted hands, she was grieving even now—not out of hatred or bitterness or anger, but out of regret that she would never have a chance to know him better. She blinked painfully dry eyes and felt a sharp throb in her temples. She would not weep. She did not dare.

Ailsa sat in darkness, her bare feet cold on the bracken, the sound of the river filling her head. Tonight the water did not soothe her. It was not only the knowledge of Charles's relapse that made her grieve. She had told the truth when she said she was happy for Jenny, but the pain of Ian's loss was strong within her just the same.

She put her head in her hands and rocked, but the anguish did not ease. She heard nothing, sensed nothing, saw nothing, yet suddenly Ian was there, standing above her.

She raised her head and felt that he had touched her hair, though he did not move. Even in the darkness, she saw that his eyes were open, that the veil of distance had disappeared.

"I've waited a long time to see your face among the night shadows with the sound of the water ripplin' by," he told her. "A long time to say what I've come to say now."

She only nodded, in case he was an apparition. If she spoke she might break the spell and he dissolve into the circling mist.

"The gods gave ye to me when I was a bairn so small I couldn't know what a gift 'twas I held. In givin' me that gift, they gave me the deepest joy a man can know, and also the deepest sorrow. But ye know all that, for ye've felt it, too."

"Aye," she murmured, "so I have."

"I'd have ye know, Ailsa, *mo-run*, that I'd give up neither the joy nor the pain, for they have made me what I am. They are part of me, even as ye are part of me."

After a silence so long, so deep, the sound of his voice vibrated through the emptiness inside her and she shivered.

"These things have also molded ye." He paused to look away, speaking into the leaves overhead, into the rush of the water and the whisper of the breeze. " 'Tis as well that ye went away when ye did. Ye were wiser than I, I think, though then I believed 'twas I alone who knew the truth. I loved ye too much, and ye me. I needed ye to live and breathe. Such a love would have drained us of our strength in the end and mayhap we would have ceased to love at all. I couldn't have borne that. Ye chose well, Ailsa, as did I, because ye forced me to."

She had known this a long time ago, but had not realized

how much she wanted Ian to know it, too. She did not touch him, for she was full of sorrow now, and relief, and joy, and she knew her wisdom had fled.

"Be grateful for the gift we had," Ian continued, "and know that I am part of ye and will be, even when our bodies become dust that floats on the wind like dry autumn leaves. Then together our shadows will wander the hills we loved, rememberin' the wonder and the pain we gave each other so long before."

She looked at him through the darkness and knew he spoke the truth. For a moment, as their eyes met and held, he opened his mind to her and she saw that what might have turned to dust was still vital and strong within him as deeply as it was in her. She felt the peace that had never been part of his nature and recognized that the wounds had healed, but the memory of their shared joy lingered. She saw all these things before he closed his eyes and his mind, so she and he were two once more. But the sight of a moment had been enough. Ailsa smiled her mother's smile, rose in silence, and in silence returned to the croft where the warm fire burned, as it always had, in welcome, even now.

Ian went directly to Charles's bedside. He knelt, put his hand on the sick man's forehead, and murmured. *"Deireadh gach cuinn, sgaoileadh; deireadh gach cogaidh, sith."*

"What does it mean?" Charles asked.

" 'The end of all meetings, parting; the end of all striving, peace.' "

Charles nodded and closed his eyes.

Only after Jenny, Ian, and the children had started for home did Ailsa notice Li-an was gone. She saw Mairi's apprehension and turned without a thought to find her sister. Even with the moon to help, it was a long time before Ailsa sensed the other woman's presence. Somehow Li-an had found her way to the jutting boulders at the foot of the mountains.

She sat with her back to the cold stones, her arms locked about her knees. Li-an stared blindly into the night sky—alone, motionless, contained. Ailsa stopped, her hands buried deep in her pockets, when she saw that her sister's face was streaked with silent tears turned silver by the moonlight.

Ailsa did not make a sound, but slipped away as she knew Li-an would want her to, leaving her sister to her proud and lonely grief.

◦ 8 ◦

The next morning, Genevra found herself alone at her father's bedside. Ailsa and Alanna had left together just after dawn and Li-an had gone soon after. Mairi busied herself in the kitchen, her attention on her herbs and her bread dough.

Genevra stared down at her tightly clasped hands.

Leaning up on his elbow with an effort, Charles noticed a gleaming circle against his daughter's skin and gently touched the intertwined gold strands she wore around her neck. "My gift to Emily," he murmured. "Does this mean you have forgiven me?"

Genevra hesitated. "I'm trying, but—" She broke off and would not meet his eyes.

Her father fell back among the pillows. "You're afraid to forgive me, aren't you?"

"Yes." She had meant to deny it, but somehow could not.

"Why?"

For the first time, she risked a look at his face, tinted golden by the firelight. She felt overly warm, but knew Charles was chilled, even beneath his many blankets. His eyes, curious yet dim with pain, seemed to draw the truth from her. "Because once I do that, I'll have no reason to stay away from India and Alex. I'll have to go back to him and let him break my heart." Genevra grew pale, astonished at what she had said. "I didn't mean—" she stammered.

Charles silenced her with a touch of his hand. "You've told me much of your Alex. He doesn't sound like the kind of man to break a woman's heart."

"Neither do you. But you did it. First to Li-an, then to Emily, then to me."

711

"I told you how it happened," he objected.

Genevra shook her head. "It doesn't matter why or how or if it was all a mistake or if you would have been too late, even if you'd found me years ago. It only matters that it did happen, that the scars are there."

Her father's expression was bleak.

Genevra touched his cold hands. "This place has begun to heal the scars—getting to know Mairi and my sisters, and you, has taken some of the bitter taste from my mouth. But you see, so long as I blamed you for my pain, you and all those British who rejected me again and again, I didn't have to admit that I was part of you, and of them, as Alex is. I thought I could turn my back on the painful memories, go back to Delhi, and let the Indian sun burn away every last trace of my Englishness."

One thing I learned quickly when I tried to find my true Indian soul was that I had English blood not only in my veins but in my bones, Phoebe had told her. *I couldn't have it removed or ignore it or send it back in a parcel to where it came from. I had to learn to live with it.* "But I can't do that now," Genevra continued. "Because I *am* one of them, just as I am part of you. It doesn't mean that I like the thought, but I have to accept it. *I* cannot deny the culture that has always denied me. I can't deny Alex."

"You speak as if it's a fact, as if you've already forgiven," Charles observed hopefully.

Genevra felt the raw edges of her scars, but there was something else besides. "I don't know if I can ever do that completely," she said. "It's difficult to let go of something you've held on to so tightly for so long. But I can try." She looked into her father's face, blinked, and looked again. This was the man who had changed her life, but he did not look at all like Alex with his blond hair and blue eyes. The two men were not the same and never had been. Alex was simply Alex and he loved her. He wanted to give her what Charles had finally given Mairi—a family, a place to belong. Why hadn't she seen that before?

Because she had not wanted to. She'd been too afraid that in the end, Alex would turn away from her as so many of his countrymen had. As Edward Townsend had, and

Emily, and Charles. And she had known long ago that to lose Alex would be more than she could bear. Yet her father had borne such loss and survived. More than that, he had found happiness, even peace from the turmoil inside him. If he could do it, why couldn't she? She carried his blood in her veins, did she not? But she didn't have to be like him, nor did she have to follow her mother's sad path. She was Genevra, herself and only herself.

All at once, she understood why Phoebe had told the story of her dead husband and her devastating grief. Genevra took her father's hands and whispered, "Thank you."

He gazed at her, perplexed, but welcomed the touch of her warm, soft hands. "For what?"

"For being the man you are," she replied, half in bitterness. "Whatever you've done in the past, you see, you never gave up on the ones you loved, even after they'd given up on you." She stared into the fragrant peat fire. "It doesn't matter if in the end you lose someone you care about, does it? It only matters that you do love them and they love you, even if it's only for a while. I have to take the risk of loving Alex. If nothing else, you taught me that, Father, and I'm grateful."

Alanna and her mother were alone together for the first time since Genevra's arrival. Ailsa had seen the troubled look in her daughter's eyes this morning and had known she could no longer avoid what she did not wish to face. So they had taken a walk, turning instinctively toward the precipice that Ailsa had not visited since her first day here. They climbed the mountainside in silence, more comfortable now that their feet had been hardened by the earth and rock and hollows of the glen. Ailsa saw by the way Alanna moved, agilely, without thought or attention, that she had been up this path many times. Her mother felt a weight on her shoulders and a pain in her chest, but she did not voice her feelings.

When the two women reached the top, they went to the edge and sat cross-legged, staring out over the landscape below. The sky was full of dark thunderclouds and the mountains shimmered, translucent black with a purple tinge—powerful and painfully lovely in the strange, dim light. For a long time they were silent, absorbing the beauty, the wild magnificence of the scene. Finally Alanna spoke.

"I think ye know what I have to say," she whispered. Her words caught on the wind and were carried into the lowering sky. "I've been happy here, despite all the sorrow, happier than I ever was in London. I don't belong in those twistin' dirty streets, Mother. I belong here, where the land speaks to me."

Ailsa had known it from the look on her daughter's face that first day, from the way she had set about learning the secrets of the glen. She had even known the moment when Alanna herself had recognized the truth. Yet to hear it put into words was more painful than she'd thought possible. She had meant to love all her children the same, but from the moment of her birth, Alanna had been the child of Ailsa's heart, the only one who listened with glowing eyes when she spoke of the Highlands, the only one who believed that there were wonders beyond the glitter and grime of London. She felt that her heart had stopped, might never beat again. Now, at last, she understood how Mairi had felt when she herself left the glen so many years ago.

Aware of her mother's strained silence, Alanna hurried on. "I want to stay here when ye go. I love the mountains and woods and the music that seems to fill the air. I never knew a place could speak in a voice of its own. London didn't call to me as this glen does. There I felt always a little cold, like a stranger, and ye my only friend. I didn't even know it till ye brought me here. Then I saw what I had missed. Can ye understand that?"

How could she not, Ailsa wondered, when dreams of Glen Affric had never left her and the shadows of her childhood had colored every moment since. "I understand." But she could not meet her daughter's gaze. Not yet.

" 'Tisn't only because I love this place so much," Alanna added to fill the silence that lay about them in spite of the sounds of the glen—the *me'h'ing*, the melancholy cry of the sheep; the *torran*, the murmur of distant thunder; the *caiodh*, wailing lamentation of the approaching storm. Yet in its center, stillness, sorrow, words that would not come.

"I don't think Grandmother should be alone after Grandfather's gone. She'll need me then. She's no' as strong as ye may think."

"I know. I saw it the day we arrived."

Alanna took her mother's hand and squeezed it in gratitude.

"There's more, isn't there?" Ailsa demanded hollowly.

"Aye. I had a dream that sent me often to the Valley of the Dead. One night I saw a ghost there. He told me, no' in words, ye see, but with his hands and his sad hollow eyes, that he wanted me to stay to care for the cairns, to see that the dead are no' forgotten. Ye told me that ye must do as a ghost tells ye and then he will leave ye in peace. So 'twas for me, once I decided to stay. I went there in the mornin' and felt the mist all around me, and the shadows and the wind. I heard the voice of another place, another time, a world beyond this one that brushed against my cheek. 'Twas a feelin' I couldn't resist." Before her mother could reply, she added, "Someday Grandmother will die, too, though I know ye don't wish to think of such a thing. Who will see that she's buried beside her family and her husband, with whom she belongs?"

Ailsa raised her head. "I'll come and see to it, and there are her friends." She did not know why she argued; it was too late to change the girl's mind. Nor did she really wish to. She liked to think of Alanna roving the glen when she was gone, loving the places she'd loved, learning the lessons she'd learned here. But she would miss her daughter, she thought bleakly. By the Black Stone of Iona, she would miss this fey spirit who had so often taken her home in those dreary London years.

" 'Tisn't the same," Alanna continued doggedly. "I have her blood in my veins and can't deny it; it calls to me, Mother. For Grandmother's sake, I must stay."

"I know. The glen has woven its *sian*, its spell about ye, and ye can't break free." Ailsa knew she must let her daughter make her own choice, just as Mairi had once let *her* daughter choose. " 'Tis only that I will miss ye, Alannean."

The fury of the Rider of the Storm had increased until

the sky rumbled and the trees trembled with the roaring sound. Alanna turned to her mother and asked the question that had been in the back of her mind since the morning when she'd made her decision. "Why don't ye stay, too? 'Tis where ye belong."

Ailsa shook her head. "I belong in England with my family and dear friends. I'm goin' back to a man who has loved me, waited for me all these years, though he never truly had all of me, and he knew it. But 'twas enough for him somehow. He loved me just the same, as much as my father loves my mother."

"But ye don't love him in the same way," Alanna insisted. She had seen Ian, seen her mother's face as she watched him, and she sensed the kind of love they had once shared.

Frowning, Ailsa considered. "No' in the same way, but just as much. Ye don't know how much William's given me over the years, how much he's come to mean to me. More than anything, I wanted to see the world, and he showed it to me. He showed me a great deal. I think now that I've been home, now that I've known my father and rid myself of his shadow in my dreams, I can give William more of me—everything."

"And Ian?" Alanna knew she should not ask, but the words came of their own accord.

Ailsa turned to her daughter and smiled, though the tearing sense of yet another loss was raw and painful inside her. "Ian and I have made our peace, *mo-graidh*. Our lives were bound together once and always will be, in memory, but the past is past long since. I knew that in my heart even before I saw these hills again and felt their strength and beauty flow through me. 'Twill never leave me again, that strength, no' like it once did. And I'll no' be afraid to return here anymore. 'Twill only give me comfort. It does now, as ye say, in spite of all the sorrow."

"Mairi," Charles said when he lay in her arms that night, his flushed face against her cool cheek, "sing to me."

She hesitated, wondering what words she could form without letting her tears flow. Strange how, when she was young, she had wept rarely, yet now she could not seem to stop. She grew more like a child by the day as the emptiness inside her deepened, making a warm, dark well for her grief.

"Mairi? Don't desert me now. I need your strength."

She looked up at his shadowed face. "And I yours, *aghraidh mo-chridhe*, dear love of my heart. If Ian were here, he'd play ye a *Suantraidheach* on the pipes to soothe your unquiet mind."

"But Ian isn't here," Charles reminded her. "So sing to me."

She laid her cheek on the pillow beside him, her mouth close to his ear.

> "Oh wert thou in the cold blast,
>   On yonder lee, on yonder lee;
> My plaidie to the angry airt,
>   I'd shelter thee, I'd shelter thee:
> Or did misfartune's bitter storms
>   Around thee blow, around thee blow,
> They bield should be my bosom,
>   To share it all, to share it all."

"You've a beautiful voice, lass. I hope you'll use it to sing over my grave when that time comes. I think I'll hear you, even then, and be charmed by the sound as I am now."

Mairi did not answer; she could not.

> "Or were I in the wildest waste,
>   So black and bare, so black and bare,
> The desert were a paradise,
>   If thou were there, if thou wert there.
> Or were I monarch o' the globe,
>   With thee to reign, with thee to reign,
> The brightest jewel in my crown,
>   Would be my king, would be my king."

Charles touched her cheek in awe, as if she might dissolve at any moment, like a phantom in the storm. "I feel that I'm dreaming this place, this earth wrapped in silver mist, the stars that glitter even in the moonlight, and the music of the hills. Have you any idea how much I love you?"

"I know how much," she said, "for ye came back to me and the world I knew wasn't the same anymore. Even the Valley of the Dead doesn't frighten me now; ye've taken the ghosts and buried them in the past where they belong."

"You did that," he said. "I only loved you."

"But that was enough, my Charles. Don't ye know that?

"Now hath heaven to earth descended
And cloud and clay and stone and star are blended."

When two more days had passed, the three sisters, Alanna, and Mairi sat around Charles's bed late at night. They spoke in low voices, soothing him when he awoke to cough violently, his fever high, watching him anxiously while he slept. He had become the focus of their lives, which centered now about this bed. It seemed to comfort him to see their faces when he looked up, and his eyes were clear, not dark with fevered visions. So they stayed, sharing their warmth with one another, rising by turns to do a few chores, but returning always to the man who lay huddled beneath the wool blankets.

"Ailsa," Charles whispered when he awoke once in darkness lit only by the fire in the center of the croft. He reached out blindly until she took his shaking hands.

"I'm here, Papa."

He relaxed and smiled slightly, tangled his fingers in her long chestnut hair. "I've seen a change in you over the past few days. You've discarded an old pain that was a burden to you. But you've found another sorrow."

"Aye," she said, "but that, too, will ease in time."

"I understand. I've left behind many sorrows in my life—all my burdens, guilts, griefs. Now there's only peace."

"Ye have no fear?" she asked in disbelief.

"Perhaps a little," he replied. "But 'tisn't important. Not compared to knowing you're all here about me when I wake. That's a gift I never thought to have."

Ailsa pressed her hands to his, palm to moist palm. "I'll miss ye," she said, her eyes glistening with unshed tears.

Genevra leaned forward. "I've one more gift for you, if you'll have it."

Her father turned but did not draw his hand away from Ailsa's. He liked the feeling of her skin against his, the pulse he could feel in her wrist. It reminded him that she was alive and real, not a dream he had created. "I'll take whatever you wish to give," he said to his youngest daughter.

Tentatively, Genevra reached into her pocket and pulled out a rolled piece of paper, which she laid on the bed at Charles's side. It was the drawing she had done that day by the river, the last time she had sat with her sisters and laughed. With unsteady fingers, she unrolled the page.

Mairi held a lamp high as her husband picked up the paper and looked at a sketch of himself seated in front of a canvas on which he was drawing Genevra's face. He gasped and held the sketch out to Alanna, who bit her lip at the sight of the portrait. "It's beautiful," Charles whispered hoarsely. He held the gift with great care, as if it were spun glass that might shatter at too rough a touch. "And it's of you. I don't think you can know what it means to me."

Her throat raw and painful, Genevra sank into her chair.

With an effort, Charles gripped Alanna's hand. "It's time, Alannean."

"I know." She rose and flung her plaid around her.

"Where are ye goin'?" Mairi cried.

"To get the paintin'," her granddaughter replied.

"But how will ye find your way in the darkness?"

Alanna smiled. "I don't need the light to find my way." Then she was gone. The ones she had left behind waited while Charles drifted in and out of sleep, watching the door anxiously each time he woke.

Finally the heavy oak creaked on its hinges and Alanna was there, a long, bulky canvas covered with cheesecloth under her arm. She knelt next to her grandfather. "*Morun*," she whispered, "I'm here."

Charles opened his eyes, stared blankly for a moment, then recognition lit his face. "Do you have it?" he asked.

"Aye."

"Then show them."

Obediently, Alanna propped the canvas against a chair, looked intently from her mother to Mairi to Li-an to Genevra, and carefully removed the concealing cloth.

The others sat, speechless, transfixed by the painting lit by a single oil lamp and the glow of the fire. It was Li-an who broke the silence at last. "Your work is very beautiful, my Father. It is something to be proud of."

She leaned close to examine the painting in which Charles had portrayed his three daughters as he came to know them. She was surprised and moved to see that somehow he had captured the essence of each on canvas.

Ailsa knelt by a clear crystal burn, leaning toward the beckoning water; Li-an was swathed in embroidered silk that did not quite fit her and she held a moon-shaped mirror in her hands; Genevra gazed dreamily, lost in another world as she painted a dark, mysterious portrait. And each woman held within her grasp—in the water, the mirror, and the colorful paint—the reflected image of her mother's face.

The five women sat staring in wonder and Charles fell into a deep sleep while outside the dawn began to break. The sun rose on people who hurried barefoot over the rough ground, laughing, calling greetings to one another through the rosy mist. Some carried large rocks that they placed in circles on an open stretch of moor. Others filled the circles with wood that would be set ablaze that night in bonfires built to herald the arrival of spring, the disappearance of winter darkness from the glen. The Highlanders knelt in the grass and the dew, with the first rays of sun on their cheeks, and prepared to celebrate with light and flame and pagan song, the coming of another Beltaine.